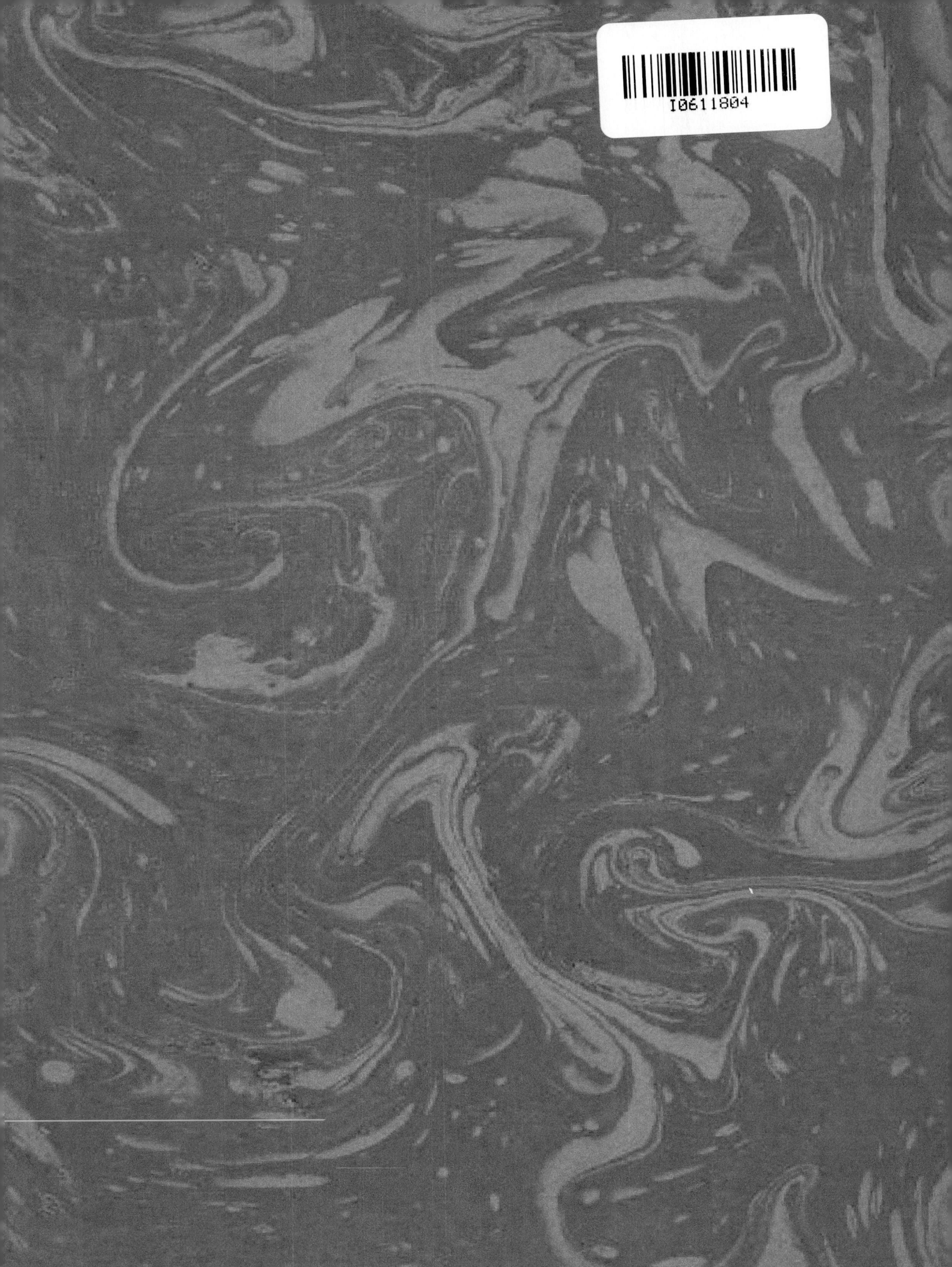

An Officer of the Crown

Bombay To Persia And On To The River Oxus

An Officer of the Crown

The Middlecombe Expedition to the Aral Sea in Turcomania and the Khanates of Independent Tartary, 1837-1838

========

Volume III

========

Chronicle of the Middlecombe Expedition in 1837, with a Full Report and Narrative on the Expedition's Departure from Bombay and travel though Persia and Turcomania to the Cities of Independent Tartary

Bombay To Persia And On To The River Oxus

Illustrated

Being a complete narrative of its inception, formation, travels, discoveries and adventures by
D. A. Driscol, Ensign
Bombay Artillery

Compiled and edited by Wayne S Rutledge

Dedication

To Master Vickery by whom our explorations were made possible and recorded

Printed in the United States in 2016
Printed by: CreateSpace, Charleston SC
Perrioe Publishing
Copyright © Wayne S Rutledge 2014
ISBN: 978-0-9969980-4-8
E-book version ISBN: 978-0-9969980-5-5
Fonts used: Century for modern American and Covington for British English,
Mangal, Wingdings, Vijaya, Vinner Hand ITC, Old newsprint and MV Boli

If one is blessed as I was to have been birthed in the paradise that is Hawai'i all other places seem rather abhorrent, malodourous, and generally beastly

MrEduard Edmund Kamali'i Kane Laanui Vickery

An Officer of the Crown

Bombay To Persia And On To The River Oxus: The Middlecombe Expedition to the Aral Sea in Turcomania and the Khanates of Independent Tartary, 1837-1838

Being a complete narrative of its inception, formation, travel, discoveries and adventures by D. A. Driscol, Ensign Bombay Artillery

========

From his personal journals and containing excerpts from the expedition's report to the Geographical Society of London

========

In four Volumes:

Volume I: Reminiscences Of An English Ensign's Journey To The East In 1836

Volume II: Suez to Bombay, A Narration of the Actions Leading to the Formation of the Middlecombe Expedition and the life of an Ensign in the Bombay Artillery 1836-1837

Volume III: Bombay to Persia and on to the River Oxus, Chronicle of the Middlecombe Expedition in 1837: with a Full Report and Narrative on, the Expedition's Departure from Bombay and Travel though Persia and Turcomania to the Cities of Independent Tartary

Volume IV: The Perrioe, The Final Volume of the Middlecombe Expedition to Central Tartary 1837-1838 with a partial recollection of what they found there, and a recounting of the engagement at the Sullen Tower of Saleh Khan, the fate of the Expedition with Illustrations, Maps, Observations, and Associated Papers by an Officer Present at its final Moments

========

With remarks and comments by
Colour Sergeant G. B. Hynes, Grenadier Regiment of Bombay Native Infantry, Indian Army
and S. P. Michaelson Assistant Surgeon in His Majesty's Indian Navy, Herr Dr. Dafydd zum Nolta, MA, MD(P) and E. K. K. L. Vickery, Esquire, Secretary of the Expedition

Written by: David Alexander Driscol, Ensign

London, Sampson Low, Son & Co, 188, Fleet Street,
MDCCCXXXXVIII

CONTENTS

========

In four volumes

========

Volume III

Bombay to Persia and on to the River Oxus, Chronicle of the Middlecombe Expedition in 1837: with a Full Report and Narrative on, the Expedition's Departure from Bombay and Travel though Persia and Turcomania to the Cities of Independent Tartary

========

========

Chapter XI

From Bombay to Bushire

From Bombay To Kurachee, The Indus River Delta, Gwadar, Ras-El-Khyma On The Trucial Coast And Bushire And On To Shiraz In Persia - Why The Middlecombe Expedition Is Necessary And The Reason To Do The Needful, An Idea Both Capital And Audacious - The Great Trigonometric Survey Enters The Stage - Determination Of Purposes For The Expedition - Seclusion Of Independent Tartary - Military Concern - Suppression Of Slavery In Those Lands - Scientific And Military Geography And Topography - Expansion Of Our Markets And Free Trade - Which Rivers Are Navigable And Suitable In Supporting Markets? - Horses For Use With The Indian Army - Conclusion - The Crew Of The *Hormuzeer* - On Moons, Night Walkers And Karachi - Dissanayake Hero Of Obscurations And Befuddlements - Scape-Goats, Cannons And The Port Of Gwadar - Amongst The Flotsam And Jetsam Of The Sea - The Home Of Pirates, Past And Present? - The Hunt - An Unexpected Visitor - Maj-Kat In Arabia - The Persian Coast And Bushire - The Expedition Arrives In Persia - Farewell The Hormuzeer And Her Finest Of Men - Remarks On The Way From Bushire To Shiraz - Over The Kotal-E-Doktar To Kazerun

========

Chapter XII

Shiraz to Teheran

A Long Week And A Longer Ride To Teheran - Many Ruins Of Persia's Ancient Past - In Mufti - Perkins Encounters A Murderous Villain - Bijan's Family And A Short Respite - Teheran And We Find Our Man - Gregory Allen François Gizhiibatoo Hynes - A Deception Revealed - The French Bank - Politics Of Herat - The Lost Children Re-Appear The Expedition Reunited - The Tales Of The Lost Expedition - Great Plans - The Expedition Presented To The Persian Shah

========

Chapter XIII

Teheran to Asterabad

Departure From Teheran For Asterabad By Way Of The Coast Of The Caspian Sea And The Land Of Mazandaran - The Mountains Of Peril - The Forests Of Mazandaran - The Caspian Sea - A Bedeviled And Thieved-Plagued Prince - The Dragoman With Eccles Cakes - God Smites The Land Of The Unbelievers - We Come To Asterabad And The Steppes Of Independent Tartary - The Day Of The Shoeless Horne And A Malaise - Preparations And News Of War - Dobbins' Chatelaine And A Persian Opium Factory - A Visitor Comes For Lunch But Leaves Before Pudding - Dining With Abu Saman And Friends - A Ragged Band Of Circassians

========

Chapter XIV

Asterabad to Turcomania

We Ride To The Gurgan River As Circassians - At The Campsite Of Turcoman 'Man-Stealers' - The Virtues And Faults Of The Turcoman - Turcoman Pilaf - Turcomania And A Description Of Turcoman Slave Taking - The Inter-Clan Conflicts Of The Turcoman - The Charge Of The 17th King's Own Imperial Light Horse Polish Lancers Of The Guard Or The Middlecombe Expedition Bares Its Teeth - Recall - A Cursory Discussion Is Held And The Attack On Our Position At Igdy Well - Melee At Igdy Well - Our Situation Reconsidered - Harvey Sauce - The Hell Fires Of The Kara-Kum - The Journey Over The Burning Sands Continues With Pain - We Come To The Dried Bed Of The Oxus - Our Old Friend - Turcoman Negotiations On The Matter Of Igdy Well -

========

Chapter XV

Khiva and the Oxus River

Khiva The City Of The Khan And A Sewer Of The First Order - A Damnable Hot Town And Veal For Dinner - The Moneylender And The Khivan Bazaar - A MOST Singular Occurrence - A Midnight's Skulking Though Khiva - Our Prisoner - Dafydd Friedrich Zum Nolta - A Ride To Nowhere - Return To The Heated Delights Of Khiva - I Deadly Discovery Made - The Foulness Of The Khivan Bazaars And The Idiocy Of Guides - We Meet With The Khan And Ameer Of Khiva And His Vizier - We Are Given A Mission By The Khan Of Khiva - Three Countrymen In The Hades Hotel? - A Voyage Down The Oxus

========

Chapter notes

========

Appendixes

========

LIST OF ILLUSTRATIONS

========

Plates

========

Maps or diagrams

=======

Artworks, plates, photographs & drawings

Chapter XIII

Chapter XIV

Chapter XV

Appendixes

Appendix Supplement

Bibliography

The consolidated bibliographies for volumes I-IV are located with Volume IV

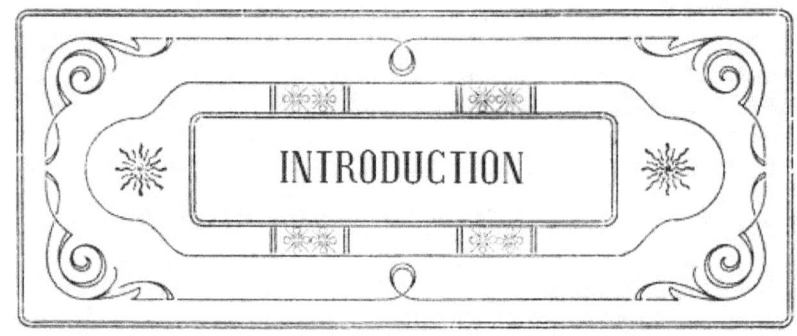

INTRODUCTION

Volume I: Reminiscences of an English Ensign's Journey East In 1836

David Alexander Driscol, Ensign of the 52nd (Oxfordshire) Light Infantry Regiment, volunteered for secondment to the India Army and after visiting his family in Eccles, Lancashire traveled to London to gain his passage east. He meets with Lieutenant Perkins who is forming an expedition to explore Independent Tartary, and as Driscol is studying Persian he is the first man recruited for the party. Driscol equips himself for travel to the east in London. In his travels, he meets Marguerite and with whom he begins a correspondence.

He takes a steamship to Gibraltar with several adventures, meeting another young lady named Millicent, then by native boat to Malta, fighting off a piratical attack off Algiers. They appear to conduct, and the record is unclear here, an outrageous prank on the Royal Navy and then make their way to Alexandria on a French sailing ship. From that city they go by canal boat to Cairo. There they assist a Maltese friend in investigating the selling of Jews at the slave market in Cairo, visit the pyramids and make their way to Suez, where they become passengers on His Majesty's Indian Navy Steam Sloop Atalanta.

Volume II: Suez to Bombay, A Narration of the Actions Leading to the Formation of the Middlecombe Expedition and the life of an Ensign in the Bombay Artillery 1836-1837

Ensign Driscol continues his voyage to India, but at Djedda becomes involved in a fracas between the Turks, Arabs and their enemies. He undertakes a mission at night in disguise into the city. Meets an Englishman named Vickery who saves his life. He then commands an 8 inch gun in sinking Turkish and Arab ships that fire on the HMIN Atalanta. He is slightly wounded in this action. The ship loaded with refugees from the fighting is turned away from Bastia in Abyssinia, but obtains supplies from Mokka. He searches Perim Island for shipwrecked survivors. In search of more of these survivors, the ship goes to Berberah on the Somali coast, where Driscol has a dangerous and mysterious encounter with the 'Grey men'. He engages pirates off the southern coast of Arabia and helps to save an Omani ship from their attack. He has a minor flirtation with an Arab Princess's lady in waiting. He arrives without further ado at Bombay, gets a dunking and is offered a position with the Bombay Artillery which he accepts. He finds lodgings and perhaps even a bibi and begins his duties as an Artilleryman in the Indian army.

Perkins and he go on a recruiting trip into the depths of India and find or are found by three more future members of the expedition. They have a run-in with an ungentlemanly officer, an issue with Indian bandits and Driscol's battery conducts a public firing and later he engages a mad elephant. Finally he and the expedition with eight men depart Bombay for Karachi.

Editor's note on conventions used within this book

I have followed a method I believe will make it easier for the reader to understand what Driscol wrote. I have inserted superscripts linked to each chapter and consolidated them as endnotes at the end of each volume. I hope that this will be less distracting than the footnotes that Driscol originally intended to use. Where I can, I explain an unusual word or description in a few words within { } and written in italics. I did this to reduce the number of endnotes. I recommend that readers take the time to read the endnotes as they greatly enhance the understanding of what was occurring in the greater world around Driscol. Where ( ) appear these are in the original and have replaced Driscol's occasional use of hyphens or dashes, some of which I have retained.

Driscol also recorded in his journals conversations by noting the person speaking by using their initials placing a = then paraphrasing what was said; so one ended up with:

DD=You find those actions objectionable Sir. DP=I do, I do indeed. Etc. I have reconstructed those into a more modern conversational style by using 'he said', 'I replied', and other conventions.

I do on occasion make editorial comments to clarify something I believe needs immediate explanation or to explain why I have redacted or abridged a section. I have done so to delete sections on matters that would be tedious to modern readers. Driscol could be quite detailed in his research. Where I have abridged, I will offer a summary and an explanation of why the abridgement has occurred. These will be noted in the manner below.

When I wish to interject a comment, I will do so using an Editor's note, as shown below:

[Editor's note: Brilliant comment on x, y, and z]

Missing pieces of the journal, gaps caused by damage or missing entirely will be marked by {...}

One last note: the page numbering for Volume III continues the page count from Volume II.

Volume III

Chronicle of the Middlecombe Expedition in 1837: with a Full Report and Narrative on, the Expedition's Departure from Bombay and Travel though Persia and Turcomania to the Cities of Independent Tartary

=======

Chapter XI

From Bombay to Bushire

From Bombay To Kurachee, The Indus River Delta, Gwadar, Ras-El-Khyma On The Trucial Coast And Bushire And On To Shiraz In Persia - The Great Trigonometric Survey Enters The Stage - Determination Of Purposes For The Expedition - Seclusion Of Independent Tartary - Military Concern - Suppression Of Slavery In Those Lands - Scientific And Military Geography And Topography - Expansion Of Our Markets And Free Trade - Which Rivers Are Navigable And Suitable In Supporting Markets? - Horses For Use With The Indian Army - Conclusion - The Crew Of The *Hormuzeer* - On Moons, Night Walkers And Karachi - Dissanayake Hero Of Obscurations And Befuddlements - Scape-Goats, Cannons And The Port Of Gwadar - Amongst The Flotsam And Jetsam Of The Sea - The Home Of Pirates, Past And Present? - The Hunt - An Unexpected Visitor - Maj-Kat In Arabia - The Persian Coast And Bushire - The Expedition Arrives In Persia - Farewell The Hormuzeer And Her Finest Of Men - Remarks On The Way From Bushire To Shiraz - Over The Kotal-E-Doktar To Kazerun

========

From Bombay To Kurachee, The Indus River Delta, Gwadar, Ras-El-Khyma On The Trucial Coast And Bushire And On To Shiraz In Persia

[Editor's note: Driscol used five different variations of spelling for Kurachee (Karachi) and three for Ras-ul-Khima (Ras Al-Khaimah) and to avoid confusion, I will use the modern spelling of the cities from now on]

Saturday 8 April {the day continued from volume II}

Bombay had been a wonder to see when I sailed into her harbour in December and I was even more impressed to sail out of her on our way to Persia. We lay becalmed, just off the port, for some hours, as the wind had died just after our departure. As it is Pentecostal Sunday, we feel it is an auspicious day and Dissanayake hosts a short service. It was an impressive one, for, despite the man's unimpressive outer appearance, he has a strong, inner keenness. Soon after, I wrote down his speech:

[Editor's note: Driscol wrote out three different versions crossing out each in turn. I suspect he asked others and perhaps the speaker himself what he had said. Only the last version is reproduced below]

...Only God, whose forbearing and forgiveness is given us in defiance of our folly and weakness of man, can bring goodness out of maliciousness, grace out of blackness, mandate out of misperception, and understanding out of irrationality. His wisdom is infinite, His ways unsearchable and past discovery. Let us pray that He will do so for us and grant this expedition God-speed, and his gracious blessing and good will for its success. This world is a place of imponderables and workings we cannot always comprehend. It, doubtless, may be that all these indecipherable things that we do and he causes, work together for the good of mankind at large, by opening a path. We proceed on this pathway by our good works and deeds to His glorious word, to interchange and civilization, by the means of his agency and wealth as well as that of others.

One chief moral we must hark back to, as we leave the shore of this heathen land, a fact at least the Indian has learned if not the British man, *videre licet {Latin for viz.}*, that there is no help in the idols, whom they worship and in whom they trusted, nor in their deceiving priests and let them, the Indians, Mohammedan, Hindoo and others well weigh this, that our God, the only true God, is one of strength and of battles won. He, whom we worship, hath given over to us the wealth of India and to the idol-worshippers and followers of false prophet nothing but disarray, dismay, conquest, domination, and loss. We go now to survey a land not well known and we pray that in time, it too will come under our direction, and therefore will blossom under the hands of the believers in Jesus. Amen.

Our ship, in some ways, reminded me of the Speronara, but it was larger and built for the horse trade. Below decks it had forty stalls for horses, now filled with our own herd, and eight matched ones for a customer of Mr Wadia in Karachi. She also carried with her in the unused stalls our equipment, such as it was, and a lively collection of goats, sheep and fowl for our mess.

A tarpaulin had been stretched between the area of the two masts from just behind the galley, a brick lined place of cooking to the mid-deck, here Arab style cushions had been placed for our comfort and a Le Hunte[1] canvas bag set up to provide easy access to drinking water.

We sat on the provided deck cushions while Perkin's scanned the area with my binoculars to make sure Husher made no trouble by coming out in a native boat. Seeing no such effort by him, for he limited his actions to prancing back and forth at the dockside, seemingly uncertain what to do. Then, after nearly twenty minutes, he rode off. Thus relieved, we settled down to discuss the situation with the expedition members. Dobbins and Horne most kindly volunteered to throw him overboard in the event he try to come aboard after finding natives willing to row him out.

Perkins, having given up his sentry duty to Vickery, informed us of his plans. It was his contention to make for Karachi for two reasons: one to be agreeable to Mr Wadia and allow his Captain to complete his commercial venture and two, it would also make it difficult for Hymison to find us. Perkin's explained we had three 'suggested' ways to conduct the expedition: one to go to Persia and proceed from there; second to journey up to Afghanistaun and depart from there; or an even a third more fanciful submission that we begin our excursion from far Kashagare[2]. It was, of course, our intention to go with the suggestion made by London and to ignore the recommendations for Afghanistaun and elsewhere, which had come mainly from the HEIC. It was hoped that the disagreeable Mr Hymison would only know about the directive from the Honourable East India Company to proceed by the latter two.

There is no specific image of the horse transport Hormuzeer that Driscol and the expedition took passage on out of Bombay but the ship in the centre of this drawing may have been very similar to it. Illustration III-XI-1

Bannington added at this time that he knew of this Hymison, for he and his mother were cousins; Distant ones fortunately, but he did not consider him a relative of his by his own choice! He was, as Bannington said, a 'bad sort', a trouble maker and no gentleman and he did agree that his family connections could, if utilised in a political manner cause difficulties for us.

Perkin's added that it was his wish to avoid getting London and Calcutta involved in a long, distant and time-devouring exchange of letters[3]. We would make our way to Bushire, a port of Persia on the Persian Gulf. From there, we hoped to obtain leave from the Government of the Shah to enter his territory for this undertaking, travel to Teheran and then, based on advice from the ambassador, the members of the British Army training mission then in Persia, and the natives, make our way to the Persian frontier and enter Tartary.

This last part was met with three cheers. Beer and champagne were produced from a basket hung over the side where it was somewhat cooler. I had some water from the Le Hunte bag. Perkins produced his papers and every man read them in case we became separated or, heaven forbid, suffered losses during our travels. All were impressed by those men who had 'signed off' on our journey most notably the King, Lord Wellington and others.

It was early evening when a steady wind arose and, with a large number of other craft, we left Bombay behind. My last sight of it was of the signal tower on Malabar Hill. I realised that while I found India at times depressing due to the press of people and its squalor, I also found it fascinating.

Our dinner that night was goat kebabs with rice, flavoured with onions, garlic and God only knows what spices. Our *bewarchee {cook}* was a talented man and we watched him at his task. It was a promising beginning.

Horne took me aside at one point to tell me the momentous news from the battery. Much had occurred in the few days I was not there. Most were of trivial nature, for Horne thought a bout of shouting between sergeants or a fistfight amongst the men to be of great importance but I did not. However, the last item WAS both momentous and decidedly strange.

Masson, Ensign Masson, our housemate and fellow battery officer, whom I had never met had fallen into extreme disflavour at the Fort William's Language school *{in Calcutta}*. This was firstly due to his poor performance and secondly by the strange occurrence of him not knowing a man he should have known from his time at Haileybury before transferring to Addiscombe. It was now thought that he had been a 'replacement man' or 'purchase man[4]' who had taken up the name. The man had been placed under house arrest, under the parole of his word, while being investigated. He had proven he was no gentleman, for he had disappeared. These things had happened in late February.

Mrs Hoary had been informed and Masson's property removed from the house to the battery - she could of course keep his paid rent. His Bibi was distraught of course, and I could imagine the scenes there for Jonaki was close to her sister. For the first time I was happy to not be there.

We all decided that the deck was the place to sleep, but during the night, Perkins, Horne, Vickery Michaelson and Dobbins became seasick; Bannington, Dissanayake, and I remained unaffected. Some of the horses were affected also and they too were sick. Sour hay is not well smelt in the early morning and our grooms were kept busy seeing to the comfort of ours and the ship's cargo horses. Blonde did well and I kept her well satisfied with carrots and the small onions she favoured.

Bannington brought out his lovely double rifle for us to view. It was a thing of absolute beauty and the finest looking gun I had ever seen, an admirable Holland & Holland, double barreled, percussion rifle. It was finished in the best style possible. We took turns handling it and Dobbins, even in his illness, announced it the most exceptional gun he had ever seen. He turned somewhat greener when told its price. I noted that such a fine weapon should be kept in a velvet-lined box and a locked cabinet. Bannington's reply was that his family had gifted him with it before his departure from England with the admonishment to use it well; they wished to have him back and not a well preserved weapon.

So, with vomiting horses and men, we made our way at 4½ knots to the north-west, headed for the Indus River delta.

Another possible image of what the ship carrying Driscol may have looked like. A common French style brig seen at night. Illustration III-XI-2

[Editor's note: I will now interrupt Driscol's journey to suggest to the good reader that he next reads a brief document written, I believe, by Driscol and Perkins and containing what was known of Tartary, and the reason for the expedition. This was edited by Father Brennan, so how much of this document is his, and how much is Driscol's and Perkins' is not presently known. It seems to have come from material contained within the journals lost at sea with Father Brennan. It came to me as a yellowed, folded, brittle and laboriously typed document, made in early 1941. The good Father had many worthy and upright qualities, but as a typist, he was lamentable incapable. See Appendix supplement one page 1100]

The Crew Of The *Hormuzeer*

Today is my first anniversary of my entry into the army. We have sixteen hundred miles to go to Bushire, Persia *{Bushehr, Iran}* the wind had died during the night leaving the ship to wallow in the swell leading to an increase in seasickness. Horne declared in his distress that on the completion of the expedition he would ride back from Persia to India. Several other sufferers of Neptune's upset supported this idea.

Perkins remarked to all that he was quite pleased to have quitted Bombay, as the politics there had made him uneasy. He never knew, when speaking to an official, if he was the man of Hymison and whether he would help or hinder.

This drawing by Perkins reflected his view of his passage among the hallways of power; and having met the King and those who were the powers behind the throne and parliament, he felt like a 'baby midst poisonously opinionated cobras', even more so when dealing with the officialdom of the Honourable East India Company. Illustration III-XI-3

By mid-morning, a steady breath of air, a strong sun and numerous native craft laid out provided us with a magnificent vista to enjoy as we made a steady six knots on our course. The Hormuzeer is a lively craft and therefore a dullard of a horse transport. She had been built at the Wadia yard of teak. That oleaginous wood is very durable and while this ship is some thirty years old she seems very shipshape to me. Perhaps any deterioration being hidden by layers of paint for this ship, unusual for an Eastern vessel, is freshly and correctly painted. I asked the Captain why she had a European's brig rig instead of a native one. He noted that being a brig announced his ship to be European - even if it officially was not - and therefore kept pirates away. The ship is just a bit younger than her Captain who I might add was neither covered in paint nor dirt and grime, a rare sight among native seamen. He did instead, have plenty of body art done in black ink which mainly took the form of swirls and other scroll work.

Dissanayake, Bannington and I enjoy a late breakfast, taken at the stern with our Captain to avoid upsetting our seasick passengers. Vickery joins us, having recovered somewhat, but he does not join us in our repast of chutney, un-leavened bread and fruit. The language of the crew is Urdu, which Bannington can speak to a certain level of competence, as he described it. He knows only a few hundred words, but they are enough to gain a great deal of information on the ship and crew, by listening to the words being thrown about.

We study our Persian; nothing is better for those who are seasick than to practise constructing sentences in Persian. We discuss the subject-verb-object *{SVO}* change in Persian, which is subject-object-verb *{SOV}* distinct from English and many other languages. Dissanayake brought up the matter of which was used in the language of the Bible. Hebrew is VSO and Greek is SVO like English. The discussion then changed, when Michaelson noted that Jesus probably spoke Aramaic which was SVO. A long debate followed over whether Jesus spoke Hebrew or Aramaic, it being decided by democratic vote that he spoke both and perhaps some Greek and Latin too. I was glad to see that debate, while spirited, was conducted in a proper manner and no bruises were left, for we would be together for some time and no rifts must be allowed to grow.

We denounced Michaelson for having no elixir to cure Neptune's contagion. He remarked contemplatively that if he did, he would be very rich and eating at this moment in a restaurant on the *Ile de la cite {an island on the Seine in Paris}*.

We found out tonight that I was not the worst snorer for Dissanayake and Bannington sounded like mills cutting iron bars with blunt blades. This can be troublesome, as at night a snore can bring raiders down on you, just like a lit fire.

Monday 10 April

We are passing the Gulf of Khambhat and our good *Nakhoda {captain}* or Muharram is a Gujarati of about forty years of age and without question a man of the sea. He speaks his own language, Urdu, some English, Hindustani and Arabic. He and Bannington are the same height, and as his Lordship can speak the same language, they, as all smaller men who are in the presence of larger men, become instant companions. Whit Monday.

[Editor's note: Driscol wrote the following later in the voyage but it seems more appropriate to place it here]

The rest of his eighteen crewmen may be divided into seven classes, though, it must be admitted, could be further divided if one took into consideration each individual's place of birth and method of upbringing.

Purwarries: two men, they are called the *Goomtee*. These poor fellows hold the lowest jobs aboard the ship. They are not quite untouchables or classless men but are beheld with contempt by the Hindoos aboard. It is their duty to carry burdens, clean the heads *{Toilets}*, sweep and mop the deck, butcher animals for us - a great sin for a Hindoo - and to bring up the anchor from the depth - they do this as the other Hindoo hold that there is a great chance of a demon or two being attached to the said anchor. The Muhammadans, on the other hand, do not raise the anchor, as it is just too hard a piece of work for them. Both Purwarries are strong, well-formed lads and cheerful. They are friendly with the non-Hindoos, and it is said that most Muhammadans in India were once of this class. When they convert or revert as the followers of the Arabian prophet call it, they go from being the lowest of the low to having a rough equality with the others with whom they nestle together within the warm bosom of Islam.

The Purwaries who did the duty of the Goomtee or the unpleasant tasks of the ship. Illustration III-XI-4

Catholic from Malabar: a single man of whom I knew little about as he was tight-lipped. He was our cook and appeared to have come from a lower-class of Hindoo. He was remarkably clean but much too fond of drink, and when not cooking, is seen to be talking to himself in the tongue of Malabar and drinking from his own supply of

liquor. He spoke Urdu badly and some other private gabble-twaddle beside his proposed Malabar language, although we could never determine what language it was nor would he tell us. He was, what is called, 'a follower of the Malabar rites of Popery'. This was the name given to certain heathen and superstitious practices, which the Jesuits of past at the Madura, Carnatic, and Mysore Missions permitted to their converts. It is the inclusion of these Hindoo rituals and beliefs into Eastern popery that adds greatly to the mighty canon of error that holds these poor souls in the land of errant men.

One of the two Gujarati sailors who act as the Sukangeer or helmsmen. Illustration III-XI-5

A Bombay Jew: who looks and dresses like the others, if slightly finer, although he has a paler, smoother and clearer skin. We found he was of the Jewish religion only when told so by the first mate, for we had thought him a Hindoo by his dress. He was a singular fellow, liking strong drink like the solitary Christian, but without the strong pride and insolence of some of the Mussulmen. He spoke Mahrati and came from the Jewish clan known as Bene Israel. He does, by agreement with the others, no work on Saturday, his Shabbat day, but does double duty on Friday during the times of the Mussulmen's prayers. He acts as the *Nakhoda-Knesheb* cargo master, *Keranee {Clerk}* and *Bhandaree* or purser. Because of this, the others called him Shanivar *{Saturday}* and he has a fine sense of humour. He holds all these positions due to his being the only man aboard who can read and write, and in four languages: Arabic, Persian, Urdu and Hindustani. His Persian is 'commerce' Persian and rough in speaking, but he can read it quite well as we tested him on this. During this, we observed he had an affliction and Michaelson removed a carbuncle from his foot, which made him the surgeon's friend for life.

Six Mussulmen: three each *Shoonee {Sunni}* and *Sheea {Shia}*, like many others of this religion, we find them bigoted, being openly contemptuous of the Hindoos. By contrast , the are more accepting of the Christian and the Jew, but often intolerant and vain. They are active stout men. Born seamen, they come from seacoast villages to the north-west of Bombay, and they speak Gujarati, Mahrati and Urdu; none speak more than a few words of Arabic or Persian. One of these is Tahir a Soonee who is the *Maullim {First Mate}* of the ship. One of the Shia, Saish is the Tundeil or Second Mate and chief of the seamen.

Purdeesses seamen. Illustration III-XI-6

Two Gujarati Hindoo men: koolies they are called, both were tall, nearly six feet, thin with fair skin with stout muscles. They were well made and of cheerful dispositions, were abstinent of all vices and the two best seamen aboard. They knew only their own language and Urdu. They are prized Sukangeer *{Helmsmen}* and one of them is always at the helm.

Three Mahrati *Kerhwah:* these are sons of the soil. They were like landsmen in our fleets, doing the heavy tasks well and following the directions of the

757

First Mate and the Gujarati men. They are not good top men, but like their horse-mounted brethren ashore, they move well and can climb ropes with astounding ease and skill. However, they lack the skills to mend rope and other acts of seamanship. Being of a lower rank within the Hindoo caste system, the sudras or farmers are not burdened by numerous restrictions on what they can and cannot do. They are small, compact, well-sinewed men, all-around good fellows to have aboard, and excellent singers.

The final three fellows were Purdesees or 'foreigners' Hindoos: Despite being from families who had lived on the West Coast for, quite possibly, centuries, their origins on the East Coast led them to being called foreigners.

Of a sailor class called the *Khelasses*, they have mild dispositions, are handsome men with clear features, the blackest hair and darkish skin. They have about them a romantic air and often rest their hands on their hips in a cavalier stance. They are sometimes referred to as Lascars, but that term is more correctly assigned to the southern men of India who are even darker and smaller. One is the ship's carpenter, another sail maker, and the third is our rope man.

That then is our crew: a likely looking group of men. The crew did have one trait I found disconcerting. The crew would sit quietly in great vacuity when not tending to the ships or other duties, while at other times they would chatter amongst themselves in Urdu and other tongues. It was in those quiet times, I thought them like dolls or toys, for they could sit unmoving, eyes staring straight ahead and doing nothing for several hours.

On Moons, Night Walkers And Karachi

The Hindoos of the crew conducted a religious service this night in the stern worshipping Chandra *{The Moon}* in some noisy fashion. In my imagination, I could hear and see them as a form of fantastical penumbra fanned by the fleeting shadows. We could see glimpses of movement from their fires and lamps; scents of incense wafted back to us, and I could imagine them committing a human sacrifice to some gory nocturnal goddess.

Our moon, which in England inspires lovers and poets, would fail in producing such effects in these seas. Its glare there is considered to be painful and dangerous and communicates feelings so disagreeable, that at night, a native may be observed sheltering himself from its rays with the same care as we would in the day from those of the sun. The effect of lunar rays, it is said by them, in producing the speedy decomposition of fish and animal substances has never, as far as I know, been explained scientifically. It is a fact that all who have been in the East and West Indies can bear testimony to these occurrences and singularities. These same rays sponsor the creation of new creatures by anomalous or equivocal generation *{spontaneous generation}*.

Michaelson disagreed, saying that experiments have been done showing that the theory of spontaneity of creation *{sic}* was not the correct line of thought on the corruption of flesh and the rise of new life. He spoke of the experiments of Lazzaro Spallanzani[5], which had given rise to doubts about these theories. I considered his reasoning fine and must probe this at another time.

That night, I observed Bannington securing his foot by a cord to his sleeping mattress. I had to ask why and he sheepishly observed that on occasion he would sleep walk and, that by tying one foot down, he had found that this would wake him, as it would impede his motion.

Tuesday 11 April

The Gulf of Kachch: Michaelson, looking to be more relaxed, as his duty ashore had been one unrelenting fight against disease, has slept long into the morning. I did bother him to look at one complaint I had for some months, nearly from the day I had set aboard the ship in London. A small red dot had appeared on my left ear between the antihelix and the fold of the same name. It had grown slowly and now I could feel it. It had, on the back part of the ear, protruded out and was hard and becoming both redder and more painful. He examined it and thought it best to lance it. He did so and the most disgusting thing occurred. The pressure and the pain ceased instantly after the flare of the steel thrust and the sharp pain from the penetration. From the spot sprang a curled and twisted hair some six inches long, slick with yellow puss and blood, so tightly packed had it been in that sixteenth of an inch mound. He pronounced it an ingrown hair and of no consequence. I apologised, nonetheless, for having put him through it, but he said that in the last weeks he had removed a dead foetus *{fetus}* and cut off gangrenous toes - this was but a trifle and he was glad to serve.

Michaelson then did a round of inspections on the crew, fixing a number of small medical emergencies and removing one tooth from the First Mate. He had the head of one of the Gujarati seaman shaved to remove head lice and performed a number of other valuable medical interventions. He also removed some burrowing worms from the leg of Vickery's horse-rat *{Horse-rat more of Driscol's humor}*.

Wednesday 12 April

A day spent at sea. We exercise the horses by walking them up and down the lower deck. Blonde, I can see, is glad to see me. We increased their grain a little that day and I gave Blonde her favourite of a carrot with a lump of *gur {a portion of Indian cane sugar}.* We are all recovered now from the seasickness that took some of the expedition, all are good sailors now, if only Landsmen.

Thursday 13 April

We arrive at the mouth of the Indus, where for some hours; light winds frustrate our attempts to move toward Karachi, which is just over the horizon. Persian and Arabic practice; Ah for a proper steam engine!

The entrance to Karachi in the moonlight. Illustration III-XI-7

Friday 14 April

As morning broke, Karachi appeared to us out of the morning mist. As Sol rose on our right hand, we knew we were in the outflow of the Indus and still at a distance of some miles from Karachi. To us, it initially appears merely as a larger island amongst several others, but we soon sighted a white tomb and the western fort. This town of twelve thousand is located at 24° 46' north and 66° 55' East. The land's colour is an off-silvery, bleached white. It rises to a considerable height beyond the shore, and some further distance away, a larger chain of hills stretches from west by north. The land around the harbour, however, is mainly *aik drakht {Urdu for mangrove}* swamp.

We were making some eight knots with a quartering *brisa,* a Spanish term I had heard for a waft of wind, *{By the 20ᵗʰ century the word Brisa would become Breeze and enter the language}* and we were soon past the outer bar at high tide with two or more fathoms of water beneath us. We anchored quite smartly, the Captain bringing the fore sails about to halt our progress and skew us into his favoured anchorage. The town is three to four miles away up a small creek.

The western fort was built by the rulers of Bahrein *{Emir of Bahrain}* and King of Muskat, when they traded with this city. The old fort is of unusual construction and is framed by palm trees, which gives it an un-military character. It shows to the seafront a curtain wall of little strength, but every seventy feet there is a cone-shaped tower, larger at the base and narrowing to the top, where only a single piece of artillery can be accommodated. A large square tower stands to guard a gate to the land entrance, which is connected by an eight-mile long sand spit to the mainland. Near the fort is a small fishing village called Salehabad. To the East of the fort are three rocky islands of fantastic shapes, one being a pyramid. Even the ancient Macedonians, when they were here 2,000 years before, mentioned them. They called this place Krokola and here they prepared their fleet to return to Babylon, led by Admiral Nearchus.

The actual coastline is a monotonous, low-lying, green, line and to the north of us, are low, sandy hills, covered by creepers and short grasses. Beyond that, the Captain said, was more mangroves,

that salt-water loving tree, which grows in the low-lying swamps surrounding the town.

Mangrove swamps near Karachi where Driscol noted Cormorant nests. Illustration III-XI-8

The Captain asked us to accompany him into the town, and taking the larger of the two ship's boats, we proceeded to shore. We found an entrance to the Chinna Creek passage that goes through the mangrove swamp. The swamp was only a few feet deep and alive with riparian life, white birds, plentiful fish and all manner of other sea creatures; I could see large crabs sitting on the mangrove and viewing us with some distaste, I must say.

We sighted some Cormorant nests and those of many other birds, which at this time of year are laying their eggs. From these sightings arose a debate as to what some of the species were; the names bandied about were: sand larks, sand plovers, sand pipers, button quail, sand martins, kingfishers, river terns, common snipe *{Gallinago gallinago}*, and little stints *{Calidris minuta}*.

As with most Mohammedan towns, the first sight of the town is a minaret associated with a red brick mosque. Beyond 'Kurrachee town', as the Captain calls it, is a Faheer tank *{the meaning of this term is unknown}* and the ruins of the English factory *{trading post}*. The factory had been built here in 1799 but closed down after disputes with the rulers of this land.

The fishermen carry out their occupation, not from boats, but by lying atop a large squat earthen pot called a *mati*. They float upon these *mati*, and from them, they hunt for *tenualosa ilisha*, a type of freshwater shad. This type of fishing is called *Pala*. When a fish is caught, it is placed into the pot beneath them.

We were all in civilian dress. I had of course brought my pistol, but the Captain advised against bringing any long arms with us. He was to meet with a representative of the ruler here to complete the transaction over the matched eight horses he carried. The bazaar was covered by a roof of wood, daubed with mud and thatch, which covered a bustling trading space.

Karachi fisherman who float on special pots to catch fish. Illustration III-XI-9

Here one could obtain almonds, cattle, copperware, cotton, dates, ghee *{clarified butter}*, goats, hides, oils, pepper, raisins, rice, sugar and all the spices of India and further East. It was here that we saw both kinds of sheep for sale, British and Asiatic.

The people were civil and would smile when we greeted them in Arabic for they knew the basic

BRITISH.   ASIATIC.

words of the language; Bannington did better speaking his Urdu.

The difference between British and Asiatic sheep. Illustration III-XI-10

Their headdress is peculiar; the men wear an odd piece of headgear which looks like one of the new experimental, rimmed metal cartridges set atop their heads: a stove pipe with a thin flattening at the top. It is made of a species of thick paper and is painted, or covered with cloth. I thought it ridiculous, as it did not shade the eyes from the pitiless sun. We saw no women, but those enveloped in a fully encompassing 'bag'; the men wore a pair of loose muslin trowsers and a short colourless tunic. Over the tunic, when in the open air, they wear - no matter how stifling - a thick kind of shawl, which they throw around them, like an Iberian, wears his cloak.

The water is indifferent, and I suggested that Horne lead expeditions inland to obtain some, which led to him having to tell his story about getting water at Mokka, to the delight of all. The Captain had left us in the market, but all the men had seen such sights before. He returned with the agent of his buyer, who was Mir Ali Murad, a brother of the present ruler. As he made these arrangements, we walked out to the ruins of the English factory followed by the family and supporters of the purchaser's agent. As they talked, we discussed what we knew of this ruler and it was not favourable. The present town owes allegiance to the Talpur rulers of Sindh, who overthrew the earlier rulers of the Kalhoro Dynasty at the battle of Halani in 1783. Taxation, which had paid for that matched team of horses, fell heavily on the trade here, but the farmers were especially squeezed. We found from those about us that, while the Indus River provided copious water brought to the fields by the use of the Persian wheels, no grain was grown for the reason that the cultivator would gain but 25% of the profit; the rest was seized for the use of the ruler. I am sad to say that the terms, 'good governance' and 'a happy people' are not used here.

Finally, a deal was reached. A great shout went up and many muskets were fired into the air. As they fired, I did calculations on whether the balls would come down and strike us. I decided that, since they were being canted at all angles, this was improbable.

Having exercised ourselves and sweated off $^1/_5$ of a stone's weight in water, we made our way back and watched for a time as the sold horses were delivered by the casual method of driving them into the sea and having them swim, by instinct, to shore. Considering the presence of sharks, I thought this a poor way to do business. Yet it was a hamfatter's *{inexpert or amateurish}* performance worth viewing. We then made our way back to our ship and were glad that we would not be departing here to start our expedition.

A hand drawn map of Karachi Harbor by Alexander Baillie & Lieutenant Garless from the year after the Perkins expedition passed that way.
Illustration III-XI-11

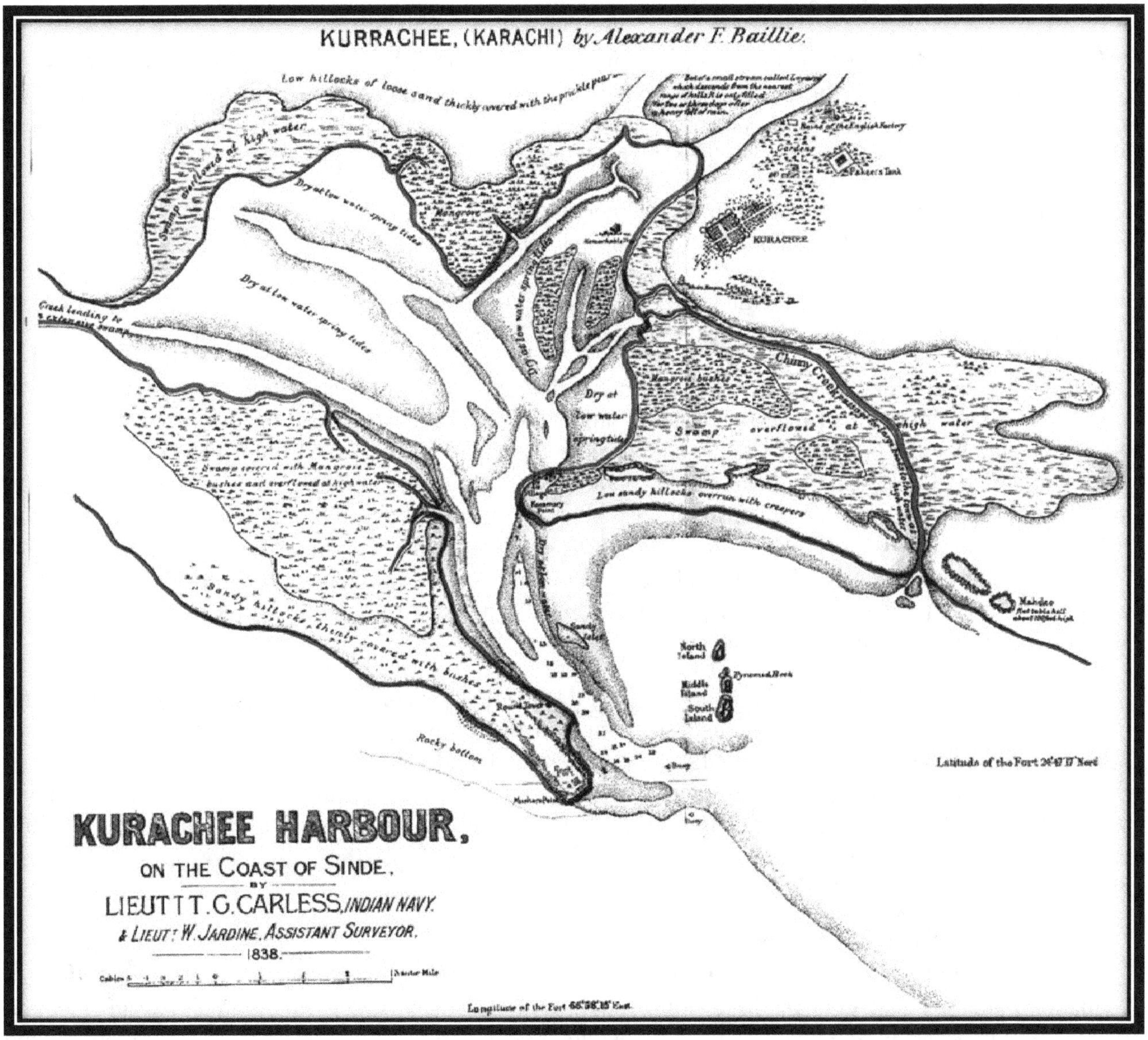

KURRACHEE, (KARACHI) *by Alexander F. Baillie.*

KURACHEE HARBOUR,
ON THE COAST OF SINDE,
BY
LIEUT. T.G.CARLESS, *INDIAN NAVY.*
& LIEUT. W.JARDINE, ASSISTANT SURVEYOR.
1838.

Dissanayake Hero of Obscurations and Befuddlements

Dissanayake was an interesting fellow, I must say, and our first characterisation of him as a dull blade was mistaken. He had no idea how to fence having never held a sword before, not even having swished about with a branch as a child. He had rarely fired a weapon, but his mind was keen to a frightful degree. Therefore, he gladly took up the task to learn these arts while, at the same time, he told us the secrets of officialdom and paper shuffling.

He explained that when he received a written directive from his superiors, who were a thousand or more miles away, that he did not agree with, or which would take up too much of his time, he simply threw it away. A month or more would pass, before a query would come along asking about his progress, on the matter with which he had dealt in such a perfunctory way earlier.

[Editor's note: Driscol wrote the word 'proscripously' regrettably there is no such word so I have no idea what he meant. I have instead placed 'perfunctory' as a replacement]

He would reply that he knew nothing of the matter and month or more would pass, as it took at least that time for the posts, or a messenger to move from his location to Calcutta and back.

Dissanayake would then receive a letter saying that on said date one *{native name unreadable}* assistant to him had signed for such a letter and what had become of it? He would reply that that assistant had been a blackguard and scoundrel, and had been dismissed from his service, and he knew nothing of the document in question. A month or two would go by and a new version of the same request would arrive, again signed for by his native assistant, who by arrangement changed his name every month or so, when signing for arrivals. He would then wait a few weeks before replying, indignantly, that he had completed this task sometime before and sent it to Mr X on such and such a date. Several more months would pass, and a letter would come saying that Mr X knew nothing about that document.

He would then reply after a month or so, that Mr X most certainly DID have the document, and that, unfortunately, due to the refusal of headquarters to approve his budget request for an insect-proof container, that white ants *{termites}* had eaten his original and the second copy of the letter of instruction, and could they send another? By this method, nine months or a year would be taken up and, by that time, the man making the request would either have been promoted, died of fever, or returned to England, and the matter would be dropped, all to Dissanayake's great satisfaction.

For such demonstrated valour on the fighting fields of administration and civil obstruction, we awarded him, that evening, the roasted eyes of our supper goat. He declined to eat them however, requesting instead instructions, in writing, on how to eat said eyes, the quoted paragraph, and queue of the order that mandated such. Plus, he wished to see the oath of office taken by the man making the request, and he also wished to query the suitability and authority of said requester for making such a presumptuous demand. Vickery and Dobbins ate them with gusto and Dissanayake contented himself with the tenderloin.

As we ate, our man of the hour, Dissanayake, told us also how his first supervisor in India had noted in writing that he was, 'too odd and too practical in nature to ensure the prosperity of this department'. He laughed a little too loud and too long over that confession once said.

The ship remained in harbour during the rest of the day waiting for its return cargo. Perkins told the Captain that we would delay our own departure to shore also.

Two gentlemen of Karachi with the 'bullet' hats Driscol found very diverting. Illustration III-XI-12

Saturday 15 April

In the morning, Perkins handed his letter to the Captain who took this change to his orders in his stride. He provided Perkins with a military salute for now, by the direction of the owner of the ship, Mr Wadia, Perkins was its commander for the rest of the voyage - and no we would not being off-loading here. I was amazed the Captain could read. He had only been told he was going to Karachi to deliver us, and then on to a port on the Trucial coast and not Bushire.

Having taken on a boatload of fruit, then several hundred and score jars of vinegar, we prepared to depart from Karachi. Our Captain said, with a longer journey ahead, and given the prices of provisions on the Trucial coast, that he would like to stop along the nearer coast at another location where cheaper supplies could be had.

A fresh water carp caught by Driscol in Karachi harbour. Illustration III-XI-13

When questioned why he could not do so here in Karachi, he explained that at the next port he was owed a large amount on credit, while here he must pay with silver, which he did not have. Perkins advised him that he had 500 silver rupees, but the Captain thought it best to go to the next port, as feed for our horses could be more easily obtained there, and so we agreed.

Besides men in comic hats, a demonstration of swimming horses and lots of flies, there was little to cause one to care for this place.

We did some fishing, practiced Persian and took lessons from one another on fencing. I caught a lovely fish, a Barbus Tor, a type of carp. *{Probably a Barbus Khudree described by Sykes, 1839}*

An off shore whiff of wind sprang up, as if by order, and we left behind Karachi, thankfully. We made our way back out into the Arabian Sea and, steering due west, we joined the stream of native craft with the same heading. So filled was the sea with trade, that we were rarely out of sight of another craft during the rest of the day. We did more fencing and Persian adjectives.

Sunday 16 April

We instituted a new regime with King-Admiral Perkins in charge. His only order of the day was that for each day, a 'scape-goat' officer be named, based on a roster maintained by Vickery. This exalted man would act as the 'officer of the day' and deal with the necessary tasks of maintaining our existence aboard the ship. He would also be blamed for anything that went wrong - any wave over the bow, a lack of wind, a spill, a poorly cooked cut of meat or a paper cut. All difficulties would be his to solve, explain, and most assuredly, ensure that they did not happen again, on pain of mockery being directed at him. The first on the list was picked by cutting cards, and I lost, but exchanged my duty with Dobbins, whom I bribed with a vial of ink scented with magnolia, given me as a gift. We believed he desired this so he might write fragrant letters of love to Miss Penelope - a charge he blushed at.

As it was Dobbins in charge, our day was thus one of training and exercise. First off was pugilism, the *Pygmachia {fist fighting}* of the Greeks. Dobbins was familiar with Broughton's[6] rules

and had with him three pairs of mufflers *{padded gloves}*. Perkins pulled rank and modified the rules - no hits above the neck, his perfect face must be preserved.

Bannington engages what may be Horne in some boxing. Illustration III-XI-14

I had no skill at this form of exercise at all, and had had my last fight when I was nine, which I won against my classmate Tolbert Smith, by kicking him rather hard where my mother said I should never kick anyone. I remember it was over his attentions towards the lovely Sally Turtle. She, being feckless, ceased to be my friend from that moment until she forgave me a few years later.

After several hours, we had established our pecking order in the manner of fist fighting.

Dobbins of course, with his powerful frame was first but Horne could, and did, give him quite a beating, as he was nearly half as strong and quicker.

Perkins surprisingly, was next. He had some skill with this art. Bannington was very good too, having a combination of punches to the stomach that was hard to counter, and was small and quick. It was Michaelson who surprised us all in man-to-man combat. He had French training and could avoid both Dobbins and Horne quite well and deliver some good blows too. However, he had a weak stomach and would lose his breath easily if hit there. Dissanayake also was fairly good, being hard to hit as he moved well. The rest of us were just not very good at this action *{that would have been him and Vickery}*.

Michaelson took to teaching us some of the moves of *Savate,* the French art of kicking. He declined a match against Dobbins, fist versus feet, as he felt someone would be injured - mainly him - and, as he wittily said, he did not trust the assistant surgeon aboard ship to set his broken ribs. We decided one of the un-eaten goats would be said assistant surgeon, should he be deceased or deprived of his senses.

Part of the coastline from Karachi to Gwadar. Illustration III-XI-15

Scape-Goats, Cannons and the Port of Gwadar

Monday 17 April

We drew cards again as Vickery, who had been detailed to keep the 'scape goat' roster, had decreed that it be done by chance each morning, to which all agreed. Everyone drew face cards, and I the three of spades. Oaths and damnation!

We continued that day with Savate and boxing training, made more interesting by the movement of the boat in the sea. That afternoon, I took them though cannon drill with the ship's diminutive 18-pounder carronade, which weighs $\frac{1}{4}$ of a full sized gun. I found that our good Captain, while a good seaman, was not so good at keeping his artillery in the best of shape; two of the carronades had stopped vents, which I quickly fixed. His breech bolt on another was cracked and for that, I could do nothing. Nor could I do anything about a marring to the elevation bolt of another that would limit its up and down motion: affecting its effective range. They were of the 1809 model, so not hopelessly obsolete, but nearly so. Still, against a native craft at one hundred yards, they would slash and smash through both sides without any great difficulty, if we could, by God's good grace, hit them.

There was only enough equipment, rammers and other tools, to man three of the four guns with a full complement. I silently cursed myself for my slipshod inspection, which I had made a week earlier.

The ship's obsolete 18-pounder carronades. Illustration III-XI-16

We carried per gun: 28 round shot, 5 bar shot, 10 double-headed shot[7] and 15 charges of double grapeshot *{36 pounds of small shot or musket balls}*. Much to my surprise, they used woolen wadding, which is more expensive than other types, but is a good value, as it reduces the chance of fouling during a fight.

The carronades were mounted on wooden, pivoting slide-pedestals and fixed firmly to the side of the ship. Additionally, ropes were available to secure the gun, if the slide failed.

We did well in our exercises and I had Horne act as my sergeant, a role he is a natural for. It did, however, take us all a bit, to get used to having only a four-man crew, versus the larger crew for a cannon. Four men sufficed, there being no need to haul the gun back into place, as the slide on the carronade was much easier to manage.

With a small bribe to Captain Muharram, we fired one charge, but without a ball, as he was responsible for munitions. Mr Wadia's directions, placing Perkins in charge, did not remove Muharram from caring for the equipment and stores of the ship, even if Perkins was in charge; nor could I convince Perkins to charge the expedition to pay for four, iron, 18 pounder shot.

Bannington, I noted, was quite taken with this exercise, and he found it useful, for as he said, if he ever charged artillery, he could, by watching the evolutions of the crews, tell at what stage of their loading they were at. We, at this point, delved into a discussion on the power of artillery, as

Horne and I had not been covering these carronades with praise. Horne called them 'castrated cannon' and I 'baby guns', and generally we did not treat them with the greatest of respect. Indeed, we alluded to the fact that if they were men, they would have frustrated wives and no children forthcoming.

I advised them that a 6-pounder shot like that from our battery in Bombay, at full charge and hitting a formation of infantry at five hundred yards, would have the following effect: said ball could penetrate nineteen men or six feet of earth or a one foot thick, stone wall. I did not know the exact power of these 18 pounder carronades, which is designed to smash up wooden ships, but I thought despite its 3 x heavier hollow shot, it would penetrate only a half or a third as much. Its utility was in splintering wooden ships at close range, killing the crew with said splinters and allowing smaller ships to carry heavier armaments. I thought the muzzle velocity of the hollow shot fired with 4 pounds of powder, would be around 1200-1400 feet per second and have a range of around 1,000 yards, with an effective range of a quarter of that.

Tuesday 18 April

Arrive off the port of Gwadar[8] or Cape Gwadel or Ras Noo, which forms a peninsula some six miles in length in the form of a giant 'T', the base being only a half a mile in width. On it are stone built ruins of some previous town from an unknown civilization. Beyond it, there is a remarkable cleft in the mountains a few miles inland, which marks this location to the seafarer. There is a good anchorage here, no rocks and a sandy bottom. The shore is rugged but of medium height above the sea.

There is a small village still remaining here and under the sovereignty of a *wali* or governor appointed by the Sultan of Muskat *{Muscat}*. Oman had gained control of the village and the peninsula when, in 1783, said Sultan took refuge in this part of Baluchistan. Here, he appealed for sanctuary from Mir Noori, the Khan of Kalat, who gave him Gwadar for his support and sustenance; there he lived until he returned to his homeland and took over the Sultan's position in Muskat from his own brother.

Once we had anchored, we were approached by small boats, whose occupants knew our Captain, and all was prescribed and jovial. In a few hours, the village's debt to the Captain was paid, and out to us came several boatloads of fresh hay, some bags of millet, plus several additional boatloads of small carpets. The Captain had paid the people last year to produce them, and I must say they are fine indeed. They are of the size known as prayer rugs and each Mohammedan must have one. These carpets are of a type of Persian carpet with the colours of brown and blue predominating and he most kindly insisted we take one for each of us as no gentleman travels without one.

We could not, however, top off our water, as they have little and must dig holes on the shoreline to obtain it. We have two weeks left of water and did not pursue this purchase.

Wednesday 19 April

We depart Gwadar and it is a beautiful day at sea. The water is nearly smooth and calm but a good waft of gusty wind moves us along splendidly. I thought of Millicent and grew very sad, so I forced my thoughts to deal instead with the wanderings of the crew of the Odyssey and of Sindbad's often-frightful voyages.

Thursday 20 April

Blonde, Driscol's horse which he purchased in Bombay and was quite fond of. Illustration III-XI-17

One of the mares came into heat, which makes Perkins's stallion difficult to handle. Later that day Blonde comes into heat also adding to the commotion below deck. Perkins tried to convince me to let nature take its course but I remind him that with an eleven-month gestation period we would be somewhere deep in Tartary when my horse would give birth; no I do not think so. Blonde showed signs of being marish, *{'Swampy' or out of sorts}* so I avoided her. It is also noticeable that Blonde has become the lead mare or boss of the other horses.

Dissanayake again told us of his paper warfare, which crossed into legal matters in one case, and he told us why British judges sitting on the bench in India did not wear the traditional white wigs. He said he had been in a session presenting testimony on a complicated case on native land usage regarding a *disseisee {the correlative, is the party put out of an estate, unlawfully}* and a party's loss of property due to an adverse possession. During this session of the Calcutta High Court, the discussion was warm but the room was hotter still. It was particularly hot, for Dissanayake had insisted on the right of 'closure' that is, closing of all the windows and doors to prevent any possibility of the sensitive case being heard by outsiders. This was his right to do so, but as it was a 101° outside it soon made the interior of the building hotter than a bread oven.

This stifling heat continued until the Chief Justice rose up and threw his sweat soaked periwig to the floor, where it splattered causing sweltering clerks to scatter. All other members of the high court followed his lead, as did all those in the legal profession within the room. Splattering wigs struck the floor. The case was deemed 'un-hearable' and returned to a lower court. Dissanayake's superiors ultimately lost this case, but he personally thought it a victory, for since then, just ten years ago, the practice of NOT wearing the periwig had spread all over British India. This decision, while causing great loss to the manufacturers, *{of periwigs}*, was very much to the comfort of the bar and began the decline of the wearing of wigs in Britain or so our man claimed. None of us had any dealing with the court, so we could not challenge this assertion. Some of us claimed Dissanayake was telling a tale, but as we were on a ship at sea, we could obtain no satisfaction in disputing it!

Amongst the Flotsam and Jetsam of the Sea

Friday 21 April

I was in the bow for I enjoy the up and down motion of the sea, the spray, and the general sense of movement, when I caught sight of something to starboard something that was red.

I could not see it clearly, and Vickery had my binoculars, for he enjoying searching the sea for whales, and I called him to my assistance. He came, and we soon found the source of the red within the sea to be a drowning man.

The Captain put about as, in our discussions, we had passed him by and we soon came up on the poor soul. He could wave weakly at us; it was his red and white head cloth I had seen. He cried weakly '*Allāh Akbar*' as we approached. He was too exhausted to take up the offered rope, so two of the Mohammedan crew jumped in and assisted him to come aboard. He was not only exhausted, but was wounded; having some three spear wounds in his leg, stomach and shoulder. Michaelson soon had him in his care. He was a strong man and spoke with us as he was treated, grimacing at times from the pain.

He was an Arab from Ajman, one of the Trucial coast ports, and spoke Arabic and some Persian. After a half gallon of water, he realised that he was saved from drowning, and wept in happiness as he was alive by a miracle, and he poured out his thanks to us and Allah. He then told us how he had come to be afloat in the middle of the Gulf of Oman. He thought we might be Djinn, as he had never before been in the presence of Englishmen. We fed and watered him as he told his story.

He was on his fourth voyage on a slaver, most recently out of Zanzibar, carrying a cargo of one hundred and forty black wretches to the port of Basra to meet their fates at the head of the Persian Gulf. All were non-Muslims, he insisted repeatedly, as if that would have been some concern to us. They came from a people who would not pay the legal tax *{jizya protection/subjugation tax: if not paid they could be enslaved based on Islamic jurisprudence}* and they were on route to a place of *Khasi* - this word I did not know, but soon heard its meaning - near Baghdad. They had a crew of nineteen, but Allah had forsaken them on entering the Gulf of Oman. The crew was struck down by a terrible illness, which weakened them all, but did not touch their restive cargo. A day later two strokes of misfortune had made a mockery of their control over the slaves. The first misfortune had been a worsening of the disease, disabling many of the crew. The second was that the cargo had included a man who could speak some Arabic and he had overheard his captors discus the slaves' horrible fate: to be castrated and put to heavy labour on sugar cane plantations in the marsh land of the two rivers *{Tigris-Euphrates}*, and that the expected life span of slaves who toiled there was but three years.

This intended destiny caused them to revolt, when they were being fed, as had their forefathers in the Zanj rebellion[9]. In violation of their own rules, the only man strong enough to carry food to the slaves had done so alone and he was seized and torn apart. Before the sickened Arabs could struggle out of the stern cabin the majority of the slaves had risen and a fierce melee occurred. The slaves had not been chained, as Negroes were usually docile once captured, unlike the fierce Gallas and Somalis.

This fearsome fight had turned rapidly against the outnumbered and weakened Arabs. Cannon set up to fire into the revolting slaves had done so killing two dozen, but had not stopped the assault. Finally, the four last Arabs, all wounded, were hemmed in at the stern of their ship. Now, facing death from weapons captured from their own dead companions, in desperation they leaped overboard. Two had drowned, as they could not swim, and another was taken by a great fish; only he, Muhammad, had survived to be rescued by us for, which he was greatly appreciative.

Muhammad saved from the sea from a later image of him made in 1840. Illustration III-XI-18

His name was Muhammad, Muhammad Hassan Ali Al-Sakri, and he claimed to be of good family, despite his disreputable employment. We fed him some more and he slept the rest of the day unbothered by our practice of Persian, an arm wrestling contest won by Dobbins, and several games of chess.

The face of our rescued guest is an elongated circle, the forehead high and flat, the nose prominent and slightly hooked, like that of a Hebrew and with a retreating chin so that his profile is of a rounded aspect. The complexion of this nearly drowned slaver is light, a healthy, milky, coffee colour, more deeply seen around the eyes and neck. His beard is of a deep black hue, worn untrimmed and about a foot long. His eyes are dark brown and bright, deep set beneath his brow and the expression on his visage in general is of one that speaks of harshness and gloominess. His behaviour reflects deeply the general character of this type of coastal Arab. In our long conversation with him, he displayed an utter contempt for all frivolous pursuits, and of what are styled the comforts of life by us.

Dissanayake, seeing Mohammed's earlier distress at not having a Qur'an and with none of the other Muhammadans on board having a copy of their holy book, due to their inability to read Arabic, gave him a spare of his, written in both English and Arabic. This book was an unauthorised reprinting of Gustav Flugel's 1834 Leipzig one, with English on the affronting page.

[Editor's note: I can find no record of such a dual language book being printed, however such a Qur'an may have been printed in German and Arabic, and Driscol misunderstood, or an Arabic-English one printed but now unknown to scholarship]

Dissanayake also asked him, when he awoke if he knew about the General Maritime Treaty of 1820. He did not of course, as he did not know our way of determining years. For us, it was the fourth month and 21st day of 1837. For him, the date was 15th day, first month *{Muharram}* of the year 1253 in the Hijri calendar. Once we had arrived at a common understanding of the date, we found he had no idea about the treaty, or so he said. He *{Dissanayake}* explained that, after an outburst of Arab pirate outrages against Indian sea commerce, the British had come and destroyed several harbours including the one we were headed to, Ras al-Khaimah, in 1809 and again in 1819. The Arabs had then signed the treaty noted above. Muhammad had heard of those attacks, but he knew nothing of a prohibition against taking blacks as slaves, for such was condoned by the Qur'an and therefore no law of man could contravene it.

Our cook made an Arab dish for the man, it was a curious recipe. Our cooks took up some sun dried fish, beat it very small in a mortar, and afterwards sifted it through a fine cloth, formed it into cakes, and then baked it like bread.

This recipe is ancient, for the people of Babylon also prepared their fish in the same manner as Diodorus described.

We tried some of it and only I, for appearances' sake, did not spit it out. Horne, with his Portuguese background of using dried cod in *pasteis de bacalhau*, should have been used to it, but having tasted this food, he remarked that his mother use to restore the dried fish before placing it in the cake. When the cooks and Muhammad went for more, we tossed ours over the side, in a harmonious and unrehearsed disposal, that brought great laughter to us all. The cook believing we had enjoyed them brought us more. Fortunately Muhammad was more than happy to wolf them down for us, and did so with great relish, for a quarter day in the sea had made him hungry.

Saturday 22 April

At about one o'clock in the morning, a gust sprung up from the southward and the Captain told us that we had entered the Strait of Hormuz. He pointed out to us the high land of the Arabian shore, terminating in a lofty and marked peak; it is the land about Cape Musseldom *{Musandam}*. The Hindoos, when they passed the promontory, threw cocoa nuts and fruits into the sea, to secure a propitious voyage, while our Mohammedans offered up a special prayer of the traveller. Our native Christian had a drink and our dour Hebrew had a nap. We had curried chicken for our tiffin. While eating these, Dobbins, who was talking in earnest with Dissanayake, brought us all into their conversation. He related something he had learned when he fought in the Caffre war *{Kaffir war}* and which would have some bearing on our expedition's success in Tartary.

> In the course of a trial that took place in Caffreland, it was stated that to seize the cattle of a native chief, under any pretence, was, according to Cafferene custom, a declaration of war. This throws light on the commencement of the late war, which broke out immediately after the seizure of a chief's cattle by Lieutenant Sutton, who did so based on a warrant, produced by a magistrate, to compensate a settler whose cattle had been stolen by persons unknown. This shows the importance of studying the customs of one's neighbours.

We conducted musket and rifle firing; Bannington is a superb shot while Dissanayake cannot hit the ocean.

The chess games continue: I defeated Horne and was then placed against Michaelson who I narrowly defeated having only a rook, two pawns and my queen left. I was then defeated by our champion, Bannington, who destroyed me with a clever trap, that cost me two bishops and my queen, and from that disaster I could not recover. Bannington is crowned our king of chess.

This day, I also draw the card for scapegoat - again - for tomorrow. I suspect mischievousness with the cards.

Sunday 23 April

We pass nearly a hundred small ships this day: none of which pay any attention to us. We fly three flags: that of England, the Company and the Wadia family flag, which is of yellow with a

Parsee symbol in the centre, and a green and red stripe at the right end. The first commands fear, the second respect, and the third envy.

Muhammad, our sea guest, is made our tool this day, and we practice our Arabic on him. He is still weak but does his best to keep up with our questions; even asking some in return.

We practice loading bar shot into the carronades.

The moon was up tonight, and I drew many a picture of her, thinking of faces, real and imagined, from Eccles. Driscol often drew pyramids and placed within them faces. At this point in his journey he did something different he placed a large amount of circles with faces. See the ornament below.

The Home of Pirates, Past and Present?

Monday 24 April

Arrive off Ras al Khaimah at 28° 48' north 56° 4' East. We found that Captain Sealey of the Bombay Artillery made it 56° 0' East in 1819.

[Editor's note: for once Perkins and Driscol did a poor job in taking their positional sight. The actual location for the modern city is 25°47' N 55°57'E Althogh the location may have changed somewhat in two hundred years, our heroes put the city some seven miles inland!]

As you come into the port, you see the ruins of an earlier town located on a sandpit. This was destroyed by our forces, after the town had become infamous for being a harbour used by the Joasmee pirates to harry Indian commerce, when the local Arabs took up the bloody red flag of piracy. It had been condemned, and twice attacked, by British forces in 1809 and again in 1819. The present ruler is said to be Sheikh Sultan Bin Saqr Al Qasimi a vassal of the Sheikh of Sharga {Sharjah} a seaport further south.

Ras Al-Khaimah.
Illustration III-XI-19

Ras al Khaimah, or the place of tents, is built on a low, sandy, projecting peninsula, about three-fourths of a mile in length, with its breadth not exceeding a quarter of a mile. The town has around it a high wall, flanked by several towers extending along the sea-coast.

The harbour is formed by this peninsula and the opposite shore. It is about half a mile broad, with a bar at the entrance, only admitting vessels at high-water. There were some twenty native craft in the road outside the town. When any danger threatens the town, they bring their vessels up onto the shore.

The town now consists of a collection of poor dwellings. These 'houses' are no more than huts made of palm leaves; the hue of both differs but little from the surrounding desert.

Beyond the town are extensive groves of date-trees; this is their main source of wealth and the location of their water source. Beyond them, at a greater distance, runs a range of mountains, elevated to $\frac{3}{4}$ of a mile. At the termination of the high land beyond the town, on the Arab side, are low hills, and to the south a low, flat, sandy shore. There is scarcely a hill intervening until one arrives at the Syrian and Taurus ranges, a distance of a thousand miles.

This was a former home of pirates, and from the Captain we found that, in his opinion, it still was. Indeed, he had a long list of complaints and stories about these pirates who studiously avoid attacking any ship carrying the flags we did.

He told of Indian craft not so protected by said flags, or those who falsely carry them and whose fabrications are found out. When captured, the pirates conduct a ceremony designed to hide their devilment. They do this with horrid solemnity, which gives the deed the appearance of some hellish religious rite. After a ship is taken, she is purified with water and with perfumes. The crew is then led forward singly to the bow, their heads are placed on the gunwale, and their throats cut. All this happens with the same exclamation used in battle of *Allah Akbar* 'God is great'. This was known, as some Indians with useful skills, or females are taken instead as slaves, and a few had escaped. The Company has so far ignored the claims of piracy still being practiced, as the Company viewed military expeditions as expensive and generally bad for business.

We asked if his *{Wadia}* ships were ever attacked. He answered no, for he brought the natives of this place what they needed: gunpowder, lead, rice, spices and alcohol. If they were to cause him harm, this would disrupt their supplies of these needed items.

A boat came off and we found they offered supplies of bullocks, fowls, butter and vegetables and at reasonable rates. While the coastal area appears sterile except for, in the distance, thin and scattered date plantations, the interior is fruitful and provides for the wants of the inhabitants. It is recorded that the custom for the majority of the population is to live by the sea during the 'winter' and inland during the heat of the 'summer'. It is not unknown for snow to fall, briefly, in the mountains of the interior.

From the boats that came out, we found that a nearby ship was one from the home city of our guest Muhammad, and we shipped the poor man over to that ship as soon as we could. He was, I am not afraid to say, a reasonable and fine companion for a slaver, and we shall miss him for his Arabic lessons. He was full of thanks for our saving him, announcing as he left that we were all part of his family and that what was his was ours. Considering he had nothing, his offer was both null and rather un-compelling.

Fencing bout or 'assault' between two members of expedition. Given the thinness of the far competitor it may be Driscol and the other Horne or Perkins. Illustration III-XI-20

The Captain went ashore after suggesting we would find nothing here to interest us. We took that as a warning that it would be safer to keep our British selves aboard ship. We did so, and by late afternoon he returned and we stood out to sea.

We had a fine curry that night, our usually silent cook saying it was one he learned from a fellow cook from Madras. With that speech, our cook

had doubled the amount of words he had previously used.

Fencing practice: Dissanayake still hopeless, Horne and Michaelson have an epic match lasting some minutes before they scored at the same time on one another. Had a bottle of wine, a Cos d'Estournel French Bordeaux, which had been cooled in the sea by lowering it some sixty feet down into the sea on a rope. It was Vickery's opinion that a shark would take it but no, his dark thoughts and wishes were not answered or affirmed.

The Pearling ship with luminous wake. Illustration III-XI-21

Tuesday 25 April

That evening we were treated to a magnificent display of nature's own maritime lights, the entire sea being covered with a pale greenish light. We used a bucket and brought up some of this water and in it we found, after some effort as it was quick and moved to avoid my hand with adroit manoeuvre, a type of insect resembling a woodlouse. It was $^{1}/_{3}$ inch in length; it appeared to be formed by sections of a thin crustaceous substance although under lamplight, it was difficult to ascertain, and while any fluid remained in the creature, it shone brilliantly like a firefly. This was the *Limulus Noctilucas* first described in 1798.

As we discussed this, a fully rigged European ship passed us, clearly showing its luminous wake. Our Captain said it was a Company ship coming from al-Bahrayn {Bahrain} where it had purchased pearls. This ship did so thrice each year and was rightly named the Pearl or in French, *Perle Orientale*. The Captain added that it carried a frigate's armament and a full complement to ward off any pirates who might wish to take hold of their treasure, which he thought might be worth £10,000 Sterling.

[Editor's note: Around one and half million in 2016 USD; however uncultured pearls would be much more valuable now than then]

Michaelson complained mightily tonight about the difficulties of learning Persian. As he notes, the lack of capitals, pauses, sentences, paragraphs, commas, full stops {periods} and other useful things, make it a dreadful nuisance for a new learner to attempt to read.

[Editor's note: Modern Persian, or Farsi uses punctuation but the language as learned by Driscol and his associates did not]

Wednesday 26 April

We sighted the first ships of the Arab pearling fleet. They do not take well to strange ships approaching their pearling beds, both from fear of our poaching their oysters, and also of piracy. It is their season for fishing and three to four thousand 10-50 ton boats come to these shallow seas of four to twelve fathoms in depth. There are three pearling seasons. First, an early one from March to April, after which some ships depart before returning for a second session from August to September. Some pearlers do not bother to leave and stay the entire time. It is said that some sixty five thousand rupees *{£6,000}* or more, in pearls, is taken out each year; many believe it is far higher. Most of the pearls are sold in Bombay and transported around the world. The good captain steered away from this vast armada of ships, when their guard ships headed our way, raising flags and firing blank charges.

The captain mentioned that last year oysters of the same type as in the Gulf had been found off Karachi and a small harvest had taken place.

Thursday 27 April

Another beastly hot day! Caught a six-foot long barracuda, *Sphyraenidae sphyraena*, which we added to the pot. Its face reminded me of one of my childhood friend's grandmothers, like her, it having only one large incisor on the right side of its jaw.

Friday 28 April

Horne very despondent today, he misses his children and bibi. He had been considering abandoning his life in Europe and marrying Catherine *{Catherine May Sajni Hoary daughter of Mrs Hoary and his bibi's sister}*. Not sure why he would he abandon Europe for that, I reminded him that his own mother had not been purely English. Yes, he said, but she had been white. He would not mind staying the rest of his life in India but another complication had arisen. He then greatly disturbed me by saying, in full confidence, that our going to Lady Moira's Orphanage has been his undoing, for there he had met that Portuguese-British-Indian girl Abigail, blonde freckles, a high nose and blue eyes. She did not seem part Portuguese or Indian to me, but he insisted he had found she was indeed a $\frac{1}{4}$ Portuguese, $\frac{1}{4}$ Indian and $\frac{1}{2}$ English. Now HER he could bring home to England, for despite her lack of dowry or family, she was whiter than him. He thought what he might do is marry her and change Catherine to his children's governess. I told him it was preposterous that he would image a Hoary (dear Catherine) would agree to this, as I knew her and her sisters well, too well to think such a course would be successful. I suggested instead, that as his children, while darker than English children, were certainly not darker than an Italian or Iberian so, he should send them to England to be educated while remaining in India with Catherine and properly married. He said that was also a possible plan, but if he married Catherine would I marry Jonaki? I would not I said, and I was saved from further discussion in this vein by the arrival of our expert on womanly subjects.

Perkins joined the conversation and added more bile to the mix. He suggested that Horne take Abigail to Europe, marry her, leave her there after starting a family and return to India and have Catherine as his 'Eastern' family. I thought this abominable and pure Perkins. I left the discussion at this point as Horne and Perkins went into the details of how such a course of actions could be done.

Saturday 29 April

No entry

The Hunt

[Editor's note: Driscol wrote this the following morning after the event but I have placed it in the day it occurred]

Sunday 30 April

We were off the coast of Arabia; skirting the Pearling fleet for all strangers were considered to be pirates if they approached unbidden. Indeed, with night coming on, we did not wish to encounter any other ship that might fire first and question us after the fact. We were running at some two knots, in a light wind, in an area where the sea was full of sea grasses *{sea weed}*. It was early evening, with the sun just touching the horizon, when a distinct and quite perceptible squeak was heard, coming from the port side, like that of an enormous mouse. Vickery sprang to the side of the ship, hanging onto the rigging, as the swell was some three feet or more and he peered intently out to sea for some time, seeming to stare into the coming darkness. This manoeuver had gained our attention, but all we received for our questions on this, was for him to raise his hand for silence, which he received. Our good Captain silenced his crew with a gesture also. Only the creaking of the boat, the sound of sea and wind, was heard for some minutes.

Suddenly he leaped back on deck his eyes and body animated and he cried to the Captain, 'TUCASH, come to and lower a boat'! In so commanding a tone, was this given that the Captain leapt to obey. The *Hormuzeer* carried two boats, one a small craft to carry some five men and a larger boat, hanging off the stern, which could carry nine or so. It was the larger that was selected. I had no idea what was going on, so I stood quietly, with my hands in my pocket holding my pistol not quite sure what was afoot.

Vickery gathered up his harpoon and two spears then cried to us in an excited way.

'DUGONG'! he cried, hissing it as loudly as he might. He added that a large male was close aboard.

The others rose and Horne expressed his deepest concern, 'Is it good eating'?

'Like the finest beef'. Vickery whispered, again over his shoulder. 'No guns, they will not penetrate its hide but you good fellows can row me'. And so we did. *Dugong Dugon* the sea-going mammal he had hunted for his livelihood in his time on the Red Sea.

All of us were in the boat, now lowered by the Captain, but he did insist on sending his First Mate Tahir to steer it. Vickery also requested and received the carpenter's largest wooden mallet.

I had not rowed a boat in some time, but we were soon in motion. I was sitting in the front, right side of the boat just behind Vickery, who was standing at ease holding his harpoon, to which he was affixing a stout line.

He again cautioned us by hand to row quietly, except for 'Yake' {Dissanayake}, all the rowers were military and we took up the demonstrated cadence provided by Dobbins, who was across from me. He was hunting and he had a wide smile on his face.

Vickery knelt and said to me in a coarse whisper, 'He has sounded; we must wait'. I knew the term from my whaling days, punched Dobbins and gave him a signal to halt and we up oared and waited as directed, except for Dissanayake, who was a bit of a tarty {tardy} in his doing so.

The sea had the swell I spoke of, and it rose and lowered the boat in a rhyming way. I hoped none of the others would have their seasickness aroused by this motion.

Behind us, the ship was three hundred feet or more away, and from her, we heard the faint sound of a horse neighing and the slap of sea against boat.

Bannington, who was behind me, had out his watch and was saying quietly, four minutes, five minutes, Vickery said they could stay down up to eight.

To our front, I heard a rustle in the water and a snort, the Dugong had risen and taken a breath. Vickery motioned for us to continue rowing, each holding his breath, and trying not to make the least sound. Tahir followed Vickery's hand motions to steer as he directed.

A sea bird flew down to investigate us, but finding we were not something good to eat, merely a boat full of men, it flew off squawking.

I could see the sea dimly and then I saw it, a lump on the water moving away from us. We were some thirty feet away. Then, as we came up slowly at twenty feet, Vickery hoisted up his harpoon ensuring the line was free of obstruction. From my whaling days, I knew how dangerous a line could be when attached to a whale. In this boat we had no rope track so I had to watch it carefully.

At fifteen feet, Vickery began to draw back his harpoon and the Dugong flipped up its tail and fled underwater.

Had he seen us, or had he taken his breath and gone down to seek more provisions on the sea floor? In this place, the sea was only some twenty feet or so in depth I thought. Bannington brought out his watch and began to count the time as before. I looked behind me and, as it was quite dark, I wondered how he could possibly read the dials of a watch in this light. To my utter amazement, his watch glowed dimly making it possible to read the darker number on the lighted disk. He whispered that it was an Italian device, a pocket watch with the addition of what in Italian meant 'Stone of Bologna[10]'. I had heard of this but not seen it before.

After six and half tense minutes, our prey surfaced some distance ahead. We could not see him clearly, so we rowed quietly ahead. We turned slightly and came in at him from his rear quarter. He was swimming lazily but still matching our speed and it took us some time to come up to him. Finally, we closed to within striking distance just as his head went down; he was sounding again and at that moment Vickery shouted, 'SLA'!

The harpoon flew out and struck the animal cleanly in its lower back as its tail came up to dive. There was no reaction at first, but the rope straightened quickly and began to run out. Unlike a whale that usually takes off at speed, the Dugong was no speedy creature. Slowly, however, its speed increased until we were making some six knots {7 mph or 11 km/h}.

Vickery was cursing that he had made a hasty attack to avoid it sounding. He turned and shouted to the now dimly seen ship to raise a light. It took two shouts before a blue light flared forth to mark her location.

We were dragged for some hundreds of feet by the rope attached to our bow, then suddenly the line slackened and the boat came slowly to a stop. All we could hear was the whisper of the salt laden wind across the water, and the slap, slap, slap of the sea against the wood of the boat.

Vickery now hefted one of his spears up. It was seven feet long in total with a foot long, two-edged steel blade at the end. He intended to use it as a lance.

He said to us conversationally as if asking for the pepper at dinner, 'He is coming up and he may be somewhat cross'.

He did and he was! He surfaced just ahead and some twenty feet or so to our right flank, snorting and splashing. We could see the harpoon had struck him about a third of the way down his body, which I estimated was nine feet long.

We rowed in with Vickery, poised again, in the front of the boat.

Vickery cried that we would come right up to the beast, and he would search for its heart with his lance. We came close and nearly touched the thrashing beast. He made a violent motion and hit our boat with his tail. Without a cry, Vickery went over board and the boat was drenched in seawater by the wave created by the creature. Bannington was behind me and I could hear him sputtering and spitting out sea water. Dobbins grabbed Vickery, who had surfaced but was facing away from the boat, and began to drag him aboard assisted by Perkins, who was behind him.

The lance was left floating in the sea. At that moment, there was a disturbance in the water next to me and a large, dark face came out of the water to peer at me. I was greatly startled and half rose up; for I thought a sea God or monster was rising up to chide me for attacking one of its children. It was not our Dugong either, for he was still thrashing about having freed himself from the harpoon. No, this was another. I suppose it looked at me and I looked at him and then I yelled out. Bannington saw him and bolted up right, nearly tipping us over, and then it sank away. The tipping of the boat caused Dobbins and Perkins to be pitched over into the sea taking Vickery with them.

As I had some small boat experience, I took command yelling rather brusquely to all to sit down. That accomplished, we brought up Vickery, who was as mad as a Frenchman who had dropped his baguette in a sewer. Next, we dragged Perkins aboard, who was now in one of his rare states of non-perfect coiffure, which disgusted him thoroughly. Finally, we hauled in Dobbins. That took two of us, with four others leaning over the far side of the boat to counter his weight!

Behind us the harpoon bobbed up to the surface, the quarry had shaken it out.

We lay there, three of us soaked, the rest wet. Then Vickery said, 'Well that went well, shall we try again'?

'Huzzard'! We cried.

We gathered in our harpoon and lance and then waited. Vickery whispered to all, after I had told him of the second beast, that Dugong mated for life and it was probably his wife. Also, as a couple rarely separated we should also be on the look for a possible pup.

Michaelson asked if we were winning, which brought a subdued laugh. He redeemed himself by wetting a handkerchief with fresh water, so we could clear our eyes of the sting of the sea salt.

It was fully dark now, with the stars just beginning to display their diamond-like brilliance. Behind us there glowed three blue lights that marked our ship. Occasionally, a horse's cry could be heard. They knew we were away and wanted to know where their masters were.

Vickery arose with harpoon once again in hand. We waited; the only sound being heard was the slap of the sea against the boat's side. A warm current of air blew over us giving a sensual feeling against our damp clothing.

Suddenly the boat rose up, the bow coming up some 4 feet and then slammed down sending up a great spray of water, one of the Dugong had come up under us. Vickery once again was propelled into the sea. He retained his grip on the harpoon this time, however.

Horne shouted do these beasts bite people? I was glad to hear Vickery spitting and answering no, but they do have tusks and great strength.

Gasping, for he had, by his surprise of being pitched into the sea, swallowed some small portion of it, he was, once again, hauled-up one-armed by Dobbins. The sopping wet Vickery regained his position, placed his harpoon and himself in a throwing stance while Dobbins and I by joint inspiration grabbed each of us one of his legs. Vickery said good to this. We waited, the night was clear and being wet we were nearly chilled, a delightful feeling as we had been overly hot for days. At one point Dobbins whispered to me that, as we each held one leg of Vickery, we should perhaps treat him as a wishbone and make a wish! Those, and other rude, ungentlemanly comments, made me laugh out loud only to be silenced by sounds like that of a tea kettle hissing. Vickery motioned for us to come forward again; we rowed slowly along with the other five. Our seaman Tahir had said nothing all this time, and I wondered what he might be thinking of our exhibition of hunting skill.

The Dugong rose up out of the water, snorting and taking a breath next to us. Fifteen feet beyond, his mate rose up also. It was not possible to tell which was which, but we slowly drew up on the closer.

SLA

The harpoon thrown from fifteen feet away, stuck into the animal with a wet 'THUNK', and it gave out that squeaky sound again. We saw its tail poised upward, as it went deep into the sea. We had only seventy feet of line, which was soon reached, and we moved forward, then pivoted. Dissanayake reported the other had gone down too.

The tension of the line remained for some minutes, with us being slowly pulled around in circles, and then the line slackened. Vickery stood, and we grasped his legs, as he remained poised with lance ready. The beast came up behind us and, with some effort; we turned our boat to face it. We were only ten feet away.

The animal thrashed one more time then lay still but continued making snorting and squeaking sounds. Vickery struck, but his lighter lance did not penetrate the creature's outer skin. He tried pushing it in, but only succeeded in pushing the boat away. His thrown fifteen-pound harpoon had struck the animal near where its shoulders might be in a terrestrial animal. The heavier harpoon could penetrate the skin while the light lance could not.

Dobbins suggested that he try the lance with his superior strength, but Vickery, his humour restored, said that he would probably snap it.

Vickery then shouted that we must secure him, take him back to the ship, and there peg him. We turned the boat again, gained his tail, looped a rope over it, and secured it to our stern. Then, with the harpoon still in him we turned. Everyone ducking the harpoon's rope, we headed towards the blue lights of the *Hormuzeer*. Sometimes, our prey would struggle, but he did not escape us. Horne reported the other beast following us some thirty feet behind. After what seemed an impossibly long time, we came up to the side of the ship. The crew praised our hunt greatly, the cook had the fires going, and we put a tackle on the lateen yard and hauled the tail out of the water. The dugong, Vickery explained was to be dispatched by bringing its tail up and, as it could not bring its head out from the water, it would be drowned. Vickery said the other way was to drive a stake up its nostrils, which is why he had taken the carpenter's mallet; this method was called 'pegging'. Usually when hunting them he had not had the luxury of a larger ship to hoist the tail. Being able to drown the beast was good as it allowed the preservation of the animal's skin, and pegging the animal was always dangerous as it had those tusks he had spoken of before. The animal weighed, I would guess, some six or seven hundred pounds.

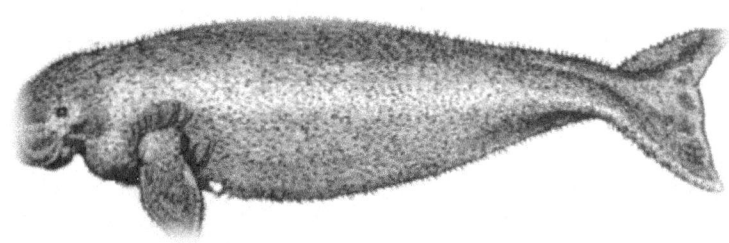

The boat was secured and we regained the deck. A tarpaulin had been placed on the deck, and we were going to use the lateen spar to hoist it up, and bring it around and onto the deck. The poor beast struggled no more and we raised it up.

A dugong like the one hunted by the expedition in the Persian Gulf. Illustration III-XI-22

The head was some three feet above the water, and blood was streaming down it into the sea from its two wounds. Then, in a white flash, something light-coloured, illuminated by the flames of our lanterns, attached itself to the animal in a great fury of splashing water.

We thought for a moment that it was the mate, but bringing the lanterns near, we saw that a great shark, bigger, in my estimation, than the nine feet of the Dugong, had seized the Dugong's head and was shaking it to and fro, thrashing to bite it off!

An Unexpected Visitor

It was an enormous hammerhead shark of the family *Sphyrnidae.* Dobbins was the first to react. His four-bore, hand cannon was nearby, but unloaded, and he demonstrated what he had once described as his rapid re-load. He plunged his hand into his pocket, brought forth a white capsule, and dropped it down the smoothbore barrel and a moment later a four-bore shot. It already had a percussion cap in, and, after tamping, he shouldered the weapon, aimed at the shark and pulled the trigger. I heard the cap fire but nothing happened. He stood still aiming for a moment then, with a tremendous bang a shower of sparks shot out. Immediately, the shark stopped its watery dance of biting and twisting, and hung there. Then, slowly, it slipped back into the water, taking with it the head of our prey.

There was absolute silence for several moments, then a concerted effort to do our duty.

After a great deal of congratulatory comments, we hoisted the Dugong in and laid it on the deck. Vickery instructed us on how to butcher it, and with great difficulty, he and Dobbins sawed though the tough ¾ inch skin that was as hard as cured leather. Dobbins thought it tougher than that of an elephant's. Our Dugong was first sliced open from neck to tail, then with great effort, and assisted by the crew, we peeled the skin back and off. The animal had a great deal of fat, which Vickery said tasted of pork and he declared that the best meat was on the back, along the spine, on the belly, and around the base of the tail. Horne had cried out in delight at the description of the meat tasting like pork. However, he cried out in disappointment that we had no parsnips, just dried legumes and onions.

I found, in the darkness and light of the lanterns the sight of the blood had much less impact on me, and I avoided, but not entirely, the worst of my weakness.

Our cook had prepared the fires, and we began to cook the creature's flesh. I estimated we obtained some four hundred pounds of meat. So, with some seven and twenty men aboard but, of who a quarter were Hindu that left about 18 pounds of flesh per man. Some would be roasted now, some plunged into a barrel of vinegar we had, and the rest smoked. Vickery had suggested we bring up the sea grass that grew here to make the smoke. We did so. The shark's body, had disappeared, his body unfortunately, sinking out of sight.

Dissanayake reported, as he guided the crew to throw the un-needed parts of the offal away, that he had seen the other Dugong, next to the boat. It had given out a particular squeak then dived away.

I had seen whale fleshed and the blubber boiled down, so this smaller operation was in, some ways, more intimate.

Dobbins and Vickery were covered in blood, as was the deck. We got the seawater pump going, and set about to clean the ship. Soon, the deck was cleared, and the cook presented us with chunks of roasted flesh, well strewn with rock salt and freshly cracked pepper. It was, as Vickery had said, a delicious steak, and being in a primitive mood, we ate with our hands. I observed Bannington, a member of the aristocracy sitting on a cushion by a lantern, tearing the meat with his hands and teeth, examining it and eating it with un-disguised delight. For it was good, very good. Scrawny goat can become tiresome to eat after a few days.

The cook then brought out some of the belly meat, fried like rashers *{bacon},* and indeed it tasted like uncured pork belly.

Off the side of the ship, during this time, the smaller creatures of the sea also ate of the remains of the Dugong and the hammerhead. All those aboard ship, who had partaken in the feast, announced this the finest piece of meat any of us had had, for we had had no pork or beef in many days. I ate my fill and then some more.

Vickery told us stories about dugong, for he had hunted them for some months in the Red Sea, with this one being one of his more difficult kills. Some Arabs would not eat a dugong's flesh, as they said it was too near that of human. He was asked about that, and he told us something inconceivable, that humans tasted of pork, and parts of the dugong taste of pork. I asked him how he had come across this exceptional piece of information. His next statement was chilling, he said that in the past, Polynesians had partaken of human flesh and pronounced it to taste of pork; one word for a stranger being 'long pork'.

That was grisly indeed. Michaelson asked him if he had participated in such gross delicacies. He told us quietly, that no, this was the modern nineteenth century and such actions belonged in the dark past of Hawaii, in the time before Christianity came to them. Speaking of which, he gave us another piece of information about the dugong.

In the King James Bible, Exodus 26:14, the people of Israel were instructed to build the first Tabernacle. The tarpaulin of the inner tent should be made of the hide of a certain animal by the name of *tachash* or Arabic *tukhash.* Luther called this a badger, but others say it was a porpoise, but he held it was the dugong, that was granted the right to provide its skin to protect the Tabernacle.

Michaelson and Dissanayake agreed with this, as they seemed to have a great deal of knowledge about the Bible in its original Greek.

Vickery added that some would not eat its flesh, as the animal is ugly, because its female holds its baby like a human child.

There was a general discussion about whether dugongs were the source for mermaids. Perkins said no, as he wished to believe that mermaids were real. That is why he spent so much time, on the first day of the trip, hanging over the rail, he was looking for mermaids!

The crew was most appreciative of the meat, and I would estimate we ate some fifty pounds of it that night; the non-Hindoos joining, as did our Jew, to eat with us. I harboured, but scuttled the idea of asking the Muhammadans if eating this beast was against their principles, as we had not followed the correct procedures of butchery, Halal, in dispatching it.

A last tale was told by Dobbins, who said that a Mr Boverie had seen a fight between a manatee and a land beast; the manatee is a cousin of this creature. He said it had been foraging ashore, for a manatee will eat from the shore at times, when it was attacked by a tiger. It had beaten the tiger so furiously with its tail, that it had disabled it. The tiger's teeth and claws had had little effect on the dense skin of the sea creature. The manatee had then killed the tiger by simply crushing it beneath its huge form. This manatee had been some seventeen feet in length.

Vickery said the largest dugong he had taken was twelve feet four inches. He regretted not securing the tusks, as they could be sold as ivory.

When he was wandering about Persia, earlier in life, he came to the southern coast, and had been introduced to a Sheikh, who had asked what he had done in life, and Vickery had told him that he had hunted the great beasts, the *Nahang* in Persian. The Sheikh had then commanded him, 'Please my good man, and please serve us up a gutted, cleaned and whole fried whale.' In addition to this, he wanted it for his next dinner. Vickery was given a boat and a scurrilous-looking crew. It was only when at sea, that his crew gave him to understand that the Sheikh was speaking of dugong, and not of whale. The confusion arose as the people used the same word for both. It was in this way he took up the trade of dugong hunting. He did say that he had found a bronze coffin of some earlier age deposited by its former owner on the ground (as he had not objected to its being taken) and was thus able to fry a portion of the dugong, in many gallons of olive oil and the beast's own fat, for his royal patron. He did so, much to the full satisfaction of the Sheikh.

I wrote the above, in consultation with the others, the next day. Vickery did complain however, that he had not sputtered and cursed, the second time he was taken into the sea! But he had, and it was confirmed by all but him.

We later spent some time examining the Captain's Arabic language, compass board. He then brought out, unused, an amazingly beautiful Arabic-made astrolabe. We discussed for some time how he did navigation. He had made this voyage so many times, that he no longer used these aids to navigation.

Our good Captain's Arab style astrolabe, which seemed remarkably fine for a horse transport. Illustration III-XI-23

Maj-Kat In Arabia

Monday May 1

In Denmark, and my home in Eccles, this day is known as Maj-kat, and is a joking and pranking day, like the English April Fool's day *{Driscol used the Danish term Aprilsnar}*. The tradition is to ask someone to deliver a sealed message requesting help of some sort. In fact, the message reads 'Dinna laugh, dinna smile make the gowk run another mile'. The receiver, upon reading it and understanding, will act as a deceiver, and send the dupe to another person, with an identical message, with the same results[11].

We figured that Dobbins, never having lived in England, might be unaware of the common types of pranks pulled there, and Horne, Perkins, Bannington and I arranged the following: we painted on the goats below the numbers 1, 2, 3, 5, 6, 7, 8 and 9 missing 4. We then brought up the fact that we did not know where the fourth was, and as it was Dobbins' day on duty it was his task to sort this out. He fortunately had not noted that the goats had not previously been numbered - for they were only 3 inches tall, the numbers, not the goats. He searched diligently, roping Vickery into the search too. They searched high and low, questioned as best they could the crew, asked all of us, some of whom were not in on the joke. They spent a good five and forty minutes at this task, which was very gratifying to us. Vickery and Dobbins took it very well, and we had to explain the concept of the prank and this day. Of course, it was pointed out that April first was the appropriate day for such high jinxing but I stated, correctly, that no one can be fooled on that day as it is too well known, well except for Vickery and Dobbins of course!

There was much good spirited palavering today among ourselves and the crew. I told my old story of the great scrumping on the local demesne, when I was a boy *{To steal fruit from a mansion or landed property - regrettably Driscol doesn't tell us the story}*.

Tuesday 2 May

Sighted the island of Bahrein *{Kingdom of Bahrain}* to our south, called Awal in some sources, it is some thirty miles in length and ten in breadth. At the southern end, is a volcanic mass forming a, more or less, square lump, which we sighted while some 20 miles out at sea. We passed close enough to see the Sheik's (*sheikh*) house sited in the town of Manameh *{Manama}*, and some three miles from there, a dilapidated Portuguese fort, long since abandoned. We were in need of water and came to anchor to the northeast of the Sheik's house. We were soon visited and good water was procured. One can see from the ship, date plantations, and poor fishing villages, and no more. It is said by the Captain, that on the island are thousands of tombs, belonging to the ancient heathens, who lived here before the Prophet came. He also told us a strange narration:

[Editor's note: Driscol came back at a later date, and attached a note about the Qaramita (Qaramations); I have placed it here instead of chapter notes as Driscol seemed to think it germane to the narrative]

> The Qaramatah were a utopian group of Shia heretics, who revolted against the Sunni tyrants of the Abbasid Caliphate. In Arabia they are best known for being vegetarians and for attacking and sacking Mekkah, and their theft and damage to

the sacred, black stone of the Kaaba. *{Driscol also noted they were cockwombles or complete idiots}*

We did not go ashore, as it seemed a desperately poor, dusty, and unpleasant place. However, we did view their ship yards, where several native craft were being constructed on shore: all with wood and nails from India.

Wednesday 3 May

At noon, while doing our positional shoot, we showed Bannington and Dobbins how it is done. Bannington was quick to learn the procedures, Dobbins not so much, and his tail was quite down *{to give up or lose courage}* by the end. We sighted dense, dark clouds appearing low in the atmosphere. We discussed for some time their formation, and as the clouds approached us, the Captain prepared our ship for a squall. The clouds were filled with electric fluid[12] and we could see distant flashes and rumbling. As they grew near the skies darkened, until, to our northwest, the entire sky was covered with this black cloud. As we observed, a portion of the cloud descended down to the sea, stretching into a conical shape. At the same time, the sea became agitated. We were struck by a cold wave of gale force, which heeled over the Hormuzeer, even with her sails down, riding the ocean with bare poles.

A water spout in the Persian Gulf. Illustration III-XI-24

======

A display of the different types of clouds in the atmosphere, Illustration III-XI-25

The dense cloud all at once transformed itself, from a black cloud, to one of white vapour, from the centre of which a small cone proceeded upwards, until it united with the black cloud from above. In this way, a water-spout, or whirlwind, formed before our eyes.

It was at a distance of some two miles, but it gave out a threatening aspect, as it seemed a stream of water was ascending into the heavens. This proceeded towards us and to get out from its possible course our captain partially raised the fore sail. The spout, swirling still, passed behind us, not more than a half mile away. We were lashed with cold winds and torrents of rain, but with its passing, the sky gradually cleared, and a half hour, later the sea and clouds were as they had been before. The followers of the prophet and the Hindoos beseeched their God and Gods, while our servants as one ran below deck. As good Englishmen, we stood and watched the event.

We discussed for some time weather and in particular clouds.

The hottest day so far, it reached 100°, which is the most trying thing imaginable. Although, being at sea, it is not un-healthy. This intense heat is aggravated however, by the humidity of the atmosphere, and dust raised by the wind and borne out to sea. We find that when we are near a coast, it is often obscured from us by a brownish, dusty, haze. Clouds are rare, and one has only the excessive heat to look forward to. Our Captain told us that this, the Arab coast, is hotter and less healthy than the northern Persian side and the southern end, where we still are, is hotter than the northern portion, which we are now entering. When asked why he sailed along the south instead of the north coast, his answer was simple; in the south, the sea bed is sand to the north rock, so his choice makes perfect sense. One can wreck up north, but ground only in the south.

This day Dobbins took the time to show our sail maker a better way to do a locking stitch on his sail repair. The crew was amazed at this and gave him the title of *Dirgee {tailor}*. This sparks a contest between him and the man to do up a canvas bucket with handle in the shortest possible time. Dobbins wins easily and he is then named *stultz nugee {European or great tailor}*. Of us, only Vickery can sew. This useful skill was taught only to the women of our families. Dobbins, the son of a great tailor, thought this was nonsense, and he took it upon himself to show us how to do the task. I found it quite interesting, from threading a needle, to the various stitches. In a few hours, I could sew on a button and change the length of my trowsers.

A useful skill.

Even Perkins accepted it as something that someone should know, especially as we would need to do so. It was odd to see a group of men sitting and sewing. My father, I know, would have laid down his knife and fork *{Died}*, if he had seen officers busy at sewing as he had always had very definite ideas on what kind of labour was suitable for a man, what kind for a woman, and what kind a soldier, sergeant or officer should do.

The Persian Coast And Bushire

Thursday 4 May

The atmosphere in this lower portion of the Persian Gulf is so exceedingly sultry and insalubrious, that we could never, for any continuance, maintain ourselves here for long. Those who have been long in India do not mind it as much; Dobbins observing it was a tad warmer than usual. It did not discomfort him to the extreme that did so myself, Bannington and Michaelson. The old hands of India, Horne, Vickery, Perkins and Dissanayake, while finding it horrid, also found they could withstand it. I could do no more than lay myself under the tarpaulin and sweat and think of cold, delightfully wintery days in Eccles, and the sharp cold on the Greenland Seas.

This morning having not seen land for the past few days, we approached and sighted the Persian coast without incident. Bannington viewed the coastline with great concentration; his knowledge of the work of the naturalist Smith[13], whose natural sciences *{we will call it geology although that term was not in common use at this time}* came to his tongue. He explained to us what the shoreline was. It was not grey cliffs rising most abruptly to a majestic height; it was instead, grey calcareous rock exhibiting horizontal ledges of a darker hue and resembling buttresses and columns. He went on about the geology of this coast for some time, but I was too hot and bothered to either remember it all, or to write it all down.

A cry is raised up by the crew and we crowd to the side of the ship, for we have arrived near our landing site in Persia. We crept along the coast, for as we neared our objective of this voyage, the wind began to falter, but not die away completely. We sailed on, willing the wind to keep blowing, until we had come up to a peninsula. We marked some ruinous walls embosomed among the date trees. We sighted a boat carrying wood and spoke with her crew; all is well in Bushire, no wars, confiscations, plagues, preternatural trepidations, or riots are reported.

We were now approaching the principal port of Persia, situated on the extremity of a low headland, formed on one side by the Persian Gulf, and on the other, by an inlet terminating in extensive swamps. The whole peninsula seems to have risen from the sea, and with the coming of the spring tides, it resumes its original character as an island.

Bushire, Persia modern Bushehr, Iran. Illustration III-XI-26

Its first appearance to us was the extent of its hilliness. Rising conspicuously from the surrounding dull flat that is now the coast, and changed from the earlier more attractive cliffs, it is singular, but far from inviting, even to our sea-tired eyes. We sight the city and are not impressed.

Busheer, Persia also known as Bandar Bushehr, Bandar-e Bushehr, Abuschehr, Abu Shehr, or Bandar Abu Shehr *{Bushehr, Iran to be called Bushire in all future spellings}* is situated on the north side of a low point. On the tip of the peninsula, lies the city, built on several conical hills, and cut off from the rest of the island by a land wall. Little grows here, but the town is well supplied from the hinterland. The water, the Captain said, tastes like horse stale, *{urine}* but is healthful. The walls and towers of this habitation are in many places nothing but ruins.

We came to anchor in the inner road between Colunna point and the town, and we did so without a pilot, as the Captain has been coming to this port to gather horses for return to India for some thirty years; his father taking him to sea when he was eight. On the seaward side, there is no suitable methodology for anchoring. Larger ships have to drop anchor three miles offshore and transfer cargo in by boats. On the bay side, where we anchored, there was good anchorage near the city, but a high sandbar prevented access for ships drawing more than ten feet; we drew but eight.

The land around the port is high, consisting of a series of hills called the Halihah; one is dynamically pyramid-shaped. From a modest building in the town, sourrounded by a white wall, we could see a British flag flying from the home of the consul. We were glad to see it; and much cheered by its appearance.

We are at latitude 29° 0' north, longitude 50° 51' East, with a magnetic variation accorded to the magnetic compass of 5° 0' west. This is the first location recorded for our expedition and will be our base line of calculation for how far we travel officially. Vickery will keep the diary marking the progress of the expedition.

[Editor's note: Perkins and Driscol redeemed themselves at this location, getting it exactly right but three miles from the center of the modern city. They probably did it at anchor, but other comments show they were close enough to view the city with some ease]

One hundred and twenty English and Arab ships a year came here to trade from India and elsewhere, bringing the products of Europe, Africa, India and China. The items most traded here are cloth, indigo, iron, pottery, porcelain, rice, spices, sugar, tea and wood for shipbuilding. Persian exports are asafetida, carpets, grain, dried fruits, especially their esteemed apricots, nuts, silk, Shiraz wine, saffron and of course, horses. It is here that caravans make their way into Persia, and from there all the way into Independent Tartary.

There are several European ships in the harbour and in particular a large country *{HEIC}* ship, the *Rao's Surprise* at nine hundred tons, a Royal Navy cutter of ten guns, and the HMS *Viper* of ninety tons with 12 pounder carronades. There is also the HMIN Brig, the *Tigris*, with ten guns: 8 x 24 pounder carronades, with two long 24 pounders for the bow and stern chasers; at two hundred and sixty tons. Along with them, were some one hundred and ten or more native craft.

Perkins borrowed my binoculars and, looking in the direction of the town, explained what he saw to the rest of us; who were so distracted by the heat, which at this time was 98°. The infrastructure of the city consists of large caravansaries. On the whole, the town, which was in summer, crowded and stifling, despite the forest of wind catchers crowning its roofs, had nothing to recommend it; for even its bazaars are limited.

[Editor's note: The 'wind catchers' were tall chimney-like structures that like a chimney create a draft and cause the air in a house to circulate an early form of a non-mechanical fan]

I was drawn to look in the direction of Perkins, when he made a sound, stood up straighter, and shouted my name; all without taking the glasses down from his eyes. I came at once thinking Husher or Hymison were standing there waiting for us, but no Husher, or the other was there. Instead, he pointed out towards another man, at the far end of the stone landing place, and handed me the binoculars. It took some effort to find him in the bustle, but there he was. a man in a white suit like any English gentleman might wear, only perhaps not as clean as it could be. I could see nothing of note, as he had binoculars of his own up, and he appeared to be looking straight at us, with his hat pushed to the back of head. I stared for a moment then he put down his glasses, turned his back, pulled his headgear down to his brow and melted into the seething throngs of natives.

The sight left me puzzled, I seemed to know the man, but who it was did not register in my mind. I turned back to Perkins and asked who it was; his answer daunted me to my bones.

Was it not the long-haired blonde man, who we had seen on the Chilean's boat? The man who had seemed to be in charge? When he said that, I knew in that instant that it was true. I was sure - or was I? I looked at Perkins, and he looked at me. I searched the dockage further with my glasses, and he found his eyeglass, but we found no trace of the man again. Had we been mistaken?

The Expedition Arrives In Persia

As it was late afternoon, and as we were very comfortable aboard ship, and in an admirable defiance of the heat, which we knew would be worse in the town, should we think to stay here. Although tired of the sea Bushire had little to recommend it to a traveller, so we stayed aboard.

Despite the views from the anchorage of the city that were encouraging, the town had a certain charm: indeed the charm of a ship cast up on shore, a bullock dead in the road, or a house falling to ruin in one's neighbourhood. The appearance of Bushire from seaward is that of a narrow, whitened strip on a low, projecting front. Brown and yellow sand, or grey clay and rock, meet the eye in every direction, un-enlivened by the smallest portion of green vegetation or trees. At a distance, it resembles a city half-built and the rest in disorder.

The houses are in ruins, or built shabbily, of either clay, or of a soft white stone. They have with flat roofs, which, rising to heights of from 60 to 100 feet, as seen as many as nine square turrets or wind-chimneys; each the mark of a great man's dwelling. The houses topped by wind chimneys *{Badgirs or windcatchers}* resemble a myriad of small minarets.

Yet we knew, from earlier travellers, that squalor was its chief delight for the unsuspecting visitor. The town looks nearly triangular with its base towards the southeast and the apex pointing to the north. There is no true sea wall. Only the land side is protected by a line of twelve towers, which at a distance seem solid, but under the binoculars' searching vision, are revealed as being tattered and forlorn. The wall itself is some eight and twenty feet high, but only five feet thick, and terribly vulnerable to modern cannon shot.

On the land side, the town is built of a soft sandy stone, incrusted with sea shells, which Bannington says is evidence on the one hand of the Great Biblical flood, and on the other hand is thought to be ancient creatures embedded in a mixture, a sediment, that has over time hardened, such are the competing theories. This stone is taken from the ruins of Reshire, a town four miles to the southward, which, in the time of the Portuguese, was a place of considerable consequence.

Our Captain told us that some six thousand people lived here. Horne noted that the term 'live' was probably incorrect; they probably only survived. Yes, indeed, and as the question of but whether it was a good life, I would say based on the surroundings that the answer to that was a resounding no.

I could not but think, with a certain thrill, that Alexander's fleets are said to have once moored here.

There was civilization here unalike the other ports we had visited. A doctor and official came out to see to our status. This brought us in contact with a Frenchman, two Persians, an Arab and a German doctor. We were deemed acceptable to drop our anchor here. Michaelson spoke with the German, a native of Emden, Saxony about health matters in Persia and the news was good. The fever season had not begun and if we could make our way into the hills as soon as possible, it would be best, as the town was known to suffer small pox and cholera in the summer's heat.

We found out that the acting British resident *{Captain S. Hennell of the 12th Native Infantry, Indian Army}* was in Teheran, and his deputy was at a small village to the south, dealing with intransient natives. However, the French Consul would be able to help us, as the two nations assisted one another in this foreign port.

Another boat appeared this one containing Mr Tartters, of Somerset, England; and the East India Company's assistant resident who had been attracted by the Company flag. He was amazed to find a party of Englishmen on the ship: six officers and two civilians. He explained he was temporarily in charge; with all the principals departed on various duties. and that we were most welcomed. After he examined Perkins' extensive paperwork. He then asked if we were the men for the expedition.

We were, and he said the most interesting thing, that in summary was, 'ah yes we were and that they had been informed that London would be sending such a grouping some time ago and that the Persians were awaiting you'.

We had been standing talking with the port doctor and we observer that the distinguished looking Frenchman knew our Captain well. Finally the taller of the Persians stepped forward, begged Mr Tartters' pardon for interrupting, and inquired if we were the expedition too: he did so in Persian.

Again, so much for secrecy!

Perkins was shocked that our business would be known to the natives. He, Mr Adoul, with a long name and title I did not remember, presented to us passports from the ruler of Persia, granting us full permissions to travel anywhere; he needed to only add in our names to make it official. He also had letters of introduction to the Walis {Governors} of a number of the main cities in Persia and of the provinces, all demanding their aid to our purpose. Our consul, it would seem, had done is job most proficiently. Our expedition was welcomed officially and we were informed that quarters had been arranged for us in Kazerun, in the hills, at which we could stay as long as we liked, until moving inland to the Capital. It was also made clear to us that we MUST see the Shah before crossing the northern border into Tartary. We agreed. The second man was to be our guide in Bushire; a ratty looking fellow. I thought him a Persian at first, and his beard was some two feet long and dyed red with henna, but when he spoke, however, I could hear in his Persian the accent of Ireland. He was a Donegal man, who had come to the East and taken it a bit too much aboard. He was a *muhtadi* or a renegade to us and an infidel come into the light for the Muhammadans. He declined to speak English saying he knew only Gaelic, French, some Arabic and the Persian tongue. His name was Basir {wise}, just Basir Muhammad. He would not give his previous Christian name.

We gave Mr Aboul letters from England. These letters all contained the simple statement in Persian, that the writer had arrived as Envoy Extraordinary from the King of Great Britain to the King of Persia, in order to confirm and augment the amity which had so long existed between the two countries, and that our party wished to exit his lands to the north. He read them and handed them back saying we should present them ourselves to the Shah Mohammad Shah Kajar for his preview.

The Sheikh of the Bushire would greet us tomorrow as it was late. Perkins asked how many Europeans were in the city and was told it was some one hundred or more. He asked about the long-haired blonde man, but none of the men on our deck had seen him, and none knew of him.

We found that another British Explorer had arrived here recently, after completing an expedition down the Euphrates. this was F.R. Chesney[14] and who had left for England some weeks before we arrived.

The visitors would not take our hospitality as they said a storm was on the onset, and they were right; the wind was picking up. As the Irish Persian was the last to go, he turned back to us and asked in French whether the man Perkins was looking for was a German with long blonde hair. It was and it seemed our man had not understood our earlier query. That man he did know by sight, but not by name, and he had come down from the north a few weeks ago, but appeared to have no business with anyone. He had come down with the messengers who were bringing the document for the expedition from the Shah.

Our compatriots asked us about this blonde-haired man, after our guests had departed. Perkins and I spoke together, keeping our consul private and decided that we should explain, in part. Perkins stated that the man we had been talking about, had been, perhaps, aboard a ship, which we had seen in the Mediterranean months ago. Our men took no additional interest in that man, as we did not associate him with the pirate ship, not wishing to open that box of weevils at this time.

The weather was rather brusque, but no storm came, just a hot wind, and some swell from the northwest, but it was a comfortable night and the last of the food was eaten. We posted two guards that night, for we knew not what Persia would bring, and we rotated each hour. I had by luck a shift that allowed me to see the sun rise.

Friday 5 May

The weather moderated in the early afternoon, and we began our transfer of luggage and horses to Bushire. This being the Muslim Sabbath day, the workers were sluggish, and it is also the Ascension Day for those practicing Christianity and the end of Rogation tide. We would not allow our good Captain to land our horse by throwing them into the sea, and fortunately horse transport was common, here and they were brought to dry land with only some difficulties of management. I could tell Blonde was quite upset by her journey. The secretary of Mr Tartters arrived bearing for us official post.

We had official post for the expedition, which had come from Europe to the Levant, then down the Tigris-Euphrates route. It contained more ideas and directives from armchair explorers and geographers sitting in comfortable clubs and offices in London, another draft of money, and a confirmation of Perkins to be the leader; but with a proviso that he name *{officially}* the expedition after one of the leading members of the Royal Geographic Society.

[Editor's note: British expeditions tended to have several names, its official name, the associated name of its patrons and perhaps a leading notable, and then the name it was actually referred to, which by tradition was its leaders last name; in this case Perkins. At this time, the official name of this expedition was as yet not stated. This was because it had no official patron or notable individual designated; as of yet, amongst the expeditionaries, it was called, in classic British understatement, 'the stroll']

The letter explained that we would be greeted officially today and that we must wear full dress at 10.00 o'clock. Oh hell and damnation.

We made our initial farewells to the crew and bid them to stay in harbour until we released them. The Captain was ashore busily bargaining for a new cargo of horses to take back to India.

We landed finally, getting our feet on Persian soil. We entered the town through a dirty, broken and shattered stone portal.

The point in Bushire where Driscol would have landed from a photograph taken some sixty years after the event. Illustration III-XI-27

On either side of that were some half-clad ragamuffins, with matchlocks by their sides, and the water-pipe, with its everlasting gurgle, in their mouths, armed with dim looking gazes, but who gave us European salutes that had they been taught by a British soldier. I would have had him shot on the spot, after personally strangling his sergeant.

Once on land, I borrowed Blood-Thirsty's *{Nickname for Vickery}* spear for a small ceremony, taking it I plunged it into the ground, emulating Alexander the Great's action when he first entered Asia to make it 'spear-won land'. I had of course been in Asia for some time, but here it seemed appropriate. The others appreciated the act, after I explained my actions. Vickery was concerned that my striking the sand had inflicted a salacious indignity on his spearhead and its point would be dulled.

A Persian water pipe. Illustration III-XI-28

These lions of Persia protect a place that is a shapeless mass of buildings that lay before us; on one hand a wretched hut, and on the other hand, a half-ruined tomb, exposed to the footsteps of all, and everywhere, broken stone walls, tilting stone building, and over this strewn layers of dust, encrusted dirt, the utter wretchedness of the narrow streets of this town expose to our view. We paused here with astonishment and to the God of rhetorical questions. Is this Persian city of twenty thousand souls, the principal sea-port town of a great nation? It was Horne and Vickery who said that if we wanted fine towns, scenery, or an inkling of what Alexander the Great had come conquer, we must go inland; for one does not find it here, at all, under any pretext.

The alleyways are not wide enough to call streets, as two men cannot pass one another without turning sidewise down those that we travelled on. These narrow pathways offer no protection from the sun, as the buildings here are sunken into the earth; some few feet leaving one's head fully exposed to the actions of the sun's rays. The sanitary arrangements of the town are non-existent and therefore our first impressions of the sights and smells of the place are terribly offensive. Towards the land side, the alleyways become true streets, but choked with filth, dirty sand, and decomposing dead animals, over which mangy dogs fight over for grisly remains. As one enters deeper into this place, one comes to the poorer section, where the buildings are not made of the local sandstone, but of date tree branches.

There are seven mosques, four for Shi'a and three for Sunnis and two large, but damaged, caravanserais. Over all this wretchedness is the all-encompassing dust, a fine and gritty mixture that gets into everything and resists, like oil, attempts to wash or rub it away. This dust is a soiled, unclean dust not the cleaner particles of a desert.

Horne made note that this part of Persia is labelled *Dashtishtan {Dushistan which means plains}* the last person to mistakenly call it that was Marco Polo himself; while Horne's irreverent variation was 'Dust-i-stan'. The people here are of the Bushebris, Shambadis, Behbehanis, Kazarunis and Khanasiris tribes. I did not ask which were of Persian or Arab blood, so as to not offend, but I believe all of these are of good blood, i.e. Persians. I was told too that there were a few hundred Jews, a handful of Armenians, two families of Indian - Portuguese Goans - who dealt with matters of trade, mainly bringing in rice from India and some 'foreign' Arabs and Turks. I was also informed that seven Arab Christians reside here, and two hundred and forty two Gulf Arabs the exact number being known as they are registered and kept track of by the Persian officials. There were also two Frenchmen, one Russian, 2 Belgians, a Greek and one thoroughly mad Bavarian. Additionally the Saxon doctor and five stalwart Englishmen although one rumoured to be Welsh.

If it be permissible, I believe I will note that while the people live in this degraded place, they are physically well-developed, mentally quick and intelligent; despite their slothful appearance. Their dress is usually an unclean robe held at the waist with a multi-coloured Kashmir shawl. That is their outwardly presence. However while naturally well-bred, and having agreeable Islamic manners, these conceal an unreliable and ungrateful disposition. They are inclined to be uncivil to foreigners, though less so than formerly; when killing Christian foreigners was a sport. This uncivility is also directed at those Persians not from the coast. Those 'inland' Persian return the dislike and refer to the Persian here as 'Saltwater Arabs'.

Vickery wandered off and sold his dugong skin for six and a half rupees, a good price, but then he was used to living in Persia and found no harrow in entering the streets of this town. I had asked him if there was any difference in a Shia land versus a Sunni one? 'Different scene same odour', he replied.

Basir had arranged for us to depart inland as soon as we could, for as noted before, there was no reason to stay in Bushire. Our luggage was troublesome, due to the lateness is getting off the ship, and we were not able to depart inland, as we were obliged to wait for the ceremony with local dignitary, and we received word that he had been detained.

We therefore found ourselves with our equipment and luggage on shore, but no place to stay until the event occurred. We decided not to return to the ship and leave our belongings on this strange shore, so Basir found us a place in an abandoned warehouse of the Dutch trading company, and we made ourselves comfortable, In some ways it reminded me of that barracks I had stayed in at Corunna. It had been a long day and yet it had barely begun. On the door was a sign in Arabic which said;

الباقي or Al-Baqi one of the ninety nine names of Allah, which means 'eternal' or 'everlasting'.

We were finally alone, no servants, crewmen or others; it was the first time for the men of the expedition, who had knitted well together on the voyage, to be here by ourselves. We sorted out our luggage, played some whist, and went to sleep in the heat, which makes one drowsy. As usual I was, by the draw of cards, assigned to guard duty; curses being the junior officer. I did enjoy waking up the others at odd hours, telling them to go to sleep. It was rather amusing, for, as a man, they would wake befuddled from my shaking and ask what the matter was. I would tell them they needed to go to sleep, all would agree and then do so, and none remembered it.

The time came, and we dressed but ate nothing as Horne and Vickery were well aware of what was coming and said we would best be hungry when the event began.

Basir appeared at 10.24 to tell us there would be a small delay in the ceremony.

At 11.47 our guides arrived to take us to the Sheikh. We proceeded in a cloud of dust, and through streets no more than five-feet wide, to the Sheikh's house. We entered it by a path covered in filth. Finally, we beheld a disreputable door, set in the wall, so poor, and ill-looking, and unguarded, that it might more properly have formed the entrance to a leper's hovel.

This led to an open area, where our guard of honour was lined up. This was the armed militia of the town who serve without pay. They even bring their own arms and create their own uniforms. The uniform's main ingredient seeming to be dirt, gold braids and vivid silks; and in that order. They presented to us, in the European manner, using a collection of antique matchlocks. Perkins returned the salute. They shouldered the weapons and drew off their backs a shield and sower {*It is not known what Driscol meant by 'sower'*} and gave us a loud roar; not so much of a lion but that of cat, whose paw has been stepped on. Such was our greeting; we were led into a large, cleaner, and airy room, filled with notables.

The inhabitants of Bushire are principally Persian, as I had noted earlier but have the blood of the Arabs from the opposite coast, who came originally from the Arabian Trucial coast, but by their marriage with the Persians, they have lost many of the distinctive characteristics of that race. This Arabness is shown in the title of the ruler here, Sheikh instead of the more common Persian term *Wali*.

We saw here the other inhabitants of this land, who, besides the Arabs of the coast, are the Iranians or Persians; plus others called the Farsi, Kurds, and Tartars. The actual Persian is always noticeable amongst these other types; due to their superior and symmetrical figure, and pliant, graceful and noble carriage. Oval faces framed by black hair, if baldness, which is common here, has not robbed the man of his head coat. Brown eyes, aquiline nose, a small but well-shaped mouth, and their true pride, a wavy jet black beard. I saw no women of course, but Horne and Vickery say they are quite handsome, except for a tendency to be hairy; especially having only one long eyebrow, which can be disconcerting, as plucking is not thought a proper thing to do. All of this perfection in appearance is marred by a haughty expression, as if they were affronted by not being the masters of all; and are the only people in the world, who do not hold the memory of Alexander the Great in reverence - obviously for reasons of history.

We were halted here for some time, due to some delay, and spoke with the men of the militia and other notables, who were working men attached to different trades: for we found a dyer by the black hue of his hands, the tinker by the smut on his face, the tailor by the shreds that had adhered to him from the clutter of his shop, and the pimp by the lingering odour of some sour worrisome perfume.

After a time, we were let through another door. This door introduced us into a small courtyard of some improved look, on one side of which was an apartment. There we seated ourselves on chairs, placed on purpose for us; fine things too, as chairs are solely a western contrivance, and they are not used by the Persians. A visit to a Persian, when the guest is a distinguished personage, as it appears we are, consists of three acts:

Firstly, the water pipe

Secondly, sweet coffee made with rose-water and sugar

Thirdly, sweetmeats

I was able to successfully hide my distain for the first two, but did find the third very nice. Vickery said more would come, but I took a number of bites.

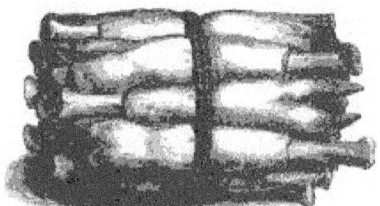

Having been refreshed, we met the Sheikh, who was an unimposing figure of a man, and rather sad looking.

A package of cooked sheep trotters. Illustration III-XI-29

Our dinner was excellent despite poor surrounding. The food was magnificent khoresh-e bademjan; or lamb and aubergines or guinea squash *{eggplant}*, made with plentiful spices, only some of which I could identify: cardamom, lemon peel, nutmeg, rose petals, and many others. Each of us was presented with a local delicacy, a 'package' of cooked sheep's trotters to take on our journey; and which here are given to anyone who is fleeing from Bushire as a token of good luck.

There was much rice and fruit, but not a fish of any kind, a peculiar thing for a seaport. We ate long and hard enjoying a *cinq a' sept {the two-hour meal beloved by the French, figuratively,"five to seven"}.*

[Editor's note: Driscol's use of this term is not exactly correct, but he probably meant they had a long leisurely meal]

The air tower above us acts like a chimney to draw up the hot air and create a flurry of air, a warm humid current, but any motion of the atmosphere is appreciated. I was drenched in sweat, by the time the meal ended.

The good Sheikh had us inspect his fortifications, and a poor thing they were. The town straggles over many hills, occupying a considerable extent of ground. The wall on the land side protects it from the un-healthy incursions of the robber tribes; who are constantly roving about in formidable bands in the vicinity. To seaward, it has neither fortifications, nor any other protection; other than a few pieces of artillery, so old and honey-combed with red corruption *{rust}*, that it would be dangerous to fire them. These cannon were, all in all, inoperable; not only being rusted, but cracked, with one having a bird's nest in it. A French gunboat with a drunken crew could hold this town to a Barbary ransom without difficulty. *{Force it to pay a sum to not be fired on}*

We had returned to our place of rest, and there were sent gifts. The Sheikh sent to us trays and boxes filled with nuts, fruits, sweetmeats and other gifts. These were toothsome, but the manner of their delivery irksome. A great man in Persia does not pay his servants he sends them on errands, such as taking presents to visitors; and by tradition, the visitor must present the carrier a present in money. We had exchanged our money and lost a number of coins to these presenters. Among the gifts, were suits of clothes in the Persian manner, fit for a gentleman of that race.

This was also Vickery's birthday and we gave him a suitable present; the rather disreputable end of a goat, not well dried but well wrapped up in netting that had seen better days. He was most appreciative and we suggested that as entertainment; he might mount the roof and harpoon any natives moving thought the narrow alleyways, and then we could render them up whaler wise.

[Editor's note: This was a spoof on his whaling adventures, 'rendering' was the process of stripping off the whale blubber and boiling it down to obtain the oil]

He was twenty this day.

The doorway in Bushire where the expedition first rested. The Arabic on the door is one of the ninety-nine names of God. Basir Muhammed the renegade Irishman is seen standing at the door. Illustration III-XI-30

Farewell The Hormuzeer And Her Finest Of Men

Saturday 6 May

Perkins and I went back to the ship, paid the good Captain, and tasked him to make sure our two helots and the rest of the servants returned to safety in India. They were bid goodbye and well paid for their services too. The good Captain asked if it would be his pleasure to take us back, and when would that be. In a great piece of theatre Perkins took out his watch, consulted it for some time, and said that we should be back here in about two and twenty months. The Captain took that as a command and replied that he made the journey here nine to ten times a year. We agreed that we would look for him and hoped that providence would grant us a timely meeting. Perkins and I both had enjoyed our journey on the Hormuzeer, as it had been as intimate as, and more pleasant than, our adventures on the Speronara *{See Volume I, Chapter III Gibraltar to Malta}.*

They were already loading their cargo of horses. These were fine animals from the interior, which they purchase for forty or fifty rupees a head and will sell them for two-hundred and fifty to four hundred rupees in Bombay.

Our official and unofficial post was given into the custody of our servants plus a substantial bonus for their selfless service. Only Dobbins' servant was somewhat unhappy, as his share of the bonus was less than the others, as he had been quarrelsome during the trip.

Arrangements were now commenced for our departure. Basir had been arranging our transport north, prior to this. He had wanted to provide a Persian, expensive, cavalcade of monstrous size. However, Perkins, backed by Horne's experience here, would not have it. It would be grand, but too slow. He wanted fast, we wanted fast, for we wanted to move with all dispatch out of this hot dusty place - this coastal plain of dirty desolation. The average Persian or Arab in Bushire is so superstitious, particularly when they have any undertaking of consequence in view, that it is difficult to bring them to commence it. Our caravan men would not be paid until we should move, but not even the force of interest, could prevail against that of superstition, which was that the number seven is a controversial number seen as a bad omen by the Arabs. As the scholar Ibn Shaheen stated it referred to Hell, in view of the Koranic verse that says:

It hath seven gates, and each gate hath an appointed portion

As this is a description of the hell of Islam Surah Al-Hijr, verse 44 it is mightily unlucky in the Arabs' mind.

It was pointed out to Basir, that May 7th was our date, and for him and them, it was the 1st day of Safar. We would leave today, or we would dismiss them. We told Basir, in no uncertain terms, that we would depart this day, even if we only got a few miles.

We had lunch at the residency with Mr Tartter. It was extremely luxurious to sit down at a table for the first time in four weeks and enjoy the customs of civilised life.

Roast beef much appreciated by Driscol. Illustration III-XI-31

He had an unspeakably fine silverside {roast beef} for us, blood red in the centre and delectable. This transition from that which most men would find to be unpleasant, crude fare, exposure, and lassitude, to the comparative indolence of comfort, and luxury, which we now enjoyed, was sudden and striking. As a result of their indulgence, together with the delightful and intelligent society with which I was surrounded, I passed several agreeable hours there. Bannington played the piano with great skill, and to our great applause, however his singing brought great pain to our ears. Mr Tartter was a sponge, who wanted every scrap of news from the world of India, for he had served three years there and was thoroughly deprived of all manners of news. Descriptions of beautiful women and parties brought him nearly to tears. He was in need of a wife.

We emerged from that social occasion back into the vile misery of this accursed town. In making our way back, I observed some of the natives and what they wore in more detail.

A man like Basir goes about in an open shirt of unbleached cloth, covered in dust and stained with years of sweat, which lies tight around the neck. Cinched at the waist is another cloth; the multi-coloured Kashmiris being for the wealthier only. In this he kept his tobacco, lead and flints along with their daggers, which served him not only finish off his human prey by cutting their throats, but also for domestic devotions. On a shoulder he hung a brass-studded powder-horn, enclosed in a leather bag and a matchlock of great length; no less than six feet long in this case. He also carries a prayer rug with him at all times, even if it is rarely used. He wore no sword, while the other men of Bushire wear a formidable sword at their side which is a thin, straight, two-edged blade, with a long handle without a guard. Some also carry a small, circular shield, about twelve inches in diameter. In some manners, his costume and arms resemble that of an old style Highlander.

We found Basir had our mule caravan all but settled and loaded by this time. There was, divided into sections, a tent large enough for us to all fit in, and a smaller one for the Persian servants and Basir. Our retinue was completed by eight horses, four and twenty mules, Basir on his own horse, and our newly-hired six, Persian servants mounted on mules.

The mules are from the island of Bahrein, where that breed is of superior size, and of better temperament and endurance than the common Persian ass. An ass can be had for thirty rupees, but a Bahraini mule can cost you nearly a hundred rupees. But ours are the best animals for the long walk to Teheran. They are hired and so we need not worry about the trouble and injury they may suffer or endure during their tenure with us.

As we were preparing to depart, the British deputy consul just then returned to his duties came and found us to wish us luck, and we in turn complimented him heavily on his office, and his excellent work in obtaining all the necessary permissions. He seemed puzzled by this and said;

'It was all done by your man, I forget his name who came last month, and he went with the consul to Teheran to prepare it all'.

But no, he did not remember the man's name as he had not met him, as he was at other work away from Bushire at the time.

It was Perkins' considered opinion that it must be Hymison-Cecil. He was in a rage over this but there was no denying that the paperwork and arrangements had been done and well done indeed.

With that sour note, at 3.23 o'clock the expedition took its first step; some twenty or so, when some of the servants remembered something and headed back. We continued on, as the road could not be wandered off, as it led south, and then turned in an Easterly direction to cross the swampland that links the island to the mainland. We headed into the looming hills of Dushistan, towards the area of Khisht, where our first station on our trip to Teheran would be found.

Blood-thirsty will run the goat bag, the unofficial money for off-the-record expenses that comes from selling the skins of goats, sheep and other animals purchased at government expense for feeding ourselves. By custom, we retain any value from selling the skin, hoofs and other parts not used by us. Into the goat bag will be entered any returns, payments or other monies found or earned in anyway. *{In modern terms, petty cash}*.

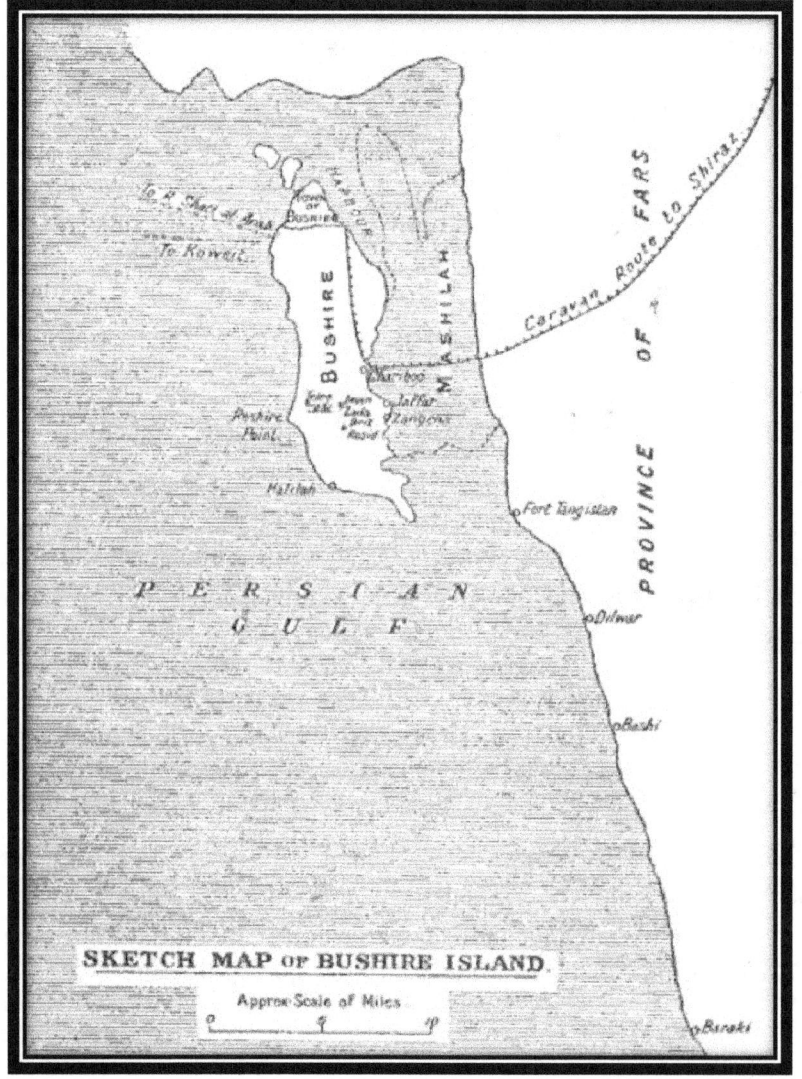

We did a final review of ourselves; weapons secured, instruments safeguarded, Vickery and Horne leading, as they had both ridden this way some years ago. I took up the rear of our party and behind me were the braying mules. We gave a salute to the British flag atop the Residence's house, salaamed in the Eastern method - while on horseback - the emblem of Persia flying from the Sheikh's house, and we were off followed by the bevy of servants and finally Basir, a lost Irishman lost even more now in the East.

Local map of Bushire and the initial route into Persia. The expedition would have followed the caravan route to Shiraz marked on the map. Illustration III-XI-32

Remarks On The Way From Bushire To Shiraz

We travelled down the East side of the city and out the southern gate, along the rocky essence of the peninsula and plunged into the swamp that separates Bushire from the continent of Asia, and making our arrival there in some hours. The soil over which we passed was a mixture of sand and broken rock, covering in patches the solid rock beneath; this gave the world a broken and un-connected appearance. Nonetheless, once we had left the town, the terrain improved remarkably and we came upon standing fields of barley and wheat and various grasses for animal feed. They are sown in December. After the winter rains had fallen, it would be harvested in another month. Also of interest was the odd way they grew grapes here. Viticulture, with the vines planted within pits, and draped over stones: all of these are located in circular enclosures around sixty feet in diameters and surrounded by low walls, which dotted the landscape. The Persian method of handling the important task of growing grapes is such that any good Frenchman would become apoplectic at the sight. Basir insists this method delivers large amounts of eating grapes. Young boys are given the never-ending task of keeping away the birds, beggars and goats. Twenty thousand date trees are dispersed here and there. My temperament was improved greatly upon leaving Bushire and seeing nature resplendent again.

A view of Bushire from the land side from the road to Shiraz. Illustration III-XI-33

Some of our caravan men may not have given the word that we could speak Persian and Arabic. I heard a few comments by one man, a Persian speaking poor Arabic to another that gave me concern. I shouted for Basir but gained his attention too late and the villainy was done.

One of our mules being deliberately tripped up, the man in charge of him had boasted he would rob the pack, while recovering the mule. He made a genitive construction {a grammar mistake} mistake which had gained my attention, when the Persian had tried plotting in Arabic. Instead of our luggage being his prize, I presented my revolver and told him in his own language that he was dismissed and without pay.

A mule takes a tumble in an attempt by the caravan workers to rob the expedition. Illustration III-XI-34

Basir tried to smooth this over, and the thief was all smiles and pretended innocence, but Perkins not only dismissed him but placed him in charge of two mounted militia men who had been escorting us and sent him well bound as a thief back to Bushire and the Sheikh. One item I found of interest was how he had caused the mule to stumble. We found from another man that the mule was trained on pronunciation of a word to trip itself. This was demonstrated for us and we rewarded the man who gave us the secret. The word was in Arabic, and quite foul, so it will not come up often. Clever these Persian muleteers! *{The word Driscol wrote out in Arabic is noted below}*

كنت القرف

We have some seven hundred and fifty or more miles to travel north to the Capitol of this Kingdom, some say Empire, but a fading one at best.

We made it but five miles further, once we had crossed to the mainland. We then settled down for the night, after our late start, near the village of Khogadak *{Choghadak or Chagadak}*. Having made a poor first day's journey from Bushire, on account of our late start, Perkins was not pleased, and gave a speech, a fine one, to our caravan and Basir. He told them I was a mad killer and that I had a magic weapon. I took his words to heart and the moment he stopped speaking I drew My Frenchmen brandished it about, and fired four rounds into an unassuming, and presumably innocent, shrubbery. Our Persian friends had never seen a repeating firearm before, and their shocked expressions and cries of alarm were quite appalling. Just in case the Persian message had not been understood I repeated the speech - with a few improvements in Arabic.

Our dinner that night was tolerably good; three dishes of rice, one made with mutton and berries, one with the roasted flesh of a Bushire fowl, which are famous for the taste of their flesh and size; and it, did not disappoint us, and the third sweet rice was mixed with all manners of nuts and fruit. To accompany this was a bowl of black grapes and sliced melon, protected from the flies by a diligent servant. We ate in the Persian manner with our hands; this being a decision made on the ship to adapt as much as possible to the Persian custom, as to become accustomed to it. One does this by bending down near the food and scooping up the rice or victual into your mouth with three fingers and the thumb of your right hand, never the left, in which you do your toilet. This proved to be difficult. I found I needed to hook my left thumb into my belt to prevent me using that ill-considered hand by mistake. Eating rice was easy. Tearing or pinching meat from the bone was a difficult task. We watched Horne and Vickery to see how this was done. It took some time, but we ate that evening in the Persian manner. Basir said we had done well.

Our dessert, as it were, was a delicate sherbet, and with that, fortunately, we were given wooden spoons.

[Editor's note: Sherbet is not the frozen delight of the modern world but in Driscol's world a concoction made from milk, dried fruits, and nuts, flavored with various fruit peels or rose water]

The water of Bushire is very bad, despite what we were told, and we had avoided it as best we could, but several of us, to myself included, were granted a demonstration of its purgative effects on an honest and trusting Englishman.

Sunday 7 May

Our *charwardar {muleteer man}* and Basir are at odds on almost everything. I believe the problem is that our muleteer is a dishonest scoundrel and Basir is just the latter. We have a simple divine service this day and move out just before dawn. We are all determined to drive ourselves and this caravan north as rapidly as possible.

Vickery recorded at noon: Cooling wind from the NW, 90° in the shade.

[Editor's note: Driscol wrote out in a letter to his mother and Karen the following which I will include at this point]

On the matter of measurements:

I had earlier neglected to record the money system of Persia, or as the natives refer to it as Farsistan or Iran. They use as coin the Piastre, Qiron and Dinar. A Piastre equals ¾ of a rupee or about 2 shillings, with 1 Piastre equaling 1,000 Dinars. They once had a coin called the Rial which was worth 1,250 Dinar but stopped minting it in 1825 and replaced it with the Qiron which is now considered equal to the Piastre.

As with many places in the East, there are many types of coins; in use with some of the names being the Beestee, Shahee and Ashrefee, all small bronze or copper coins of little value.

Our caravan leader gives distances in '*Fursungs*'.

A fursung is a method of land or distance measurement in Persia, said to be nearly the equivalent of four English miles, but in fact it is an indeterminable distance meaning almost anything, from 'perhaps that far', 'to over there at some distance' or 'a short distance out there somewhere', and in fact varying from 2 ½ miles to 6 or more.

We made our way across the dusty plain, which is white with salt, crossing a dry river bed near Ahmadi, and then passed through the plain going by low hills to our right following the caravan trail to Shiraz.

On our way, we went besides blackish swamps, and naphtha springs, whose smell can be, detected miles away.

Bannington found this geologically of interest, and fell in love with some samples of gritted asphalt mastic *{sediment with bitumen in it}*, composed of mastic, broken to small pieces less than one half inch in diameter. He melted some in a pot and found about 7% percent was pure bitumen and 40% percent dry grit. These are our first official samples taken.

Near the town of *Borazdjan {Borazjan}*, the aspect of the country changes and date and tamarisk tress appear.

Village of Borazian.
Illustration III-XI-35

We are met by a delegation of *Istakbalk {honourary assembly}*, notables who come with a detachment of irregular cavalry.

Bannington and Horne are dismissive of their equipment, order and weaponry, but are admiring of their horses.

We had travelled that day some ten and a half hours; coming into the village to stay at the old caravanserai. These places for the weary traveller have, within them, cells for wayfarers, and are made of burnt mud brick or real brick in some places. The resting place is a raised platform some two and half feet high. This can be swept and *nummads {traveling carpets}* laid. The walls are of course filthy, dirty, and blackened by smoke. I am told that if a rain comes, and the roof leaks and the walls are cleaned in this natural way, a man will come and splatter the walls again with this special décor, so the native Persian traveller will feel at home. We decide that this is unacceptable and move on.

We ride on; our caravan men protesting loudly. A Persian Jew comes to us to sell watermelons which are excellent, and we have them with our mutton, served this night with boiled wheat, dates, sesame seeds and a type of red fruit I do not recognise.

We made our way up an incline, and came to a site of elevated rock, that completely commands the road. A well serviced battery could hold this road against a division - until such time that light infantry - with souls of mountains goats - or pursued by a fiery sergeant hell bent with a stick - should turn the position, it was a Persian version of Thermopylae.

A fort, much ruined with square towers, blocks the pass and overlooks a lovely place to camp. The muleteers, still protesting, go back to the town while we remain here.

We have continued the scape-goat and it is I once again. We run a roster of one of us awake, for two hours each night, beside the native guards; who appear steady, but we are un-willing to risk a surprise.

As we set up camp, several Persians approached us and asked for our assistance in a matter of health. In Persia, and indeed all the Orient, many consider *fringees {foreigners}* to be both magicians and *Hakims {medical men}.* One of their own, for they were merchants had a badly fractured leg. The Persian, as a whole imagines all kinds of fancied disorders, brought by witchcraft, sin or the overwork that comes from irredeemable sloth.

Michaelson was presented to them, and he was treated as the wisest of sages. The Persians had come into Bushire just before us and had left, but had been moving slower, and had suffered the accident that had caused them to turn back and attempt to return. The bone of the leg had penetrated the skin and Michaelson set about his duty aided by Dobbins. Their leader was named Assadollah, the rest of his name I have forgotten for it was complex. We found they were a party of merchants just returned to Persia from a pilgrimage to Kerbal in Mesopotamia. He was well educated for a Persian and knowledgeable of our world. For one, he knew where Manchester was. He knew the superiority of western medicine and he could speak some French. The man with the broken leg was his son-in-law and cousin; for a Persian marries his first cousin at all times. He was tutoring the young man in the way of merchants. They had accompanied a body of pilgrims to that city, for in Shia Islam, there are three great places of pilgrimage for a Persian. Those are Mekkah, which is of course the most merited, and those that have been, there are granted the title of Hajji, the second most is where they had been and they are deemed Kerbelai, The lesser of the three is a visit to Meshed, and one who has done that is a Meschedi. The commoner and noble alike take these titles very seriously and anyone who purports to have done these pilgrimages, and has not, is considered a liar of the first degree. Some have been slain for claiming to be Hajji when they are not. Some men also journey to Jerusalem and Medina, but these are considered lesser places.

We invited them to dine with us, but his knowledge of western ways would not allow him to overcome his reluctance to actually eat with infidels! He offered us silver after Michaelson had conducted his operation under the fading light, aided by our lamps. The young man took his pain well and was commented upon by all of us. They were sent off, with the young man in a well-made splint. We were well thanked and Michaelson, being as it was his profession, took a token payment of one hundred dinars. Vickery tried in jest to enter this as a profit to the expedition, but Michaelson would have none of it. He reminded us of the many exams he had taken in cold halls, boring lectures in Latin by fools and too many views of corruption to go unpaid. He said that his patient had a 30% chance of not dying from blood fever, as the wound had been exposed for too long before treatment. We wished the brave young man well.

Monday 8 May

Vickery recorded at noon: haze in the morning with a fresh NW wind during the day, 91°. We were at 29°15'' north 51°12'' East and by our estimation, some fifty feet about sea level.

Nine miles to a place called *Daulakee {Dalaki}* and we began to enter the Zagros Mountains. It is here that a pass begins. On our left, is the river named for the place, whose water is brackish, but we are promised good water in Konartakhteh, some fourteen miles further on. We pass over many dry stream beds, which are rocky in the extreme - this is the main road to their Capital? The mountains rise about us in fantastical forms, their strata of great interest to Bannington, who announces we are in a folded belt, land risen up and tortured into the shapes we see. The rock is soft and crumbles in your hand, making one ride well away from the edge of a ledge.

Dissanayake falls off his horse, the heat and the motion of the ride seems to have put him to sleep. We do not notice initially, as his horse is a small mare named Betsy, and she will follow us even if the master is asleep. We were only alerted by the shouts of the fallen man and our servants. Blonde and Betsy get along well, and will often approach one another and travel and 'talk', as horses will do for, some time.

We pass two springs of brimstone *{naphtha - crude oil seep}*, the scent of which neither man nor animal entertains with any enjoyment. This black pus as Michaelson calls it is a poison to life, but some say it has healing properties. It is nearly dark, when we make it up the tiring switchbacks to Kunar Takhteh *{Konartakhteh}*. It has been twelve hours in the saddle. The caravanserai; a neat little building, is full so we camp to the side of it. As promised, there was a well-constructed tank full of good water for the horses and men. It was noticeably cooler that night and very refreshing.

Today is marked as the birth of Perkins, who is now a venerably nine and twenty years of age. We make him a present of a somewhat aged and unhappy looking fish head, wrapped in some fluctuant *{I do not understand Driscol's use of it here; it means unstable}* burlap. He is greatly pleased at our gift, and our heartfelt sentiments in which Horne, as our spokesman, expressed the thought that at his arrival to this great age, we hoped his virility was not impaired and that perhaps a session of love with one of the more comely mares might be in order?

Perkins rather unsportingly threw Horne into a small pond upon his saying the above, and earned our pretend rancour, for attempting to prevent our rescue of the honest-speaking man sent overboard. We attempted to rescue Horne, while at the same time yelling out over the small pond that dinner was served to any shark that might be about. This resulted in a melee of pushing and wrestling; with only Dobbins not ending up in the pond. We thought this rude and rushed him *en masse* and all but drowned him. The natives thought this all complete lunacy of course.

During this boyish parade, Dissanayake was singing the *{Thomas Best Jervis}* Jervee hymn 'Sweet is the friendly voice':

> *Sweet is the friendly voice which speaks, the words of life and peace;*
> *which bids the upright heart rejoice, and sin and sorrow cease.*

> *{Written in 1795}*

The Kotal-e-Doktar pass between Shiraz and Kazerun. Drawing by W. Kleiss. "Fortifications." By permission from Encyclopedia Iranica, online edition. Illustration III-XI-36

Over The Kotal-e-Doktar To Kazerun

Tuesday 9 May

Vickery recorded at noon: ground fog, then a hazy day, but cooler 84°, 29° 35'' north 51° 22''' East. We start out early but everyone, Englishman, Persian, horse and mule is tired. Perkins is adamant that we push on to Teheran at all speed. I feel he intends to shoot Hymison-Cecil on sight when we get there. We do twenty grueling miles this day. We made the crossroad to Shiraz. There is a route that goes directly north, but Basir is against going that way, as it is a rebellious and bandit filled country, and a very difficult ride. Instead we will turn towards Shiraz, which is to the East.

The ride is along a rocky path with fearful plunges down the side. My fear of high places is in full force and I spend the day sweating profusely. Betsy, who enjoys walking by Blonde, did so today trying to walk on the inside of Blonde, which caused some disturbance, as I would not be pushed to the outside. A terrifying and vertiginous day, and my hand shakes as I write; we did, however make it over the Kotal-e-Doktar pass.

We passed vistas of great natural beauty. Basir said that a great ruined city lay to the north of us *{the Sassanid city of Bishapur}*, and that great art had been carved into the sides of the mountain, and in a cave, a great stone giant resides *{the twenty-two foot high statue of King Sapur}*.

Vickery as usual was leading and we neared a small walled village. Each village in Persia that we had seen so far has the appearance of a stronghold, surrounded by high mud walls, and in each of the corners there are towers. They are built thus not to keep enemies from killing them, but to keep strangers from viewing their women. This voluntary confinement, some say, is a consequence of their frequent wars, revolutions and raids. I, and those with whom I ride, ascribed it to their jealousy and envy of their neighbours and an overpowering passion and fear that someone will steal a look at their women. It is a reasonable thing to fear this happening as a Persian spends a great deal of his time trying to do just that. They are susceptible to the wildest extent of violent bloody action against any man who might, in some remote way, threaten or be capable of seeing, their women. A woman drowning, or on a runaway horse, is left to her fate; for to rescue her is to see her and to be killed for doing so. That said, we were amused when a young girl, who could not have been about but four or five, came out to us with a kitten in her arms.

Kazerun. Illustration III-XI-37

This she offered to Vickery, who declined the honour. Perkins gave her a coin, and I some of the sweets that had been given us in Bushire; ones that would not melt. Vickery told her to keep the kitten and raise it for him, for he would be back when she was older. She agreed and asked the name she should give the beast. Vickery replied, 'Sperm whale', to which she agreed. We then rode on. After an exhausting day, we came to the town of Kazerun, set in a valley between two high limestone crests running northwest by southeast.

We ended the day by boiling water, and found that it came to a rolling boil at 208 ½ degrees, indicating an altitude a little over two thousand eight hundred feet. Basir promises us a steep climb again tomorrow.

We stopped at the Caravanserai, but found it full of contentious merchants and instead rode a bit farther and camped by a delightful lake *{Parishan Lake}*; paying a small amount to a farmer for the use of his fallow land. This was a pleasant green spot near it, a former garden perhaps, planted with cypress and orange trees.

We give Basir a drink, which he will not touch in front of the other Mohammedans. He does so in the security of our tent, and is soon drunk and asleep, as we did not wish him to listen in our council that night. We tested his insensibility by touching his arm with a burning brand, to which he did not react. Perkins and the expedition review the situation. It is Bannington and Dissanayake who provide the most distressing information. Our man of concern is known to Bannington, and he reports to us that just a week after we had left Poona, that man had taken a leave of absence. That in our estimation would have given him enough time to beat us to Persia, but how had he known to come here? In retrospect we found our own tongues may have given us away. We had spoken of Persia to five people during our recruiting trip and anyone could have relayed that information to him. Perkins is inconsolable as to this misstep of ours, for which he takes full responsibility. I made a suggestion that our passage might even have been arranged by the blonde haired man. Perkins and I, after this discussion, could see no reason for him doing so, unless he was an Englishman with the appropriate papers. We dismissed my idea together and he added later that he thought the man he had seen in Bushire had NOT been the man on the Xebec which had attacked us off Algiers.

Horne suggests that he and Vickery ride separately north. He had spoken with our drunken friend Basir in the day to confirm that he could obtain permissions for us to make use of the governmental messengers' *Chapper Khaneh {post station}*. Just two men could make Teheran in ten days or less.

The mountain passes of the Zagros Mountains, Illustration III-XI-38

Perkins seized on this idea and made it his own. He asked Dobbins if he was prepared to take the expedition up to Teheran without him? He confirmed that he was. I was miffed as I had considered myself as the second in command, although outranked by nearly everyone; he then turned to me, and asked if I cared for a long hard ride. I did and was well mollified that he had picked me to accompany him.

The Governor of the area came in the early evening and had tea and coffee with us. He seemed an empty headed man, as he talked of local politics, which meant nothing to us. He did note that I had walked by his house from our campground and he asked why I had done that? To a Persian, a man should be on horseback, as soon as he passes the door of his house. To take a walk is considered highly bizarre, and even ill-mannered. When the Persians see a person walk backwards and forwards, they conceive it must be on a sort of business that is either erotic or exotic or they look at him with far-reaching astonishment, and will even think he is out of his senses, or ill.

We had that night *Khoresht-e Chaghaleh-Badoom;* a stew of almonds and lamb, finally lamb and not tough mutton. These were spring almonds, still in their green outer shells, and a taste that was enjoyable to hungry men. All ate well; our appetites sharpened both by the hard work we had done and the coolness of the atmosphere. We eat all that there is. I am so enchanted with it, that I spend some time to draw out the recipe from our cook, who demonstrated by miming his actions in some cases.

Khoresht-e Chaghaleh-Badoom

3 pounds of lamb shoulder or shanks, 1 onion well chopped, ¼ pound or thereabouts of butter, a small bunch of parsley and mint, a spoonful of the Indian turmeric spice, some salt, a sprinkle of crushed pepper, a teacup of lemon juice and one of water and one pound of shelled almonds crushed or whole as you like.

One cooks the onions, mint and parsley in the butter and you then add everything else for an hour of cooking and then add the almonds.

Wednesday 10 May

We do our sighting this day; 29° 37' north and 51° 39' East it is 59°. This morning is brisk and such a delight after the suffocating heat of the Gulf and Bushire. Basir is appreciative of our gift last night, and even while befuddled, he does agree that yes, if we can reach Shiraz, he can obtain for us permissions to use the *chapper khaneh* and he can provide as a guide one of the messengers. He has no intention of joining us on such a ride himself, as he suffers from haemorrhoids, and while he can ride along as we do now, a hard ride would disable him.

Blonde is weary, as we all are, but the local mules are quite content. We set out, as again as we have a short time to wait as water is obtained. Bannington leads us in practicing some cavalry evolutions, going from column to charge and other manoeuvers, despite the tiredness of ourselves, and the horses, this acts as a tonic. Perkins decrees that we shall do so, whenever the land permits. We begin a horrid climb this early morning. There are times I just dismount and lead Blonde, as I am so terrified she will pitch over the side of one of these narrow passes, which sometimes narrow to a few feet.

As we climb, one of our mules brushes up against the rocks, and loosens its pack and it fell to the ground, releasing one of our luxuries: a nine pound round Double Gloucester. This cheese, on the steep incline, began to roll and rolled down unerringly some half a mile, magically bounding and turning to stay on the road, and not be lost in the ravines below. It was recovered, in a broken condition by the *charwardar,* we parceled it out and had a good meal of this piece of England, and Basir even liked it. This reminded us of the tradition that arises near Gloucester England in the May of each year on Whit Monday *{Pentecost Monday a Christian feast day},* where the cheese-rolling festival takes place at Cooper's Hill, which I had attended once as a young boy[15].

Soon after this cheerful event, Dissanayake fell off his horse again.

Bannington jocularly suggested that he had not joined the expedition to climb mountains! As we reached the worst part of the Pira-zan Pass, the temperature has risen up to the eighties and there is not a breath of wind.

[Editor's note: The creation of mountaineering as a sport had not quite occurred at this time, only a few eccentrics climbed mountains in Europe at this time, climbing a mountain for 'sport' was seen as a great folly and the exhibition of a questionable mind]

We arrived broken in body, but not spirit, but we made it only to a lovely flat place called Dast-e Arzan *{plain of the mountain or bitter almond}*. There is a lake here in this mountain basin, fed by springs, which give forth wondrous cool water. There are oak and almond trees here and good grazing land. The horses are hobbled and allowed to roam a bit amongst the ample pasturelands.

At the end of the day, we boil our water again and the thermometer reads 202 $\frac{1}{4}$, establishing an altitude of 4,900 feet above sea-level. It had been a strenuous climb and we all congratulated ourselves. Basir said this area once held lions and wild boar. That night we hear the sound of said boar too, but no lion's roar. Dobbins said that if he was not so tired, he would stalk the boar but instead went to sleep despite Horne's offer of a reward for its meat.

I found out from the *charwardar* that the nearby village is the birthplace of a man from the Qur'an, Salman the Persian who was a companion of the Prophet.

Thursday 11 May

Vickery reports it is 54° degrees today; a frosty morning. My arse and legs are in a painful condition, everything is raw and hurting. The horses, while tired, seem otherwise immune to this torture. The horses seem unaffected by the colder weather too. We travelled mostly over a country of ascents and descents, and on a better road than those of the preceding days.

There is nothing of interest to see this day, as we ride towards Shiraz, which is some five and thirty miles away. All are too tired and even Perkins agrees that we must rest some, and we do. After two and twenty miles we come to rest on a ridge, where in the distance we can just make out Shiraz an enchanted city of folklore.

A Persian gentleman. Illustration III-XI-39

I have a conversation with Perkins again over my situation with Jonaki and Millicent. I do my best to explain my now obviously bad decision in this regards. Perkins placed his hand on my shoulder and said,

'You misunderstood me Driscol; I said that you were living bloody dangerously but not incorrectly. If you felt the need for the Indian woman, perhaps Millicent is not for you'?

We have passed many other travellers, when up from Shiraz came three young Persians, what we would call 'gentlemen' whom Basir called upon. For five and thirty dinars, they will gallop this evening into Shiraz, taking a message to the *chapper khaneh* commander. It is paid, and they are on their way, happy as larks, young men on a mission for foreigners and being paid to do so; a rare treat for the Persians who talk loudly between them about using the money for wine and discreditable and appalling liaisons.

Friday 12 May

As we arise on this day, it is 60° in the morning and the mountains are shrouded in shifting misty clouds. One would think we were on Olympus itself; we have Herakles, Apollo, Ares, Hermes, Poseidon, Asclepius, Pallas and Hypnos here.

[Editor's note: This intrigued me as Driscol never explained fully which of his companions were associated with which god but he made a number of margin notes. I believe that he associated them in the following manner]

Apollo = Perkins, probably because women called him that - or so he claimed

Ares = Horne, the god of war

Asclepius = Michaelson, the god of healing appropriate for the good surgeon

Herakles = Dobbins, a strong man, Herakles was crossed out and Artemis noted down then crossed out again, and Herakles circled, Artemis being a great hunter but not acceptable as she was woman, Driscol must have seen his error and corrected it

Hermes = Driscol, a traveller, trickster and patron of knowledge

Hypnos = Dissanayake, name for the god of sleep, his ability to fall asleep anywhere and everywhere had been mentioned several times

Pallas = Bannington, this was hard but then Pallas was a titan, a giant and Bannington was the smallest in stature of the companions so perhaps it was a satire on his small size

Poseidon = Vickery, was a god of sea considering his earlier life as a whaler, he was the tallest of the companions, so perhaps Pallas should be awarded to him?

We rode towards the city, and were some miles from it, when we encountered large quantities of pheasant, *Phasianus colchicus*. Basir announced them a very rare sight in this part of the country. We secured a half dozen, with Dobbins' medusa bringing down three.

We had only just gathered up our prey, when we were approached by party of hard riding Persians, one with a large feather flowing from his turban. This turned out to be the *Chapper-Bashee {commander}* of the *chapper khaneh* come to aide us.

A conference was held. Our bona fides established and directions considered. There was a *Barid {Baird is the former name of the chapper-khaneh from the early days of the Persian Empire and still commonly used}* post just to the northeastern point of the city; near the *Darvazeh Qur'an* gate. We would make our way there, and begin our journey the next morning, when our guide, a man called Bijan Firouzabadi. All was agreed and they galloped off.

We came to a point where we could see the valley in which the city lies. It was a brownish, white city and as we rode towards it, there even being at times the hint of going downhill.

The approach to Shiraz.
Illustration III-XI-40

We made our way into and though Shiraz; the first city of any size we had seen in Persia. Shiraz has six arched gates set in a much collapsed, mud brick wall, set with semi-circular towers that barely rise above the parapet. The town is divided into ten quarters or parishes, in which there are fifteen considerable mosques, besides many others of inferior note; eleven colleges of error {religion}, and a central square which holds a large bazaar.

We passed through many streets to the Bazar-a-Vakeel, a long and spacious building, the shops of which were all laid out with their choicest merchandise to display, on this occasion, the plenty and prosperity of the country. The city's buildings are constructed with of an un-lovely, yellowish, burnt brick. My dreams of it being an enchanted city are somewhat dimmed by this.

There are several mausoleums in Shiraz; the most distinguished of those within the walls is that of Hafiz: the poet whom all of Persia loves. Of the three great poets of Persia, Firdausi, Hafiz and Sadi two of these were natives of Shiraz. All of this has caused the people here to consider themselves to be the greatest and most 'prime' of all Persians speakers. The fountainhead of pronunciation and grammar, they say that their spoken words are like honey to the ears of the other rough sorts, who make up the rest of Persia, and their elocution is always correct. They often spend a great deal of effort in making light of the speakers of Koom {Qom}, Teheran and Ispafan. It is like the people of Shakespeare's birthplace taking the Bard's birth as an indicator that they are the focal point of English in Great Britain' when it is well known that it is Eccles, Lancashire {Where Driscol was born}.

The tomb of Hafiz is to be found placed in the back court, at the foot of one of the cypress trees, which he planted with his own hands. It is a parallelogram, with a projecting base, and its superficies are carved in the most exquisite manner. One of the Odes of the Poet is engraved upon it, and the artist has succeeded so well, that the letters seem rather to have been formed with the finest pen than sculptured by a hard chisel.

The Arg of Karim Khan is a fortress with a wide ditch around it and the first usable fortress we had seen. It is a square with eight and thirty foot high curtain walls, but Basir did not know the thickness of the walls or the details of the round towers at each corner.

We paused for a few minutes at the tomb of Claudius James Rich, former British resident at Bagdad and explorer of Babylon and Kurdistan, who died in Shiraz in 1821. He was saluted.

We asked Basir about *mey {the word for wine}*, the most noted product of Shiraz is its wine made from the famous grapes of the Khullar vineyards, 30 miles from Shiraz, but only a very small quantity of it is exported, and religious scruples still prevent its manufacture on a larger scale. The wide use of wine, by this nation of supposedly non-drinkers, is well noted as is the fact that the most famous Persian literary character is that of the *Saghi*, the wine pourer, who has been a central motif within Persian poetry for more than a thousand long years.

I had heard one story from the Qur'an in that a man had been drinking wine when he heard the prophet had proscribed its use, and that he immediately spat out the forbidden drink. The Arab version of this story is added to with this comment, that when he spat it out, a Persian immediately fell on it and licked it up. The Persian version has an Arab diving for, and successfully intercepting the spat out wine in his hand before it hits the ground and his sucking it from his filthy left hand.

We found the post-house and made our arrangements. Perkins and I will travel as lightly as possible, and I reduce my luggage to my dress uniform; and on an inspiration I took with me some of the materials given me by Catania, and the gift of a Persian outfit by the Sheikh of

Bushire. I left behind both my books and the majority of my medicine case, which caused me some concern.

The Persian post house where officials and messengers could exchange horses. As guests of the Shah Perkins and Driscol made use of this perk. Illustration III-XI-41

That evening our guide presented himself: Bijan, a tall dark Persian, with a certain wit about him. He joined us to share our *Charghavol ba Khameh {pheasant with double cream}*. I nearly broke a tooth on a leaden pellet, which I threw at Dobbins, as it was one of his. I knew this, as the great hunter uses pellets with a portion of copper mixed with the lead, to give it a coppery sheen to allow him to identify that which he has shot from all others.

Bijan is conferred with. He never asks WHY we must ride with haste to Teheran; he is only concerned with getting us there. He explains how it will work. Perkins and I agree that should one of us falter, or a horse be lost that the other will press on. Bijan agrees for he knows that on coming into Teheran, he will receive a munificent gift for bringing us to the Shah: for such are our directions - to report to the Shah as soon as we arrive. That is our public stance while I know our private one is to confront Hymison, and prevent any further interference from him. I expect a frightful row *{argument}*.

The Persian post rider Bijan. Illustration III-XI-42

Bijan himself is young by action, but a rather old looking man; wiry, sturdy, with the complexion of an old, brown, leather boot, covered here with scars and wrinkles. He says he is two score old but he looks three. His body looks old, as I noted, but his eyes are of an eleven year old, full of mischief yet undone. His clothing is rough, as he is no dandy. He wears a Manchester made coat of coloured cotton that was perhaps blue when I was born. Green baggy trowsers and a frock of red calico makes up his attire topped off by a ragged skull cap of some cotton stuff over which he winds a cashmere shawl that has seen better days and atop all this he sometimes sports a lambskin hat. He is from Qom a place on the road ahead. Such is the smart uniform of a Persian *Chupra {Post rider or courier}*. He is an employee of the Post-master-general of Persia who is given the authority to oversee the lines of communications between outlying cities and the Capital of Teheran.

Chapter XII

Shiraz to Teheran

A Long Week And A Longer Ride To Teheran - Many Ruins Of Persia's Ancient Past - In Mufti - Perkins Encounters A Murderous Villain - Bijan's Family And A Short Respite - Teheran And We Find Our Man - Gregory Allen François Gizhiibatoo Hynes - A Deception Revealed - The French Bank - Politics Of Herat - The Lost Children Re-Appear - The Expedition Reunited - The Tales Of The Lost Expedition - Great Plans - The Expedition Presented To The Persian Shah

========

A Long Week And A Longer Ride To Teheran

Saturday 13 May

We rise at 4 o'clock and secure our Persian horses. I get a lively one. We enjoy waking everyone else to see us off. I have left Blonde in the care of Horne and threaten to cut off his legs if he loses her.

It is a custom of Shiraz to give charity to the poor to gain merit in the eyes of God to bless one's trip. One does so just outside the post station. There were many aged men present, who had had their eyes gouged out. I asked why there were so many, and was told about the siege of Kerman in 1794, by the present ruler of Persia's ancestor. In his revenge against the city for resisting his Majesty's mandate of kingship he had a pile placed before him of twenty-thousand detached human eyes and had the city razed.

The leader of this revolt was worse treated, and an English reader would be revolted at the tale of his treatment, which surpasses all human decency.

By tradition, a post rider goes twice through the Koran {Qur'an} Gate, and we do so mindful to follow local custom. It was built long ago and in a small room atop are placed two famous Korans known as the Hifdah-man. These books bless travellers passing underneath the gates, where it is believed pious travellers receive the blessings of the Holy Books as they begin their journey from Shiraz.

In the intense darkness we ride northwest. I regret not seeing Shiraz in the daylight more fully, for even in the shadows, I saw much that would draw my attention. We pass the river by a fine bridge and enter the city. Bijan speaks a clear form of Persian which we can understand quite well. He also speaks slowly and uses common words; we appreciate his courtesy in this. He tells us of the city in some detail, about the Armenian and Jewish quarters and the many buildings put up by the great men of the past. Few lights can be seen and we soon pass out of the city, which seemed to pass before me as an apparition.

There are posts for horse exchange every 18-20 miles and he feels we can make the first by noon, a bit of food, then on to stop the night at the second. This way we can make forty miles a day; if we wish to go sixty we must travel at night.

The horses are trained to move at a trot or cantor, which is good for the horse but punishing to the rider.

The plains of Zergoun and a caravan. Illustration III-XII-1

We made our way north and to another pass that leads out of the Valley by a narrowing of the road. We descend that pass in the morning light, into a pleasant valley, and then up another ridge to see before us larger grasslands stretched out before us: and our guide pronounced to be the plain of Zergoun. We head for a gap in the mountains many miles away. We come to the Bend Emir River and crossed it on a four-arched bridge and were now, accordingly to our guide on the plains of Mervdasht.

Bijan informed us that of the four and twenty posts before us from Shiraz to Teheran each had its own version of pillau or rice dish. We had a meal of just such, at the first post where we exchanged horses: with rice, chicken, dates, apricots, peaches and currants in it. This dish was called *Dami Ghalebi ba Morgh*.

In selecting a horse, Bijan instructed us on the way to do this as you must be aware of the bias and prejudices of the *chapar-shagird {post-boy}*. I will also remark that, though called a boy, the *chapar* is a man, usually an elderly one of great experience. The rider may select any of the horses he chooses, from a limited set of usually not more than five or six, and usually a bad lot. The *chapar* will try and steer you to the animal he does not want or whom he wishes to get rid of. After a selection it is a time for a discovery, good or bad about the horse, once a horse is taken, it cannot be exchanged unless it is utterly un-rideable and even if both front legs break off, you will have a two hour argument to obtain another. With your new horse, you mount, and in a few steps, after a period of acute suspense, you know whether your ride will be pleasant or torture. The horse is trained to either trot or canter, alternating with a walk. While Bijan seemed to enjoy a bone-breaking jog-trot, it must be said that is excruciating painful. We also have to take with us a brutish looking whip made of twisted leather with a plain handle. In the skilled hands of Bijan, it makes the most appalling whacks, but in true Persian style, it does not raise the faintest response from his hardened mount.

Perkins, as we slashed around with our new whips, made comments about how I could use this to tame a 'hoydenish' Danae. This was a word I did not know and he said it was used to describe girls who acted thusly; wild and boisterous, tomboyish, or those who expressed themselves with logical clearness of their arguments; in other words, women who thought and talked like men. I thought it most appropriate for her description. I suggested we should have brought her along. To this he thought a little then laughed and said she could have probably outboxed Dobbins. We discussed this further and decided she would make a good match with Dobbins; much more so than fair and dainty Penelope.

I then replied he could try to use it to tame Prudence, but he would probably end up being strangled with it. We did agree that if we tried that, the one who faced Danae would surely die an embarrassing, painful, crippling at her hands; while he who faced Prudence would be whipped out of her presence. While Millicent would just smile at you and you would then whip yourself to entertain her.

[Editor's note: Driscol wrote a page and a half about his feelings for Millicent but as they are a repeat of what he has written before, I have summarized them as: he loved her madly yet he could not put his finger on exactly why]

Driscol's idyllic view of Millicent. Illustration III-XIII-2

If not from our urging, our Persian post rider either likes to ride at neck break speed galloping, or a speed we call the Persian shillyshallies; a walk as slow as a man on foot, with a pace showing that he has nowhere to go - that or the bone breaking trot-jog. This must be seen in comparison to a post-rider who rode eighteen hundred miles in seventeen days, to alert the country of the death of the previous ruler. He told us this story in the two best known versions, a raucous and pious variety.

(...)

These modern Persians are cowards at the best of times: but a Persian post-rider is all together more the weakling than his fellows or any other man in the vicinity. Thus, if a province next to another province has a hint of Turcoman raiders about, he ceases to be anything but an old woman. He thusly does not like to ride at night, or considering his profession, alone, or on any path that might, be even possibly, dangerous. Bandits know that to find a post-rider is to find a man who will gladly hand over whatever he carries without the slightest hesitation or show of fight or flight.

Another characteristic of the Persian post horse is its tendency to misstep; the horses' legs show the scars of this behaviour, which rewards them harsh punishment on the ground of Persia. I found that nothing I did would cause them not to stumble two or three times in an hour. It seems they have some need to stumble and are compelled by some law of nature to fall enough times to complete some unknown, but measured quantity, to complete that which was demanded of them by some Persian god like the Romans had had *Epona* who weighs how many times they fall down versus whether they shall enter a horse heaven filled with grain fields, no wolves or men and plentiful sugar and salt licks. *{'Great mare', Driscol was wrong here the goddess was actually a Celtic or Gallo-Roman spirit}*

Knowing this from Bijan, one looks for a horse with un-scarred knees, but as Perkins remarked after we had exchanged several horses, searching for such was like looking for an honest man in Parliament or a virgin among the daughters of a Guard's Regiments' Corporals.

At one point I encountered a procession headed by pilgrims, in which were blue and green turbaned Sayed's; or direct descendants of the Prophet. All behind a retinue of white-turbaned Molaahs *{Shia priests}* following them, was a long queue of the King of Spain's trumpeters

{donkeys, a British insult to Spanish nobility}, carrying on each side of them a long object wrapped in black felt.

A pilgrimage of dead Persians on their way to their final resting place at the Holy city of Meshed. Illustration III-XII-3

There were some score of these, and I found as I pass them what they were; rather dead Shia's on their way to the city Meshed, the blessed 'City of the Silent' where all the faithful wish to be buried. Some, however, had not been embalmed, and this brought forth a repulsive cadaverous stench, some of the bags were also not fully sealed, and they revealed the presence of poorly dried human bones. Wealthier dead men were carried by horses that looked decidedly unhealthy themselves.

I went to a gallop at that point. Noting that the donkeys were all jacks and no jennets *{male and female}* for no Muslim man can be carried or accompanied to his final resting place by a female human or animal!

There is scarcely a green shrub to invigorate the brown mountains which rise before us; the *Mist Rahmed,* which here and there are varied by the starkness of their varied forms, as extravagant and shocking, as they are uncongenial to view. Large flocks of bird's flew over our heads at times, and the road here and there was strewed with ruined castles, towers and fortifications.

At the end of our day, and two miles from our post, lay the remains of fabled Persepolis, the ruined capitol of the ancient Achaemenid *{Persian}* Empire; destroyed by the hand of Alexander the Great my namesake *{Driscol's middle name was Alexander}.* Although very tired, I need to see this, and I left Perkins to sleep as he had little interest in stones. I walked to the city my legs in need of a different type of exercise.

My first and indeed lasting impression was astonishment at the immensity and an admiration for the Persians to have built such a city. I had previously borne a great number of emotions to be here at dusk in Persia, when but a few short months before, I had been in England. I was enraptured, enthralled and sad. For here had stood the famous city of Persepolis! A group of walls still rise, with a series of columns. Many are the cuneiform inscriptions on the walls, but what they say is unknown to the people of our day. Many of the inscriptions are un-finished. Alexander is said to have burned the city, but I saw no sign of this; but after two thousand one hundred years what could one expect? Some of the stone, which I examined by lantern, was as smooth as glass. Islam has left its mark on the city, with many of the faces of men and monsters chipped away, for they hold that no face should be shown in art. So the faces of even the winged bulls are missing. I tread upon a terrace built of black marble and counted some two and seventy surviving columns. Some of what I saw seemed to me to be Egyptian in style, but mostly I saw a type of Greek architecture. There were sphinxes on which Europeans had left their mark. I saw carved there, the names of several noted explorers.

I wandered for some time, but the darkness made me grip my Frenchmen and I soon made my way back to the post, becoming lost for some time until I found it again, much to my relief.

It seemed I had but a moment of sleep, when Perkins was up and it was time to ride again.

Persepolis; Driscol saw it at dusk and during the evening he would have enjoyed it even more in the full light of day. Illustration III-XII-4

Many Ruins Of Persia's Ancient Past

Sunday 14 May

We had slept an hour later than we had planned and one delay after another kept us at the post until dawn had well broken. From us to the north was a noticeable hill, on which was a fortress.

My enthusiasm to see more of the great city overwhelmed both Perkins and our guide, who grudgingly diverted to take a look at it. In the end, Bijan was unmoved and Perkins enchanted.

The gateway of Persepolis with Bijan presumably standing before it. Illustration III-XII-5

We diverted somewhat again to view in passing the tombs of the Persian kings at Naksh-i-Routem *{Nagsh-e-Rustum}*; these consisted of a cube-shaped building and four magnificent carved tombs, cut into the living rock of the Gonbaden Mountains. Perkins regretted our inability to stop but did say we would stay some days in this spot, once the expedition was completed, and we were on our return journey. We went through a pass of sorts and turned to the East. We rode some six miles before turning to the northwest up a narrow, torturous, valley. We saw few people, but did sight a large herd of gazelle on the far horizon. Nothing helped to pass the monotony of the journey. Boredom was the king of this day, until we made the next post, where we had more rice; this time rice mixed with aubergines; called *Dami Eslamboli* by some, slimy and tasteless by me.

We passed the gorge of Sivend, whose walls rose above us like the walls of a house would seem to a long sighted mouse.

We crossed a stream at a poorly maintained bridge and came to a solitary spire, a Doric style fluted column, with a double-headed sphinx for its capitol and around it, laid many of its brothers and sisters. They were similar to those I had seen in Persepolis. Perkins was dismissive of these mere rocks and said, 'think instead of the trophy we can make of a *{Hymison-}* Cecil's head'. This was a good joke and he indeed was envious of my night time journey to Persepolis.

Bijan called this the Column of Cyprus but I found in questioning him about Persepolis, that he had never gone there, and his general view of the world was locked onto this road; what might be fifty feet away from it, he was completely, and happily unconcerned about.

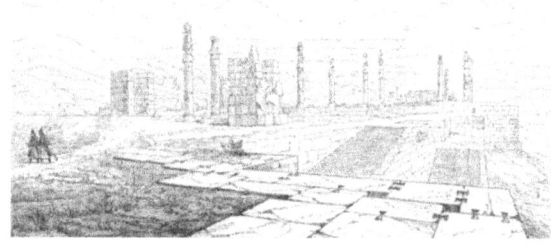

Persepolis in the dawn's diffused light. Illustration III-XII-6

We pushed on into the mountains, passes and valleys passed us in succession; here and everywhere laid ruins and broken masonry. The main reflection on this day's ride, as I write this, was two-fold; pain in the my nether regions, and this evening's rice was a kind that came interlaced with a yellowish bean called *dampokht,* and was quite tasteful.

Monday 15 May

To make up for yesterday's delay, we awaken an hour earlier, and are away. I am amused still by the fact that I, in the early morning, am immediately awake, while Perkins, and to a lesser extent Bijan are groggy for ten or so minutes. We ride through countryside; all shades of brown. In making a turn we found a refreshing wind from the north. So delightful was it that we rested there a luxurious ten minutes and had the heat and dust blown away with, but for a short time, our many concerns, discomforts and cares.

It is my legs, buttocks and lower back that are in near agony now. We sup on rice and noodles, some kind of meat and plentiful dates for tiffin. I get a very lively horse in the afternoon that cannot be held back and I outpace my fellows.

The pass through the mountains, from a military point of view, presents the most admirable means of impeding the progress of an enemy, and Perkins and I pass the time in discussing how one could defend or assail it.

Bijan took us off the trail somewhat to bring us to the Tomb of Cyrus the Great, this surprised us, but he had learned that we liked such sights, and would give him a gratuity if we were gladded by what we were taken to view. He told us to rest, and rode off returning in less than an hour with our change of horses. Several persons were in the vicinity, who came to talk to the foreigners that had been deposited in their midst. We were a third of a mile off the main road, and it was as if we had entered a different world and time. One elderly Persian we found was a Mullah and well versed in the history of the land. He was very happy to find that we knew Persian and Arabic, as he had learned that Holy language himself. He knew the tomb as that of the great king, but the natives call it *Mashad-e Madar-e Solayman {the tomb of the mother of Solomon}.*

A view of the Tomb of Cyrus also known as the Mashad-e Madar-e Solayman - the tomb of the mother of Solomon. Illustration III-XII-7

He said the natives had called it that when the Arabs had come to bring them the warmth of Islam, but they had wished to destroy the tomb, as it was of a heathen king, and it was against the tenets of Islam to have a marked burial; but the women of the town convinced them it was the tomb of Solomon's mother, and that the Arabs felt it was something that should not be destroyed.

It is a simple tomb set, on six courses of ashlar masonry, atop of which sits a rectangular stone tomb with a curved roof.

Nearby, the learned man said, was another ancient city called *Pasargades,* which I had not heard of.

[Editor's note: The learned man was correct in both cases. It is thought to be Cyrus's tomb and the city of Pasargad. As for the story about the lie to the Arab raiders - well it's a nice tale and of course it could be true - or not. Later Driscol came back and noted down in this journal that the great Strabo, the ancient author, had written about this city, but Driscol had drawn a blank about it at the time. [Editor's note: Driscol seems to have greatly liked this monument and recorded the writing that is on the structure. ꜰ꜓꜓ ꜷ ꜒꜓꜓ ꜷꜰ ꜰꜱ—꜒ ꜱꜰ꜓꜖ ꜷꜱ꜖ ꜱꜱ ꜷ (I am Cyrus, who founded the empire of the Persian); of course at that time it could not be read, and its translation was to be in the future by Grotefend in 1847]

He told us of what lay ahead in more descriptive terms than Bijan. He gave all distances in Persian fursungs, which we have found are estimates, more usually over-calculated than underrated. Bijan returned to tell us that this tomb was the greatest tomb in the entire world: a typical example of Persian exaggeration. I asked if he had seen the pyramids of Egypt. He had not, nor did he know where Egypt was, or what I meant by a pyramid! I suggested that when he went to Mekkah *{Mecca}*, he should take the time to go to Cairo.

He did tell us to be careful when passing through the next town. I was told in whispered confidence that their local mullah not only suffered from meager sacerdotal qualifications, but had an unlimited capacity for marrying, then divorcing young girls. He also drank and inspired his followers to raid and kill other Muslims with whom he did not agree, over what the Qur'an said. I thanked him for his warning and we skirted that town by riding around it.

After this cross-country ride, we ate our tiffin as we rode, which is a good way to consume rice, for it was always rice at the post. This time it was peas and lamb and was called *Nokhod Pollo.* One spills food over everything, but several small birds of a species I did not recognise, were brave enough to land and did a fine job of finding and eating every lost grain of rice.

When a good Persian needs to swear something is true, or to curse an enemy he has a delightful palate of words and phrases, which he uses the most common words uses. The most common words used are the Almighty, Allah, the Prophet, Ali - very popular - Houssein, beard, his life, his death, his father or grandfather and various variations of this, or comedic combinations.

He might come out with, 'By the prophet's beard, what I say is true'; or, 'I swear I have never touched wine, on my grandfather's grave', etc.

One can learn these and express them virtually with no English accent, my three favourites are, 'By my grandfather's beard you art the fool', 'If I lie may the Prophet keep me from heaven', and the always useful, 'Tis true, I swear by the truth of Ali's martyrdom'.

During our interminable ride, we came across many Persians riding the trail. One notable was a Persian officer of the camel corps, who came promenading along with a detachment of his soldiers on foot.

He returned our greeting in great style, but would not speak to us at length; obviously an uncivilized, superstitious, misbegotten, and mongrel individual.

Persian camel corps with infantry support. Illustration III-XII-8

Bijan apologised for this rudeness, saying he must be from Qazvin, a place where the men were not manly. He noted also that Isfahani men act like greedy Jews, Rasht had women who looked like men, and Shirazis were just foul and slothful. He then told us a story about the Qazvin, who are so degenerate that they execute woman; something the Persians very rarely do, even for murder.

If a woman is to be executed, no man will do it, so the countryside must do it. She might be force to step into a well, poisoned by her own hand, or crushed. He recounted the case of a lovely girl from the lower classes of Gazvin. She was very pretty by all accounts, and had a certain reputation for immodest talk and actions. One of her actions was to draw the interest of a top Mullah's son. This gained the anger of said son's grandmother who did not want her grandson to marry beneath himself, so she approached the senior Mullahs to deal with this outrage and to point out the girl's un-Islamic escapades. The lovely girl was sent for and she demolished the charges by the adroit use of the Koranic scriptures, reason and logic. The grandmother was outraged and she worked for some time to gather to her all the woman of the city - they then ambushed the girl in the bazaar, wrapped her in a carpet, and had every female of the city walk or jump on it until it was flattened. The murder done, the grandmother was praised and never charged, and it would not have excited much consideration at all but for the beauty, and notoriety of the target and more importantly that a perfectly good Kerman carpet was ruined.

In his journal Driscol listed the members of the expedition and rated them in accordance to their loyalty to Perkins versus H *{most probably Hymison}.*

Perkins & Driscol solid
Bannington did not like Hymison and had nothing to gain from him and was a complete gentleman.
Dissanayake seemed as unlikely to turn against us as anyone.
Vickery had no wants and was a completely loyal fellow but had not met Hymison.
Michaelson struck us as completely loyal but he had also not met Hymison.
<u>Horne might be tempted by offers of patronage to gain a Cavalry commission and money. Concern.</u>
<u>Dobbins, the man with the least political power or money and was not a true gentleman and he had questioned Perkins' orders at times. Those two we would need to be watched.</u>

[Editor's note: the sentences underlined in the original, single and double lines]

In Mufti

Tuesday, Wednesday & Thursday 16-18 May

[Editor's note: Driscol wrote about the following three days at a later date for the reason noted below]

Another day, we are in a more isolated area and there is a problem with my horse, who is both lame in the left foreleg, and has an addlepated twit for a master. The one I rode yesterday is exhausted, so as we agreed, before we began, I must remain behind while Bijan and Perkins move on. As soon as they are gone I find we have been deceived the animal is not lame, but instead is unlucky. A horse had been sold to the government with the very luckless mark of a white foreleg, but this was covered up by a stain, which the station master had discovered, after several weeks when washing the animals for the first time. He certainly could not send out a guest of the Shah on an inauspicious horse. He is now off to exchange it for a horse in the nearby village. A post such as this should have a half-dozen horses but Bijan says the men who run the stations hire them out to farmers for commercial work.

A minute after he leaves, I am asleep on the *sukoo {raised bed}* at the station. I awaken at late morning - he has another horse and more *Nokhod Pollo*. I take both with thanks.

I ride through a number of small mean looking villages. Dihbeed *{Modern Dehbid the village of willows}* was one. Every house is covered by a rounded roof made of thatch; an approach to building probably forced on the natives by the scarcity of large pieces of timber in this sparse region. This matter of construction was common in all the places which I have seen so far in Persia and the doors and porticoes are universally formed with a pointed Saracenic arch *{seen below}*. The caravanserai here is in near ruin, and no potable water can be found, except in scrummed over pools that are vile, yellowish green. I survive by obtaining milk from herders for a trivial sum.

The road was monotony itself with no fellow travellers; not even a single blade of grass or a view of middling interest.

I did have one piece of excitement, when I came to a small town of perhaps a thousand inhabitants; the path around it was rough, so I decided to ride through. I was near the centre, when a rough-looking fellow, both ragged and forward-looking came up and began to demand who I was and where I was from and why did I think I was going to ride through his town; or so I was to understand from his rapidly delivered Persian.

I replied that I was an Englishman, a guest of the Shah proceeding on his ruler's business and who was he to obstruct me. I did not offer him any of the documents I carried, as he did not resemble a man who could read.

He could tell of course that I was no Persian, and some sort of foreigner, but he dismissed my explanations and demanded that I come and explain myself to the *durkhaneh {mayor or official}*. He was joined by several others, who insisted it was not safe or prudent for me to ride through their town, without being identified.

Making sure My Frenchman and Ascalon were within easy reach I directed them to lead me to such man as they wished. They did so and I felt more like a captive in a Roman triumph, than a traveling Englishman. We came to some ruined little place, I kept on my horse while they ran about trying to find an official, and they found one, a greasy, fat one, who was not happy to have been awoken from his daily nap. I showed him my papers which included papers, with the signature and seals of the Shah's Vizier. This he read, read again then folded it up quietly, kissed it and handed it back to me with a small bow. He then turned and slapped the first man so hard, that he fell at my feet, causing the horse to jump back. For one horrible moment, I thought she might start kicking, like Blonde might have done, but she did not. I thanked him for his kindness and suggested that the first ragged man might enjoy a turn in the Shah's transportation corps, as he was a *korreh khar {son of a donkey}*. This pointed jest brought forth a mixture of laughs and scowls. I turned and rode out of that town at a trot to depart the vicinity as soon as possible. I, for several miles, examined the road behind continual but there was no one following me.

In another village, a side show of some sort was being acted out and a large Negro drank three large pitchers of water and then for nearly four minutes he spouted it out in a never ending fountain of water. While so watching, I became aware of stern and hard looks directed at me, and I quickly left the show.

I passed the high point of the trail which rises a mile above the sea. Here the road is marked by ruts and rubble of brown limestone making detours necessary. The last two incidents had demonstrated to me the idea of traveling alone as an Englishman was perhaps not the best solution to my present situation.

Driscol's brand of Ink which he added to his beard's dye. Illustration III-XII-9

Having ridden well beyond the village I went off the road to a secure place among some large rocks and changed into my Persian clothes given me by the Sheikh of Bushire. I also used my small silver mirror to apply the black dye Catania had taught us.

Hair dye; one part ammoniure of iron, sulphate or iron one part, gall nuts two
parts and eight parts of distilled water

I found that this was not quite thick enough for my purpose and added some Sanford's ink as thickener the same in which I write this.

So I went off the road as Ensign David Driscol and came back to it as an *Adyghe {Circassian}* mercenary, from Kuban and a speaker of Kabardian, a language I knew not a word of and my explanation was that I was on my way to seek employment in Teheran. Feeling more confident, I rode on, and having gathered plentiful dust from the road I rode into the first settlement, where no notice was taken of me, I obtained some fruit and made my way back to the main road, confident in the quality of my disguise. I was greeted in the Muslim fashion by many, who in the past had only grimly saluted me, if at all.

I passed by travelling merchants; from a single itinerant, to a half mile long *tukhi-e-rawans {caravan}*, *abbas douzis {beggars}* at whom I always throw small copper coins. I bought small items from the *Eeliauts*[1].

I listened for some time to the people in the small bazaars I passed, but it was all *guftigu {bazaar talk or in modern parlance, gossip}*.

I was caught by a splendid little dust storm that blew up, assaulted me thusly, and then departed as fast as it had risen. I found myself coated in a yellowish-white dust neatly calsomined.

[Editor's note: Calsomined means whitewashed but the word is sloppily written, and the word I think it is, is not attested as being used before 1860 so what was the word?]

More rice for my supper. I forgot to record its name, but it had lamb, yellow peas, turmeric and a taste of lime and cinnamon. I slept well for a few hours, then decided to push on at night. I believe Perkins and Bijan passed though some eight hours before me. The post keeper tried to persuade me not to attempt it but the moon is at $^3/_4$ full and the night is clear. I set out determined. Persia at night under the moonlight takes up an ethereal unreal look.

I worried that in his passion Perkins might actually do harm to Hymison, so I considered ways to 'put him out of the way without the need for strife and foul'. I believe the best way is to subdue him, and place him under the forced care of a Christian order of monks, as an insane person. The good brothers would then keep him under control until we return. It could be done with a sufficient lubrication of rupees, and if we can find the proper, pitiless, Godly men. The only possible difficulty might be if he has supplied himself with supporters. In such a fight, I believe

we could, barring any refusals or changes of stance, overwhelm them as Michaelson, Bannington and Dobbins would all three act, and be as two men each.

The interior square of a Persian Caravanserai. Illustration III-XII-10

I remembered well a game of Paille-maille *{Pall Mall, a lawn game that later evolved into croquet}*, I was in as a child where due to some blatant cheating a struggle had ensued with the mallets swung and balls thrown, but it was more shouting and threats. I recalled that tumultuous juvenile broil when thinking of our men meeting those of Hymison.

I now stand in the saddle for minutes at a time to relieve my pains and sore spots. A post horse is to be ridden the full time, but I took to walking the beast for ten minutes or so an hour. I stopped also and made a remedy of talc triturate *{Talcum powder}* and tease *{tea?}* oil. This works to a minor degree. I am happy to make the next post. I ride on after many mouthfuls of *Sabzi Pollo*, or green rice made with butter and spices. I do not find it to my full liking however. I strive forward having placed a purchased coverlet over my saddle for more comfort.

The land I rode over was part wild mountains then desolate plain, then manicured lawn, then again more steep, narrow, passes within the mountains of Mayeen.

These plains of Kooshkizerd are where the King of Persia keeps his horses and where some of the post horses are bred; as well as the plains of far and fair Mazandaran to the north.

The plains to the northward of my route are bounded by a flat horizon, from which every successive ridge, hill, mountain, village or building rose, as I advanced, like ships seen at sea.

The land is of stone, then gravel, small forts and caravanserai appear and are visited, horses obtained, a dish of rice eaten, and then I am off. Sometimes the master of the post is talkative and asks me about the reason for my haste. Some are silent and morose, some are energetic, some are impertinent and slack in their duties and one is treated to my whip for his insolence.

They ask because haste in the East is associated with insanity, murder, adultery, theft and war

and the last is reason for both haste and sloth too.

A Persian Caravanserai and post house photographed by Captain Crookshank, R.E. who retraced the expeditions route through Persia in 1937 for the Hereford Times, which published a two paragraph story of the expedition in 1937 on its 100th anniversary. Illustration III-XII-11

What misery I am in, as I pass through the fortified village of Abadeh, with its cascading stream where I sit, fully -clothed in its passage; soaking my body entirely. I am much refreshed by its cold water. I purchase *zerd allou {apricots}* at those villages where the land has water; where there is water, the barren land blooms. Walled villages are the norm now and I skirt them, not wishing to be questioned or delayed. At the village of Soormek, the *Khad-Khodah {head man}* flags me down and is delighted to find I am no Persian for he has an affair that requires a man like me to accomplish. There is a murderer in a valley to the East of the town. None of his relations will bring him in or pay the Qisas[2], but they have agreed that if no town man is involved in his apprehension and execution, they will not object. He offers up a fifth of a Toman, a gold coin worth some 2,500 dinars or roughly a two shillings and four pence or perhaps 2 rupees. I respectfully decline his offer, but did suggest that they wait for a party of foreigners coming up behind me and ask for a man called Blood-Thirsty *{Vickery}* or Dobbins who would be willing to do it. He accepts my declinement and said that another foreigner had said the same thing earlier in the day. I take that as a sign of Perkins.

One village seemed to have suffered from an infestation of *moolah {Mullahs}* for next to the caravanserai and the post station was an *Imaumzadeh {shrine}*. Touts came to me short of the town to have me worship the ashes of Mohammad, a son of Imaum Zein-ul-Abideen *{A great-grandson of Prophet Muhammad}*, whom I

had never heard of. I made my excuse with the classic Arabic word of delay and procrastination *bukra inshallah {tomorrow God willing}*. I was not about to tempt my novice skills at Islamic prayer amongst those faithful, especially alone.

The village of Yezdikhaust.
Illustration III-XII-12

I came, I remember as I write this afterwards, to a remarkable ravine that had at its bottom a beautiful stretch of green, spanned by a bridge of unusual aspect and a wonderful town; a fairy town in its appearance.

The fantastically situated houses were mud and stone buildings sitting atop a great rock which rose out of the dry river bed. The village's perch was some two thousand feet long, but only one hundred and forty wide. It could only be approached by a narrow and not very strong-looking bridge. I longed to visit this village, which seems like a great ship petrified to stone in this ravine, but fear and the pain in my arse prevented me. It was here I understood was Yezdikhaust *{Izadkhvast}*. There is a proverb in Persian that I learned while traveling on the William Fawcett.

> *There are three good things in in Persia, the wines of Shiraz, the Ladies of Yezd and the bread of Yezdikhaust*

By the road was a marker of sorts; noting that in a year I could not read, and so could not determine the date in our AD calendar; for I had not learned how the years of the Persian calendar are translated. It stated that in 1158 by the *Jalaali* calendar *{Persian calendar for the year 1779 AD}* the men of Zaki Khan had slain their leader due to the atrocities he had attempted here.

I passed this interesting place and increased my pace and was rewarded by a squall that passed me, leaving me wet and refreshed.

As a general rule it is difficult, if there is light, to miss the track; for the route is not simply a mule track which crosses plains, climbs mountains, and descends gorges. Sometimes, so to speak, it is instead a single rut, and sometimes a wide belt of parallel paths, yet the passage of countless animals has left such impressions upon the soil that the direction to be followed can often be traced in advance for miles. At night, a stranger would be lost at once, if this worn path was not there, I suspect that these routes have been used for thousands of years and are antediluvian in age.

I lost my horse only once, one great fear when riding alone in a foreign country, is that the horse not being your friend, will take off when you are off her, it or him, when answering nature's needs. In this specific case while buying some fruit, my scheming horse seeing her chance to be free, bolted away jerking the reigns from my hand. Away he plunged deep into the convoluted alleys of the village I was in. We had quite a game of 'approach and run' before we could drive him out again. I say we, as I hired on the spot five young men, and offered a princely sum to the man who could grab her bridle.

A Persian woman in her full glory and a bevy of beauties. Illustration III-XII-13 & 14

In the chase the beast burst through a gate, with me and two of the men in hot pursuit we set off a bombshell of excitement, as a bevy of young Persian girls were

scattered; who went screaming this way and that, trying to fashion their veils, which frighten the horse so much, that it stopped its run completely. Unfortunately I was unable to savour the experience of the rare and forbidden spectacle of all these lovely faces as I had at that that moment run chest first into her, the horse's, less interesting part.

A Persian peasant girl in her working clothes and no veil. Illustration III-XII-15

Nothing is more feared or fearsome than a dozen screaming Persian women, and having faced it myself, I can assure you I would rather face the charge of a company of bayonet armed Prussian Guardsmen, with a rage on, instead. It ended up that I was the one who secured her but I gave each the amount of 10 Dinars worth; perhaps a pice and a half in Indian currency or in total $^1/_{32}$ of a rupee or a pence and change, they were quite delighted at these riches. I was sure as I rode out of that village I would be ridden down and shot for seeing some faces I should have not.

In another part of my ride, I surprised a peasant girl newly risen to do her chores; she did not hide, but gave me a thrilling smile. I remember it well.

The night Sky of Persia. Illustration III-XII-16

One of my clearest memories of riding at night was when I had noted earlier an occultation of the Pleiades by the moon, the cheery and bright moon now set and dark was the night. I was beset by unreasonable terror; a terror of sound, sounds with no knowledge of what might be making them plagued me that early morning. The most particular that I remembered came at first from the back of me. I heard the peel of a bell, and then soon after, I heard it again. I stopped in the middle of the road to listen more closely, my hand determining that both Ascalon and My Frenchman were at easy reach.

The sound was sorrowful and pleading, and a perfect consistency of iteration, gradually growing nearer to me, swelling in its intensity, nearer and louder, and perhaps, I thought, intermingling with the tones of many smaller bells. I could make no sense of it and left the pathway and rode out into the plain some distance. On a flat stony plain, there is no place one can hide and I did not relish the thought of trying to get this unknown horse I sat astride to lay down. So prepared for the worst, I waited. Dim shapes resolved themselves before me, for by now the moon had set over an hour ago and all was dimness and shadow. Suddenly out of the darkness loomed a slow moving light-coloured mass, like a ghost ship on a shadowy lake, moving with a slow flowing motion and then to this ghostly vision were added the sounds of a soft shuffling, the great ghoulish procession moved on past me lasting many minutes. It was disappearing into the darkness and was about to be swallowed by the night, when a voice, loud and clear, said in Persian, 'The worst day for a cock is the day when his feet are washed - for then he knows he is to be eaten' and the caravan, for that is what it must have been, disappeared into the gloom of the night. Caravan, of course! Why this simple explanation had not come to me at the start, I did not know, but I blamed my weariness and my fallacious knowledge that caravans did not move at night. Well at least one did! I often wondered during my ride what had been said before and after that peculiar statement.

I arrive in the morning at a place called Qowmsheh *{Shahreza}* and find that Perkins and the guide are but an hour ahead of me, as they had spent the night but had moved out before dawn. They offer cold *Albaloo Pollo*, rice with sour cherries and chicken; probably the best I had had so far, and I consume two pounds or more of it before the master brings me another horse to continue my journey.

The caravanserai where Perkins confronted a ruffian and nearly shot him. Illustration III-XII-17

I press forward at speed and arrive at the next post which is Mahyar, which has a strong wall in good repair - but only one side exists; the other three are complete gone. The village lies beneath the shadow of a great rock. The gate is unguarded and consists of an arched portal, well covered in green, lacquered tiles and splendid brickwork, from here; one enters a large square, which was unpopulated when I arrived. The caravanserai is off this square, along with the Post area. The building is extensive, with a veranda built under lofty arches, and I find, to my shock, that my companions had not arrived.

I feared at first I had missed the road, but no, I am correct, I am still on the road from Shiraz to Teheran. Somehow, we had missed one another. I am utterly spent. I am so tired I am unable to eat. The water here is so detestable that I cannot drink it. Instead I purchase a large draught of fresh goat's milk. Drinking this down, I buy another which meant the man had to find another goat. Finally another was secured and my thirst finally quenched. I take a bench outside under the arches and wait with my weapons and luggage about me. A Persian of the better class rode by me, attended by a servant on foot. He kindly acknowledges me, but hearing in my reply that I was a foreigner, his look took on a stern expression and he rode on. I said to him in Danish, *'Din lille lort'* *{You small piece of shit}*. I knew Danish cursing well from my summer with Onkel

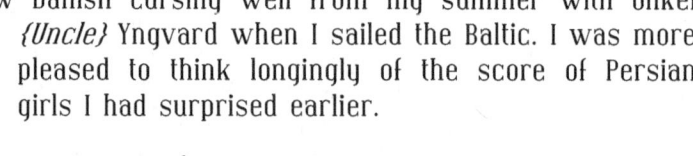

{Uncle} Yngvard when I sailed the Baltic. I was more pleased to think longingly of the score of Persian girls I had surprised earlier.

A group of Persian women gossiping. Illustration III-XII-18

[Editor's note: within Driscol's tattered notebooks are bits and pieces of paper, stray sheets, items torn from other journals, etc., one such fragment torn from a magazine or newspaper and yellow with age. I will place here. It is not noted when or who said

this; or if they are Driscol's comments put into print: ...such surroundings, one would expect to find cultured and witty girls, if not beautiful ladies, for all beautiful women are witty, for they have the wit and wherefore all to be beautiful. In Persia, the latter is rarer than a unicorn, and the former long since extinct. The Persian woman is by her nature still a child. A poorer class woman works all the time, the middle class are raised as children, and like the rich or noble classes, do no real work, for they have slaves and servants for that drudgery. They spend their time in endless gossip changing clothes to impress one another, and doing nothing whatsoever to educate the mind or spirit furthermore.....]

Perkins Encounters A Murderous Villain

I awoke suddenly sprawled on the ground, I thought I had fallen from my perch, while asleep, but it was Perkins! He was standing above me, demanding to know where I had obtained that rifle. He was speaking Persian, and had a very large Colt revolver that I knew very well, pointed at my head. I am bemused and befuddled but finally, I was able to swallow and speak in French.

Une femme est un diable tres perfectionne
{A woman is a very perfect devil}

This being one of his favourite and oft used phrases, he stood dumbfounded for a moment. So I fired another volley, as I dearly wished for him to not fire that revolver. He was a poor shot, but not too bad at a range of two feet. So I added in haste another of his favourite saying, not thinking of the simpler path of simply announcing who I was.

Friendship is more to be valued than love, for love is a thing a man can buy and a woman can
get for nothing

He still kept the pistol pointing at me, the confusion in his eyes growing, and so I kicked him in the shin and told him in English that I was Mr Driscol. That cleared the confusion from his eyes.

He cried at me, 'damn your eyes Driscol, it is you, and I nearly shot you. I thought you some Persian bandit who had taken Ascalon from you! How in God's name did you get in front of me dressed as a Persian pimp'?

'I am terribly clever', I replied to which he could only nod and grin, 'And I am a Circassian'.

Bijan has come up and declares *furdah, ispahan, inshallah {Tomorrow if God wills it, Isfahan}*, and says my disguise had fooled him completely, helped no little by the layer of dust that lay on my features.

[Editor's note: Driscol's beard would have been several inches long by now, and if dyed black, with well, sunbaked white skin he would have been the picture of middle-eastern manhood; if overly tall and having hazel eyes, which while rare, were not unknown]

We are all tired, and Perkins says that perdition might claim him, but he must break his own word to himself and me. With that declaration, we spend the rest of the day here and also stayed the night to rest. Bijan pays for a different meal, as we are in a more fertile area, so no rice tonight. We have *Koofteh-ye Sabzi* or parsley meatballs, which are quite good. I sleep on my side and stomach this night. I find that he and Bijan had gone off the road to seek nature's comfort at one point and had been off the path for a half hour and somehow we had missed one another during that time. Given the wide expanses we had been traveling our good fortune had deserted us that day.

Friday 19-22 May

We rise in the pre-dawn, stiff, tired, and saddle-worn but we ride on, and we decide as one to push on at all speed. Perkins, inspired by my dressing as a native, takes it up too.

We have both become accustomed to the trot of these horses, are backs and stomachs more ready to deal with the two-beat gait it performs. We decide to push on as far as we could, as we were paired up again and experienced in distance riding now.

Isfahan. Illustration III-XII-19

We previously caught glimpses of the city in the distance, when all at once, we emerged from a small wood on top of a hill, There, lying before us, was the grandest type of panorama of ruins, bridges, domes, blue tiled mosques, minarets, palaces, well-tilled fields and gardens, all of which are surrounded by a wall which runs some twenty or more miles to encompass this great space. The mountains, which bound the plain to the Eastward, are the most distant; and those to the west are most strongly marked, and all are dark without any verdure. The general appearance of the soil in the town is light, and nearly of the same colour as the houses.

We have come to fabled Isfahan {Esfahan}, once the royal capital but now a faded provincial town; a mile high and so cool to our delight despite the intensity of the sun. This once great city is no longer 'half the world' as it was formerly known. The city was destroyed by the Mongol Tamerlane, who rose up his infamous pyramid; the structure built of skulls torn from seventy thousand inhabitants who had resisted him. Its recovery was badly delayed again by the actions of the Afghans and the long civil wars of the 18th century. So damaged was it, that the Kajar Shahs moved the capital to the less-damaged Teheran.

Bijan noted that a town before the city was inhabited by Armenian Christians. We passed a deputation of Armenian clergy, *Parska-Hye* composed of their Bishop and attendant priests chanting this and that and who carried flags on which were shown the passion of our savior.

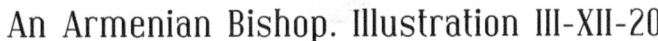

An Armenian Bishop. Illustration III-XII-20

We spoke to them in Persian and they were very happy to find two foreign Christians on the road. They made no mention of our dress. We were blessed, sanctified; holy-watered and otherwise made whole and safe. Perkins remarked that his father could have learned some things from them on show and pageantry.

[Editor's note: Perkins' father was the Bishop of Westchester]

We crossed a river, whose name I do not recall, as I write this later, on a great bridge with four and thirty arches. We passed gardens and pigeon towers on a great road that stretched out in front of us, and it pierced the wall at a ruinous gate. There we entered onto a great space of open ground, which Bijan said was the *Chahar Baghe*. The road here was lined with plane trees. Beyond the trees, were great gardens that were called at one time the eight paradises, these well-watered oases are surrounded by the tattered ruins of palaces and pleasure houses. So we walked our horses though the ruins of grand Isfahan. We crossed the Zayanderud {River} on the famed Khaju bridge-weir.

The bridge-weir of Khaju. Driscol crossed this while going into Isfahan. Illustration III-XII-21

I regret I cannot write with accuracy of what I saw. I was overwhelmed, as I had been in Cairo, by so many sights to see; the blue of the building tiles, the twisting pillars, walls covered with writing. Much I could not read, due to the distortions of the script to meet an artistic need. The domes of the mosques are covered with green or sometimes blue-lacquered tiles; with ornaments in yellow, blue, and red. The inscriptions are in the same colours. They are crowned by golden balls and a crescent, with the horns of the crescent bending outwardly.

Bijan sang as we went, for he spoke of the poet Kama Ad Din, martyred here on Azar 6, 616 JA *{Jalaali calendar or December 21ˢᵗ 1237 AD}* by the Mongol hordes. One of these songs reminded me so much of Millicent:

'Thou art serene and silent as the night, and yet thy very calmness wounds the most, and he that might defy thee is a ghost – dead is the heart that can resist thy might' The LXXV quatrain of the Rubaiyat of Kamal ad-Din of Isfahan.

'Downtown' Isfahan. Illustration III-XII-22

Bijan insisted we eat at one of the kabob shops *{eating houses}*, where we picked up a number of these easy- to-eat-on-a-horse morsels. They were, I must say, the best food I had had in Persia since landing. The bazaars were busy, and in these crowds of hundreds of people, not a single one paid us the slightest attention. Perkins and I discussed this in French. For some reason I did not wish Bijan to know our thoughts.

Isfahan as seen by Driscol as he rode away to the North. Illustration III-XII-23

I wondered would it be wiser to enter Independent Tartary disguised as natives, instead of as Englishmen? Did we not seem to be able to pass as natives? From our experience here, I suggest that our expedition should not be an overt one, but covert. Perkins thought for some time and finally said that he mostly agreed. He said he had been thinking the same thing and that we should not go openly as Englishmen, due to the attentions it garners, some of which would not be to our liking. He granted that we both could go in mufti and had proven its efficiency, but could the others? I thought Dobbins, Vickery, Bannington and Michaelson would have no difficulty; Horne, due to his nature, might seem not like a native by his manifest mannerisms and dislike of most locals. Dissanayake, we could not agree on whether he would be good or bad at the game.

I agreed that as Englishmen and infidels, we would be instantly noted, but as natives, we would go unhindered. We had seen and understood that trade was brisk in the region; could we not go as traders of something? However our horses would mark us as foreigners, but why not as Circassians such as my present disguise was? Circassians resembled Europeans in skin and eye colour.

Perkins suggested we might take him along as our resident madman {Horne?}. Dissanayake would need some training and motivation also. We considered all the points during a long discussion on the matter.

For had Catania not showed us the way? In the Mohammedan world, Circassians and other Mohammedans of European blood were known, and respected as fierce warriors. We could pass as these. This would also cover the defects in our Persian and local knowledge, but we must become more knowledgeable of the practice, ritual and forms of Islam.

It was Perkins who gave the answer to what we should trade in. We shall go as traders in horses, for that is the one thing they export in great quantities; and with Bannington and Horne we have horse experts. We shook then on this idea and had a great laugh at the idea of Horne taking on 'nigger's robes', none of the others, we thought, would object at all. We agreed his expression of being told this would be worth the effort alone. Horne would obey orders I was sure.

We made our way out of the ruined city with its great buildings, beautiful mosques and continued on our way north towards Teheran.

Around the city are four post stations, as the place is a crossroad, and Bijan suggested we exchange horses and ride the new ones from the Eastern station to the northern, and then change again. We did so, and had a wild gallop, then cantered for some seven miles. This was a great respite after the monotony of the post horse's trot. The northern post master was not amused, when we turned in three, sweating, exhausted, horses and there was a shouting match who Bijan won by presenting our permission, which I suspect the master could not read but who knew them by their seals and ribbons. We rode on greatly refreshed in mind if not in body.

A discussion arose about the Persian's use of the preterite for we had observed that Bijan often used the past historic instead of the more common present indicative.

[Editor's note: I have deleted two pages on this question which deals with how the language of Farsi (Persian) handles graphic narration the sentence above is provided as evidence of why I did so]

We made our way from side to side, of a great, melon-growing plain but they were too green to savour. The ground changed to soft and crumbly from the harder argillaceous soil *{made of clay}* of before, dust devils excited our admirations and we found that Bijan was truly afraid of them, as he thought they were actually some of the invisible folk called the Djinn within them and they were not to be viewed and under no circumstances allowed to come near. He demonstrated his resolve by galloping away at one point when a small one neared us.

We crossed a summit and found ourselves in another dry valley, and on we went until we came to Kashan in the evening, changed horses, ate some rice with stringy mutton and bitter fruit, and continued on into the dark, it was a full moon now, and it lighted our way. We sang Persian and British song, but mainly we just rode in silence. At one point, the trail had moved to the East and we rode into a glorious sunrise and we found we were coming up behind a group of Persian lancers who formation was, to say the least, ragged. We came up to them and found they were the noted Nizam-Atli, who had been formed in 1835 by Major Fernand *{A British officer with the team sent to help the Persian army which Horne and Vickery had been part of}*. They bore with lances sported red caftans, but only 30 men were left of the original 120. They were out for their monthly 'ride'.

Their commander was a Persian of the better class but he had no time, in a featureless plain, to speak to 'Circassians' or a mere post rider. We were delighted that he thought of us as such.

It was late on the afternoon of the next day that we reach Qom, home of our guide.

Sunrise with the Nixam-Atli Lancers. Illustration III-XII-24

Bijan's Family And A Short Respite

Bijan begged of us a short stop that he might visit his family. Perkins and I agreed, as we were in need of rest ourselves.

My entire lower body was numb to any pain at this time. I suffered not so much from that numbness, or from a lack of sleep, but from pain high up on my back and neck, which vexed me greatly. Each horse is different, some smooth, some jarring; sometimes we went to canter or slow them to a walk, but as their training is to go at a trot and that is what they do. Damn them.

The land is poisoned with salt and has no water and there is some mud from the rains that occasionally splashes us with moisture, but they do not last more than a few minutes until they travel on. We pass ruin after ruin, caravanserai, towers, fortresses and hovels, all in various phrases of decay, destruction and destitution.

One structure was in fine shape the shrine of Fatima al-Masumeh a notable Imamzadehs or sister of the eight Imam and daughter of the seventh. Illustration III-XII-25

We finally come to the holy city of Qom, which Bijan has told us a great deal about. We find that it is full of saints, mostly dead. We could see for some miles away the golden dome of the tomb of Imaum Reza.

The town was like Isfahan, half ruin, the other half full of people. We stopped for a moment at the shrine of one of the notable *Imaumzadehs {relatives of the important twelve Shi'ah Imam's}*. His family lived on the northern side in a small walled villa. We came there and he greeted his family, his parents still living, and his wife and five children. We leave our boots at the door of the house, as per custom.

The house was smoky, crowded, and made no better after several rounds of horrid-tasting, sweet, tea that I felt obliged to try; and finding no way of disposing of it, did so by drinking it down as quickly as possible. The houses of Persia are not well constructed. The main ingredient for a Persian house is, of course, mud, mud made into sun-burnt bricks or sometimes stone is used, or both. Bijan's house is made up of rubble covered by a layer of this dried mud. It consisted of several rooms, mostly open towards the north. These openings, which we might call windows, but they have no glass in them, are shut during the night with a wooden hatch, but left open during the day; rain or shine, heat or cold. In each room there is a chimneypiece, generally opposite the largest wall openings. The floor is of rough stone, covered by reed mats. The roof is made up of thin wooden poles, covered with thatch. The inside has neither chairs, nor tables, nor any article of furniture whatsoever. The good Persian sits cross-legged on the ground. Their meals are served upon trays; and when a man is tired, a pillow is brought to him, and he sleeps on the same spot. The house is divided by a curtain of sorts; one side is the public half in, which we are in and only the men and guests reside here. Bijan's mother, wife and two daughters we had seen only for a moment, as Bijan had surprised them by bringing foreigners. They reside on the other side of the curtain and that place is forbidden to any other to enter but the females of the family and when necessary, the males.

Bijan's father had been a cavalryman and post rider in his time and he was a right, proper, gentleman for such mean circumstances.

Unusual for a Persian, he had only one surviving child, Bijan. As we talked, and his father was somewhat amazed that we could speak Persian, for while we were dressed as pseudo-Circassians, he could tell by our way of speaking and mannerisms that we were not of his world; this small insular place that was his universe.

A sound was made from behind the curtain and we were invited to stride outside, There we stood for several minutes. Then were bidden to return and found a large meal laid out for us by the mysterious and hidden women of the house.

They had laid out on a new carpet, the only true 'Persian' carpet I had seen in the house, a large flat piece of bread, which not only covered the whole rug but hung over it onto the mats, and it serves the Persians both for bread and napkin; on top of this had been placed the leg of a sheep, along with a separate dish with various roasted sheep offal, a dish of stew sprinkled with saffron, and a large metal bowl of boiled rice, two shallow plates of sour milk, and a large jar of fresh water; but with all these, there was neither knife, fork, nor spoon of course.

We had had some practice at eating with our fingers and were soon at the hard work of tearing, teasing and wrenching the cooked flesh off the sheep's leg.

Bijan's father was a study in gentlemanly ease, with his left hand resting on his thigh, to prevent any hint of it touching the food; as the left hand is used to clean oneself after nature release is done. He slowly stretched out his right hand and plunged it wrist deep into a dish of greasy rice, moved his fingers to take a small portion with three fingers, and conveyed it, with slow deliberation into his mouth; seldom did he drop a grain neither soiling either his beard or his moustache. He repeated this manoeuvre many times in the same manner, then poked his greasy hand into a variety of the other dishes which he fancied; taking a morsel here or there and, at last, seized a goblet of water and drank it down in one dash. He did so with the air of a King of France before his admiring nobility. Finally sated, he broke off a piece of the bread 'table', and having wiped his fingers with it, rolled it up and swallowed it with an air of placid satisfaction. There is nothing more efficient and practical than eating one's napkin; it is the height of efficiency. He next found a bowl of water and washed his hands but did not dry them as the Persian allows their hands to dry in the air alone. Having done that, he leaned back and having dined, smiled all around and belched loudly. Bijan had earlier fallen asleep while eating and was left to slumber.

Perkins and I gladly found the ground outside in the garden to be warm and comfortable. Nothing is seen in this garden but vines growing on lattices against the walls, and stunted fruit trees. Flowers are not considered important and are treated as weeds would be in an English Garden. I found a soft log for a pillow and was soon asleep, despite my many bodily pains.

We were awakened by Bijan who never seemed to sleep much. He had brought our change of horses, his mother sent us a large *baqlawah {baklava}* with pistachios and we ate it with gusto. We found from our watches that we had slept but four hours but were greatly refreshed. I spent some time picking pieces of pastry from my moustache and beard. I would long remember that pastry; for which we had left his mother a gift of gold, which brought tears to her aged eyes for

the salary of a post rider was modest by any definition and we were greatly honoured by her appearing unveiled before us.

The countryside past Qom showing the line of 'head' poles.
Illustration III-XII-26

By the customs of Islam, an aged woman need not be veiled, only those I would consider to be 'nubile' must be, or such is my interpretation.

Perkins entered this gift as a payment in our accounting book for the expedition; as an expense for a 'banquet' for the 'merchants and notables of Qom, who rendered us a great welcome and drank toasts to the good health of the King and Parliament'.

We ride on, passing a stream of salt water, in which we did a quick French bath to clear our faces and hands, This was followed by wet ground, and then a desert of sorts made up of soil mixed with crystals of salt that annoyed one's eyes and lips when the winds whip them up and onto you. We changed horses, and we found the travellers around us were from Teheran, but they had not the time for our questions. As we travelled we noted a line of poles set in the dusty soil here; and these stretched for some miles. Bijan held the answer. At one point during the recent Civil War, the heads of eleven hundred men were placed upon these as a warning to Qom to remain loyal. They had heeded the message.

We came upon another regiment of Persian cavalry at practice, forming columns of threes then to troops, and then to squadron, wheeling left then right. We left the road to see them more clearly and we saw that its officer in charge was a European. He was in Persian dress but had on his head a rakish European hat and as we drew nearer, noted that he had European boots and spurs on too.

We greeted him in the Persian manner, and he observed us with little interest. He was Russian and an officer in the service of the Shah. We found he was a Volga German *{A Russian of German descent}*. He seemed annoyed at us for interfering with his observations, so we left him in peace.

Had he known we were English his greeting would have been different, I do believe.

A detachment of Persian irregular Kurdish cavalry as seen along the route to Teheran. Illustration III-XII-27

Perkins and I were very happy to note he had not thought that we were Europeans, but of course his own Persian had been poor.

The cavalrymen themselves wore long blue capes; green pantaloons, leather boots and a yellow blouse and were well mounted, and wore either a brown hat, like a thin backwards *mitre {the hat worn by the Pope or grenadiers}*, or shapeless turbans of a disreputable look.

They held ten foot lances from which small flags fluttered. Their manoeuvers were at best un-expert. We later found that this was the Shah's bodyguard of irregular Kurdish cavalry, which is recruited and is said to consist of two thousand four hundred men. They are admirable individual horsemen, from what we had seen, even if they could not perform well in formation riding. It is a truism in the East, that holds that a true cavalier cannot be broken by discipline, which is considered as detrimental to his ability to fight and so Eastern cavalry fights as a body of individuals and is so often charged and broken by a body of European trained horse that fight as a unit.

We carried on crossing more salt-laden streams every few hours; we came to Kinar-e-gird and changed horses for the last time; for it is only some sixteen miles to the capital now. We trotted on and after a few tedious miles, we came out of some small hills, and there Teheran lay beneath us. It lies in a great bowl, the sides of which are a lofty range of mountains to the west and East. The mountains are the Elbourz *{Alborz}*, and are well tinged with snow and cloud. It was a memorable sight. Bijan pointed out the greatest of them, Mount Damavand, 18,600 feet, the highest mountain between the Hindoo Kush and the Atlantic. It is the highest mountain I have yet seen; outshining the Alps by no less than a third more in height. No other of the peaks tower over its brothers, and from our location, the summits of the range seemed nearly level. These mountains lacked any great beauty, no fabulous spurs or squarest tops which make mountains interesting. The front rank of these mountains shields the others behind them from sight so one does not see them as they are; a mighty range of mountainous layers, receding into the distance.

We passed more ruins that Bijan did not know the name of. We rode over many dikes, which are next to the road, to avoid other travellers and the great holes and ruts in the road. It is gratifying to be here. I told Perkins that my back wished to thank him for this memorable journey. Perkins, who was I believe, discomforted as much as I said that his arse and thighs had more pain than my back. We argued back and forth over who had the worse pain. As we neared the city, we could see that outside the city walls stood a palace. On an eminence to the north, the *Kasr-i-Kajar*, built by the former ruler Fath Ali Shah, was the sole object that relieved the brown monotony of the surrounding plain.

Teheran {Pure} is a rough and fortified polygon when viewed from the hills above it.

Eastern gate of Teheran. Illustration III-XII-28

The circuit of its wall, which we understand is of poor construction, and ruined in parts, is some four and half miles long and it is made of mud brick varying from eighteen to one and twenty feet in height, studded with circular towers, and fronted by a broken down ditch, some five and forty feet in width, and five and twenty feet deep. There are said to be six gates covered with the Persian style blue tiles, but we could see only four from our vantage point. Bijan said the roads were narrow and filthy; having a drain running down the middle of the street. The best part of the town is to the north, where the city's mud and thatch built *Arg {citadel}* lies.

There lies the *Kakheh Golestan {Royal Palace}* of the present ruler who is Mohammad Shah Kajar. From the ramparts, flew the red, white, and green banner of the Lion and Sun; the proud flag of Persia.

As we came closer to the city, it presented to us no glittering domes, towers or other great constructions. Only as we neared the walls, could we make out the finely made gates. These were adorned with enameled tiles covering the pointed archways and columns and fanciful decorations. To Perkins, who said to me in French, 'It seems like an effort by a patissier *{French pastry maker}* to put frosting on a trash heap'.

We checked our watches; mine said it was exactly 4 PM on the 22nd of May, his 3:55. We settled on four as it is easier to remember, as we had left Shiraz at 4 AM on the 13th of the month: some five hundred and twenty-five miles behind us, an average of nearly ninety miles a day *{from Bushire}*. It was an accomplishment for those not trained as long distance horsemen. We shake hands and enter Teheran and as we approached the gate, we are approached by a mob of men, who come at us boiling out from the gate. They have demands. They want to know if we are Amir-Haydari or Ne'mat-Allahi[3]? We were alarmed by this threatening mass and I had my hand on My Frenchman. Bijan appeared unconcerned saying he is from Qom, and a post rider, and has no place in their quarrels, he tries to answer for us, but the crowd insists we answer ourselves - as we were dressed in the Circassian or pseudo Persian manner. Perkins says 'neither' and I say, 'we support the one who is right'. They can tell by our voices that we are neither from Teheran, nor even Persian, and surge by us yelling and screaming. From Bijan we find these two groups are involved in public fights and disturbances. He does not know why they are ill disposed towards one another but so it has been for centuries. I said they sounded like Montagues and Capulets, or perhaps an Eastern Irishman's way of having a good bout. They were certainly no gentlemanly as some of their comments were contumelious.

Teheran And We Find Our Man

We came into the town feeling much like conquering heroes, but we had many things to accomplish, so we could not engage ourselves to a parade *{I take this to be more Driscol humor}*. We had to make our way to the British Legation to find the British Ambassador and present our passport, permissions and letters to him, in addition to finding Hymison, and as Perkins stated it, making him aware that his presence would not be accepted. We then had to gain an audience with the Shah, to report to him as he had ordered, and give him our communications from London. The post station was near the palace and we rode there post-haste. We explained our needs to Bijan who knew a small Hammam *{bathhouse}*, where for a price we could take a bath, as it was used by Armenians, and others not of the Muslim faith. We would not be welcomed in one used by the Shia here. We rode through Teheran and found the station and exchanged horses, They were for our use here and not for riding on. A few small Shabi coins silenced the station master's complaints on this matter.

We accomplished this, and as the hour was becoming late we were now in our undress uniforms and rode to the southern part of Teheran and found the Legation. It was built in the Italian style, with portico and pillars; a small part of Europe in this Oriental city or a small counter to what the French call the *maussade, morne* and *tenebreux* of this place *{desolate, joyless and gloomy}*. The mission as it is called is located on grounds which originally belonged to one Mohammed Khan, the *Zamburakchi {Zanburak or little bee} Bashi*, or *{Commander of the camel battery}*. His story I have noted down.

The Persian Corps of cannon armed camels. The artist has given the poor creature an armament much larger than he actually carried. Illustrated III-XII-29

Needing a site to place the British legation, it was this lucky individual whom his sovereign bequeathed a special confidence on him that none may decline, by inviting him; *suo motu {describes an act of authority to part with his property}*. This was which was forthwith transferred to the English Sir Gore Ouseley, who built upon it a commodious house spending some £8,000 to do so to act as our nation's legation.

We had been most amused to see this unit, perhaps still commanded by the man, who had lost his land to us, at its training task in the great square, whose name we do not know. This ceremonial guard unit of the Shah is made up of camels, on the back of which is sited a small cannon, a half pounder perhaps. The captain of this gun sits behind his piece, and loads and fires it, without any great difficulty, as it is stubby tube. He wears orange clothing and a helmet of black sheep skin, with a copper plate on which his rank and unit are emblazoned; all adorned with red feathers.

Besides the cannon, the camel carries with it a ten foot pole, from which a large green and red triangular flag flies. This peculiar unit has some eighty men in it, and they fire salutes to the Shah whenever he mounts or alights from his horse. *Zanburaks* were often fired from a kneeling camel, but could be employed from a trotting or standing one as well. The origins of this oddity are ascribed to the Afghanis, but there is no proof of this. I find the idea rather ridiculous but Bijan informs us that the Russian, Ottomans, and others, are all in dread fear of this camel-mounted cannon. I think not, as the only damage it might cause, would be the discipline of a European unit as they would be unable to hold formation while convulsed in laughing.

We found at last the mission, and here we met Mr William Taylor, military secretary; it being unusual to find a civilian with that title.

The British Legation in Teheran.
Illustration III-XII-30

We find that Ambassador McNeill[4] was neither in Teheran, nor Gulchek, his residence outside the city, but instead is north of the city in the Lars valley under the shadow of Mount Damavand.

Taylor gave us a hearty welcome, as if we were long lost family, for he knew of our coming, as the expedition's arrival at Bushire had been reported, but he knew not our names. He also invited us to dinner, and said our companion was awaiting us here. We steel ourselves for the encounter to come with Hymison. Our weapons and our tongues are prepared, ready. Good sense absent, as our anger was foremost, and we were resolved to end his attempt to join or take over the expedition. It would be ended this night, one way or the other. I did not expect us to shoot him, but I did expect to have a most violent verbal display. Our knowledge of him led us to believe that he considered himself a dueling man and he had a hot temper. Thus we were prepared for anything.

We had argued over who should restrain him and who should shoot him in the leg - by accident.

We came into the dining room, and there he was, for he had heard us approaching. He was standing there in complete insolence, hands on his hips, dressed in civilian attire, long hair flowing, with a knowing look on his lips, a good growth of beard and his whole presence in the room one of dominance. There was also a mischievous look in his eye, as he knows he knew he had us at a disadvantage and had outsmarted us completely.

He said loudly, and it still rings in my ears now, hours later, as I write this, 'I see the young gentlemen have arrived, late, very late indeed. I would have thought you would hurry here faster with the arrangements I had made'.

Perkins and I were both overcome with the intense emotions of the moment. We were constrained, for he had picked his ground well, for gentlemen and ladies were present for the meal. Nothing untold could happen in the dining room of the British Legation in Teheran, Persia. There could be no outbursts here, no expression of emotions. The plotting swine!

We both strode up, I took out my hand, not holding My Frenchman, and coming up to him brought it up and returned his outlandishly grand salute; for we were in uniform.

For before us, standing in civilian attire, was a bearded and broadly smiling Sergeant Hynes; dressed in a form of Persian attire. Perkins had lost his voice it would seem. We stood there looking at him, amazed and befuddle, in complete silence. He stated coyly,

'I have been given the understanding that two young officers are desirous of making my acquaintance'?

We shook hands again, vigorously like the almost American he was. My comments were something to the effect of how could you be here? Had he taken *Filer à l'anglaise? {to take leave English style, the French version of the British phrase to 'take French leave' or to desert}*

How could he be here, we both said again? He asked why we were so shocked to find him here. Had we not wondered who had arranged and prescribed our travel across Persia? We stumbled out that we thought we might meet another.

This puzzled him, then he bristled somewhat, and voiced his dismay that we could have thought that popinjay *{Hymison}* could have done what he had accomplished?

'Gentleman, I know that creature, and he works hard to just fail at being a muttonhead'. He made an exacerbated sound and smiled at us, as all good Sergeants learn to do when faced with young officers who have made an amusing mistake. He could not chide the officer too much but both of us knew the meaning of the look. Fortunately it was directed at Perkins, and not I or I would have melted with shame. Perkins took this downgrading very well and launched into a list of things that had NOT been properly arranged. After having counter-struck, the two lay down their arms, and we begged him to explain how he had come to stand here; something that filled us with unbelievable joy.

He picked up his neglected glass, took a long drink, and told us just how he had come to be here. He had been greatly vexed by his not obtaining the position he felt he deserved; especially being annoyed due to the complications caused by Hymison. As he had many friends, one of these, a medical associate, had conspired with him unofficially of course. He had been diagnosed with a bruised spleen; taken as damage during one of his very physical bayonet drills with the men.

He added, in a poor attempt at an East London dialect, 'it was me spleen, governor, it was all swollen, painful and puffy it was'. He has many talents; but acting and accents were not one of them. Hynes made a valiant attempt, to make out that he was one of the twelve out of every one hundred Englishmen who speak that way, was a glorious failure.

We found it hard to believe that this description and deceit was believed, but the Colonel, with a wink, had approved a medical leave of one year, and up to two more years, depending on what was said in London about his condition. Hymison had heard of this, and not believed it and had protested; but as it was not his bailiwick, he could do nothing. So Hymison had taken leave to actually try to follow our good Sergeant, who initially said he was going to Calcutta and from there into northern India to rest, instead of London. As far as he knew Hymison had gone to Calcutta also.

Instead, our companion went to Bombay, dodging Husher by way of a series of midnight rides through the Dekkan. He had to ignore our expedition officially, but he did speak to Vickery for a time *{March 2nd}* in his guise as a merchant seaman, and of course Vickery had no idea of his true identity. Since Hynes was going on medical leave, he had decided that a nice sea voyage and a change of scenery would do him well; him being in such a delicate condition.

He had the misfortune to run into Lieutenant Husher, in Bombay who knew him, and insisted he go aboard, as his medical leave dictated, or he would report this violation of his medical leave, for he was there to make sure he did not join the expedition. He felt he could either disobey the young officer, or out fox him, so he did the easier of the two. He had taken up a position of passenger on a ship, ostensibly for a return to England, and onwards from there to Canada.

That evening, he went over the side of his ship and into and into a small native boat he had hired at dusk; from the many that hovered around ships in the harbour, selling fruits and all others things that a hearty man might need. Leaving on his door a note that he was indisposed, and back on shore, he had taken up a landsmen's *{amateur sailor}* position on a ship going to Bushire. He then handed us the bill for his passage, and the passage he had arranged for but not taken which Perkins agreed to pay as the representative of the expedition. It was a trifle, as he had paid up to Suez only.

Thus he had arrived. He quickly made the arrangements in Bushire for our expedition. Then he had then talked his way up north to Teheran, speaking Persian he had joined an Armenian's caravan going north, disguised as merchant by the name of Omar Al-Muhammed, and had made it to that place a month before we had arrived. To the Ambassador he had told the story that he was the vanguard of the expedition, but had lost his papers in a boating accident at Bushire *{a not uncommon occurrence}*, and as McNeil was told by the staff that they knew the good Sergeant from his earlier time in Persia and he was well aware of the expedition's purposes, he was accepted as such. He had seen that all was arranged.

A LUSTRED TILE. "HAIL OMAR!"

Perkins offered him a warrant billet in the expedition but he declined as he was on medical leave.

Instead he would join as a volunteer only. So at that point, he joined the expedition un-officially. Since the pretence of the viability of his medical leave had to be upheld, he asserted, he stated quite clearly, that a month at sea and in Persia had worked a miracle and he was now healthy - Praise God!

Gregory Allen François Gizhiibatoo Hynes
Grenadier Regiment of Bombay Native Infantry
Drill master of the Poona Cantonment
Sergeant, Infantry
Presidency of Bombay, Indian Army

Gregory was born March 30th, 1813 as the third and only surviving son of Mister Robert Chrissenwheat Hynes a former American Loyalist from the island of Nantucket, Massachusetts colony transplanted to the northern colony after the American War of Rebellion. His mother, Valentina was a *metis* the daughter of a fallen Jesuit missionary and newly minted fur hunter and a *Mississaugas* First Nations mother who herself had previous French blood from the first settlers of that far land. He was born in a temporary fur trading camp of the North West Company amongst the Chippewa Indians of the Great Lakes Region and his Indian name was *Gizhiibatoo* which meant runs fast or light of foot. With his family, he travelled to the far Columbia district *{modern British Columbia}*, where he developed his hunting and forestry skills. His schooling was rough and informal, but he had developed a passion for reading and had been well instructed by his mother and father in the necessary matters. He learned not only French, but several native Indian tongues and a smattering of Latin and Greek. He read every book he could lay his hands on and would speak at length with any traveller with pretentions to knowledge or experience.

He had not wanted to be a fur trapper and had gone first to America, then Nova Scotia, doing what needed to be done, seaman, servant or timberman and then joined the British 95th Rifles in Halifax Canada. He had joined the depot for the regiment which was sent to England for reasons of recruitment, and stayed at various places in the sainted lands of Devonshire. He volunteered as a 'fill man' or 'topper', an enlisted man added to a regiment going overseas to bring it to full establishment, and had come out to India. From there, he had joined the group who had gone to Persia to train their army.

In Persia his skills in learning languages stood him well. He was also beloved by the Persians; and in one notable instance, a Persian general, and cousin of the Shah, had refused to cross a stream while leading a division of infantry as he did not want to wet his slippers; a monumental failure of his duties. Hynes had picked him up by the neck and robe and thrown him in, the man was immediately swept downstream, and only by a prodigious display of personal bravery and strength, did Hynes regain him and return him to command the troops, who had of course crossed the stream to watch the rescue.

Upon his return from Persia, he had been volunteered to assist in the formation of native Infantry regiments and his command of drill and native languages had led him in time to being selected as the drill master of the Poona cantonment, which held nearly twenty thousand soldiers; British and native.

His first Colonel, in noting his early rise to the rank of Corporal, and then Sergeant, noted that on parade, Hynes would make a Guards' Regimental Sergeant Major look awkward and unpolished and he had a knack of training new officers and native troops to their duties with a mixture of patience and sarcastic wit. He had the knowledge of exactly how far to go when castigating a superior officer over his lack of performance, in such a way as to instruct and gain the man's full allegiance. He was in the opinion of all a most honest, intelligent, tireless, zealous, and most deserving soldier.

He was described as being 5' 10", fourteen and half stone in weight (205 lbs.), solidly built, a fair rider, excellent shot, and an acknowledge master of bayonet drill. He was also known as a man who knew how to do anything; a true Jack of all trades, and contradictory to the cliché; he seemed to be able to master them all. He was also an accomplished musician and able to play well the violin, piano, clarinet and classical (Spanish) guitar and well-practised in the music of Antoine de Lhoyer.

===

A Deception Revealed

We could talk no more as supper was being served and guests must be met. He informed us where we would be living and that we would be eating out at Gulchek *{modern Gulchek, Turkish for little lake}* after tonight. He went to his supper and us to ours.

[Editor's note: The above is a good example of the class system in Georgian and soon to be Victorian, England. A Sergeant didn't eat a meal with officers in a formal social setting; the idea of doing so would have been inconceivable. However given Driscol's middle-class upbringing, he would not have thought anything of it if he did, whereas Hynes would have thought it decidedly off-putting. Officers and Sergeants could eat together when in the field, or when they invited one another to visit the others messes]

We were both absolutely elated to have him here, and it not being Hymison. A wave of relief overcame us both, and we became as giddy as girls. We took this all as the best of omens, and found delight in knowing that we had bested Hymison; his beard had been pulled. Had it been Hymison, would we have shot that man and been cashiered and hung? I do not think we would have, but it would have been an unpleasant scene nonetheless. We did not even mind the long rides, now seen to have been unnecessary. We found that Hymison had been misled and gone to either Karachi or Calcutta. I wonder why he had done so, and looked at Perkins accusingly.

[Editor's note: a journey by land to Calcutta would take six weeks at a normal pace of a waggon as it lay some 1,000 miles from Poonah, depending on how fast one wanted to move. However a lone rider, who could exchange horses, could travel much faster, like Lieutenant Preston who rode from Bombay to Calcutta in 8 days and 14 hours with the news of the victory at Waterloo. If you changed riders, also it could also be done in half or a third of that time]

Later, Perkins tapped me on the shoulder, and bent over to me, and told me why Hymison MAY have gone to Calcutta or Karachi. Obviously Hynes' comments might have sent him to Calcutta, while.........It would seem that he and Vickery had sent out two packets of documents. The first one had been sent to Hymison, for he had formally requested them, and the request had been counter-signed by the man we knew to be a senior official at Poonah, and the second one another to his *{Perkins'}*, Engineer superiors at the Survey of India. To both, he had sent copies of the papers from the East India Company, stating that we were directed to set up our expedition at Peshawar by way of Karachi and to enter Independent Tartary from Afghanistaun.

He had then added another letter to each packet; one to Hymison and another to his, Perkins', superiors. In this letter, he said that he disagreed with the order to go to Peshawar and instead will follow the orders of London to go to Bushire. Unfortunately, Vickery had somehow, inexplicably, foolishly, unaccountably, made the mistake of putting just one copy of that letter in the packets; the one going to the survey, while the other packet, to Hymison contained a letter, an older one from the time before we had changed our minds. The letter had said that pursuant to these orders, we were moving to that location in Scinde {*modern southern Pakistan, i.e. Karachi*} and then, logically, on to Afghanistaun. Thus, Hymison would believe we were going to Karachi, as previously directed by the HEIC to use that route.

Now Vickery took the blame for failing to put the correct letter of going to Bushire in the envelope to Hymison; purely a mistake by our overworked secretary, damn the luck. When Perkins had found out that Vickery had done so, he of course had sent a correction. Awkwardly, Vickery had only remembered this error during our later sea voyage. He reported that he had accidently addressed it to another Hymison in Ceylon. For these grievous errors, Vickery had had to eat a fresh and luscious mango, while standing, and without a proper napkin, plus having to promise not to make such mortal error ever again. He had done both penances with some sorrow and had spent much time reflecting on what he had done wrong, or so his official journal showed, to include a note of a rebuke and official caution from Perkins. Dissanayake might be a Prince of paperwork, sleight of hand but Perkins and Vickery were certainly Dukes.

I had some difficulty containing my laughter at all this; I later reflected on how Perkins, the son of a Bishop, had done something so ungentlemanly, dishonest, calculating and deceptive, it was worrisome.

There were some two dozen people for dinner that night at the legation. It was for me a lonely feeling, as it made me think excessively of home, for one could feel as if one were back in merry England; in a wood-paneled room with a chandelier, servants in proper livery, including Indians and one Persian. We dined on: smoked, tinned, Scottish salmon; tinned lobster; potted Cornish crab; potted shrimps; a leaf salad; Persian spring fruit; a Bakewell pudding; Keen's cheddar; and stilton cheese with actual baked bread. A loaf of bread was something I had not seen for months, that and a tub of butter I made them my special friends that evening and kept him close until he disappeared down my gullet.

I met Lieutenant Todd of the Bengal Artillery, who had recently returned to Teheran after doing a journey of exploration along the southern shores of the Caspian Sea. He held the local brevet rank of Major. Another graduate of Addiscombe of 1822, he knew some of the members of the Bombay Artillery, as they had of course, gone to the same school. His was a common romance; born to a Yorkshire gentleman of good family in London, his father had lost his fortune in stock speculation, and he was consigned to the care of an uncle. He was most interested in our coming expedition, but was now assigned to the legation. He suggested that if we wanted to get to Tartary, the best way was the way he had just explored, and not the road to Meshed. I introduced him to Perkins, and we had a long discussion on how to move about in Persia, and the best way to go to where we wished.

In our conversation, he made a pithy remark. Mr Taylor opines the Persians think we are quite mad, but we have the advantage over them, for we know we are mad, while they are not aware that they are much madder than us.

I also met the secretary of the legation Captain Justin Sheil and his wife Mary Leonora, an Anglo-Irishman of the Waterford family. He had gone to Haileybury and had been one of the elite Eastern

Cadets[5]. He had joined the 3rd Bengal Infantry and had come out to Persia with the same group Horne and Vickery had been a part of. He was very pleased to know that both these men would soon be here. It would seem that Horne owed him £2 10s and Sheil intended to collect! He seemed a very well-informed and sensible man with a mild temper and the skills of a diplomat. He found the Persians to be both equally interesting and infuriating in equal doses, and his greatest question was just how such people had ever been able to form a kingdom, let along an empire. He would next week be going to Alamut and Khurrem-abad[6] and we were invited to join. We could not of course. He remembered something, left the table, and when he returned gave us four items.

These were four new Kater's[7] or prismatic azimuth compasses in sturdy boxes. These were azimuth compasses with a finely built in sight within a wooden storage box with a sliding lid. The compass consisted of a cylindrical metal casing with a glass cover. Through the glass, a circular base plate made from brass, with an attached, printed, card can be seen. There were numbers written around the edge of the base plate. A hinged arm was screwed to one side of the casing, the hinge allowing the arm to rest on the glass lid.

On the opposite side to the hinged arm was a bracket for the sight to be attached. The sight consisted of a metal frame, holding a lens angled over a mirror; one of the four having a cracked mirror. The wooden box was lined with green baize. The lid of the box was made of wood. The magnetic variation of Teheran was written on them in pencil; it being 2° westerly. These were superior to the ones we had found in Bombay and they were now ours.

There were a number of European business men at the dinner representatives of the companies then in Persia doing business; the Swiss concern Ziegler & Co, Ralli & Angelasti, Gray, Dawes and Company, Hotz & Sons, Persian Carpet Manufacturers, exporters and importers. There was also a member of the French Bank, the *Banque des Prets {later the Banque d'Escompte de Perse}*, where our financial needs would be met. Todd introduced me to the French manager, who assured Perkins and me that any bill or order we produced from London would be instantly filled. It was, I was told, in a conspiratorial whisper, the custom to not use the Russian Bank, as we were in tense times with those people.

I had the enjoyable situation of being paid more attention to by Mrs Sheil, than Perkins received; aided perhaps by my early mention that Perkins was a polygamous reprobate of the first order. However, she interjected I need not say that, as she had already heard about him. She gave me an exhaustive description of the Persian culture, which I had hitherto not observed, with the result that I was overwhelmed and promptly forgot much of it. I had not spoken with a woman for two months, so I found this older lady's attention very pleasant. One thing I do remember was that the Persian throne, the lovely peacock throne, was the best looking thing in Persia. This was in stark contrast the poor taste in which the Shah of Persia stocked his harem. It would seem he was interested in the weight of his brides and not their beauty. Gossip indeed!

It was a long dinner, and passable, despite the tinned nature of most of it. I ate an entire loaf of bread with as much butter as I could slather on. I noted that I wrote of this earlier, but that may have been because it had been such a pleasure to savour it, that I mentioned it twice. The last toast was made and the dinner broke up near midnight.

Hynes was outside, well fed himself, pulling at a large pipe and prepared to take us to our lodgings. It was then we both notice that he carried a musket, but it was an extraordinary looking one, for he had been working on it when we came outside to find him.

It was the most prized and wonderful weapon I have ever seen a man have and he told us that his aunt had married a *Tryolese {Austrian}*, who had migrated to Quebec, and he had turned the weapon over to him for he wanted nothing of war anymore. This man had become intensely religious and regretted his killing of so many men during the Turkish and Napoleonic wars. I had heard of the weapon, but Perkins had not, for it was an Austrian military repeating air rifle invented by the Austrian army *{Bartholomäus Girandoni, Vienna, Model of 1780}*. It was a marvelous machine; a breech-loading repeater, having a two and twenty shot magazine, filled with lead shot of .46 calibres. The air reservoir is cleverly designed to serve as the butt stock of the weapon, which resembles a regular musket. He would not fire it on the grounds of the legation, so there was but one thing left to do on this heavenly night.

Led by Hynes, we took that night a wild, moonlight ride to our home-to-be Gulchek. Hurdling over the landscape, made fantastic by the shadows cast by the orb above, we followed Hynes, which was not easy, as he rode very well. we were forced to ignore our many pains as we galloped at full speed to that town in the hills above Teheran. We vaulted a dry stream and headed uphill, nearly due north. We came and passed by Kasir Kadjar, or so I thought he called it, as he shouted back over his shoulder. On we flew into the night, passing two ruined towers. Two dry and rocky, stream beds challenged us, but we sped over them following the sparks of Hynes' horse as the horse's iron shoes struck the rocks which cover this area. We saw glimmering lanterns ahead, which he declared was our home to be, and more above it, in the hills beyond the town itself. Those lights blazed forth from the metropolis of Roustamabad. One drier stream, that was not quite dry, gave us a refreshing splash and we flew into the village of Gulchek. Exhilarating!

[Editor's note: modern readers may not be aware that a horse in good condition can gallop at up to 50 mph (88 km/h) or at a sustained canter, a horse can move at 30 mph (50 km/h)]

The whole village has been set aside for us and for our comfort *{British Legation & Mission}* and Persian law no longer applied here. Here the Ambassador and staff lived, out of the squalor and flies that are so prevalent in Teheran. The village is referred to locally as being the countryside headquarters of the British mission.

We found a rough but comfortable spot with new mattresses with no obvious hint of vermin within them, and were soon asleep.

Tuesday 23 May

We arose early, as we have grown accustomed, as we have much to do. Hynes, we find, is up and chopping wood with a large axe. He finds the exercise fits him. We are beside ourselves to see how the air gun works.

He brings it out and we examine it at detail. He has four reservoirs for the compressed air; two air pumps, and four magazines. We examined it in detail and I recalled that in London I had passed a shop that had several air rifles made by a maker named Staudenmayer and it was my impression that Hynes' weapon looked similar to it.

He demonstrated the working principles of the weapon and fired off three shots, which he could do in a few seconds, with great rapidity and ease of motion; having only to tilt the weapon up and pull the hammer back to cock it, aim; and engage the trigger. The weapon made a loud, CRACK, CRACK, CRACK sound as it fired. The most remarkable aspect of this was that there was no smoke or flame from the barrel. It was truly almost magical. Hynes said that he could fire all two and twenty shots in less than a minute. We were then concerned with the penetration and accuracy of the weapon. We found the weapon's discharge was such that it was more powerful in penetration that my pistol whiles it and had about ¾ the penetration of Ascalon. It was in fact a carbine, from my point of view, with an excellent accuracy due to its rifled bore and good penetration out to 150 yards. After that, it seemed to become more inaccurate than a powder-driven ball.

Each butt reservoir required over four thousand strokes of the hand pump to charge it to its full capacity. This was clearly a major difficulty with the design, a flaw, as it would take nearly an hour and three-quarters to pump up one to full capacity!

A lovely, black wood, cleaning rod with a bone tip was provided too, and I found the workmanship on it exquisite.

Hynes lamented that it had no bayonet lug and its fragile butt magazine made it a poor weapon for hand-to-hand fighting which is why he always carried a rifle musket to which a bayonet could be fixed. I showed him my fitting for a bayonet on Ascalon and he was full of praise for it, but did note, correctly, that my bayonet needed cleaning, and had I been his soldier, I would have had four hours punishment as a reward for my slovenly kept weapon. Once a sergeant always a sergeant!

After that exciting spot of firing we rode back to the markets of the Capital: seeing clearly for the first time the barren lands we had careened through last night without a care. It seemed to us impossible, in the clear light of day, that we had not come to disaster in any of the abandoned irrigation ditches or pitched down an open *qanat {underground irrigation canal}*. We marveled at our luck in not having killed ourselves.

We went first to the French Bank, where our credit was established, and an account established for the writing of the necessary documents we might need if we were to purchase large amounts in Persia. We also exchanged some £100 pounds into Persian gold Tomans, silver Qirans and copper Dinars.

The manager there told us why our bills would be so readily acceptable in Persia. It would seem that a past British envoy, Sir John Campbell had found that British bills were not held in esteem but were viewed with contempt; as various British adventurers, explorers and ne'er do wells had given out such pledges - without authority - and they had not been accepted for payment by the mission. To restore British prestige and national honour, he had bought up all these unpaid bills and settled them with extra payments for their being late and thus he had made British letters of credit and other instruments trusted throughout Persia.

Persia has no true banking system. If gold or silver is not available, the Shah issues *berats* or bills on the provincial governors for the payment of his creditors, and to provide for his army his household and the establishments of the Kajar tribe.

However as the issues of these bills exceeds by twenty-fold or more the actual amount of the money available, no one, but a fortunate few, ever received full payment. The Shah's credit is rated according to the position of the holder of the bill, from worthless to par. The latter is its worth when held by a European or noble and the former when the beneficiary was a common merchant.

Where the British held sway in Persia the village of Gulchek and also where the expedition organized for its movement towards Tartary. Illustration III-XII-31

The French Bank

We found at the Bank a Swiss merchant to whom we spoke for some time. He exported rugs to Europe and had lived in the country some twenty years, having taken a Georgian wife. As he seemed very knowledgeable of the trade and country, we solicited his advice in entering Independent Tartary after we had spoken to the banker.

The banker was running a ruse. In my opinion, he was just a European face to an effective operation run by Hindoo Indian Bankers from our colony in India and whose true backers were the exiled Persian Parsees and some Jews who were able to gladly accept our HEIC and London bills and issue ones in Persian and several other languages.

His first advice was in German, which was an exclamation not to go. He said we would not do well there. We asked about going in mufti. He knew not that word and we spent some time in French and my limited German explaining the concept.

He said that if we must go, that way be wise. He further advised that we enter the place by going to Meshed then to Merv then onto Khiva or Bokhara.

We asked about markets for horses within the area of interest. He thought the one in Asterabad {Gorgan} was the closest but Meshed and Merv and the other cities would be better. Perkins asked him about Caucasian mercenaries and traders.

They were uncommon as trader but more common as mercenaries, but expensive and not always deemed reliable and were better known as Circassians in Persia. Their particular brand of Sunni Islam gaining them no friends in Persia, but they would be more acceptable in the farther reaches of Central Asia. I then asked if he knew of a blonde man, with long hair, unhappy looking and medium height, perhaps a German speaker? He did not, but we did get an invitation to dinner; the bachelor's way to free food, but we had to decline. He was an interesting man and resembled, in a way Schaffhauser Bock. *{This man was probably Stanislaus Greisbad from Schaffhauser and the 'bock' was the canton's goat; more of Driscol's humor}.*

This gentleman took us on a mounted tour of the city, and we noted that he was greeted warmly by many Persians. We came first to the Meidan-i-tup-Khaneh or artillery square, which is a park holding collections of old rusty cannon; and as Perkins unkindly noted, just the place for me to spend some time loving them. There were some modern French and English 24 pounders and a few 12's but most of the artillery was broken and obsolete. I found cannons stacked like cord wood and in these piles I found Portuguese tubes from 1622 and a few Russian, Ottoman and German made guns.

I had heard from Todd that Persian artillery corps consisted of some nine hundred men and that most of the cannoneers were actually Georgians and not Persians; as Persians have no head for the business and science of artillery.

I did find one British made gun brought here I suppose in 1812. This gun was a fine 9 pounder, disfigured by a cracked muzzle swell. I had a momentary velleity *{a wish or inclination}* to bury the poor thing. This place was a gloomy cemetery of dead and wrecked guns. To me it was a sad place. I remember Horne speaking about a battle in Persia where the English trained artillery had done well at Sultanabad, I believed it was called, but then was defeated at another battle later in the same year - 1812. The Kajar {*Qajar dynasty 1785-1925*} army was outdone by the much better trained and equipped Russians, who attacked them at night and defeated them even while being outnumbered 10 to 1. After the defeat, the Shah declared that the ancestral lance was still the best weapon and thought the musket and cannon were not.

There are two other large *meidans* {*open squares*} worth seeing. One is the Meidan-i-Mashk, {*Champ de Mars or parade ground*} an open space inside all the ruins of Teheran, over a $^1/_4$ of a mile in length, which is used by the garrison for its parades - or 'jumbles' as those who had witnessed them had so named them.

The other square is reached by a street, which leads from the northwest angle of the 'Gun Square'. The remaining square, called the Meidan-i-Shah {*Square of the King*}, is next to the Arg {*citadel*} and has a large pool in the centre that is filled with fetid water and sports a large brass gun, known as the Tup-i-Murvarid, or Cannon of Pearls, which has always been an especially sacred *bast*, or sanctuary, for the fugitive criminal, a veritable 'horns of the altar,' in Teheran.

[Editor's note: Driscol wrote, B K 1/50-51, which I have decided means a reference to the King James Bible Kings 1: 50-51 which deals with the taking of sanctuary by the 'taking hold of the horns']

> *And Adonijah feared because of Solomon, and arose, and went, and caught hold on the horns of the altar*

> *And it was told Solomon, saying, Behold, Adonijah feareth king Solomon: for, lo, he hath caught hold on the horns of the altar, saying, Let king Solomon swear unto me today that he will not slay his servant with the sword*

Tehrani women, wishing to get married or obtain a child, climb on the cannon or duck under it hoping that their wish will come true. It is said it was once studded with pearls but I don't know the veracity of that claim. I will ask about it.

[Editor's note: Driscol added a note later in pencil saying 'information from mission on cannon' and added the comment below in the margin of the journal]

> There are many stories about this cannon, which to my eyes looks too thin in the barrel to have been successfully fired more than once. Some say it came from Delhi, where it was originally decorated with pearls, others say that it was cast in Persia, which seems unlikely. Some also said that the gun was cast in Shiraz by a King of the Zend dynasty for his wife, and that, having been kept for some time under cover in an Imaum *zadeh* {*religious school*}, it became considered as an object of sanctification.

We next rode to the Arg; the central mud walled fortress where the Russian Embassy is. The Russians came here for greater security after the assassination of Grebayadoff {*the Russian ambassador in 1828*}.

The following tale was told to me by Taylor at the Mission.

> The Russian had come to Teheran as an envoy, and had set himself the task to ascertain which harems contained women from the territories recently captured by the Czar from the Persians. It was his duty to return them to their newly

liberated Russian homelands if they so wished. This interference in the order of the harems had enraged the Mullahs, who declared that their sacred rights were being degraded, and a mob stormed the Russian legation. The building had well-fortified walls and entrances but the mob entered by tearing up the roof. They killed every Russian soul they found; the Ambassador dying from a knife being driven into his side. The bodies were degraded and thrown into the street. The Shah's men did little to defend the mission. Disaster, and another war with Russia, was only avoided by the fact that the Czar was about to attack the Ottomans, and accepted apologies and money instead.

As we rode, on we saw a regiment of Persian infantry at their drill, and found they were armed with matchlocks; a completely obsolete method of war. Our knowledgeable guide told us that the Persians, having learned to make matchlocks, would not change the industry, which was sited at Shiraz. One munitions factory in Yezd produced the Kingdom's saltpetre. Supplies of French and English muskets were often kept in storage. Indeed it was said were often sold by nobles to various tribes, thus leaving the army bereft of their use.

Having viewed the delights of Teheran, we made one more detour to view the horse markets of the city, and having seen what we wished to see, made haste back to the hills. It had been a terribly hot and uncomfortable day in that dirty city, yet the flies had mainly kept their distance.

Wednesday 24 May

We made our way this morning to the mission to complete our arrangements. We gave in our papers and documents; from London, Bombay and the French Bank, to the clerks who run the mission. One was a tiny, little, man with long hair and a fancy goatee with pretension to be a Van Dyke named Truscan, who insisted we call him Mr Truscan; an un-likeable gnome who was all fuss and bother about the quality of our expedition's paperwork. He wanted this paper signed in front of witnesses, even though it had already been done in London or Bombay and it would be impossible to now do that. This clerk was completely pompous, and he seemed to think each pound of provisions, each blanket, or instrument was to be torn from his bosom and squandered in front of him. We soon found that all the paperwork that Perkins and Vickery had done in Bombay would need to redone; and in a manner according to Middlecomb, (...) the erstwhile Mr Truscan - who it must be said could back up his demands by pointing to this or that policy. We needed Dissanayake but he was somewhere to the south of us, probably falling again off his horse as I wrote this.

[Editor's note: Why Driscol and the others called him Middlecomb will become clearer later in the narrative]

Mr Truscan, or Middlecomb, as we insist on calling him to his distaste, did tell us two tales of interest from his life in Persia. He was once chased for some time by a colossal starved boar that followed him over hedge, rock and valley, and he insisted that he barely escaped with his life. He had escaped only by abandoning his lunch to the creature's hunger. He also told us in great circumspect style that while everyone knows the Muhammadans may not taste pork, and that it elicits from them disgust if even discussed, he knew that members of the Royal family often dine here and at the French mission on the forbidden meat.

Despite his bemusing stories, we left terribly frustrated and we agreed that we must find McNeill to bring his dog to heel. To do so would entail a long day's ride from our present quarters, as he was still in the mountains above us.

Hynes was pleased we had met the 'bloody fool in administration'; he had made our arrangements with McNeill and the others, instead of that man, whose sole pleasure seemed to be in making demands that were neither practical nor possible.

Thursday 25 May

With Hynes and one of the Gulchek men to guide us, we left early this morning to make the ride up to the valley of Lars. We did so, taking with us each an additional horse, to ride through the rocky, barren, terrain that surrounds Teheran. We then came to green, alpine meadows; alternating red with poppies, or yellow with another flower, whose Latin name I did not know. Next were lush woods and the rippling Lar River; and after some scanning of the terrain with my binoculars, I found a hint of smoke and a yellow-striped tent. We arrived in the light of early evening, just in time for dinner, and it was a fine one indeed; a bear had been successfully hunted and was on the menu. We met here two outstanding persons, the giant Sir Henry Lindsay-Bethune, an Englishman nearly seven feet tall, an artillerist and general in the Persian army, in the company of the very man we sought, the ambassador himself, along with three Anglo-Indian servants and no more. We were made most welcome and found we had come at a trying time for the Ambassador and General Bethune.

Bethune was glad to meet me and I had to go through, again, my experience at Djedda.

Hynes and the General knew one another well, having served together in Persia before, and they shared a Falstaffian exchange of hilarious comments, ribald insults, vile observations and remembrances. It was quite unnerving to watch Sergeant Hynes gravely insulting a man, both way beyond his rank, and class standing, and who also towered over him. It would seem that Hynes was in no way cowed either by this man's giant size or rank. He might not be, but I certainly was.

Hynes had told me that a good Sergeant was always in the superior position with any officer, whom he let THINK was in charge, while in fact the Sergeant ran everything. A good Sergeant ran and directed, officers were left to think, and usually they thought they were in command.

The Ambassador to Persia, McNeill shoots a Persian bear at point blank range.
Illustration III-XII-32

Politics of Herat

We were told that a crisis was brewing in Teheran, which is why the ambassador and the senior English officer in the Persian army had come to this remote place with English *(Indian)* servants only.

The story was recorded later, as it seemed impolite and unwise to write down what were confidential statements of these two men, so I took the precaution of committing it to memory and to disguising the message.

[Editor's note: Driscol did take precautions he wrote the following using the Arabic script but using Danish as the language. At first I thought it was gibberish as neither I nor native Arabic or Farsi speakers could make any sense of it, and I had to write it out letter by letter, then reverse it to discover it was Danish, I suspect that few, if any one in Persia would have both the skill of reading Arabic and Danish. It should be noted that Arabic is written right to left and Danish, like English is written left to right]

The Shah had foolishly decided to attack the Afghani city of Herat.

When Fatah Ali Shah Kajar *(the former Shah of Persia, 1772 - 1834)* had died, the present Shah had been his grandson. His father Abbas Mirza had been selected as the heir of the above Shah, Fatah Ali, but he had died before he could take up the accession. Abbas Mirza had picked his other son, Muhammad, to be his heir, before he died, but this did not sit well with the more senior members of the family. Other sons, including the present Shah, rose up to claim the throne and a civil war ensued over the crown. The brothers and other sons of the previous ruler had been numerous, brought up to be independent, and skilled in war, and governance, many declared they were the true Shah. Worse still, they were surrounded by many contemptible sycophants, who in order to gain advantage for themselves, provoked unceasing war between uncles and nephew and half-brothers. What was a miracle was that only two competitors had seriously challenged for the kingship, from the two score or more most of the pseudo-Shahs were too lazy to make the attempt.

The first to declare he was Shah - and act like he was - was the brother of Abbas Mirza, who held the powerful position of governor of the Arg *(fortress)* of Teheran and the title of Zil-i-Sultan. The second was a wealthy Prince of Shiraz who had money but no army to speak of, or a commanding presence to gain more.

Mohammad our present Shah was in Tabriz *(northwest Persia)*, but without funds. The English ambassador *(Sir John Campbell)* wished to avoid a destructive civil war that would weaken Persia, when England needed Persia to halt the Russian advances against Central Asia. Campbell advanced Mohammed a large sum, to allow him to pay his army to advance on Teheran *(a sum of £80,000)*. He did so, and the first usurper from the Arg, who had held nominal power for forty days, was swept away. The army had marched under the direction of General Bethune. Having secured Teheran, he marched on, to crush the small insurgent army of the rich man of Shiraz, and took him prisoner. Mohammad instead of staining his hands with blood had these pretentious relatives retired to obscure places with small pensions and a guard of honour, to make sure they did not stir up trouble. He ensured this stability; it was said, by simply making it known that anyone visiting these men would have their hands cut off and tongues cut out in order to prevent people from taking messages to confederates outside, and starting conspiracies against the present Shah.

The new Shah had selected as his Vizier, or Prime Minister, Hajji Mirza Aghasy; his former priest *{Imaum}*, tutor and valet, a *sufy {Sufi}* devotee and a supporter of Russian interests. It was he who had flattered the new Shah into regaining the city of Herat; for the land had once been Persian and the people of that district spoke a form of Persian *{Dari}*.

His detractors held that Aghasy had led the Shah into Sufi mysticism, and the two men came to be known as the two 'dervishes' in Teheran. It was thought by the both the French and British that the Vizier was attempting to use Sufism as a weapon against the growing power of the mullahs, who were opposing both modernization and foreign influence, especially in the areas of military, political and economic development.

The other actor is this play was Comte *{Count}* Simanovich, a Dalmatian, formerly in the French service who had been taken prisoner in the rout of the *Grand Armee* in 1812. He had switched his allegiance and in time became the Russian Minister to the Shah *{Ambassador}*.

The Shah was also encouraged to act, by the outright violations of an existing treaty between Persia and Afghanistaun, by the Afghan ruler of Herat, a fool named Shah Kamran. He had invaded Persian territory and raided villages there and gave to the Persians an excuse to offer up a counter-attack, for they clearly had right on their side as the attacked party.

It had been England's position that the Shah should focus his attention on the repair and rebuilding of a Persia that lay in ruin, to build up her industry, arts and people; for a strong Persia would be able to dissuade all foreign attackers.

What Count Simanovich played at was to put the Shah and Persia in a position that if they took Herat they would come into conflict with England and if they lost they would be weakened and poised once again to suffer Russian advances. The Russians had freed all the Christian provinces of Persia but they could still advance further to encircle the Caspian Sea - or to make it the 'Czar's bathtub' as some claimed.

At the present, the Shah was gathering an army to take Herat. If he did so, this would cause problems for both our expedition and England.

The threat of Herat to England lay in the city's strategic location; placed as it was in Sistan, a province between Persia and Afghanistaun proper, and on the border with Independent Tatary. It was an important crossroad as all the great roads of Asia met there and it had the resources to feed an advancing Russian army. If one advanced towards India from the central part of Asia, one path lead directly through Herat and it is one of the finer and direct pathways. It was that passage that worried us, and sparkled before the Russians as their goal. It was a way for the Russian bear to strike at England, untouchable at present to the bear for we stood safely behind our wooden walls {Royal Navy}. Frustrated by this, the Russians could not attack us directly, but they could invade the crown jewel of our colonial holdings.

A war would confuse the issue of our expedition, but Hynes says that we could use it as an excuse to travel about looking for horses, as they would be needed by both sides. A nearby war would tend to 'stir the pot', but perhaps it would be a good thing.

The bear roast was superb if gamey, and the cool atmosphere invigorating. We took a bath in the icy, cold, stream and got a good look at the scarred body of Hynes, who had, as he said, taken abuse to his body from arrows, Indian short axes {tomahawks}, knives, grapeshot, musket balls, and various manners of cutlery, to include a large, carving spit. However, we had learned that some of these stories were just that stories: told in jest. I had naught to show, as the scar on my upper lip was well hidden by my moustache. I had only the shot marks earned from the Chileans off Algiers, and the Turks and Arabs off Djedda, and the Grey men off Africa. My 'pucker' wound in my right hand, which bothered me still, was not very impressive. The only other 'medals of scar' were various scratches I had earned in service, plus several small, honourable, wounds from my life as an adventurous boy.

We aided them in cleaning the skin of the bear, a somewhat loathsome duty, and drying the rest of the meat over a low, smoky, caliginous fire.

A drawing from McNeill's journal of the Campsite with MG Bethune the Giant stirring the pot, Hynes (?) cutting something and Driscol is carrying water. III-XII-33

We asked them what in their opinion would be the best way to proceed. McNeill thought it best to go the Caspian Sea route and take a boat up $^3/_4$ of the way along the Eastern shore of that Sea, then disembark and proceed directly to the Aral Sea, and then to the Oxus and the cities along its shore.

Bethune thought it would be best to go first to Kushan or Merv and proceed from there, after hiring an escort of Turcoman raiders/riders, onwards to Khiva and then on to the Aral Sea and beyond.

One of the older valets, a trusted Anglo-Indian, claimed to have known George Trebeck[8], who had gone on the Moorcroft's[9] expedition. He had spent part of his life in Persia and was well versed in the area. He thought our best course of action would be to advance to Bokhara {Bukhara}, as envoys of the Persian Shah, and having established ourselves and gained the friendship of the Bokharans, move out to explore from there.

Bethune and McNeill did not agree with this idea, as they said that the Emir Nasr-Allah bin Haydar Tora *{Nasrullah Khan}*, ruler of Bokhara, was a despot and unfriendly to the British, Persian and the Russians. In fact, he was pretty much un-trustful of everyone. Perhaps Samarkand would be a better place to go?

No, said the valet, *{a knowledgeable person who may have been a man named Joshua Chandra Keene}*, as the Emir of Bukhara had sovereignty over that ancient city and there was a garrison of his men holding the Registan *{public square or in this case the citadel}*.

We also discussed the explorations and adventures of Captain Arthur Conolly[10] an officer of the 6th Bengal Light Cavalry.

We finally considered going first to Kokand, Tashkent or Khiva. In the end so much was said, that I cannot now sort it out to write it now, for I must sleep. As it is 2.30 in the morning.

One final word; McNeil mentioned that he had received notification several weeks previously from London and that in his words;

> An important change had happened as the English Government transferred the control of the Persian mission from the responsibility of the HEIC in India to its own sphere. Thus McNeill was here under the authority of London, and not Calcutta, and as we were under his control, the HEIC no longer had any possible claim of responsibility or authority for or over the expedition. London had done exactly what Perkins had expected, and for once the authorities in London had been good to their word and not tardy in telling everyone.

[Editor's note: See Appendix III-II for a map showing Central Asia and four of the discussed routes]

Friday 26 May

Good breakfasts with our bear kidneys and tongue. We then rode over to the Lar River and did some fishing; and I was doing very well, catching three fish I did not know the designation of. Each creature was about eight pounds, and they were a gorgeous, golden colour. I brought these back, and found they were called *Talaji* in the local dialect, or *mahi safed daryachet khazar;* of the family *Cyprinidae {cyprinids}*, or as I described it, the *Caspian Driscolli*. As far as any of us could tell, they had not been described in the literature[11].

The general and the ambassador had decided to leave two men to continue the process of preparing the bear skin for preservation, so in the late morning, the rest of us rode off, a party of one servant, Perkins, Hynes, McNeil Bethune and I.

Hynes again demonstrated his air weapon, which on the one hand amazed Bethune, while less so the good physician, for McNeill had studied medicine at the University of Edinburgh, where he graduated at the age of nineteen, and he seemed to find little inspiration in it. I mentioned he was a healer for he had spoken out about the horrific wounds that the multiple balls would inflict. As they were not being heated by the powder, they would penetrate the body cold and thus, would more easily spread infection.

[Editor's note: this is an interesting observation in a time when the germ theory had not yet gained dominance. Military surgeons had noted that cold steel caused greater chances of infection than a hot bullet - if it passed out of the body and left no part of the victim's clothing in the wound]

Bethune wondered what would have happened if Boney *{Napoleon}* had made widespread use of this weapon. The defect of the weapon was shown him after he had two-hundred repetitions at the air pump. It was a wonderful toy, but in the field it was fragile and had need of a way to quickly fill the air reservoirs, which did not currently exist

As we rode, McNeill observed that we would need to name the expedition and establish a patron. We could not leave without doing so, for how would he announce to London that we had left? We must do the needful soon.

Perkins agreed. We arrived at Gulchek in the late evening, having been delayed in cooking my three fish beside a pond, before descending once again in the flat, plain, plains of Teheran with its heat, dust and disorder.

Persian prisoners'. Illustration III-XII-34

As we rode in, we passed a group of Persian prisoners going literally to the salt mines.

During our entrance to our habitation, we, by my error delayed the passage of some Persian, functionary who I knocked down in the street by my horse moving uncontrollably. I provided the necessary apology in Persian and in return the man, cursed me in Persian calling me Omar the Shimr *{slayer of Al-Hosayn a notable of the Shi'ah religion}* and a deadly insult among the Shi'ah. We found this amusing. It was likened to an Englishmen calling a Persian the 'son of a Frenchman', or of his having 'Italian courage' or 'German *Kultur' {culture}* all very insulting to an Englishman, but meaningless to a Persian.

Saturday 27 May

We continue our frustrating dealings with Middlecomb, as he refuses to believe that London would want us to purchase examples of unknown breeds of horses in Tartary; despite the letters stating so clearly. His argument is that if they KNEW that horses could be bought anywhere, India, Arabia, even Persia, why would they want stock from Tartary?

We spoke with McNeill later and continued our complaints against the man. While in Lars valley, our Ambassador would not take up the subject. We again pressed him on this issue asking him why he had Mr Truscan, for he referred to him by that name exclusively, in his service. He took us to the garden to explain

[Editor's note: Driscol took scribbled notes but instead of reconstructing it as a discussion I have placed it as paraphrased paragraph]

'He is a bastard', he said, and we agreed with him on that, unanimously. But no, he meant in the more infamous way, and looked at us knowingly. 'Why do you think he is in Persia in my employ? He, I must say, keeps the accounts very well, but he is an impossibly vain fool and poltroon too. I just have him do up the accounts, and then do as I wish. Have him, make a list of his, ah, er, requirements, and I will address them, one by one, and dismiss them without your need for future concern'.

[Editor's note: The clerk in question was indeed the rumoured illegitimate son of the Earl of Rutland and later in life he would make a claim on his alleged father's estate, but was defeated in a series of public law suits in the 1840-50's. He was unsuccessful, as English law of that time was very indifferent to such assertions]

We plunged back into the accounts. I remember at one point this man looked at us and said, 'My dear gentlemen this paperwork will just not do. What will the Emirs of Tartary say when you dare to show up without a properly franked and certified copy of your transport cost from Bombay? Dare I say they will not be impressed'?

We were certainly not impressed.

Sunday 28 May

We returned to the hills and worked on our accounts.

In working on our papers, Perkins said two things of great wisdom and humour.

'Attempts at economy are the thief of time, which is more precious than Sterling' and 'the boundary between a humble income and boundless wealth is suspicion'.

Dinner and supper is not more bear, but a chicken, well stewed with yellow peas.

Monday 29 May

Perkins and I are both unwell from a congestion of the stomach; perhaps the bear would have been better?

Tuesday 30 May

Good Lord very tired from our illness, and sleep the day away. Bethune visited and told me an account of his early days in Persia.

> When he had become a Persian general, and was commanding their best corps of men stationed on the Ottoman frontier, he was invited to dinner by the governor of the adjoining Turkish province. The latter had pretenses of knowing about the west and the likes of Englishmen. Music was provided and it was comprised of cymbals, drums, flutes, tambourines, trumpets, and other clangorous instruments, which had been scraped together somewhere out in this wilderness. Upon taking leave, and thanking his host, Bethune invited the Turkish officer to come to his camp on the following day, and he said he would return the Turk's gift of music with his own melodious counter-gift. Supper was a great success and then a select band of four Europeans, who had some skill, performed some the best works of Italian, French, Austrian and German composers. At the end of this display of Europe's best tunes he asked the Turk what he thought of the music. He replied that he preferred his

own as the Frankish *{European}* musicians played music out of a book, which he had heard once before in Constantinople, while his musicians played a different tune every time.

I thought it a very quaint and witty tale.

Haviland Middleworths Truscan, bastard son of the Earl of Rutland (Dalhousie Hector Middlecombe) who always insisted on being called 'Middlecomb' without the 'e' for reasons known only to himself. Illustration III-XII-35

The Lost Children Re-Appear The Expedition Reunited

Wednesday 31 May

We heard early in the morning, from a post rider whom we had bribed for advanced intelligence, which our expedition arrived at the final post station prior to Teheran the night before. So we rise up from our death beds and rode out to meet them in the morning. We will go in mufti to confound them.

We saw them as a brown smudge in the distance, and came towards them on horseback: we being in mufti, and riding unknown horses, we expected to surprise them. Dobbins and Vickery suddenly spurred their horses and came towards us crying our names, for our movements in the saddle were too well known. It was a joyous meeting. All the others came up. Dissanayake stopping his horse too violently and was thrown upon its neck and then slowly slid off onto the ground, landing on his feet, I must grant him.

All were well. Michaelson could tell we had been ill, but we pooh-poohed his concerns. They of course wanted to know what we had done about Hymison. We had thought to deceive them, but having had our disguise penetrated so easily, and as Perkins had observed he was a poor liar when the audiences were men, we told them Sergeant Hynes was the culprit, and we hoped that Hymison was in Calcutta, Karachi or on his way to Cabul! Blonde is quite happy to see me, and I have brought here some of her favourites to nibble. She does not take kindly to me riding the other horse and begins to push at her and I switch to her for the ride back some twelve miles. Dobbins relinquished his independent command with a salute and received compliments for having brought it forth without loss or incident.

Horne was quite pleased to know that Hynes was here and that we had met several other members of the earlier military mission to Persia. We told him of Captain Sheil wanting his debt paid. This statement caused him to launch into a long tale relating how he could not possibly owe him anything. It was amusing in its impossibly complex layers of odd happenings, miscommunications and lost chances.

All members of the expedition are in good shape; and Bannington exhibits to us the skills of riding and formation that he has drilled into the organization during their passage. They do quite well. He and Horne have whipped them into a passable cavalry troop.

The legation had prepared an entertainment for when they arrived, so we make them ride all the way to Gulchek, by passing Teheran altogether for no European stays in the squalor, stench and heat of Teheran in late May, unless he has pressing business there. There is an artificial pond on the property of Gulchek, which had been screened off and the men, horses & pack animals obtain a much needed bath.

Persian Musicians. Illustration III-XII-36

An entertainment and feast has been prepared, all on the tab of the expedition, to both welcome the main body, and to thank the Mission for all it has done, which I am sure will cause dismay and consternation to Mr Truscan later on, who, I might add was not invited. We have a typical Persian display of what they consider entertainment, to my eyes it was indifferent, and to my ears an insult.

We were given two episodes of so-called; the first was music of a sort which I would describe as hogs being dropped into boiling water, and fat women being told there is no cake. The second occurrence of music, or what Horne called 'a tune the old cow died of', occurred during what might be called 'dessert' and this consisted of a concert entailing the screams of what we supposed was a vocalist. The orchestra played in a manner to suggest not so much music but a pack of monkeys being skinned alive. Western music is based on polyphony, harmony or a contrast or counterpoint to harmony; it is organised, and this 'music' displayed none of these mellifluous characteristics.

Their dancers were clothed in robes of silk, from which gaudy ribbons of different colours were attached in no discernible pattern, and from close observation, we decided there must be five boys, as we could not imagine girls exposing their unveiled faces to foreigners.

Persian dancer who caught Driscol's eye. Illustration III-XII-37

A new group of female dancers appeared and these were fairly skilled and even seemed to somehow follow the discordant sounds made by the orchestra. They began dancing, and throwing themselves into various attitudes. After a change of costume, our dancers reappeared being bare bosomed which drew an appreciative and ungentlemanly roar from all.

One lovely dancer had a face and bosom which reminded me of Karen, and I reflected long on the idea if she might look like this uncovered, another of Millicent, and yet another of Marguerite.

Of more interest were Persian wrestlers, who were quite good. Each man, after a hard tussle, would come to obtain a small coin from Perkins.

Dobbins and Hynes both challenged the larger of them. Hynes went first and took him down twice out of five times. Dobbins beat him three times in row, his strength being unbeatable. Another of the Persians challenged Dobbins and he, again defeated him twice when the Persian took offence to this action and struck Dobbins in the stomach, which to the horror of the Persian Dobbins only smiled, backed away, and told us this man could not put a dent in a pound of butter with his fist.

The fight that occurred, for it was no wrestling match, was something to observe, the Persian trying to get Dobbins into a position and hold to force a submission and Dobbins avoiding this and pounding his body with loud blows, which the Persian would have done well to avoid, but did not. At one point the Persian wrestler got Dobbin's left arm behind his back and looked like he would win, but Dobbins reached over grabbed his hair, which shaved to prevent this but he did anyway and bent forward throwing the man forward. Finally Dobbins ended the match, for until then he had landed blows only on the man's body, but he now hit him sharply in the ribs, and then to the temple, and the man went down. Dobbins put the smallest of our Dinar coins on the man's forehead, before he was carried away.

Persian wrestlers from a photograph seventy years after Driscol viewed them; but the costume and shorn forehead would have been the same then. Illustration III-XII-38

The other Persian wrestlers were quite happy with this, as the other man was no friend of theirs. Dobbins suffered no ill marking from the contest and I observed he had only the sheen of perspiration on his brow, and was not breathing hard after what I viewed as a hard contest.

He did later remark that his knuckles and wrist were sorely tested by the blow to the man's temple. McNeill was quite happy, as Dobbins had defeated the best known wrestler in this part of Persia, and there was nothing that McNeill liked more than was to put the Persians in their place. Bethune of course challenged Dobbins but he, tired from his previous excursions just bowed and said he would not even attempt it but perhaps later? *{Bethune was a head taller and weighed about one hundred pounds more than Dobbins}*. I wondered how a Lieutenant and Major General at fisticuffs would look. I truly suspected that the giant Bethune would be unable to defeat Dobbins.

Vickery tried his hand, and quickly defeated a much heavier opponent by applying a submission hold on his leg; it was quite impressive. He said he had learned it all from an old *Olohe {A master of the Hawaiian martial art called Lua or Ku'ialua}*.

After this excitement a dancing bear was not at all amusing, and then a wrestling bear without teeth or claws but even Bethune would not take on that challenge.

Rams were next; and I thought of the Roman Coliseum and those legendary gladiatorial contests. The rams butted heads in a lively contest; the sound of their collisions made my head and teeth ache.

A lion and oxen were next brought on, and I thought, to my horror, that the lion would stalk and kill the ox. Many of our expedition had never seen a lion, which was a female and the act considered of the lioness leaping on the back of the circling oxen and doing other simple tricks. I do hope they keep the lion well fed, for the oxen's safety.

The ubiquitous Persian water pipe.
Illustration III-XII-39

More bad music and singing, then food; various types of stews, mutton in a dozen guises and various dishes, some good, some indifferent. The evening came to an end with the men drinking forbidden wine and taking long draws on the Turkish pipes. I withdrew at this point.

The Tales Of The Lost Expedition

[Editor's note: Driscol at this time wrote that Vickery had kept the spare log of the second part of the expedition. This consisted of a location by latitude and longitude, an elevation and estimate of the miles travelled. He also noted any expenses made, the price paid, what was obtained and for what reason; dull stuff. I have left this out, except for a few samples, as it covers an area already commented on by Driscol and I have left in the personal stories noted both by Vickery and Driscol that took place during this time, even if recorded days or weeks later, and included those noted to have occurred during this time. Each day Vickery would write a similar entry to this one below]

May 18 we are at latitude X, longitude Y elevation Z, cloudy day with a mean temperature of 86 $\frac{1}{2}$ F and have travelled 14 and $\frac{1}{4}$ mile over rocky terrain

> Purchased additional fodder for animals: $^1/_4$ Quiran (400 Dinars)

> Sundries: watermelon seed, roasted, approximately 3 lbs, 2 Dinars

> Fruit: Dates, Ganthar style, 41 Dinars

> Beggars: 2 Dinars in small change to scatter them

> Haddad (Blacksmith): 90 Dinars

[Editor's note: Vickery used the Arabic term for blacksmith, haddad and Driscol wrote down the term kaveh, who was a famous mythological Persian blacksmith while the actual term should be aahangar]

Observances from the journey made by members of the expedition:

Bannington: Spoke for some time with a Persian astrologer, who was delighted to speak to a foreigner for the first time. Bannington mostly noted that the man seemed shocked that we had departed on a journey without asking the aide of one of his kind and that we had no knowledge of Persian astrology; for no Persian of any consequence will step outside his door without a reference to the acceptance of the stars of his action; whether it be for a new wife, a new robe, a war against his neighbours, everything is filtered through an analysis of the stars.

This knowledge of the stars seems limited, as the man knew little of European astronomy. His knowledge of the heavens is limited to what he needed to know to conduct and construct verses for use in judicial astrology. If he knows the names of the planets, and carries with him the Persian equivalent of an almanac, and can spout some technical sounding terms, he has a well-regarded lively-hood. Bannington was pleased to note that the man did know that the earth went around the sun, but shockingly also believed that the other planets and the stars went around the earth in turn. The phrase 'don't you know' was Bannington's comment on this and it was repeated a great deal. How this cosmology would work was not a question the astrologer had either seriously considered or if he considered, or if he had decided it, he had decided it was of no importance.

He also noted that enemies of a man can get to him by way of his astrologer; for the astrologers can be bribed to give false readings. In such a way, one businessman was warned not to not trade in this commodity and that for months, while his competitors, had for the price of a small bribe to the other man's astrologer, had kept him locked in inactivity by the words of a false predictions of eminent peril should he make any move at all.

Dissanayake: observed and discussed with any learned Persians he came across to understand the way the law worked in the country. He found that '*urf*', or customary law, as administered by the Shah and his minions, ruled the land. Thus the men who enforce the law, the magistrates consider themselves to be above this same law, as do all members of the Kajar family. The same goes for rulers of provinces, governors of cities and other authorities, *urf* is what is used to decide matters dealing with those who are not so privileged. The only check on the activities of those that are not constrained by the law is the dread of a superior taking offence or being bribed to act against a lower man. In such cases, the lower man has no defence except to flee, plead for mercy, offer a bribe, or seek sanctuary.

The magistrates exercise the law quickly, and with great dispatch, often ignoring any evidence that is germane to the question. Such is the way in Persia. Your fate is consequently decided by a man who by nature is either vigilant and virtuous or avaricious and tyrannical. To his judgment there is no appeal unless one can gain the ear of the Shah, for only he can overturn such a judgment or unless it can in some way be made a religious question, which a fair amount of life in Persian can so be considered. Then a cleric who have a multi-layer hierarchy of their own, may intercede.

Michaelson: spoke with two Persian physicians; finding one practical and the other a complete fool. Both were grounded in the aspects of Ibn Sina *{Avicenna}*, and one had with him a copy of that book the *al-Qanun fi al-tibb {The Canon of Medicine}*, to which he referred at all times. Michaelson had seen the second volume of this book, translated into Latin, during his own medical studies. They discussed the nature of the four temperaments[12]. He also noted that the Islamic restrictions do not allow for vivisection with the consequence that little is known here of the inner workings of the body.

Dobbins: had a chance to speak with a hunting man who was using a goshawk to hunt for bustards, but the pressing need to push on prevented him from witnessing any display of its skill, or the master's technique of directing it. He also mentioned the grasping custom of men who lurked about the caravan route. Perkins and I avoided them because we were on official business and when I travelled by myself I simply rode around their stations. Dobbins noted that as a group, they had penetrating eyes, a nose for that which is hidden, and an insatiable curiosity.

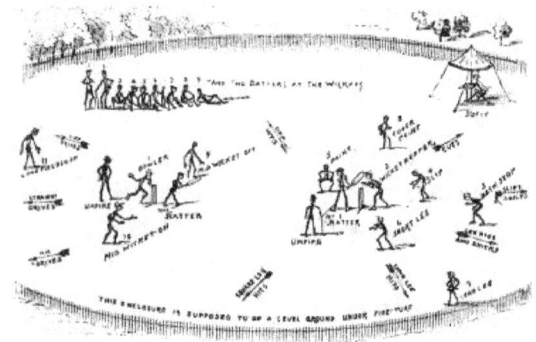

One of two diagrams found in Driscol's papers drawn by Horne they show the position of players in cricket, this one has the players' positions written in English the other in Persian. Illustration III-XII-40

Horne: found no place that would grant him a demanded meal of cold, greasy, pork with buttered parsnips, despite asking in several places. He had nothing further to add about the journey except a discussion he had about the game of cricket, apart from casting detailed and damning aspersions on all Persians present, past and future.

Vickery: was stopped by the man I had previously encountered, who wished to hire him to search for the murderer in question, but Vickery gave him instead a 1 Dinar coin and suggested he buy a musket, a bottle of wine, and a burial shroud, to be ready for all eventualities-when he did the business himself.

[Editor's note: Driscol added in the following reminiscence as a separate sheet]

Vickery had said to Dobbins at one point:

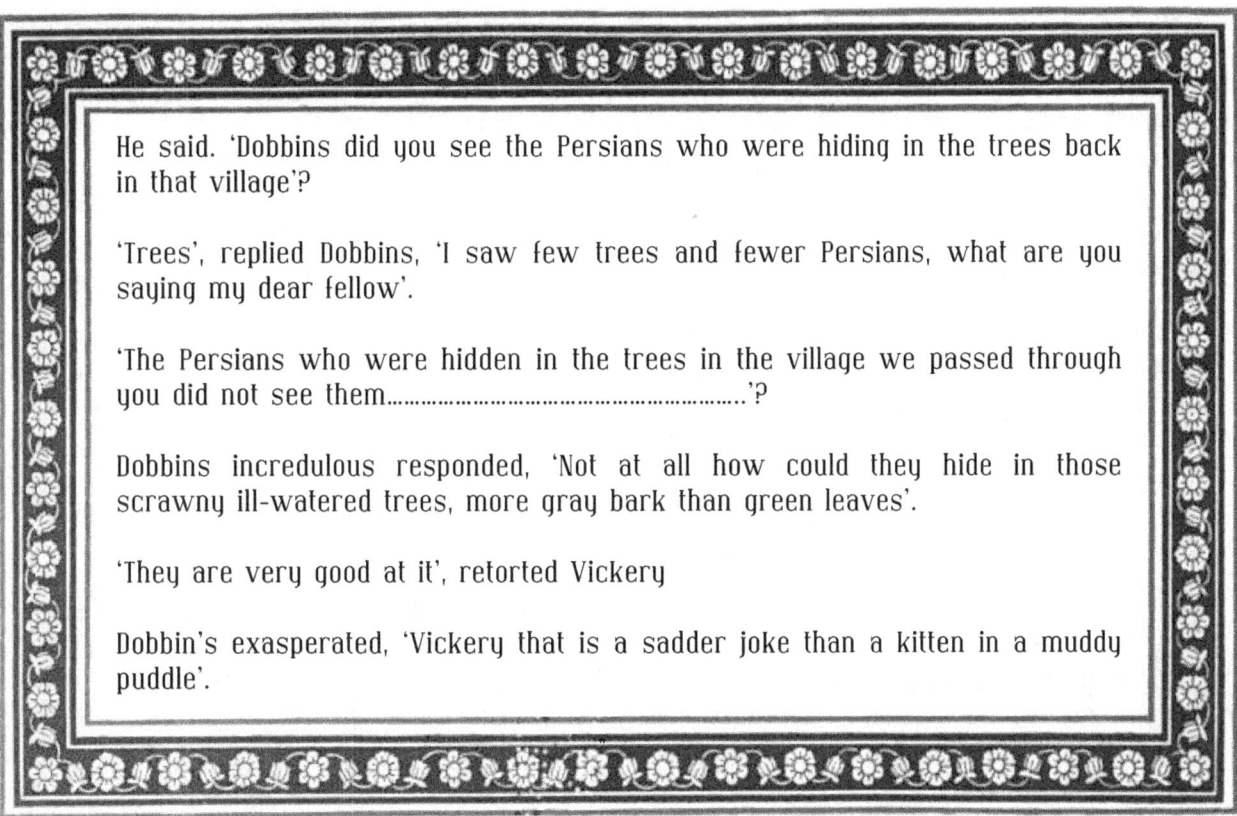

He said. 'Dobbins did you see the Persians who were hiding in the trees back in that village'?

'Trees', replied Dobbins, 'I saw few trees and fewer Persians, what are you saying my dear fellow'.

'The Persians who were hidden in the trees in the village we passed through you did not see them...'?

Dobbins incredulous responded, 'Not at all how could they hide in those scrawny ill-watered trees, more gray bark than green leaves'.

'They are very good at it', retorted Vickery

Dobbin's exasperated, 'Vickery that is a sadder joke than a kitten in a muddy puddle'.

Great Plans

Thursday 1 June

I noted today that it was the 43rd anniversary of the Glorious First of June and the death of Uncle David, I made a silent toast to his memory.

[Editor's note: A naval battle between the Republican Navy of France and Great Britain and an English tactical, but French strategic victory on June 1, 1794. Driscol's Uncle David Jeremiah Driscol, who was the sailing master of the fifth rate HMS Phaeton, a 38 gun Frigate, lost his head in this battle to a French round shot. Driscol, in Volume I, had stated that another Uncle David, lost at the battle of Maida, was the one for whom he was named. Hence it would seem he had more than one relative named David who had died in battle and after whom he was named!]

The men rest, as we, and the legation servants, and staff, see to the horses. After fulsome tiffin, we meet in the garden to discuss that which must be decided; how we will now proceed. We had come out to Persia earlier than initially planned, to avoid any interference from persons who would not be named. We had lots of options to consider: we could either conduct ourselves here, or as we had been advised, summer over on the Caspian shore. or up in the cooler mountain villages near Teheran or we could do one of the many options previously considered.

We spoke together for some hours. Bethune and others came by at various points to add information or to see to our needs. Perkins treated our discussion like a meeting before a great battle, when a general or admiral gathers to him his key commanders and staff, and asks them their opinions. We had before us, a large map of Persia and Central Asia, noting the many white spots, not known to the cartographers. Despite the knowledge that we would ride into the intense heat of the summer, all were for going forward immediately; the method and manner of doing so, however was more contentiously disputed and debated.

Just before dinner, an agreement was made. We would travel to Asterabad as Englishmen, observe the trade there, and obtain additional horses, for we had decided to travel very lightly with only one tent, no servants and only a guide. We would then, transform our guise to that of Circassian mercenaries looking to purchase horses for a regiment of the Turkish army *{in Tartary the Ottomans were respected, as they were Sunnis, while the Persians, as Shia were considered enemies and loathed}*. We would travel to Merv, then onto the Oxus *{Amu Darya River}* and proceed by boat or horse to the Aral Sea; investigating the city of Khiva as we passed her. After conducting a circumnavigation of the Sea, we would then either follow any outlet to the Caspian, or if finding none, we would inspect the markets of Bokhara, Samarkand, Khokand and Tashkent. We would winter in Tartary at a place we would decide on later, and then make our way up the Jaxartes *{Syr Darya River}* until we made contact with Russian patrols. Then depending on the situation, make our way to the frontier lands of Seres *{China}* and the rivers there. We intended to stay in Tartary until late spring of the following year, hoping to this same garden one and half years thenceforward.

[Editor's note: Based on later explorers' experiences, this plan was bold indeed]

We also discussed an official name of the expedition and several notable figures were proposed. As we were London based, any suggestion of a person connected to the HEIC would not be considered. We considered a wide range of notables, military, scientific, political and noble, but no agreement could be found.

We had a formal dinner party that evening, but all British, no foreigner was invited. McNeill, who had been in Teheran all that day, brought us word from our Swiss friend, who had obtained the name of a recommended guide. He was a man with many years of caravan and war experience in the region, but who had retired, it was said to a town north of us Meshed-e-Sar *{modern Babolsar}.*

Horne embarrassed us all, by his usual tactic of crying out for his greasy pork and parsnips, which the ambassador took in an amusing way. Nonetheless he did not take well to Horne's next public announcement, for we had been fed small sweetmeats and French style delicacies at the start, then finally a good sized, British style, roast beef was brought. It was five and sixty pounds of roasted, steaming, hot meat running with redden juices, to which upon seeing it, Horne stood hastily, hoisted his glass, and proposed a toast, 'By Jove, finally something to eat at last'!

Perkins and I were seated on either side of McNeill, and we were speaking of the expedition, when he asked if we had arrived at a name and patron?

Perkins, for I know the tone of voice he uses when he jests, said we would call it the Middlecomb expedition, after that meddling clerk, but that part went unsaid. McNeill did not laugh; instead he leaned back and seemed in deep thought. I thought he had taken offence but instead he rose up and called for a toast.

'Gentleman, Lieutenant Perkins has just told me the name for your expedition and I must say it is brilliant, truly appropriate. I would not have thought of it, and it is rightly inspired. For many years, the man so named, has worked hard for the advancement of geography and knowledge, yes he is shy and lacks the social graces, but I do know that he was one of the silent backers of the expedition'.

Seeing that the ambassador was mistaken, Perkins tried to lead him away from it. However, we soon found that he was thinking of Lord Middlecombe, a quiet, little known man, and member of the Royal Geographic Society. He thought it most capital to name it thusly and he added that Middlecombe, who by the way, was a cousin by marriage of his, would be most appreciative and as he was vastly wealthy from West Indian sugar money, we might expect a hefty honorarium after the publication of our report.

As I sat there, I remembered something Lieutenant and sometimes Major Todd had said to me days earlier, 'there are four great powers in Persia, the Shah who had some power over the nobles and people, the British resident who had command of the greatest empire in the world and barrels of money, the French counsel who thinks he has some influence, but in reality does not, so we will not count him, the Russian resident *{minister}*, who might be a threat to us all but a distant threat, and Mr Middlecomb, aka Mr Truscan who actually could kill us all, by a mistaken entry in his books'.

Perkins looked at me, I looked at him, and he shrugged his shoulders; for neither of us had ever met this Lord and I had heard of him only on rare occasions. The others did not give away our jest, as only Hynes knew who Middlecomb actually was.

Afterwards, Perkins said OUR Middlecomb, Mr Truscan, the clerking bastard, must be a true bastard of the eponymous Lord Middlecombe in London. If so, and he is rich and powerful, then he is a fitting patron. I agreed. All the expedition found our misstep amusing, as all knew that in reality the expedition would not be remembered by that name but instead, tradition would hold true and it would be known as Perkins' expedition.

[Editor's note: as the title of this book demonstrates they were greatly mistaken]

==

Dalhousie Hector Middlecombe
Earl of Rutland

The Earl was the second son of the previous holder of the title, Lord Morris Johnston Middlecombe and his wife the Lady Angelina Beatty, and he was born in 1773 at Casterton house, Northamptonshire. He was a sickly child, but lived, much to the delight of his parents. He attended The University and King's College of Aberdeen, but left before finishing his degree, because of ill health. He did take a Lieutenancy in the Yeomanry *{militia cavalry}*, but it was found that his sensitivities *{allergies}* to horses made participation impossible. He later purchased a Captaincy in the local Militia, but served less than a year, when he found that walking more than a half mile, or riding more than two, would prostrate him for the rest of the day. Later he rejoined and travelled around in a carriage, as he needed to avoid direct contact with horses. His carriage was drawn by trained zebras, which avoided the sneezing he suffered in the company of equines. Unable to stand outside journeys, he settled into becoming an armchair naturalist, reading all the available materials of the day. He was a member of the Linnaean Society and Athenaeum Club of London, although he never attended them in person and was a founding member of the Geographical Society of London *{later to become the Royal Geographical Society}*.

In lesser matters, he held that Newton had been right, and held that the Bible was written containing enigmatic codes, which could predict the future. It was salaciously rumoured that he had illicit relationships with his household staff, with several illegitimate children being the result; Mr Truscan being one such result obtained with 'flat faced' Abby whose surname was Scullery.

He also supported William Herschel's contention that the Sun was inhabited and that the light we saw came from the ignition of the clouds about the planet Sun, which did not harm its inhabitants because of an opaque layer of clouds above them that separated them from the flames above.

He also toyed with the idea of bringing back the phlogiston theory, not as a fire-like element, but holding instead the idea that it was a chemical released during battles between the agents of Lucifer and various unidentified angels. These actions produced the blue colour of the sky, in a manner he never quite explained. He fortunately never wrote down this theory.

He did, however, do a great deal of solid geographical and geological work and was also fond of snails and fought a long, antagonistic battle by post with a number of scientists over the true nature and name of the *Vertigo substriata* and *Vertigo angustior*. These Vertigo were a genus of minute, air-breathing, land snails, terrestrial pulmonate gastropod molluscs or micromollusks in the family *Vertiginidae*, or the whorl snails. He held that instead, they were partially aquatic in brackish water and he fought over this matter with a scientist named Jeffreys for twenty years. The matter was particularly distasteful, as he had taken as his wife Jeffreys' sister Maude in 1803. This may explain why he felt that the *Vertigo sustriata* should have been named the *Vertigo maudiata;* at least he felt this must be the name and he petitioned the scientific community to do so, six times. In 1835, he would be a major contributor to the pressure on London to conduct an expedition to the Aral Sea, for he and others held, in spite of accounts to the contrary. He felt that the 'balance' of Tartary could only be obtained if there was a flow from the Aral Sea to the Caspian.

===

The Earl of Middlecombe's descendants in a zebra drawn carriage photographed a half century after Driscol's time. The Earl domesticated the breed and his success later led to the Penicuik Experiment[13]. Illustration III-XII-41

Friday 2 June

We could not depart until we were presented to the Shah and his court. We studied Persian and spoke with many on the aspects of Islam and culture in this country. This day I went to the city to purchase some items, and while doing so, I sighted a man in Persian costume and it was obviously Horne. I followed him for some time to see what he was up to. He was up to nothing, and after a half hour of this, I came up and thumped him on the shoulder and asked what in God's name he was up to? I did not receive the answer I expected. The man swirled and although looking like Horne, was not he at all. He was a Persian and wanted to know, with hand on his dagger why, I a foreigner would strike him. I apologised and said I had mistaken him for my colleague. He was soon mollified, his resemblance was terrifying. I soon found why he resembled, in a way, our Mr Horne; he was a *Jonubi {southerner}* from the south coast of Persia, from the borderland between the provinces of Kerman and Laristan, near where the Portuguese had had a fort. Some of those Iberian gentlemen had left a mark on the inhabitants, and he was the result. I invited him to visit us that day.

His visit was a great success. side by side, one could tell they were not an exact match, but that the same blood did flow between them. Horne, for once, was a complete gentleman and greatly charmed by this unknown, near twin. The Jonubi, named of course Mohammad, was a merchant, and we had a long discussion about the ills of Persia, the poor roads and the hope for more trade. His full name was Mohammad Abdullah bin Mirren Kouk.

محمد عبدالله بن ميرين كوك

[Editor's note: The man signed his name in Driscol's journal and offered up good wishes for their time in Persia]

Saturday 3 June

We conducted survey practice at the ruins of Raghes[14]. We have been invited to a party that evening, given by the Italian painter, Riccio, who makes his living creating indecent paintings to decorate the walls of harems; and so he is of course, very rich. The party was a success as all the European or Christian ladies in Teheran had been invited. The food was plentiful and well prepared; the music admirable, one of the Dutchmen playing a clarinet with some skill. My parents had decided, against my will I assure you, that I should play the clarinet; despite the failure of my entire sibling suite, with the exception of Zoe, to exhibit the slightest musical aptitude. After two years of torture they gave up, but I had given up but two days after beginning.

[Editor's note: Driscol wrote about this for some time and in summary he was, and much of his family appear to have been, tone deaf and couldn't hold a tune if it was stapled to them]

I had the great misfortune of being seated for dinner between two men; the first was an unemployed missionary, who suggested that our expedition would be aided by the all mighty if we were to make a vow of celibacy. I did mention, that based on the circumstances, I did not think that would be necessary, as the nature of land, its people and our duty would naturally prevent any reproduction. The other man was even worse; a Frenchmen who was from Cevennes[15] and naturally an idiot. There is only one thing worse than sitting next to a boor is to sit by a French speaking one. Naturally he found piddling faults with my French and I returned the comments with remarks concerning the failures of French politics, Empire and their poor cuisine.

I did not get to speak directly with the painter Riccio, who had some interesting points of conversation, one, which I overheard; he said in French to someone else, and I paraphrase,

> ...he wondered if the members of the Royal family, envious and covert enemies of the present ruler, the Shah, picked his wives for him or does his highness have poor eyesight, or just simply suffers from monumental bad taste in the fairer gender?

This was the second time I had heard this, and I wondered why it was such a popular sentiment? I had to presume that discussing a ruler's family life was something that we shared with the Persians as I had heard stories about the FritzClarences my whole life

[Editor's note: King William the IV had a relationship with Dorothea Jordan an actress with whom he had ten children. They were given the family name of FritzClarence. This was all very scandalous, yet the laxity of the 18th century still pervaded and the prudish Victorian era lay in the future]

There was much dancing, but as the men outnumbered the European women by eleven to one, this would have been unworkable had not the Italian also invited a large number of Armenian and Georgian women, all Christians, to attend. I had not seen so many white women in some time, for In Persia one does not see women, except in the distance and usually covered up, although working peasant women were not so constrained, and I had seen a few pretty faces in my ride up from Bushire.

Now these women were female, I can attest to this, and dressed in a fair resemblance of Europeans, but they had not been, well supplied with pretty. One outweighed the largest Scotsman I've ever seen. Another was a dwarf or midget and only 4 feet tall; more like a child than a woman. Another, I am sure, had a mother who had had indecent relations with a wart hog. Perkins, Horne and I used our Persian to try and describe the women, an area of nomenclature we had not concentrated on before. Perkins came up with the best one *golabipestaun*, *golabi* meaning pear, *pestaun* mean bosom and we all thought that an accurate description of ones woman's most attractive trait.

Entertainment was later provided by a Persian, who was wearing a caricature of western clothing; red trowsers, a green coat and a blue shirt with no buttons or collar. He was a notable figure, however, in Teheran as he was the current 'teller of stories to his majesty the Shah'; a job with many good points and requiring a man of great wit and entertainment acquirements. The man, some centuries before, would have been the court jester of a European monarch.

Persians love street exhibitions, but their culture sorely lacks any formal theatre; a great failing of most Mohammedan cultures. This failure to develop a canon of plays is countered by a rich supply of myth, folklore and legends; such as the stories, which were told by this man, with great elegance. He was quite skilled in the manner in which he altered his appearance and his tone of voice; at once an angry and pompous official and the next moment, speaking like a frightened maiden. He told several stories in Persian but I could not follow them, as they were in an older form of Persian; which must be like us listening to Shakespeare and puzzling over its use of terms and metaphors.

There were some five and thirty Europeans here and I had not met them all. One, a tall man, looked vaguely familiar and as he had come after the dinner, I knew not his name. I do not normally introduce myself to those I do not know but I did so in this case.

I was astounded to find that his name was Phileas Vickery, a naturalist, who had been in the Ottoman Empire looking at their birdlife, who was now on his way to Bushire and home, to write his book on Asia Minor avians; and that he had been in Asia Minor for seven years.

I introduced him immediately to my Vickery, who had attended, but had spent his time on the dance floor, and had not met guests, and it was a sight to see. No he was not his father, but the man was the first cousin of the man who was. They had a resemblance in height, receding hairline and as Vickery described it 'piercing good looks' or as Perkins observed a sublime beauty that only a sperm whale, one that was out of print *{dead?}* at that, would appreciate.

He did know of Vickery's father, for the family had received a letter announcing his marriage to 'A Sandwich Island *{The English name for Hawaii at that time}* princess and the birth of a son'. This was an extraordinary stroke of luck, a coincidence of the first order. To balance this good fortune, he was unlucky, for the man knew nothing of his father's journey after that, only that he had not been heard of for many years, and was feared deceased. He did welcome Eduard *{Vickery}* to the family and with the party breaking up; they departed to discuss family matters. Vickery and he decided to have a portrait[16] made of himself by Riccio, but he was busy and instead suggested a Dutchman in residence at Teheran, who had made a private fortune by painting the catamites of the local Persian notaries.

This joyous party was brought to a crashing end by the arrival of the Armenian Bishop, who came in thumping the floor with his Saint Peter's staff, and announced that it was midnight and therefore now Sunday, and it being a Sabbath day, it was improper to continue. He had no influence on the Englishmen and the other Europeans, and was soundly boo'd and hissed at, but the few Armenian men were under his authority and with them, their wives, who were the chaperones of the other ladies, departed and the dancing ended and the party died. the dancing ended. Moreover, the light had been dim, so I had, for once, felt free to dance and as the evening ran on, my boots, as it was 85° or more in the room, became so saturated with perspiration that later I could not get them off without the greatest struggle of my life. I thought for sure my heart would burst during the fight, but to my immense relief, I removed them, with a long sloppy slurping sound that sounded more disgusting than I can write and the smell would have struck a maggot insensible.

We continued to have difficulties with Middlecomb, whose interference and insolence became unbearable once again. We were set to speak again with McNeil, when Dissanayake joined us and listened for a while to our gnome's endless demands for paperwork, signatures and seals. Dissanayake interrupted and asked our 'man' for a copy of his franked and attested oath of commission. Truscan attempted to change the subject, but was brought up shortly, and Dissanayake began to ask dagger-like questions and in a few moments, our former tyrant was squirming like a worm. In less than three minutes Dissanayake had completely crushed him and our last words from him were that, 'all will be done as you wish'. We asked Dissanayake how he had done this. He replied that it was simple, the man was not a Crown employee but held a sinecure by the sufferance of McNeil, and he lacked the papers he had requested, for he held his position by favour and not by official appointment in accordance with the Parliamentary directives that would have governed his appointment as a support to an embassy. He was nothing but an unofficial toady loaded up with self-appointed powers.

We pronounced Dissanayake to be our sovereign prince for the day.

[Editor's note: Driscol wrote out two pieces of Danish with translation in English but there is no explanation as to why he did so]

Hvor skal De hen? Whither are you going?

Meget vel, til Tjéneste. Very well, at your service.

The Royal Audience Hall At Which The Expedition Was Presented To The Shah. Illustration III-XII-42

The Expedition Presented To The Persian Shah

Sunday 4 June

We are on this day to pay our respects to the King of Persia. The procession, proceeded through miserable streets, having started at the legation which were crowded by the curious, until we came to the large maiden, at the entrance of which were chained a lion and a bear, to which, I am sure, that when out of sight of Europeans a screaming Sunni Arab is fed to teach day.

There were troops on both sides, and cannon in several parts, and when we reached the first court, two very thick queues of soldiers were ranged to form an avenue for us. They were disciplined and dressed something in the manner of western troops, but with a black sheepskin hat. They went through their martial exercises as we travelled between them, with some passing resemblance to order and efficiency. Hynes and Horne were both snorting with derision however, fortunately with some discretion. Horne had been threatened with instant dismissal from the expedition if he did or said anything unseemly; Dobbins strode by him with secret orders to punch him if he slipped from his word.

When we had arrived before the Imperial gate, we stopped and dismounted, and the British ambassador and Perkins advanced took out the King's letter announcing his wish that his brother *{the Shah}* allow us to travel in his lands and beyond them into Tartary. We proceeded through darken passages, until we met *Ish Agassi {Master of the Ceremonies}* and the Lord Chamberlain. Our presentation was to take place in the *Khalvet Khonélz {Hall of Audience}*. We were told by the Chamberlain that the high King of Persia paid his respect to his Britannic Majesty; the *Ish Agassi* also informed us that the King was ready, and we proceeded along the hallways again. We entered the great court, the *Dewan Khoneh*, in which stood the men and officers of his personal guard. In the middle of all this was a small marble throne and from there, we came to another small, and mean, and poor looking door. I thought for a time that if everything kept shrinking, we would soon be crawling. This Lilliputian doorway led us to another dark and intricately carved hallway, and on to the *khalvet khonelz*.

Here our Persian guide arranged us in proper order and a proclamation was made to us and the crowds of Persians about. It was a bunch of meaningless phrases, which I do not recall, but I did remember his making mention of the Hijiri date Yekshanbe 30 Safar 1253 A.H, our date and then the Persian date of Yekshandeh 14 Khordad 1216. I find it odd that the Persians use both the holy Arabic calendar, which is lunar based and therefore woefully inaccurate, and their own solar calendar the Jalaali or Maliye. I have been keeping track of the Hijri date since arrival off Djedda some months before.

The order of the procession was as follows:

General officers of the King of Persia with swords drawn, native officers of cavalry, infantry, camel artillery, and artillery all with swords, Persian officials of the Shah's household, in scarlet and gold, dismounted, the Persian colours displayed on a large silk banner carried by a gigantic Negro slave. Then it was our turn, following with one of the Ambassador's servants holding up our flag. The ambassador led the delegation, followed by Perkins with the King's letter. We then followed by order of rank with Dissanayake bringing up the rear, as he has the lowest rank within the King's forces. I stood behind Dobbins and Horne. A flunky came to say we could advance and a damaged, silver-covered door was opened and we marched in military style into the court. This was graced with splendid fountains and trickling false streams in which stood the nobility of Persia, richly and barbarically outfitted or at least those nobility with nothing better to do. Then a trumpeter inside the building gave a good rendition of God Save the King.

The point of all this was at the far side of the room, there sat his grace the Shah. We marched up and were signaled to stop and bow, which we did with little precision or grace. Our guide then announced in much too loud a voice;

> 'Your most mighty Monarch of Persia, Director of the world, the light of Islam and the embodiment of fear to the Russian, Afghan, Arab and Turk I present the ambassador McNeil from your Majesty's brother, the King of England, who has come to beseech you to grant this group of men the right to travel in your house for the greater glory of Britain and Persia. May the dust at your feet rejoice in being walked upon by your utter greatness'.

We then awkwardly removed our slippers for we were all forewarned of this step and none wore boots.

Once properly unshod, the Ambassador came forward with the letter and placed it at the feet of the Shah, the Vizier, or Prime Minister, a sinister looking fellow known then as Hajj Mirza Aghasi, with a split two forked beard. Took up the letter, broke the seal, glanced at it, as it was in English, and handed it to a young Persian next to him, who was the translator.

After a moment's hesitation, he began to translate, 'Letter from the King to his Majesty the Shah'

[Editor's note: a copy of the letter was found in the Royal archives of England, see Appendix III-III]

The Shah nodded to all of this that was read to him in Persian. He then asked of the health of our King, for he had heard from the Russians that he was dead and that a small girl had taken up the reigns of dominion.

McNeill informed him that no, the same King reigned, who had dealt with his predecessor. Our ambassador was motioned to a chair that had been brought out for him.

The Shah mentioned again that the Russians had spread the rumour that the King was dead and his place taken by a girl, which to a Persian would be ridiculous, as women had no minds or thoughts worth noting, and they certainly could not lead a nation. Does not the Qur'an say so?

[Editor's note: Driscol at some point wrote in the margin in a later hand with a different pen the following hadith or saying of Muhammad]

> It was narrated that Abu Bakrah said: When the Messenger of Allah (peace and blessings of Allah be upon him) heard that the people of Persia had appointed the daughter of Chosroes as their queen, and he said, No people will ever prosper who appoint a woman in charge of them. Written by al-Bukhaari

McNeil said that the Russians often told untruths as it was their nature, as the cold of their lands unbalanced their minds. The ambassador and he chatted for some time about the evils of the Russians, then the Ambassador stood and presented each of us to the Shah; Perkins as leader and commander of the expedition, deputy commander Lieutenant Dobbins, Horne as the adjutant, myself as head of science and survey, Hynes as quartermaster, Vickery as secretary, Michaelson as surgeon, Dissanayake and Bannington as naturalists.

When our names were called, we stepped forward, if military we saluted and bowed, and the others just bowed.

The Shah himself wore a short trimmed beard, unlike many of his people and courtiers, who sported 'rat nests' as Horne called them. His dress was also more like that of a European. To greet us, he wore robes of black, with some silver adornments. He has a reputation as an honest man, keeps but three wives, and directs that simplicity rule in his court. He did seem somewhat timid and unwell, and travels by carriage instead of horse. To me, sitting on that throne was a man who was an actor who was bored with the part, but his audience would not let him go out of character.

As I was also bored with the endless prattle that the Ambassador and the Shah got into about Russian evilness, Turkish cowardice, Arab piracy, and the outlandish hereticism of the Imaum of Muscat and other trivialities *{Omani's follow Ibadhism, a denomination or sect of Islam}*, I studied his throne, the famous *Takht-i Khurshad*, but I could see this was not the famed throne of legend *{The Peacock Throne}* but a lesser replica. It resembled the original, but is called by the Persians the Sun Throne. However it shines with gold plate, enamel panels and is encrusted with emeralds, rubies and diamonds.

It was the opinion of McNeill, Todd and others, that the higher ranks of the Persians are hampered by an energetic desire to plunder anyone and everyone, and are also apt to speak ill of each other, which is their principal source of recreation, with the results that a constant stream of men are being executed for speaking against the Shah, others of importance, and those religious authorities, who should not be challenged. Persians delight in turning one in for speaking against what I wrote about above. Of course slander and deception are also high on the list of good characteristics for a successful Persian courtier.

A banquet was held outside, under a large Asiatic style pavilion, where the Shah presented a *Kalaat*, a dress or robes of honour, to Perkins, and we were all given lesser clothes that must be semi-honourable or so says Horne. I asked how he defined 'semi-honourable'?

Horne said an honourable man challenges his enemy to a duel and shoots him under the rules of the Code Duello, a semi-honourable man challenges his enemy to a duel and shoots at him under the rules, but he also has a friend with a rifled musket some distance off, just in case he is needed.

But, I countered, if the challenged man, who has the right to pick the weapon to be used in a duel, chooses sword, what happens then? Horne was unfazed and replied, an honourable man uses a sword of the same length as his opponent, and if he disarms him by skill or by chance, he steps back until the enemy is ready to engage again; while the semi-honourable man does all that, but instead of stepping back, steps forward, places his foot on the dropped blade, smiles AND has a friend with a rifled musket some distance off, just in case he is needed.

Monday 5 June

A large garden luncheon is being given by the Mission and set in the Persian gardens. Most of the noble Persians and lesser Europeans in Teheran were invited to include Comte *{Count}* Simanovich and the staff of the Russian mission. The Count was a short, stout man, coarse looking, and he had an assistant who looked like him, but limped, due to his meeting with an unruly Persian musket ball at the siege of Ganja in 1803, when he led the Russian Grenadiers at the storming of that city and put its defenders and helpless residents to the sword. I knew this, as he had also been shot in the head, and part of his skull had been carried away, and it had been replaced by a silver plate with this information inscribed on it in Russian and French. It was the first time I had read a man's head before.

I never had an opportunity to use what little Russian I had to speak to him or his staff. He seemed a frightful man and I thought it best to avoid such a person - besides reading his assistant's head.

One story I heard was told me by Major Todd, who in his early days of working with the Persian army had operated against the Turks. He had heard this one from an Italian mercenary in their employ, who had been an artificer of muskets and cannon in the Neapolitan army, a Mr Gagliardi, who held an *Arghadh {Castellan or commandant of a fortress}* commission in the Persian army. During the Ottoman-Persian war in 1822, he had been leading a column, when they came to a large stone which had borne the following inscription in both Turkish and Persian;

> *Whichever of the two powers, Ottoman or Persia, shall seek to extend its borders at the expense of her neighbour, and first passes this stone, shall be damned forever to never enter paradise.*

The Shah's general, a man who was the father of the present Shah, paused sometime before this stumbling stone, but soon recovering from his surprise, having forgotten that these stones had been placed in the previous century, and he ordered that it should be placed in a large waggon, and carried before the army, until he had reached the limit of his planned conquests, where he had the stone set up again.

During the actual luncheon, I made a social misstep. I had been eating lustily, when I noticed that the entire table had gone quiet and was staring at me, which caused me some confusion until I noticed that in my boredom with the conversations around me, I had put my elbow on the table. I had to issue an apology, removing the offending joint and I kept my eyes firmly fixed on my plate for some time afterwards; being thought of by all at that table as some sort of ill-mannered lout.

After the luncheon, I wandered off into the gardens, and this was well worth the diversion; in it were rose trees some fifteen feet in height, fully covered in fragrant flowers. Persians love roses, while disliking other flowers. Not only was my sense of smell enchanted with this place, but so too my ears, for within it were numerous nightingales whose calls seemed to mingle and flow with the scent of the roses. I can see why so much poetry deals with roses and the varied calls of these birds. I resisted a temptation to lie in the short grass here under a rose tree and to listen to the birds. I nearly did so but was interrupted by some blundering Russian under-secretary.

The party continued for some time, but without any number of free ladies, it was not much of an affair and I left as soon as I could disappear without being noticed.

Later that afternoon, being in a jovial mood, we played a game of war by sections. In the game of sections, one takes command of three others, while another takes a similar group and you start at the ends of a flat space cleared for easy movement by military drill. The object of the game is to march your men, at a steady one hundred and forty steps per minutes with military drill commands, only to intercept the 'enemy's' section on his flank or rear.

The great challenge is to do this using only the proper commands, usually in haste you give the command on the wrong foot or otherwise make an error. Hynes is a master of this, but Dobbins and Horne can give him a good fight. I am terrible at it, as is Perkins. Vickery and Dissanayake do not know the commands, but learnt them in several hours and Dissanayake became a formidable player. Bannington is mediocre as he cannot get the timing right. Michaelson is incapable of marching. He keeps leading off with the wrong foot. I ended up being marched around a lot that day.

Flank march is a great escape as is 'To the rear'. The only way to win was for the enemy to make a mistake in his commands or his section to get out of step. One could win conventionally, but you had to cleverly trap the enemy against the side of the parade field and bring the head of your section to intersect his flank or rear; a very difficult task.

In the game, a variant is blind sections. In this your men must close their eyes. This prevents them from aiding the order giver. Some watching Persians will certainly add their observations on our actions as proof that Englishmen, along with all foreigners, are completely insane.

We do receive by messenger, who must be well rewarded for delivering it, a Royal Firman {passport} from the Shah, dripping in seals and ribbons, that is addressed to all the chiefs, khans, emirs, functionaries, do nothings and bureaucrats of the Shah's provinces, districts, villages, towns, etc. demanding they provide us with horses when requested, food when demanded and lodging at no cost.

Persian lawn entertainment such as Driscol attended. Illustration III-XII-43

Chapter XIII

Teheran to Asterabad

Departure From Teheran For Asterabad By Way Of The Coast Of The Caspian Sea And The Land Of Mazandaran - The Mountains Of Peril - The Forests Of Mazandaran - The Caspian Sea - A Bedeviled And Thieved-Plagued Prince - The Dragoman With Eccles Cakes - God Smites The Land Of The Unbelievers - We Come To Asterabad And The Steppes Of Independent Tartary - The Day Of The Shoeless Horne And A Malaise - Preparations And News Of War - Dobbins' Chatelaine And A Persian Opium Factory - A Visitor Comes For Lunch But Leaves Before Pudding - Dining With Abu Saman And Friends - A Ragged Band Of Circassians

========

Departure From Teheran For Asterabad By Way Of The Coast Of The Caspian Sea And The Land Of Mazandaran

Tuesday 6 June

Our expedition departs from Teheran. We have hired for our trip to the Caspian Sea and thence on to Asterabad, eighteen mules, four horses and six men to carry the necessary equipment. They are led by a one armed man named Muhurem, whose appearance is marred by a cleft-palate, who defies tradition and does not wear a moustache with his beard, perhaps to highlight his distortion and who has unsightly clumps of excrescent white hair growing from his head and neck. We are joined by an official escort of four rather unlikely looking Persian stalwarts. The start-up of the mule train was one of unbelievable pandemonium; braying beasts, upended mules, spilled loads which burst open scattering cooking pots, bags of flour and salt onto the road in a discordant symphony of human, mechanical and animal noises. Hynes is at these disorders in a moment, and he neither shouts nor strikes but directs and comments using the sharp idioms of Persian perfectly. All is soon brought to order by his calm hand. Asian mule drivers have five things in common; they are usually incompetent with mules, they do not know where they are going, they are always petty thieves, they are filthy, which leads to their smell, which need not be mentioned. Our present crew fits this common description perfectly.

One of the muleteers with our lead horse. Illustration III-XIII-1

The first was proved by the poor state of the train when we tried to move; the second by their lining up to head towards Shiraz, their third taking the spilled foods and placing them in their own luggage (which we recovered later) and the last were no secret to anyone within five and sixty feet.

Driscol's Persian escort, Zaan, Basim, Vahraz and Betty. Illustration III-XIII-2

Our escorts were introduced to us as Zaan, Basim, Vahraz and Betty; or at least the last name seemed to sound like Betty from the way the man pronounced it. They would accompany us until some undefined point was reached.

We were but two miles out, when Major Todd galloped up and presented us with the greatest of all gifts, post to include newspapers from Bombay and London!

The Middlecombe expedition immediately and informally disbanded our Persian mule drivers were left to camp by themselves. As the rest of us, we all had received post, even Vickery, although his alone was official correspondence. We all sat by the side of the road reading these precious deliveries. We found by shouting comments to one another that our post had arrived in four and sixty days from India, two hundred and forty one days from England - on average.

I had letters! One and thirty private pieces for me, sixteen from Millicent, four from Marguerite, two from Karen, single ones from my brothers Mark, John, Stephen and my Frenchmen firearm manufacturer and PRAISE JESUS AND HIS CHURCH! with an extra cylinder for my pistol and a charge sheet for fourteen francs and a letter thanking me for my comments and five letters from my parents, in which I found comments from all my sisters and other brothers.

Truly I love that French cylinder. Perkins shouted back to me that NO the expedition would not pay for my new cylinder.

There was a piece of official post to Ambassador McNeill which he had forwarded to me, a letter from the Bombay Presidency commending me for my actions off Djedda and recommending to the Governor-General that I be promoted. That is excellent news. I went to show the others but they brushed me away as they were intent on their own post. The indifferent barbarians!

One part of that letter said:

> *His perilous actions seem on first glance to be those of a reckless swain....but these actions, while spiced with risk, flavoured with official orders were effortlessly washed down with the nectar of cleverness and a good eye for the target'.*

I found a twelve page letter from Millicent and another of one and twenty pages the others were just a page or two.

[Editor's note: With great frustration I can assure the reader that Driscol made no detailed mention of what was in these letters, nor did they survive, and he also did not note what he wrote back. However, later in his journals, he did make four references to what was written in these letters that may reflect on either his concern for his bibi, Millicent or Marguerite and these are noted below (and not repeated later in this or volume IV)]

...I must resolve to gain a command of a battery as soon as I can for even only with a Lieutenancy I will have the resources to marry and have outlined that clearly to her...

...if she does not wait what shall I do? It will be a bitter pill. *{I'm unsure if he was referring to Millicent, Marguerite or Bibi in that comment}*

...what shall I do if I find a baseborn *{bastard}* when I return? *{this would apply only to his bibi at this time as far as we know}*

...come live with me and be my love, and we will all the pleasures prove, *{by}* Christopher Marlowe[1]. I shall write such to Millicent.

Driscol makes no mention of the contents of any of the other letters, other than those noted above, except the following items.

Letter from the Swiss missionaries I had met on the Canal boat in Egypt and whom had been left on the coast of Abyssinia saying they were soon to have a child whom they have decided to name Nile, whether boy or girl and the boat cat they had adopted had had a litter too and now sported the grandiose name of '*Tres Beau Chat*'.

Dobbins was beside himself, as he had over fifty letters from Penelope and he sat and read each one out loud, so sentimental were they that I had to shift my position so I could not hear all that romantic nonsense, for I had my own to savour.

I did note the contents of a letter to Dissanayake from his brother; a man of, 'a peculiar colour of mind' *{addled or insane}*.

Dearest brother! I have finally done it. I pray you take steps to make known, but at the same time you must preserve my secret that yesterday, glorious yesterday, I completed my invention, as I have long written to you about my plans. A new age for the world has come on my invention's completion; the long sought in vain 'Perpetual Motion' as some scathingly call it. I am fully supported at this time by the King and the words I find in the Bible. These are my convictions. Although my machine at this moment only exists in my mind it is complete there. I have built it there, I tell you, so that none can steal it from me, as there are spies and witches everywhere, everyone strives to take it from me. I have certainly fixed the principles in nature and once built in a safe place where none can find me....

There were also a number of letters to Perkins about the expedition or personnel.

A note from Mr Middlecomb, our beloved legation clerk, saying we needed to precede immediately to his desk to draw up, draft, edit, write and have signed, witnessed and stamped our collective wills before we departed on our expensive lark spending the monies of the King. Less we go intestate *{dying without a will}*. We started our fire for tea with that one.

Three were from various minor officials in the HEIC having no authority to do so but demanding that Hymison be taken on the expedition or placed in its command and referring to various circulars, rulings and higher officials that we were in danger of falling afoul of, if we did not obey.

Two were from other officials, informing us that any orders regarding Hymison were to be ignored as being private pleas, and having no authority or basis within the HEIC.

Two were from the Bombay Presidency, one for a meeting dated two days after we had left to discuss our plans, and another from a head clerk asking why we needed naval transportation to go to Afghanistaun. The man writing that was geographically challenged as he also said that we could not go to Central Asia because, I quote, 'we were not properly invited'.

One letter was from HEIC revoking his *{Perkins'}* leave of absence as he was now assigned to an expedition, and must go to Central Asia, as he had been ordered to do so. He was glad to accept such sage advice.

Another was very welcome; it was an official notification from London and the Corps of Royal Sappers and Miners *{CRSM}* and the Board of Ordnance, authorising Perkins to grant to 'Englishmen and those acceptable foreigners' who will be brought into the expedition, the same status as men of the CRSM and not previously commissioned or enlisted in our corps.

Perkins read this letter out to everyone and we performed the acts to bring Vickery and Dissanayake into the Corps of Royal sappers and they learned the two mottos; *Ubique {Everywhere}* and *Quo Fas et Gloria Ducunt {Where Duty and Glory lead}*. Dissanayake was given the rank of Private soldier and Vickery, due to his prior experience in Persia, was made a non-commissioned officer with the rank of Corporal. Dissanayake was inordinately proud to be a private soldier! Hynes thought Vickery should start as drummer boy, to which Vickery replied with a very disreputable comment involving a door knob, a keyhole and a sponge. Hynes reminded him that he, Corporal Vickery was now a subordinate non-commissioned officer and he would not suffer such allusions again. Vickery told him to go kiss the caravan leader.

[Editor's note: This is a bit of pre-Victorian skullduggery and considered at the time an acceptable practice, as Vickery and Dissanayake were already being paid as the secretary of the expedition and the other retained his resident's pay from the HEIC. Their additional payments from London and the Corps of Royal Sappers and Miners would not be noted or commented on by the HEIC. It also brought the two men under the provisions of military discipline and would also provide a pension if they were disabled, or a death gratuity, should they be killed in the service of the expedition; in the case of Dissanayake, it would go to his parents but I'm not sure who would have obtained it for Vickery, probably his mother on Kauai]

There was one letter to Perkins from his mother, wishing to know who were all these women writing to him at their home, and demanding to know where he was, and that his behaviour was shocking to her and his father, and that he should explain himself forthwith, and that he should visit them once he was finished with his infatuations with India when he had finally decided to enter the church. He showed me that and I had to undoubtedly ask, why those women WERE writing him. He thought for some time and he said finally that he was weak with women and would sometimes mention that he was interested in marriage; unfortunately he tended to ask nearly everyone he knew. This was something I had heard from other sources, but it was a nice confirmation. I suggested he should never go home, to which he looked at me and nodded. 'Another expedition to Arabia after we finish this small one', he asked? We agreed.

He later came to me and added that his relationship with women was one of flirtation and not seduction, for some reason I find this believable.

Eleven additional letters concerning other matters more in the line of Vickery to look at these were correspondence about various expenses involved in setting up the expedition from Bombay but addressed to me - I sent them to the new Corporal to deal with.

There were also letters from Hymison to Vickery. This was quite amusing as he offered Vickery substantial compensation if he would relinquish his secretarial position to him. He then made vague threats against him if he failed to do so; of such a nature that no sane gentleman would put on paper. The content of Hymison's letter fluctuated from a tone of un-failingly politeness and correctness, to taunting curses and unmanly threats. His best one, and one that Vickery enjoyed from his sailing days, was that Hymison referred to him as the son of a Portsmouth fire ship[2] how droll! Vickery saved that letter for future reference.

It took some hours to read and write replies out, but some of us did not finish, but the good Major Todd agreed to accompany us for a day or so to allow us to return responses with him, for which, needless to say, he was most heartily thanked and toasted as a true gentleman for this kindness. It was noted however, that he questioned each of us whether if we had marriageable sisters or cousins who might be available when he returned to England next year! I thought him a good man despite his squint, atrocious skin, blacken teeth and most damning, no private fortune, and therefore not suitable for Zoe or Lauren *{Driscol's sisters}*.

I spent some time reading and writing, while watching one of the mules eat his guide rope. It consumed some five feet before its meal source was noticed by the muleteers. Its action reminded me of the fate of Ocnus the Greek, who was condemned to spend his immortal life in Hell, endless weaving a rope of straw, which a mule eats as fast as it is made. Ocnus to me reflected the fears, frustrations and delay caused to the expedition setting out by Hymison's actions and impertinence. Nonetheless the rope had now been pulled from his mouth and his plans deflected.

I read in one newspaper, with some delight about the Royal Vauxhall balloon, which had been taken aloft on the day after my birthday *{21ˢᵗ September}* and landed in Nassau. I found the details on the craft and its journey a great wonder.

[Editor's note: Driscol misremembered this as there had been an ascent on the 21ˢᵗ but the longer journey to Nassau (in Germany) did not take place until the 7ᵗʰ of November]

Wednesday 7 June

No entry

Thursday 8 June

We awake and I hand my post to Major Todd who has been the perfect gentleman in waiting for me to finish my two and fifty page epic to Millicent. Vickery and Perkins finish the official correspondence, and Todd is sent away with a large load of post. Before he leaves us, he asks us all to consider service with the Shah's army, once we return from our meander into Central Tatary and looking at Dissanayake and Vickery, 'or other service' as the Shah had said he would reward us with appropriate positions upon our return. We thank him, we all shake hands, and our goodbyes are sincere and long and then he is gone, but as he leaves he gives to us in French some final advice.

> *The Persian can be scrupulously trusted to be untrustworthy, unless it serves his*
> *own interest or his family, and any consideration about whether the might be loyal*
> *to Persia or the Shah or to us was not worthy of a moment's deliberation*

That was certainly a bitter morsel of words to consider. However, I spent several hours thinking about gaining a brevet rank of Captain or Major while serving in Persia.

The path we will take will be along a narrow river valley up into the Elburz Mountains, which we can see are dry blighted slopes showing little vegetation and no trees. The colour of the rocks is reddish, with large chunks of greyish stone interspersed. We move between nearly perpendicular heights up and down broken and jagged ravines, cut by rushing streams. The path itself is of broken rock, gravel intermixed with bones of those poor creatures, four and two legged, that have perished on this pathway before us.

One incident on the road was of interest. Our lead mule, who has an unprintable Persian name, was making its way up a steep gradient and had nearly reached the top, when it lost its footing and toppled back down the slope, missing every other mule, horse and man and most remarkably of all, despite spreading it load across the mountain side itself, was unhurt, and as soon as it had stopped its downward passage it regained its feet and started back up the slope, and had to be restrained from its heroic action and repacked. From then on, we called that mule 'determined' instead of it gross Persian name.

[Editor's note: Driscol at some point wrote the name in Persian ☐☐ 'chos' which means a particularly obnoxious fart]

Another sombre incident occurred as we passed a small village, where a thief was being dealt with. They did so by *yaching* him, this is done by lashing him to a stout pole and building around him a cocoon of mud brick and once up to his neck they pour in liquid lime. If he retains his

sanity and life for some six or more hours as measured by the estimate of the executioners he is then dispatched by being shot.

Bastinado directed at a Persian man who assisted a thief. Illustration III-XIII-3

Mount Damavand.
Illustration III-XIII-4

At the other end of a village, one of his co-conspirators was being dealt a less lethal punishment of being beaten on the soles of the feet.

In the night, we hear the scream of a *Panthera Pardus {leopard}*, much to the discomfort of the horses; the mules do not mind the sound at all. Dobbins patrolled the edge of the camp with his hand cannon, but the leopard came no nearer.

Friday 9 June

At dawn we find that heavy dew has completely saturated ourselves, our tent and bedding, and we awaken amongst the billowing clouds. We find from our mule leader that the natives are very careful to avoid exposing themselves to this wet as they believe it harbours disease, madness, and the power to instill unnatural lusts in a pious man.

Certainly I never thought of dew as so dangerous. Dissanayake remarks that good English dew would never be so improper.

Quite!

Dissanayake also expresses his desire after the expedition to travel to Mount Ararat to seek Noah's Ark. I knew of one expedition with a similar goal by James Morier in 1809 and an earlier one sanctioned by Peter the Great of Russia more than a century before that. I knew that the Russians claimed, and they have a tendency to claim to have done something first whenever they can, to have been the first to the top of the mountain in October of 1829, by a certain Professor Parrot.

Dissanayake seemed well up on the history of such expeditions, and we found that five more had occurred; all without success; one by the Englishman Rawlinson, two by the Russians, for the Holy Mountain now lay under their dominion.

We continued our travel up the Haraz-rud, or Lar River valley. Above us towers the immensity of the Damavand volcano, which stands nearly eighteen thousand feet, capped still in snow during the summer heat. We sight, on the steep ridges above us *Capra Aegagrus {wild goats}* and *Ovis Orientalis {red sheep}* with their reddish coats and fine brace of horns.

The pathway gradually became narrower, dearer, then steeper; so much so, that we had to dismount out of regard for our own safety and out of concern for our tired horses and laden mules. We took to clambering on foot up the mass of rock and mingled weeds, which in spring forms a torrent's bed. Sometimes, our confidence in the presumed pathway was sorely tested; for it had become very dubious whether it was a path or not, as these hard rocks did not well preserve the passage of tens of thousands for thousands of years.

Once on top of one of these walls we had climbed, the side of which we had expended so much effort to scale, we now found ourselves, looking over a scarped rock of seven hundred feet in height, on the other side of which was a dark gulf, which none of us could see down into. The glooms of night had begun to fall round us, and our native muleteers, with certain nonchalance, took us to a narrow ledge, where the marks of fires showed that many had sheltered there in the past. One mule was found by us to be carrying firewood and soon it was ablaze. I shudder now as I write this for the recollection of the sight of an endless pool of darkness and depth into which I had looked had awakened my anxiety over height more so than any other time yet in my life. That evening, I wedged myself well in-between two rocks, to prevent me from rolling off the ledge on which we slept. I did rise however several times in the dark to ensure that Blonde was well secured.

The mountain passes north of Teheran where the expedition
passed through on its way to Asterabad.
Illustration III-XIII-5

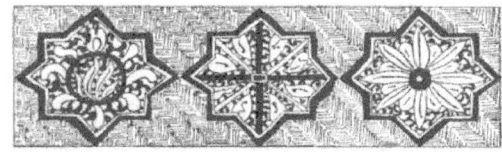

[Editor's note: Two additional images that I believe are associated with the expedition and their passage of the mountain passes north of Teheran. To the right, the image is captioned, "a journey through the high pass called the 'impassioned daughter' showing the Persian muleteers passing the half way stone between Teheran and the (Caspian) Sea". The image is from Richard Hobson's rare book, "The deeds of gallant gentleman," page 142]

Illustrations III-XIII-6 & 7

[Editor's note: At the left is another orphaned image which I believe shows Dissanayake, who having been thrown from his horse, is nearly pitched into a 'bottomless ditch'. This is from a collection of newspaper and magazine pictures that a person interested in the expedition collected but unlike the majority, he did not state on the back what publication he obtained it from or the date. The only marking was, "'D' at it again," the other figure may be Horne or perhaps Bannington]

The Mountains Of Peril

Saturday 10 June

The morning was cold and dreary and the beginning of our day's work was a hard one, for we had to go down the other side of the rock we had climbed the day before. The road was more tormenting than the day before, both from its roughness and its constant glimpses of death-defying depths. It consisted of one mass of large rocks and stones without any intermixture of earth, and from the intermediate crests, we could see ahead of us a wild and jagged country as ever foul Lucifer's mind could ever have imagined; not a tree nor bush was to be seen, just short weeds between the rocks, which were nibbled at by the mules and horses.

The road continues on a steady incline, we trudge by a deep ravine in which the Dhalichar Stream rushes with great violence and sound. Our path is some 1,300 feet above the water in that stream, which seems a distant ribbon to us above. Here and there a spare juniper tree struggles to survive, as do I, as I must not look down. This is a challenge, as the way is blocked by loose rock and gravel, we must often gather together to urge a horse over a dangerous bit. I notice that Dissanayake may also share my fear of the heights, but he hides it well, but not well enough.

We were cheered by Blood-Thirsty's sea shanties and Horne's renditions of English pub songs, of which he had an endless repertoire, and Perkins added in the few bawdy Tamil songs he knew.

We were singing one of these when Vickery came to a stop ahead and raised his hand. I suppose he shouted, but his voice was lost then to the wind. The others and I hurried forward, and before us lay our first sign of civilization.

Ahead of us lay the mountainside village of Ab-e-Ask, that lies at the latitude of 36° 0' N, longitude 52° 8' E at an elevation of 5,900 feet. We determined the altitude using our Casella's Hypsometrical Apparatus, which we confirm with the boiling water test. We had secured this mountain barometer in Teheran, where it had been left by an earlier explorer. It will be returned once we come nearer the desert. The Haraz River runs below the town through a deep and narrow channel of rock, crossed by a well-made wooden bridge, an unusual thing to find in decrepit Persia and here especially, as there are no large trees. It is the capital of the mountain headman of the Larljan. It contains many reddish, brown houses that sit on shelves of rock, which rise up the steep sides of the mountain for several hundred feet. Here there are green trees, bushes and grass and it is a delight to the eye. There are more than two thousand inhabitants. It is an extraordinary place, situated as it is on one side of a great mountain. The village is surrounded by immense mountains, which shut it in all around excepting where the river Haraz has formed a rocky and narrow egress and ingress, pre-eminent amongst which is the great pyramid shaped Damavand. Near the town are sulfide fumaroles and deposits of tan travertine *{a form of limestone deposited by mineral springs}* produced by the geo-thermally heated, supersaturated, alkaline waters.

From a military point of view, only light infantry, trained for mountain use, could approach this place and only with great difficulty. Small cannon would discourage any attempt to advance up the valley. I would think that only *Gebirgsjäger {Austrian mountain infantry}* could be effective here; or irregular infantry of well-motivated mountain natives commanded by Scottish officers.

I had the same fear that night, that I had had before, that I would roll over in my sleep and down the slope. Bannington fearing his sleep-walking as always secured both his leg and one arm something he had been doing since we entered this vertical land.

Sunday 11 June

Perkins wakes up with a *Phalangium opilio {daddy long legs for Americans, harvestmen for the rest of the world}* sitting on his chest looking at him. In my mind I imagined it was considering whether it could eat him, for if it could would it not eat like a king?

I was not carrying a fishing pole, but created one from the sprouts around me; given the lack of suitable wood in this route, I decided to keep this one. I did so by cutting down a young springy poplar, which grew along the river's edge. I made the fishing pole by notching the top of the pole for a line, and to this I tied a sufficiency of my stout line with a sailor's knot, and to the line I attached a piece of split lead bird shot and a brass hook. The river here formed pools, and in these I decided, with the confidence of a veteran fisherman, that there lay a great number of fish. I threw in my baited line in a fever pf optimistic expectation nothing happened. It was not until our head mule man came and explained that the non-sportsmen rapscallion troglodytes, who live here, discovered that with a net you can catch more fish, and much faster, than with a pole, bait or fly.

So during the day, as we rode along, I would venture ahead of the column, fish for some ten to twenty minutes as the rest passed me by, and then catch up again. The stream foamed and thrashed about, and still provided the signs of good fishing places here and there, but it was not until we had come to rest for tiffin, that I providentially caught a fine two pound brown trout which struck after my hook hit the water, but I was not rewarded with any other riverine harvest that day, notwithstanding, I did have one roasted fish for my lunch which I shared with all a small tidbit. We headed down a steep slope towards the sea. We entered in the afternoon wild chasms and I cannot, for the life of me, imagine why the great-grandfathers of the Persians thought they could put a road there, but they had. We found surprises at turns in the twisting, climbing, plunging trail, when, all at once, we came to a point where we could clearly see the northeastern slope of the mountain, which we skirted. I learned then the Persian word for 'ice' and 'snow', two words that while on my voyage had not come up often of course. I found out from our head *charwardar* that in the snows of the mountain lived a rarely seen but deadly creature, ice worms, which he describe as nearly invisible, transparent, but only a few inches long and which cause the burning sensation when one's plunges his hand into ice by the action of their toxic touch.

We pass several ruined towers or fortifications; small and badly made, and I could not see why any fortification would be needed in terrain like this, as God's hand has made it impenetrable to all but heroically inclined Sappers - and such people did not exist in Persia or anywhere near it.

It was here that our heroic escort suddenly announced that we were at the said point where they would leave us. We bid them a tearless goodbye, as they were four fine eaters, but had contributed nothing else. They rode off and we saw them no more. Perkins unhesitatingly declined to offer them any gratuity but did compliment Betty on the cut of his blouse.

That evening we had our night's rest in a commodious cleft in the rock, while I spent a restless night worrying about it collapsing on top of me. I gave a sigh of relief when we awoke this morning, uncrushed and still alive.

Monday 12 June

More stony paths and we had some difficulty with the inhabitants of a small village. These mountaineers seemed to think we were Russians and as all good Persians hate Russians, they disputed our passage. It took some time to convince them that we were instead good, wholesome, beloved, and honest Englishmen and not the evil, scheming, men from the north. I thought it all an act and they charged us high prices for the poor provisions that they could spare.

At one point Dissanayake horse took off, for no particular reason, and ran away with him. Normally this is dangerous, but on a three-foot pathway, with a drop of a several hundred feet on one side, it was deadly. Incredibly he regain control, halted the animal, but while dismounting, he tangled his foot in the stirrup and fell heavily to the ground; gaining himself a cut to his head and a bloody nose. We congratulated him on mastering the horse, and bringing it to a halt, but took him to task for his dismounting skills.

While chewing incessantly on a ghastly, and grisly, piece of dried, and very dead, mutton, I read the London Times, dating from September of the previous year which had been dispatched to me by my brother Stephen and given to us by Major Todd. My good brother had sent it, as it carried in it the announcement of my going overseas on secondment to the Indian Army. Those two lines were my only mention and the rest of the paper was full of political nonsense and scandal. Perkins commented on some of the material about a certain wife of Lord F_____.

A lovely cat may have nine lives but the scandals she starts number in the hundreds

We played cards around the fire until Vickery lost a card, the ten of diamonds, in the fireplace. We decided to hate him for several hours, as that card, is as we were told by Bannington informed us, foretells good fortune in travel; so much for our good fortune indeed!

Dissanayake brought up an interesting subject this evening, while discussing military terms and their meaning, when he wondered why there was no other word for synonym. To this, Hynes asked why the word abbreviation is so long a word. None had any answer to these clever observations.

Tuesday 13 June

The track now followed the rounded stones of the riverbed, and nothing could be more painful or dangerous to both horse and rider. The river had to be constantly forded, and as it was ice cold, this was a sorrowful chore. Occasionally, the river could not be forded, and we had to make our way over difficult rocks, along terrifying and horribly narrow ledges.

At one point, Blonde became, I believe so frightened by the roar of the river in some narrow crevasse, that I was forced to both muffle her ears and blinker her. This eased her plight and I was able to lead her to safety. This occurred just after one of our mules, carrying a load of fodder for the other animals, plunged off the trail and was dashed to pieces on the rocks below; leaving a scarlet stain across the rocks. It took some hours to recover her luggage, which we had the animals eat, to save us repacking it. We all declined a meal of scrambled, bone broken, mule.

Later that day, we came to a small village and asked where we might water the horses. The people became agitated, and we found that we could not use their well, but must instead go on, a half a mile to a stream. This seemed unwelcoming and we presented our letters to the Imaum, the only man with any semblance of knowledge in the village, showing we were guests of the Shah. We supposed their reluctance to grant us permission to take water was because we were foreigners.

This was not the case. It seemed the well was presently poisoned. Who had done this we asked? It was an old woman who was a witch. How did they know it was poisoned? When they pushed her in, she had died, and the water is foul to drink, thus and thus proving she was a witch. This had been done by a few days earlier. We rode on in some haste.

Pass in the Alborz Mountains which the expedition went through in June 1837. Illustration III-XIII-8

The Forests Of Mazandaran

We came at last to a vista, from which we could see the summits of verdant mountains, and the heavy mass of vapours that hovered over what our charwardars said was the *Darya Khizer* or *Darya Mazandaran {Caspian Sea}*. Ahead, beyond the wooded mountains, lay a plain of glorious green, which was a treat to our eyes, which had grown tired of the oppression of endless grey rocks. It also brought flies, flies in the thousands, large ones and small ones, some greenish some brown and some black, which who bothered us to no end.

One of the annoyances of Persia.
Illustration III-XIII-9

[Editor's note: Driscol had collected this image from Volume I of James Bruce's work on trying to discover the source of the Nile and he labelled it 'Persian fly' while it is in fact an African Tsaltsalya a large, venomous, two-winged fly, native to Abyssinia. Driscol made this mistake early on in life]

We descended and found the going downhill to be extra hard on one's knees; whether mounted or dismounted. As we went down in height, the heat rose up until it became distressing to both man and mount. This was compounded by the humidity in the atmosphere and the lack of elasticity in the air, which constricts the lungs, and produces a sense of uncomfortable suffocation. Our perspiration n did not evaporate but adhered to us, leaving us feeling uncomfortably wet; with everything we touched feeling moist and clammy.

[Editor's note: the journals reflect this moisture with running ink, smudges, and several cases of fungus growth, later arrested by applications of alcohol and other remedies as noted by Driscol whenever he applied it]

Our Indian veterans said it felt like Bengal or Bombay at the height of the monsoon.

Wednesday 14 June

We came in our journey to the town of Amol *{Amrda}* latitude 36° 30' N, longitude 52° 23' E at an elevation of two hundred and fifty feet, *{Perkins and Driscol were once again off their game: the actual location is 36° 28' N 52° 21'' E}* We are in the province of Mazandaran and inhabited by a people called the Ghilani. The town was dispersed in the dense forest and orchards and was difficult to see as a whole or gain an overview of. The town had no need for the surrounding walls, gates, and other fortifications characteristic of more traditional cities of the Persians. The abundance of these dense forests led to the use of wood as a building material, a practice rare in Persia, but this has also led to repeated fires and the town burns down once or twice a generation. The city is also home to various epidemics due to the unhealthy climate. We entered this forested town and found poverty, decay and gloom. We passed a large and spacious mausoleum. It was said to have been built by Shah Abbas, to commemorate the remains of some past luminary. The town seemed unoccupied; a ruin spread across all its nine famous quarters, once known for their beauty, size and population, are now destroyed and depopulated. We rode through streets, which were overgrown with thick brush and weeds. Roofless walls, broken tiles and bricks marked former houses that often had small trees growing out of their inner rooms. What had been the cause of all of this? It was the three curses: disease, tyranny of inaction, and war. The raiders were not Turcoman, who we were traveling to visit, for they produce some of the best horses in Central Tartary. The destruction had been caused by other Persians; from rival factions to bandits, during their long series of civil wars. With centuries of experience, the Persian Shahs had a simple way of dealing with these types of raiders; they did nothing.

The dilapidation and dirtiness of the town was terrible, but it was less terrible than what the people seemed to have smeared on their faces. We rode for some time until we found the remains of the bazaar, in which now only three or four shops were still occupied by listless, unhappy, people. We procured the few supplies that could be had, and of these, excellent watermelons were most inexpensive and welcome. The merchants told us that the damage and dismay we see was caused by the plague of 1831, which killed over half the inhabitants, and drove a large number mad from grief so much so that some set fire to large areas of the town.

There is supposed to be a cannon foundry in the area, which used water to drive a powered drop hammer, but no one we find has heard of it. The place is governed by a man, who is said to be a Prince of the Kajar bloodline. *Per contra {Italian, contrary to, nevertheless}*, he rebuffed our attempts to see him and our letter from the Vizier, signed by the Shah was returned to us without comment; so much for the power and writ of the Shah.

We spent the night in a flat space, by a ruined building, well covered by grass. The animals were happy with the browsing and Blonde was once more a friendly horse, as she had been both tired and terrified in our journeys along the rocky and dizzying paths.

I suggest to all, that perhaps when we return, we NOT take that pathway again. This was agreeable to all but Dissanayake, who had rather enjoyed the scenery. I thought this a sign of bravado on his part, due to the fear of heights he seemed to have. Considering he had nearly plunged to his death several times, I found his position unexpected and inconceivable in the least.

That night we hear the roars of a *Panthera tigris virgate {Hyrcanian tiger}*. We have our first true argument that night. Dobbins' blood is up, for he wishes to detach himself for a few days to hunt a Turan tiger *{another name for the Hyrcanian}*. Perkins will not have it. The debate is intense. It is agreed then to push on to Meshed-e-Sar and find our guide. If any time can be allowed there, he may have a day or so to hunt. Perkins annoyed, Dobbins was unsatisfied and his behaviour was bordering on insolence.

Thursday 15 June

We are now in the province of Mazandaran proper. Ahead of us, or, so our sources have told us, lie forests, swamps and the shoreline. The place is insalubrious. We are cautioned by Michaelson. He informs us that said while the mountains were healthy; by contrast, where we are now is notorious for its ill health. He likewise said that when in Teheran, he had asked several of the other physicians about it, and had been told there was a Persian proverb that says;

> *Whenever one becomes tired of life he may go to Mazandaran to expire with ease*

With that chilling thought, we rode on, passing in the early morning fields of sugar cane and plantations of mulberry trees raised for the eclipse *{flock}* of silkworms that were imported from China long ago and thrive here and support the silk industry.

We pass at this time a village that the *charwardar* hurries us through after suggesting we keep our arms close by. He will not tell us the reason until we have passed it. It would seem it is a place, where a holy man was killed recently, murdered so the villagers can have a holy tomb to attract pilgrims to his resting place and shrine. The holy man so slain had been from Teheran and known to our mule leader, who considered him a *pyghamer {prophet}* of the foremost rank and quality; overlooking the prophet's performance of the occasional intermittent murder, a rare perchance for seeking the close company of goats, and the infrequent thievery of other people's stirrups *{stealing their horses}*.

We had a pleasant level ride through the forest, fording several shallow rivers which after their mad rush down the mountains had become calm if swift. Also magically the flies that had tormented us for a day or more disappeared and we approached the town of our search. Both Vickery and I thought we could detect the scent of the sea but were probably mistaken.

We rode easily across the flat country, keeping the mountains some twelve miles on our right. The land here supports vast fields of cotton, along with rice. It is this rice that much of Persia delights in; especially a dish called kata, which, we are told by our guide, is so good that when the Prophet *{Muhammad}* heard of it, he stated that when he was resurrected, it would be his first meal. The dish is made with rice, salt and butter, and once cooked, is made into a loaf of sorts called *kata-qalebi*, which is allowed to dry, and then is eaten plain or with various stews. All around us were tall forests, vastly different from the mountains we had come down. There was much traffic here and we were a sight to be looked at and avoided. Here everyone assumes foreigners are Russians and Russians are not well-liked.

Like Amol, the town we sought was built within the woods and was indistinct to one approaching it; and so, we came upon it with no more warning than a slow increase in the number of farms, until we came to our goal; Barfroush or Barforus *{Modern Babol and meaning a place where goods are sold}*, at the latitude of 36° 33' north and longitude 52° 51' East and an elevation of sea level. We continued; on our muleteer asking for the location of the governing Prince. We crossed many forested paths; many had ditches, or were broken up or blocked by a fallen tree or limb. We saw buildings here and there, but like Amol, the place had also been depopulated by plague and war. We came upon found a suitable caravanserai, meaning it was not a complete ruin. Next to it was a bath and we were bidden to wait, as our man sought out the location of the Prince. Perkins had a letter for him from his cousin the Shah. Near our place of rest was a tall tower, made of brick, in an octagonal manner, with a pyramid for a roof. It had well carved, wooden doors and was inscribed to say that it was the grave of a Soltan Taher, and that the *memar {architect}* was one notable Sams-al-Din and it had been built in the year 875 *{1471 AD}*. Around it were a few merchants who sold felt, soap and horse coverings made by the Turcoman, these were very divergent in colour and of excellent design and manufacture.

It was early afternoon before our unworthy one reappeared with a reluctant Persian official, who stated that the Prince was not in the town, but at Resht, and that he was his deputy. He was a kind and helpful man, once he saw our letters, and we were granted free access to the caravanserai, fodder and provisions by the manner of a *seeoorsat* declaration *{the natives would provide fodder and provisions on demand}*. He did not know the guide whom we sought, as he was a man from southwest Persia and only newly arrived here.

There was a discussion that night about bad poetry and poets and it was decided by a vote, with a majority deciding that one Richard Savage, Englishman, murderer, poet, querulous, vindictive, criminal-minded, shady, with a character of careless wantonness, satirical writer and general reprobate, had been the worst. Horne and Michaelson knew some of his poems while I had never heard of them or him. However a few lines from his work, 'A Poem: To the Memory of Mrs Oldfield', made me glad I did not.

Had but my Muse her Art to touch the Soul,
Charm ev'ry Sense, and ev'ry Pow'r control,
I'd paint her as she was-the Form divine,
Where ev'ry lovely Grace united shine

Map of northern Persia south of the Caspian Sea, on which the expedition's progress can be discerned. Illustration III-XIII-10

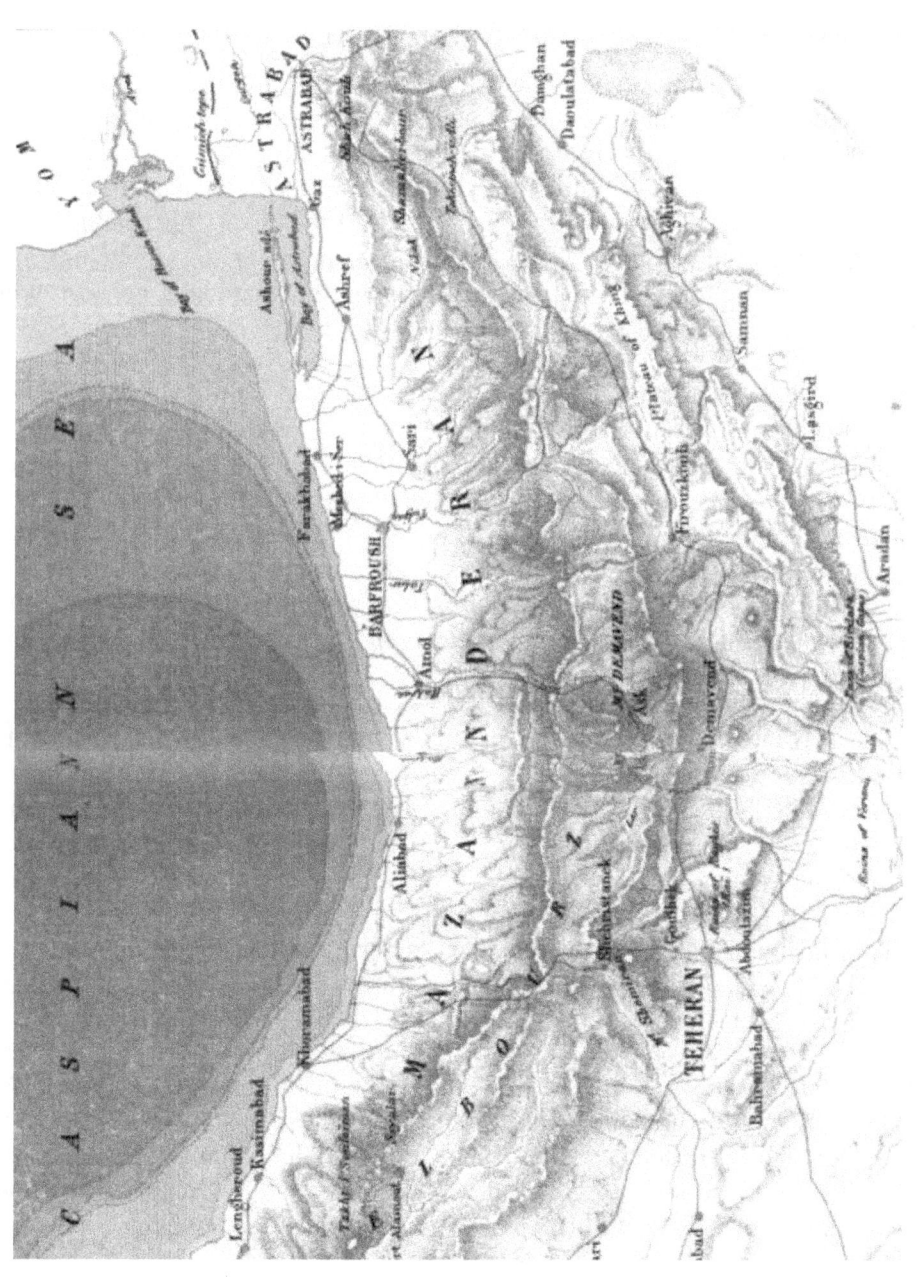

The Caspian Sea

Friday 16 June

I was pleasantly sleeping, when Hynes' voice, the man with whom it seemed that just an instant previously I had exchanged the position of camp guard, cut through the fog of my satisfying slumber with the chilling words,

THEY ARE COMING AND I CANNOT STOP THEM!

Immediately followed by the jarring discharge of his musket, a moment later, everything was confusion. It was just dawn, so I drew on my boots, for I was fully clothed otherwise, as shouts and questions flew about me, at any moment I expected muskets to flare, and I imagined a line of Turcoman raiders, swords out, and slaver irons dangling, charging down on us.

If it were not that horror, perhaps a battalion or two of Chilean-led irregular, land pirates, or a coven of maiden aunts with ugly marriage-minded cousins in tow. It could also be raving Persians, out to collect an eyeball or two, or the grey men of Somalia who had somehow found me and wished to pelt me with again with rocks once again, or who wished to bite my head just once more. My final two fearful thoughts, as I rose with Ascalon at the ready, were of the long-haired, blonde man bearing down on us backed by a regiment of decidedly unfriendly Cossacks with wielding sharp sabres, or the even worse thought of Hymison, coming with baskets of paperwork carried by sharp-minded clerks to confound us.

What I found instead, was our camp raised in a similar state of confusion as myself. Ahead of us, from the southwest pouring out of the edge of the woods, was a charging mass, there were hundreds of them, driven by the sharp cries of their leader. They came at a rapid pace and there was nothing we could do, but brace ourselves against the impact of their charge, as the light was insufficient to do anything else, or to take accurate aim. In any event, it is doubtful whether our fire would have any effect at all against such a surging, unstoppable tide. They burst in amongst us, scattering our sleeping arrangements, the sounds of their voices and calls caused our horses to react and in an instant we were all surrounded by the numberless hordes that had overrun us.

Damn sheep. A herder had moved his flock of several hundred head and they had run right on and over us. Hynes showed his displeasure in this, for he and Dobbins grabbed the insolent sheppard and threw him into a nearby bog and gave him a violent flow of Persian; for Hynes could curse very well in that idiom. We spent some time chasing and scattering the sheep away from us. Horne, Bannington and Perkins were beside themselves as the pot of water that had been set to boil for tea and been knocked down and the tea itself cast down and scattered onto the soil an insult to an Englishman that can never be forgiven. To knock over his morning tea, is no less an insult than to suggest his sainted grandmother sold her charms for half a pence at the local pub for the amusement of scurvy landsmen.

In spite of the disaster, I was pleased, at this time, to note that everyone was speaking French. We did to prevent any of the muleteers from understanding us, as a few had a smattering of English and we worried that a Russian agent might be amongst them. I had noted that the use of the formal term 'vous' in French, while addressing one another, had faded away and that everyone now addressed the other with the more familiar 'tu'. I stated this later to Perkins, who was elated by my observation. as the men being constantly together, nerves had occasionally begun to fray, on one another and a sign of friendship was encouraging. Dobbins' French was improving too and he could use it more now.

As we were all awake, and the tea was ruined, we decided against breakfast and rode out earlier than usual and made our way towards the port of Meshed-e-Sar. The Babil River was crossed by a bridge of masonry with eight arches and in excellent repair; certainly an unusual occurrence in decrepit Persia. It was so atypically remarkable, that Perkins had us stop and examine it. We observed that it was perfectly placed and both well made, and maintained. No one could explain this oddity. Just when you convince yourself that the Persian is completely inept and incompetent, he surprises you.

Ahead of us now stretched a ride, I would say, of some thirteen miles. As we rode, Michaelson was approached by mothers, who like many in Persia, think all foreigners are devils, magicians or physicians. Her son had signs of infantile imbecility. For this he could do nothing, however another woman, emboldened by the act of the first, came forth with her son, a Cyclops or so he first appeared. This Michaelson could do something about, as the poor child had a growth of skin across his left eye. We halted for a while, and he with a few deft strokes of his scalpel, and a touch of medicine here and there, and the eye was restored, with very little loss of blood, and remarkably no brawling by the child who was, at a guess, five or six. He had me caution the mother to keep the eye covered so that it was exposed each day for one hour longer until the eye had adjusted to the sunlight. We received large amounts of food in repayment and ate well of bread, sweet cakes and other delights[3]. Michaelson said it was the first time he had ever been so promptly paid for his services.

Our road lay through a continuous line of houses, half hidden among the forest; this was a mixed wood of elm, hornbeam, oak, sycamore and wistful willows. Almost everywhere one could see grapevines and various berry bushes, plus each house always had a fig tree for a Persian loves his figs. Each house has a well laid-out garden, rich in melons and other fruit. One had to wonder why a Persian would want to live anywhere but here, and especially not on the forbidding, dry, central plateau; of course the reason for this was disease and the proximity of cross border raiders.

A sounder of wild boar crossed our path, which necessitated a pursuit, but without dogs, we could not track them in these unknown woods. We lost nearly an hour trying to regain the road and did so only by hearing the braying of our mule train.

We rode down the East bank of the Bawul River and came in time to the straggling village of Mashad-i-Sar {modern Babolsar}, which means the martyred head, and this comes from the fate of Imaum Zadeh Ibrahim, a relative of the famed eighth Imaum[4], who was made a saint by the Arabs, and who having gained possession of the country {of Persia} struck his head off for being a heretic. The river finds the sea, here and this is Persia's only port on the Caspian Sea. It is a poor harbour at that, one that no ship of any true size can approach closer than two miles, due to the extensive shallows. All cargoes are transferred by flocks of small boats.

It was good to see the sea again I tried the water, and as the ancients had written, it was much less salty than a true sea, but has a bitter taste, said by some to come from the naphtha which rises on its shores. One would not want to drink much of it. Camels and mules will drink the water, but horses will often refuse it. Blonde did quite strongly.

There is neither a noticeable tide in this sea, nor any regular current, for it is more a lake than a true sea. It is shallow; being no more than one hundred fathoms deep *{600 feet, 183 meters}*. Navigation on this body of water is not however easy, as there are violent winds that come without warning from the East or west. Its shallow coastal areas are full of sand bars. Some have theorised that at one time, the Black Sea and it were joined, and that may be so. We conducted our elevation experiment and determined that this sea was seven and ninety feet below the average surface of the world *{the modern measurement is -91 feet or -28 meters}*.

The markets here are livelier and this place has suffered less than the other places of Persia from the ills of war, disease and bad governance.

Persians discussing swords in the market place, which led to confrontation. III-XIII-11

Some swains were grouped around one of their cohorts examining blades, when like young men everywhere; they started swinging them in what we took as a mock fight. After several near misses of standers by, one misguided youth swung one at Dobbins, who moved back to avoid it, then stepped in, grabbed the man's wrist and in a remarkable display of strength, bent and swung him over his back and then proceeded to literally fling the astonished foe no less than twelve feet into his compatriots. The group was shocked at this, and stopped their mayhem, and before any more could occur, an older man, an Imaum came up and berated them. The crowd was quite bemused by all this and Dobbins was the centre of attention and his excellent command of Persian allowed him to thank his many newly-acquired admirers. One Persian man asked him how he had become so mighty. Dobbins foolishly replied,

'I believe in the power of Jesus Christ and I eat *Suyorera Mansa*' using the Bengali word for pork. Fortunately, the man could not speak Bengali!

This caused a conflict between Perkins and Dobbins, as Perkins rightly felt those actions could have led to an attack on us all. Dobbins strongly defended his actions under the pretence of *oderint dum metuant {Latin for let them hate, so long as they fear}*.

Michaelson was happy to find here *Bedornah*, the pips of the wild quince, much used in medicine.

We purchased here some sturgeon's flesh for our meal, and returned to our camp, and we found it capital eating. The black eggs *{caviar}* of this creature are said to be a great luxury and we secured some, but found them to have a strong fishy taste. They were a novelty, but I did not care for them. Without regards to my opinion, Bannington, Perkins, Horne and Michaelson found them delightful, so much so, that they purchased more, sending one of our Persians to obtain it. I noticed that all the 'higher class' members had liked the food, while those of us of a more middle-class background, Dobbins, Vickery and Dissanayake, did not. This brought up a discussion of who was of what class. Obviously Bannington was nobility, Perkins was a Bishop's son and Horne from a well to do family, but both insisted they were middle-class too. Michaelson also said he was middle-class but his education, accent and breeding said otherwise. Vickery was nobility by birth, but middle-class by choice, and he took no part in the debate; stalking instead the seashore for fish to spear. After much debate, it was decided that all were middle-class except Perkins, Michaelson and Bannington. This annoyed Michaelson to no end, and we had to massage his character to return him to his normal good temper. One unstated aspect of this discussion was whether Dobbins was middle or lower-class. I suspect we all avoided that specific area.

One of the aspects of Michaelson, who had spoken against his being of a lower class, was shown to be wrong not only his European exposure in education, but his knowledge of the going-on in higher society. He had once mentioned that he had seen Lord Shaftesbury's son die of a blow to the head from a fist, during a quarrel over a game; and that had been at Eton. We felt his sensitivity was due to his families fall to this lower strata, and that it had anger him. He was certainly upper-class by breeding and education, despite any financial lowering that may have occurred to his family, due to his father's mischances.

The village has some two hundred buildings; none of any value, except another brick tomb with a conical spire. This we found was the burial place of Imaum Ibrahim, a brother of the more famous Persian known as Imaun-i-Jawab *{Imam of the answer}*, he gained this name by claiming that while visiting Holy Mekkah, he had greeted the tomb of Mohammad, their prophet, upon first seeing it, with the traditional Muslim greeting, *Salam Alikum* and that he had received an audible answer from within the tomb, saying of *Alikum Salaam* in return; or so says Islamic folklore.

The place is surrounded by a swamp, and as a consequence, we were surrounded by buzzing annoyances.

We found a place to camp along the shoreline the caravanserai looking very uninviting, and we set out at once our mosquito netting. We could see from the shore the mountains to the south, and after some time, we made out the great volcano we had skirted the week before. That evening a humid mist came in and surrounded us. The heat is oppressive here and reached 87° this afternoon.

I contributed to our bounty by walking along the beach using one of my wooden ramrods to probe for turtle eggs. The method is simple, plunge it into the sand, and if it comes out sticky, you have found eggs. I found some after only twenty minutes, as one of the men at the legation party in Teheran had mentioned that the turtles of the Caspian area lay their eggs in June and July. I found a clutch of five and twenty unbroken eggs one pierced by my ram rod and one being left to the goddess of the shore line, a Persian myth and tradition. The eggs are elongated, white and about two inches long, with brittle-shells.

The madman of the Caspian after he had been clothed. Illustration III-XIII-12

Horne and Bannington went on a mad dash. Racing their horses in the sea surf, they went down the beach and came back much slower, dragging a large log of drift wood as a prize. It fed our bonfire this night.

Vickery notes that we had come hither on land a greater distance than the length of Great Britain, for we had travelled eight hundred and seventy five miles from Bushire to this place. We were astounded that Blood-Thirsty would know that being that he had never been to England and that we have come so far and accomplished so little, yet!

As our bonfire roared up, and the sea flurry drove off our noisy, winged friends, and our evening goat was being roasted along with our turtle eggs, we received a visit from an astonishing colleague. I say colleague, as he was a traveller, and also completely mad which made him our brother.

He announced his presence by voicing dreadful cries, as if his groin was being tormented by heated tools of the inquisition. We must be forgiven for thinking he was mad, for the first impression would have made anyone take him for a madman. He showed up in front of us in a sheep's skin, which barely covered the necessary body parts; while his torso, hands and feet were naked. He wore garlands of flowers atop his head and in his left hand he held a short *doru* *{Greek for spear}*, and in his right hand he held a bowl. However, he was not entirely mad, but nearly so, for he turned out to be a dervish. He chanted for some time, during which the name of Ali continually occurred, and we were told by our mule men that he was praying for our happiness. Their reaction to him was to ignore him completely. We had a supply of clothing and finding him to be a fine old fellow, we outfitted him with some of our rougher stock, and soon he had slipper, trowsers, blouse and turban.

Although he did not beg alms, a conduct very praiseworthy in Persia, we threw some money into his kettle, which he took without thanking us. There are several different sects of these dervishes. This man seemed to be a member of the one that passes their whole lives poising as an annoyance to others, yet in this case he had not been overly aggravating.

We did find that today was the 12th day of Rabi-il-Avvel in the Hijiri calendar and therefore the birthday of the prophet Mohammed. Our caravan men were slightly impressed that I knew this; they took it rather matter-of-factly, after the initial shock had been overcome by their usual, intellectual sloth.

The sunset over the western beaches of the Caspian Sea was a delight to behold.

Saturday 17 June

In the morning we awoke to find a small flotilla of boats off shore, we examined these with our glasses and found them to be Russian. We found from Muhurem that these were indeed Russians who sought sturgeons for their eggs, for the Persian does not do so. For this right, the Russians, pay the local prince some fifty gold Tomans each quarter *{£425, 15,000 USD in modern terms}*.

Horne and Hynes are detached to go and find the man recommended to us to be our guide into Central Tartary, while Perkins and I head off to find the Shah's crumb eater *{prince}* and give him a letter from the Vizier and the Shah himself.

The southern shore of the Caspian Sea. Illustration III-XIII-13

A Bedeviled And Thieved-Plagued Prince

He was a hard man to find, for he had gone, the previous evening, to an outlying house for a wedding and we spent a morning or so searching for him. The weather was warm and the insects were insistent on gaining a meal. Obtaining guidance from Persians on where such and such a dwelling was located, was vague and misleading. We did find him finally, in a pleasant grove where the wedding party had been, and the party was in a disgraceful state of confusion. A body of fifty or so men, befuddled by an excess of drink the night before, were wandering around screeching, and all were poorly dressed, if at all. This odd behaviour was soon explained. The wedding party had been a great success and the men had drunk themselves into a stupor, the Koran *{Driscol changed from his normal spelling of Qur'an to this, for no particular reason}* having had no sway in these woods the night before. In the early morning hours, thieves had come among these Persian unseen and unheard. They had plundered them, stealing not just money, jewels, weapons and horses, but items of clothing, tents, food, and pretty much everything. We found his Excellency, in an ill-humour wearing someone else's shawl and a poor man's cap and nothing more. In summary the entire wedding party, guests, servants, and ineffectual guards, had been most completely and professionally robbed. How many men it would have taken to take all of this, especially the tents, was in Hynes' estimation no less than a score of men, who having to work at night. They had done so without awaking a single soul, or more probably being aided by some members of the Prince's entourage and their profound drunkenness.

Nevertheless, our initial estimation of the Prince was too low, for he immediately turned from being a dedicated-seeker-of-thieves-and-whose-head-would-roll-for-this-outrage, to a premier class questioning bureaucrat, who on presentation of our letters, changed again. Almost instantly, he became a flattering courtier of the finest quality. So bereft of a rug to sit on, we sat in the dirt and discussed Teheran, the Shah, the expedition and the coming campaign against Herat. This wedding had been called because one of the men had wanted his night of Eros before leaving for the war. The Prince himself would be setting out soon. We found that he had communications from the Shah that he himself would depart from Teheran for 'his' city of Herat on June 23, and he would meet this Prince and his 'regiment', or more correctly his feudal band of assailants, at Meshed in August.

Beyond this, he could do nothing for us, as his 'court' was in disorder. He gave us verbal assurances, that while in the province, we would want for nothing. We asked about the guide, but on that subject, he had no knowledge. He asked that we join him in the city of Ashraf in four days' time, and there we would be properly welcomed, entertained and equipped. This Prince, a cousin of the Shah, then surprised us by saying goodbye to us in passable French. We left this 'court of disorder' to find its way back, by walking; something no good Persian will do unless forced, as they would not ride horses that had been ridden by infidel foreigners.

After we had ridden away, we had a good laugh at the Prince's discomfort, and we decided our own situation was similarly in danger, as our encampment on the shoreline might be subject to just such an attack. Also perhaps our mad visitor had been a scout?

We arrived back to find Hynes and Horne with our guide, or I should say 'guides'. The weakness of the Persian for mendacity is proverbial, equaled only by his incapacity to do it effectually. One instance of this national weakness was demonstrated for us in our camp, and caused us some significant inconvenience for the day. The locals had determined from our questions that we were searching for a specific man to be our guide into Central Tartary. In response to this, our two H's {Horne and Hynes} had been subjected to a deluge of men claiming to be the said guide. All these charlatans wanted money in advance in order to 'prepare' the expedition. At one time, we had three men in the camp saying they were the man we sought. However, our description of him incorporated a key attribute that none of those impersonators could match; for our man could speak Arabic and was not a Persian by race. None of those who showed themselves, and claimed to be the guide had this skill or else, they were obviously Persians. Hynes had developed a technique of kicking them out of the camp, which we watched with some wonder; a partial bum's rush and a swift kick completed the operation.

It was the unanimous opinion of the expedition, that when the Persian Prince had told us 'to meet him in Ashraf', it was merely a ploy to get rid of us. It was Hynes who stated it clearly; A Persian will tell you anything to make life easier for him, and in their estimation, for you too. He noted that to a Persian.

A fiction created for convenience is better than truthfulness which causes trouble

We had of course had guards up during the night, but for the rest of the afternoon, we prepared the camp for a possible attack by thieves; but it was our view that the Prince's own people had been in league with the robbers and our danger was not as great as we had first feared.

In the evening, a youth appeared in a travesty of western dress, and delivered a message to us. It was written in Persian and announced this lad to be the son of the guide we sought. As his son reputedly wore western clothes, and spoke some English, we thought he might be legitimate. It had directions to the guide's house, which was outside the town in the direction of Ashraf, so we decided to decamp the following day and find him. This son stayed the night and was full of information about his father. The boy was well groomed and dressed, tending to fatness and of a look one would expect in Alexandria or Bombay from someone trying to sell you French postcards. He declared that his father did indeed speak the language of the blessed prophet {Arabic} peace be upon his head.

He could not tell us anything about the availability of his father, but he did ask us many questions. We found that he had spoken to various Englishmen over the years, most recently Lieutenant Wyburd[5]. He was one of the very persons we were to seek in Central Tartary, as he had disappeared some years earlier before. He in turn asked us many questions, some of which I will record below.

> He asked whether it was true that there was a large ass or horse that was white with black stripes. We told him that yes and it was called a Zebra although none of us, except Dobbins and I, had ever seen a live one.

> He asked if the woman of England walked around without clothes on. That was, unfortunately, not true, we said.

He wondered when Napoleon would come to India? He was dead we told him. But he did not believe that, for he knew, he said, that Englishmen were swarming over his lands precisely because Napoleon had defeated us and driven us from our lands far to the west.

We had that evening, after the boy had fallen asleep, a spirited debate on the developments of the Oxford movement in England, which I read about in the London Times. Michaelson, Perkins and Dissanayake seemed to know the most about this association, or conspiracy, as Dissanayake named it, to bring back into the Church of England some of the forms of Popery. I had heard of it before, but under the name of Tractarians. They went on and on about this subject for several hours; I lost interest, as did the others, with the trio denouncing me as a non-conformist. I happily concurred and confessed I was, and then went off to write in my journal the day's happenings.

I thought that perhaps the boy might be a robbers' scout, but our night passed in peace, and as was my habit, I arranged my tour on guard to be the last one so I could greet the Sun.

When we all woke and were conducting our ablutions, I found in the bushes an interesting thing. It was a black stone called by the locals a *beldashe*, or a tribal marking stone. It date back to older times, a war leader would call upon his men to gather at the stone, which was known to all, at a certain time, as a method of tribal mobilization. There were only 'symbols' carved on the stone, and I could not read them.

The stone found by Driscol and drawn into his journal.
Illustration III-XIII-14

I ventured to imagine that the Persians had used just such a stone to gather men to fight against Alexander the Great; such evidence of history just transfixed me with wonder.

[Editor's note: the symbols as Driscol drew are cuneiform and in the language of Achaemenid Elamite, which right up to this day has not been translated]

The Dragoman With Eccles Cakes

Sunday 18 June

Dissanayake led a small service for us on the shores of the Caspian Sea. Following that, one of our muleteers was found to have been stealing from the others of his race, and was driven from the camp by Muhurem at knife point, without his wages and his two mules. His possessions, well searched, were piled up and left at the wayside, for him while the two mules were kept. Muhurem explained that he knew the man and that he would return the mules to him in Teheran, someday, maybe, *Inshallah {God willing}.*

Some two miles out of the town, our party came to a small side road and there we were directed down it by the boy. After another mile, we came to a modest, walled compound. We were greeted at the gate by a man who looked neither Persian nor Arab. He was of medium height with greying hair; for unlike the Persian, he did not perpetually wear a lamb skin ha. The openness of his countenance and his honesty in his words showed the breadth of his knowledge, while his inquietude was reflected in his deep, brown eyes. He was the man we sought and he said we could call him Dragoman, although he called himself Abu Kumzar *{father of Kumzar}*, for that was the name of his son, who had brought us, and the name highlighted he was an Arab, or was he? We noted that he spoke a language to his son that none of us could understand and it was certainly not Arabic. He invited us to tea.

His home was well built of stone and wood and had, in the English sense, a parlor or veranda, surprisingly enclosed in glass within a wooden lattice works, Where he had found so much clear glass, I could not have imagined. He seemed to sense our wonder and pronounced he had obtained the hundreds of 12 x 8 pieces of clear glass from Russia - at great cost.

His son brought out tea, good English tea, and an absolute marvel that left me simply stunned to speechlessness Eccles[6] cakes. To be served such a thing in a Persia was beyond belief, and nearly brought tears to my eyes I was so moved.

He had some English but spoke Arabic and Persian well. As we thought, he was neither Persian nor an Arab he was another race, a Kumzar, for he had named his son after his tribe, who lived in isolation on the Musandum Peninsula of Arabia, in the village of Kumza, and he was a member of the Shihuh tribe[7], located at the very tip of the peninsula, that juts into the straits of Hormuz.

He had started life as a seaman and fisherman and had been forcibly 'drafted' by a Persian ship, and as he had great skills, he had come to this other sea in order to man warships that were used against the Russians and others who raided the coast. He had married and settled here; far from his lands, and had travelled to Russia, to Baghdad, to Cabul, to Tashkent, Medina and Holy Mekkah. He had known a number of French and English explorers and had met Ormsby, Wyburd, Alison[8] and even the ill-fated Moorcroft. It was from Alison that he had picked up his little bit of English and also how to make an English pastry; the delicious Eccles cakes. He had retired the previous year, as he was getting too old for these long journeys; his bones protested too much he said.

We explained that he had been recommended to us by many high officials.

'He asked where did we wish to go'?

'The Aral Sea'.

'Why'?

'To see it'.

He had seen it and it was, 'nothing to write home about'. He said that in English, having learned the phrase wholeheartedly, with a Middlelands *{Midlands}* accent. This caused us all to laugh.

We talked for some time, and came to an agreement. He would not enter Central Tartary again. His bones, as he said, were tired, but he knew other guides, men he had worked with, and trained as his assistants, who could be found in Asterabad, and whom he could guarantee to aid us in our journey.

We discussed routes into the area. He quickly told us that we would face many obstacles, as Englishmen, and he was impressed by and supported the idea that we would go in disguise, but said that even that was no guarantee of success, and mentioned that Wyburd had come to him in disguise as Hajee Ahmet Al-Arab.

We asked him if he knew the fate of the man. He had heard stories that he was taken and slain by the Emir of Bokhara, who thought he was a Persian spy; also that he had been killed as a Russian spy by a Turcoman chief, while another rumour held he had been embraced by the light of Allah and lived as a sheikh amongst the Turcoman tribes. Further stories claimed that a tortured, dead man had been found on the banks of the Oxus and when examined it was found that he was a white man and that he had been slain by the Russians, another held that he had ventured into the land of the dog-faced men, that he had captured by them and had thereafter disappeared from this world.

We asked for details of all these, but he had none, as all he had were such rumour to repeat.

I asked who the dog-faced men were, for I had not read or heard of them before. I saw fear in his eyes, and he explained that within the deepest desert, men and entire caravans were known to have vanished; their sad fates associated with legends and myths about 'dog-faced' men who lived in the desert. He did not seem to like the subject and would not provide more information, despite all our attempts to gain it.

We offered him a large sum to come out of retirement, but he pointed to his house, his son, spoke of his other children, and shook his head. He would, for a much lesser sum, join us at Asterabad to make introductions to other guides he knew. They were men who had been his trusted assistants in the past, and who were now experienced guides themselves. He would join us there in some days. He said also that he had sickness in the house, and because of it, he could not bid us to stay for a meal.

[Editor's note: Driscol made a note in Arabic 'hayz' which I believe was noting that the Dragoman's house was ritually tainted by a female in her menstrual cycle and therefore not fit to host guests for a meal]

The Eccles cakes had been an unexpected wonder, and seeing that I loved them, he gave me all he had, a full dozen. Dobbins, having not been to England, asked where Eccles was and I explained. He then asked what other thing Eccles might be famous for, and that I had to think for some time for an answer, as the village was not famous for much of anything. However, but I did recall an incident from my youth, which I related to all as we walked to our rides.

I remember an accident, which I had witnessed as a boy of twelve *{1830}*. The railroad from Liverpool to Manchester was making its first run and I and some of the members of my family, had gone down to the tracks to watch it come by. They did and the train it stopped at the Parkside railway station, to take on water for the locomotives, which were very thirsty beasts. One of the trains, we were told, carried the Duke of Wellington, but the cars were well surrounded by well-wishers and my father who had known the Duke in the wars *{Napoleonic wars}*, could not approach close enough to shake his hand. A cry went up, for another train was coming up on the parallel track, and the crowd had to scatter. I was off to one side holding hands with my sister Zoe. A gentleman I did not know was talking adamantly with a man in the coaches, and did not see the approaching train, and the noise of it prevented anyone from warning him. At the last minute, he noticed his danger, and tried to enter the Duke's carriage, for it was he, but the door swung open, leaving him dangling over the track, where he was hit and his leg severed. We later learned that the man so injured, was a Mr Huskisson, the Liverpool member of Parliament, and the train that struck him was the Rocket, driven at that time by its builder, George Stephenson, whom Karen's family knew. He died in the Eccles hospital. Much later it was realised that he was the first man ever to be killed by a locomotive.

I ate six of the cakes while telling this story, and by the time we had arrived at our horses, there was nothing but bits of pastry left about me to tell the story of their existence.

We rode for some time between the lush jungled lands, broken here by huts and rice fields. The road was a causeway of some three hundred miles, built by a wise, famous, former King of Persia *{Shah Abbas 1571-1629}*. It was well constructed in parts, and these were dry, while in others, it was completely ruined and overgrown by the ever encroaching forest or undermined by the rice fields; in which cases we rode in mud and we forded a shallow river the Torlod *{Torlor River}*. We came at last to the village of Aliabad that was surrounded by trees and had in it a number of houses NOT in ruins, well-built, and having red-tiled roofs; however this was just an exception, and most of the people here seemed to live in rude huts. Few people were seen, and those that were, tended to be vagrant dervishes like our previous visitor at the sea shore, looking for handouts. A few dinars thrown here and there cleared them from out of our path.

An etching from the Swiss newspaper, Neue Zürcher Zeitung recording the expedition's crossing of the Torlor. Probably based purely on artistic license. Illustration III-XIII-15

The only clean and cleared area we could find to have our modest tiffin was within the gateway of the local cemetery. We rode on, making our way down the broken causeway, fording shallow streams whose bridges were down. The causeway widened here to some eighteen feet, with a ditch on each side, but was in poor repair, especially near the rice swamps *{paddies}*. Having passed these, we bypassed the broken causeway to ride through the forest over wonderfully smooth turf at the edge of foothills, passing several small villages on our way. Nearing Sari, we heeded the advice of other travellers and rejoined the causeway to avoid the bogs along the way. The causeway here becomes like a good English dirt road and is appreciated by us, as the land here is perfectly flat, and to our northeast and southwest were the mountains.

We decided to stay at Sari or as some call it Sira, or one of its many other names. It was at latitude 36° 30' north, longitude 53° 10' East. We took our measurement near the town's wall, which is a laughable affair, not higher than Bannington's head, and fronted with a partially filled-in ditch that we estimated to be at sea level. The wall is of clay and mud brick and has square towers, none of which were in good repair. We had found that doing our navigation duties attracted attention, so we had devised a way to do the necessary movements and gauging. While surrounded by the others, from a distance it looked like a group of men involved in an intense debate, if a native approached to within one hundred and fifty feet, we would not attempt it or discontinue our task. This did not apply to our own mule men, who had been told that these awkward gatherings were religious in nature.

Sari was entered by a ruinous gate, which was a pile of rubble brought down by an earthquake, which had once been covered with beautiful blue tiles.

Three scenes from a Persian market. Illustration III-XIII-16

It is now adorned with nothing more than beggars and rubbish.

The city was the same mix of ruins and livable dwellings; many with green tiled roofs, that we had seen in other Persian cities. The bazaar was livelier than any other we had seen since Teheran.

There were several caravanserai, and we picked the one that was the largest, and in fair repair. It had a neat garden, no nearby dead animals, a water tank and functional fountain in the central court. There were several public baths, but their owners seemed unwilling to admit us, and we decided not to make an issue of it. One of the other names of the city is that of 'the yellow city' attributed to the many groves of citrus which surround it. We obtained some juice from green oranges, unimaginably tart but refreshing nonetheless.

We walked around the city, enjoying the coolness of the shade trees after the soaring 100° of heat we had endured on the causeway. We visited the Aga palace and saw a cylindrical tower with a cement top about one hundred and ten foot high and two and thirty feet in diameter. We also obtained some ice from the Persian ice houses[9] and we found a vendor who supplied us with *faloodeh;* an iced noodle dish flavoured with lime juice, pistachios, rose water and sugar.

Our muleteers and Muhurem became involved in a shouting match and some fisticuffs with the locals over some trivial matter. As a result, Michaelson needed to close some wounds and staunch some blood. The fight was ended by Perkins firing five shots into the air rapidly from my Colt. That demonstration of a repeating arm gained him immediate attention. Blood-Thirsty observed that he should have shot into the townspeople and not into the air. I held his comment to have been in jest and not recommendatory.

Monday 19 June

We rise later than usual, as Muhurem informs us that it is but a half days ride to Ashraf. Our breakfast consisted of chunks of the sheep left over from our supper, which was warmed on the fire using our ramrods, as our cookery apparatus had already been loaded. One had to be careful to not burn one's wooden rod. We noticed that the muleteers used an iron ramrod which to us was a thing that might be considered as unduly rash to the point of insanity. Hynes noted that he had once seen a man load a musket with an iron ramrod, as he had been doing for many years, but this time, the rod struck a spark, and the musket went off with the black powder charge only; but even with no shot in it, the rod hit the man in the face. Under the cheek bone and passed out though the top of his head. More remarkably was the fact that the man did not die. He recovered to a degree, but while he retained his life, he had ceased to be the man he had once been. He became ignorant of those around him, antagonistic and argumentative; so much so, that he was court-martialed, dismissed from the regiment, and was killed in a pub during a fight some weeks later.

[Editor's note: This was similar to the case of Phineas Gage an American who survived in 1848 a much larger iron bar passing through his skull. The man Hynes noted may have been Sergeant Warden J. Wade of the Bombay 2ⁿᵈ native Infantry, however his case was considered to be one not of brain damage leading to personality changes but death by use of excessive alcohol]

The way ahead was wooded and swampy. Dispersed among the forest and fields were clumps of isolated fruit trees, secluded houses, and land in cultivation mainly of barley, wheat, rice and larger orchards of citrus. We came again to the ruined causeway, and followed it for some time, passing various nondescript ruins. One of these, just near the village itself, had been a great palace, but had alas fallen into ruin both by neglect and continual Turcoman raids.

When we came to more open fields, we deployed and practiced our cavalry movements, to the delight of the horses, who like to canter and gallop, nearly as much as their riders.

We found the caravanserai not to our liking, and befouled too much with manure, human and animal and so took up residence in a disused orchard, the trees being overgrown and unpruned. Here the foothills came down close enough to us, so we could ride again among hills, a pleasant change from the sameness of the flat that we had experienced over the previous few days.

Andre Yves Saint Vuitton a visitor. Illustration III-XIII-17

While there, we met an interesting fellow; a Frenchman, dirty, disheveled but quite happy. His name was Andre Yves Saint Vuitton; former traveller, merchant and *homme du monde*. He had voyaged to the East to avoid conscription, during the Napoleonic wars, and had just stayed. He was quite pleased to speak French again. In speaking with him, we discovered he was a simpleton, and it was the opinion of Bannington, who had, the best command of French, that he had probably not returned to France because he had forgotten where it was. We fed him well, and gave him a good supply of food, tobacco and money, and he wandered off - truly a lost but happy soul.

During the evening the rain came and it was throwing it down for an hour or so.

Horne, myself, and Dissanayake have developed a rash or inflammation of the skin about the toes. Our good doctor treated us with Brown's impregnated blistering tissue.

[Editor's note: Driscol made some cryptic remarks later in the journal, which I translate as meaning that the treatment was successful. Brown's mixture was made with cantharidine one of the most poisonous substances then known to science in 1837]

We engaged in some fencing, and then cleaned all of our weapons thoroughly, as we had been near the sea, and salt water is the enemy of all iron and steel.

The party riding through the foothills of Mazandaran. Illustration III-XIII-18

God Smites The Land Of The Unbelievers

Tuesday 20 June

I was sleeping soundly, when I heard the mules and horses making a great noise. I thought that a predator was in their midst, or that raiders or robbers, had come. I sought to rise, but suddenly found myself enmeshed in my mosquito netting; the framework of branches I relied on having collapsed. As this had happened before, I began to mend it. It was then that I noticed that the entire world was moving. It was the oddest sensation. Several cried out to ascertain what was happening. Vickery on guard duty at that time shouted that it was an earthquake, or the end of the world. Bannington announced, in a loud and cheerful voice that yes it was an earthquake, and was it not a delight? So at three o'clock in the morning, in a Persian lemon orchard, I experience my first moving of the earth. It felt as if a great wagon was passing near me at speed, everything shoo. I tried to rise, but felt as if I was at sea in a great storm. I groped my way to my feet and made for Blonde, but I did not reach her and the ground came away from my feet. I found it best to sit in the darkness and let it shake all around me. I found My Frenchman, and sat there in the darkness, as the ground shifted beneath me. I could hear my friends cursing and shouting. Horne was wondering who the bastard, was who was shaking his mattress. Then it stopped, the fire was nearly out, but our lanterns were lit. All looked normal; the trees had not fallen. It was Dissanayake who pointed out that fire had taken hold in the village of Ashraf for we were on the hillside above it. Down there, fires had begun and wailing and other noises, told us the people were in distress. Muhurem said this happens often in this land, and that is was Allah's anger at the drinking of wine, blasphemy, and not enough attention given to the five periods of prayer. I did not feel that it was worth pointing out to him that I had yet to see him or his men do their prayers.

We had with us four lanterns, and all were now lit. Bannington and Horne agreed to stay and guard our camp, and we made our way down towards the village. We came to the first house, which we had passed just the day before. It had been a typical Mazandaran house, made of wood, and it had collapsed like one made of cards, the whole thing crumpling inward, and the roof falling intact atop it. We shouted, but heard nothing in return, and headed for the village proper.

We had nearly come up to the village, when we were all knocked off our feet, as the ground shifted violently beneath us again, and the ground heaved and rumbled for nearly a minute, before calm came again to this tortured land.

We found the villagers engaged in pulling people out of fallen houses. Not all the house had come down; some stood unaffected, some stood but were twisted or leaning, a mosque's minaret had fallen across one house and we found a Imaum dead under the fallen masonry; a certain irony was evident there. We found that the villagers were hostile to our attempts to aid them, and we returned to our camp, where Muhurem could not understand why we had gone. His men were from Teheran why would they help these people?

In the morning, we went down and observed the bodies of many; and I would estimate the death toll at one hundred, being washed and wrapped in accordance to Islamic rites, while a large grave was dug into the ruins on the west side of the village.

It was mid-morning when a crowd approached our camp, shouting and gesturing. Muhurem said that they blamed us for Allah's anger and that we were sorcerers. A demonstration of our arms made them return to their damaged village.

Seeing that no good would come of trying to deal with them, and despite the Prince's promise to meet us here, we decided to move on. One of the muleteers, who declared he was somewhat ill, decided to stay behind and also to await any arrival of the Prince, who would probably be delayed by this disaster to his land and people.

We were soon ready to go and headed cross-country to avoid the villagers; a few of whom followed us for a mile or more, shouting things we could neither hear nor understand.

We rode rapidly, with those villagers behind us, and regained the causeway, the mules jangling away as they ran to keep up with us. The road entered a great forest, and here and there, a tree was down, after two miles, the dirt road became a stony pathway, set with large rounded stones which were difficult for the horses to manage. We rode for an hour and were approaching what we were told was the village of Rekiabdin.

As we approached the village, a monstrous sight affronted to us, for we were on a slight rise of some around eight and thirty feet and could see over a plain towards the village, which was dotted with trees, fields and the road, which led straight to it. The village 'jumped' or moved as we watched, and towards us came the most remarkable thing; a wave, a wave of earth moving through the soil. It was like a ripple in a body of water. I knew not what to do, but dismounted immediately, gripped Blondes traces, and knelt down. Some of the others did so too. It came at us like a mad thing and struck. All were thrown from their feet; the horses screaming, the mules giving forth their cries of fear, the mule men all shouting for God's mercy and forgiveness. All about us was a great rumbling, like a drum the size of the Moon being beaten endlessly. Dissanayake was giving out a prayer, as was Michaelson, which sounded odd, and about us was that grumbling roar, as soon as it had come, it was gone and I found myself on my back with Bannington horse fallen across my legs, it was my luck to be on soft ground or I would have taken an injury.

Vickery announce it was like taking a thirty-foot sea wave in the surf. We struggled to our feet. We found Hynes and Dobbins also trapped by fallen horses and gained their release, all the horses were fine. One mule had broken both her hind legs and was dispatched by a shot from Dobbins' Medusa. We stood flustered, stunned and amazed. The mules were a disaster. All their packs were off or skewed. We left them with Vickery, Dissanayake and Hynes to sort out and rode on to the village, which we found completely destroyed. Dazed villagers were screaming for help and these souls did take up our offers of help and we found ourselves shifting timbers. I gathered up two children, out from under some wood, and returned them to a screaming mother, an old man was rescued, and so it was that we spent the rest of the day in this small village doing what we could.

We would shout in the vicinity of each destroyed house, 'Is there anyone alive here'? Once we heard movement and dug down to find four small goats. I found an elderly woman in tears atop a demolished home. I asked her if anyone was inside. She said yes, her money, and she would pay us 1,000 dinars {less than $^1/_6$ of a pound sterling} to find it, we left her to his ruin. At another ruined house, we found a groom who had lost his bride of four days. He was the personification of misery. Here and there were demented people. One woman was wandering, shouting and dragging her crushed, dead, daughter by the arm.

It was precisely 2.24 when another shock hit us. I knew this as Horne and the others had come up with the mules, and he had his watch out and was seeing to the time, when it was jolted from his hand. Found the only rock in the area and was shattered. He was rather annoyed I would think. The mechanism still worked by the crystal was reduced to splinters.

The village was small, perhaps of seven or eight hundred people, and we searched on until night time. About a score of houses had remained partially upright but one of these fell down in a cloud of dust but for no apparent reason. The ground was not shaking when it fell. The head man and Imaum were gracious in their thanks. We had even managed to inspire the muleteers to assist in a way; by having them not engage in looting, and staying out of the way.

We decide to move on Hynes and Michaelson both said that disease follows earthquakes, and it was best to be away from the dead at this time. As we rode on in the late afternoon, most of the men and me were pleased that we could help. We also endlessly discussed, defined and described the nature of the 'earthen wave' that came towards us that day. The road is no better or no worse, we turn aside at points to avoid gaping holes in the causeway, one mud hole, we decided, was so deep that it could have swallowed up a camel without difficulty.

We came to the seaside town of Bandar-e-Gaz by nightfall here the damage had been slight, and no sea wave {tsunami} had disturbed the town, which is sited overlooking a tranquil bay, on the Caspian, and is surrounded by wetland filled with wild fowls. It is a seaport of sorts, but no large ships were in the offing, and we retreated somewhat to a hill near the village, as we wanted nothing to do with a building this night. Our concerns were not warranted, as no shocks occurred.

We purchased for a small sum some ducks, which our men managed to overcook and somewhat burnt, but they were a welcomed taste after a steady diet of eggs, sheep, chicken, mutton and more lamb.

[Editor's note: Driscol had the misfortune of being at the epicenter of the 1837 earthquake, which devastated this small area on the southern coast of the Caspian Sea. However, the damage just a few miles away was minimal. Driscol and the men of the expedition had no idea that in England, King William the IV had died at the age of 71 and that his heiress presumptive, 19 year old Victoria had become Queen Victoria, as of twelve minutes past two in the morning English time or that he was now in what would later be called the Victorian age, and that he and his story would be categorized as "Victorian" and he a Victorian age explorer]

Wednesday 21 June

We rode steadily on and found that we were climbing uphill again; a change, if not a welcome one, from the sameness of the flat plain. We passed several burying grounds, which were filled with fanciful headstones, some coloured red, blue and green. We passed several mountain torrents as the mountains were closer now to the shore line. We came to, and bypassed, the village of Koulbad {Kordkuy}; for a party of villagers met us a mile from their rude village and demanded a ridiculous sum to enter it. We went around though the wheat fields, some boys chasing after us yelling for money. They threw rocks but were rather poor at it; Dobbins, Bannington and Perkins had all played Cricket and were expert bowlers. They had no difficulty beaning a few miscreants and discouraging their pursuit.

We came, after a time, to a great ditch, some twenty feet deep and marking the border of Mazandaran and the new province of Asterabad. We crossed it and kept going. When we came to the narrow but deep stream, we crossed it on something only a Persian might call a 'bridge', but I would have characterised it as a pile of broken masonry topped or repaired by timbers poorly laid.

I had heard of this bridge and its repair in Teheran. The Shah had sent money, worth some three thousand pounds sterling, to have this critical bridge repaired and the Governor had instead laid some planks down and kept the money to pay the soldiers of his guard; consisting mainly of his family members.

The conveyance of a disgraced Persian official having been recalled to face the Shah. Illustration III-XIII-19

I remembered this tale due to what we next saw that day on our march.

We had stopped on the other side of this bridge, as a curious column appeared. It consisted of a Persian palanquin, with its long pole-shafts saddled upon the back of a mule at each end, numerous servants on foot, and a bodyguard of eighteen mounted soldiers; all armed with flag draped lances. The great man, who occupied the palanquin, remained concealed throughout the pandemonium, which our appearance, or more correctly our baying mules occasioned among his hearse-bearing mules. The commander of the guard was acquainted with Europeans, and greeted us warmly, and we found that he did not guard, but escorted the disgraced former governor of the city of Asterabad, who had been found to be gaining wealth from the sale of information, {black} powder and people to the Turcoman raiders.

That a Persian official will steal is considered normal, that he would plunder his people by taxes, extortions and brutal robbery is the way of the Persian world, but to deal with enemies in such a way as to lessen what is stolen by a <u>higher</u> official, is an action punishable by death. He was therefore not condemned for dealing with a national enemy but for undercutting the profits of a prince of the Royal family, who by tradition had the monopoly on such traitorous dealings.

In Persian law, any crime can be bought off; even murder can be dealt with by the payment of a suitable amount of blood money, but in this case, the man accused, and found guilty by the same denouncement, was unable to pay the high price of the pardon that was demanded. He was therefore seized, and placed in that palanquin, and would remain there until he approached Teheran, where if the Shah had decided on mercy, he would be granted his freedom, exile or blinding. More likely, he would be met by a messenger, who would bring him a choice of a poisoned cup of cold coffee, a dagger - if sharp a sign of respect - if dull one of gross disrespect, or a knotted rope fixed with a noose. From these the man must choose, at that instance, with no delay, the method of his doom; for if he failed to do so, he would be is dreadfully tortured, until he expired or agreed to one of the proffered methods. So he passed us by on his fateful journey to the capital, which few, if any, ever came back from whole or alive.

[Editor's note: The Persian traveling to Teheran may have been Golab Farahani, whose family made a partial payment of the money demanded for his life. The Shah graciously had only one eye gouged out, which was returned to him on the payment of the remaining funds. He was exiled to the island of Kish in the Persian Gulf, where he was forced to wear a noose around his neck for the rest of his life, to remind him his life belonged to the Shah, who could take it at his will. He was later executed by hanging, but by another noose made by HEIC officials in India, for the murder of the Italian tourist Geovanni del Carpine and his valet in 1851, after he had fled from his exile in Kish to Bombay]

Asterabad, as seen by Driscol approaching from the West
Illustration III-XIII-20

We Come To Asterabad And The Steppes Of Independent Tartary

Asterabad arose out of the green meadows, which is a fixture of this fertile land a square shape on the flowing land, and behind it, rose up the green and forested mountains of the Alborz Mountains.

Asterabad *{Modern Gorgan}* is situated along the River Astar and its tributaries, which flow around the city, and down to the Asterabad Bay, and the Caspian some twenty miles away. We are now at a latitude 36° 50' north and longitude 54° 26' East, with an elevation of four thousand feet. The city sits comfortably at the foot of the northwest slope, amongst the foothills. From the western side, a ridge line runs, ending in a type of acropolis, this is topped by more ruins. One can see its twenty foot high crenellated, mud wall some distance away and this wall runs some four miles around the city's circumference. It has round towers that surmount it at measured points, but most are in a state of partial or full ruin. We come towards the city on the road that leads to the western gate, which is roofed and in better repair. The so-called Mazandaran gate was closed to us, and the guards would not open it, so we went with other frustrated travellers around the city to the southern gate, called the *Chehl Dukhtar {Forty virgins}*, so named for the forty women plucked from the city by Turcoman raiders a generation ago.

From my studies of Greek classics, I knew this place to be Hyrcania, a fabled province whose capital was fair Zadracarta, but that city is lost now, having been conquered by Alexander the Great, and I wondered if it may lie under Asterabad[10]?

Once inside the city, we found the same spectacle of ruin and hovels we had seen in the other places of Persia, while here and there gardens had sprouted on the ruins of the city. The buildings are made of dried mud brick, which the trees, that grow thickly here, use as rooting soil. Accordingly there was a denser forest within the walls than without; the forest having been driven back a mile or more by the success of agriculture and the constant need for wood to fuel fires.

This town is where the noble Kajar family of the Shah arose but it seems not to have profited from this relationship, except perhaps as Michaelson observed to have a cleaner type of dirt than other Persian cities, which was actually a true statement.

Our long suffering guide Muhurem is happy to be here as this is where we contracted him to take us. He was under the threat of the Shah to get us here, and he had done so without the loss of a single European. He praises the Prophet's beard for this, for his favourite and oft time repeated phrase had been for every conceivable situation, 'by the Prophet's beard'. We go to a caravanserai, also in ruins, but nearly clean, for we cannot camp outside the town as the chances of a Turcoman raid are too great.

As our place of living is near the Eastern gate I go there as I am bored of riding and my good companions and wish to be away.

Hynes and Bannington have charge of the camp tonight and I have, as usual the last guard time. I always insist on that as I enjoy the peace of the early morning before dawn, and the rising up of the followers of Muhammed to their call for prayer. I find the roofed gate to be a complete ruin. Sadly, atop the gate are two sleeping guards, and a position for artillery, where two neglected guns, with their wooden carriages all but rotted away, sit, forlorn in the extreme. One is a finely made French 8 pounder cannon with a wide crack down its length. Its presence here seems mundane {archaic sense: futile}. Another piece was a Portuguese-made 9 pounder captured some time ago, as it shows the date of manufacture as being in 1587, one year before the Spanish Armada sailed to defeat against England. I wish I could adopt the poor things, but they each weigh eight hundred pounds, so I must leave them here. I think again that someday I will have a great estate, and on it I will bring one of every type of cannon known, and make there a place; a museum of cannons. From the gate I can see northward, and over and across the steppe, which goes on to the horizon. It is into that land we shall go.

I walk out into the bazaar, where an Englishman in civilian dress garners no interest or respect. I saw some men playing the game of *As*, which I watch for some time. Eventually I was asked to take part. As it was not for a large amount of money, I joined in, learning the rules as I went along. They thought it peculiar that anyone, particularly an Englishman, did not know the rules. 'Does not everyone' was their communal thought. They were greatly entertained to know that others in the Dar al-Harb {house of war or the west} played cards, but not *As*, but some did not believe that we had other forms of cards and games instead.

Of the four men I was playing with, one was the son of an Imaum and he was here in the city studying to become what his father was. Another was an older, better dressed, man who was a trader in spices. He knew the long road to Bushire well, for he had travelled there five times a year ever since he was nine. He complimented me on my Persian, and we joked for a while at the expense of the native Bushirean, whom Persians consider as trash, being as they are of Arab blood and not true men like themselves. I agree with him both to be social as he was right.

While the Persian is generally superior to a city Arab, I feel the native, desert dwelling, Arab is grander and more civilised in actions that a Persian. I base that on my reading and not from personal knowledge - something I will correct in the future. This made me recall Hayathem, whom I must say, is a fine example of an Arab.

The next man was of an indeterminate age. He was also something I did not know. What he said he was in Persian meant nothing to me, and he and the others declined to explain, even though I asked twice for a clarification. The last man was an officer in the Persian Infantry of the equivalent rank of Captain I believe. He had a fine scar on his left cheek, which accented his face in an extraordinary way - any European Hussar would die to have it, for it made his face dashing in the best sense.

The rules were similar to American poker, as taught to me by that scoundrel of an American, Mr Vadeboncoeur, on the William Fawcett. There are no flushes or straights and there are five 'colours' or suites and only five and twenty cards. The cards were small; being about $2\frac{1}{2}$ by $1\frac{1}{2}$ inches in an oblong shape. The back of the card was covered with a flower design, the front was coloured in a way to show its value; the lowest being the harlot in red, second the knave or soldier in yellow, third the queen in gold, fourth the king in green and finally the ace in black, which is called *As*, which is where the name of the game comes from. It portrays a lion eating a gazelle, the king is seated on a throne, the queen is shown seated with an infant, the knave is shown as a soldier, and the finally the harlot is shown as a dancer in an exotic and erotic poise.

Given the Persian's ability in deception and perfidy, bluffing is the main tool in the arsenal of the *As* player. I lost a few dinars, perhaps twenty in all, worth nearly a pice in India or $^1/_3$ of a good English pence coin. The game was ended by the calls of the *adhan {call for prayer}*, 'Allahu Akbar' resounding through the market to herald the fourth prayer of the day. Some of the people in the square ignored it, but the small group I was with were prompted by the soon-to-be Mollah to answer its call. He invited me to attend, but I demurred.

It was interesting that the Shia Persians hold that Muhammad, who by God's command, ordered the '*adhan*' as a means of calling Muslims to prayer, while the Sunni hold that Mohammad's colleague Umar had dreamt of the call, and having liked it, adopted same. It is said that he held that a man's call was preferred to the use of horns by the Jews or bells used by the Christians.

While many, if not the majority of the men, in the bazaar interrupted their trade to go to the mosque, many did not. I found one group of these. I studied them from a distance and determined, from their appearance and manifest sloth, that they must be Turcoman. They assembled in several groups in the bazaar, and were speaking a language I did not understand, and I understood, from what I had heard of them, that they enjoy speaking endlessly of their own cleverness, their feats of prowess, and their defeat of enemies and the taking of plunder.

Those visible clues, derived from their dress and presence in the Asterabad bazaar, suggested that they were most likely a breed called the Chomeur, or civilised Turcoman, who live on the border of Persia or within it along the banks of the Gurgan River. There they farm the land, as do the Persians and they sell grains in the markets here; mainly barley and wheat, butter, beautiful carpets, felt, sheep, and of course horses. Their stable domestication does not, however, mean that they do not rise up at times to commit plunder or do man stealing. They are apathetic to the forms of Islam, and are weak Sunni, as compared to the majority Shia of the Persians. This would explain why they would not enter the mosques, here as no good Sunni would dare to enter a Shia one, not that he would be permitted to do so in the first case.

Those Turcoman were amusing themselves, by playing what I took to be chess on fabric 'boards'. interestingly enough, it did not have the different coloured squares of western chess, just plain lines. They use for chess pieces the following; a piece of cow horn for the king, a smaller one for the vizier *{queen}*, the knights are pieces of bone with notches, the bishop is an elephant and represented by a vaguely elephant looking piece of bone, the rook or castle has the form of a mushroom, why I have no idea, and pawns are made of a sheep's feet bones.

These men were not as Mongol looking as I had been led to believe. They did have a slight appearance of an Asiatic, especially around the eyes, which are black or dark brown, and which are somewhat slanted, but the nose is sharp and sets off the face well with the higher cheek bones and high forehead. His body and limbs are slender; he is tall on average, a trait they share with the Persian. His head sports puffy lips and black hair shown in sparse beards and stray strands from beneath his notable head covering.

They all wore the same costume, a flowing robe, called the *jubba*, itself a voluminous affair, fastened with a sash, in which is held their dagger. The robe is often a dirty brown colour but a few brave souls sport what might have been green or even a dark blue to the world. Many are striped with cotton or silk layers of different colours, such as green, blue, red or purple. Some of the lower sort of Turcoman wear robes not of silk or cotton but made from camel hair. On their feet, they wear a style of Persian slipper of no great notice, and on their heads, the ubiquitous conical sheepskin cap in black, grey and few that may have once been white. A few sported turbans of various colours or simple caps. I had been told that the year before, a Persian army had striven to chasten them, and a large party of settled Chomeurs and their nomadic brothers the Chorwa, who are pastorals, had been driven away and had taken refuge with the Khan of Khiva. This to me illustrated the frustration that the Persian military has with the Turcoman; they will not fight a war. They will only raid, and if pressed, simply use their superiority in mobility to disappear into the Kara-Kum desert ahead of the Persian columns and seek the aid of the Khans of Khiva or Bokhara, who greatly hate the Persians.

I was not brave enough to approach these men, and set about to wander the nearly deserted streets, for in a purely Mohammedan town, all the men SHOULD disappear at the time of the call to prayer call for forty or so minutes.

I wandered the streets, with my hand always in my pocket, resting on My Frenchman. I came to a Polygonal shaped, baked brick, tomb or *bog'a marqad {revered mausoleum}*, which I entered after removing my shoes, and found in it a prayer book in the name of Emamzada Nur, an honoured descendant of the Imam Musa al-Kazem[11].

Some say the city was named after a mule, which is *astar* in the older versions of the language. Another name of the city is Dar-al-Momin or the gate of the faithful; from the many Sayid who live here.

I wandered the markets, and began speaking with the owners of stalls and shops, as they returned from prayer. In it were many things of European manufacture: things like knives, scissors, mirrors and the like. From India, came spices and tea, from Russia, the great enemy of the Persians, there came sugar, weapons, cloth, glass and boxes. China provided pottery, which was of the delightful blue and white pattern, which my mother had always loved, and even tea. From Khiva came hides, from the city of death, Meshed, came cloaks and from the devils themselves, the Turcoman, came horses, horse furniture, salt and naphtha. A common article of trade was also slaves. The Turcoman raids both Persia and Russia, and sells slaves from the one place to the other. A suitable Russian girl can be purchased for as second, third or fourth wife or as a domestic servant, for just one hundred thousand dinars or about half a pound Sterling. A strong working man, in the prime of life, might go for 2½ pounds Sterling.

The Asterabadians produce oil of sesame, dried fruit, grains and soap, and they are well armed. Every Persian I saw since I arrived, except clerics, carries a sword or at least a wicked curved dagger; but here everyone also shoulders a matchlock, but most of these are no more than gimcracks *{badly made, worthless}*, with flintlock not being often seen, and if seen, they universally have a broken lock. As to why they carry heavy, ineffectual weapons about, I do not know.

The people here greatly esteem rice, and will not willingly eat anything else. One must be very poor to eat bread. I purchased some bread and found it the equal of the flat breads of India. A mother of this land will threaten a child with the withdrawal of rice and substitution of bread if they are bad. I am led to understand that this threat alone is enough to make even the greatest hellion become quiet and respectful.

I spent some time watching the sellers and buyers in the horse market, where some hundreds of animals were for sale, very cheaply from the standards of India. The horses seemed to my distant eyes to be a fine lot. However I was more interested in viewing HOW the horse trading occurred; noting how a breeder was approached, what was said, gestures, what people wore, how the animals was inspected and what was discussed. I found that if I stayed a certain distance away from the market, none approached me, but if I advanced to around five and forty feet away, this would trigger a tout to come up to me with an aggressive pitch of his wares.

I found that Horne and Dobbins had also wandered and had come here too and they entertained the bazaar by a game of Jan-ken-po. They were doing so to determine where to go, and they collected quite an attentive audience, and before I showed up, had taught a number of young boys how to do it.

[Editor's note: in Driscol's time this was stone - knife - cloth instead of the modern rock, scissors and paper or even more contemporary rock, scissors, paper, lizard, Spock]

I was faced once again with a change in currency. I made some notes, and found that in Central Tartary, that four and twenty gold coins of Bokhara is worth, perhaps a pound sterling while the Khivan coin called the Tenghes takes forty to be equal.

The copper coin is called a Shaie and is twenty to one Krans, which is made of silver, and ten Krans equals a Tilla, Ashurfee or Toman. Beyond that I could make no sense of it as each city issues its own coins. The moneylenders are Jews mainly, and they make a good living sorting out this mess of coinage. I did show the coin that Vickery had given me some time before. The Jew said it was very old, dating back to the time of Alexander's successors. I amazed him by use of some Hebrew I had learned from Catania. He turned out to be a good fellow and was helpful in his advice and knowledge. He did ask if I had been to Jerusalem. He was genuinely sad that I had not.

I wondered why the people of this city stayed here? I could see that in parts, the city was as lovely as a favoured mule, or perhaps it was that they were just a stubborn people; living here, at the foot of the mountains, with greenery all around, looking out over the drier plains, and being subjected to the incessant raids of the Turcoman. Perhaps it was that stubbornness that kept them here, or perhaps, as the Jew had suggested, they would not be welcomed anywhere else.

As I wandered and thought, I recalled England in June, and what would be in its markets: asparagus, carrots, onions, peas, radishes, and spinach would be ready for purchase, as well as Fruit: apricots, currants, gooseberries, nectarines, peaches, raspberries, and strawberries. All manners of fish, flesh especially wheatears *{modern genus Oenanthe but in Driscol's time considered a thrush}*. Leverets and poults were also turning prime now *{a young hare and turkey under one year old}*.

The Day Of The Shoeless Horne And A Malaise

I noted that Horne was sporting a new pair of boots; of Russian manufacture no less. He disgustingly explained that they too had found that polygonal brick tomb, and had entered it and that when they came out, Horne's and not Dobbins' shoes had been taken. He had unpleasant things to say about the thief. I wondered who would have wanted well worn, smelly, English military style; stovepipe boots that reached nearly to one's knees and were wide enough for the trowsers could be tucked in. Given that the Persian did not wear trowsers, what would they do with them? We put it down to the mischief of children. I later found out that Horne had kept two, good, gold guineas in the boots as a hidden reserve.

That night, my mosquito netting fell down around me, and I thought it another earthquake. But no I had fallen asleep with my journal on my chest, and Dissanayake had moved to place it in its carrying case. As he was doing so, and I was sleepily thanking, him for he was on guard duty, he had knocked the net down upon me. As we spoke and sorted out the tangle, there _was_ a sharp secondary earth tremour, a shivering of the ground for a few seconds, then silence, but it was enough to disturb the horses, and set the town into a frenzy of shouting and the sight of lights moving to and fro.

Thursday 22 June

Muhurem is eager to be released, for his men wish to leave this place as soon as possible. We agree that they may go tomorrow, depending on the outcome of our meeting with the local governor. Persians officials are infamous for making people wait to see them, but we are backed by his Royal Sovereign, and we soon have an appointment with him. I let Horne, Dobbins, Hynes and Perkins do the visit, as I have much to write.

A messenger brings a note from Perkins to me to come, as there is a difficulty. When I arrive, for I have flown there, I find that the governor is frustrated and had demanded money from us. Next, he demanded, as was his right, that we officially bless him in the Shia way. This would normally mean that we would have to do as requested and as he calculated we could not, we would have to withdraw until we could hire a Moolah who could carry out the needful and only then could we return, another day, to continue our discussion. He was clearly trying to end the discussion by employing this tactic. He did so because he was a new man, for we had seen the previous governor, on the road, riding to his doom. This new governor had not yet determined what he should do. He probably needed more time to determine how much he could steal from these people, as he was from Shiraz. He was amused, said Perkins, to hear that the ruler of the province had been robbed and even more bemused that an earthquake had shattered the villages and towns to the west. His reaction was to do nothing and await orders from Teheran. We too are to wait, for what, he does not know, but seeing his predecessors' fate, he is cautious but grasping. Perkins has declined all his hints at presents and bribes. Perkins had sent for me, as I had researched and practiced the Shia method of official blessing, as we had been told of this irksome tradition in Bushire. I had practiced the necessary actions during our ride up from the sea after learning it from N.B.B.

[Editor's note: what N.B.B. is or who it was is not known]

I begin immediately, as I had already been introduced, and made my homage to the governor. I boldly stepped forward raising my hands and recited a surah from the Qur'an. I selected the second shortest of them all; the 113 An-Nas (The Mankind); 'Say, I seek refuge in the Lord of daybreak, from the evil of that which He created, and from the evil of darkness when it settles, and from the evil of the blowers in knots, and from the evil of an envier when he envies'. I said it in Persian then Arabic. This is taken well, and I add in two *Rabbana Wa lakal-Hamd {Our Lord, all praise is due to You}*. I followed this with the Arabic *wayajuz alnnazar salati {May my prayer be heard}* and the translation in Persian. The great man and his aides answered this, as they must, by repeating it. The governor extended his hand to me, and emboldened, I strode forward and grasped it, and performed the *musafaha {shaking of hands}*, which he extended into the *Mua'naqah*, a type of hug where the necks met, for he had risen. The governor smelt of rose water, tobacco, *bromhidrosis {body odor}* and a hint of garlic.

I then took a step back, wondered what I smelled like to him, blessed him again and then made a mistake with one of the phrases I had memorised saying one instead of the other. I foolishly said,

لباسهایتو در بیار {*Take your clothes off}* instead of

بهترین آرزوهایم را برای تندرستی تان بینید {*best wishes for our good health}*, how and why I made that mistake, I am not sure, but I blame Perkins, who had been teaching me 'useful phrases' for highly improbable meetings with Persian women.

The governor and his men roared in laughter at this, and I later found that that phrase 'take your clothes off' meant to 'be a man and not a governor', or in other words, be helpful and not an arse. My error had worked in my favour. I was not amused that our people had also laughed at my error too.

Perkins, Hynes and Dobbins later praise me greatly for my performance. They do not seem to realise I made a mistake, instead considered my repost *{riposte}* to be masterful stroke - I shall let them continue to think that.

[Editor's note: Driscol wrote the above in Danish probably to keep Perkins, who sometimes read his journal, from understanding it]

I feel unwell and am not hungry and go to sleep early that evening.

Friday 23 June

All of us are ill by early morning. The symptoms are tightness in the chest and weakness in the bowels and blood. Michaelson has the worst of it, and he is of no use to us. Our muleteers seeing our incapacitation take their leave. As we do not control their pay we have no way to restrain them. Our equipment is nicely piled up in the large thirty by twenty foot room we inhabit. The horses are well situated in the caravanserai stable area. Later that evening the man we had left at the court of the ruler of this land shows up. He says that the Prince is concerned with the matter of his robbery and the damage to his lands by the earthquake and he has no time for us now. It is suggested that we contact him again in a few months, Mashallah!

A man of the caravanserai offers to assist us for a small sum, as we are all taken ill. Only Bannington seems to still be mobile to some degree. I am too weak to rise up for more than a few minutes at a time. We can talk amongst ourselves and the main product of this is quibbling, doubt and qualms about the future.

[Editor's note: Driscol makes a long list of mistakes in French said by Dobbins, but as these are obscure, I have deleted them, and leave just three for the reader to ponder]

(...) at one point we abuse Dobbins for his poor French and the many mistakes he makes. Saying things as, '*une jambe*' instead of '*une cuisse de poulet*' for the leg of chicken, he had also referred to our '*la salle a coucher*' instead of '*la chambre a coucher*', '*salle*' is a public space versus a *chambre* which is private place to sleep or referring to Michaelson as '*un physician*' {*meaning a philosopher*} instead of '*un medecin*' {*a medical doctor*}.

Michaelson in the morning cures himself, and has returned to us once the sickness has passed. He is now the best of us in regards to health. He lists the symptoms of our joint case:

> A general malaise of spirit and strength

> A hot uncomfortable pressure behind the eyes and face centred in the sinuses

> Sharp random pains in the head for all but me

> A racing of the *praecordia* {*heart*} at the slightest exertion

> He thought we were in for a course of fever and that some of us might have fits

> Our new assistant was directed to make us all tea with five grains of calomel each {*a diuretic and purgative*}

Michaelson is of the mind that as we were struck, and not the muleteers, or as far as we can tell, the inhabitants of the city, it must have been something particular to us alone.

Once we have enjoyed the effects of the calomel, he gives us from his store of medicine a large dose of *elixir salutis,* made of aniseed, brandy, cochineal, elecampane, fennel seed, jalap, manna, parsley seed, raisins, rhubarb, saffron, Spanish liquorice and a touch of caraway, salt of tartar and scammony as a follow on. He said it was good for convulsions, agues, and piles. He also said while pointing to Hynes, that it would cure surfeits, vapours of the spleen, green sickness, distempers, worms, rickets, stony gripes, the King's evil, crudities, gout & rheumatism, griping of the bowels, dropsy and scurvy PLUS the Asterabad fever, which we all seemed to have now.

Bannington and Horne both protested that we could not have scurvy, but Michaelson silenced them with a knowing look. The elixir was rather tasteful in fact, yet Horne noted that if he had a choice

between eating sheep dung and this, he would select the manure hands down, as long as he had gloves on.

One of Driscol's dreams was of a naked woman, with a staff, tormenting a lobster. We too are unsure of what this might have meant, yet he obtained an etching of it. Illustration III-XIII-21

The night was a sordid, restless one; I being feverish and tormented by bouts of nausea. I resisted the urges of nature, until compelled to rise.

Sleep came in waves, which when it came, contained both riotous and repellent dreams, which just as suddenly turned pleasant and idyllic, then once again changed to nightmares, inflicting the grossest anxiety. One such dream was one in which I seemed to watch a cavorting woman prancing around a distressed looking lobster holding a staff or spear. I awoke with a start having been aroused both in my hunger and dark desires, unsettling. I later made the mistake of telling Perkins who seems to take great joy in my description of it.

The awful night dragged on endlessly. I had pain in the limbs but I continued my childhood resistance to pain in the head, which all the others complained of greatly. There was concern for Bannington, who had seemed at first to be the least affected, but who had now taken a turn for the worse. The matter is made no better by the heat of the day, which must have been in the high nineties. We repaired at dusk to the roof, where a light wind could be felt. By dawn I was tired, but alive, yet obstinate attacks continued to assail me, and mad dreams tormented me. In the late morning, I fell asleep and woke to the sounds of activity all around me. I found myself to be downstairs again. Surprisingly, Bannington had recovered fully and Michaelson was up and attending to us. Everyone appeared to be better now. Hynes was most annoyed at our illness. He and I took what seemed to us to be a long, dreamy, walk to where the horses were. In reality it was but fifty feet away, but it seemed more like an hour. Amazingly, in the circumstances, they were well groomed and fed. We had paid in advance for their care, and for once, Persian inefficiency had not raised its ugly head.

We both make our beds just in time as fatigue nearly crumples us to the floor.

Saturday 24 June

I wake in the darkness and feel fully well. I bathe myself in the water I find; the water in Asterabad being the best we have encountered recently, as this comes straight from the mountains and is most refreshing. I find my watch has run down and I have no idea what time it is. It is very dark and I look in on the horses. All is well with Blonde and the others. I become bored as I have nothing to read so I go to the station's fowl pen and secure one at a time eight chickens, the commotion of the third raises the master of the station and I pay him well for the pleasure. I get a fairly clean copper pot set up; a fire built, and am now aided by Hynes who has risen too. We clean the chickens, something I had not done for some time; the blood of it and the smell nearly unmans me again, and I believe Hynes notices it. I pass it off as weakness from the illness, but I am not sure I am successful in deceiving him and his all-knowing eyes.

There were no vegetables to be had, but some spices are obtained from our stores and the eight chickens are soon at a boil. I also placed on skewers theirs livers, kidneys, gizzards and hearts and plan to serve them separately mainly because I do not like the taste of liver in soup. When finished, I enjoy waking everyone and giving them bowls of *soupe au poulet {chicken soup}* and a skewer of sweetmeats, they are greatly appreciative. I eat several bowls myself. By the breaking of dawn, all are awake, and we spend the time eating the soup and walking about and discussing this illness, which has been defeated, it would seem.

Horne and Vickery started an escalating battle of flung chicken hearts, which was soon joined in by all of us. Soon our room was spattered everywhere with bits of chicken heart. Nevertheless, our spirits were lifted, and I was given much praise, and I felt for a time like 'Ude' *{Louis Eustache, a famous French cook at Crockford's, a private club notably earning a salary of £1,200 yearly during Driscol's time in London}*

Sunday 25 June

Dissanayake has become our vicar by public acclaim, with his popularity based on the shortness of his sermons and the directness of his ceremony. I enjoyed at times his short sermons the last had two good quotes;

> *Moreover as for me, God forbid that I should sin against the Lord in ceasing to pray for you: but I will teach you the good and the right way. I Samuel xii, 23*

> *For to do whatsoever thy hand and thy counsel determined before to be done. Acts 4, 25-28*

He also notes that yesterday was the Nativity of St. John the Baptist, and Horne suggested that we obtain a sheep's head on a platter for our supper. He was soundly boo'd and hissed for that remark.

It rains this day, so we stay in, killing pests and cleaning our luggage of the grime accumulated in our journey from Teheran, and in some cases, from the trip from Bushire and Bombay.

We had some soup for tiffin, and Horne noted that it tasted of horse. Michaelson observed that the French held horsemeat in high regard, and told the folkloric tale of the French army surgeon, Dominique-Jean Larrey, who at the battle of Aspern-Essling *{1809, Napoleon versus the Austrians}*, had the wounded fed from a bouillon of horse meat, seasoned with gunpowder.

Dobbins said that on occasion, he had seasoned meat with gunpowder. The fire burns away the powder cleanly and leaves a salty taste from the nitre, our two cavalry men, one real and one wishful, Bannington and Horne, not to be outdone in a discussion of eating their favourite animals, noted that saltpetre had another effect on a man's plumbing. There was a great amusement about this.

Somehow the dialogue veered off onto a discussion of the Catholic relief act of 1829, which allowed Catholic Parliamentarians to sit in Parliament. I remember my father being adamantly against it. In our group, Horne, Dissanayake, Perkins, and Bannington were against it and the rest for it. This was lively debate indeed. Horne's position however, I found both sacrosanct and sanctimonious. Bannington switched his position after some consideration and after one outrageous comment on the *recreancy {Unfaithfulness or disloyally}* of Catholics to the Crown. He observed that he must soon write to the Royal Society of Linguistics on the insufficiency of the parameters within the tone of voice in English. To wit, it's in communicating to others a sense of irony, when someone speaks of duplicity in others, and demonstrates that they have not the brains God has seen fit to gift to a chicken. He made this statement after Horne had added to the debate the following, which I wrote down, so as to not miss its delicious words.

I am not so young as to not remember some of the learned men of the county and especially the Vicar who remonstrated against teaching the poor to read and write, and they were right in my opinion to have done so.

After Bannington's comment, Horne made a rude noise, and Hynes observed that a certain gentleman's reasoning were not the caricature of reason, but an insult to the caricature of blunder.

I tended to avoid the conversation, but was brought into it by Hynes, who wanted to know what I thought on the matter? I said I thought it was dribble.

This brought up a storm of protest; did I not mean 'drivel', instead? No I meant dribble as drivel is a singular term for a poor statement and dribble is the plural meaning of a great deal of said poor statements. This was all grammatical nonsense, as I well knew, but it brought the debate thankfully to an end.

We had noted that it was impossible to approach closer than seven feet to Hynes, before he would wake up. His watchfulness was unusually acute, Thus, Bannington and Horne contrived to

challenge the proverbial 'piss in the ear of sleeping weasel' by making a certain amount of background noise and having Bannington, barefooted, slowly approach their prey. In his hand he had a particularly loathsome insect to place on Hynes' forehead.

He got to within an arms distance of the sleeping Hynes, as we all held our breath, but as he bent slowly down, Hynes without opening his eyes stated;

'If Mr Bannington wishes me to observe him eating that thing, I would pray he continue'.

He did not.

To the right is a scene from within the Caravanserai, and above outside it, where a mosque and its comings and goings caught Driscol's eye. Illustration III-XIII-22 & 23

A street scene in Asterabad; showing the many trees that grew
within the walled city. Illustration III-XIII-24

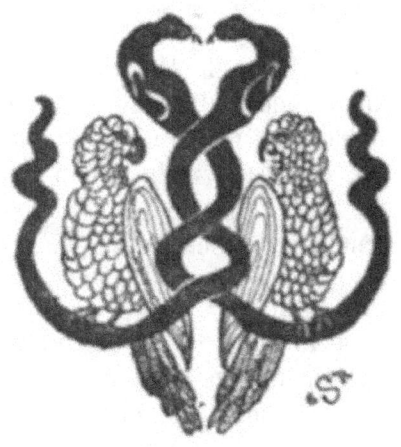

Preparations And News Of War

Monday 26 June

Having recovered our health, and seeing no sign of our guide as of yet, Perkins decrees that we must prepare ourselves for our journey. This is to consist of gathering as much information as we can, from the locals, on the nature of the Turcoman who control the entrance to Turcomania and Tartary.

Perkins and I are entertained, as we see now the reasoning behind the HEIC wanting us to go by way of Afghanistaun. From there, we could have made the upper reaches of the Oxus River by going north of Cabul. Thence we could have gone down river to Khiva and on to the Aral Sea. However getting to Afghanistaun might have been much more of an effort than traveling through Persia. Whereas here we had the great support of the mission and the invaluable aid of the Shah himself, whose directions and words seemed to motivate even the most languorous of his subjects; usually, but not always.

A Barid rider has come in from Teheran, with the news that the Shah has left with his staff to bring war to Herat, and he has brought orders for the governor of the province and city to bring their forces to the border of Afghanistaun forthwith.

All of this I find out in the bazaar, for the stalls are full of men speaking of this matter. I come, by chance, to find Saman, the studying son of the Mollah I had met before at the game of *As*. He is troubled by this news, as our friend the Captain, who was also at the game, is in the bazaar. That soldier is making purchases, for he will join the army going to the East to engage the Afghanis. Saman is like most young men.

[Editor's note: Driscol underlined the words 'like most young men' and put several examination points, obviously he felt the same]

He is considering putting off his studies to join the war, and I support his eagerness. I am joined by Dobbins and Saman. Finding that we were a party of foreigners, he invited us to take supper with his family the following night. Saman's father, or so he says, is always eager to speak to foreigners on the matters of Europe, religion and science.

Perkins and the others have now shown up, all but Michaelson and Vickery who are on guard duty of our horses and property, something one must always do in Persia.

So it has happened; Persia will be at war with Afghanistaun. Perkins and I had discussed the possibility of this, and it is both a hindrance and a help. It is trouble, as the Crown supports the integrity of Afghanistaun. Nothing noble will come of Persia taking the city. It is good for our cover story, as it will mean that the country will be in an upheaval and our idea of posing as horse dealers, not only for stock for our supposed homeland in the Caucasus, but also for both Afghanistaun and Persia. War is cruel on horses, and their casualties many, so our quest for them might not seem in anyway unusual.

I accompany Bannington as he and I go to banter with the natives about horses. The others go on about their various tasks. I have a fair appreciation of a horse, but Bannington is by far the greatest expert I have encountered; overshadowing Horne's abilities. He seems to be able to pick up a harrowed or ill horse at fifty paces. That one has colic he would say, that one has a disturbance in its blood, which he can tell from the consistency of its droppings, another has yellow mucus around it eyes, another has a higher than normal body temperature, which he determines by feeling its feet. Yet another he decries as temperamental by the way it stamps its hoofs, he detects laminitis in another, while a third has an infestation of ticks. A few horses had been dyed to hide various colourings that the Persians don't like. Some parts of the horses we examined had been henna'd, imparting that orange colour that men like to dye their beards with in the East. I am told that women do so to their hands. Henna is said to make the horse nobler, and as it can be expensive to do, is a mark of a leader or wealthy man. I leave him at the market, yelling back and forth with dealers. His Persian is good enough to point out the deficiencies of their stock in great detail to the sellers, who are taken aback by a foreigner speaking to them in such a way. As I left I could hear his strong tenor voice telling one dealer.

> 'This horse, this horse my good sir is *bee namak {humorless, dry not good}* and you *khar bar sar-et {dirt on your head - you should die}* for trying to sell this to a *ba namak {salty or good}* person like me'.

Having made some purchases, I planned out what we needed to do for the next few days. We were guideless and the officials of the town were running about like Arabs with their heads cut off due to the news that the Shah had moved to attack Herat - despite their having been warned of this months before. Incidentally, a Persian will substitute the term 'Arab' in the phrase above instead of 'chicken' as we know the idiom.

We are left to our own devices in all things now. I determine that the best way is to use Saman's father to gain access to information on the Turcoman and on the best way to pass the Persian frontier and into their country.

[Editor's note: However, Driscol doesn't tell us how he plans to do that!]

Half of the expedition does not smoke; myself, Perkins, Vickery and Michaelson. The rest did and they had come to the following conclusions.

Based on their avid sampling of Persian wares, and in spite of the various fancy names applied to them, there were in reality only three grades of smoking products available in the bazaars. The medium brand consisted of $\frac{1}{4}$ to $\frac{1}{2}$ of dried horse dung, while the premier products had the same proportion of said material but from a sheep, while the common folk must make do with that from a goat. Hynes and Dobbins, however, only rarely smoke cigars, as they are devotees of the hookah or water-pipe. None of the others find it approachable for entertainment or enjoyment. When I discussed this with Hynes, he corrected me on my error. He did not use a hookah to produce smoke, as did Dobbins, but instead he preferred to use it to melt the tobacco mix which produces a vapour. Thereby it is called a *nargile*, which he takes into his mouth but not his lungs, while Dobbins takes the smoke internally.

We have moved to a larger room in the caravanserai, and by our efforts, and those of the man who we had hired, we have made it cleaner. The Persian makes no use of tables or chairs, so none are to be found, but a chest, boxes and other objects are used to make our furniture. That night, we have our dinner, a fine dish of rice and 'splintered' pigeon.

[Editor's note: despite an exhaustive search, I could not ascertain what 'splintered' meant in this context but I will advocate for it being deboned and shredded]

We play cards, and noticed that we had made a mistake in our planning, which we by a unanimous vote, we blame on Vickery, who is on guard duty, and so he cannot vote against it. The complaint is concerning his not having the foresight to bring more decks of cards, as those that we have are starting to wear out, and he had, of course, dropped one card into the fire earlier. I have noted that the Queen of spades has a slightly curled tip, which being a complete middle-class gentleman I feel I do not need to mention to the others.

Many are the subjects discussed at the card table, as during the day, the men had made many inquiries. Dissanayake suggested that as opium grows in these parts, we should gather to us a supply of the pernicious article; to which Michaelson agrees, and we plan an expedition to a place where it is manufactured. This brought us to a discussion of what were the gifts that the three wise men or kings brought to Jesus. It was decided by our First Council of Asterabad that;

[Editor's note: I believe Driscol was being droll here and he was referring to The First Council of Nicaea where the tenets of Christendom were hashed out in 325 AD]

That the men may have been Persian Magi, but they represented Christian thought, held that they were the King of Arabia, Melchior who brought the gold, Caspar the King of Tarsus, who gifted Jesus with Frankincense and finally, the King of Ethiopia, Balthazar who brought myrrh. Dissanayake's suggestion that the latter had brought opium was dismissed as nonsense and we outvoted him. He responded to our intellectual tyranny against him by winning four hands in a row, and taking control of our supply of small, worthless, bronze coins that we carry around for this purpose.

It was at this time that we all began to become ill again. Michaelson thought it must be the pigeon, which had been purchased by Horne, who declared that said the merchant had claimed that they had been fed on figs, and indeed they had been very sweet and toothsome. Our physician thought instead that they may have been like *Coturnix coturnix {quail}* that eats hemlock and sickens the man who eats them. We all found that our water *{Urine}* had turned green, which frightened all of us, but the discomfort left us after an uncomfortable few hours, and before Michaelson, his eyes bright in anticipation of an experiment to be done, could dose us with his purges and scald our insides with his mixtures.

Having recovered, and drunk the last bottle of wine, the others said goodbye to that happy spirit, that they seem to worship, and which is nearly impossible to replace here. We have some other spirits but that was the last of the European wines. Perkins, also much to his regret, drank the last of his own private wine supply. He did, nonetheless, convinced me and the others to share the last of it. I dutifully obeyed and sipped it and found it would, if aged ten or more years, make a fine start for a lethal rat poison, but I am a hater of fine wine, or so I am told. The others however found it most delightful, with a wonderful flavour of fruit. They spoke happily about it for fifteen minutes or so and chided Perkins for not having shared it before.

Perkins' last bottle of Lillet. Illustrations III-XIII-25*(C)* TheWhiskyExchange.com by their permission

So I happily said goodbye to the Lillet wine of *L'Hexagone {France}* while the others thought of it as the loss of a newly found and aromatic friend.

[Editor's note: Driscol calls it Lillet while present day Lillet came into existence in 1872. I have not yet found an answer to this conundrum but believe another unrecorded wine of that name existed before the current version]

Tuesday 27 June

Bannington made an extraordinary find this morning when he was in the stable. He found on the wall a small inscription in a place where a man lying down might easily reach. How he noted it is remarkable in itself for it was in English in ½ inch letters.

'WYBUR# IX-IX-XXXV TOM##ROW WOULD BE #WEET IF W# COULD KILL YESTERDAY'.

[Editor's note: I have place # symbols where Driscol placed a combination of an ☠, !, and § mark for missing letters. Emails to Iranian officials determined that the caravanserai was torn down in 1947 and there are no records of the inscription]

We all found this of the greatest curiosity and searched the building thoroughly but found no more markings, nor did anyone at the caravanserai, among the staff remember him. We imagined a situation where he bedded down and scratched the above while unable to sleep. His comment drew from us many hours of discussion over what it might mean.

(...)

I had the opportunity, while we were checking our horses' hooves for thrush and stones, to examine in detail Dobbin's chatelaine, which he had kept well-wrapped in our journey up to this point. It is a fine device. It is a strongly made and undecorated attachment to his belt which hangs down on a chain and ends in a leather bag where the device is hidden from dust and insult.

CAPT. HAYES'
HORSEMAN'S KNIFE.

Dobbins' device sounded similar to Captain Hayes' Horseman's knife, which is shown in this advertisement from 1883. Illustration III-XIII-26

These are an assortment of interesting and useful devices. There are:

A vinaigrette or scent holder. Illustration III-XIII-27

A small knife, A small hoof pick *{for cleaning stones out of a horse's foot}*, Nail knife *{clippers, as we have now, had not been invented yet}*, Tweezers, Ear scoop, His seal, Scissors, Thimble, An awl like device, A small vinaigrette.

[Editor's note: Vinaigrette; no not salad dressing. In the early 19th century vinaigrette stood for a small bottle that held perfume or other liquids]

His vinaigrette he shared with me and one sniff brought forth a flood of thoughts of Penelope; for it was a container of her perfume. I told him that I was envious of him and regretted not having such a reminder of Millicent. I thought too that had I obtained such, it would have been of hyacinth and lilac a mix of scent she preferred versus plumeria *{did Jonaki, his bibi, like plumeria or is this reference to his mother who loved the scent also?}*

The big man mentions that at their last meeting, he had given her a nosegay *{a posy or tussie mussie a flower with herbs and dolly}*. He was quite pleased, that upon its presentation, she had held it at heart level, which indicated her acceptance of his love. Had she handed it back or pointed it to the floor, or worse yet thrown it to the floor, his heart would have been crushed.

[Editor's note: The Europeans of this time, and the British in particular, assigned all matters of importance to flowers; floriography was the study of the secret meaning of flowers, herbs and other scents. I deleted several comments by Driscol, which showed that his understanding of this 'code' was at best, incomplete, if not entirely lacking]

Perkins was full of information about the meaning of flowers, and I chide him for not sharing with me this important wisdom. He is quite amused to find I know nothing of it, and he promises, in our future dull rides, to inform me thusly.

It is a hotter today, as we ride out to a place some three miles from the town. We take with us our live tiffin; some squawking chickens, one of which, Hynes says, sounds just like Hymison.

We came across the opium factory behind a stout wall, on a rise off the road to Meshed, sited on a sharply raised hill. Several hundred feet from it, the wind shifted, and brought to our noses the not unpleasant smell of its product. This pungent, sweetish, smell hung over the place, and grew stronger as we grew near.

There were guards at the gate, who were to say the least, astounded that six foreigners, with permissions from the Shah himself, had shown up to see them. We in turn were surprised to find an Indian face in command of the guards, the round face of a corpulent Bengali it seemed to me, a man from Orissa *{Odisha}*.

He was less than happy to see us, but his Persian was excellent, and he knew well the seals on our papers. I suspected at once that he was an exile from the sub-continent, and no supporter of the HEIC. However he took us in, although we had to disarm before entering, as we were entering a treasure trove.

The building had once been a proud house, I suspect, destroyed by Turcoman raiders or during the civil wars, and it had been rebuilt with a concern for structure, strength and survivability and not for beauty. Amartya Banerjee, or just Banerjee, was our host. This period of the year was the time that the containers of raw opium came down the road from Afghanistaun, from the Eastern border of Persia, where it grows. They came in crude brown earthenware jars; ones I had seen in many a Persian, Indian, Turkish or Arab bazaar. They contain the brownish mass, which is the juice of the poppy pod from the plant known as Persian white or *Papaver somniferum*.

We found that this 'factory' was here, instead of the more logical location of the Eastern border, due to a decision taken a generation earlier by the governor of that area, who had been a Kajar.

Being a member of the ruling family, and having decided to retire, he had brought the enterprise here to keep it firmly under family control. The handlers and workers were all Orissians and Bengalis. They were Muhammadans but not Persians; with the exception of the guards who were from the Dari {a dialect of Persian} speaking Tajik people - as the Tajiks do not divide themselves into tribes, but by their provenance, and these came from the Panjsheri Valley.

Each year, one-thousand to two-thousand five hundred tons of the brownish sap comes to this place. Here the Indians test it for purity, for the chances of adulteration are high. Michaelson found the testing for this of great interest. They detect impure opium by testing each vessel with sordine {Iodine?}, which will show it has been it has been adulterated with arrowroot, and by dosing a sample with alcohol to see if another plant secretion has been added to cheat the buyer. If this is found, and each jar is marked from where it came from, the payment to that organisation is reduced.

Once the purity of the opium has been confirmed, it is mixed with other batches. The approved supplies of the substance are then poured into a large copper kettle, where some five hundred pounds of the substance is then mixed and pounded with long wood mallets.

There were four Indians, whose sole duty was to scrap every morsel from the delivery jars. These scrapings are then taken to dry. The question as to why they dry only these scraping was not answered and the look on our guide' face when we asked it was one of a parent being asked by a child why the sky is blue for the thousandth time.

That dried material is then used to make opium tea. We were offered some, and a more vile drink cannot be imagined, however Dissanayake found it somewhat palatable, but you would have to be utterly desperate to drink that swill.

The primary product is repackaged into the jars, which are sealed with gutta-percha, and a label is placed on it with a cord, saying when it was made and where. It is these jars that I had seen in the market places. A seller then scoops out of it the amount his customer might want. Each jar holds around eight pounds of the substance.

Michaelson asked our irritable guide if he knew of the work of Serturner and the product he had refined from opium which he called morphine[12]? He did not, nor was he interested in finding out about it. He was following a method of production that his father had taught him, it was all HE was interested in. Other than the revolting opium tea, he offered us no refreshments. He would not sell us any, and were told we could buy it in the market place.

Having completed the tour, and seeing that our host had tired of our presence, we made our thanks and departed. I was glad to get away from there, as that scent had begun to make me feel unwell.

Our tiffin was our next concern, and by going south, off the road towards the tree line, we soon came to a woodcutter's yard, where fallen timber had been left unfinished. There was of course plentiful wood for a fire, and sections of logs, some two to four feet in diameter to sit on. Our hired man was preparing the chickens in an unusual way; having dispatched them in the Islamic manner, instead of burning off or plucking the feathers he simply skinned the birds. It was faster but one did lose the taste of the skin. As he skinned one, he placed it on a cleaned plank on one

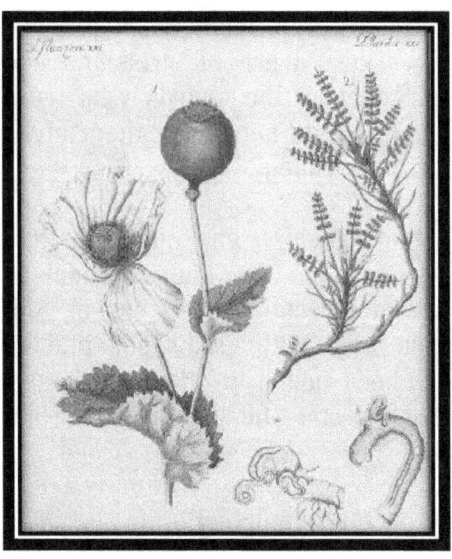

of the larger logs that lay there. I was sitting comfortably writing down these lines, when a movement in the corner of my eye caused me to look to my left.

Opium the 'beneficial plant'; or so it was called in the 19th century. The storage of the prepared drug, as seen by Driscol, in the factory outside Asterabad. Illustrations III-XIII-28 & 29

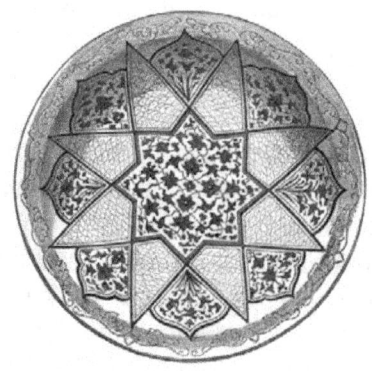

A Visitor Comes For Lunch But Leaves Before Pudding

Behind the labouring mess man, his hand drenched in blood, was the log where three stripped chickens lay on the plank, but they did not garner my interest, it was the head that now rose slowly above them, the white and orange of a tiger. He was looking at the man, and I froze. Living in Eccles, one is not prepared to meet a tiger, while waiting for lunch, and when one does,

one is somewhat confounded. After a long moment of confusion I decided not to shout and reached for My Frenchman.

A Turanian tiger.
Illustration III-XIII-30

The tiger turned his head to my movement, observed me a moment, gulped down one chicken, and seizing a second, turned and plunged away.

I stood up and finally was able to shout TIGER and ran past the astounded cook to the log and saw the tiger in full run, some hundred feet away. I got of one hurried shot before he was lost in the wood line nearby. Dobbins ran up, and looked on in amazement. He had his double-barreled rifle up, as did Horne. He immediately vaulted the log, was tripped up by a stray branch, fell over a slight embankment, and landed in what must have been a depression that had been filled with the leaves of the cut down trees. His weight caused him to crash down into it, releasing a cloud of insects which came at us from the rotted leaves with a vengeance, for we had disturbed THEIR luncheon it would seem. Dobbins was hip deep in this soft and rotted mass of wood and leaves and it took us some time to recover him. He made his displeasure well known. What bothered him most was how had the tiger come across it? To that we had no answer.

Dobbins had sighted the tiger at the same time as I had, and had been slower at reaching for his gun; so slow that the tiger had not even looked at him, but it had taken off before he could get it to his shoulder.

Our Persian helper, now recovered from his shock, said that the tiger had been a spirit one and not a real one. The fact that two chickens were missing did not change his mind on his declaration.

For a few minutes, everyone talked at one. I was relieved that they did not think me mistaken or flighty, for Dissanayake and Bannington had also seen the tiger as he ran. We were flabbergasted; half of us chattering like children and the others speechless.

Dobbins, Bannington and Michaelson cautiously followed her trail, for Dobbins had announced our tiger a female, probably recently delivered of a whelp, and that the first chicken had been a *hors d'oeuvres* for her, and the second for her young charge.

Dobbins was all for going after the beast, and could not be dissuaded by the lack of beaters, no useful knowledge of the local terrain, no dogs, or the lack of proper arms for the rest of us.

It was about two minutes after this encounter that out of the woods came a great roar. I remembered the old myth that the roar of a tiger; that is close and hungry, is enough to causes a disturbance in the blood and bowel. I found this myth to be no legend.

It was Hynes who broke the spell with a contemptuous grunt and reminded us that the 'kitten' had relieved us of two thirds of our rations and he had. Our resolve began to recede, assaulted by the tiger's roars and a sergeant's disdain and our pledge to Perkins. He and Vickery were on guard duty back in Asterabad and Perkins had agreed to our side trip, but only after he had insisted that we agree to come back that afternoon, with no excuses. We were on our honour to return, so we desisted from embarking on the hazardous hunt as we were to have dinner with the Sayid that night that and our horses were nearly mad with fear and wished to be gone from this place.

Dobbins could talk of nothing but tigers during our limited lunch, and he told us several stories of the tigers he had hunted in India.

It was Dobbins' opinion that all men should hunt tigers. Those who did so successfully could be counted as men of greatness. He was awarded for this statement with thrown chicken bones, and general abuse, as by implication he was suggesting that we were lesser creatures for not having shot tigers.

We arrived back in Asterabad, where Perkins and Vickery did not believe our tale of the tiger, pointing out that we were probably addled by the opium tea and the toxic atmosphere of the factory. Secretly, I found that theory plausible, but then rejected it, as we would all have all had to have the same, shared, delusion of losing our luncheon chickens.

Dobbins did advocate that once we returned to India, we should all go on a tiger hunt; Perkins thought this a capital idea and declared it to be one of our post journey objectives.

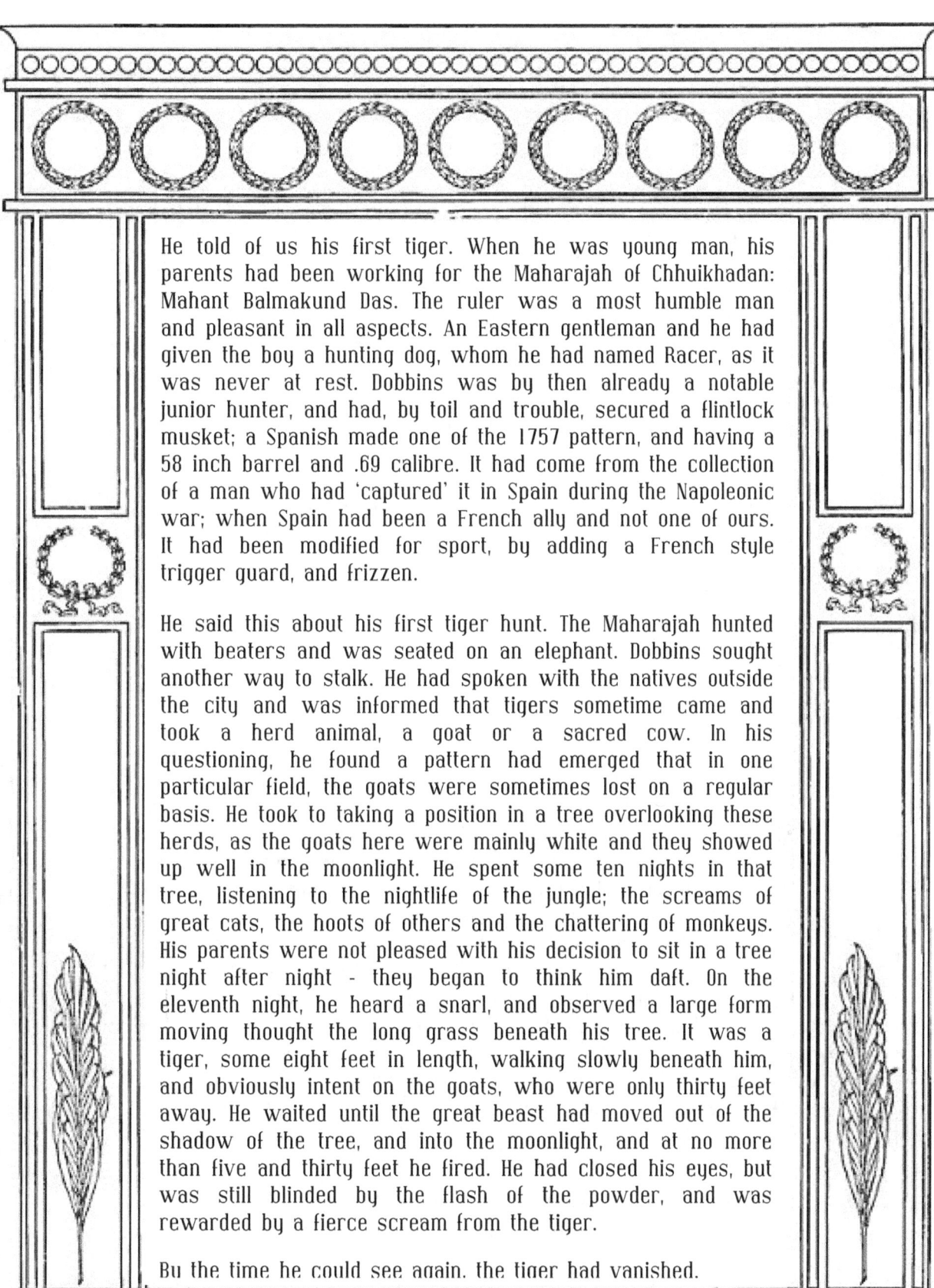

He told of us his first tiger. When he was young man, his parents had been working for the Maharajah of Chhuikhadan: Mahant Balmakund Das. The ruler was a most humble man and pleasant in all aspects. An Eastern gentleman and he had given the boy a hunting dog, whom he had named Racer, as it was never at rest. Dobbins was by then already a notable junior hunter, and had, by toil and trouble, secured a flintlock musket; a Spanish made one of the 1757 pattern, and having a 58 inch barrel and .69 calibre. It had come from the collection of a man who had 'captured' it in Spain during the Napoleonic war; when Spain had been a French ally and not one of ours. It had been modified for sport, by adding a French style trigger guard, and frizzen.

He said this about his first tiger hunt. The Maharajah hunted with beaters and was seated on an elephant. Dobbins sought another way to stalk. He had spoken with the natives outside the city and was informed that tigers sometime came and took a herd animal, a goat or a sacred cow. In his questioning, he found a pattern had emerged that in one particular field, the goats were sometimes lost on a regular basis. He took to taking a position in a tree overlooking these herds, as the goats here were mainly white and they showed up well in the moonlight. He spent some ten nights in that tree, listening to the nightlife of the jungle; the screams of great cats, the hoots of others and the chattering of monkeys. His parents were not pleased with his decision to sit in a tree night after night - they began to think him daft. On the eleventh night, he heard a snarl, and observed a large form moving thought the long grass beneath his tree. It was a tiger, some eight feet in length, walking slowly beneath him, and obviously intent on the goats, who were only thirty feet away. He waited until the great beast had moved out of the shadow of the tree, and into the moonlight, and at no more than five and thirty feet he fired. He had closed his eyes, but was still blinded by the flash of the powder, and was rewarded by a fierce scream from the tiger.

By the time he could see again, the tiger had vanished.

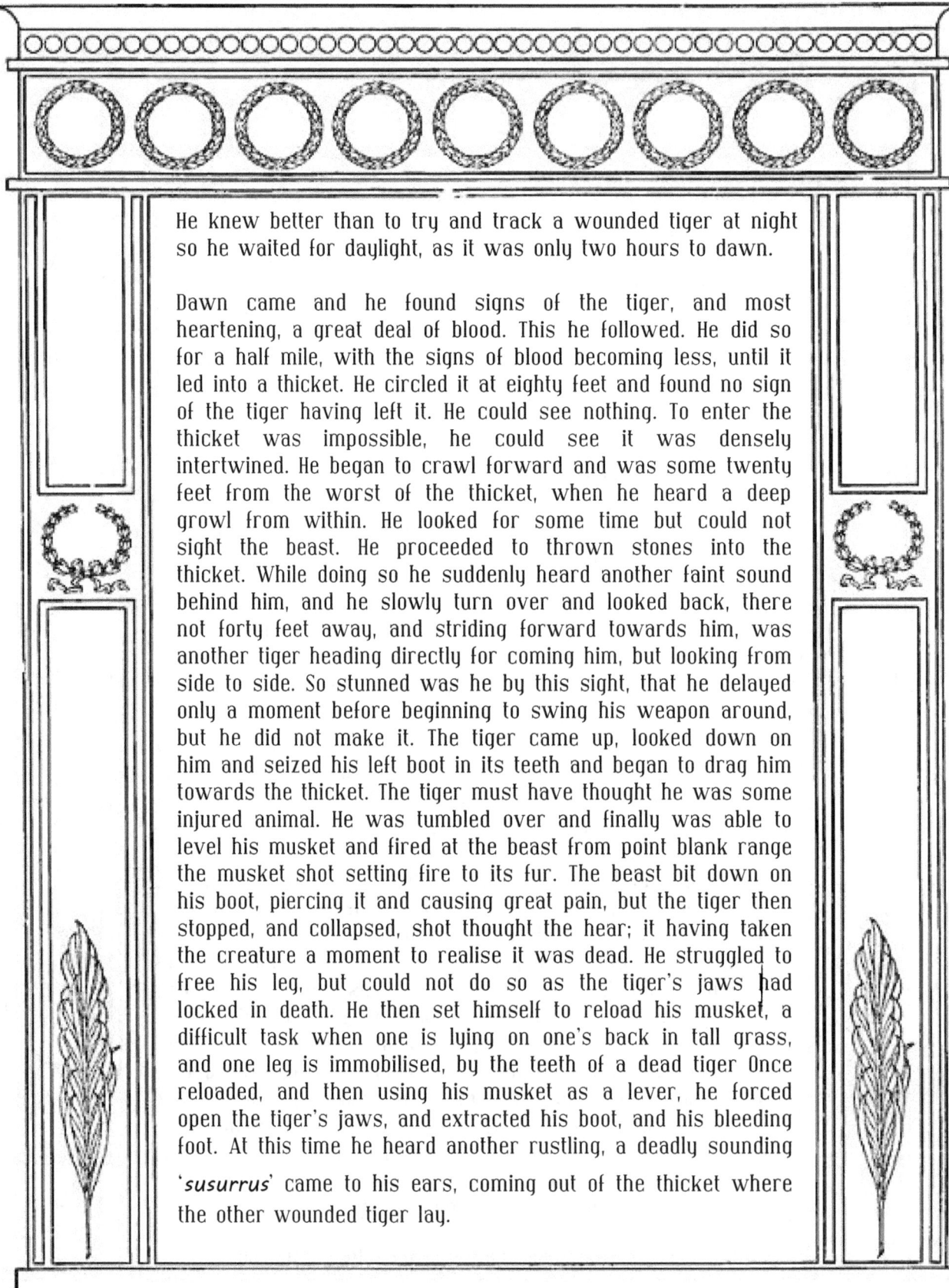

He knew better than to try and track a wounded tiger at night so he waited for daylight, as it was only two hours to dawn.

Dawn came and he found signs of the tiger, and most heartening, a great deal of blood. This he followed. He did so for a half mile, with the signs of blood becoming less, until it led into a thicket. He circled it at eighty feet and found no sign of the tiger having left it. He could see nothing. To enter the thicket was impossible, he could see it was densely intertwined. He began to crawl forward and was some twenty feet from the worst of the thicket, when he heard a deep growl from within. He looked for some time but could not sight the beast. He proceeded to thrown stones into the thicket. While doing so he suddenly heard another faint sound behind him, and he slowly turn over and looked back, there not forty feet away, and striding forward towards him, was another tiger heading directly for coming him, but looking from side to side. So stunned was he by this sight, that he delayed only a moment before beginning to swing his weapon around, but he did not make it. The tiger came up, looked down on him and seized his left boot in its teeth and began to drag him towards the thicket. The tiger must have thought he was some injured animal. He was tumbled over and finally was able to level his musket and fired at the beast from point blank range the musket shot setting fire to its fur. The beast bit down on his boot, piercing it and causing great pain, but the tiger then stopped, and collapsed, shot thought the hear; it having taken the creature a moment to realise it was dead. He struggled to free his leg, but could not do so as the tiger's jaws had locked in death. He then set himself to reload his musket, a difficult task when one is lying on one's back in tall grass, and one leg is immobilised, by the teeth of a dead tiger Once reloaded, and then using his musket as a lever, he forced open the tiger's jaws, and extracted his boot, and his bleeding foot. At this time he heard another rustling, a deadly sounding

'*susurrus*' came to his ears, coming out of the thicket where the other wounded tiger lay.

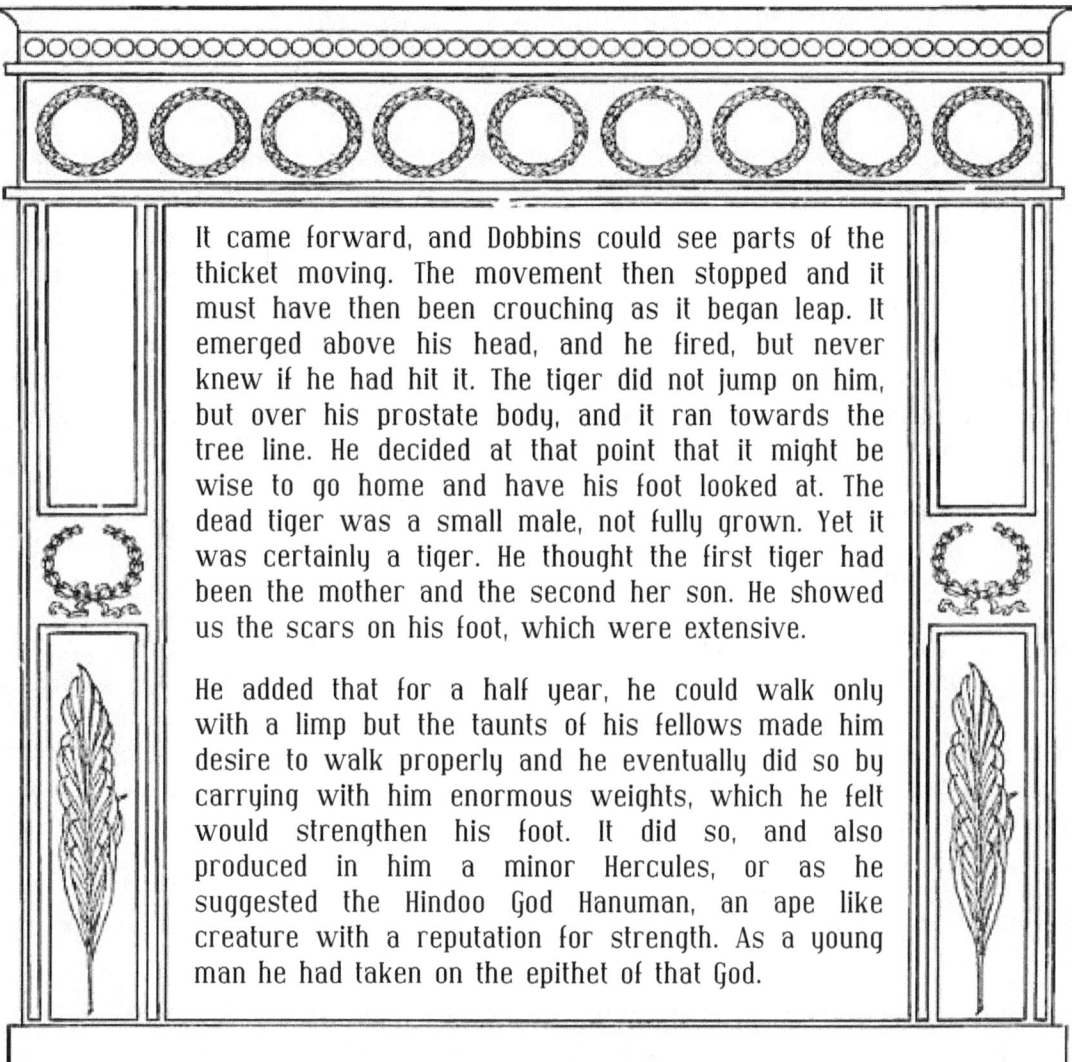

It came forward, and Dobbins could see parts of the thicket moving. The movement then stopped and it must have then been crouching as it began leap. It emerged above his head, and he fired, but never knew if he had hit it. The tiger did not jump on him, but over his prostate body, and it ran towards the tree line. He decided at that point that it might be wise to go home and have his foot looked at. The dead tiger was a small male, not fully grown. Yet it was certainly a tiger. He thought the first tiger had been the mother and the second her son. He showed us the scars on his foot, which were extensive.

He added that for a half year, he could walk only with a limp but the taunts of his fellows made him desire to walk properly and he eventually did so by carrying with him enormous weights, which he felt would strengthen his foot. It did so, and also produced in him a minor Hercules, or as he suggested the Hindoo God Hanuman, an ape like creature with a reputation for strength. As a young man he had taken on the epithet of that God.

Dining With Abu Saman And Friends

We had some difficulty in finding the Sayid's house, but arrived fashionably late, as timeliness is not a trait one can note in the Persian race. Our (in my mind) shameless tardiness was overlooked as unimportant, as it was of no matter. Had we shown up on time, this would have been deemed decisively unusual, if early, insulting and a sign of folly. We were graciously welcomed to his dwelling, which in the front had a pleasant garden, and we were brought into a room, where we passed the time. There were the six of us; Michaelson had volunteered not to go as his Persian would not be up to the challenge. The same excuse applied to Dissanayake but our subsequent experience showed he could have easily followed some of the conversations. We left them on guard and looking forward to a meal of cold flat bread and well-cooked mutton.

There were some twenty Persians there. Saman's father insisted we call him Abu Saman {father of Saman}. The son and father greatly resembled one another, or as the Persians would say, 'He had fallen from his father's nose' their way of saying, 'A chip off the old block'.

We talked of nothing for some time. The Persians were all his relatives and colleagues. All had come speak to and see the foreigners who could speak Persian. A Persian is not amazed that a foreigner would speak his language any more than an Englishman is at all awed that a Frenchman speaks English. It is considered a normal thing. He should understand, shouldn't he? That is the way the world should be, but an Englishman is always interested in what an English speaking foreigner might know.

[Editor's note: Driscol use of 'shouldn't' is interesting as he normally avoided contractions this is one of his few times he did so]

After a short time learning names, which I immediately disregarded, we were taken into another room; a mighty dining hall some five and thirty feet in length, with a beautiful carpet down the centre, resplendent in pronounced, coloured, geometric, patterns and around it cushions of the finest silks. On the walls, hung more carpets, in the colours of red, blue and brown.

The clerics of Shia Islam do not traffic with ideas of poverty being an achievement or wealth being a sin.

In the centre was laid out a feast, two great platters heaped with rice, and atop them each a half of a large sheep, displayed with fruit; and so the evening began.

So much was said, and I must say the fellowship in the room was quite inviting. I can only remember a fraction of what was discussed. Most of Abu Saman's colleagues and relatives were Mollahs and were in what Perkins dismissingly called the 'God business'. As most foreigners do, they asked questions about Europe and Christians.

Some of the idiosyncrasies that came out in these dialogues were that these men held; (for their scientific knowledge was replete with opinion but barren of fact), that the moon is the image of the Earth, and is not a solid body. It is a reflection of some sort. They used a number of Persian terms I did not know, but I learned this after from Hynes, who is our best for understanding their morphology. One aged relative understood that Europeans held that there were lands in the West. Yes we told them: two great continents. The man dismissed this as impossible, as he had seen maps made by noble Muslims in past centuries. How could Allah and the Prophet not know of these lands? This 'Americas' cannot exist, he declared. We said nothing to this bizarre claim and I noted that Hynes, our 'American' smiled broadly during that time.

The Persian cosmology was a thing of unthinkable construction, and amongst themselves, there was great disagreement, a mixture of Hebrew and Babylonian mischief.

In Driscol's collection is this image which he labels as the Persian cosmology

but it is not. Instead it is the much earlier Hebrew cosmology, perhaps adapted by the Persians through the Zoroastrian tradition. See Appendix III-IV for discussion of Babylonian Cosmology, which the Persians also believed in. Illustration III-XIII-31

Another Mollah demanded to know if it was true that the English red coats came from the blood of slaughtered Hindoos? He did not seem to believe us, when we said they were simply dyed. Another, his uncle I believe, as they had a family resemblance in ignorance, had heard that British officers and officials were made smart by drinking a sorcerous brew that came from the collected and decanted brains of African slaves. I nearly laughed at this one, but it was asked in all seriousness.

They were all in favour of the Persian attack and war with Afghanistaun over Herat; for the Herati spoke Dari, a variant of Persian, should not all Persians be one?

I reflected that this was also the call of the German and Italian speakers that the reciters of the same language should all be in the same nation. While there is some value in this thought, there is also the reward or necessity of constant wars to achieve it.

They had the greatest hatred of the Russians and only slightly less so the Turk, and were utterly contemptuous of the Arab and Indian, but they did hold the Afghani in some regards as a fighter, but hopelessly barbarian and Sunni. They thought the loss of the Christian provinces to the Russians was a sign that the world would soon end; for how could Allah allow such an insult to his people and religion? They did not in any way fear the Russians coming into Tartary. They had been fighting the Turcoman, the Uzbeks and others there for hundreds of years and could not defeat them, so how could the Russians?

Perkins fielded all questions on Christianity; these men had mulched together a whole slew of strange ideas about Christians, mainly influenced by the idolatry of the Eastern Christians and Catholics. We surprised them by demonstrating when we opened our blouses; showing that, we did not wear hair shirts or have crosses tattooed around our necks. Nor did we worship women and yes we thought women have souls. I was able at that point to say that the Bible was in agreement with the Sura-An-Nisa {Chapter of woman} in the Qur'an where the term of soul is used. I was greatly admired for having known such. None of the men in the room had read the Bible of course, so they had no idea what was in it.

We discussed the various similar stories in the Bible and the Qur'an, Cain and Abel or Qabil and Habil, Noah and Nuh, Moses and Musa and several others.

We were, of course, asked if we had tasted pork. We had discussed that one question in depth between ourselves, while afloat in the Persian Gulf. Horne, naturally nearly undid us but Perkins interrupted him to say that we had 'heard' about it from the lower classes, for only the most base people eat it, and that it tastes of veal.

Wine, contrasting with its wide usage at the Shah's meals, was not served. Instead we had sherbet or water with lemon in it.

After a time, we came upon a subject of great interest to us; the Turcoman. I made the observation about what I had seen of them in the market place.

Abu Saman told us, aided by shouted comments from his relatives that the Turcoman was one of the four plagues upon the honest Persian. The first is the Sunni, who spoils the perfect religion of Allah, the second flies who spoils a man's meal, the third Jews who spoil his making of money and the fourth these mounted tribesmen who spoil ones contentment by constant raiding and banditry.

With him leading, the Persians gave forth with a prayer, which in part said;

> *We beseech God to devastate the infidel Turcoman, to have their dwellings burn,*
> *their flocks scattered and taken, their honour abased, and may they find their*
> *horses lame and their women to be unfruitful and untrue*

He said that five great tribes of Turcoman existed to the north, but that these tribes were split into smaller ones and the power and size of some of these smaller divisions equals that of the traditional five tribes. These he listed;

The Saloo *{Salu}* who are considered to be civilised, partially, among these philistines - or so I took his words to mean - barbarians, who live in the area between the borders of Afghanistaun, Persia and the Khanate of Bokhara.

Another grouping called the Sarik Turcomans inhabits the area around the ruined city of Merv. These men control the direct route to Khiva over the desert to the Oxus. They often threaten the holy city of Meshed and are a most cursed race of men.

The largest tribe is the Tekke who live in the desert region to the northwest of Meshed. They are the most nomadic and the most violent of the man stealers.

The Yomuts *{Yohmuds}* to the north of Asterabad between the Caspian and Khiva and north of the mountains called the Khrebet Saandak, they also live on the banks of the Gurgan River which lies just eleven miles to the north of the city.

To the East of them, and between the Tekke, are the Goklans and it was these that I had seen in the Bazaar. They are the most civilised of all the Turcoman. The land they live in is bordered on the south by the Alborz *{Elborz}* Mountains of Persia; to the west by the Caspian Sea, to which they are prevented from going by the great hatred of the Yomuts, who live between them and that sea; to the north the Kara-Kum desert goes all the way to the Oxus and Khiva; To the East is the Khrebet Saandak and they live to the south of it, which separates them from the more dangerous Tekke tribe.

The Persians took a moment out of this discourse to curse them *{the Turcoman}* in the vilest way; it was like hearing Church of England Bishops using the vilest language possible to describe Methodists or Quakers. Mohammedans grudgingly accept the people of the book, but hold the Jews in great contempt, Christians too at times, and they wholly loathe the Hindoo polytheists, but their greatest hatred is towards their own brothers, the Sunni. In this, their eyes will blaze when they talk of it. I was reminded of the 111 Surah of the Qur'an, where the uncle of the Prophet, Abu Lahab is cursed to hell for his slander of Mohammad. Arabs are a hot blooded people, like the Latins, and they take better the insults of those outside their family, than the trespasses of those within in.

Abu Saman also explained why the Persian, did not wipe out these pesky flies *{Turcoman}*. He said that the recruits used for the army are not Persians, but others who suffer from cowardice and are of little worth in waging a war of offence. The Turcoman can choose the time for a raid, are cognisant, all the while, that their families and flocks are safe from a counter-attack. Besides this, the lack of Persian willingness to attack is the fault of the Persian leaders themselves. All along the frontier, men are assigned to command garrisons, and head the militia protecting the population. If the Turcoman would be tamed or driven off and permanently ceased their forays, the Shah would put an end to their commands, and worse yet, take away their salaries, and perhaps send them on military service against the Ottomans, Afghanis or Russian, where a man might get killed for the Turcoman avoids fights with the Persian military, and attacks the civilian population wherever possible. It is due to these facts, that there is every probability of a continuance of the Turcoman raids for eternity or until the world ends. It was my opinion, not expressed openly, that the Persian system of government mingled tyranny with greed and imbecility.

Besides these five main tribes some of the sub-tribes of the Turcoman are of interest for there are four that claim to be descendants from four great men of Islam; the Makhtoum-Khuli are said to be the sons of Abu Bakr; the Khoja clan; who are reputedly the sons of Ali, nephew to the prophet; the Atta, the children of Umar and the Shikhs, the progeny of Osman. It is these smaller sub-tribes that use their influence, and special stature, to move between the other tribes, which are in constant war with one another, and act as merchants, messengers and peacemakers; quite safe from the molestation of the larger tribes.

[Editor's note: the men named above were all notables in the early history of Islam]

I saw that Perkins, Bannington, Dobbins and Hynes had all picked up on this key point, for this was a way to proceed to Khiva and the Aral Sea.

We were disappointed to hear that the Yomuts conducted piracy against the Russian fisherman of the Caspian, having all but destroyed the Persian industry generations ago. We also had not realised our danger in camping on the shore line when we did days ago. Yet now Russian warships had all but swept them from the sea, within the last generation, but sporadic raids, especially in the area we had camped, still occurred.

For good qualities, these Turcoman have some, but are given no credit for them by the Persian. They are considered evil in general, and are only brave in raiding and ambushes, and they will not stand in battle. They prefer the blade and spear and will not often face the matchlock's ball.

951

Their greatest sport and desire is to plunder, all other instincts are subservient to that goal, and his first objective is to loot the Persian, if unable to do so he will target the much more dangerous Russian. If he cannot do that too then he attacks his fellow Turcoman who are even more dangerous and finally against the Osbegs {Uzbeks} of Khiva or the other cities to the East. However these are of even greater danger to the Turcoman, as they have horses as swift as their own. Their next reigning urge is for revenge, not usually for any honourable goal but for sordid gain, they cry they want revenge for this or that but in reality, they want a reason to attack their own, even their own family.

Their main source of income is from slavery; they are expert at this. If a large ransom is not paid immediately for a person so taken, they are sold in the slave markets of Khiva or Bokhara, or are kept to work for the Turcoman. They often seize members of their own tribes and use them to gain horses and sheep from other members. This constant kidnapping is always roiling the Turcoman tribes. Often times they raid the people on their borders to gain the funds or material to ransom someone from their own family taken by a neighbours or an unfriendly tribe or sub-clan. If threatened by a Persian, Khivan or Russian force they will, for a short time join forces to harass it until it withdraws then they will fall out and begin their incessant raiding against one another again. We also heard that slaves from India, especially women were sold there.

As they live in tents, their ability to move quickly is remarkable.

The origin of their name is in dispute but Abu Saman held that it means 'Turks of purity', which caused a great laugh amongst his countrymen. He withstood this and after a time raised his hand for silence which was given him. The Ottoman Turk he said has bred so much with those he has conquered, that he no longer seems an Asiatic, while the Turcoman has not done so to the same degree.

Perkins next asked for clarification on the Shia opinion of Caliph Harun-al-Rashid, the man who is revered in the west as the famed father of the classic 'One thousand and one nights'. We found that their hatred of him was strong, as he was also the father of the murderer of their creed's founder, and all Shia will lay their feet {an insult in the East} on his Tomb in Meshed or if his name is spoken they spit. The Shia who heard his name mentioned in this discussion all spat into an emptied bowl for this purpose, issuing forth a curse. Perhaps it is similar to the way Christians view Judas.

Several times in the proceedings, the Asiatic delights in strong perfumes; musk, civet, ambergris, attar of rose, oil of jasmine or aloe wood, extract of cinnamon were expressed when a man would ask us to rise and spread this scent over us by lighting a brazier or sprinkling us with a mixture of it. Some were enjoyable; others needed a female to accompany it.

We talked about many other topics, and one and all, with the exception Horne, came away from the evening with a better appreciation of the Persian, for these had been religious men, bigoted against Christians, with not a scientific bone between them, and yet I found they were gentlemen in the broadest sense.

[Editor's note: Driscol pasted the above into his journal but when he actually wrote it is not known, but I would say it was within a few days of the evening in question; see also a timeline Driscol wrote on the subject in Appendix III-V]

We arrived back after an unusual walk without lights though the darken streets of the city and in spite of some misdirection, we found our compatriots at last. Here we had a good surprise; in that our Dragoman was here, full of compliments, excuses for being late, and with a plan.

Our Dragoman Abu Kumzar. Illustration III-XIII-32

He had been delayed by the earthquake, the rising of troops for the war and the difficulty of finding his intended guide. The guide was a man whose brother had been of service to Captain Conolly, who had come this way some years before *{1829-1830}* but who had not been able to travel to Khiva due to Turcoman treachery and instead had gone on to Herat.

His brother Orauze Kouli Agha, who would be our dragoman, was an Asterabadi with close contacts with the Goklen Turcoman and he had agreed to take a party of 'Circassians' to Khiva across the Kara-Kum desert.

Our Dragoman had been in the city some days before, and had found us, but as he had not completed his tasks, he had not spoken with us until now.

It was very early in the morning once the plans were set. We would move the next day, in the general direction of Herat, to the East, beyond the opium factory we had visited, telling all and sundry, that we were on our way to the city of Merv, but instead would move to an abandoned farm called 'Alaman' in the ridges south of Feyzabad *{Fazelabad}* a small hamlet some two and twenty miles away.

There was much to do.

I write now in the early morning by the lantern, a long day for all. Clothing and materials have been secured. We have given up all, or most of, our 'Englishness', which will be left in the care of our Dragoman; some five mule loads of it. Our greatest remaining load is scientific gear which we cannot go without, this has been dispersed among us, another difficulty are our weapons, which must be disguised, as they are unlike the weapons one sees in Persia and certainly not in Central Tartary. Hopefully this will not arouse suspicion as we are considered to be foreigners: Muslim foreigners. Therefore we will keep them out of sight and as for our long arms; they will be 'uglified' by the use of cloth, paint and dirt. Another difficulty is that of our horses. They are of breeds not seen in Central Asia and it is hoped that their being unusual will not be a demonstrable sign of our 'outwardness' other than being Circassians.

The Dragoman had purchased for us eight additional horses to carry our food and equipment. He bought them, as horses have identities, and the locals, loving horses as they do, can tell where they come from, who sold them and who bought them. These were by luck, Karbardin pack horses from the Caucasus. I found one that Blonde would not immediately kick and named her 'Dune' for the light reddish colour of her coat, which reminded me of the sand dunes that I had seen in Arabia. She was fourteen and half hands high, a compact well-muscled horse, with an obedient temperament and a Roman profile. She resembles, in some ways, the steppe horses of the Turcoman, and they are probably cousins; one for the desert and the other for the mountains. Having horses like this, we hoped would balance the oddity of our own horses which were clearly not from this region.

[Editor's note: Driscol went on and on about this and to summarize his comments; in a modern sense he was stating that people then could tell that the horses they rode were very different, like the cars one sees in India being different from those in Europe or the Americas. The sight of them would immediately tell someone that they were foreign, something that could not be disguised]

It was a hot day, cooled by a gentle wind off the Caspian Sea. Dobbins still wanted to hunt that tiger but we have bigger game afoot. We depart Asterabad late, dressed in a mix of Persian and European gear. We have left late, so when getting to our destination it will be after dark and less people will note our passing. We have told anyone and everyone that we are on our way to Merv.

The student Saman's goodbye. Illustration III-XIII-33

One complication was that Saman, having heard of our departure, came to bid us goodbye. He rode with us for a mile, until the lateness, and our constant warnings that he would be taken by the Turcoman if he delayed turning about, eventually sank in. He finally weakened and was gone.

It is an uneventful ride, but we did pass several columns of the Persian army on their way to Herat. A fine 'regiment' of Azerbaijanis passed us, well-horsed and having some resemblance of being a disciplined force. Units of 'less fine' groups were 'assembling' also but in name only.

They are the best cavalry that the Persians can assemble, of non-Persian blood of course. We then came upon a force of infantry. I dare not say a regiment, as it seemed more a gang that an organised group of men. They had, on the other hand, been awarded new uniforms which at least made them look like a military unit, instead of wretched beggars. Like most men on a route march, they are friendly, and we shared their camp for a while for our delayed tiffin.

The men were attired in light blue coats, over dark blue trowsers, and leather boots, which laced up to the mid-leg, and they all, of course, sported black sheepskin hats, shaped like a Bishop's mitre. They do not carry knapsacks, but instead their equipment is carried by mules. This seems a bad thing, and was much commented on by Dobbins, myself and Bannington. To separate a soldier from his supply of food, cooking gear, shelter and ammunition, seems a foolish thing. Their weapons were in sad shape, flintlocks some of French and others of British manufacturers with some 'sergeants' carrying Russian made trophies. All are in poor repair and their way of handling them is shocking. I suspect their misfire rate would be in excess of five times out of ten.

Persian 'Regiment' assembling. Illustration III-XIII-34

They were, as a group, surprised by Persian speaking foreigners, and their officers thought we might be Afghan or Russian spies, but our Firmans eased that worry. With our tanned but white faces, we could and would seem like Afghanis to them.

In speaking with them, I found that a private soldier gets a little over three pounds of bread or cooked rice a day, nothing else, and is paid a wage of two pounds ten shillings a year.

These underpaid unfortunates are drafted almost entirely from the wandering tribes, and are not true Persians at all. Our identification of them as 'Persian' was mistaken, they were just landless peasantry. These fellows were Azeris from the area around Tabriz, but all could speak some Persian. The Persians have a habit of organizing regiments by the tribes, which of course means in time of civil strife, they often fight for the causes of their tribes, and against the Shah. The historical fighting quality of these men is strangely good, why they fight is a mystery. If properly trained and officered, they are equal to a European force, or so say Hynes and Horne.

As the Persian infantry soldier is a good man, so the officers, in all the branches are worthless; excepting those of the artillery or those who have been trained by Europeans. One becomes an officer by favour, not unlike our British method of obtaining infantry and cavalry officer positions; and bribery and flattery is the pathway to promotion. There is in no sense a corps of officers, military professionals, or a sense of national duty. The sergeants are in general slack and unknowing of their duty. It has been observed by Horne, who taught the Persians before, that if they were given good officers, the Persian could stand up to French Grenadiers or Prussian Guardsmen for some time - before giving way and surrendering. I mean one must be reasonable in these things.

There are some, who say the Persian lacks the will to die for his country or as it is written,

'They are greatly deficient in the soldier's first art, the art of dying gloriously for
their nation'

[Editor's note: This was said in the book 'A second journey through Persia' by James Morier, Longman and Co., London 1818, I believe the quote came from Hynes and Driscol recorded it]

They follow the old custom of seeking their own safety, first then look for ways to safely slay the enemy. It is said that a Persian will fight hard and resplendently, if there is no chance of his dying. They look upon courage as a quality, which a man sometimes has and sometimes he has not; all by the will of Allah.

The Persian cannot stand with the leadership and training they have against well trained Europeans, but they can easily defeat local tribal groups, Arabs, Afghans and Turks as those armed forces are no more organised than they are, and as equally badly led, although man to man, the Afghans are much more capable.

We were also passed by two Persian artillery batteries. They were organised and soldierly looking; active fellows, well dressed, all mounted, with the cannon drawn by horses. It being the practice to crew cannon with upwards of five and twenty men, most who are there to defend the guns; as Persian generals tend not to provide infantry support to artillery. In European armies, the infantry protects the artillery, while the artillery kills the enemy infantry. In the Persian army the artillery protects the Infantry, while he offers himself up as a target to the enemy infantry. They were 9-pounders cast in Tabriz, they said, but they went by us without stopping, and with only a quick exchange of words. The officers were notable mercenaries; a Calabrian *{Italian}* and a Transylvanian *{Romanian}*.

We came to the caravanserai of the town that we sought in the gathering dusk. We watered the horses until the evening star could be seen, and we then moved south. In time, we came to an isolated farm house with a serviceable wall about it, standing next to a mosque that was in ruins. We came across our first obstacle in the performance of our plans. Within the house, was a group of Kurdish beggars, *banu sasan*, who claimed, with much passion, demands for our pity, and that they were the descendants of the dispossessed Sasanian house[13]. An hour or more of discussion, offers of money, declarations of our having legally rented the house, all were dismissed by the band of five. The negotiations were ended by Horne, Hynes and Dobbins, who threw them out bodily, after having exhausted every other reasonable means of persuasion. We soothed their wraith by a payment of some dinars and a skin bag filled with spirits.

They went down to a nearby stream, and we could hear them yelling and hooting for some hours. We put up two guards that night, and as is my habit, I elected to guard in the early morning hours.

Friday 30 June

One of the new horses was found to be lame, much to the unease of our Dragoman, who took this as a personal insult. How dare an animal become lame! Indeed.

He took her back to town and sold here and brought us back a serviceable donkey.

There were no neighbours that we could see, and we spent the day changing our appearance. Our eyebrows, beards and hair were dyed. I however, went for a complete dye job, as my body is covered in blonde hair. We donned our Eastern clothing, a short coat with wide sleeves, over a short-sleeved shirt, baggy trowsers with laced up boots.

I chose dark gray trowsers and blouse, and over it I placed a longer than usual brown coat of the Circassian style. For a hat I took on the flattened cone of black sheep skin, but thought its rimless manner would not shelter my eyes from the sun and wore atop of it a reddish but limp turban which well sheltered my eyes, for as a Circassians, I would not be able to wear my coloured spectacles.

[Editor's note: Driscol had not mentioned before that he wore them. In amongst his boxes was a pair of battered, red coloured spectacles that may be the ones he wore at that time]

The social classes of the Circassians are of five orders; the peasants who are called the *Tchokotl*, then the common freeman or *Begualia*, thirdly men who are vassals of nobles, called *Uork of Uork*, then there are then two classes of nobles; Princes called *Pschee* who have risen by recent actions - usually bloody - and those nobles of ancient nobility 'the first blood', called the *Uork* who rank beneath the princes.

We had decided, based on the information we had, to divide ourselves in this manner. Being as we

[Editor's note: it is uncertain what the source Driscol and the expedition used in knowing about the Circassians, several books had been published by English, French and Russians who had lived with the Circassians in their native land. It is my belief that the British library at the Legation in Teheran, and its staff was the source of this information, which is fairly consistent with what is known today about them]

Intent to act as men in search of horses we had to be in the service of a noble and Perkins was selected to be so. He would be a *Pschee* or son of a Prince and would wear white the traditional colour, myself, Dobbins and Bannington would be Uork and would wear something red or grey, Uork of Uork would be Horne and Michaelson who would wear brown, and Begualia would be Vickery, Hynes and Dissanayake who would wear black.

We considered making Bannington a Prince also, as his manner of walking, his proud carriage and whole nature bespoke an assumed authority. He did his tasks like the rest of us, but you could tell he was different. He was also, in our chain of command, fourth after me. He was a 'natural' noble.

[Editor's note: Driscol never defined the chain of command but by this and other comments we can suggest that the chain of command was Perkins, Dobbins, Driscol, Bannington, Horne, Hynes, Michaelson, Vickery and Dissanayake - although Michaelson technically outranked Hynes, medical officers at that the time and in the present do not sit in the command line. That said Perkins commanded the expedition, but Hynes ran it, nothing was done without his expressed agreement]

In Circassian social order, which is feudal, the Prince is supported by the lower orders however Perkins made the point, when no native was about, that he too would take guard duty and other tasks on. We disagreed and had an argument it being decided that he as commander should not stand guard instead he should wake every two hours to CHECK the guards.

He gave us a classic look, an established moue *{a grimace or pout}* which he often affected when presented by something so outlandish or childish he could not respond to it and retain his usual Perkinseque reserve. He then replied that yes he would wake every two hours and tell someone else to check the guards.

One item we could not find in any supply, was the traditional swords of the Circassian people, the *shashka;* a short sword with no guard and a single edge. We could find only three of these, and four of the straight daggers they always wore. These were given to Dissanayake, Hynes and Vickery. As for us, our story would be that we carried European weapons taken from Russian dead. If anyone noted we carried French or English swords, we intended to say that they came from the Napoleonic wars, and even in Persia, and we hoped Central Tartary men here knew of the loss of the French army to General Winter and the Cossacks *{campaign of 1812}*.

Our Dragoman had had difficulty finding even these, as the items of the *Carkas* as the Persian styles the Circassian, is not an item of great interest to them.

Between us, we learned several phrases in Adyghe *{West Circassian}* and hoped to God we did not encounter a man who could speak it. We thought that unlikely, and decided that for us, French would be our language of choice. English was known to some within Central Tartary due to contacts with the Hindoo and Indian Muhammadan traders who had encountered Sahibs before. We also had Latin and Greek, but our different levels of understanding of those ancient tongues made rapid or instructive conversation difficult if not impossible. We found that Michaelson, who had learned his Greek from a Frenchman pronounce the language completely differently than us poor British trained linguists.

[Editor's note: Each nation in Europe pronounced Greek differently, and during the Greek War of Independence (1821-1832) against the Turks many well educated notables made mention that the Greeks of that day could not understand their hard learned ancient Greek]

We could say easily in Greek, 'the day is hot' or 'lets us go there', but to convey, 'there is man with a musket, two hundred feet to our left behind that tree' was nearly impossible with any speed or efficiency. I can say with some pride that of our expedition I had the largest and most useful command of Greek, with Michaelson the next best.

Later photograph from 1889 of a typical Turcoman village
that the expedition would soon encounter.
Illustration III-XIII-35

A Ragged Band Of Circassians

When our Dragoman returned from one of his purchasing outing, he brought us our fresh food for the day and he was met by us in full costume. He was complimentary in his view of our efforts. He adjusted a number of items that he found wanting, such as our saddles and how our horses had been fitted was not correct. He had only been able to find two proper saddles and these were not liked at all, with it straight cantle and rounded horn, limited gullet and their manner of cinching. The best we could do here was place Turcoman style horse blankets and cover our English style saddles with textiles, suitable dirtied and torn.

One thing we could do was to replace our traces and reins with iron chains; in order one to be more in the manner and custom of this area, and to protect them from being slashed. Blonde and Dune, of course did not like them, but Dune took to them after a short time while Blonde continue to fret over them for a few hours.

Standing in a circle, we observed one other, seeing that one could swagger with hand on sword. I had placed Golden in a small leather pocket on my belt. I had a Persian belt of Georgian manufacture that fitted well, over this; I placed an outlandishly-coloured, silk, sash. I also found I could not get My Frenchman securely under the belt, so I had made a holster, adapted from a typical, Persian, holder for a balled, butted, flintlock by adapting it as necessary and aided by Dobbins' significant sewing skills.

Ensign David Driscol of the Bombay Artillery disguised as a Circassian. Illustration III-XII-36

We had a good meal that night; a Persian stew of goat meat, limes, chickpeas, apricots and plentiful garlic and black pepper.

We ate in the Mussulmen's style with our fingers, not an easy task, as the fingers are more sensitive to heat than the lips; that and the stewing had not loosened the meat from the bones as well as it should. But we did the best we could, cautioning several people who forgot and used their left hand, a serious breach of etiquette in the Mussulman world, as the left hand is to be used only for the toilet.

In selecting to be these people, we did so from what we considered to be their many advantages:

Firstly, they were known and feared warriors, and much used as elite troops by many Muslim despots. We hoped that the news of a party of us would halt any petty attempt to molest or hinder us.

Secondly, the Circassian is in all respects a European, with dark hair but having a multitude of eye colours, something we too all had. They were also thought, by non-Circassians, to be of rude, and known for their unusual actions and manners; such that our mistakes of usage and custom might be excused, like a Londoner would view a rude country Scotsman from the far north.

Thirdly, they were Sunni, and that sect predominates in Central Tatary, unlike the Persians, whose Shia'ism is a source of separation, disdain, and a reason to be attacked.

This drawing was done by Hynes and appears in Vickery's journal. Upper left Horne, to the right Perkins, lower center Bannington. Illustration III-XIII-37

Fourthly, their Muhammadanism was wrought with contradiction and local variation, which would be our excuse for any non-Muslim act we might commit in error. That Circassians followed a much splintered version of the faith was well known, and an object of ridicule, but also of sufferance, the common saying was;

What do you do there, are you Circassian to pray in that manner?

This phrase was often spoken in the western region of the East.

The practice of religion by these Circassians is a mix of paganism, Christianity, and Islam, for the true faith this is limited to a reverence for the cross and to give it respect at all times to those of our true faith. Yet, the men we would pretend to be are said to show an acceptance of the concept of a spirited fight between good and evil in a matter like the ancient Persian religion. There are inwardly Christian with pagan influence and outwardly Islamic.

The latter is at best a nominal faith and their knowledge of it is limited and fragmented. The true subject of study for such a man is war, robbery and revenge and it is this knowledge that makes the first of my observations so formidable. We cannot be tested or tripped up by not being able to read the language as it has no alphabet and few outside speakers.

Fifthly, it is the nature of the Circassian to keep all family communications under the greatest secrecy. It is a great insult is to ask a man, of this race of men, about his wife and family. This we felt would protect us from too close a questioning of our backgrounds. It was no one's business and Circassian prickliness, and tendency to draw his knife on this subject, is well known in the East.

Sixthly, their past history gives us a good reason for why we would be in Tatary looking for horses as they have been resisting the Russians for generations and although partially tamed, they are still in constant revolt against them. Therefore, the fact that we would be searching for horses would be a commonplace action for them.

Seventhly, the lands of those people have been torn asunder by another series of conflicts over the rising of a man, who claims to be the second prophet of Allah, a man named Shamyl, who has brought extermination and a new intensity of war to the region. For this reason, many men have left the county, after their families have been destroyed, or the noble or prince who they supported has been killed.

Eighthly, should we encounter another Circassian, he will be most unwilling to approach us, in the fear of his life; as he would not know which side of the conflict we are on and it is also a damning custom amongst this society to take prisoners and to hold to ransom anyone outside his own family, clan or vassalage, should they be encountered in a situation where they can be taken.

Ninthly, these people, and to the great perplexity of the philologists, have a secret language, ostensibly a barbaric gabble, a language of war, used by them chiefly in their wars, each group is said to have their own, we could therefore speak amongst ourselves in a language others could not understand. Besides this war language, they have some one hundred or so distinct *patois {dialects}*, which are often not understandable to someone living in the next valley over, let alone from farther afield. So if we encounter a man who knows a trace of a Circassian language, we shall have good reason to decline to know it.

We decided that the following day we would ride out and camp nearer the Turcoman and our Dragoman would then bring us the guide, and introduce us to him, as being band of Circassians, seeking horses in Central Tartary, wild men but in his estimation pacified enough to be guided safely.

Saturday 1 July

My last entry in this well filled journal. I worry that it will be lost but our good Dragoman has sworn,

> *Behser e Jeddam (by the head of my Grandfather) that it shall not*

That our property will find its way to the British legation, I can only trust and hope that it shall be as we planned.

[Editor's note: In this Driscol was rewarded for his trust, this sixth of his journals did make it to the legation, however there is a story behind what happened to them then, which is covered in a later volume. Our man then wrote in his full name, the location of his place of residence in Bombay, his regiment, the location of his brother John in India and his parent's house in Eccles. He then began his Central Tatary Journal, as he called it, these books were manufactured in India, and were of inferior binding, and paper, and in the twenty first century had become very dark, making reading them difficult at times, and the leather bindings had disintegrated, leaving the pages unbound, and held together only by the original silk threads. I have also taken entries from Vickery's Expedition diary, which offer, on occasion, some greater insights into the occurrences and happenings within the expedition]

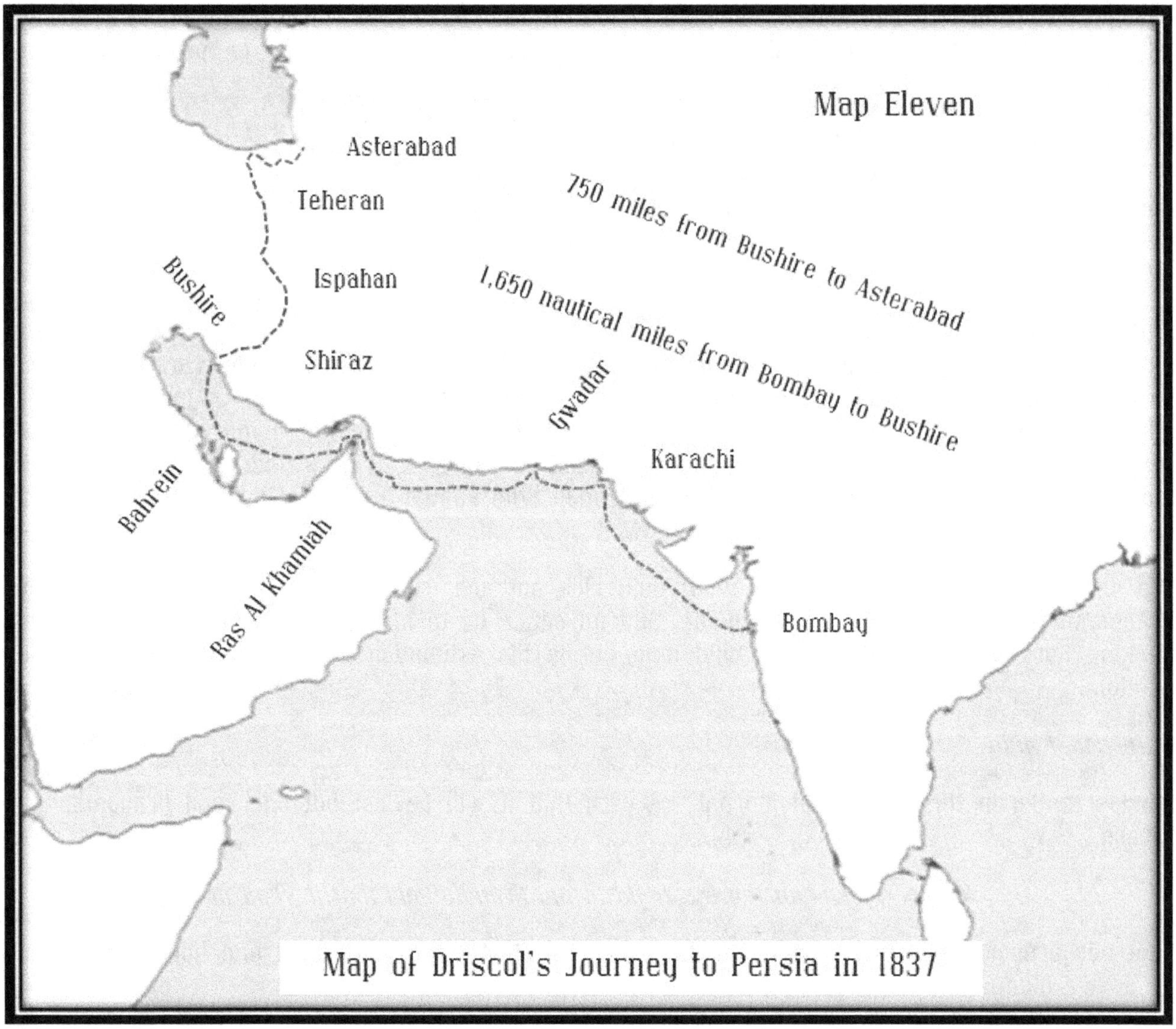

Map Eleven

Asterabad

Teheran

750 miles from Bushire to Asterabad

Bushire

Ispahan

1,650 nautical miles from Bombay to Bushire

Shiraz

Gwadar

Karachi

Bahrein

Ras Al Khamiah

Bombay

Map of Driscol's Journey to Persia in 1837

Chapter XIV

Asterabad to Turcomania

We Ride To The Gurgan River As Circassians - At The Campsite Of Turcoman 'Man-Stealers' - The Virtues And Faults Of The Turcoman - Turcoman Pilaf - Turcomania And A Description Of Turcoman Slave Taking - The Inter-Clan Conflicts Of The Turcoman - The Charge Of The 17th King's Own Imperial Light Horse Polish Lancers Of The Guard Or The Middlecombe Expedition Bares Its Teeth - Recall - A Cursory Discussion Is Held And The Attack On Our Position At Igdy Well - Melee At Igdy Well - Our Situation Reconsidered - Harvey Sauce - The Hell Fires Of The Kara-Kum - The Journey Over The Burning Sands Continues With Pain - We Come To The Dried Bed Of The Oxus - Our Old Friend - Turcoman Negotiations On The Matter Of Igdy Well - Turcoman Courting - Khiva The City Of The Khan And A Sewer Of The First Order - A Damnable Hot Town And Veal For Dinner - The Moneylender And The Khivan Bazaar - A MOST Singular Occurrence - A Midnight's Skulking Though Khiva - Our Prisoner - Dafydd Friedrich Zum Nolta - A Ride To Nowhere - Return To The Heated Delights Of Khiva - I Deadly Discovery Made - The Foulness Of The Khivan Bazaars And The Idiocy Of Guides - We Meet With The Khan And Ameer Of Khiva And His Vizier - We Are Given A Mission By The Khan Of Khiva - Three Countrymen In The Hades Hotel? - A Voyage Down The Oxus To Khodjeili The City Of Hajjis And The Disaster That Befell Us

=======

We Ride To The Gurgan River As Circassians

Day 1, Sunday 2 July [Vickery kept track of the days the expedition moved and the count is taken from his accounts. This day was deemed the first day of the actual expedition]

We depart the green hills that nearly surround this pleasant place where we have stayed. Certainly it reminds one of England, with its green fields of grass and splendid trees. It is at latitude 36° 51' north, longitude 54° 46' East and it has 73 degrees of heat at an elevation of 450 feet. We are all in good spirits. Dissanayake has led us in prayer for our success; we are nine men, and two and twenty horses, not counting our Dragoman, who has gone ahead. We are dressed as villains, and if I had been riding in Persia, and encountered us, I would have left the road and kept my hand on My Frenchman until we passed.

Spit but no polish, Hynes' motto for the expedition, which at this point found all of us disguised as natives. He wore a haggardly *posteen*, an afghan's outer garment.

[Editor's note: with the starting of the new journal, Driscol also began to write his entries in a way to make it harder to read, should his journals be taken and read by a Russian or Central Asian. He did this by writing in the Arabic script, but in the language of Danish, much interspersed with English, French, Greek, Hindi and Latin. Consequently, given his poor hand writing, and the cursive nature of Arabic, and that he was writing English and the other languages backwards - and sometimes forward - it has given me and my assistants the great of difficulties in translating it. I would estimate that one out of every five words that Driscol wrote we had to guess the meaning of]

The Goklan district is a dangerous one for wayfarers, and the inhabitants are only too ready to indulge in crimes against persons and property. As, however, this state of things is common to every part of Persia, the conduct of the Goklans is regarded with indifference by the ministers of the Shah.

We encountered a mounted Persian woman with child, and the father walking next to them. He had just ransomed her, and his child, from the Turcoman, who had taken them a week ago.

A Persian returns with his family ransomed from the Turcoman. Illustration III-XIV-1

He was bitter, for he had had to sell his land to re-purchase them, and now had no home. Perkins gave him the equivalent of five pounds, a small fortune, and his tears of joy were hard to watch. He volunteered to join us but we sent him on his way, as his safety of passage would last only this day. After that, he or she could be captured again. With that amount of money he could buy a shelter and farm without difficulty. Perkins is often cold to suffering but in this he was munificent. We also suggested he leave this area and go to a safer area deep within Persia, he said it would.

Our passage forward is downhill in a northwesterly direction. We are searching for the specific place by a lake, where we shall meet with our prospective guide. As we rode over the green lands here, they were so flourishing that our horses wished to stay and graze, like I would before a cake shop. I frequently looked back at the verdure of the hills behind us, and rising past them, the grey blue of the Alborz Mountains, with the white snows of Damavand that showed us where we had come from. For once, our group was quiet. Everyone reflected on our mission, perhaps on what we were about to do, his part in it and the danger that it all entailed.

We passed through these fields and woods, emerging out onto a large plain that is crossed by irrigation ditches, and the land so enriched by this water, that we thought we had entered Eden itself. We had not come across any villages, when we realised, almost instinctively that we were now in the land of the Turcoman, which lay not six miles from our former abode in the city of Asterabad. Around us, we could see their felt tents in groupings from ten to fifty, and large herds of animals; horses, oxen, sheep, goats, even camels were to be seen. All these were watched by children, but we could also observe armed, mounted, men at intervals, with lances at hand.

Three of these converged on us, and in a manner neither friendly nor hostile, enquired as to whom we were, and what was our business for entering the lands of the Goklan Turcoman? We were asked this in Persian and Perkins rode forward and stated our mission to find the tents of one Orauze Kouli Agha, the noted and famous guide.

They conferred and told us to wait. Two men rode off, each in different directions, while the other stood astride our path between the canals. There was nothing to do, but have our tiffin and tend to the horses. We adjusted straps, as we had done before, as our movement shifted loads, and we grew more knowledgeable in the type of horses we now had as pack animals. Hynes' experience in these matters was important; our two cavalrymen were less knowledgeable in packing the load of a horse than one would imagine.

We had a silent meal of some cooked goat, cheese (horrid stuff) and the flat breads common to this land.

[Editor's note: Driscol references a table that he had written earlier, which lists the duties, abilities and skills of the expedition by man. When he may have made this, is unclear. Of great interest is that he included Hymison & Husher at the bottom of the table, but how could he have known about some of the characteristics he noted? See Appendix III-VI]

We were soon summoned, for two men had come back, and one was different. He was taller than  the average Persian or Turcoman we had previous seen, but was dressed as a Turcoman, except for the glaring exception of wearing a bright pink turban and a golden chain about his shoulder, like a French fourragere or aiguillette. In fact that is what it was, for it turned out to be a military award of Russian manufacture, which I would have imagined had been taken in battle as a trophy perhaps.

Expedition guide one Orauze Kouli Agha, Photographed in 1858. Illustration III-XIV-2

A party of Turcoman cavalry photographed in 1908 in the same location where the expedition rode seventy years earlier. Illustration III-XIV-3

We were greeted as conquering kings, and led a mile or so to his village, which was a scene out of a comedy; or so it seemed to my eyes. His dark, brown felt tent was set up by the banks of the river. There were gaily clad children running about covered with jackets of every imaginable colour, skull caps of contrasting colour, sewn with bits of metal and coins, flags fluttering from lances driven into the ground, and all seemed astir.

Unalike the dour Persians, this Turcoman's wife was at the door, unveiled and greeting us with bowls of *Calleon*, consisting of fresh milk with sour curds, a type of butter milk in taste, thickened with rice and pieces of bread, along with wheat bread and cheese. We happily broke our riding fast and accepted the kind welcome. Even though we had just eaten, we were still appreciative of this demonstration of hospitality, and with the exception of the sour milk, we enjoyed a very tasteful tray of savoury treats.

I now felt safer, as we were now, having eaten from her freely given food, guests of these Turcoman, and by their laws, untouchable.

Around us gathered a crowd of laughing, happy, people all uncouth in manner, man and woman intermixed, with children screaming, and the youngest coming up to point and pull at our dress, all with the perfectly set smiles. Perkins said in Greek to me that he felt we were surrounded by the wildest description of Hungarian Gypsies, and his comparison was apt. Our greeter's tent sat in a general square encampment, with some thirty other like tents, all with their openings pointing to a central 'square' or broad street. Around all of this, was a wall of cane some six to eight feet high, more to keep horses and children in than petty thieves out, as it had no defensive value.

Turcoman tents the famous *kibitka* showings it manner of construction and how it would have looked inside. Illustration III-XIV-4

At The Campsite Of Turcoman 'Man-Stealers'

The horses and packs were secured in a guarded tent. We then all entered his family tent, with his children and wife having departed as we filled it up.

As is the Oriental fashion, we did not speak of our purpose, but instead of everything else, mainly about the war between Afghanistaun and the Shah; actually the war had not started yet and would not until the Persian sovereign crossed the vaguely defined border, but everyone knew there would be a fighting war, after the many weeks of travel were completed to gain that far frontier. Who would want to declaring war, then traveling that far in the summer heat, and not having a nice battle?

We had to drink 'caravan tea' or 'desert tea'; a tea particular to the Turcoman and Central Asia. It is made of black looking tea, which comes from a dried brick of tea from India or China that is crumbled away to form a fist full of tea dust. It is boiled up until it is well dead, with a pint or two of salt-laden water, occasionally sweeten by a fist-full of sugar cake *{hard sugar in a loaf}*, more commonly left plain, but on rare occasions made worse by adding cardamom, pepper, mace or nutmeg to the mix. This bitter, sweet brew is then shared with all. I need not comment on its strength of taste nor on my drinking little of it.

[Editor's note: Driscol at some point came back and wrote in pencil, in Danish, 'I have vowed that in my travels I will, I must, find a people and a land, who do not drink tea and coffee all day long. Such a place must exist, and if it does, I shall find it and make myself king!]

More about the tent or *kibitka;* from the inside it was held up by four saplings, each an inch in thickness, bent in such a manner as to support the walls and attached to a wooden circle through which the chimney also passes. It is over this thin framework that the panels of thick black felt, which they call *nummud,* are laid, and then tied to the support poles. On the outside, a framework of wicker is used to hold the nummud firmly; this is made of split reeds and dried vines. The side of the tent has a lintel, placed between two of the supporting poles, and a flap of sorts is constructed. On the floor, another felt rug is laid. Within this space, a place is made for the fire in the centre, and a wicker-like wall is emplaced to separate it into men's and women's quarters.

We found that the tent we were in was an *akoy* type, for it had within it, an interior felt that was pure snowy white, while a more typical *karavy,* or black tent, was black due to the influence of the cooking fire.

The furniture consists of saddles, horse and camel bags; often made of richly made carpets. The weaponry of the family then decorates the walls. The wives' weapons of domestic activity are all made of wood or clay; for they will not cook food in metal pots, as it is a superstition amongst them that it takes the courage from a man, and the fertility from a woman to so do. However, this misconception has yielded to necessity, and in the tent is a large Russian made, copper pot. The entire arrangement can be packed on two horses, three mules or one camel.

This compactness allows the Turcoman his mobility and is their secret to avoiding avenging, military columns.

We left the tent to observe the ceremony of a young camel being slain; his throat cut in the way of *Zabiha {Arabic for slaughtered}*. I managed to stand in the background, which due to my height, I am usually placed anyway and I avoided viewing the majority of the act. The beast was cut up, and during this process, a great cry went up for a large tumour had been found within the beast; such a discovery was a great omen for success, and for our future culinary delight.

Having seen our dinner being sacrificed, we returned to discuss the matters of the day with our host; the weather, the crops, the accursed heretics *{the Persians}* he having ascertained that we were Sunni, why God was great, why women are a curse, when would the world would end and why it rain?

Our camel re-emerged as large steaming chunks atop a plain wooden tray, brought in by four women; for it was some forty pounds of meat and an equal amount of rice, mixed with nuts and fruit, and tinted with saffron. This was placed atop a cloth, which was spread before us; which was such a horror to a European that it is hard to write about. It is their custom, we had been told, to never, ever, wash a table-cloth, as it was thought to be very unlucky; so our trays of food were placed on this greasy and stained sheet, which well showed what the family had eaten in the last few months, as the crumbs and stains from those meals were embedded in it.

I noticed that Michaelson, our doctor, all but turned turn as white as sheet.

Each of us had placed before us a slab of coarse bread nearly an inch thick and two feet in diameter on which was placed a portion of boiled rice. This would serve as our plate. Our drink was a thin, unpalatable mixture of camel's milk, brackish water and even more salt. I drank none of it after the first taste. I was later saved from choking to death from a dry throat, when a skin of *chaal* was passed around *{fresh camel's milk}*, which is delightful. On another tray, atop some shredded green vegetable, came the well-cooked *neoplasi {tumor}*.

The Arabic blessing for dinner, the *Bismillah*, was worded out. Not in the best pronunciation of Arabic, for I am sure he had no idea what he was saying. He was just repeating what he had been told to say by his parents, as they had been told by their parents and so on, back over a thousand years.

This was the first test of our ability to eat in the proper way. The camel was full of flavour, and I must admit to having a reservation on tasting it but it was like a cheaper and stringier cut of beef.

I tried some of the tumour, for it had been the size of an eight pound swede *{rutabaga}*. I found it tasted of camel, but had the texture of a chicken's craw or *ventriculus*. It took a great deal of mastication to dispatch it. A good beating by a strong armed-man with an iron mace would have greatly improved its chewability, nevertheless it was indeed tasty and something I had not previously savoured.

Our ability to eat was meagre in comparison to our guide, who with finger and thumb, could in some skilled way that I could not master, tear off large portions of meat from the bone, with no effort, or so it appeared to me.

We had the highest compliments for the meal, and I noted only one error in our men's actions, at one point Horne wiped his mouth with the back of his left hand; a gross social error but fortunately our guide was discussing horses with Hynes and Perkins at the time. Our best Persian speakers were Hynes, Perkins, Bannington, Dobbins and I and we carried the conversation.

As we ate, the purpose of our trip was discussed. Our guide had been told by the Dragoman that we wished to cross the Kara-Kum desert to the horse markets of Khiva, Bokhara and other sites.

This our guide agreed to. There was some discussion of leaving the horses, and taking camels, which are faster and less dangerous to take across the desert at this hot time of the year, but horses can do the journey, if at a slower rate of speed. The manner of doing so would be that he, a Turcoman of this tribe, must gain acceptance from one of the four gifted tribes. Those tribes were the ones described to us by Abu Saman, and those who are allowed passage anywhere within Turcoman lands would take us. To go by ourselves would mean a very probable encounter with the enemies of his tribe, who were all the other tribes of Turcoman.

So he said that the Turcoman between the old bed of the Oxus and the north Persian frontier could be passed this way, and the trail would by a more westerly trail from the Attrek River to Igdy Well, and then on to Khiva. The exact path taken would depend on which of the four gifted tribes we made an arrangement with, and that would be his honour to arrange. The price for all of this was two and twenty thousand dinars or some twelve pounds sterling. Camels would be added to our mounted array to carry the necessary water and fodder for the horses, for no proper fodder could be found on the trip. The journey would be of some three hundred miles. The majority of the trail to Khiva would be over the sands of the black desert {Kara-Kum}.

As it was still light outside, he asked if he might view our horses, for he had seen they were dissimilar to his own type. He was most appreciative of the different types, which we accounted for by saying they had come from Turkey, Arabia or were captured Russian trophies.

We spent the rest of the night discussing horses, and ate a desert of sweetened nuts while being entertained by the screeching of a *bakshi* or Turcoman minstrel or poet. He was a terrible singer, as he did more through the nose than mouth and on rare occasion strumming the three strings of a large instrument whose name I did not bother to determine, as it was made of gourds. Our guide later said it was a great song. The man was reputedly an artist of the greatest fame, and the tale he sang about, concerned a great horse, a raid, and a captured Uzbek Princess. The others enjoyed smoking from the simple Turcoman pipe which is nothing more than a common reed which they use to suck up smoke from tobacco spread over hot coal. They call this 'drawing a draught of happiness from the breath of paradise'. It smelt like burnt straw, with a touch of manure, to me.

Smoking had been one area where our Circassian guise might fail, as four of our expedition were heavy smokers; using pipes or cigars, with Perkins and Hynes occasionally bowing to this habit. Horne smoked cigars and Dissanayake smoked dainty French *papelates {cigarettes}*. Michaelson, Vickery and I did not smoke, while Bannington and Dobbins rarely do and had pledged to avoid the vice while on the expedition.

[Editor's note: the widespread use of cigarettes would come after the Crimean War, when French, Italian and British soldiers brought back the custom of their allies, the Turks, and their enemies, the Russian, both of whom were reduced to smoking tobacco rolled in newspaper and not proper cigars or hookah. If Dissanayake was smoking papelates at this date, he was truly one of the first to do so, a pioneer indeed. Of course they were not paper wrapped, but with a maize (corn) skin]

The smokers had agreed to take only a few cigars, and free tobacco, and to make do with the local versions using the manner of smoking common to the land; which tended to be various styles of hookah, as they are called in India. I can see that Dissanayake is the most distressed by this lack of burning weed, as he also had chewed tobacco on occasion, when more conventional methods could not be found on our trip.

The Turcoman loves his horses much more than his actual family; certainly more than his wife. The true man within these tribes spends all his leisure time with his horses, or with men discussing said horses. Not even a first son, a true *Baba Jan {father's soul or dear one}*, a title given by the Turcoman to their eldest sons as a term of endearment, can tear a father away from his horse. There are stories that if a man stealer takes a man's son, he may pay to have him returned. If a favoured horse is taken, a large ransom will be paid and the man who took the horse will be forever watching his back, for he will have gained some gold, but also the unrelenting hatred of the horse's owner. In short, Turcoman culture is defined by the unquestioning fact that they love their horses more than life itself; with the possible exception of the pursuit of unlawfully obtained plunder.

I mentioned sons, as his male children joined us and Bannington showed us an unexpected ability, by the light of the lantern - a Russian made one of excellent quality - he made shadow puppets on the white wall of the tent. The Turcoman had never seen this and they were both quite scared and entertained by this. They pronounced our man to be a true wizard.

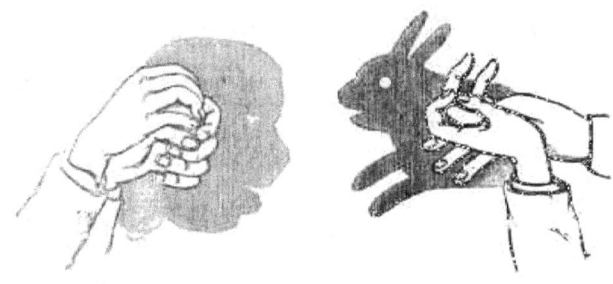

Shadow puppets by Bannington.
Illustration III-XIV-5

Having eaten and discussed our business, and come to an agreement, we retired to our camp, which was next to the tent were our equipment was. We then spread our blankets on the ground and went to sleep; after a long, whispered conference between us; in Greek and French. We kept guard here, having three men up instead of our regular one. I took as usual the dawn portion.

The Virtues And Faults Of The Turcoman

Day 2 Monday 3 July

I thought during the night that I ought to make an effort to escape future reproaches for garbling and colouring facts with unsupported rumour and geographic gossip by the learned men in London. To do so I would keep a more detailed account than I had first imagined I would of the expedition, when I had first heard of it. I will do so by recording some facts about our hosts the Turcoman.

We had been warned by many that the Turcoman while he has the virtues of all unsettled people, like the Arab or Red Indian, in that they hold embellished ideas of hospitality and martial gallantry. The other side of the coin are their vices, in that they are greedy, thievish and even if they often keep good faith, with their own clans or guests, they will also frequently try to find a way to allow them to plunder a foreigner, guest or clan member using religion, race or supposed insult to grant them an excuse to indulge their interests in loot. They are by any word or measure, shrewd, and alive to their own interests, which are always paramount.

Thus, we were on constant guard, but as we were nine in a sea of hundreds, what could we realistically do? We had to cross the desert to accomplish our tasks, and in that mission, we could not and would not fail.

Dobbins, Bannington and Horne were of the mind to exam the tents of the Turcoman more thoroughly, and did so with great diligence. It being their idea that those types of tents would be of use in India. The lack of need for guide ropes and tent pegs would greatly facilitate their being set up quickly. The felt does not burn; it just turns to carbon, so tent fires, which were a common occurrence in our armies, would cease to plague both soldier and quartermaster alike.

We were joined by a number of Turcoman and we found them to look more Asiatic and not able to speak Persian well. We found that our guide was the son of a Goklan chief and a Persian slave, so he both looked less Asian, and spoke Persian well. We all found this odd as we knew that Persia lay but a few miles away. How come the woman had not escaped or been taken back after payment of a ransom?

We had of course taken on Circassian names, nom de querre for our stroll. We had chosen names that somewhat sounded like our real names, or had titles that we thought supported our respective roles.

I had written out the night before our new names and identities so that I would be able to remember them;

Perkins:	Pshimide, 'The Prince that does not agree'
Dobbins:	Dzedzn, 'Brave Knight'
Driscol:	Dizchin, 'Silver'
Horne:	Heshir, 'Puppy', we did not tell Horne that, instead we told him that it meant 'great warrior'

Bannington:	Blaneshu, 'Valiant Cavalryman'
Michaelson:	Maxweqwe, 'Happy healer'
Hynes:	Hetsu, 'Master'
Vickery:	Wizche, 'Crafty Weasel'
Dissanayake:	Dzeghaschte, 'Scares the army'

We found from our guide that he would go to make our arrangements. He stated that we had the freedom of the camp, but to not venture any further, as we might invoke a clash with his neighbours.

Vickery asked why I had been so restless the night before, and I said it was Horne's fault, for our gear had been piled up all around us and as it had been Horne who had directed this 'construction', I felt it would collapse on top of me, which caused me to feel claustrophobic during my sleep.

The Makhtoum-Khuli conducting the morning ritual of loading the horses.
Illustration III-XIV-6

I then explained how as a child playing at sardines[1] I had been trapped in a small work room above our main barn in Eccles, seven lads and I had become trapped there, and since that time, I had not liked anything to loom over me.

A messenger arrived from our guide with instructions to follow, and we dutifully did so.

We could not, of course, pay our host for our keep, as it would be considered part of his duties as a host, and of course he was being paid to guide us. We had brought a gift for his wife with us, for we had been told of this by Abu Saman and the Dragoman, that it was customary to reward the wife of the man who provided us with hospitality. We did so by presenting her a shawl of the finest Chinese make silk, a bright blue with a crimson three clawed dragon rampant upon it. She was most pleased, as her broad smiles showed, and her quickness in showing the finery to all her, soon to be envious, neighbours.

We crossed the river at a ford, and a mile or so on, found another Turcoman camp called in their language an *Oubeh*. Here we were introduced to a party of Makhtoum-Khuli, the descendants; it is said of Abu Bakr the great, rightly guided Caliph. They are one of the four tribes of Turcoman who may journey between the five major groupings without hindrance.

They had with them six camels and four men, so with our guide, we found we would be taking the more westerly pathway, the one discussed before, though the Kara-Kum to Igdy Well and onto Khiva.

I then asked our guide, for he had mentioned the night before, a dry river bed, and yes we would come to it, for it was the bed of the Oxus, although he knew it by another name. I questioned him on it, and his description was that a great river had once flowed there. I spread this information to all and it evoked great excitement in the ranks of the expedition.

We would be going along, on this trip, with a party of Yomut; so at first we would head west for some miles. However all of this action came to nothing and we ended up camping there, as some arrangement or so had not un-expectantly fallen unfulfilled.

The Yomut are the enemies of the Goklan, but these Makhtoum-Khuli explained that trading must be done, and by arrangement, they could do so without interference from others, just as we had been told. I was not convinced that this was true. However there was no other way to cross the Kara-Kum, for we did not know the way except by following a compass. That is our backup.

Day 3 Tuesday 4 July

Words were exchanged between Horne and Dissanayake over some matter. Perkins and Dobbins intervened and the matter resolved. Perkins stating firmly that any anger or argument would be allowed only by his sufferance, and that he would not provide it. They had also spoken in English.

We left mid-morning and headed north by northwest. We had had for our breakfast a type of wheat noodle mixed with dried curds, horse milk, and a stew of mutton fat, marrow and dried bread, which was better tasting than it sounded.

Our escorting party was armed with ten-foot lances, swords and daggers. Those Turcoman are the *beau ideal* of an irregular horseman, a natural, light dragoon. Our guide had shed his pink turban and is now displaying a puffy looking, lambskin hat on his head and he holds, what might have been at one time, a Russian made musket. It had been a flintlock, but it had been adapted in a crude way to a matchlock. He let us examine it, and we found his weapon had been cut down to some four feet, and that it had an enlarged vent drilled at the location of the pan, to allow a matchlock to function. It was the opinion of all of us, expressed secretly and diplomatically in French, that the weapon was useless, more like harquebuses for display than for fighting.

Dobbins allowed our guide to examine, not his hand cannon, but his regular double-barreled rifle.

Planta Tartarica Boromez the Barometz or 'Tartarian lamb' as imagined by gullible Europeans. Illustration III-XIV-7

He was summarily dismissive of our percussion caps, but then admitted he had never seen one before. We told him that they were the newest adaptation for war from the Ottomans. We asked about his fine hat, which was a good example of the hat making process. We had seen these although Persia and had found out that they were made in a barbarous way, by slaying the ewes to obtain the fleece of the unborn lamb; the earlier this is done, the finer and softer is the fur of the unborn sheep.

That is the reality of the trade, but for many centuries, the origin of these fine hats was steeped in mystery; some holding that 'Tartarian lamb' was actually a plant and a sheep shaped one! This fabulous plant was called the 'Borametz or Boranetz', and sightings of it had been reported for centuries, by dimmed minded and sighted Europeans.

The camels in our caravan were fine animals and of a type I had not seen before; as they differed from the camels I had seen in Arabia and India.

These were dromedary with two humps and they are the animal that is most often used for transport, while the more commonly known, and larger, single-humped camel is used for the purpose of riding. Each of our dromedaries was carrying from four to five hundred pounds, for the younger males and females, while one fully grown male supported the mighty weight of seven hundred and fifty pounds.

The heat is not unbearable as there is a cooling wind off the Caspian.

The 'Wall of Alexander' this British newspaper image of it is wildly inaccurate making it many times larger than it is. Illustration III-XIV-8

We came to a ruined wall, which I presume is the Wall of Alexander. *{The Gorgan Wall was built during the Parthian and Sasanian period, 163 BC to 637 AD}* I had previously read about, the Persians call it the Sadd-i-Iskandar, while our guide gave it the name of Qizil Yilan.

Our path ran along it for some distance, allowing me to examine it more in detail. Our guide had little information on it, other than the vague assertions that it ran to the East for 'a far distance' *{120 miles or 195 kilometers}*, it was in a ruinous state but at one time had been eighteen to two and thirty feet wide, five to fifteen feet in height and we could see the larger square ruins of intermediate forts along its course. It is made of burnt red bricks and the construction is of good quality, but it had never been repaired during our modern era. On the north side is a ditch, now filled in with debris and sand.

We came after some time to the end of the wall, which ended in a fort. We could see clear evidence that the Caspian had been higher in ancient times. This made me remark to Perkins that perhaps the dry bed of the Oxus had run into the Caspian in the past, and that now it ran into the Aral Sea. This might explain the lower shoreline. He liked the idea and we discussed it with Bannington, who thought it most probable. We knew that the old riverbed lay to our north but we had not shown any excessive interest in it, in order not to excite the suspicions of our guide as to our true attentions. The natives of this part of the world have a habit of paying no attention, and having no interest in geography and they find that an interest in such things is a peculiar addiction of *ferenghi {foreigners}*.

One good point of the Turcoman is that their devotions to religions are very weak, so we do not have to pray. These new Turcoman seemed no more interested in the aspects of their religion than were the Goklan.

Hynes mentioned that this day in America was a holiday for a number of the states, a day to celebrate their 'Day of Independence'. We drank a toast, wishing them confusion and disaster in their future. Horne and Dobbins were of the opinion that the United States would fall into war between themselves, and would, in their distress; call upon a branch of the British Royal family to re-establish a proper government. Some held that the Americans would re-institute a monarchy using a prince from the Swedish or Danish royal families. We all felt that that large land of tiresome and wayward Englishmen could not possibly continue as it was, however none held that this would happen within our generation.

That evening, we camped on a small rise to the south, where we could see the ruined line of the wall, and beyond it, the snow cap of Damavand and to the west, a hint of the Caspian. To our East, lay open pasturage, dotted with woods, and to the north, more of the same.

Our cook for the evening meal allowed me to follow his method in making the meal. He used a large copper pot, which I noted was of Russian manufacture, and which he said was NOT metal, in order not to invoke the superstition concerning the use of metal tools to make food. To him iron was metal and copper was, well - copper. As the pilaf he made in the 'non-metal' copper pot was one of the best I had encountered, I will provide the recipe he followed:

Turcoman Pilaf

A good fire is built up and some sheep fat placed in the pot, some previously cooked mutton is thrown in to brown. When they seemed well cooked, he added enough water to cover the meat and left it to boil. Once in a good boil, some salt, a few peppercorns, and some slices of carrot are added. Once they have cooked for a short time, a portion of rice is added and the mucilage well mixed in. As the water is absorbed by the rice, the pot is moved farther from the fire, more water added and the lid is put on and it is left to sit for about half an hour; it being dangerous to examine one's watch, but I managed to do so in this case.

From the pot was produced rice well flavoured with sheep's fat, carrots soft and tasteful to eat, and small bits of mutton, once well cooked, and partially dried, now soft and easily eaten.

Day 4 Wednesday 5 July

We set out for the river and the ford at Bairam-Olum, the ford itself is easily passed as the water flow is slow, and the stream width is eighteen feet and a piddling depth. The river's bed itself is one hundred to a hundred and five and twenty feet in width, with sharp banks twenty to thirty feet high. We forded this muddy Attrek River and having passed into Yomut territory, which appeared to us as a plain, studded here and there with mounds. I think the mounds may have contained tombs or ruins, but it was unwise to show any interest in them. Once we crossed, we were met by one of the Yomut, and our passage agreed to by an exchange of words between the guide and the leader of our guardian clan with 'border guards' who consisted of a sole youth of fifteen. I would have imagined him, nevertheless to have been well-armed with a broken spear and a matchlock with no lit fuse. We found that these Turcoman do not settle along the banks of the river and their agriculture is of a spotty nature.

We came to graveyards where the tombs of great men were pointed out, as were the graves for slaves and Shia, which are called 'dog ditches'.

Turcomania And A Description Of Turcoman Slave Taking

Day 5 Thursday 6 July

I thought that I would describe in this journal the people, in whose land we have entered, in more detail, as I am considering writing a book on this subject once the expedition is complete.

[Editor's note: I deleted here a repeat of some earlier material but have retained the following paragraphs despite it being similar to some pages in the appendixes, but it is in more detail and somewhat different in scope]

Turcomania is comprised of that land which lies within the borders of the Caspian to the west, to the north it is bounded by the Aral Sea and the Oxus River, while to the East the land goes until lost in the foothills of the Hindoo Kush and the trailings of the Himalayas, to the southwest it is hemmed in by the mountains and hills of Persia and two rivers the Attrek and Gorgan, while farther to the East, the border becomes a flat and dry land; a true desert. Several small rivers flow from the mountains, but none have enough force to avoid being evaporated by the desert, and these do not join the Oxus. The desert makes up the greater part of this land. This dry land has no cities or towns, and it inhabitants live in tents and they move their villages as they see fit. Their lives are a cycle of continual search for grassland and water. It is their proud claim that they have neither shade nor king, and for the latter they are grateful, and the former they rue.

Our guide described the method of the Turcoman's man stealing raid on the Persians. A notable leader will announce that a raid will be done or a group of family members will discuss the same. Each man comes with his horse and some rations, some cooked rice, a bit of wheat flour, other grain for his horse, some slabs of cheese, plentiful water and his weapons plus his slaving irons.

Slaving irons. Illustration III-XIV-9

They then move towards their goal at what we would call a trot. They stay at this pace for long periods of time, stopping only for short periods to let the horses graze on any grass that might be found. The man himself eats little and sleeps less. They are supported by their companions, who treat what they are doing as a bit of a lark.

They look at a raid on the Persians with the same gravity, as young boys who take the risk of raiding a neighbour's apple tree. They are completely disdainful of Persian strength, and well know that no organised opposition will be offered, for they say the Persian is a 'weak body with no head'. Having been in Persia and among the Persians for some time, I can agree there are no real adults in charge within that kingdom.

Their usual method of attack is to come in at dawn, either on a party along a road, or to take farmers going out to tend their fields or flocks. Sometimes if the wall of a village is in ill repair - a universal problem in Persia, they will enter to steal children and women. If the wall is complete, they steal the herds. They take the strong and beautiful into their slavery. All others are slain. A Turcoman claims he can defeat eight Persians by simply appearing before them. So in awe of these raiders are the Persians, that they often offer no resistance at all. I wonder what Xerxes and his Immortals would have thought of such modern Persian cowards?

If they secure men of a suitable age, or a woman, they swiftly secure them with irons and attach them to their horse by a rope. The Turcoman never intends to fight and is quick to leave the area they have raided. The captive is forced to run along while the Turcoman flees the area. If the captive cannot keep up, they are slain. Occasionally if the captive is a young and beautiful girl she will be tied to the back of the horse, but this is rare.

The Turcoman retains captives in the hope of obtaining ransom for them. As, however, the Persians kidnapped are mostly poor, the ransom money never amounts to much, and is often not obtained at all. To stimulate the relations of the prisoners to send money for their release, the Turcoman subject their captives to torture, immersing their legs in boiling water, placing red hot embers on their stomach, and so forth.

One aspect of the Turcoman that is surprising, is their dedication to their own freedom, which contrasts with their properly endowed title of 'man-stealers'. In their devotion to liberty and equality, no Turcoman is above or below the rest, nor is any man a master of another. Each Turcoman is the king of his own tent, family and herds, and they pay homage to no nobility, governors, chiefs, ruler or magistrate. Respect is given to the elders who give guidance or entreat a course of action, but it is only that; advice. Some respect is also given to other family members, but even this fades away, once the man is married. It was said that among them, the rarest thing is to find a man who thirsts for power, and rarer still, a man inclined to follow him.

What rules the Turcoman, is not law, nobility or mother but *deb*, the customs, morality and rituals of his people and they

(...)

[Editor's note: Driscol stopped abruptly and did not restart on this subject. Instead he turned the page and started on another subject]

Much to my regret, I had not been able to fish in the local rivers, as I had not seen any native doing so.

I heard a shout, and a bevy of horse cries from behind me. I turned to find that Dissanayake had been thrown from his horse, and that it was standing next to him, looking at him with a disapproving eye. It is where our man lay that was the cause of concern; he was entangled in a large *kar-e-sotor* as the Turcoman calls it, of the family *Papilionaceae {camel's thorn}*, and he was thoroughly entangled in the thorns of that suffrutescent *{slightly woody or shrubby at the base}*. It was hard to keep our laughter at bay. It was found impossible to cut away the bush without jabbing more thorns into him and the guide had a simpler solution he brought up our camels and they proceeded to eat the bush away from around him. We chided him on not being tasty enough for a camel to eat. Michaelson found him hale and hearty beside the two score or so of thorn pricks and a few sharp thorns, which we plucked from his nether regions.

Horne says to me in private that he believes that Dissanayake falls because he is in a daze, and that he is lost and might as well be locked in a lavatory in Timbuktu for he is certainly not here paying attention, making light of his inability to maintain his seat.

After this incident, one of the Turcoman came up behind Bannington, and shouted at him in a language I recognised as Russian; but what he said I had no idea. Bannington just looked at him in puzzlement. This led me to believe that some, if not all the Turcoman, might think we are Russians. I warned each of our men in turn over this.

Our animals were being fed with *juwaree*, or barley straw, which is chopped into small pieces and given to horses instead of hay. Blonde would eat sixteen to twenty pounds of it in a day.

Vickery's horse Akua whose haggard look was considered a source of amusement by the horse loving Turcoman. Illustration III-XIV-10

The camels would also eat it, but as a ball mixed with a little sheep fat, but even this they do not require each day like a horse. They were happy to eat any indigestible bramble or dried bush we came across, as the lush lands of Persia were being left inexorably behind.

The Turcoman has found our horses fascinating, for they love horses, and ours are both mysterious and strange to their eyes. Bannington's mount is the most respected, Perkins' is next and the one that most laugh at is Vickery's. Blonde, being a mare, receives scant notice.

Bannington's white Arabian stallion garnered the utmost respect from the Turcoman. Perkins' black stallion was also admired greatly. Illustrations III-XIV-11 & 12.

Day 6 Friday 7 July

We begin the morning with *coppok*, or whipped camel's milk; a thick and pleasantly acid drink, that I have come to enjoy. Given that this is a Muslim holy day of prayer, we expect some religious action, but it is not a concern to the Turcoman. I ask about this indirectly, and our guide claims that Allah allows them to pray by riding. This seems sensible to me, and pragmatic. Dissanayake is beside himself in wonder at this skewed, moral, compass and temporising.

We have been climbing upwards again into some nearby brown hills. This feature stretches from the northwest to the southeast in a nearly straight line, from what we can see. It is 97° this day, and coming down the northern incline, we see the desert before us, the Kara-Kum which the Turcoman calls the Garagum which means the black sand desert.

It is not truly 'black', but in parts it is reddish grey with tinges of black. Beyond us, we can see dunes lining the horizon, with their indescribably graceful, sinuous, concentric curves. There is little green to be seen, brown predominates. We had started before dawn and make a long trek that day. I would estimate that we went five and thirty to forty miles, and I will write no more as I have fallen asleep twice while writing this. Yet!

I have become an explorer and my ecstasy at this is beyond measure.

Day 7 Saturday 8 July

Our movement has begun to become a pattern, for we must rise early in the morning, an hour or more before dawn. The guide's men keep guard, but we do also. They show no annoyance or acceptance of our doing this. As I usually elect to stand guard for the last period of time, I am always ready to go.

I write up the previous day's incidents in the morning, if I did not do so the night before. I make the pretence to take out my Holy book, light a candle and place over me a covering held up by sticks. I leave the Qur'an open, along with my Arabic dictionary and take out my journal. I also lay My Frenchman next to it. God or a bullet will greet the man who disturbs me. In this manner I can write without being suspected by the Turcoman not that I would think they are in anyway suspicious of us being anything besides Russians.

We came in the afternoon to a slight rise, and when crossing it, we come across a great feature in the land. It is obvious what it is at first sight. It is the foundation of a dry river; the bed is four to five hundred feet in width and filled with loose sand. On our side, the bank of the river slopes gently down to an embankment of ten feet, while on the other side, the banks are much higher; perhaps forty to fifty feet. The sand is arranged in dunes, and if the embankments had not been in place, one might not have noticed the dry river channel at all. All over this area are spots of green, showing that tamarisk and other thorny brush can live here. Our path continued along the southern bank until we came to and went past a marshy area, where the course of the former river is filled with water. Our guide explained it was hopelessly salty, even too much for a camel to drink. We passed at one point a body of water that is of a livid, purplish pink, colour and well encrusted on all sides by salt; the pink and white making for an interest contrast.

We went along and turned sharply to the west and came up to some ruins, and within the bed of the river was a pool. Our guide announced this to be Igdy Well, which consisted of several wells that are bored down through the clay to the clean water; the water in the pool being encrusted with dried salt as usual.

At the wells were crumbling ruins that were some three to four feet high. A number of rectangles were all that remained of what I suppose had once been a village. Here and there, stones had been piled up to form pillars, and in other places, pits were seen. This desolate scene of a once thriving site of habitation disheartened me, as I counted some thirty ruinous places in this apparition of a village. We descended into the bed of the river to obtain our water, all around was the white of salt, then the grey of the sand, and above that, the partial green of sturdy plants that somehow grow here. The bed of the river could be seen to have cut into the soil and there is rock here also. All about were the bones of camel and horses, but I saw none of man.

Our water was renewed here and I found Blonde was suffering much from the heat. I covered her with water. The horses had had a hard time of it in the dunes, where the clay floor of the desert had been covered over by the ever shifting sand. However this path is thousands of years old, and nearly forms a trench, and is impossible to miss, even if covered here and there by a dune.

A shout went up from Dobbins and I found him pointing to the north, dust was tinging the horizon; a clear sign of a disturbance. The Turcoman took no great notice, but our guide and the head of the Makhtoum-Khuli clan did ride up and met whoever it was. Above our heads an animated discussion took place. This went on for some time and I stood near Blonde during these exchanges. I did note that they never looked our way, as far as I could tell, but the sounds that came to me made me think they were having a most energetic discussion.

The Sparse vegetation of the desert. Illustration III-XIV-13

The Inter-Clan Conflicts Of The Turcoman

The newcomers in the number of five then rode away. Our two men came down to us to say that we would spend the night here. Perkins and I had to press the guide for an explanation, and the best we could get was that the clan which we were under the protection of, was in conflict with the men who had come to see us.

We expressed our concerns, but the guide was nonplussed. He did say that we had nothing to be concerned about, and that his clan would not be hindered by any of the larger tribes of Turcoman. However in this matter, it was one of the other gifted or special family clans like the Makhtoum-Khuli who 'our' clan was in conflict with; specifically the Atta clan who are the children of Umar. This was merely a disagreement over a previous trade that had become, as he said; 'complicated'.

We camped within the ruins of the village. We had our own discussion. The Turcoman seemed to go about their duties in the normal way, but it was sharp-eyed Dobbins who noted that the men with matchlocks now kept them in their possession at all times, and flint and steel for igniting the matches was always at hand. Swords and spears also were seen to be kept close at hand.

We settled ourselves into the ruins as best we could and decided to be at the ready at all times and that we would all rise at four in the morning to forestall any early morning attack to overwhelm us; a well-known Turcoman tactic.

Our supper was meagre that night it consisted of *korot*, which is made of salted curds, rolled into balls, and dried in the sun, which keep for a long time. It is eaten by breaking it up into water or milk, and with it we have the usual flat bread and a touch of mutton fat for our butter.

Day 8 Sunday 9 July

I spend a fitful night waking every few minutes, to check the position of the moon and estimating the time. We all awakened as we had planned, and formed a rough square within the ruins and had another discussion. The Turcoman showed little interest in what we were doing and made no comment, but the head of the Makhtoum-Khuli came to us with the guide and said that we were obliged to wait for a resolution of the disagreement before we could safely move on. Perkins asked if it would be safe for us to see the area around the wells. The Turcoman thought we were mad but the guide explained - or so he told us later - that he had informed the man that we Circassians have a need to wander that cannot be controlled.

We left our luggage, except for what we would need, in the camp, and decided to scrutinise the bed of the Oxus and obtain a longitude and latitude for this location. Thus, resolute and determined we marched out and down into the bed towards the west. As soon as we are beyond their sight, we posted guards and set up our survey equipment. We determined after one false start, caused by sand in the instruments, that we were at latitude of 39° 90' N and a longitude of 56° 90' E. It was very satisfying, for this was the first time in over a week that we knew where we were exactly.

We settled down and cleaned our weapons and instruments, something we had also not done, as the sight of so many exotic weapons might have caused undue interest. It was at 11.43, for we were all in a group bringing our watches into agreement, when we heard the distinct sound of firing to our west for we had gone around a dog's leg to the East of Igdy Well. We heard more shots. Our concern was for our luggage, pack horses and supplies.

We were mounted quickly and found a way up the bank of the river and began to cautiously ride in single column in among the dunes that come up to the dry river bed, then came to a halt.

Dobbins and Horne rode forward to spy out the land. We remained mounted and with our weapons at the ready.

I removed the cloth disguise from my sword, checked Ascalon and decided to fit the bayonet. I took out the Frenchman, which I leave with only four cylinders filled for safety and added another round. I ensured my other two cylinders were in easy reach. I attached a lanyard to my pistol and looped it over my right wrist. I had decided that in any action, I did not want to lose her. Golden remained in her leather carrying holster. Everyone else armed in a similar manner.

[Editor's note: see Appendix III-VII for a partial list of the armament of the expedition in which they were designated as the '17th King's own Imperial light horse Polish lancers of the guard']

I would have liked to have had some men from the battery of the 1st of the 2nd here, disregarding their gypsy-like taste for colour and luridness; they being half-savage, indolent, recklessly wild, uncertain of morals and steeped in superstition. I would have wanted some here, those artilleryman, faults and all, none the less. Perhaps even Guerts who hopefully not shoot himself in the foot again.

We could hear the firing and it was our opinion that some six weapons were being regularly fired. I began to sweat and compulsively checked my weapons again, dismounted and checked all of Blondes fastenings. I helped Dissanayake disentangle his musket from his robe. Michaelson had taken on the role of warrior surgeon and was looking grim. Vickery had taken on a visage of a stern warrior. Of us, only he carried a weapon made for mounted warfare; his lance and he had five of his throwing javelins, across his back and he had placed his musket in an elongated leather pouch to keep it readily at hand, and at his waist he had secured the second Colt.

Horne came back to us at a trot, doing well to raise no dust. His training had taken hold and he saluted, and reported to Perkins that a group of men, some six or so, had the camp under fire and beyond them, out of the sight of the camp itself, another body of men, estimated at twelve or more, were mounted up and in his opinion were circling the camp to attack it from the northeast. Dobbins had sent with Horne his opinion. He recommended that we either; rest here and let the Turcoman sort out the difficulty, or that we settle the matter by moving to engage the larger party. This started a strong debate, which quickly came down to our group not wanting to become involved in a matter that did not concern us - directly. So it would have remained, had not our guide come hurtling down the dune behind us, then seeing us, he attempted to change direction so rapidly, that his horse stumbled, an indication of his panick and haste, for a Turcoman is a master of his horse most of the time. He came up to us and he told us quickly what was happening. A parley between the two clans had taken place after we had left. The discussion had failed when the Atta clan had suggested that the caravan be placed in their hands for the payment of a delivery of slaves that had gone awry in some fashion. The Makhtoum-Khuli had of course refused to do so. The others had left, and sometime later the camp had come under fire.

Perkins asked what he suggested we do; the guide recommended that we pay the amount - which was some two and half million dinars, a preposterous sum, ride away or join with them against the party of Atta - who, he took great pains to explain, were a single family and not all the Atta and that their actions were against *deb {Tradition}*.

A board of war was quickly held in French, Bannington led the war party and Dissanayake suggested we get the hell out of here. I went with Bannington, although my heart nearly failed when I so voted.

Perkins turned to our guide and announced, we fight, and he did so in French and had to repeat himself in Persian, showing perhaps evidence of his own unease.

Perkins turned to Bannington and appointed him acting commander for this action until we came up to Dobbins, for Perkins had no mounted combat experience, nor did he know how to handle what would, under Bannington, be a mounted cavalry action or would Dobbins go for dismounted?

I thought this remarkably wise of Perkins.

The Turcoman is well known for avoiding fights, unless their lives are in danger. Our guide stated that a show of force, and our use of our firearms, would cause them to quail before us. I did not believe him in the slightest.

We were soon off, Bannington leading, following Horne back to Dobbins, then Perkins and the guide and the rest of the men with myself in the rear, Vickery being just to my front.

We came to Dobbins, who was dismounted and lying just at the crest of a sand dune. He rolled down to us. War or peace', he asked?

'War', said Perkins and added 'with capers on it'. We all laughed at his wit.

The enemy is about to charge, I suggest we let them, and counter-charge into their flank. He pointed at Bannington and it was done, he, our noble companion would remain in temporary command.

Bannington gave the order and we moved at a trot to the north for some nine hundred feet. The firing had continued unabated during this time. Dobbins pointed to a peculiar shaped dune and said the enemy was there. We formed in line abreast, my position being to the far left of the line with Vickery to my right. Perkins and Bannington were ahead of us, the guide behind us with Dobbins. Bannington drew his sabre. I drew mine and then thought it would be better to charge pistol in hand. I changed my mind several times as we crested the dune ahead of us but no enemy could be seen, we moved forward. Blonde grew taunt beneath me, for she knew something was happening. One reason I had elected to be to one side, was to keep her from kicking our own horses, the nag that Vickery rode not counting, as I considered her well worth kicking.

We struggled up the sand of the higher dune, and Perkins and Bannington signaled to stop, and we tried to straighten our line. Hynes was doing this by stretching out his arms to signal that we should come up to them and line up properly.

Perkins and Bannington seemed to be discussing the weather, when the firing stopped and ahead of us, we heard then a distant shout, Bannington head came up, the enemy was in motion.

We too moved forward, struggling up the last few feet, and as we came over the top of the dune, the situation became clear to me.

[Editor's note: Driscol drew a sketch map which is in the shown below]

A mounted party of Turcoman Atta was to our left front, some six hundred feet away in a ragged line. There were some twenty of them, moving away from us at a trot, directly towards the camp, which was a half mile away but it was still out of sight.

Bannington turned and made the signal for silence and we proceeded to follow the Atta, who disappeared over a dune ahead of us. Our horses could move silently in the sand. All one could hear, was the movement of horses, the faint jangle of our chain harnesses and the creaking of leather.

As we came over the next dune, I feared the enemy would be at the base, matchlocks raised for a volley, but they were not there. They were closer now, and just disappearing over another dune ahead of us. We picked up our pace coming to a brisk canter at fifteen miles per hour. I finally decided to go with My Frenchman and placed my sword in my left hand with my reigns.

Up again another dune, we came over and I could see the camp a third of a mile away and the Atta some two hundred yards ahead of us. I had placed my spectacles on and had tied them by a cord around my head to ensure I did not lose them. On the expedition I had not used them as they are unknown to these people so I had for most of the trip been riding with distant objects only being a blur to me.

The Atta ahead slowed then gestured, we had been seen, they are good horsemen but we caught them on a dune and that slowed their turning and only half did so when we were one hundred yards away when Bannington turned and yelled.

Map Twelve: Sketch map of the mounted engagement between the expedition and a contingent of Atta Turcoman at Igdy Wells on July 9th, 1837

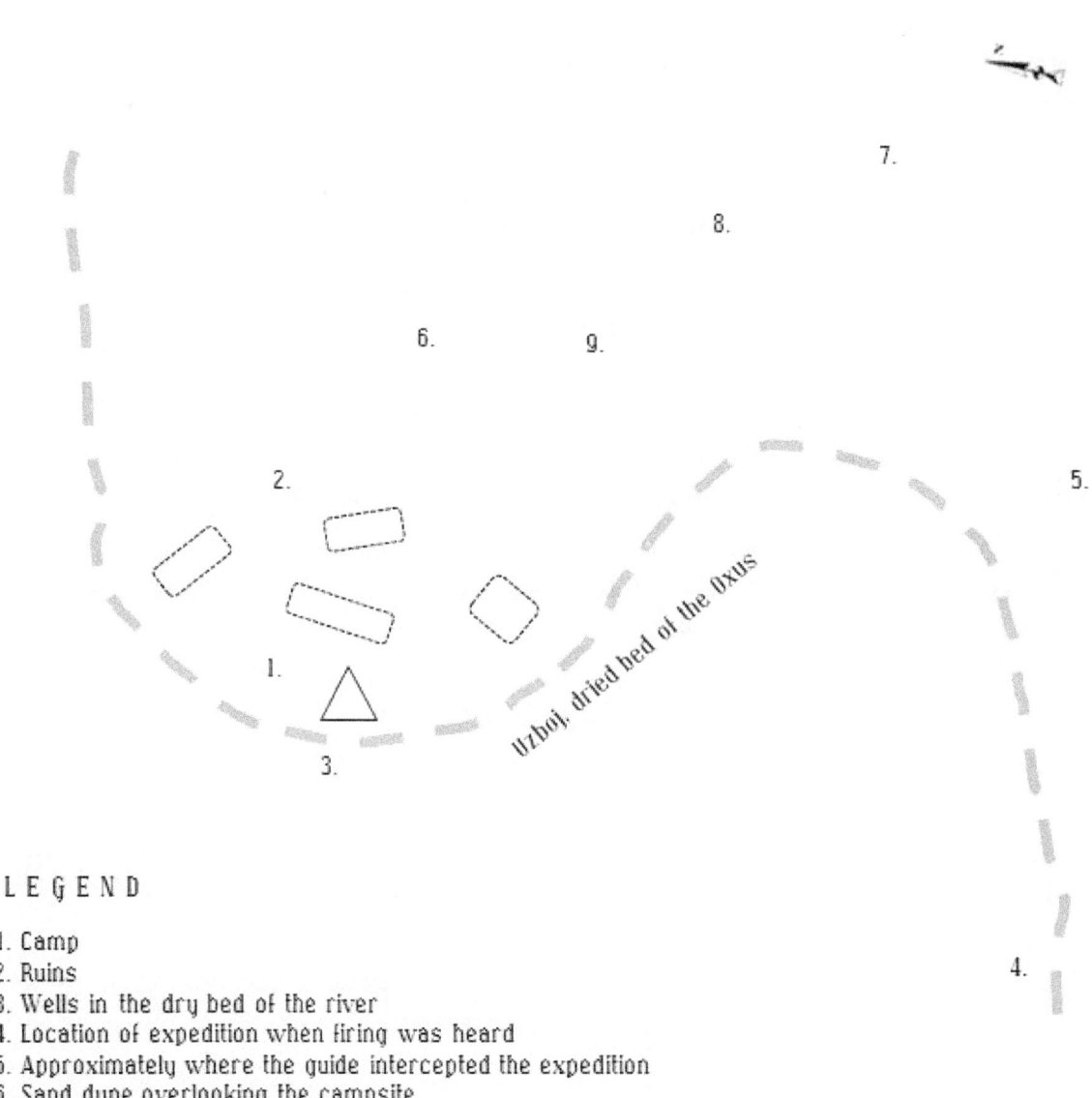

LEGEND

1. Camp
2. Ruins
3. Wells in the dry bed of the river
4. Location of expedition when firing was heard
5. Approximately where the guide intercepted the expedition
6. Sand dune overlooking the campsite
7. Turcoman horsemen sighted
8. Expedition follows the Turcoman
9. Expedition charges into the rear of the Turcoman formation and routs them

The Charge Of The 17th King's Own Imperial Light Horse Polish Lancers Of The Guard
Or
The Middlecombe Expedition Bares Its Teeth

CHARGE!

We yelled in unison, HUZZAD, I could hear Hynes voice above all yelling, 'drive home, drive home', Horne was yelling something too, but I could not make it out. Blonde had started her gallop a moment after all the others; even Dissanayake was ahead of me. I could not but think of Alexander the Great and his companions and their charge to kill Darius *(at the battle of Gaugamela in 331 BC)*. Vickery had crouched down, and like a medieval knight had his lance pointed. Some three or four Atta had spears and rest sabres. We came on as a wave, the groups practice in our ride up through Persia coming to the fore.

That we had surprised the Turcoman was evident, as they began their counter-charge far too late, and those on the side broke away, I thought to flee, but then saw that they were moving to envelope us.

In a moment we hit. Blonde is a large horse, not as large as Dobbin's monster but we collide for she had taken to aim at a smaller Turcoman horse certainly not by my direction which was to avoid such a strike, it was glancing blow, but sent the smaller slower moving animal to the ground in a spray of sand. I took no notice of the rider. To my right, Vickery had skewed his man; his sickening squeal of horror cutting through the sound of the battle. I could not see what happened as I was mindful of the men coming around our flank. There were three circling around and headed for me I decided. I dropped my reigns and held up my sword as a guard and with Blonde now circling back towards them at a cantor, I engaged the first man at twelve feet, and shot him directly in the chest. If he felt it at all, I could not know, as he swung at me strongly, which I parried with my left held blade and gave him another pistol ball *en touche*. Another blade struck along my back, but in the man's eagerness, his blade had turned, and I took no hurt from it, yet it frightened me greatly. The next man was even more unlucky; his blow missed me and sliced into Blonde's rump. I regretted having dropped the reigns for Blonde went wild, lashing out with her rear legs and turning a circle casting destruction all around and throwing me into the sand. I did a fine landing, rolling as if I had planned to do so and came up kneeling in the sand I fired a shot into the side of the second man whose blade whistled over my head. I sabred his horse in the ribs and she jumped away, the third man's horse had been kicked by Blonde with such force as to break her ribs and she went out of control, unlike me the Atta kept his seat. The first man was slumped over his saddle and his horse was trotting off. I could not remember how many shots I had fired but pulled the trigger until my pistol did not fire I did so at the second man with the sabred horse.

All about me was chaos. Shots were being fired, men were yelling, someone was shouting 'FOR ENGLAND'. Blonde was still rearing and kicking in all directions and no sane man would approach her. My first three opponents were down or busy. I found I was not alone, the man who I later determined must have been the rider of the first horse Blonde had overturned, came at me, he was a poor swordsmen, but I was fighting left handed.

I threw My Frenchman in his face, and changed my sword to my right, and took up a proper stance in the soft sand of the desert. All around me, I could now hear more firing and shouting, men and horses screaming. Beyond the approaching Atta was Vickery, sitting on his horse and rummaging around himself, in some panic or haste.

I parried several strong blows, but with my height, and longer sword, I began to thrust at his face; something he did not like at all. His face was a fierce one, and his teeth were clenched as he glared at me. Another mounted Atta came in from my right, but he turned sharply away, as I heard a Colt begin to fire. It was Vickery. We had between us the Atta I had been exchanging strokes with, and he moved to face us both. Vickery came up on his horse leveled his pistol at him, just out of sabre's reach and shot him twice. I heard the distinct sound of the bullets hitting the man and a gasping scream that did not quite leave his lungs. He collapsed, but when he hit the sand, a long high scream came from him, muffled by the sand as he pitched face downward.

I ran and regained Blonde's bridle. She who had recovered her senses but had a blood stained rump. All about me was the devastation of the battle, men and horses were down, horses and men were screaming this and that. All this had happened in less than twenty seconds, and it was another ten seconds before I was remounted, remembering my pistol which by some miracle was at Blonde's feet and visible in the shifting sand. I looked around, and assembled on Perkins and Bannington, who were standing in their stirrups yelling, 'recall, recall, rally to me'.

The Atta had scattered, broken by our unexpected charge into them. Hynes, Michaelson and Dissanayake could not be seen. Some of our men were wounded, but none seem seriously hurt.

Perkins commanded that we go to the ruins and I wondered if we would come under fire. As we rode up the dune, I found that my breathing was still rapid, and my hands and legs shaking. Blonde still seemed like a wild thing beneath me. As we crested the dune, I drew forth Ascalon with her bayonet fixed to find our camp as we had left it, with our Makhtoum-Khuli standing about in a casual manner. Our guide reappeared and stated the obvious; the Atta who had been firing had departed. He gave out a speech to his men that must have been about our charge in their honour and support, and leaving no one behind, they came with us to see the carnage. It was only then, that I realised I had left my Frenchman lying in the sand somewhere. I remembered with some shock that I had looked at it, but I had not recovered it! I suffered a momentary fear, greater than that of the fight, that it might be lost. We came over the dune again and found our other men gathered about, they had separated in the fight. Michaelson was hailed.

I found, after some anxious searching, my beloved Frenchman. This greatly relieved me. I also became more aware of the pain of the blow across my shoulder. I had Hynes, who was grimly smiling, to check me. He found only a thin line of blood going from the right shoulder down to the spine. So part of the enemy blade had actually found me and split my costume. I was well suntanned, as were all of us; on the face, neck and hands, but my pale flesh was a concern. Meanwhile, our Turcoman allies and 'friends' were busy checking the other fallen Turcoman. The butcher's bill was seven Atta slain, and two badly wounded. For us, every single one of us had taken a wound; none serious. Dissanayake's horse was dead, speared though the chest. Despite the animal's obvious hatred of him, he had tears in his eyes for the beast. He was also extremely proud of himself, for he had faced war for the first time, and no man knows how he will fare, until he does so. Horne said quietly to us that Dissanayake had killed two of the enemy with his sabre, and that he had fought like a tiger; he advised us, in muted tones, that our mild mannered clerk had become a warrior. He still stood ten minutes after the fight, with his bloody sabre in hand; he seemed both elated and stunned, unable to stop his tears for his beloved horse; or did he cry for the dead, or himself?

Bannington and Horne had set out almost immediately to scout the area to ensure we would not be counter-attacked. Before they left, I clapped Horne on the shoulder, and congratulated him on his charge. He still had a wild, distant, expression in his eyes, but he looked at me in some pain, and confessed that he had killed a man, and it did not sit well with him; not that he had killed him, but that he had enjoyed it so. I said no more to him, and watched him ride away.

The two wounded Turcoman had both lost their right arms to Hynes swordsmanship; to swing a blade at him was to lose the arm. The other Turcoman would not allow Michaelson to bind their wounds, for what Turcoman would want to live without his right arm? Seeing the blood from this wound suddenly left me in the full horror of my unmanning weakness. I had to sit a moment by the man whose life had bled away from him. By the time the dimness of my vision had cleared, and I could stand, bathed in cold perspiration, he was quite dead.

The Turcoman count heads after the battle. Illustration III-XIV-14

I found that I had been discomforted for less than a minute, something I had experienced when I was younger. As had happened then, too, I felt very refreshed and invigorated once it had passed.

Recall

The Turcoman slashes and does not use the point of the sword. As a great swordsman once said, cuts wound, thrusts kill and great cuts end the matter. The light sabres of the Turcoman had not been effective against our clothing and leather accoutrements. The battle had been won by our surprise attack, but more so by our use of firearms. Turcoman do not like to face firearms, and they had probably never seen a repeating arm before, nor did they like to fight when it was a matter of choice. Their choice was ambush and raid, not a straight up encounter.

Perkins had a cut to his head, along the right side, and almost to the temple - I told him it would leave a fine scar. He had his mirror out, and found that his beauty had not been greatly marred and was he consoled with it. Horne had a slash to his left forearm. Dobbins had taken a spear to the right thigh, but it had not penetrated; only opening the skin. Vickery had blocked a blow, and the enemy hilt had broken two of his fingers on his left hand. Hynes had a bloody cut to his left shoulder, Michaelson 'an enlarged paper cut' he called it, to his left foot, that had torn open and ruined his boot. Bannington had two wounds, both slashes to the right and left upper arm; neither of which was deep or dangerous. Dissanayake had been cut across the upper chest, and had it been several inches higher, and given with more force, it would have cut his throat or removed his head.

Besides Dissanayake's horse, four Atta horses had been killed. Three wounded horses were taken as prizes. The bodies of the Atta had been looted by the Makhtoum-Khuli, who left them naked, they beheaded them, and carried their heads in a sack back to the others. However, they obtained nothing from them but sabres, daggers and bloodied clothes. The horses were another matter. Perkins claimed one horse as Dissanayake's prize as he had lost his own. The Makhtoum-Khuli gave it up with ill grace.

Our Turcoman were rich in their own praise, for they consider themselves masters of mounted combat, but Perkins just told them that Circassians conduct mounted combat when they are eight years old. I think they believed him. The bodies were left behind. As they lay, a large portion of one of the horses was cut away and brought back to camp as horse meat is a favourite of the nomads, but not often indulged in, unless an enemy's horse can be used. His own horse would <u>never</u> be so used. It would be like eating your brother, one of them said to me in broken Persian.

My own wound was stinging like a thousand bee stings, as sweat got into the wound. As my wound was minor, Michaelson got to me last. After having examined me with the help of Dobbins, they reckoned that a patch of collodion would not be sufficient and so Michaelson decided it would have to be stitched up.

[Editor's note: It is unclear what Driscol meant here, as collodion was not invented until 1846. It is thought that he may have been referring to the use of wet paper as a bandage, which was also called collodion]

The cut was some twelve inches long, so he put in fourteen of the wretched things, and then painted the area with lunar caustic *{silver nitrate}*. He went at me with a curved needle and a silk, cotton, line *{thread}*. I suggested, in my intense pain, that he use the Roman method of closing wounds with white hot irons, but he said he was a modern medical man, and if I did not like his treatment, I was free to take my wound elsewhere. Dobbins held my arms, and in his grip, I could not move, and I went through it as best I could. I thought of a time when I had broken my forefinger in playing with wooden swords, and how the tip of my finger had been twisted around so it looked decidedly strange. I remember Zoe and Karen crying out when they saw it. It had not pained me at all, until the physician came and whose remedy was simple. He twisted it back. That brought forth from me a very loud whelp of pain.

We had barely finished, when a shot drew our attention. It was Bannington and Horne flying back with muskets out. They came in at a gallop and reported to no one in particular;

'Cavalry, fifty men, a quarter mile behind us, coming up at the trot, and armed to the teeth'. They repeated this in Persian for the guide.

Our guide demanded to know if they were Atta.

Horne yelled back, 'How the hell would I know'? He did so in English, but Hynes informed the guide in Persian, that Horne was not a native to these parts, and regretfully, he was unable to give a definitive answer to the very valid question. Horne could not explain. The Turkman and our guide could of course tell, at a glance, who someone was and what his affiliations were, by sight. We, of course, could not.

To meet this new threat mounted was impossible, our horses were down at the wells being washed and treated....nor could we face that many; even with revolvers.

Dobbins and Hynes quickly conferred, and they pointed out our position in the ruins. I, shirtless, ran to a place where the wall was highest; some six plus feet of stone, so that I could stand behind it, thus we took up our positions. I replaced the Frenchman's cylinder, reloaded the empty one, placed Ascalon within easy reach, stuck my bloodied sword in the sand, and laid out ball and powder for reloads of Ascalon. We were all in the same rectangle except for Vickery, who had taken a position just to the left of us.

Hynes tells us to hold fire. He and Dobbins will first open fire at longer range, due to their weaponry. He would then give us the command to fire. Hynes asked the guide if he could identify the leader.

The Turcoman have no leaders, there could be a *Sardar {raid commander}* but he would not be marked in anyway.

Horne yelled, just shoot the biggest ones.

Hynes turned to Horne, who was behind him, and said to him in English, 'Sir, I would appreciate that during the coming action, you do not shoot me in the back of the head by accident'.

Horne replied with all graciousness bowed and replied, 'I will endeavour to accommodate that request, Sergeant, to the best of my very limited ability'.

Hynes retorted, 'You are a good officer Mr Horne, and should you shoot me nonetheless, in spite of your assurances not do so, we shall have words together, afterwards'.

'I look forward to it Sergeant', and he gave him a mock salute.

'Right then let's deal with these bloody buggers then we will be ready for some luncheon'. Said Hynes before he turned back to face the enemy.

We could see some dust from the north and it came up to behind the dune, where we had engaged in the mounted fight not five and twenty minutes earlier, the dust came on and billowed over the edge of the dune.

Perkins rhetorically noted to all that they were probably reviewing their dead, that seemed probable or else, they were moving to encircle us at a slower pace to prevent dust rising.

A whimsical engraving printed in The Times of London to illustrate Bannington's part in the cavalry charge at Igdy Well. The only detail the artist got right was that he was indeed riding a white horse. Illustration III-XIV-15

A Cursory Discussion Is Held
And The Attack On Our Position At Igdy Well

After four or five minutes, three men appeared over the dunes; one signaled with a lance in a circular motion.

This was a call to conference. Our Makhtoum-Khuli elder returned the motion with a stick and two of his men rode forward with him. They were met just in front of our position by three of the enemy. The first man was the *Sardar* of this family clan within the Atta sub-tribe, the second man paid no attention to the parley, but instead studied us and our position, the third kept watch, to ensure none came near them from the flanks.

The summary of what they discussed was given us by the guide as they rode away obviously unsatisfied.

'The Atta wanted to know who had killed their men, and for what reason'.

'They had been told horse merchants'.

'Horse merchants did this'? They replied as they did not believe me.

'Yes' by Allah I speak the truth.

'Who are these merchants'?

'Circassians come to buy horses to fight the Russians and gain profit from the coming war between the Afghani and Persian'.

He added that the other, hearing the word 'Circassians' had widened his eyes

[Editor's note: In the context of the time, Circassians were noted for being deadly fighters, like in modern terms hearing your foe was an American Special Forces, British SAS or Russian Spetnaz]

They wanted blood money of two hundred thousand dinars from the Makhtoums, and all the Circassian horses, trade goods and themselves *{to be slaves}*. The Makhtoums would be spared their lives and enslavement and no more.

This was rejected of course. We were guests and customers of the Makhtoum and could not be given up, even if they paid for it with their blood, such was the obligation of *deb*.

The two men went over the ridge, and a moment later the dune was lined with horsemen. Hynes observed to Bannington and Horne, that instead of fifty, there were no more than four and forty; typical cavalry over-estimation, he and Dobbins both snorted in derision, to which Bannington replied with an interesting gesture of agitation.

'Forty four, fallen sons of Adam, doubly in sin, by following error and determined to commit robbery, murder or worse', stated Hynes, 'At a range of three hundred and score of feet'.

The *Sardar*, we could see, was in earnest discussion, shouting orders perhaps. From what we knew of the Turcoman, his 'orders' were suggestions; for each Turcoman thinks and decides for himself. These accursed *adamferoosh {men-sellers}* were a determined lot, but would often not engage in a real battle, preferring *chepawuls {raiding or forays}* and the ambush.

Hynes suggested that they would fix us to the front with a few matchlock men then ride around us, and attack at dawn tomorrow.

As if they could hear him, four men with matchlocks dismounted, and wandered about the top of dune perhaps looking for likely firing positions; turning occasionally to speak, actions that they kept up for some time. There was a very adamant discussion going on up there.

[Editor's note: This might seem an unwise move to a modern reader but a smoothbore matchlock could not hit a man at a 320 feet more than a football field, at that range they were safe from any accurate fire of course they didn't know that the expedition had with them some rifles that could easily hit them]

Vickery suggested they were discussing who would get to torture who, and with what.

'That is whom', remarked Perkins, his attention to grammar never undimmed, no matter the gravity of the situation.

Vickery then suggested that, like an abscess perhaps, instead of waiting for them to surround us, we should just lance it by shooting them, and start the fight at our advantage, instead of waiting for it to burst on us. I seconded the idea and an argument began but ended as soon as it started.

For one Turcoman had spurred his horse, bent his head behind the horse's neck, shut his eyes, or so I imagined he had done, yelled *Ya Allah* and pointed his lance in our general direction and headed down slope in a mad charge, screaming as he came towards us. He gave another yell that we could better hear, then two more joined him, then five, then twelve more, until the full force, with the exception of the dismounted men, was boiling down the dune's slope in a reckless charge towards us. I sighted first on the lead man, decided with a moment's hesitation that others would shoot him and fired at the left hand man of the two who had followed him. A fusillade of shots resonated in a crash of noise. I could hear the distinct CRACK, CRACK, CRACK of Hynes' air rifle, over which the thunder of Dobbins' hand cannon they closed to fifty feet at which point Hynes ordered all the others to fire. I did not, holding Ascalon's 4 bore as a finally measure of defence. The lead Atta had been unstruck and with such luck that favours the foolish, he vaulted the ruined wall of our rectangle, sailing over Dobbins' ducking head, with his horse landing near Perkins, who was in the centre of the walls. His horse had jumped at a full gallop and careered to its knees when it was stopped by a two foot, stone, wall that caught its lower, front legs. The youth, for that was what he was, hurled over his mount and struck like a projectile the stone wall beyond and next to Horne. His impact was such that the wall was demolished, along with his head and shoulders.

An Atta reigned in his horse, just in front of me and leaped to the ground, in a well-practiced move, only to be met by the full force of Ascalon's lower barrel. He fell back his upper chest and lower face shattered. His horse that was also touched by pellets ran off screaming its displeasure. Some half dozen horses had jumped into our hasty fortification, or so it seemed to me. I could see Hynes, crouched down behind the wall, firing back into them, CRACK, CRACK, CRACK. I was at them with my bayonet, running it into the lower backside of one man, whose horse was struggling to find a footing in the rocky remains of this peasant house on the side of the dried up bed of the Oxus. Another party of the Atta had headed for our horses and over to where the Makhtoum-Khuli were with their camels. Another group to the left had disappeared into the dust. Dust was everywhere with lead balls filling in spaces between the motes. I continue to try and bayonet the man while trying to avoid his spinning horse, He fell, the horse fell, and I fell too.

Melee at Igdy Well

I had thrown down Ascalon and now had My Frenchman out and my sword dangling from my left wrist, which in retrospect is not a good idea as I cut my own left knee several times on the razor sharp blade.

Two Atta came from behind me and I brought My Frenchman up but the one climbing over the wall sprouted a bloody point from his chest and fell the other turned and took a second javelin from Vickery into his belly, his shriek cut thought the cauldron of noise that was this rectangle. Perkins was wrestling with an Atta who was on top of him with upraised dagger, I dare not shoot him, so I brought my blade down left handed across the narrow of his back which so distracted him that Perkins cast him away and I shot him, with Perkins adding a shot from my borrowed Colt. I heard Michaelson's pepper pistol go off that rage of fire silencing all other shots at that time, what his target might be I did not know but I felt if it were a man, he was rather un-happy at that moment. Then Bannington backed into me knocking me down again, although I did not at that time know it was he and I found myself under a man. Who rolled off before I could position my pistol to shoot him - it was then I discovered I had tangled with Bannington!

Our rectangle was cleared now I stood and went to reload Ascalon as Atta were riding this way and that and Hynes weapon was still going CRACK, CRACK, CRACK. I obtained Ascalon and was about to reload when I next.....

.....found myself on the ground facing the sand with a taste of blood in my mouth and a terrible thirst. I had Ascalon still in my hands beneath me.

It was strangely silent, my ears were ringing. I was struggling to get up when I felt the firm pressure of Dobbins' strength, I knew it was he, from the times I had wrestled him, both lifting me up, and keeping me from any action.

'They are gone', he said in a tone as calm, and conversational, as noting the time of day.

A pain shot through my head like none I had had before. It reminded me of a tooth I had had removed as child. It caused me to catch my breath. Perkins appeared his face clean, his previous wound hidden by his cap, and half his beard sheared off by some rascal's blade.

I was seated on the wall, where I had started my defence, scattering my carefully laid shot and powder cartridges. I felt faint, and had a great desire to sleep. I looked about me. I recognised everyone. No one seemed to be dead, but all around us were Atta, very dead Atta.

My thirst overcame the pain in my head, and I ventured to feel the back of my skull. I did so gingerly, and was shocked to find a mass of dried gore, and sticky hair there, and a racking, savage, searing, pain. I drank deeply from someone's water skin. I had some difficulty and much of it ran down my face, neck and chest. Vickery came and kindly assisted me.

Have we won I asked him? I found I knew the words, but they came from me slurred, and hard to understand, even to myself who was saying them.

'Yes, rather handily. What do you remember'?

'You had speared two men, then the world went dark for me'.

Vickery whose voice now seemed far away told me the following, 'they broke just a moment after that, as if by signal, they rode like the wind. Vickery emphasized this by throwing his arms out wide. They must have realised then, the casualties they had taken. I drank a gallon or more of water. Michaelson came and seemed concerned, as he stared into my eyes and told me not to move, and under no circumstances, to remove the scab on the back of my skull. I promised I would not do something so foolish, and then slid off my perch on the stone wall, flopping like a wet rag onto the sand beneath. I could do nothing to prevent it.

Vickery helped me to lie as comfortably as I could in the heated sand and rock, and then told me the saga, as I used one hand to shade my eyes from the sun's brightness. As he had mentioned, they had broken, again our modern automatic weaponry {By 'modern automatic weaponry' Driscol meant repeating, and double barrel weapons, and most assuredly, Hynes' repeating air rifle}.

They had probably never experienced such fire power before, with the two colts, my pistol, Michaelson's pepper pot, Horne's double barrelled pistol and Dobbins' Medusa; not to mention Hynes' repeating air rifle. All the others, besides Dissanayake and Perkins, carried double-barreled muskets, and Perkins his shotgun. The fire power of Hynes' automatic air gun had been devastating. Vickery helped me to turn about, and I viewed carnage on the slope, where some eight horses and nine men lay motionless.

Within the rectangle, another five men lay with two horses, and further afield, another two, to include the poor fellow whose face and chest I had removed in a rather frightful way with my 10 bore.

Hynes and Horne walked by me, bid me a good day, and continued their discussion; for it was a vigorous one. I heard them as they walked off, until their voices were lost. However I could make no sense of what they had said, thinking at first it was French, but realizing it had been English, but that was no help in understanding it until, in a flash, it came to me like a snap of one's fingers.

...well yes', Horne was saying, 'they were cavalrymen, but undisciplined and they had failed to advance as a whole'. Hynes interrupted him to ask, 'you are saying they are cavalry. With so many of them now gone, I suspect that the average human intelligence level of this world has gone up the teeniest bit'. To which Horne replied, 'that at least they had died as cavalrymen, wait what are you saying about intelligence....'

I next awoke again, and it was early evening. Michaelson was bending over me, and a small shade had been erected over me, for the heat was still great, and the sun beat down on my body, but for some reason I did not care.

All he said was, 'good you are still with us'. I replied that, 'I had an appointment with a young lady at the Cafe Procope {then the oldest and most fashionable restaurant in Paris} but I thought I might tardy here awhile', at least I tried to say that, but I found while I knew what to say, I had the greatest difficulty pronouncing it properly.

He smiled at me and I was able to say, after the third attempt, 'If it were up to me, you would not get your fee, as your bedside manner is atrocious'. He shook his head and said, 'It is lucky you have me here at all. He held up his left arm which was bandaged. Hynes shot me.'

I said that, 'I knew he did not like you, but I thought he respected you as a physician'. I added, 'wait if he shot you why are you alive'?

'Ah good you are making jokes. No he shot a man, and the shot went through him, and into me, most unlucky, especially for the first fellow'.

'We are all badly cut up. There is little I can do for you; you must heal yourself with rest. I can do no more'. I found my head and neck had been bathed in water to keep me cool, and he had applied mustard plasters to my calves.

Was I hit by a sword or a mallet wielded by Hercules?

I found that neither was true. The men on the dune had started firing at us when the attackers broke away. I was confused and Michaelson arranged himself as best he could at my side trying to avoid his previously injured foot. I did not see it, but Dobbins and Hynes said that as we shot down the first ranks, the men in the back broke away and rode to our left and right to get away. They also said that once we struck down the few men who had ventured up to our rectangle, and seeing them cut down, they, the ones dismounted on the dune, open fire, one of those shots had just clipped the back of my skull, probably after a ricochet.

'My brain is still inside then?'

'If you have one, it is still in there', and he tapped my head which caused a wave of nausea and pain.

He apologised for the touch, and added that there had been eight wounded Turcoman; all but two died, as they would take no attention. One rode out a few hours earlier, taking a message to the clan elders of the Atta to resolve this. It was the *Sardar*, so he may wield some influence; the other is still here. Michaelson waved over in some direction I did not see. The wounded Atta would take no aid and he had exchanged his dagger for food. He was shot thought the lung, and he didn't know why he was still alive. He had lost too much blood to be alive. Michaelson believed that the Attar was too dim-witted to realise that he should be dead by now...or that was his medical opinion.

I requested he bring me my medicine kit. He knew where I kept it, and had helped himself to it as we had agreed. I secured one of the tablets that contained the goddess of the poppy. Michaelson added that the Sardar himself had come into the rectangle, and he had emptied his pepper pistol into his horse, killing it and wounding the Sardar in the leg, breaking the lower bone he thought,

but the man had mended it himself, before he rode off.

Driscol dreamed of flying as a Prince of Arabia in his opium driven dreams. Illustration III-XIV-16

I was soon carefree and thinking of a lovely creature who was neither Millicent, bibi, Danae or Karen, who stroked my hair and murmured sweet things to me, that made no sense, but which I liked to hear nonetheless. I had no appetite and went to sleep, where I dreamt of the 1001 nights and of steering a bird powered flying carpet through the starry heavens.

The desert from the vicinity of Igdy Well showing the secondary camp, the dry bed of Oxus was just beyond the smoke and before the low hills. This image is from 1881. Illustration III-XIV-17

Map Thirteen; Turcoman attack on the camp at Iqdy Wells

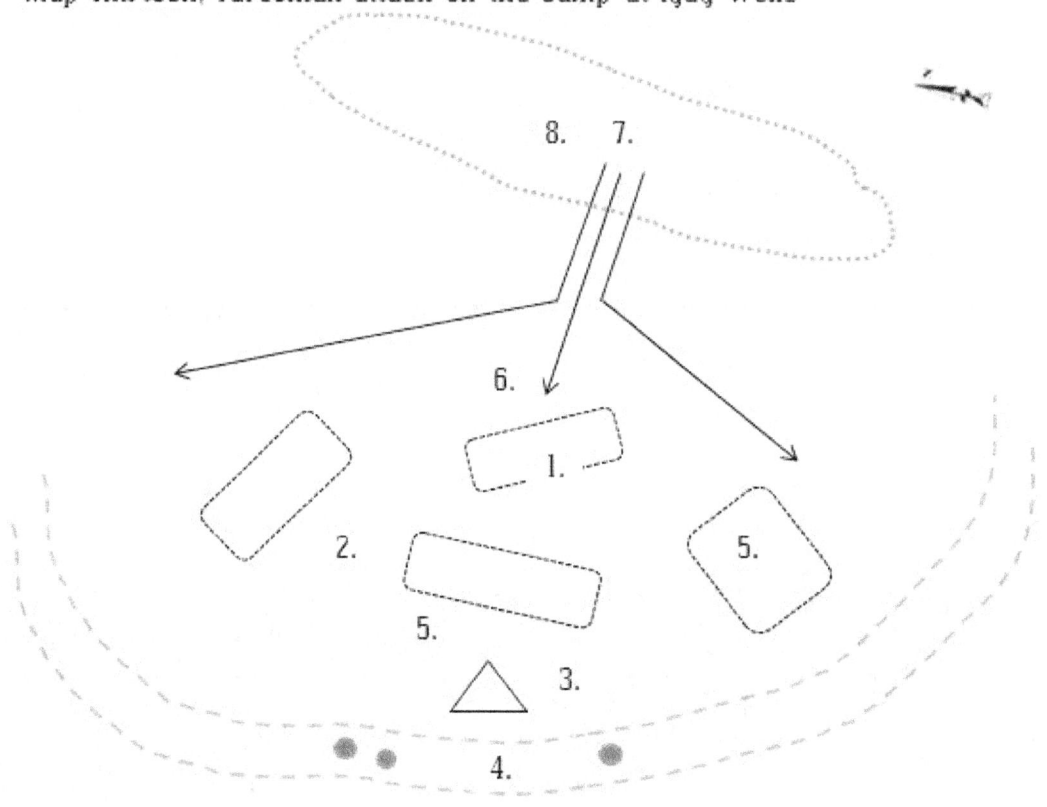

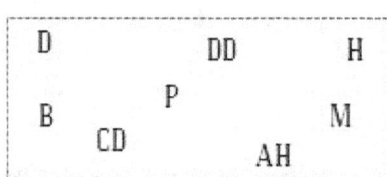

Diagram showing
where the men of
expedition set up prior
to the Turcoman attack

V

D		DD		H
		P		
B				M
	CD		AH	

1. Location where the expedition took up their positions
2. Ruins are shown as rectangular dotted lines
3. Tents and camp
4. Wells and where the horses had been moved
5. Where the caravan men took up their positions
6. Parley took place
7. Main Turcoman attack and showing pathways taken by them when leaving the sand dune
8. Where Turcoman matchlock men took up position one of whom shot Driscol
V=Vickery, D=Driscol, B=Bannington, CD= Dissanayake, P=Perkins, DD=Dobbins, H=Hynes, M=Michaelson,
AH=Horne

Our Situation Reconsidered

Day 8-10, 9-11 July

No entry from Driscol. Vickery's official notes on the Expedition for these three days;

> Expedition re-supplied to the members 1½ pounds of powder and two one pound bars of lead, for shot expended in defence of the position at Igdy Well.

> A supply of weapons, clothing and horses lost by the force that attacked us has been given to our escort. One horse was retained to replace that which was lost to Private Dissanayake, due to enemy action. We also purchased the life of one wounded attacker and sent him away on his horse, as he would have been killed by our guide's men, had he remained.

> 1 jar of Harvey sauce was taken from the collective stores for expedition use.

> A map of this area has been completed with three observations of its location, by star and by sun shot.

> Dissanayake is charged with the destruction of our only Réaumur scale[2] which he dropped. The full cost of fifteen shillings will be deducted from his private soldier's salary, but he protested that it was an accident and that the accident had been caused by his being jolted by Dobbins' horse. Perkins reduced the charge to one shilling as the scale was used, and it was the opinion of many in the expedition that it was inaccurate.

> A/S *{Assistant Surgeon}* Michaelson and Ensign Driscol reimbursed in the accounts for drugs secured for use of the wounded to a sum of five shillings eleven pence

Day 11 Wednesday 12 July

It was in the inky darkness of the unawaken day, that I arose and watched as dawn came to us from the East. It would be a beautiful day, I thought, if a little hot, and it beckoned me with its light to stride forth and do great things; not only for myself, but for the expedition, my family's honour and for England. However, I decided that this greatness would wait patiently for me, and I slept another hour or so.

We are still in the vicinity of Igdy Well, only now we are at the other side, and up wind of the well, pool and rectangle, the carnal display made from the binnacle list there *{naval term for sick or dead list}*, made staying anywhere, near impossible from all the unburied corpses lying there. Numerous bodies' horse and man emitted an *effluvium* that offends one senses. The Turcoman uses the term, 'they have planted their horseshoes' to refer to death. Our Turcoman would not bury the enemy dead or their horses.

Horne rose up, and in the finest of counterfeit Shakespearean voices, expressed those immortal words of the Bard in his play Coriolanus;

> *You common cry of curs! Whose breath I hate as reek o' th' rotten fens, whose loves I prize as the dead carcasses of unburied men that do corrupt the air*

Dissanayake was being Biblical, when he thought it smelt like the Devil's own bodily wind. However he made it a point to declare that we all must surely have seen the hand of God in our victory without loss?

Hynes and Dobbins had both been greatly amazed, and astonished by our lack of casualties, given the size of the party against us, the rapidity of their attack, and the closeness of the melee. Bannington put it well when he said that;

Our pluck and lead was found more worthy because of the ill luck of the enemy

I was reminded of the Spartans 'no shed tear victory' when they had slain countless Arcadians for the loss of none of their own *{the tearless battle of 367 BC}.*

I had taken a dream like ride on little Dune from there to this new place, Blonde is fine her wound has no depth, bloody but not dangerous for her. I feel much better and my appetite has returned but I have deep flashes of pain at times and at other times feel nothing but my gait is unsteady and sometimes I find it difficult to focus my vision.

I have gathered notes up, and I have written up what I understand to have happened at the charge and the subsequent stand.

[Editor's note: I have placed what he wrote above and not here but in day 8 when it occurred]

After much discussion, my first recollections of the fight were misplaced. It was the opinion of the whole group, that once the first brave Turcoman lad had charged, about a quarter of the enemy had followed him. Then the *Sardar*, followed by another quarter of them followed the first. Meanwhile the two other quarters began to attack, but seeing the effect of our fire broke left and right and rode away to safety. Only the first group of men and the one man from the second quarter actually approached our position. The few that entered our defences were all slain or wounded. It is the opinion of all that had the enemy pressed the attack, he would have overwhelmed us - at a terrible cost, but he would have done so, and nothing we could have done would have repelled it. We are fortunate that the Turcoman would not willingly face musket fire, unless compelled to do so, and in this case they felt no such compulsion.

We have been remarkably lucky. No one has suffered a disabling wound or death of course. How we avoided that, bearing in mind the number of assailants, is a miracle of sorts, as Dissanayake has expressed in his own inimitable manner. Our guide treats us with awe, as do the other Makhtoum-Khuli Turcoman. They believe Hynes is a first order magus, for they saw how his weapon fired, giving no smoke, and firing without stopping, and marvelously quick. The phenomenon of our revolvers leaves them thunderstruck too. In the fight, Horne lost his two barrelled pistol, but it was found by one of our men under the body of an Atta. Double barreled weapons are not common here and few if any carry a pistol, except effete Persians.

I wake again at mid-day, ravenous and consume some previously cooked horse, liberally dosed with Harvey Sauce, which does not compare with Brand & Co. sauce, but nonetheless, was not bad at all.

My victory meal was; tenderloin of horse, previously cooked and re-warmed, with a refreshing side dish of stale and iron hard biscuit, crushed with a rock and moistened with salty tasting 'fresh' water.

Harvey Sauce

This was not English made Harvey, but some concoction made up in Madras. It was made, I believe, by dissolving six or more anchovies in a pint of the strongest, wine vinegar and then adding to it some Indian soy mixture, a measure of mushroom catsup, two heads of garlic and an ounce of cayenne pepper, plus enough cochineal dye to colour it red. The container is pottery, covered in leather, with a cork well-sealed in wax.

[Editor's note: see Appendix III-VIII for a modern version of Harvey sauce recipe]

Our guide was of many minds; the two clans were in conflict, and outright war now and the Atta would be very driven to obtaining revenge. He advised that we should either return to the Persian border, or make our way to Merv. If we waited here for a discussion to occur, he warned us, the Atta could raise a force of some one hundred or more men and they could attack us again. Alternately, we might proceed to Khiva, by the route we were following, but we would most certainly encounter the Atta again, as by tradition, this was 'their' route. Lastly - and he did not advise this because of our horses, we could leave the known trail and cut across the Kara-Kum to Khiva OR go to the northwest and intercept another trail and its wells that goes from the Caspian Sea to Khiva.

Perkins would have nothing to do with either staying, or going back. We had a discussion on this and it was decided that the last option was our best idea. It would mean crossing 90-100 miles of highland desert, rocky and not as sand-strewn as the Kara-Kum, but still a severe trial for our horses. We would, for this reason, travel this coming night and we would have left earlier, but I had been, as Perkins called it, 'out of my head'. I contested this, but all agreed that for some hours, I had been speaking with myself, and had not been aware of those about me. I had no memory of doing so and this worried me greatly.

The weather supported our move, for steady sand moving wind was coming off the Caspian from the west and it would help to cover our tracks.

Above us was a vast azure blue vault of the sky, cloudless with a faint, brownish, haze at the horizon, which stretched all around us and beautifully framed the deep blue of the sky above.

Two hours before sunset, with the temperature at 92°, we set off; each man carrying an extra water skin, appropriated from our former Atta attackers. Our greatest concern would be in encountering sand that the horses would have difficulty in. Our guide said he knew not this route in detail and only by description.

Day 12 Thursday 13 July

We travel during the night for the moon was going from first quarter to full, the Makhtoum-Khuli seemed to be all hudder-mudder, while we were all hugger-mugger *{secrecy versus the expedition's spirit of careless frivolity}*. We had crossed the dried bed of the ancient Oxus again, and found the soil beyond to be white, and very reflective in the light of the moon. However, the light was deceptive, and one could not tell a tamarisk shrub from a rock at times. This same soil was firm, and gave little to the horse's hoofs. At times, we encountered patches of salt, and some hours into the journey, found broad ridges of sand blocking our path and several times we had to change direction. I kept a knowing eye on the North Star to maintain our general course. We encountered grass wilting under the heat, but at least it was something for the horses to nibble at. Behind us, two of our men dragged a *beefroum*, a drag made of a vine called *taukh* that is used to help cover our trail in the sand. The wind also picked up, and around midnight, it switched from the west to the East.

[Editor's note: beefroum, I could not find this word or any reference to it so we must trust Driscol in this matter. It was probably a Turkmen word he did not write down correctly]

We stopped at around one in the morning. I had had a great deal of sleep and was far from fatigued, but my back wound burned still, and I found myself, at times, light headed. I had taken my normal position towards the rear of our party. We halted in an area of dried grass, where the animals ate as we did too. We used no fire but feasted instead on smoked horse and the stalest of bread.

We pushed on into the night going up an incline with the ground becoming rocky. Some of the rocks were difficult to see in the high, dry, grass. Blonde was having difficulty at times finding her footing.

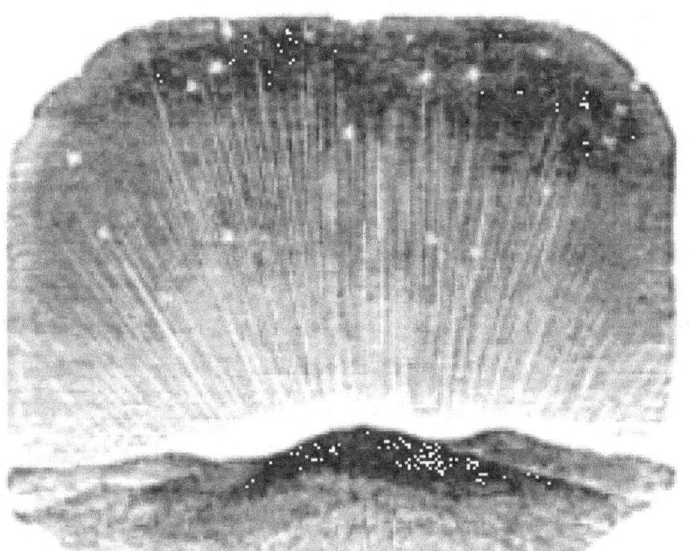

It was after dawn that trouble came.

Dawn in the Kara Kum Desert. Illustration III-XIV-18

The Hell Fires Of The Kara-Kum

Day 13 Friday 14 July

It came suddenly, with the wind masked from us by the rising of the sun. We had been discussing where to halt, but all such talk ceased. The horses, Makhtoum-Khuli and Dobbins all smelled it on the wind at the same time.

FIRE

From the East, it came skipping across the desiccated grass, and shrubs, the *astragalus* and *salsolarichteri {saltwort and other common bushes}*, dried to perfect tinder, and had taken afire. The flame, feeding on this dry fuel, was soon a streak of dancing red and yellow; perhaps a mile off, but driven by the wind, which on the Beaufort scale was perhaps force 4, a moderate whiff of air. Above it rose a whitish, grey, cloud backed by the rising sun. At dawn, such an inferno presented a fearful appearance; when far and wide the horizon was lit up in a sea of flame, hidden from us in its details by the rising sun. Even the bravest heart, for Dobbins was our bravest, cried out at the appalling sight as it moved towards us.

The guide was undecided for a long moment, then we headed parallel with the fire, to reach its edge, and we moved due north as the slope went down in that direction. One of the caravan men's camels stumbled and it crashed to the ground. This delayed us some minutes in righting a camel - a task in itself, and the fodder it carried. Once again, we set off, first at a walk, then as the sun rose and the fire came closer, at a trot, and then a canter. We could smell the acrid scent of the smoke. It rolled on towards us like red water flowing over a parched land. Its sound of roaring and crackling began to surround us. The horses' fear was beginning to mount, as was my own. The fire was now a half mile away, speeding towards us. We came to a flat plain, dotted every few feet with brush, in a nearly perfect arrangement, and by no man's order but in unison, we went to the gallop amid this two-foot high dried grass; the camels beginning to immediately pull away. The wrath of the flames came nearer. I could see we were approaching an edge or so it seemed. Blonde was well beyond my full control, as she ran in the light of morning I had to keep her from running away from the flames, and to keep to trying to reach the edge, where it did not burn, but that edge seemed to stretch out beyond our possible reach.

The scanty frondescence *{foliage}* seems to be urging it on to burn faster. As we flew at full tilt, a fall now would mean a man's death. There was much to see and be concerned about, the flames to my right, my companions around me, the camels pulling away and my path. Suddenly the camels began to disappear we had come to that previously seen edge. It appeared it was a gulley or wadi in the desert floor. It was some five and thirty feet wide, and the same in depth, with crumbly soft sides, but having no vegetation in it. The fire now was only some hundred or so feet away and cinders flew over us and the smoke choked us. We plunged down the steep sides of the chasm, so steep I knew we would tumble, but Blonde, beautiful Blonde, kept her footing till we had slid safely to the bottom, and came to a stop, sweating wildly. I dismounted. The horses, camels and men knew we would not leave this gulley, and that our fate was in the hands of providence. Behind me, others spilled down the slope. Horne and Bannington were shouting something, which I later realised meant that we should set a back or counter-burn, but there was no time. I was near Vickery and he and I upset his horse, then he and I did the same to Blonde. I covered her head and prayed she would remain down. At the last moment before the flames burst over us, I covered my head and hers with my bedding, and then it was there. A sudden blast of noise and a feeling I had experienced when I opened up the furnace of a steam engine once; intense suffocating heat, a great roaring, like a waterfall or the howl of a great storm at sea. I felt Blonde struggle beneath me.

I knew not how long this moment lasted, for it seem longer than a dull talk by a Vicar, or one of my mother's tales about her relatives that involves dull husbands and bright-as-a-new-pence wives.

Then it was gone. I found it hard to breathe and threw off the blanket and found a world of black, greyish, smoke everywhere. Men were coughing, but a tentacle of wind had come down the gulley, or as they call them in the East, a wadi. Slowly, the smoke thinned, and then cleared, as all around, I could hear men coughing. I could see Blonde was still breathing hard from her run, and I knew it was not good for her to be still so suddenly, and so I brought her up. Dobbins was also up coughing and spitting then the others got up. I climbed up the side of the wadi and found that the wind had died, as it often does at dawn, and the fire had halted and was burning some two-hundred and fifty feet from us. The wadi had been wide enough to prevent it from jumping over us, while from the direction we had come, the grass was charred, smoldering and burning here and there. A few white saxaul had survived due to their greater content of water.

As one, we decided to remain where we had come. It was a bad place to camp and stank all day from the smoke. Some items had been lost in our haste, but none of great importance.

Vickery had cleaned my weapons when I lay under the spell of the pernicious article *{opium?}* and my wound, but out of habit, I did so again.

We had all been very silent in the aftermath of this traumatic flight. For some reason, I felt my alarm had nearly overcome me. In the two fights with the Atta we had some ability to counter their hostile actions, but what can one do again a flying wall of flame that appeared to be a mile in length?

The guide came to me and asked if I and Perkins spoke Arabic. We used it when we did not wish the others to know what our exchange was about and it was intended to be *sub rosa {Latin for communicated in secret}*. I admitted that we did, and he asked how we had come to know the holy language. I said, quite truthfully that I had been to Cairo and Djedda. He knew nothing of Cairo, but had heard of Djedda and asked if I had done the Haj. I told I had not, but planned to do so in the near future. He asked if I had read the Koran, I had I said in Arabic and produced my copy, which he reverently took, opened, but could obviously could not read, as he had it upside down, and he handed it back to me with great care ,after he had first kissed its cover. When he left, he bowed towards me, with his hand over his heart.

I noted that Perkins had taken out his mirror, and had finished trimming his beard, for it had been uneven from the stroke of an Atta sword, which had cut off the left lower side. I told him that it made him look like a billy goat or a Spanish Grandee. To this, he saluted, in mock acceptance of my high praise.

At this time, I noted that my vision had grown indistinct and that I could not seem to focus on that which I looked at, and I had to turn my head or eyes to one side to see what I wished. This was disturbing, along with what appeared to be flashes of colour on the outside of my eyes. I remained immobile until this had passed. It was indeed strange, but I decided not to mention it to anyone.

Perkins and Dobbins, the perfect leaders, walk about with us, for our spirits were low and they attempted to inspire us to keep our stiff upper lip. We dined solemnly with one another on old, rancid, cooked horse, and staler bread than before, under a pale of smoke and under circumstances of extraordinary importance, or so we imagined. As we ate, our *tristesse {melancholy}* lifted.

Bannington suggested that we use this ready-made canal, become *navvies {labourers}* and dig through to the Caspian. Hynes laughed at this, coming temporarily out of his facade of a laconic figure, with an indifference to suffering, fear or doubt, but then I considered that it might not be a façade and that was the true Hynes, an Englishman gone somewhat feral in the wilds of Canada with a Cromwellian heart and a Wiggish head *{brave and thoughtful}*.

Horne raised the alarm in the late afternoon, crying out that some fine looking men, gentlemen by the cut of their coats, along with their pretty wives, were coming to tea.

He had been somewhat over-stated in his observation, for it was four camels, with two aged men and their crones who passed not fourteen feet from us. The guide pronounced them to be of a sub-clan of the Tekke Turcoman, so we hid our presence and delayed our talk until they had passed from sight.

It had been a hot day, and the horses had suffered, for it had been airless in the gulley after the wind of the morning.

We moved out, and headed in the same direction we had taken originally; to the right of the setting Sun and towards the northwest. As we rode on through the last, fading, glimmers of daylight, Michaelson and Bannington began a game in French. They would name some feature of a letter and demand to know all that would be part of that set.

The first question was; what letters looked the same upside down or up? That took some dialogue to resolve. The next question was harder, 'which lowercase look like their capitals?' The final question was which letters also signified numbers in Latin. I had thought to ask my own question, which was; what letters enclosed no space? *{see for the answers[3]}* However, Perkins forbade further talk, as it had grown too dark, and the Moon had not yet been raised up by the hand of God. Thus chastened, we rode onwards, and in silence, into the gathering mirk.

Day 14 Saturday 15 July

Early this morning, we came to a brightly, shining, flat and ghostly, white plain, under the risen Moon's light. We found it was a hard crust of salt. The horses made a great deal of noise on this surface, the camels none at all, we passed some shadowy shapes that marred the perfect white of the plain, and these turned out to be the dried remains of former camels. Our guide said that he thought this meant we should soon reach the trail that led northeast to Kazakly Well. We ran on for some time, then when dawn was breaking, we halted the caravan. The men spread out all around us, and we were left alone, for they had gone in search of the trail. The guide found it, and led us to it. It was easy to miss. We decided to push on to the well. Whether it was behind us or ahead of us, we did not know but we carried on northward. It was mid-morning when we sighted, not Kazakly Well, but an approaching caravan of some two-hundred camels, with a few riders. They were Turcoman and they were bringing a caravan of flour, salt and slaves to Goklan and onwards into Persia. The unfortunates who were enslaved were some score or so of dejected-looking Asiatic women, young girls and matrons, tied by their hands to camels and walking under a pall of sadness behind them. Our guide announced them to be Kirghiz. They had been taken in a raid several weeks ago, he later added.

They brought news that we had missed the well we sought, but that we would find the Uzunkuyu Well some miles ahead. We purchased, from another passing caravan, a few live sheep, for they had a herd of some hundred with them. This raised a faint cheer from our expedition, as the horse meat had not been popular.

We made the well at noon with the heat at 101°.

Horne observed to us all that the heat this day was enough to make sacks of flour sweat.

As we proceeded on our course, we were presented by an alluring vision ahead of us at one point. Before us came a shimmering body of water which turned out to be a mirage, quite believable when first seen. I learned from our guide that one name of this is the *suhrab {as noted; but this was not a Persian or Turkic name but the Baluchi term}* and means the water of the desert.

The two small towers seen by the expedition, probably tombs seen as they cross the Kara Kum, the artist's depiction of the sand dunes behind are rather inaccurate! Illustration III-XIV-19

I find from my companions that they hold that an animal will never be deceived by a mirage and if you believe it is water and the animal does not, believe the beast and not your own eyes.

Before we had come to the well, we passed a pair of unusual looking small towers, which I thought might be tombs. I rode around them but there were no inscriptions. I put them down as another mystery of Tartary.

The Journey Over The Burning Sands Continues With Pain

We came to the Well and found it deserted, except for a solidary figure, who acted as some sort of guardian. He showed us, for a few dinar coins, where to find the best water and a place to camp that was not covered with camel dung. The water here tasted of camel urine.

We had a most interesting discussion about medicine, in which we found that Michaelson was of the mind, that sedation of a patient by any means, and the pernicious use of alcohol or opium to do so, stole from the man his pain, which is known to be one of the most powerful stimulants to life.

He did not hold that cholera came from injudiciously eating fish and meat in the same meal, but instead held that what you ate had no effect, but that it was where and when you ate, and whether you would be overstimulated by the effects of the sun.

Michaelson also noted to us that present medical thought, that held that a man in the hot areas of India or the Orient were not healthy because of the said heat, was not in any way correct; and he hoped to prove this by more research once we returned. *{the British had yet to make it into the foothills of the Himalayas and build the wondrous hill stations, those would come in another generation, along with the realization that untreated sewage was the cause of many of the illnesses of India}*. He thought instead that the consumption of claret or port, in its recommended medicinal quantities of two or three bottles a day, might be excessive and this, tied with contaminated food, were the leading cause of illness in the sub-continent among Britons. He thought it would be best to take only one bottle a day with your well-cooked evening meal.

The burnt horsemeat that we had dined on for several days, had led to un-comfortable complications, which our medical stalwart *{Michaelson}* treated by dosing us each with the Blue Pill *{pilula hydrargyri used to treat constipation}*. We spoke about what it contained and fortunately Michaelson was a conscientious physician and made his own using a mixture of 35% mercury, 10% glycyrrhiza *{liquorice}*, 10% glycerine, 20% sugar, 15% Althaea *{ground marshmallow - the plant not the candy}* and 10% honey of rose *{a fluid extracted from rose petals and honey}*, that pill was followed by a spoonful of the dreaded Black Draught, which he did not make himself, but used the standard Royal Navy recipe taken from Naval stores; consisting of a tincture of Egyptian senna, Epsom salts, cardamom, coriander, ginger, spirit of lavender with a touch of Hartshorne *{ammonium carbonate}*.

It happily produced the predicted results, but at different times for all involved, much to hilarity of all, as one after another, the others sought privacy, in a place with none.

Michaelson observed that out of every one thousand seamen and soldiers, seven would die each year in India, but just 5 women; showing that they were the stronger of the gender.

Dobbins disputed that, but Michaelson won the contest by observing that woman can, repeatedly, survive any wound a man can take, and also give birth - repeatedly. Dobbins admitted his defeat with his deep, jocular, laugh.

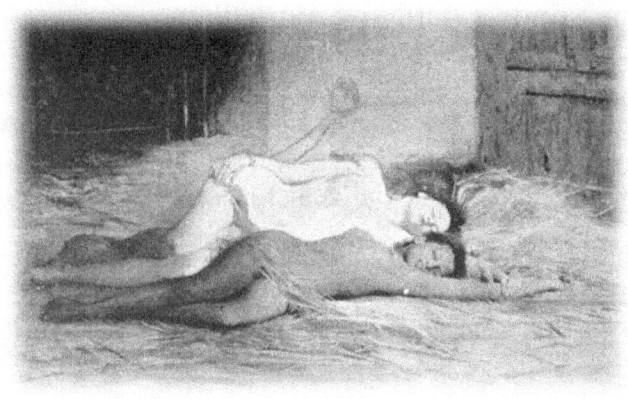

Another opium & injury induced dream for Driscol. Illustration III-XIV-20

My back wound itched the entire night, and I kept waking when I rolled over on my back and the rear of my skull touched the ground. Each time, I would turn on my side, only to be taken again by the sharpest pain, like a hot needle entering the area of my soul each time it occurred. I took more opium, Perkins and Michaelson are concerned that I might become like a Chinese opium addict; an unpredictable fiend. I had a series of fantastical dreams.

One stood with me two lovelies; one of ivory, the other of chocolate, who in my dream I found sleeping, and so enchanted was I, that I stood and watched them in my dream, until a hot needle penetrated the back of my head and stole the enchantment from me.

I puzzled over this in the early morning, unable to sleep as the scene had seemed familiar to me.

It was some time later, as I continued still to be mystified over it, that I realized it was set in my family barn, and it was a distortion of a time when I had found a white and a brown kitten in there asleep. It would seem I had grown up, and after, I wrote this. I shall try to sleep again. I reflected that my mother, while she allowed me to keep the kittens, would not have allowed me to keep the two young women.

One of Driscol's more vivid opium dreams, his sister Zoe and her friend Elizabeth Maloney. Playing with a rather large fantastical butterfly. Illustration III-XIV-21

Day 15 Sunday 16 July

More maddening dreams during the day; one of these poppy driven dreams involved my sister Zoe, and her friend Elizabeth {Maloney}, who were often tasked to take care of me. They often went to a field near our home, where I would run about and catch butterflies, and bring them to them to admire, then release them unharmed. In my dream they came across an enormous butterfly - the size of a large dog. I found that odd, and woke with a jolt, as if I had touched a Leyden jar {an early form of *battery that would give an electric shock or spark}*, but it was just the back of my head yet again.

We discuss changing back to moving in the day, but the guide says it is best to do as we do, until we reach the banks of the true and wet Oxus.

It is a long ride this night, and I still feel I am not myself. My memory has become extremely sharp, and during the day when I cannot sleep, I record what discussions occurred during our ride.

Blonde stumbled badly at one point, having stepped into a *Lepus Tolai's {Tolai hare}* underground lodge; my fears of having to shoot her with a broken leg were quickly dispelled. Dune is doing very well and is a fine horse.

Hynes commented on the noxious American notions of liberty and noted that many in Canada resembled the Jonathans in their ill-conceived presumptions, ignorance of politics, arrogance towards the rights of property and the conceit of being somehow above the true Englishman in his thoughts and that these particular Jonathans were the Princes of creation. We took a vote amongst ourselves as to whether we or the Americans would win a contest of war. It was decided, after much debate, that Lower Canada might be lost to them, but that we could with our superior navy, take and hold several of their ports and force surrender. However, our merchant commerce would suffer heavily, as it had in the past, for the Jonathan was at heart an Englishman and therefore a lion at sea, and our maritime commerce but sheep.

Horne made an astounding comment about my trusted batman, Guerts, whose help had been greatly beneficial to me in my time in the 1st of the 2nd. He stated that my man had once told him that he had thought of committing an offence against Crown property, so as to be transported to the penal colonies of New South Wales. There he said that after serving his time in the service of the Crown, he could easily have picked up several hundred acres of land. I noted this, to question him sharply on this proposed felony, once we returned.

Dobbins spoke of a time in India, only two days after he had become an Ensign, that a mad dog had attacked him. Dobbins, who was unarmed, allowed it to fasten its teeth onto his leather boot, adroitly removed his uninjured foot from said boot, then reached down and throttled it, as it savaged his empty boot.

Bannington told a story of his uncle, who was traveling in northern Lombardy, and had un-expectantly come across a traveling English family, that had a very suitable daughter - and his Uncle was on the prowl for a wealthy wife. He had obtained an invitation to dine with them, when to his horror, he found his butler, a chap he had once trusted, had only placed in his luggage his morning dress and his formal evening dress and that there was no afternoon tea coat. He sacked the man immediately but what was he to do? He was in a rural part of the Kingdom of Savoy. He thought of begging an Italian gentleman for his coat, but there were none to be found. He did find the residence of one Italian gentleman, but his staff said he was in Leghorn *{Livorno}* and would not be back for some time. Desperate and knowing well the manner of Italian servants, he took the valet aside and tried to bribe him to obtain one of his master's coats. He was successful in this, but found that the gentleman must have been a dwarf, and the coat would in no way fit him. The valet was hungry for money and suggested that the house seamstress could perhaps make him a coat?

He agreed and the seamstress was produced. She had the skills, but not the materials. She could not touch any of her lordship's clothes, so he was reduced to walking through the house with the Italian staff, looking for something that could be made into a stylish jacket; but nothing was there, the drapes would not do, the linen was lace, he looked at some golden coloured pillows with an evil intent, but no they would brand him a dandy - or worse. In desperation he found that the man had a billiards table, a table the staff said he never used. The green baize of it was taken up and made into an incommensurably bright but stylish jacket. His coat was made, he made the tea party and he found the daughter, while she was a jewel to look at from a distance, she had the teeth of a British coal miner, and he was disappointed greatly in love; but he had obtained a gaming jacket of some repute!

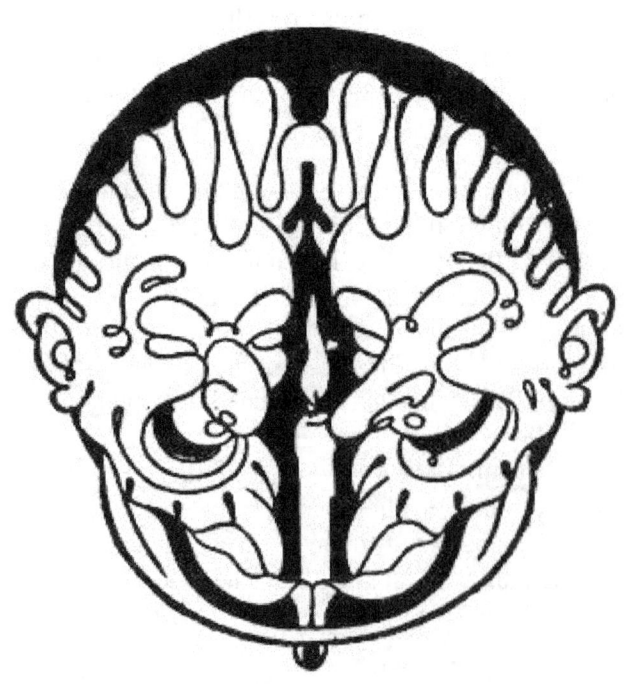

We Come To The Dried Bed Of The Oxus - Our Old Friend

We came again to our old friend; the bed of the dried out Oxus, but here it was wetter and there were numerous brackish pools, some green with algae some red by other means. The water here was poisonous. We found from the Turcoman, who for once offered up a geographical comment, that in this place, the dry bed was called the Uzboy[4] and that for some miles, there would be both sweet and salt lakes. It is here that the former river re-enters the Kara-Kum, and sand dunes can be seen on both sides of it and the bed is well filled with sand. The direction of the former river is to the north and it was in this direction of travel, that we came to the large salt lake called Betendal-kol and nearby were the wells of Sarakamish and Dekcha, where we obtained brackish, but drinkable water. I could see the Blonde relished it no more than I, but Dune drank large amounts of it.

Bannington demonstrated his knowledge of geology in pointing out that in the northern hemisphere, the rotation of the earth influences the flow of water, and that the right bank of a river will show more erosion than in the south by the action of rotation of old grape[5].

Perkins came to speak with me that night, as we rested and ate. I was removed from the rest of the men, as I was hiding the fact that I was writing from the Turcoman. I did so using one of our rare pursers's toothed glims *{a candle made from spermaceti, costly but giving more and better light than tallow}*. Perkins wanted to discuss Dobbins and his leadership and what I suggested he should do about the trouble brewing. Perkins' comments and complaints were but thin gravy to cover the meat of his argument, which was that he was afraid of Dobbins' influence and attempts to undercut his leadership, and that if this continued, he must take sharp measures against him. I said that I understood his concerns and position. He uncharacteristically replied abruptly.

'Driscol you say you understand my position. My position you say? Only six people might or could understand my position; a king about to lose his throne, a general to be relieved of his army, a husband his wife to a seducer, a German Professor who has unfortunately gone mad and who can recite my apprehensions and distresses backwards in Latin, God almighty, and the Devil, who knows that no matter what he does, he will lose in the end.'

I had noted of course that Dobbins had continued to overstep the bounds of the hierarchy, for he was a formidable leader and had a dominant personality, matched by that of Hynes, but Dobbins knew his position, and in reality - and I did not say this to Perkins, Hynes ran the expedition, while Vickery kept the paperwork straight; Perkins commanded it and Dobbins directed it. I did say to Perkins that Dobbins was within his rights as second in command to act as he does. If you thought he was overstepping his bounds, you should tell him.

Perkins said, 'I have and he was neither apologetic, nor forthcoming with any statement to moderate his ways'.

After an awkward silence, we discussed the other members of the expedition. Of the many things that he said, these few have stayed in my memory as I wrote them down immediately after Perkins had left.

> He said of Vickery, if one were to throw him, tied up into the sea, he would emerge with a fish in his mouth. Most assuredly!

Dobbins he said wears his silence nature like some knight wearing a suit of armour - what lies beneath, no man can tell. He is not a true Englishman or a gentleman.....he lacks a generosity of spirit that is hard to define, but he is not like an English bred man. Agreed!

Horne, he noted, is like a dry reed, which seeks the company of a fire, weapons ready and good sense absent. Quite True!

He is a clever fellow that Michaelson and he told me this account the other day;

> Michaelson noted that he was once asked by a wife if he could improve the civility of her husband, who had the habit of constantly spitting on the ground, rugs and floor, by the application of some herb. He said he could, and later told her, that he had operated on her spitting cobra of a husband and had shortened his tongue, so that while, in the past, he used to spit all around, he now but dribbled on his breast - he said this in jest of course. What alarmed him was the wife seemed to think this a sensible solution and wanted it done post-haste!

Perkins then said a most shocking thing, for he asked me in all seriousness, if I thought Michaelson might be a Russian spy? Michaelson seems to be a man with a notable background, but what is a man with such family doing as an Assistant Surgeon in the Indian NAVY? I began at this point to worry about Perkins, thinking he might be becoming imprudent from worry and his concerns for both the expedition and his position at its head.

Perkins observed that Bannington had probably never done any physical labour in his life more demanding than self-abuse, and seducing oafish servants, but that he had shown himself to be diligent, and a clever lad nonetheless, and a man to be relied on in all things. I agreed completely.

Hynes was our stalwart; there was nothing this man seemed not to have done before or that he was unable to do himself. He is a godsend.

I suggested we should recommend him for a commission, but no, Perkins did not think this a good idea, as the problem with Dobbins was that he too was a good man, but no gentleman. I replied that Hynes was a true gentleman. On this Perkins thought for some time and said that yes, in a rough way he was much more so than Dobbins.

> Perkins' take on Dissanayake; he does not have any disreputable vices - how can a man trust another man with such a lack of enthusiasm for life? He then told me that our man had said the following to him a day or so ago;

> > I find it to be child's play to resist the temptation of other's vices, especially if that habit makes them unpleasant.

I reminded him that we had discussed, many months before, the idea of splitting the expedition. It was one reason we had taken on so many men, good men. So it was decided between us, that once we reached Khiva, the expedition would split; one party going up to the Aral Sea, the other to trace the former bed of the Oxus and back to the Caspian Sea. This was a legitimate goal and it would serve to set Dobbins and Perkins apart for some time. The problem would be who would go with which section? The only known part of this idea was that Perkins would be in one section and Dobbins in the other. I made it my goal to be with Perkins.

Day 16 Monday 17 July

The guide says now that we are four *mezil {Turcoman for a day's march}* from the pleasures of Khiva and that in two more, we will arrive in paradise.

In the early morning, just at dawn, they came before we had camped for the day. They came into our camp, emissaries, for we had not run far enough, or fast enough, to avoid those we had engaged at Igdy Well. They had come to talk of peace between the two sub-tribes of the Turcoman. This was accomplished after much discussion. The thorny issue was us; we were guests of our sub-tribe, and therefore under their protection, while their enemies were ours and vice versa. As they had a duty to protect us, we also had a duty to respond to any attack on them. Pledges were made, fines were established, oaths made and the matter to our observation resolved and the emissaries departed well satisfied. We were now at peace with the Atta Turcoman.

Sarykamysh Lake or as the Turcoman called it the Sarygamys Koli, from which the dried bed of the Oxus, called then the Uzboy, once flowed to the Caspian Sea. This lake may have been the source of the rumours concerning a lake that flowed into the Caspian. Illustration III-XIV-22

Turcoman Negotiations On The Matter Of Igdy Well

Our Guide came to us later and explained all this in more detail, as we had not been involved in the discussions, which had taken place in their Turkic tongue. He said to us what I had noted above, but added, 'at this time the matter has been resolved, but I must warn you, as you are my guests, once you have left my protection, the families of the men you killed may seek their own revenge. The enemy leader's son died in the fight, and he is resolved to take his vengeance out on you. The tribe is at peace with you now, but not his family. I suggest that you do not return to Circassia by the way you came. We did ask how there was a leader in a people who had none. He explained that the term he used described the man selected by consensus at that time to make decisions of an immediate nature, *id est {Latin, i.e., that is}* a war party leader and not a leader of the Atta and of that particular family.

He turned, but then turned back to us, and told us also that, we had been referred to as the 'magicians'; for the tale of the breaking of the attack was being spread all over Turcomania and afar. It was said that we had black arts in our power, weapons that fired endlessly and without smoke. In his eyes, I could see that he feared us, and I wondered perhaps that he carried a snake in his pocket *{feared the expedition and secretly wished it ill}*. He said that once we arrived at Khiva his commission with us would be ended, and he would be done with us.

Horne, who still holds that we should travel as Englishmen, took this as a time to voice his long held opinion, oft-times expressed, that a man should, no matter what the situation or the happenings around him, keep to his own race, breed and religion. If these rascals had known we were Englishmen, they would have kept their distance.

That was so, said Hynes, but we would have gathered about us even more enemies and perhaps ones that were larger and more dangerous. Hynes also remarked that perhaps he should have scalped all the men he had shot that day. We were horrified by this as it was certainly cricket to put a piece of high speed lead through a man's body and slay him, but not to removed his hair as a trophy, Dear God of Heaven! I do not believe Hynes was serious about this, but he did explain the method and science of scalping; Dobbins and Horne finding it fascinating.

It was another hot march that evening. As we moved at night, the days are dreadful; full of suffocating heat and flies and my Indian mosquito netting is a great comfort. I wonder what the Turcoman makes of it, for they have nothing like it, as they rely on their beards and dirt to keep the insects at bay. We travel through a ghostly landscape, past sculptured acreage and pillared rocks; as odd in their shape, as to make one think he travels in the ruins of a great city: a city of ghosts. We come in time to Ortakui, or the inner or middle well. Here we encounter four large caravans, all preparing to move in the day over the route we have come. They use mainly camels. Our guide has insisted that we move at night to spare the horses, and I could not agree more, as Blonde sweats gallons during the night her blanket being drenched by the end of our 'day's' march. Dobbins' pack horse has gone lame in the front left pastern *{lower part of the leg}*. He has had her pack removed and she suffers along.

Dissanayake comes to each man in turn and gives each a small dose of religion that he had been unable to do on Sunday. I would have preferred a drink of cool water more; especially one that did not taste of salt or ammonia *{from camel urine}*. We watched for some time the manner of the caravans at this well. A caravan of fifty of so camel came in after we arrived and the men remove the camel's packs, while they make known their wish to drink. Once relieved of their packs, they move with some speed to the well and drink their fill. As they do so, they relieve themselves at the edge. This accounts for the taste of the water.

During our trip that day, there was this incident with our guide. He has a habit of beginning our night's march with a grand set of gestures, but invariably after no more than a half-mile had been travelled, he stops to make water in the trail side bushes. This time he disturbed a snake, which instead of going away from him, went around him and onto the road and began to cross it. This can be a very bad omen, to have a snake cross one's path, but our guide was quick witted and sliced it in half with his sword while giving a thunderous *bismillah!* He then did a bit of dancing with his men joining in; having celebrated his victory over the snake he remounted and in his movements brought his horse to where the snake lay. It had been several minutes since the serpent had been cut in twain, and it still twirled and twisted, but with the horse there it somehow, in some unfathomable way struck out taking the poor creature in the leg just above his hoof and into the fetlock. The horse reared and our guide was thrown to the ground. The still living snake was dealt with but the damage was done.

We found the snake which was only three feet long and yellowish brown colour, none of us knew, I thought it might be a *Gloydius halys* but this was disputed, but we all agreed it was some manner of *Crotalinae {pitviper}*. That it was venomous was soon demonstrated as the poor horse, such a fine beast, was soon shivering, foam came to his mouth, then his bowels became un-settled and within twenty minutes he collapsed on the road. The guide sent us on, he was quite sad as he had raised this horse from infancy. This was a true demonstration of how these men loved their horses. He stayed behind with another horse and came up to us several hours later. He related that, sadly, his snake bitten horse had not survived.

Day 17 Tuesday 18 July

This night we passed a great ruin, which we find to be the ruins of a Khivan fort called the Ismukshir; we are now encountering small groupings of the Turcoman known as the Yohmuds, who inhabit this plateau, for we have now left the fringes of the desert. Numerous are the ruins here; many of the names are forgotten, but our guide speaks of a few of them he knows. There lies the dead city of Tarpakkala, and then there are the twisted ruins of a city whose name is no longer remembered except for the title of its leader, the three-finger ogre. I believe that this region was once the great kingdom of Khwarizum, now lost to time, and to the blood lust of Jinghiz Chan *{Ghenghis Khan}*. There is no more sand and the horses have a much easier time of it. At the ruins of Akchegeli, we pass another caravan and the men of these two share greetings as they are of the same race.

We came in time to a place where the sparse and brown grass of the plain gave way to greenery; we could tell that even in the dark of the night for we could smell the living lushness of it. We soon entered an area with another well. We would rest here some hours, and then proceed again, for we would switch over to day travel again; but Perkins decided to rest the day here and we took up our camp and had a good rest in celebration of having successfully crossed the Kara-Kum.

Dobbins took with his rifle, at a range of seven hundred and sixty feet for we measured it, a *Gazella subgutturosa {goitered or black-tailed gazelle}*. However the shot took the animal though the hind quarters, and he had to be chased down. It was a much appreciated addition to our larder, despite having a rather gamey taste. He remarked at the time, when questioned why he had taken so long to take the shot. He said that, in aiming at the creature, he had for some odd reason, a quirk of his mind, delayed. The matter of this was that he had considered for a moment about waiting for it to move slightly, in particular to move its front leg which was nearest to him which was set back. He considered waiting for it to move the leg forward, something he would have done if it were an elephant or water buffalo, which would have allowed him an unobscured heart shot - but of course it was not a large creature and the strange thought had delayed him a few moments. While an elephant's leg could absorb a shot a small gazelle's leg could not of course. He thought his momentary pause to be a demonstration of the advent of old age and the confusion of the mind that occurs when this happens. We all thought it was the heat which had in some ways affected us all.

After this Blonde is sweating so much that I later dreamt of drowning in an inky dark sea of horse sweat. It has been my habit, when arising for guard duty, to give her more to drink and a bit of sugar or root, if it can be found.

I could not sleep, of course, and went to view a tower that sat a mile away. Vickery was game for the exercise, and we went by way of the ten toed horse *{they walked, horses have either four toes if you count the hoof as one or if no, none, men have ten of course}*; something I had not done much in the last two weeks or months even. Michaelson also came after us and joined us; later Bannington and Hynes came out too. It was to view a ruined tower that rose above the ruins of a large city, the city had been built of mud brick, and it had all but melted into the plain, but this cone-shaped tower was of burnt brick and some one hundred and five and eighty feet high. It was ringed around the base in a language of unknown meaning, with the letters being as big as Bannington was tall[6].

Staircases of dubious stability led us upwards, where we found it had become a boarding-house for birds and bats. One did obtain an outstanding view of the surrounding area. I found this useful for over 240° degrees of my view was greenery, and the other 120° was the seared lands of the desert. We saw other ruins of interest, but it was revoltingly hot now and we walked back slowly, everyone speaking of their mock hatred of me for having dragged them out on this promenade. We came back to a fine meal, and had I not been sweating so much, I would have enjoyed the food even more.

Somewhere to the north East of us was the town of Khodjeili; a place said to have been established by those of great purity after having done the Haj to Mekkah. Their descendants all live there in a great city - or so I am told.

Turcoman Courting

On the outskirts of the remnants of this city, were some Turcoman, who seeing we were from a caravan, paid no mind to us. We soon found out why. With much shouting, a young woman mounted on a horse and clutching a sheep went tearing past us at full gallop shouting to the winds. In a moment she was followed from the village by a hooting and shouting mass of young men, led by one with a certain quality of leadership. We knew not what to do, for I felt a knightly urge to help the young woman, but were quickly cooled by the firm voice of Hynes, who restrained both me and the others to not interfere, as we knew not what was going on. We watched her exhibit some excellent horsemanship, avoiding the men, and in time, it became clear it was some game or exhibit, and was not real, and she was in no danger as she was full of laughter. Later our guide said it was part of their marriage ceremony. The bride to be is pursued and 'kidnapped' and taken as a prize back to the groom's home. There he agrees to a bride price, and until he pays it, she stays with her parents; while he keeps the sheep. Once paid, he goes to her home in a mighty possession and takes her up and the two set up their own felt tent, leaving the sheep with her parents.

So what we had seen was the start of their 'courtship'.

I had at first been annoyed by this halt, as I had wished to get to Khiva, but I soon felt the wisdom of it. It had been more recommended by Hynes and supported by Dobbins,

Turcoman courtship, the groom chases his bride to be on horseback while she carries a sheep, once caught they can marry. Illustration III-XIV-23

and Perkins had decided that in fact it should be. I spent the afternoon, opium free in going over every inch of Blonde's harness and my own gear *minutieusement {thoroughly}* cleaning out a pound or more of sand. I also give her a bath of sorts, carrying water in our canvas bucket to wash her down as she was coated with dust; sand which had stuck to her sweaty hair. She soon looked like a presentable animal again. The others slowly did the same. There was no way to properly wash ourselves, as a Turcoman never bathes and our pale white bodies might elicit comment.

Perkins was in a poetic frame of mind and made up a verse treating our recent conflict as a romantic dance; rather unseemly, and shall I say specific, in the manner of its warming qualities, which I have had him write below. It was both full of humour and erotic allusions. Dissanayake thought it disgraceful for an officer to have written such, while Bannington and Horne took great delight in it. Bannington with his musical talents associated it with a popular ballet.

[Editor's note: this is missing, the upper portion of the next page is torn away taking with it part of what was said the next day also. Some detective work on an inscription on the back of the page showed that the unknown editor had written 'remove' and left the bottom half of the word on that part of the page that was not removed]

(...)

..... the Turcoman took our example of cleanliness as a preparation for Islamic prayers, for that ablution they do do, if only on rare occasion. They had in the desert joined us but once for prayers, after performing *tayemmum {ritual cleaning using sand instead of water}* with us, or as they called in *Teharet*. I wished we could do *ghusl* or a full body ablution which is the equal of an English bath. I had a good reason, for the Islamic code holds that one must do this for a number of reasons; one's death - one must have some help for that however, and for after having lost consciousness. This I had done at the battle and I deserved a ghusl for that alone; however one was not available!

Our guide came to speak to us, and he made a startling observation to me, for it astounded him so much that he blurted it out in a way that made me feel as if the Prophet himself had appeared before him. He called all his men to come immediately. As always in such matters, I had My Frenchman near at hand, and their rapid movement and attention to me caused Hynes, Michaelson and Vickery to rally round. Vickery edged closer too. He had his spear at the ready, as he never goes anywhere without a spear in hand, and he had fashioned another after breaking his old one in the charge, although where he had found the wood to do so in that stark desert was his secret to keep.

The guide explained in his own jumbled tongue some great thing and pointed repeatedly at my arms, and the other men, as if handling the most valued relic or first born son, did stare at my arms with great interest. My arm is many things, but it is not particularly interesting. However to those Asiatics, its paler tone and blondish hair seemed to have gained their undue attention. I thought for a moment that I would be seized and exhibited in a cage as a, 'wild hairy man of Circassia'. The guide and men aped about for a while, then departed, and only then did the guide explain the wonder he had found in my arm. It took some time to explain to the others. He lacked the words in Persian to explain it but we worked it out with the help of Hynes.

A Muhammadan washes his hands and lower arms before prayers and he does so theoretically five times a day, all this washing has apparent consequences. For a Sunni all this constant washing has a permanent effect as he does it in the Sunni way which causes the hairs of the arm to incline towards the palm of the hand, and in a very orderly way. A Shia however washes his lower arms in a different way. This is contrary to the Sunni way and it causes the hair to point upwards to the elbow. Thusly, one can tell the religion of a man, no matter what he says he is. Our guide had seen that while many of my hairs pointed downwards, a few pointed up and there were a few that pointed in every direction. He found this remarkable, as he as a youth had been very observant of the religion, and his arm hairs were arranged in the finest manner of Sunni order. Those of his men, who were not so observant had a majority that pointed down also, he was glad to see I was no Shia Persian, and confessed that the men had come to think we might be Persians due to our paler skins. He was glad we were not, but did wonder how our hair had come to be so arranged. Perkins who had come up jumped in at that moment and pointed out that the Circassian's did not wash up or down they washed their arms 'all around' and were truer to the Prophet Mohammad's instruction, peace be upon his name.

Our guide, who was very satisfied with this answer, took one more look at my arms, and went away. Horne observed that we were lucky he had not checked the short hairs on his arse, as he had no idea where they might point.

What utter absurdity. We gathered everyone around and filled them in on the story, for we might be found 'out' again. We had noticed just how different we acted to these Asiatics in so many things. We Europeans defecate, drink, eat, gesture, laugh, sigh, sit, sleep, sneeze, shout, spit, stand and weep in a way different from those around us. Our notions of cleanliness are alien to these men, and our ways must seem strange to them. We are only saved in that they have rarely if ever encountered Europeans. Our having taken up the guise of Muhammadan Circassians has worked well so far, as they think we are the same religion, and as we are among people who pay little attention to it, this makes it much easier for us. Any oddity of our presence is considered normal by them, as does our talking in French or Greek. They presume I suppose that it is the Circassian language. The worst difficulty I have is not using my left hand, for it is not used for anything but cleaning one's self after answering nature's call in the Islamic world. To use this in eating or handing something to someone would be a deadly insult.

Hynes said it would be like coming up to an Englishman and offering your foot to him to shake, or to not remove your glove when taking a woman's hand. It was outrageous and simply not done. I had taken to keeping my left hand either tucked into my sash or holding something, usually Ascalon, to prevent me from making this mistake. I could see that all the others had the same difficulty; except for Hynes and Vickery, who seemed to have picked up the mannerisms much better than the others. Michaelson, Dobbins and Dissanayake also struggled at this, but much less so than Horne, who seemed out of place even to me.

Vickery told us of his great struggle with this, as in Hawaii the right hand is the hand of war, while the left hand is the hand of love and peace. To hand something to someone with the right hand is taboo, so for him, he has had to completely reorient his use of his hands, yet he had done it well.

I resisted the urge to sleep until evening, and did so and enjoyed the first night of rest in a long time; ignoring as best I could the annoyance of vermin, mosquitoes, threat of fever or ophthalmic complaints *{eye disease}*, but the heat makes it difficult to ever truly be comfortable.

Day 18 Wednesday 19 July

We are back to a world of moving, amidst a scented cloud that smells of leather, horses and men's sweat, but added to it now is the moist fugue of decayed vegetation and stagnant, still water. Endless canals, insects too, but delightful foliage and flowers are to be seen everywhere. Birdlife is abundant and that staple of the thousand and one nights, the nightingale, is here in plenty. In this fertile area, there were also many cucurbits *{gourds}* of wonderful design and shape.

I would estimate that the population of this densely populated and thronging land must be no less than a half million souls, or so it would seem to me.

Perkins at one point took me aside on the trail, pointed to the wound on the back of my head, and inquired as to my health; and I replied that I was doing well. He said he was asking as he had seen me talking to myself. To which I too had caught myself doing recently, and I had prepared a witty remark, should anyone else note it. I said that of course I was talking to myself, for I was the only intelligent person I presently knew. He gave me an exasperated look and rode on.

We passed this day the town of Yani-Urgenj, said to be the largest town of this city state, with five and thirty thousand inhabitants. We could see it only dimly as we were heading for Khiva and Perkins would stand for no delay.

I remember as a boy reading about the East and was reminded of a quote about Khiva,

> *If you wish to live well go and dwell in Damascus, if you wish to live in piety go to dwell in Mekkah, if you wish to look upon cultured ways go to dwell in Cairo and if you wish to die go to dwell in Khiva*

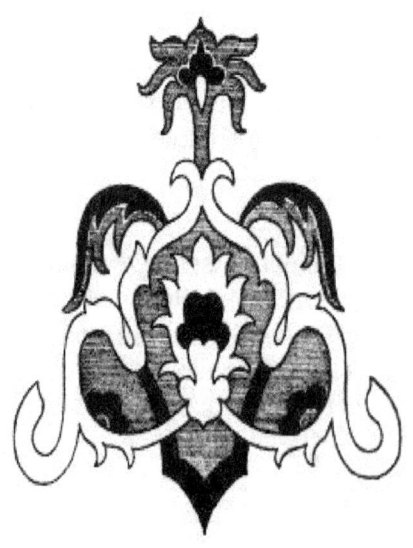

Map of Khiva from the 1880's showing the Khan's palace, the school area in which they had a later adventure and the Caravansary they initially stayed in. Illustration III-XIV-24

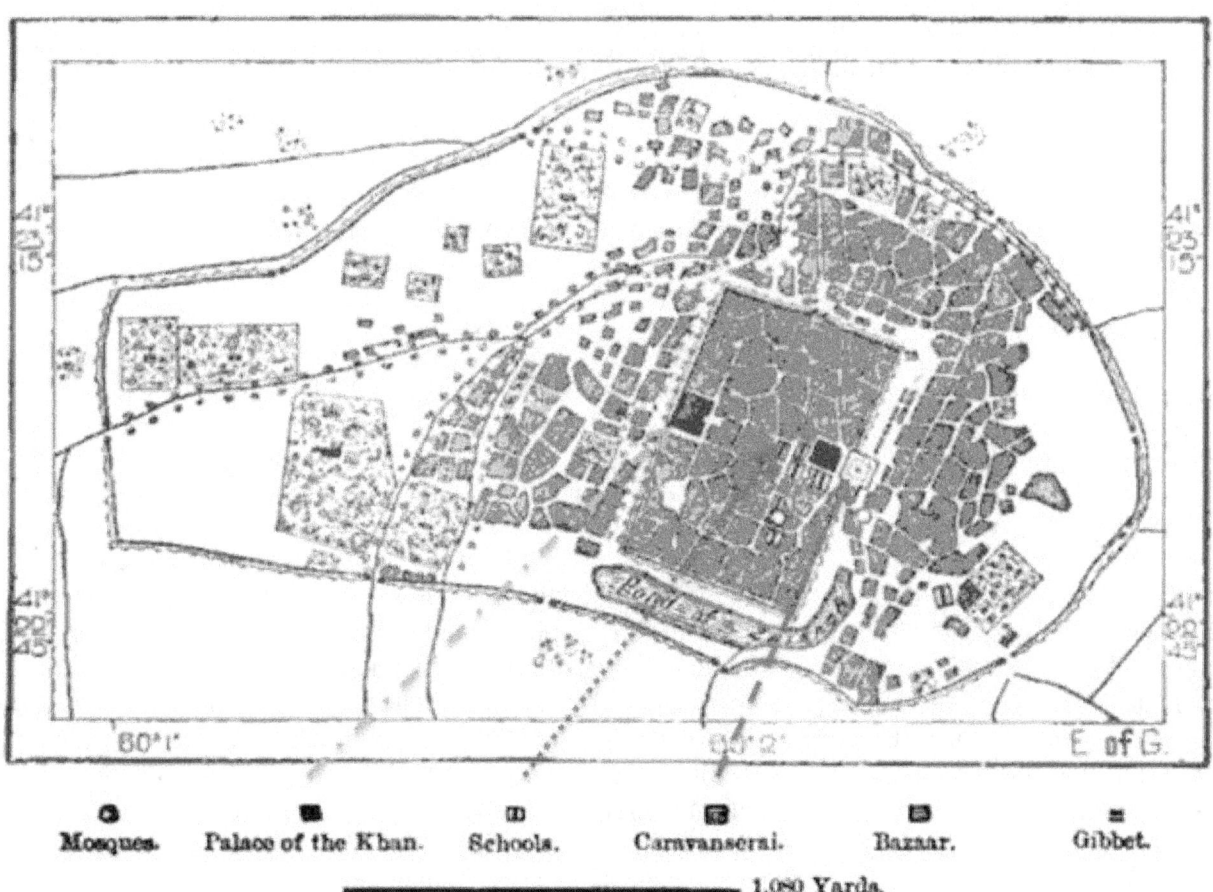

KHIVA

Scale 1 : 26,000

●	■	⊞	▦	▣	≡
Mosques.	Palace of the Khan.	Schools.	Caravanserai.	Bazaar.	Gibbet.

1,080 Yards.

Chapter XV

Khiva and the Oxus River

Khiva The City Of The Khan And A Sewer Of The First Order - A Damnable Hot Town And Veal For Dinner - The Moneylender And The Khivan Bazaar - A MOST Singular Occurrence - A Midnight's Skulking Though Khiva - Our Prisoner - Dafydd Friedrich Zum Nolta - A Ride To Nowhere - Return To The Heated Delights Of Khiva - I Deadly Discovery Made - The Foulness Of The Khivan Bazaars And The Idiocy Of Guides - We Meet With The Khan And Ameer Of Khiva And His Vizier - We Are Given A Mission By The Khan Of Khiva - Three Countrymen In The Hades Hotel? - A Voyage Down The Oxus To Khodjeili The City Of Hajjis And The Disaster That Befell Us

=======

Khiva The City Of The Khan And A Sewer Of The First Order

Day 19 Thursday 20 July

As we broke camp, word had come from passersby that two men had been caught at the gates of Khiva by the *Pasheeb {head night watchman}* and they had admitted their guilt as Russian spies. They had reportedly then been tortured and had their throats cut and their remains thrown into a central pit outside the Khan's palace as a dire warning to all other spies. This brought a certain chill to our outing.

So we came to the outskirts of Khiva, within the land known as Kharezm, where water flows everywhere and the land is cut here and there by mighty and lesser canals. The city lies to the southwest of the main channel of the Oxus River. It is a rectangular city, surrounded by an irregular series of rude villages; ten in number. The land is endlessly fertile, as the river brings both water and alluvia to the soil; in this it is like the Nile. The roads are a series of water filled holes but the roadsides are strewn with poplars, palms and elms. The vegetation, foliage and roses grow thickly and are strewn with mulberry bushes which are often found around the white painted homes of the peasants. The farmers here are famous for their pistachios and melons. A rich man in Persia when offered the choice of a pound of Indian gold, a lovely Kirghiz girl or a melon from Khiva will take the melon. I had read once that when the Chinese Emperors held sway here, that the city's melons were taken by mounted messengers to grace his table.

As we approached, the road thickened with other travellers, and it was a motley group: farmers, herders, fisher folk all on their way to the markets of the city; all were men or boys, no females were to be seen. I saw beggars, slaves on errands, reminding me of that monstrous and poisonous canker of slavery that existed here, and a dozen nationalities, some of which I had seen in Persia, but others were new to me, and I knew not who they were. There was a Jew, then a man who wore the clothes of a native of Khorasan *{Persia}* perhaps a freed slave.

A man I thought might be a Turk, Ozbegs *{Uzbeks}*, an Afghani, brigand like men I think are Kirghiz for they have a cast of their features that said Asiatic, but it does so quietly.

These men had close shaved beards, or none at all, and narrow eyes which spoke of cruelty and ignorance. Tatterdemalions flittered here and there, there were goats, horses of a dozen breeds, some the sorriest looking steeds I have ever seen while others were some of finest on this earth, camels ridden by wild looking, brown-skinned half-naked riders, one humped and two, the camels not the men, a few oxen, flocks of bleating sheep, several broods of chickens and I was surprised to not see a unicorn or gryphon amongst this exotic scene. I did see, on a tree limb that came out over the road, a rare sight, a clutter of cats, of many feline races looking down on all this riotous difference with that imperial air, which only a truly indifferent cat can deliver.

The outskirts of the city consist of no more than unsettled rows of rude hovels, enclosed by a low mud wall and an impractical moat, now fallen into disrepair and existing as a series of greenish ponds of the most offensive smell imaginable; and I have smelled some impressionable evil in the East. Here, however, my nostrils were assailed by a reek so powerful and nauseating, like a leak from a well-used outhouse at the apex of a hot summer in England. Such an outhouse would, by its singular smell, almost be considered to possess a certain beauty, compared to the scents that came from outer Khiva.

It is said by knowledgeable, native writers that when coming to Khiva, one must always travel though Persia first, if not one's nose will be shocked into insensibility, when coming to such a wretched and filthy place. Persia lowers one's expectation enough, and toughens the senses, so that you can ride into Khiva without being knocked off your horse by the stench.

In the distance, floated the great, blue tiled, dome of the main mosque whose name we did not know at that time; accented by a golden globe at the highest point.

The Khivans themselves were a most disagreeable and decrepit looking race of men, of a harsh and ill-cut appearance marred by smallpox, dermal eruptions, weeping red eyes, with a stare that spoke of an abuse of opium. They seemed to me, to be men who would take to robbery and treacherous murder, without a moment's hesitation. The city and the land is made up of five main populations, the Ozbegs *{I will use the modern term Uzbeks}* make up the balance of the population, and consist of two and thirty separate tribes and these are not just names, some of the tribes speak different languages or have diverse customs and by appearance seem to be different races; some look like Persians and others like Tartars. The Uzbek, when he does not live in Khiva, has many of the noble traits of the nomad; honesty and open-heartedness, while said heart still yearns of plunder. Those that live in Khiva are another matter, which I will write of below. There Islam is tainted with sprinkles of heathenism from the old Parsee religion and more shockingly, hints of Shia concepts.

The next group is the Sarts; an old people, some call the Tadjiks and who are considered the original race that lived here before the nomad armies came. Some probably have Greek and Macedonian blood in them. Their language is Turkic and they tend not to marry beyond their own race.

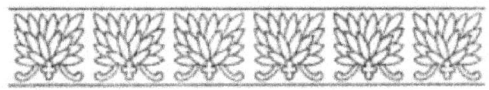

Jews, there are a few thousand of this old race here, performing the tasks that Jews everywhere seem to fill in any society; they are at times oppressed, while at others they are left alone, depending on the whim of the Khan.

A Khivan Jew. Illustration III-XV-1

Persians, mostly slaves, many of whom stay in Khiva, where they work with industry and purchase their freedom, almost all convert to Sunnism from their own Shia'ism. Their grandsons will be full citizens and the blemish of slavery removed and they are then called *Khanezad*, or house born.

Another group are the Kasak *{Kirghiz}* nomads from the surrounding deserts. They are rarely seen, as they roam as their ancestors did, for millenniums before.

Qaraqalpaqs *{Karakalpak}* are a people who live in the Oxus Delta, where they breed cattle. They are most notable for having a noble look and are said to have the most beautiful women, while the men are considered the greatest of idiots. They are divided into ten tribes. Some Europeans think they may be descendants of the lost tribes of Israel.

The Turcoman are here in small groups, mainly the Yomut tribe and they live in the area between the Aral and Caspian Sea.

[Editor's note: Driscol later wrote on the margin in pencil the following in English, all his previous comments were in Danish written using the Arabic script, I suspect this was after their 'entertainment by the Baccha boys' which occurs later in the narrative]

> Horne stated to me that the Khivans seem to be a wholly dissipated race of men, unpardonably feeble in the higher arts of civilization, amongst which, honour is given no moral consideration. They have a tenacious malevolence to disallow what they know to be the given path of Islam, for there is some good in it, and instead concentrate with great concern, on the modes of religious dogma and trivialities. They have a spiteful disregard for all others and display as virtuous, their insalubrious and wicked appetites, which degrade their own society, religion and culture so badly as to make even themselves unwilling to be a part of it.

Most wear a type of round, Persian style, black, lamb, cap, which makes their ears more pronounced and gives them the look of a vase with two handles: a vision that always makes me want to laugh at its sight or recollection and as I write this. The Mussulman holy men conversely wear a type of ragged turban. The Khivans also wear a robe of bland colours, some with coloured lines or patterns, but invariably dirty; a sash perhaps, dagger and sword, some sported chains or other devices around their necks or across their bony shoulders. One can tell the better sorts, by the simple fact that their robes will not be as filthy as those of the lower classes. I believe the Khan has issued an order, that any man seen walking about in clean clothes, should be seized and cast into rubbish.

We entered through an outer wall that was made of mud, irregular but in good repair, it was some six feet high and four feet thick, what purpose it served could not be determined, as it had no way for a man to take a position behind it and use bow or matchlock.

Bannington and Horne both said that the wall would keep out no invader, but might keep the filth and vermin within. We passed this wall by an ill-defined entry, that was gateless and that had no guards, and we kept on for some distance before coming to the centre of the city. It is in the form of a quadrilateral and is surrounded by a true crenellated wall, eight and twenty or so feet in height. It is in tolerable repair and is some fifteen feet thick at the base and of the type that swells out from the perpendicular. It had large, well-built, round, bastions every few hundred feet. The population of the city must have been no more than ten thousand.

The wall here did have proper gates and guards, but they paid no attention to us. Instead they were focused on a naked raver who was turning somersaults before them and the crowd and we were of less interest than his flops and screams in a language we did not know. The gate itself had two, smaller, round towers on either side. The heavy door was named and written in the Arabic script and read, *Ota Darvoza* or west gate. We were entering that part of the city that is called the *Itchan Kale*.

We came to a place of execution and found two men on display. If these were the Russian spies, they looked like no Russians to me. One had died horribly, his left ankle chained to a short stake in the ground and a rope placed around his neck and tied to another stake that rose some ten feet. The man would have had to stand on his right leg's toes to keep from strangling, how long he could have done that before his leg tired and he strangled I could not say. His compatriot had been placed in a small framework of iron in which he could neither sit nor stand as it was too short, and the inside studded with three inch spikes. His too, had been a horrible death. I was riding near Hynes who expressed himself to me in English that these Khivans were of the worse sort. I silently agreed.

Our Dragoman headed us for a caravanserai he knew in the quarter of the central city, where the tomb of the patron saint of Khiva, a man called Phelivan Ata, was within a great mosque. This Mr Ata it was said, had written that,

> If you are a traveller, you must look to the road. You must keep yourself from fear
> and worry

He, in my estimation, must have said that before he rode into Khiva. There is much romance in adventure stories of great travellers coming to a far city there to find some prize, intellectual, scientific, romantic or visual. Great are the rewards in other cities but in Khiva there is no such discernible prize.

The Dragoman said the markets were full, and we must take a roundabout way, to avoid the crowds. We rode into, and out of, a number of quarters of the city. The only notable one was a place called Keflerkhane, a place whose name means the 'village which eats no bread'; a dwelling of the poorest poor, or so said our guide. It looked not poorer than any other section of the city. We came to an artificial pond, surrounded by large plane trees, and resembling nothing less than a park.

Our guide, while bursting with eagerness to be shed of us, did tell us one legend about the city and that the name of the city came from Shemson of Nuh *{Noah in the Bible}*, who found a well beside the river Oxus and declared it Khi-wa! This, we are told, in the local dialect means 'best water'. He concocted a number of other historical inaccuracies, for his own amusement I would guess, and put forth these tales as we rode. He spoke of Russian Czars beheaded in squares we passed, of Chinese armies reduced by magic so they resided in a small child's box, or of great monstrous creatures chained up at this building or that, or of fountains that once sprayed so high into the sky that the water falling from them would kill a man.

We went through the city, which was besmirched in dirt, but contained a number of interesting buildings, numerous madrasahs *{religious schools}*, minarets and the like. We came at last to the place our guide sought; the caravanserai of *Allakuli Khan*, and nearby was the market he gave the same name to, but we later found the Tim or bread market, and of greater interest still, the *Anusha Khan* baths, which we could not use however. Next to the baths, was the *Sertrashbazari*, or place of barbers, who will shave your head to remove the lice, but of course, they will not shave you, for a man shaved, is a man without honour.

We came to find that the caravanserai was full to the bursting and so we moved to another one towards the north and the river. It was less filled with travellers, but as we discovered, as night fell, it was a place well occupied by our enemies. When darkness came they swarmed out; the *Blatta orientalis {cockroaches}*, they came in their hundreds, bent on an evening of annoying their betters, and of eating anything they could find. They came at us from all directions, and despite our being heavily outnumbered, we dealt them a swift defeat. Michaelson and I formed a compound of arsenic and other chemicals, which strategically placed, made our dwelling room more foes-free. The fleas of Khiva, however, proved a most formidable enemy, whom we could not vanquish.

It had been my ill luck to obtain the position of the officer of the day, or scapegoat, and I was presented with the symbol of office, a butter knife of dubious origins, that morning. It was therefore my duty to find our dinner.

The mosque that was outside the Caravansary the expedition occupied while in Khiva.
Illustration III-XV-2

A Damnable Hot Town And Veal For Dinner

It was damnably hot in the city and I walked down to the market and found a place amongst the merchants, where I could plunge my hand in to a large pond and it was uncomfortably warm but the evaporation soon cooled my arm. I tried again and at a depth of two feet it was much cooler, if not by much. My exploration brought me to the attention of the pond folk, who found the sight of a foreigner kneeling down and putting his arm in the water to be a sight rarely seen here, I would presume.

I did enter into the four centuries old Hazerti Pehlivan-ata, which our Guide had pointed out; a mosque, which is constructed of fired brick and contains the remains of the patron saint of the Khivans, for whom it is named, and who has so many variants of his name that I will not begin to list them all. It mounts a large gilt dome, and two secondary ones. It was full of Koran reciters and their rumbling pronunciations filled the dark interior to such a point as to make the viewing of the interior and its kasha *{ornamental tiles}*, a trail of discomfort, and not one of discovery. Having seen it briefly, I left, driven out by the endless noise.

I saw a herd of oxen being driven into the market. The pond was a hundred yards across and the herder foolishly drove the herd into it - why he did this I cannot imagine why - who can account for the madness of foreigners? Nevertheless he and his helpers drove the cattle into the pond; I would think perhaps to clean them of their trail dust, but everything in Khiva was covered in dust, and I could not believe that spotlessness would be rewarded by a higher price.

A side of veal: Driscol would comment on this meal several times in the future. Illustration III-XV-3

There were some antics when a few decided to swim back to the same shore but these were driven around by much shouting and the flailing of whips. One calf was not up to the task and drowned. It was brought ashore and was butchered on the spot. As it was brought ashore near me, I purchased a side with the show of a coin and I also gained a ragged but cheerful boy name Akmeed to carry it, and so, and we were to have veal that evening.

As we walked back to our dwelling, I went through a market filled with Uzbeks, who conduct all their business from the backs of their horses, never leaving the saddle. I walked through this mounted market with some feeling of dread, but they were far too busy speaking and gesturing, and doing that which Easterners do in markets, to even note the passage of me, my boy, and my veal.

I was much praised for my industry, for we had not dined on beef for some weeks. One tires of the flavour of mutton - oh how one tires of it! Horne and Dissanayake had a mock argument that began when Mr H. was complaining about the dinner, and made much of a need for some lemon for the veal, but I was not about to hunt the markets for them. To which Mr D. replied that perhaps as Horne was off the meal, we could arrange the daughter of Cimon to provide him with a more suitable suppertime? It was interesting to see who got the allusion made, Michaelson caught it first, and I did of course and Bannington. It left Dobbins, Vickery, and Hynes in the dark. Perkins was not there, at the first saying but coming in, it was repeated and he obtained a great laugh at the wit of it and then explained it to our lesser educated members. Hynes amazed us by then noting that he did know the story and mentioned two famous baroque paintings on the subject. Vickery and Dobbins took their being trumped quite well, although I suspect that some great fish *{whale}* or beast will suffer for it later in time.

[Editor's note: well Driscol would have laughed at me also as I didn't understand the comment either until I researched it, what I believe he was referring to was an ancient legend of the man Cimon who was sentenced to death by starvation and was saved from it by his daughter Pero who came to visit him and breast fed him]

Perkins had returned, and dinner was well underway, when he explained that our guide had departed, well paid and perhaps too eager to get away from us.

As I was the duty officer, I assigned Hynes to entertain us with one of his tales. Hynes this night told us an anecdote he said he had heard from a Persian noble in his first visit to that land. He told a tale of an earlier Shah.

> ....that a favoured daughter of the Shah had become uneasy at the attentions of her father's Vizier, his presence she found distasteful, and she thought he might wish to take her as his wife; something she would not consent to as he was base born. Telling her fears to her mother, the mother said, have no concern I will deal with the matter.
>
> This scheming mother wrote to the first wife of the Vizier in the guise of the Shah. She stated that she, as the Shah, desired her, but it would be an unseemly thing to take the wife of his own vizier but should the vizier be dead, his widow would become his primary wife and her son the next Shah.
>
> The ambitious wife was taken in, and soon delivered to the Shah the head of his vizier; her former husband. The Shah was horrified by this, and launched an enquiry. He soon uncovered the perfidy of his daughter and her mother. The vizier's wife was slain most cruelly and for his own wife, the mother of his daughter, he had her buried alive in a large tomb, while his daughter he confined to a ruined tower, and had her knee tendons cut so she could never leave, and there she was left to starve to death.
>
> As the Shah thought over this turn of grim events, he decided to make a trial; he summoned all his generals and said to them that he wished to have their wives for his own. As a man, they all refused, saying that their loyalty did not extend to permitting that. Ask them to die in battle for him and that they would do so, as to this other thing, no, they would not consent. Having been rebuffed, and happy with their demonstrated resolve, he wrote to each of their wives saying he wished to take them to wife - if they could arrange to become widows. All did so, and the Shah bore witness to the spectacle of the heads of his generals being brought to him on platters; many platters. To this barbarous act of infidelity, he could do nothing but marry them all then, shut them away in a small village, which he

ringed with loyal soldiers. This became the village of 'Those twice widowed' and these aged crones can be still be seen incarcerated near the city of Zehadan.

This bloody tale was well received by all.

A search for suitable toothpicks brought out from Michaelson a tale he had picked up in France about life and death in Italy. I was passing him a suitable toothpick, recently detached from a piece of fire wood, when he noted that these small helpers are rare, and hard to find in Italy. People prefer their fingers, a piece of straw that they themselves pluck from the ground, or even a dagger. In a pension *{hotel}* they may occasionally be found for foreign guests, but the average Italian will not use them. The reason for this is that one of the popes *{Clement II?}* was poisoned by means of a quill, medicated with salt of Saturn *{Lead acetate}*.

When he told us this snippet, he had started his speech with a mocking 'ladies and gentlemen'. Bannington noted that the use of that formula, with ladies before gentlemen, was a demonstration of English graciousness and showed how chivalry still stirred in the breasts of good men. Among the other nations of the world, priority in word order is still given to men, such as by the French, with Messieurs et Mesdames or the Bavarians with Meine Herren and Damen. I had never thought of this, and after a lengthy discussion, it was remembered by Dissanayake that the use of Ladies and Gentleman, instead of being centuries old, had begun in 1808, when it was done by a comedian for comic effect - it was deemed charming and has continued since then.

[Editor's note: I could find no 19th century source that would confirm this]

Dobbins replied to all this about a man named Jehonathan Toothpicke. The said man was a lighthouse attendant. It was due to his experience, that there are now always three men stationed in a Lighthouse off the British coast. In the past it had been two, but on a certain day one man died in his sleep and, as often happens during the stormy winter, no boat could come near for some time. Mr Toothpicke was obligated to keep the departed body of his comrade beside him, until it had thoroughly corrupted; a thing so horrible that it had driven him out of his mind. He had not disposed of the body, as he would in all probability have been charged with murder. Happily, owing to the measures now adopted, of a three man crew, this would not happen again. Horne knew of this and commented that one of Bombardiers was just such a man. This I found shocking, but in his case he had been charged with murder, and had escaped to India. The battery knew of this, as the man had confessed while in his cups *{drunk}*.

The Khivan market where all transaction were conducted on horseback .Illustration III-XV-4

The Moneylender And The Khivan Bazaar

That night, Dissanayake woke me in the dead of night. I thought we might be under an alarm, but he accused me of 'playing the French night horn in excess'. I told him what I thought of his accusation, but some of the others, out of the darkness, added their accusations too! *{Driscol was snoring}*

Morning came, and we were very disconcerted to find that our side of cooked veal although hung, and covered by a clean cloth, was rife with vermin. I had looked forward to breakfast of cold veal, alas! We cast it away and were treated to the sad sight of the beggars outside the gate of our dwelling fighting for its wormy remains. I had thoughts of a *blanquette de veau* I had once savoured in Paris, but such a meal was many months or years away.

We had decided, the evening before, on our plan of action in Khiva. Our main concern was to investigate the horse market here, then to make arrangements to split the expedition, with the main body moving north to study the Aral Sea, and secondary party to backtrack and trace the dry bed of the Oxus to the Caspian Sea.

Main section: Perkins, Driscol, Horne, Vickery and Hynes

Secondary section: Dobbins, Michaelson, Dissanayake and Bannington

We went to the horse market in our separate groups, with the secondary group tasked to provide our stay behinds at the caravanserai, and having changed our clothing somewhat, we had thought Perkins in his Princely white stood out too much, we proceeded. We found that our Persian could be answered by some, and we sought men who looked educated, and found a money lender who was able to speak it well. We exchanged some coins, and found out about the happenings in the city. The man, who was a Dari Afghani *{a people and dialect of Persian spoken in western Afghanistan}* was knowledgeable in the local politics and like most of the Persian race loved to gossip, we learned the following from Hynes as he was best at finding out what was being said:

> Some of what we learned was; the city was still independent, it was as free as a flightless bird in a pit it cannot scramble out of, and was surrounded on all sides by hungry cats, and the only reason it had not been eaten up yet, was because each cat thought the others would attack them, if they pounced on the tasty morsel first.

> It was the feeling in the bazaar, that the Persian move on Herat was a false one, and that they intended instead to secure the city of Merv, then attack Khiva, or Bokhara. Other parties held that the Persian attack was also a false one, and that the Afghans would meet with their Persian brothers at Herat and ally against Bokhara and Khiva. Yet another group held that the cities of Samarkand, Khokand and Tashkent were also cats, as were the Kirghis and Turcoman tribes. The biggest cat of all, the elephant sized tiger at the side of the pit were the Russians. Rumour was that a large Russian army composed of sixty thousand Cossacks and one hundred guns were marching on the city at this very moment.

We were told, with the great authority, of the common acceptance of the bazaar, that this army was coming by way of the Caspian Sea and then up the caravan route to Khiva.

Having just transversed that part of the desert, this was laughable as no source of water existed that could provide for even a lesser amount of one thousand men and beasts, so a movement from that quarter would be doubtful in this dreaded, summer heat.

A second route was proposed; by way of the desert and steppes to the Aral Sea, then by boat up the Oxus by way of the great delta, but some held that a lack of boats would prevent that, for there was no wood for boat building in the upper northern reaches of the Sea.

The same problem was held for the third route to the Aral Sea as before, but then up the Jaxartes River *{Syr Darya}*. This would also mean that at some point, the Kyzyl-Kum desert would have to be crossed, and we were to led to understand that that distance was greater than the distance we had come from the Attrek to Khiva.

The fourth theory was the one most favoured by our money lender. He would have the Russians cross the desert and steppes to the northeast of the Aral Sea, then to the Jaxartes River. Something was added to the last tale, and it was an arresting point. It was taken by Bannington and Horne to be indicative of an invasion, which was a description of a very non-Central Tartarian action. It was said that numerous caravans had seen Russian columns in the northeast, that had been building what to their minds were magazines and depots or as the moneylender called them 'places of luggage'.

Having spoken for some time with the knowledgeable moneylender, whom we rewarded well, we moved on to the main bazaar and wandered there for some time. I could see a mix of Central Asian tribesmen, with frowns showing in their eyes, as they had a cloth over their noses to protect them from the stench of a city, and in this they were correct. Khiva was one of the rankest places I had ever visited. It produced in me a racking cough, almost from the start.

The main bazaar was contained within short mud walls, some three hundred and fifty feet in length that faced one another. From those walls, smaller, more inconsequential, barriers came out to make three-sided spaces, some six to eight feet wide. Over each space was a reed matting, or torn felt, to keep off the sun's rays. All the overheads were torn, and to my eye, to the same pattern, and I wondered if perhaps they were made with the tears in them? Within these *sukkahs {compartments}*, was where the shops were stationed. The merchants squatted on disreputable looking cushions, and surrounded by their treasure, these customary traders display their wares for their patrons. Farmers, or those who are indifferent traders, have no regular place within the mud wall set up in the central open space, and were exposed to the full fury of the heat from the sun. I would say that this day some 3-4,000 persons thronged the market in the hours I spent there.

I found in the market something I had seen the Turcoman use. It is the dried powder of an herb called *kouginasse, {unknown}*. This they place in their mouth like some Europeans do with tobacco.

Some of the delights of this market were fruit, then other kinds of food, manufactures, oil and horses, donkeys and camels. One could find oats, barley and millet here, and I purchased some for Blonde. There is a fine kind of wheat here called by the local's *kourka*, bearded wheat and I tasted bread made of this and found it equal to any European baker's production. The olive oil was of the Greek type, clear and sweet and as thick as syrup. They have local oil made from cabbage seeds, but I found it had a distinct and unpleasant taste, like old and mouldy bread. I also purchased and consumed in a native manner, an utterly luscious *cauon {melon}*, some twelve inches long with a lovely golden rind, and when cut into, one finds the flesh deviously cool, despite the heat of the day, no matter how long they have lain in the hot sun. My mother would not have been pleased by my manners, but it was full of good juice and the flesh excellent. Even the flies would not face the sun's direct rays, so I stood in the central market square, spitting seeds. I wonder how the good people of Eccles would have taken to my standing in their market, dripping with melon juice, and spitting seeds everywhere? I think not! I enjoyed it so much, that I ate two more.

I bought peaches, yellow and purple grapes, some *cak*, which is a dried fruit, which tastes of aromatic quince. I saw similarly walnuts, a fruit I did not recognised called an *igde*, and small indifferent looking apples. Well fruited, and feeling somewhat like a two-legged English frugivore *{fruit eating mammal}*, I met up with Vickery; who being the tallest person in Khiva, and I being the second tallest, facilitated our finding one another in a crowded market. Our group soon gathered in the central spot and ate my supply of fruit. We soon found our brains well grilled by the heat of the day, and thought it wise to seek shelter, but there was none. We found our instruments indicated a temperature of 97° at that time. We plunged into the lanes of the city but there was no relief to be found. The heat ricocheted off the mud walls like hotshot, right into our faces and lungs, and it made one feel you were a fowl in an enclosed oven. Michaelson expressed that we must, as a matter of some urgency, find shade, and so we sought it with greater zeal. We finally came to an area of religious schools and a building two or three stories high and found delightful shade. We stood there, for one could not sag against the wall, as it too was hot, and we sweated and listened to the sound of voices reciting the Koran. It was interesting that the Surah they were learning to memorise in Arabic (a language I am sure most did not understand) was about horses.

Since I heard it thirty or more times, from multiple people on the other side of the wall we were resting behind, I remember it well now, as I write by candle light, before I sleep.

> *Surah 16 An Nahl (the Bee)...and Allah created the horses, mules and donkeys for you to ride and adornment and he creates that which you do not know.*

This droning was becoming wearisome, when from a distance, a disturbance was heard, which resolved itself in a procession led by drummers, horn men and cymbalists. They created a loud, but not disharmonious music, as they passed and were followed by some notable person, led on a horse. Behind him, came a small mounted guard, well-dressed, and behind them, more drummers.

We found that this man was the *Nakib* or spiritual leader of Khiva, a man who had greatly fallen down on the job, in my opinion. We could do no more than flatten ourselves against the hot wall, and watch them pass; the music being too loud to allow an exchange of greetings; not that the 'great' man paid us any attention at all.

A MOST Singular Occurrence

After he had passed us, the most singular thing occurred. Later I discussed what had happened before I wrote this down and I believe it is an accurate account of what happened, and the manner in which it did.

[Editor's note: Driscol wrote this section in English with no attempt to disguise it, but placed it on separate sheets and placed them at the back of the journal, in the journal itself he noted down the title above and nothing more]

We were still pressed against the wall, as a stream of well-wishers, beggars and those with nothing better to do than follow the parade. As they passed, I saw out of the corner of my eye something come falling down to strike Perkin's shoulder. It rebounded and fell onto the filthy street. Perkins did not note it, but Vickery and I did, and we in a most comical fashion struck one another's head in bending over in unison, and in a not comical way, I cried out in English, 'Damn'. Vickery secured whatever it was, as I looked around, as if someone in Khiva would have been drawn to my English expression. It was a wad of paper, somewhat soiled. We looked above us, to the three storeys building that stood there. The ground floor had no windows, but the first and second bore arches, and recessed within them, was windows behind dense, lattice works of wood.

[Editor's note: For Americans, Driscol would have called the 'first floor' in the American sense the ground floor]

We could see nothing. Perkins looked at it a moment then handed it to me. It was written in a fluid style, and in German. My German is not that good and the sentence made no sense to me, but Michaelson was standing next to me and he whispered to me in English its meaning which shocked us both by it boldness.

Sie sind Europaishchen. Helfen Sie mich, bitte! {You are Europeans, help me!}

A chill passed over me as we scanned the building that loomed above us; two men passed us grumbling to one another about some arcane subject. As soon as they were done, we heard again the memorisation of the Koran coming over the wall behind us. Out from above us sailed another note.

This one was written in flowing Cyrillic script *{Russian}*, and although I know some Russian, I could make no sense of it, and raised my face and shook my head. Sometime went by and a stick came out of the third archway to our left on the third floor and from there another message came, the third one was written in Latin.

Bring Aqua Fortis at Midnight

[Editor's note: Aqua Fortis (fortified water) is the Latin name for nitric acid]

I nodded to this and we waited, with much comment between us, for twenty minutes, but no further notes came flying down to us, nor could we see anything, not even a shadow in the recessed window.

This was unheard of, and we moved, as a compact body, back to our place of rest, and to where the other two were, and we soon were standing tightly together, in disregard to the heat, to discuss this. Perkins had lifted the requirement for Persian to be spoken between us at all times, and an animated and heated discussion took place in English.

Perkins' held that it was woman, and being a woman, she had of course thrown the first message to him. However everyone else agreed that the handwriting was male. There was great debate over what, or who, had done what, to give out we were not Circassians and instead Europeans. Some tried to blame me for crying out, but Vickery pointed out that I had done so while bending to pick up the first message that had been thrown, before I collided with his wrought iron skull.

It was then considered the man must be an educated Russian, held as a slave. An examination of the second message I found was so befuddling. I could make no sense of it, but I could tell that whoever had written it, did not know Russian very well. On a suggestion from Dissanayake, I re-read the message, and he was correct, it was something I myself had done in this very journal, for it was written with the Russian script but in the German language. Michaelson and I thought it said:

Held prisoner with others by the son of the Vizier, need Aqua Fortis

Both Michaelson and I did have some of this chemical. I carried the acid at a 24% concentration as a spirit of Niter as a final test for any gold coins I might exchange and he carried a 63% concentration of near fuming nitric acid to dissolve warts and as part of syrups for relapsing fevers. We had between us an ounce and half of the pale yellow liquid. We decide we could spare an ounce of ours if we mixed the two.

Dobbins suggested that he and Dissanayake, led by Horne, who said he could find the way back, should go back to the location, and establish where it was, for our knowledge of the city and its location was not firm in any of our minds. As those two had not been seen, they could wander the quarter, and determine the exact location of the three storey house, and a possible owner. They altered their clothing as best they could, and took on a more Turcoman look. They were off and we continued to debate our next actions.

Evening had fallen when they returned, carrying a long pole. Needed by us if we wish to move a glass container up to a third floor window. We too had obtained a slightly longer pole. Horne jested that we were now truly 'Polish', having two poles in the expedition, and Bannington noted that this would be true as our ad hoc cavalry organization the 17th King's Own Imperial Light Horse Polish Lancer of the Guard did require a 'pole or two'. This was a most capital observation.

They had found the place with some difficulty, and had also found it was a long building some seventy feet in length; of similar construction as the other Koranic schools in the area. Another street held the gate, which barred its entrance. This was ten feet high and closed with an iron clad gate on heavy timbers, topped with spikes, and painted blue. The gate and wall enclosed an area from which the tops of trees which grew in the garden obscured the second and third floor windows. In the hours they had spent, no one had gone into or out of it; in stark comparison with the busy flow of students and holy men in the schools around it.

An expedition meeting was formally held with Vickery declaring he was against any attempt to free the man, unless we knew him to be a good cook; he then withdrew to act as guard of our herd of horses.

Perkins was for it and he held that it was a woman, a European woman, and thus as gentlemen, we must provide assistance.

Horne was for it with the proviso that the expedition removes itself from the city of Khiva and that he and one other should go and provide the acid.

Dobbins thought it unwise and advised against any action, but if it was decided to do something, he seconded Horne's recommendation.

Hynes said he was no gentleman and felt no need to rescue some foreigner, and as the note had observed that the prisoner knew of other prisoners, and he was held by the son of a high official, this would bring down on a heavy retribution, should we be detected.

Michaelson thought we should do as Horne suggested, and leave a note (in Latin) describing a point outside the walls where this escapee might find us. We all felt that no Tartar would know Latin.

Dissanayake thought it imprudent and ill-advised. He did not trust the paperwork, either what was written on them or the possibilities therein, and he was highly suspicious of the entire matter.

Bannington thought it our duty to attempt to save a European, despite any risk to ourselves, for we were ENGLISHMEN and it is what gentlemen and their associates did.

I suggested that we might do so, not from any gentlemanly consideration, but in order to free the person for the information he might have.

A vote was taken, as Perkins thought he should not simply make a decision on this important matter.

It was decided to proceed with the following plan. We would leave Khiva, while two men, Horne and I, delivered the Aqua Fortis while the rest waited outside the gate to see if anyone emerged.

We would wait one hour, then make our way out of the city. Based on the distance and the need to avoid the guarded gates, Horne and I felt we would be at the 'tree of the overhanging cats' on the road just outside Khiva, that all of us remembered well, within two hours after midnight.

So it was decided, and so it was done.

A Midnight's Skulking Though Khiva

Horne had his two-barrelled pistol and sword, plus the second Colt, while I carried My Frenchman and knife. We had disguised the pole as a cavalry lance which Horne was very happy to carry about, festooned with a green banner we had purchased, 'Allah the Merciful' it read in white Arabic .

Michaelson and I had concocted our acid brew and tightly sealed it. I would regret losing the bottle, as it was gold washed, for only gold could contain the fierce actions of Aqua Fortis.

We had speculated why our mystery prisoner would have requested it, and had decided it could best be used to remove or weaken shackles, or a lock, but one ounce was not much with which to do so. Dissanayake had suggested they wanted it to kill themselves, but such a method seemed a very hard way to die.

Late night Khiva is a fraction cooler, and the stench of the city is lessened by the oily smells of cooking, of rich Indian-like spices, of streets cleared of their loads of incommodious people. Khiva has a curfew that begins thirty minutes after midnight, and is signaled by the firing of cannon from the gate before the Khan's palace. The Khivans have four Pasheb *{chief watchmen}*, who each command eight lackeys to patrol the streets after the cannon is fired. Additionally there are two and thirty executioners, who travel the streets and alleyways too, and who have the authority to execute anyone found outside. However, we knew from the market place that while that was the plan, the reality was that none of these officials were out at night time, although some of the gates might be well guarded by sleeping men.

We made first for the three storey house. Found it, the window, and the gate, then from there, we went to where we could cross the inner, higher wall, at a sally port that had been left open for a century or more, and then the main street to the west gate. We then returned along the empty streets. We knew not if there was any guard, militia or watch, but saw no sign of them, for at eleven in the evening, the streets were bare, and the only sound was the rustle of our passage through the night. We carried unlit candles and I had some self-igniting matches. We walked three times by the gate of the house in question, and on the last pass, we were awarded with flickering lights in both the second and third floors, but nothing could be seen within the slotted lattice work windows, sitting with their recessed archways at the back.

We had found our watches in disagreement, and with my temperament, we arrived early at the street behind the house using Bannington's luminous watch piece, and in the dimness with much whispered discussion, found what we thought, was the third window.

We waited, behind us there was no drone from the Koranic memorisation school - no sound came from it at all, the street had gone very quiet and there were no lights to be seen. It was a half-moon this night, but it had not risen, and would not until we should be back with our associates.

Horne's watch's crystal was on a hinge, and I could lift it and feel the raised hours - a most valuable trait in a night watch. I checked Bannington's glowing fob watch. The time came and I put the precious vial in its small, Cloth. pocket at the head of the spear. Horn advanced with his lance well poised. with bag and vial attached. I could see little of him, but heard him 'ooff' as he hit the wall, and there was some shuffling, dimly I could see the pole, which was painted white, slowly advance up the wall until it came to the third window. I stood against the other wall, My Frenchman out and ready - for what I had no idea.

Nothing happened, Horne waited a minute or so, and then I could hear that he was tapping against the window. A period of silence followed during which I could see or hear nothing then I saw the pole move and in the next instance, Horne was next to me.

It is taken!

We were off, and as we planned, we exited the street. We checked the bag at the tip with our candle and matches, but there was no message, and so, disappointed, we slowly made our way towards the front gate of the house.

A tense twenty minutes went by, and we both had our pistols out. The two lights we had seen were still dimly observable but nothing more could be seen. We waited an additional ten minutes then reluctantly moved away. Our faithful pole was left for some scalawag to adopt, and we made our way towards the sally gate.

In the darkness, and even with all our skill, we became lost, and it took nearly an hour to find the blasted door and then we found why we had missed it earlier; it was closed, and would not open at our strongest tugging.

We went next to western gate.

[Editor's note: Driscol is unclear here, so I remind readers that Khiva had two sets of walls; the twenty-eight foot inner wall, which they were trying to pierce, and a lower outer wall]

This we found to be closed and guarded by five men who looked reasonably alert and awake. The Eastern gate was the same. We tried the southern gate and found that it gaping open with no one anywhere near it, except three sleeping donkeys and a man atop them, mumbling to himself, as he lay in the middle of the twenty-foot high gate.

We passed him by without comment. We had never seen this gate before, and we only vaguely knew where the road and our companions lay. Horne resolved to cross the lower, outer, mud wall, which we did after a long walk, and then we followed it as best we could, knowing that at some point we should intercept the western road. This we did. Horne's watch told us it was now 4.10 in the morning. We headed out, moving as swiftly as we could, over the uneven surface piled with animal waste and pools of water.

We saw and heard no one, but the many sounds of insects, and the growls and grunts of animals all around us. I realised, as we walked, that I remembered the tree of the cats from how it had seemed to me when we had come from the other direction. This seemed meaningless in the darkness now. I was jolted by a voice out of the darkness.

'Horatio'!

Horne replied, 'Nelson'!

We had found our expedition, the time was 5.36. It had been a long night indeed!

For once I took an offer of a bowl of sweetened scandal-water *{tea, so named for its being central to gossiping}* and drowned it at once, as it was no hotter than the atmosphere around me. The liquid refreshed me, and then came the taste like a fist out of the darkness, horrible!

We recounted our adventure in some detail. All were saddened that no message had been given to us when we had delivered up the acid.

Perkins announced that we had done what we had intended to do and that we would wait until dawn and then move north.

Then.

A voice came out of the darkness, in English, for we had been speaking English at that moment.

Are you Englishmen? The voice was followed by the movement of a musket's lock, a thunderous flash and crack of a shot, with a blossom of light and sparks as it fired, sundering the darkness.

Driscol had collected this image and wrote on it, "a fanciful view of an Eastern city and what I would have wished Khiva to have looked like, instead of the way it did." Illustration III-XV-5

Our Prisoner

We were well ambushed, as we fell apart from one another. I was on one knee with My Frenchman out. At that point, Bannington blundered into me, knocking us both down. I knew it was him, as I kneed him in his privates before at Igdy Well, and his curse was one I knew to associate with our Lord. Chaos was about me, but there were no more shots, as weapons were being cocked. There was twenty seconds of absolute terror, in the dark of the morning, and I suspected a bandit attack of swirling savages, or troops of the Khan's guards.

Dissanayake cried out that he had been startled, and had fired his weapon by accident. Who was there?

From in front of me, a voice with some concern in it, called out of the darkness again.

'Good, you must certainly be Englishmen, for you are dangerous'.

Five of us shouted for his name, and identification, at the same time.

In accented English the voice in the darkness replied, 'I am Nolta, I am the prisoner you have saved, and I am much in your debt. Does anyone have a glass of wine, and to whom do I return this phial'?

We were all delighted. We took him to our campsite, some two hundred feet off the road. Dobbins asked our new guest if we needed to be up and about, and would there be a pursuit?

At the fire we found him to be a tall, thin, man, nearly as tall as me, but of nobler bearing, naturally curly blonde hair, unshaven with a thin raggedy beard, but with a quick smile and an outstanding presence.

He told us quickly, I had him delay his tale, as I obtained my writing instruments. He was nonplused to find we had no wine.

He did have some tea. Michaelson set to treat his wounds, which were obviously wounds caused by shackles on his ankles, and wrists. These he cleaned and bound. Nolta was very appreciative of my giving him one of my green opium pills.

[Editor's note: I have gathered up from these notes the materials to create an introduction sheet as I have done for the other notables on the expedition. That will be followed by an explanation of the more current events]

Dafydd Friedrich zum Nolta

Herr Doctor
Painter, portraitist, pharmacist, military artist and ardent Bohemian

Nolta was born on June 13th 1814, as the only son and heir to Furst *{Prince}* Adalbrecht zum Nolta ruler of the small Rhine principality of Schaestein-Noltaberg. His mother was the Austrian Grafin *{countess}* Heimke Wittgenstein. In 1806, Napoleon had mediatized his family line of nobility, and the principality was absorbed into the larger state of Hesse. His father's support of the liberal policies of Napoleon, had led to his title not being returned at the Congress of Vienna in 1814. The family did retain a large estate, despite the loss of the privileges of nobility and that of being rulers of their own small state.

Nolta received an inflexible education, which he rigorously fought against. He had demurred to his father's wishes to earn a degree in Law, but was later persuaded to begin a medical degree at the age of fifteen at Medizinische Fakultät der Ernst-Moritz-Arndt-Universitat at Greifswald. Nolta completed only one year, before moving to Leopold-Franzens-Universitat at Innsbruck, and its college of medicine, concentrating on what would later be known as pharmacology. He stayed a year, and then moved to complete his studies in Fine Art in Munich at the Royal Academy of Fine Arts, where he studied under the famous artist Hermann Anschutz, who pronounced him one of the most talented artists of his age. It was here too that he began his explorations of the Bohemian lifestyle, on the death of his father, and on coming into his limited fortune.

He stayed at the last college until 1836, obtaining a dual magister[1] in Fine Art and Medicine. He was fluent in English, French, Russian and Italian, plus Greek and Latin. His wild life style soon swept him to Berlin, where he became involved with the upper classes of Prussian nobility; doing a number of notable landscapes of the Pomeranian coast and portraits of the leading ladies and gentlemen of Berlin. Nolta also drew fantastical maps and scenes from imaginary places and times. His oil painting titled, *The Goddess of Absinthe observing an opiated Mars* was considered the finest piece of this period, and was purchased by the wife of the Kaiser herself but destroyed in WWII.

There were unsetting rumours that he was dabbling in forbidden areas, and concerns were raised to such a height, that his family greatly restricted his use of the family fortune.

He then joined the Saxon, then Prussian army, at the end of 1836, as a mapping artist and was sent to Russia as part of a liaison team. He was celebrated for winning a race in the dead of winter to the top of the highest spire of the incomplete Saint Isaac's Cathedral in Saint Petersburg. Unfortunately this was in the nude, and two young members of the Russian nobility suffered severe frost bite, and the young artist was dismissed from his position. He stayed on in Saint Petersburg until recruited into the Russian army, and went to the Caspian Sea. It was while his ship was off the Bayardi Islands, and he was sketching the Emba River Delta, his ship was attacked and taken by Turcoman raiders in a savage dawn raid. Captured, he was taken in chains to Khiva, and he disappeared from the knowledge of any European. Those with knowledge of the matter noted that the other Russians taken in the same raid were all ransomed within a few months, but that no request was made by the Khivans for Nolta, and this was noted as being most unusual.

Nolta is a thin man of six feet, ten stone, with blonde hair and a clever, and witty, look to him, and pale greyish-blue eyes that would equally grace a either God or Bedlamite.

He continued his story to say that in Khiva he had been treated well, and had been questioned about his knowledge. Few educated Europeans had, in the past, been enslaved by the Khivans, and in him, they found someone who could be very useful. They had found it hard to believe he was not a Russian; their sworn enemy, for they had heard of Frenchmen, Italians and Englishmen but never of Prussians or Germans. He was purchased by the son of the Vizier, Yusuf Kush Aga. He explained that the three storey building we saw served several special purposes; it housed a gunpowder factory in its basement and this was new, having been built up by Nolta. The Khivans were desperately short of black powder, and had taken this opportunity to build up their own supplies.

The factory was hidden, to prevent the Khan himself from finding out about, it and simply taking it over for his own use. The factory was for the profit of the Vizier, and in these lands the ability to make money would attract the greedy eye of a ruler.

The building was also used as a prison for 'special' people who were slaves, but treated much better than the common chattels. Nolta had his small room, light at night, and plentiful food. There were other special captives there that he knew: including a Persian doctor, who did abortions and treated genital congestion *{sexual diseases}* for the Khivan nobility. There were also political prisoners there, and the second floor was an exclusive male brothel, established for the leading religious scholars of the Khanate.

Horne, upon finding out that there was a male brothel in Khiva observed, 'it is generally thought that one's opinion of a native population rises, the longer you are acquainted with them, except of course when they are quite beastly swine. Here sodomy is not vice, it is a virtue, but it does seem to keep down the population, which is a good thing for such a place'.

Nolta explained that he had been in his room for his luncheon, when he had heard the same parade that we had witnessed going by us. He said that he keenly noted that two members of our group, but he declined to say which, had shown they were Europeans, when the music had gone by.

We demanded to know what this tell-tale activity was.

Two of you were tapping your feet in time with the music. No Tartar would do this. Nolta called everyone who lived in Central Asia a Tartar.

He explained that he had requested the acid, because at night he was held in his second storey room by a chain that was attached to a ring set into the floor, and then, that to his ankle or wrist, depending on the capricious will of the guards. Another chain led from that ring and held the door closed, for it was designed to swing out. Each morning, at first prayer, he was thrown the key by way of a small window. He would unlock himself then loosened the chain that held the door. He had used the acid to weaken the central iron bolt that held the two chains to the ring. This he had done. He had opened the door and found the keys, which were left at the guard's desk.

He noted that above that desk was a grisly relic, as there were nailed several pairs of dried human ears, some no more than parchment, other still drying, and others somewhat fresher and giving off the most offensive odour.

He had requested the Aqua Fortis at midnight, as he knew the guards usually disappeared at this time for thirty minutes each night. Nolta felt he visited the brothel, when the others in the house had gone to bed. He knew there were more guards, and bolted doors, with heavy locks downstairs, so he went up on the roof, found a guard there asleep, discovering his luck was good he jumped over to the next building, for there were no alleyways between them. He continued this, until he came to a third building, trying not to disturbed the Khivans who often sleep on the roof in the summer. He found a fruit tree he could jump into. Down it he climbed, dreading at any moment a cry to stop, and soon, he found the dirty streets of Khiva under his feet. He looked for anyone who might be watching the place, and spied us. He could make out that we had what he thought was a pole, that could have delivered the vial, or it could have been a spear. Too fearful to come up to us, in case we were guards, he had nonetheless followed us, as he knew nothing of the city. This he had done very successfully for we had not noticed his presence at all. He had arrived here and edging close enough had heard, to his great joy English, and had spoken up.

I was overcome by fatigue at this time. Some stayed up to speak further with our rescued captive. I felt very satisfied by the evening's events and how I might portray my heroic efforts in person to the ladies who passed by in my thoughts every day. I rehearsed my speeches as I lay trying to sleep. I heard many more comments from our German friend, and these are what I recall the next morning when I wrote this.

Our German friend wondered out loud to us. Why does one travel? Why did he travel so that he had arrived in this place as a slave? Enjoyment of the joy of discovery, a sense of duty, which is the same as lunacy to my mind, to add richness to a dull life, give a reason and topics to write on, to see scenes to paint, to escape a bad situation, to enhance one's future or to find a charming anonymity, where your previous faults are not known.

For me, he said, it was all those things. Besides, being in Russia, I met and socially mixed with those at odds with the mind of the Czar. I was picked up and given a choice, accept exile by administrative order for the safety of the Czar or face years in a Russian prison. The fact I was not a Russian, made no difference to the way they applied their strict rules. So, that is how I came to this fate. I thank you all again for helping me, and I am forever in your debt.

Nolta in Eastern dress with his beard dyed black and a much longer beard that he had in fact. Illustration III-XV-6

A Ride To Nowhere

Day 21 Saturday 22 July

We all feel the need to leave the vicinity of Khiva as soon as possible, should a general search be conducted. We have little additional clothing to give Nolta; deciding on the formerly, white, robe worn by Perkins in his starring role as a Circassian Prince. We also had to redistribute our loads, as we had to make one horse available for our new companion. However, we did not have a saddle, but Bannington that master of the horse, and true gentleman, gave up his saddle, and elected to ride bare back, for he said he had done so as a lad. It was not a surprise that he kept his seat with no difficulties at all, and his legs were like vices.

By the first prayer of *Fajr*, we were heading away towards the north, to a river side town called Gourlen, where we intended to take passage down river to another place called Tchimbar, and at that point, we would split the expedition, as previously planned. We were cresting a rise in that direction, when from behind us came a sound we all had heard before; that drumming sound of a large body of horse moving at speed. We then heard horns blaring. Other travellers began to move to the side of the road and we followed their lead. They came up from the south; a body of horsemen, traveling at a fuming pace, dangerous on such a potted and ill-formed road such as this. I had my hand on My Frenchman as they came abreast of our small party. We could have no hope of success against such a mass of men, should they attack us. I would say it was a thousand mounted men, if not more, armed with jingling scimitars, daggers, battle-axes, spears, bows and arrows and about a quarter with matchlocks or flintlock muskets, some wore brass helmets or an iron cuirass. There were many banners, flags and streamers. Their appearance was scandalous, and would have given apoplexy to any English cavalry commander or good Sergeant. This mounted force without order or common pace, they surged passed us, covering us all with dust.

After the dust had cleared, and the traveling circus had disappeared up the road, the last thing we heard of them was the sound of their horns. Hynes, Bannington and Horne were beside themselves with laughter at such a comic sight. They too had thought we were about to be slaughtered on the road, but instead, we had only been severely sprinkled with road dust. There being only one road to follow, we continued to do so. Now that it was fully light, I could see we would have a problem with the disguise of Nolta, his hair is blonde and skin very fair, and he had only a few weeks-worth of beard. As all males of age have a beard in Central Tartary, so he must be a youth, but his blonde moustache was a problem too. We stopped for a while and dyed his moustache and told him not to shave for the rest of his life. Given he was nearly my height, showing him as a boy would be difficult. Perkins suggested we dress him as a woman, who in this blighted place is covered from head to toe in cloth, when in public view. To my surprise, Nolta took no offence, and thought it was inspired, but it remained an idea only, as we had no clothes of that type.

Our luck held, for a traveling Jew came by with a cart load of clothes. We made him an excellent price for his custom, and we were soon off with nine Circassian men and one woman. Now we had no idea what a Circassian woman wore, but we figured we should follow the Persian and Arab models we had seen. He was covered from head to foot with a dark blue robe, and only his blue and grey eyes showed forth. We came in time to cross the Dailatek River. There was a ferry, but most were fording, we watched the disorder for some time, and seeing that horses were passing without difficulty at one point, we decided to cross there. As we were preparing to do so, those horns were heard again. A column of dust that we had seen earlier grew nearer. It was that same party of horsemen. Even their splendid Turcoman horses could not have kept up the pace they had held earlier and now they walked. The whole body came down to the far shore and began to water their horses. We could do no more than proceed.

We crossed without difficult and were making our way up the shore when a better dressed horsemen, greeted us in Persian, begging our pardon, and asking if we were the party of Prince Pshimide? *{Perkins' Circassian nome de guerre}*. Perkins presented himself and the conversation was over before I could arrive to listen to it.

Perkins related later what had been said after we rode on.

The Khan wishes to speak with me, in my guise *{as a Circassian prince}*, on the subject of the approaching Russian army; given my life time of fighting the Russians. We are invited to be his guests in Khiva and to take an audience with him and his officers as soon as is feasible; non-acceptance of his gracious invitation would not be accepted.

That we were not being considered prisoners was soon obvious. The officer, who was a cousin of the Khan, and five men, remained with us, to lead us back. We were given a number of presents, mainly cooked foods, which given our paltry breakfast and little dinner, was appreciated. We were fortunate that the commander, who insisted we call him Begi, was not devout in his religion, and we avoided the need to pray in the Mohammedan style.

A view of the natives fording a tributary of the Oxus. Illustration III-XV-7

Return To The Heated Delights Of Khiva

We made our way back with increasing apprehension. We had given Nolta the title and name of the Prince's wife, Gwaschenise or Princess, as we knew no female Circassian names.

Amongst ourselves, we practiced our story, like school boys building up a plausible explanation of why the neighbour's hazelnut trees were missing their fruit; we tried to think of every possible question that might be asked.

As we rode on, with a tightness in my bowels, Dissanayake circulated around us and brought us words of support, for today was the festival of Mary Magdalene and in particular his reference to Hebrews, Chap. Iii, verse 12.

> *Take heed, brethren, lest there be in any of you an evil heart of unbelief in departing from the living God*

We arrived back after a joyless trip and to our surprise were placed in a private house with servants; six of them, all slaves, and one major domo, who did not speak Persian, so his use to us was limited. An interpreter, one of the most evil looking men I have ever seen, who had a mouth like the anus of a cat, was also there to assist, and he could speak Persian, but was a first class moron, and was helpless in any field.

Illustration III-XV-8

An interesting piece of décor presented itself in the house, for over one door, was a plaque which read: *History is a mirror of the past and a lesson for the present.*

It was a Persian proverb, but by whom we did not know *{it is not known who said it}*

Bannington observed, 'The genius, wit and spirit of a nation are discovered in its proverbs' *{That proverb was said by Lord Bacon}*.

We all thought this single sign was an omen, or sign, but of what we could not agree.

Our horses were well taken care of, as we had neglected them for nearly two days. We found the house comfortable in the Khivan sense, no furniture, but low cushions on the floor, and a number of beautiful, Persian and Afghani rugs. There was one guard. We found him to be a friendly fellow, but with no common tongue, his duty was to keep beggars away from the Khan's guests and not to keep us in.

He made a sweeping motion with his arms to show we could come and go as we pleased.

We had a boiled goat for dinner and having banished the servants by smiles and hand waves, we were left alone, and we posted our own guards and discussed long into the night our situation. We must, as Hynes described it;

> 'We Must 'Clumsy' Our Way Through All That Might Come'.

Our home had butter, lard, wheat, eggs, fowl and red meat on the bone, plus rice from my parents' time in India. I found it a very different kind of rice than what is actually eaten in India, but I did not know that until I came here *{India}*. My mother served limited vegetables, which initially were boiled to a grey ooze, but later, were made much more palatable, by less cooking. My father liked liver; so 2-3 times a month, I had to choke down well fried liver; often cut into very small pieces and swallowed whole to avoid the taste of it. During this time, I learned the delights of my own sauce: made from anchovies, garlic, onions, salt, sugar, tamarind and spices, this would cover even the taste of liver. My Danish relatives ate more seafood, most of which was a delight, but I remember with the greatest dread, a type of fried fish cake mixed with pounded fish flesh and onions; utterly horrid stuff, and a thing of my nightmares. My summers at sea had seen very rough food, boiled meat, stale biscuits and dried pease *{peas}* plus some plum duff. I had tasted finer food in the army and lovely food on my trip to the continent, where I found that I favoured some types of French, German, Italian and other foods.

Day 22 Sunday 23 July

A sleepless night, and considering my fatigue, I was in poor shape in the morning. Nolta would not stir from the house. He found he was exhausted. He was quite willing to do nothing and his wounds were sore as he had not ridden for some time, and he was aching from the actions of our ride. We worked out a strategy, whereby the servants comprehended that he *{she}* was not to be disturbed; on pain of death. The house was so constructed, that we realised that we could place one of us in such a position as to prevent anyone coming by chance to Nolta. It was Horne's duty day, so he was glad to sit and I decided to walk in the town for I had to tire myself in order to allow me to sleep. I went out after morning prayers. In a Muslim town, it is not good to be seen walking around during prayers. One may even be assaulted by a religious fanatic, armed with a dull tongue or a sharper dagger; even in a city full of non-practicing men. I then proceeded on my own.

I had changed my appearance somewhat, making myself much more shabby looking. I thought this would be in vain, as my height could not be disguised. In Khiva, I felt the want of a chain mail purse; for thieves were thick on the ground here, or so it seemed to me. No one wished to go with me, so having armed myself, and lamenting that there was no way to take Ascalon with me, I took instead one of the Colts as a support to My Frenchman.

I went again to the money lender and was glad to see he did not know me. I asked him of the news, but there was nothing of importance nor new, but I did find that a Circassian Prince had come for talks with the Khan, and I was glad to hear that there was no gossip in the bazaar of a missing slave, escaped European, or anything of the sort.

I watched a fight develop between two groups of Turcoman; probably of opposing tribes that fell quickly into a sword fight; four against three. They mainly sparred with one another ineffectually, then the three attacked in earnest and in the confusion, one of their enemies missed a blow and drove his blade to the bone of his companion's thigh. That should have given the three their chance for victory, but one of them, in his movements to advance, tripped over the feet of his friend, and fell onto the side of the third; wounding him grievously. That put an end to the harebrained fight, resulting in mutual defeat. Their swordsmanship seemed to have been learned at the butcher's block.

I moved with the crowd who gathered to see the two wounded men bleed, and the enemies who were shouting at one another from a distance. I had a chance to observe their swords, or rather scimitars, which were fine weapons made of Khorassan steel *{cast in Persia and forged by Russian slaves in Khiva}*. They are expensive, and the examples I saw were held in scabbards of red and blue dyed, camel, leather. The pommels were bulbs, with silver or gold wire wrapped over skin, and a few have cheaper, coloured stones set in them.

A man in the crowd nearly as big as myself, seeing I was interested in weapons, presented me with his fire arm to examine. I dearly wished I could have presented Ascalon to him, for he would have been astounded. His weapon was a five and a half foot long, matchlock with a beautifully, twisted barrel and long butt, that was rounded and designed to be secured under the arm and not set to the shoulder. It had no mechanism for aiming, the wood was not in the best shape and the uncleanliness of the lock itself would have gained him two days additional duty in my battery. However it was a beautiful, if grimy, weapon set with silver and un-polished brass. It would have been best to just to put it up on a wall and to make up heroic stories of capturing it from desperate men, while outnumbered three to one, than to risk its use in battle. We shared no common language, but by my motions, I made him understand my thanks, and my pleasure at examining his weapon.

I ran into Bannington and helped him find another saddle, paid for by the expedition. We bought it from a shop full of Persians, all slaves and ex-slaves, who were quite pleased to help us as we spoke Persian, and gave them news of their former homeland.

A Persian run shop in Khiva. Illustration III-XV-9

A scene of a Koranic school in Khiva. Illustration III-XV-10

A Deadly Discovery Made

As we had servants now, and we were to be fed from the Khan's larder, I made no search for food. I was drawn, against my own will and common sense, to the scene of our night action. I decided to causally wander by the three storeyed house where Nolta had been held. I came into the street at a time when the local Koranic schools were taking a pause and the street was crowded with students. I hate crowds, so I moved to a side wall to wait for the 'herd' to clear. The wall was unpleasantly warm. I was facing in one direction, when from behind me I heard something that triggered my interest, but before I could turn, three men swept by me. They were in the disreputable clothing of Khiva, and seemed nothing special, but as they passed, one of them said clearly:

Wir sind gewohnt dass die Menschen verhohnen was sie nicht verstehen?

{We are accustomed to people who scoff at that which they do not understand}

This was German and I froze. Slowly I brought my hands into my robe to find My Frenchmen. I could hear the pounding of my heart in my ears. The three men were now on the side of the street away from the gate of the former prison, and they had to wade through the students and came to that formidable blue gate. One tapped and another shouted in Arabic that it was them, and a moment later a plate set in one side of it opened, a face peered out then closed just as quickly, then the gate swung slowly open. Two men entered, while the third turned around, spat in a foul manner, wiped his beard and chin for his spit had not gone far, and he surveyed the scene. He looked at the crowd of students and seemed to be speaking to the men within the gate but I could not hear them over the crowd, which had become noisier. He looked directly at me but there was no recognition in his eyes, and he paid no attention to me, looking over the crowd with an evident displeasure. I considered at that moment the idea of drawing my revolver and shooting him. He was only twenty feet away, and regardless of the crowd, I felt I should and must hit him. I was indecisive and my mind froze. I had the impulse to shoot him then and there, but for what? Was it he, or another? I could not decide. I could not see his hair, and he sported a bushy black beard, but I knew those eyes, it was he! I knew it! He finished his view, spat again, the ugly yellowish glob striking the wall and slowly, egg-like, made it was down towards the street, while he disappeared into the gate, which closed after him

I stood there some time, until my breathing had slowed, and the students had cleared away. I walked at all speed back to our new residence, which, of course, I could not find without a great deal of inner cursing, and the sweat pouring forth. I found no one there but Horne and Nolta. I had memorised the phrase, for it had been German, but the pronunciation had been odd to my ear. Nolta was the man to ask. He had me repeat the phrase several times, and he stated that it sounded like an old dialect, such as the type used in Osterreichische Kanzleisprache, or the old official language of Austria. That is what the written version was called, and he suggested the man might have been speaking Schonbrunner Deutsch; the old noble speech of that Empire, and what in English we would consider to be, 'upper-class speech'. However, unless he heard the language, he could not be sure, as German was a pluricentric language *{having several, different, standard versions}*.

Horne seemed unconcerned, but then Perkins and I had downplayed, and limited, the knowledge of that man to our expedition, even though we had explained to them somewhat at the docks of Bombay and Bushire when we had sighted him. I paced for some time, working up a fearsome sweat, but no one returned and around noon, as the prayer calls sounded, my fatigue overcame me, and I slept.

[Editor's note: To remind readers; Driscol had encountered a German speaking, long-haired, blonde, man several times in his travels. He was convinced it was the same man who always seem to show up at odd places]

I was awakened, none too gently by Dobbins, who had a bowl of some savoury stew for me. I must say, the quality of food had gone up. Overlooking the excessive fat, it was delicious; being made from sheep's marrow bones, and other tid-bits.

I found our party in the forward room. The servants had brought the meal, and we had sent them away, so instead of eating in the Eastern way, all sitting around a large tray and eating with our right hand, the food had been placed into bowls, which had been filled with fruit juice that we had drained and which now contained individual dinners for each of us. We all had a spoon somewhere, but Nolta had to make do with a fork. We had only one spoon for each member and the fork was extra. I dare not tell him where, and in what circumstances, we had found that forlorn and lonely European fork. I am sure the story of that solitary, bronze, Barcelonian-made, fork would have been a revelation.

Perkins and I discussed my sighting. He simply would not believe that that man could be here, and I was now uncertain of my identification. We asked Nolta if any Austrians had been around his prison. He had seen none, nor heard them, but he did state that nearly all the scientific instruments he had used, had been made in central Europe, mainly Austria.

After this discussion, I dismissed my concerns, as the imaginary constructs of a tired and fearful mind - but the Austrian phrase echoed through my head. I thought long and hard that night of many things, and the man responsible for the death of my friend Beer, was foremost in my thoughts.

Horne and Vickery brought up one of their favourite subjects, one we had discussed before; their evaluation scheme for public eating places in Central Asia. They and the rest had been adding rules and conditions to it for some time, and now it was felt that the time had come for official consideration, and its acceptance as a policy of the Perkins' Expedition;

Vickery's Rating, our Ten Point Guide to Fine Dining in Central Tartary

1. The outside walls of the establishment should be standing, and not more than two can be ruinous, if it is a tent, then there cannot be more than six rips in every square yard

2. The inner walls should not have blood on them, if they do, this may not extend over more than two walls, unless fresh, then that is acceptable on all four

3. Flies; there cannot be more than 100 flies x the # of customers x their fingers

4. There must be a regulation sized 6' x 4' x 2', retching trough outside the establishment, and it is considered the height of luxury, should it have cushions for one's knees

5. Dead customers; these must be removed promptly; after the contents of their pockets and bags have been divided amongst the surviving customers. Once this is done, a tasteful - but short, ceremony must be performed - then the body may be thrown into the street

6. Hanging meat; must be recognisable as to cut and kind under its layer of flies with, one and only one, pass of the hand to disperse them

7. Furnishings; must have rugs or cushions that do not have on them in Persian or Arabic inscriptions promising a painful and unnecessarily cruel death to any who sit on them

8. It must be at least one hundred and fifty feet from the nearest mosque, and said house of worship may not have an Imaum who enjoys shouting, or who more than one month a year, usually during the month of Ramadan, incites his followers to find infidels, and take slices of their flesh from their heretical, inner thighs.

9. It may not smell like a combined abattoir and pissoire on a hot day in southern France

10. The cook may not be a leper, a Hindoo vegetarian with one arm, nor a German speaking bastard, who knows only four recipes, and they all contain sauerkraut

Day 23 Monday 24 July

Perkins made one of his infrequent inspections of my journal this morning, and seeing what I had written, called over Michaelson and proclaimed I was ill. Pointing to my writing, he suggested that I had a bad case of *typophilia*, an illness that manifests itself in an undue interest in writing in odd fonts and scripts. Michaelson suggests a gunpowder suppository as my pathway to health. I suggested in turn that Perkins was an overly fastidious, fussy, old maid, who did not understand fonts any better than he did why water ran down hill, or how to charm a snake, and as for Michaelson, he was just an urbane twit, educated beyond his level of competence. We all thought Perkins' creation of the word 'typophilia' was a most charming invention however.

We still had no place to go. No word had come from the Khan as to when Perkins would meet with him, and so some varied discussion took place among us.

Horne and Nolta were arguing over the greatness of Britain and Nolta mentioned British duplicity over the treaty of Paris and our sworn declaration to free the Ionian Islands[2], the land of Odysseus, to be a free and independent state, and had not done so in the past, nor even releasing these most Greek of islands, to the newly formed Kingdom of Greece. We began to speak of Ireland and the following observation was made by Michaelson, who had dealt with 'dead drunk' Irishmen as part of his duties. He declared an Irishman is not finished drinking until he is in one of four states, dead, unconscious, without drink as he had no money and no friends left, or finally he can stick his finger into his mouth and with the tips feel and stir the drink resting in his throat before moving on to the stomach, if he can do this, he truly has had enough to drink.

Bannington added to the Irish bashing, that British soldiers in Ireland often held the opinion that the locals had pointed tails hidden beneath skirt or trowsers, proof indeed that they were devils, and certainly not quite human. He mentioned once that he had sat on a courts-martial of a soldier, who while drunk has slaughtered his Irish fellow soldier, to see in fact, if he had a tail.

He spoke of the trial in somber tones, and of his being convicted, for the evidence was overwhelming, and he was condemned, brought into a square of men, blindfolded, stripped of his uniform and drummed out of the regiment. Once no longer part of the regiment, he was then hung outside the barracks.

From this, the discussion swung to an animated scientific one on the luminiferous aether[3]. I found this somewhat difficult to follow, and no conclusion was reached as no one could contradict Newton's particle theory or Fresnel's wave theory in any convincing way.

There being nothing else to do, so I wandered out again to the markets with a firm decision not to go near that house where I had seen the blonde haired man - now with a black beard.

THE GREAT MINARET OF KHIVA

More sights from Khiva, the great minaret. Illustration III-XV-11

The Foulness Of The Khivan Bazaars And The Idiocy Of Guides

In the market place a revolting display of entertainment; a cat was spiked to a pole, then butted to death by men with their heads. This seemed to be the Central Tartar's method of bull baiting *{a bull being attacked by dogs a popular street entertainment in England}*. I for time sought a way to disrupt the attacks and save the cat but it could not be done without my being killed also.

You rarely see a deformed man in Khiva; nor a dwarf as these tend not to live; nor a man born with a crippled arm, or if they are truly cursed, without a hand *{Muslim's cut the right hand off a thief}*, as they will be thought to be thieves for the rest of lives. Some with bad legs and feet are seen, as a son is a son, but never in a woman, who must be sellable as a bride, and damaged goods are never easy to sell. Those who are deformed are always left to die. However, I rarely ever saw a woman anywhere, and if I did, they were always covered by tent-like layers of clothes.

I went to the *Kitchik {slave market}*. The first man up was an example of human wreckage. He had no right hand, no left thumb, no nose, nor ears, and the hair on his head, eyebrows, and beard had been plucked out and the skin sheared with a white hot iron; a practice known as 'scaling the fish', and as if that were not bad enough, one of his eyes had also been burnt out. I could see no way this wretch could do any work, and he was not purchased. Two younger men that I thought were Russians were sold for agricultural work. Various tribals were brought up and sold too. Several of the wretches here were obviously Dravidians from Southern India; and even lighter skinned northern Indians. I dared not try to speak to them, for my courage failed me at that point. I found this depressing and left soon afterward, as I always felt I would be seized and sold myself.

Two scenes from Khiva the inner bazaar and the appearance of Islam Hoja Street 180 years ago. Illustrations III-XV-12 & III-XV-13

I went by the main Eastern gate and heard two men speaking in Persian about the Khan's Vizier;

Is not the wisdom of God great and most enlightened? Has he not given acumen and some cleverness even to a dog? A little less, it is true, than to the woman. But a great deal more than that to the Khan's Vizier? Who can explain why the Vizier has put his own son to death. Who can understand these things?

I came across Vickery and Hynes and we eventually were recommended a guide; this was not a very easy task, as few of the merchants spoke any Persian. When we found the said person, it became immediately apparent that he was somewhat drunk, although he offered a feeble excuse of having a fever. He did at least speak Persian and we found that he was in fact a Persian, a man of Meshed who had been captured and enslaved as a boy, freed later after he became a Sunni, and who had remained ever since in his captor's city. Yes he said he was a guide, for he had been on every path, track or road that it was possible to walk or ride over in Central Tatary and he had forty years' experience of working on or leading caravans.

We asked him if he could guide us to the Aral Sea and the discussion went something like this:

'We wish to travel to the Aral Sea'

He replied with a smile, 'Yes, I can do so, yes'

Perkins asked, 'How long will it take'?

Our guide seemed puzzled and asked. 'How long will what take'?

Perkins said, 'How many days would it take for us to arrive at shore of the Aral Sea'?

He replied again with a smile, 'Not long'.

Perkins becoming irritated stated slowly, 'How long please in days travelled'?

Our guide responded, 'It would depend'.

'Depend on what'? Asked the annoyed Perkins.

'What country is it in'? Was his reply…

As we knew the Aral Sea was about two hundred and twenty miles to the north of Khiva, we were surprised that he was so demonstrably 'knowledgeable'. We left him to his 'fever' for he must indeed have had one as he was clearly not well.

The servants brought us a half a sheep this evening with plentiful greasy rice and fresh fruit.

Hynes had been making note of the expedition's interpersonal relations and he declared that for a group of mainly officers and two civilians plus a gentleman foreigner, we were rather uncivil to one another and he then went about attempting to civilise us. He proceeded to regale us with his views of proper 'gentlemanliness', which we found most amusing, coming from a Canadian, backwoods, provincial.

I can recall here just a few of the observations that he came forth with this evening from an extensive list:

Let your recreations and entertainments be manly and not those of a child, or in any way sinful, or if sinful, truly sinful; no half actions

Never start an argument at our supper table, being beaten to death by a meat bone is any way for a gentleman to end his life

Do not raise up your hands to pick your teeth with an instrument in an obvious and distasteful way, and Hynes pointed at me, instead use your tongue, and if needed a helpful finger to point, your own finger, it should be noted

When sharing a communal meal do not besmirch the atmosphere by forceful sneezes, spitting or coughing, if you must do so, use your own hand or handkerchief not your neighbour's

When a man of the world is explaining the niceties of behaviour, it is a demonstration of your lacking couth, to laugh and make light of what he is enlightening you with, as you are doing now, especially as that man can turn you on his knee and give you a good spanking

That the French serve woman's food, and nothing, yes nothing is better than a good hunger conquered with tepid ale, and undercooked, and bloody, red beef; to that statement we all cheered!

His final piece of wisdom was wise and I paraphrase it as follows.

> Nothing is more motivating to a young man's career than unrequited love. He must either go mad, become a drunk and ruin himself, and therefore help another to take his place; helping THAT young man. He may become indifferent to woman, and so armoured that he is no longer distracted by the fair gender, and instead devote himself to his career or throw himself into his work to quell his feelings of loneliness and desperation. To this we all cheered, for each of us had tasted that cold spear in the guts, the suffering that is called unrequited love. If we had not yet faced such a trial, he suggested we should arrange to do so, as it would greatly enhance our futures.

A minaret near the Khan's prison in Khiva. Known as 'the tower of last view'. It was so named, as it would be the last thing most people saw before entering the prison, from which they would never emerge Illustration III-XV-14

A street scene of Khiva near the house where the expedition was held before meeting with the Khan.
Illustration III-XV-15

We Meet With The Khan And Ameer Of Khiva And His Vizier

Day 24 Tuesday 25 July

Early that day, with our breakfast, there came a messenger to tell us that the Khan, Allah Quli Bhadur Khan, would see us this day after the noon prayers. An escort led by Begi would come for us at that time.

The Rug merchants.
Illustration III-XV-16

In the meantime, the Khan sent us a multitude of rug salesmen, with the mission to give a rug as a gift from the Khan to Perkins; the erstwhile Circassian Prince. Perkins asked them to come back tomorrow, as we had no need of a rug. Instead, the merchant, a wise little weasel, suggested we select one. He would present it to us as the gift from the Khan, then his brother would purchase it for 75% of its value, and all would be well - we did so.

Perkins had asked how many of his retinue he should bring, and he was told that no more than two or three of us, mere lackeys, should accompany him.

He decided on bringing Hynes, due to his superior Persian, and I. I am not sure I appreciated being included. We discussed at length his replies to possible questions. We would go armed, and the remaining party would stay indoors and fully armed, should this be a ruse to separate the leader, and attack us separately.

The time came. Perkins had regained his washed white, Circassian, outfit and we and Hynes had borrowed enough clothing to look rough and presentable, somewhere between a rugged mercenary and a fallen courtier.

Begi, the same officer who had found us on the road, came to greet us. His friendliness reduced our anxiety greatly. He told us to follow him, and we made our way to the Khan's palace, which was nothing to see; being hidden behind a great wall. The gate of lattice iron was opened and we were soon in a courtyard garden. We were greeted by a fanfare of horns, drums and other clashing noises.

The officer left us in the care of a very small man, who was some fussy, functionary, who gave us directions in Persian on how to comport ourselves, and described in some detail the ceremonial actions we should take. He did say the Khan was forgiving of mistakes by foreigners, and that he would be behind us all the way. He then added that while the Khan was a reasonable man, his Vizier was a stern man, religious and disliking of anything or anyone not Khivan. Both he and the Khan spoke Persian. The other officers we might meet spoke the language either not at all, or indifferently.

As for us, Hynes and I we must see if the Khan wished us to be part of the conversation, or if not, to go with that decision and withdraw.

We marched through to the chamber, which was filled with people, notables and un-notable Khivans and foreigners. These were passed by, and we entered the throne room. The Khan was seated; one twisted man stood near him, while another, who by his dress, I took as a servant, stood behind the throne. We had not been searched, but in entering the room, we found armed men to the number of twenty in the position of guards with scimitars lined up along the walls.

We had been informed of an old and stale Khivan tradition, that those coming from afar were seized and dragged before the Khan in this way, showing their submission to his greatness. This indignity was directed at Perkins only, and consisted of one man placing his hand on his arm as if to drag him forward, but he, as Perkins was a friend, had this dismissed by a motion from the Khan. That piece of theatre completed, we advanced, making sure not to do so in step which would be too European, but instead shuffling forwards in a slow, impertinent, Eastern way.

The Khan was on a type of couch and not on a true throne, and we greeted him in the Persian manner, adding some touches, which we had read that Circassians do. This was well accepted. We soon established that we could communicate well enough in Persian, and the Khan's servant and probable translator, and the man behind us, withdrew. We took our seats on cushions next to the couch while the twisted man, who turned out to be the *Kushbeghi {Vizier}*, stood and never said a word during the proceedings.

The Khan did in truth consider Perkins to be a Circassian prince and he knew of our magic weapons and he was curious to know where they came from.

Perkins replied that he had captured them from the Russians, who had many such things.

The Khan asked if we had one with us. Perkins replied in the affirmative and handed over his Colt. The Khan was like a boy with a new toy soon he stood up, having asked how it worked and fired a shot at one of the pillars. The shot was extremely loud in this room of stone and the ball bounced around for a few moments. He then asked if it was that it would fire again. On hearing that it was indeed true, he again fired at the same pillar; much to the distress of all, especially the two Khivan guards who stood on either side of it. I wondered if splinters of lead or stone might be affecting them, but they did not move. He fired two more shots into the pillar and gave forth with several Arabic and Khivan phrases of utter amazement. The Vizier, I could see, was visibly shocked.

Did we know how to build such things magical things? Perkins told him that sadly no we had no skill in that, as the Khan could see they are mechanical weapons made by men of great skill, and not magical. The Mussulmen still believe in magic, as the Koran states that magic exists, therefore it does, and one could be cut down for suggesting otherwise.

He asked us what we knew about the Russian army. From Nolta, we had updated news, not of the rumoured invasion force but of the army in general. Perkins spoke of the Russian army's infantry, in their hundreds of thousands, the regular cavalry and the Cossacks and the artillery.

The Khan said that he had a Russian man in his employ, by the name of Bel-Bel[4], who had trained his gunners to fire in the European way, and that he had four and thirty guns. He enquired how many guns the Russians might have. Perkins motioned to me to answer, as I was the artillerist.

I answered that and said four thousand or more. This Khan did not believe me. He asked how this was possible. I said that many were on ships; some carrying one hundred and twenty guns, and explained that many fortresses contain up to two-hundred guns.

The Khan did not believe this either, as he knew well the cost of casting cannon. Did the Russians have cannon that could fire like this 'revolver'? He said the word in English, as Perkins had mistakenly used that term, not knowing any such word in Persian.

No they did not.

The Khan explained that the Russian were coming and asked our advice, as we had more experience in fighting this enemy. The Khan himself had nearly a hundred thousand irregular cavalry at his call, but it all depended on the popularity of the Khan, and who wished to answer the call to arms. He also had some two thousand household cavalry, who are much better armed and mounted, as they come from his own family and tribe. it was they who we had seen on the road north out of Khiva.

He said that the Russian army was headed towards the Aral Sea, and from his spies, he felt that the enemy, who had set up depots along the lower Jaxartes, would approach from that direction.

He asked what we thought the Russian objective was?

Perkins said the Russians wish to conquer this land for three reasons; to own it, to free the Russian slaves held here, and to stop the slave trade, which was against their religion and thirdly to advance closer to the Persian and Afghanistaun borders, for Russia wished, in the future, to attack the latter or the former, to secure an invasion route to British India.

The Khan and Vizier looked at one another, and he demanded to know how we knew this. Perkins explained that we had travelled from our homes, and had stayed sometime with the Turks and Persians, and in Persia had met and spoke with many tribes of Europeans, and this was the common knowledge amongst them. In addition, we had spoken too with Russians who had informed us of the ultimate objectives of the Czar.

The Khan asked why the Russians wanted his land, for if they had such vast lands, why did they want his small piece?

Perkins explained that the Khan had many, many beautiful horses and that he controlled the river Oxus and this river could be used to move an army to the borders of Persia and Afghanistaun for the reasons explained before.

The Khan asked if the Russian would force them to become Christians?

Perkins said no, the Russians already had many Mussulman citizens under their sway, and that they were treated well in regards to religion. They treated our own people badly by conquering them, for we had no wish to be under them; however they did not try to force their three Gods on us {Circassians}.

The Khan stated that his spies said that the Russian army consisted of only ten thousand infantry, some cannon, and an equal number of cavalry. Did the infantry have guns like this revolver?

Perkins retorted that many of the officers might do, but the regular troops would have flint-lock muskets that could fire 2-3 times a minute, and that they would fight in squares. He went on to explain what a square was, and how his Khivan cavalry, noble and brave as it was, would not be able charge and break them, as the Russians also used bayonets.

The Khan said his men would overrun them, but Perkins then explained what a bayonet was and how it worked, and the Khan acknowledged that he knew of this dishonourable weapon; for his ancestors had faced them before, with ill luck, but had defeated the enemy anyway.

This seemed to discourage him, and he asked what we might suggest, having been at war with the Russian for as long as he could remember.

Perkins stated that he should start by freeing his Russian slaves. This would remove one of the main reasons for the Russian advance, and they might, just might, halt.

The Khan and Vizier withdrew for a time, and we were left to our thoughts. Servants brought in a liquid pulp made from fruit, which was very refreshing. They were away for some time, but I dared not look at my watch. The two men returned with a body of others, all well-dressed. These were introduced as the *Bey* or commander of his army, the *Atalik* his commissioner of the state, and the *Mehter*, a man in charge of the Khanate's internal affairs *{head of the Khan's spies and what in the west would be called secret police}*.

We repeated all that had been said; us speaking in Persian, then it being translated in to the Khivan language for the newly arrived.

They then had a long discussion between themselves, and a most heated one at that, for we could hear it even while they were quite some distance away. After a time, they returned and presented to us a paper written in Russian, and having a seal at the bottom. The Khan said that a man, declaring himself a Russian diplomatic agent, had appeared some weeks ago and presented this to him, and could we tell if it was legitimate?

The paper was not the best. I asked permission to put the paper in the light, and found it had no watermark

It said in part, for I could not read all of it, as it was written in flamboyant Persian

> *To The Grand Khivan Emir… long list of his titles….from the Russian Czar with his …long list of titles… seemed to demand freedom for all Russian slaves, or payment of fifteen thousand Tomauns for an agreement to hold them for ten years, and which later could be renewed every five years. I could at best read on half of what was written, but did take note of the blue wax seal on the bottom of the letter, which while elaborate, I knew came from a package of 'blue seal flour', a Russian import I had seen and bought in the markets. [Editor's note: This would have been equal to around 125,000 pounds Sterling or ten thousand less in Rupees, a large sum]*

I told the Khan that I thought the letter was illegitimate, for as I understood the Czar would never make such an offer, and secondly the seal was from a package of flour, which one could find in his esteemed markets.

This caused consternation with the Vizier and the Khan, and soon a guard was dispatched to secure a package of the flour. We passed the time with Perkins, making up a fanciful story of his lost lands in Circassia proper, and the perfidy of Russians in general. While I worried that some insane man would have, that day, bought up all the Russian flour in the market, and at any moment a breathless guard would appear and announce that no such flour or seal existed.

However, the dispatched guard returned streaming with sweat as he was wearing a steel cuirass, and had obviously run the entire distance, no less than $\frac{3}{4}$ of a mile I would suppose, and it was around 91° outside. He brought with him a slightly wetted bag of the flour and of course the seal was found to be the same. I suspect that the 'Russian diplomatic agent' might be about to have an unpleasant afternoon.

The Khan thanked me, and the Vizier, by an intermediary, gave me five gold Tomauns; worth some three and forty pounds, a fortune indeed *(nearly half of what he made a year in salary)*. I was also given *Misbaha (prayer beads)*, of lapis lazuli and most beautiful, with ninety nine stones, each to represent the many names of Allah. As I handled it, it broke asunder and I and the guards all scrambled to find the various small beads. We were ultimately successful.

A broken misbaha. Illustration III-XV-17

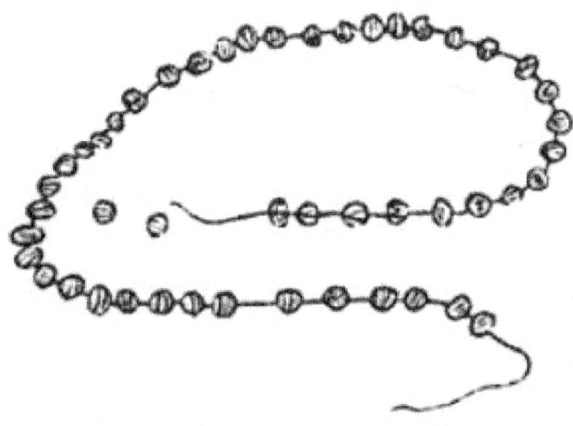

We Are Given A Mission By The Khan Of Khiva

The Khan directed that we make our way to the lower Jaxartes, and intercept the Russian column, and determine their purpose, and for this he would pay us well, but we would not have the authority to make a treaty; but simply the task to obtain information only.

Perkins thanked him for his trust in his ability, but he said we must respectfully forbear, due to our incapability in such matters, and that we were here to buy horses and not to become involved in this war. He was known to the Russians, and he might not be the best ambassador as we might be arrested on sight. I thought that was very clever of Perkins to so say.

The Khan waved his hand and pointed his finger *{a rude gesture to a Muhammadan}*, 'you WILL proceed as we direct, and upon your return, we will grant you five hundred horses as a gift. What would you do with these horses'?

Perkins' replied that, 'we sought several thousand horses, and would take them to the Caspian by way of the dried Oxus river bed, and there ship them to the Circassian regiments forming in Turkish territory.'

Our Khan said quite deliberately, 'You will not be able to do that without my permission and you have made powerful enemies amongst the Turcoman and you will not be able to return in safety to the Caspian or Persia from here. You will aid me, and I will see that you can then move anywhere you like. The Turcoman are bound to me and will do as I say'.

Persians and Central Asians have a remarkable skill in making up stories, and it is considered bad form to correct them while they do so. The story being told by the Khan was pure fiction, as he had little or no control over the Turcoman tribes, but Perkins could see no other way out, other than to agree. He was immediately handed a bag, a heavy bag which I believed contained coins, which he handed to me. I then handed it to Hynes, who grunted at its weight.

This we were told was a small gift to allow you to purchase what you may require to conduct your mission. It is my wish that you depart no later than the day after tomorrow. A party of my cavalry will escort you northward.

We thought at this point that the interview was over, and began to rise. The Vizier whispered something to him and the Khan sat down on his couch, for he had spoken to us while standing.

He asked if we would recognise Russians? He had captured two spies a few days ago and they were killed but he had captured three more yesterday but they insisted they were not Russians and did look different. Did we speak any Russian? Perkins said that I spoke some, but not very well; to this I bowed.

From behind us, a man unseen came up, and was spoken to by the Khan in the Khivan language and he then spoke to us in Persian, advising us on our ceremonial duties. He then bowed and asked for us to follow. We could do no more than follow, having made our farewells and salutes to the Khan and his officers, in the manner we had been so directed.

This officer was Mr Begi, our finder and escort from before. We again found him to be a pleasant chap of about five and twenty years of age, and the commander of what might loosely be thought of as a regiment of the household guard, which we had seen on the road. We therefore referred to him as Colonel Begi. *{In England anyone commanding a regiment was a Colonel}*

He took us out into the sun, which was blinding, and we all had to stop for a moment before we could see, then we plunged into another dark building and were blinded again, and required another moment of time to recover. We walked for some time in silence, going down one corridor, then a pathway, then a passage, and finally we came to place, which spoke of a prison, for everywhere were bars and the stench of humanity and its waste.

We were taken to a framework or iron that we took to be a type of covering over a hole in the ground, in which we could see nothing. A lantern hung over it, and it was lit by a man who would have fitted well in Dante's book, for he resembled a demon in this light, and the light was lowered down. This illuminated a vermin filled pit in which four men lay. The demon had a spiked pole and he pointed to three of the men, and Begi translated that there were locals and of no concern, but this other one was different. The pole had a hook and he brought the man face up.

The grill over the pit. Illustration III-XV-18

Three Countrymen In The Hades Hotel?

It was a filthy face, but his hair and beard were ginger, and the face pale. I took him as a Scotsman and said so to Perkins in Latin. Hynes said he thought he was a Scotsmen too, but in French. Begi made us understand that they could find no language he could speak. I tried some Russian, and the demon dumped a pot of water over all the men. The other three did not move, but the ginger haired man did and gasped and cried out

Ceart Laidir Abu
{Righteous and strong}

That I thought was Gaelic, we spoke down to the man using French but he did not respond, nor to any other European language. We were avoiding using English when he spoke to us in that tongue.

'Who are you do you speak to me?' and he did so in English with an Irish accent.

Perkins motioned us to remain quiet, and he began to speak English to him, but it was an odd version, and it took me a moment or two to understand that he was chopping up the language to make him think we were not English speakers, for if he could see us, we would have looked like Central Asians to him.

He was Patrick Fitzpatrick of Dublin, former soldier and valet, but he could barely speak, so we had Begi order the demon, for at first he refused, to send down to the man some water, which he gulped down.

He was able to explain that he and his party had been captured by raiders near Mazar-e Sharif in the territory of Afghanistaun.

Perkins asked him for whom he was the valet?

Lord Solomon, he said, and at this moment, a rat ran across his face and he began to shriek and scream in the most frightful manner. In his rant, we could hear Gaelic and English. He seemed to believe he was dead and being tormented in Hell, and considering the surroundings, he was not far off, but he was certainly not dead, unfortunately for him.

We backed away and Colonel Begi explained he had been captured with two others and they had been brought here to the Khan's personal slave market, and place of 'preparation'.

That they were Europeans was obvious, even to the Khivans, and the only Europeans they knew were Russians *{the Khivans had seen other Europeans before but rarely}*.

Perkins pointed out that how would Russians be on the other side of the Khivan world *{to the south east lay Afghanistaun}*, while all the Russian lived to the north of them?

As Patrick screamed, we moved over to another pit from which the most offensive odour came, and a light was lowered, there was one bloated and burst dead man, and next to him, another, in vaguely European clothes, but Colonel Begi noted that this was the dying pit where very ill prisoners were put to die. So covered in dirt and filth was this man, that we could not tell who he might have been, nor did he respond to us in any language, despite two dousings with water and prodding with the spike. The third pit held another solitary man, with slightly less vermin. The light was lowered, and a fine collection of British curses came up to us. Perkins told him in French, that we were friends, and asked him who he was.

He did not answer, but shouted abuse at us, our mothers, fathers, distant cousins and our future generations. Perkins tried his version of broken English and the abuse stopped and he demanded in a weaker tone who we were.

Perkins said we were Circassians who had learned some English from David Urquhart[5]. We will try to help you, but tell us your RSE *{regiment, ship or establishment, i.e. who are you associated with}*.

'Go to hell you are fools to think you can lie to me.' He shouted then began with abuse again.

We tried several times to engage him but Perkins had no intention of telling him we were English as he might expose us. He was a gentleman from his voice but he was on the edge of insanity or so it seemed to me.

We told Colonel Begi that one man was a Scotsman; a vassal of the English, the second man was probably an Englishman, and the third was English and a nobleman, and if Khiva valued its existence they should immediately release them and provide full medical care.

Colonel Begi had heard of the English, for several had passed through Central Asia in the past. Perkins put it succinctly.

Perkins turned and faced Begi and said, 'You fear the Russian'?

'Yes', replied the Colonel.

Perkins told him, 'The Russians fear the English. You will make a powerful enemy if you do not treat these men with respect; the English have aided us *{Circassians}* against the Russians'.

Perkins said this with great force of voice, and I could see that Begi was alarmed by this. We were directed out of that hell hole and were soon in the fresh air, super-heated but better than what we had been breathing. Colonel Begi bided us to wait, and we did so beneath a looming minaret. One of our guards spoke some Persian, and he made us understand that the minaret was the last part of the outer word that many entering the prison ever saw. A cheering thought.

Begi had gone to report on Perkins' comments, and he returned some time later, saying that the Khan sent his thanks and would consider our request.

We were taken back to our quarters, with no other word being spoken. Our escort did not leave, but instead took up station at our gate, and around the house; it would seem we were prisoners, although Begi would say no more.

We briefed all the others. They were all much distraught to know that three Englishmen were being so badly treated and we resolved not to surrender ourselves to such a fate. Our dwelling was flanked on both sides. There was a window in the rear, closed by wooden bars and a covering cloth, now guarded by two men and some wind chimneys. We ventured up on the roof and found three men there too. We waved and they scowled, but the only true exit was by the way of the gate and garden.

Food had been brought for dinner, and then for supper, we gained no additional information. The horses were well fed, and I brushed down Blonde to her delight. There were guards here too; a half dozen men who were bored in their duty and helped me in my tasks; for even Khivans love horses, and ours were strange and wonderful to their eyes.

We had our entire suite of luggage with us, so we had about a weeks' worth of food; enough powder and lead for approximately twelve hundred shots, and some four hundred cartridges for the Colts and my Frenchman.

It was a poor evening of conversation. Nolta observed that death was preferable to capture by the Khivans, for he had heard many tales of their unspeakable cruelties.

Colonel Begi appeared again and handed us a second velvet bag, which was heavy with coins, and explained that he had placed the guard on us as a temporary matter, and that he meant no disrespect from it, and that the coinage was a gift from the Vizier.

We found that the two bags of coins contained one hundred and twenty pieces, all of gold, and of a dozen different types and minting's. I would put the value at two hundred and ten pounds sterling. *{well over two year's salary for Driscol}*. We distributed it to the expedition, with Vickery getting the majority for the expedition's expenses. Perkins, in an aside to me, told me that I might retain the coins I had gained from the Khan for knowing about the seal. I suggested that at some future time, I would buy him the finest meal which Paris could produce. He immediately suggested the A La Petite Chaise *{the second oldest restaurant in Paris having opened in 1680}*, we agreed, and shook hands on it.

Day 25 Wednesday 26 July

Colonel Begi appeared, and again apologised for having put a guard on us, and stressed that it had been his initiative and not the Khan's.

I could understand his caution, for in the Orient, to make a mistake of judgment, or take a misstep on an appointment directed by your sovereign, that might earn you a minor rebuke in the Occident, such as a demotion or at worst a court martial and being cashiered, here it would earn you a detached head or being cast into a vermin-filled pit.

The Khan had agreed to our proposal, and the men had now been released, were being treated, and would in future be hosted as Royal guests. The Khan asked that we move now on our agreed mission to the Russian army.

Perkins and I wrote a reply of thanks, and our great willingness to do as the Khan directed. This lifted our moods greatly. Assisted by Colonel Begi, his men, and the servants, we made a large number of purchases, repacked the horses, purchased a fine beast for Nolta and eight more pack horses to carry additional supplies.

The Khan invited us to an entertainment. I volunteered to be the duty officer so that Dobbins could go, so it was I, Michaelson, Nolta and Horne who stayed back and we were glad we did.

The others returned late at night, well fed, but greatly put out by the entertainments they had been forced to witness. There was the same, horrible, noisy, music, like the cacophony we had heard in Persia; but worse still had been the small boys, dressed as women, who were dancing.

Those were the famous *baccha bazi {boy dancers}*, and they had been offered to them as 'enticements' to do the duties of the Khan well.

He said also that the Khan had asked if Perkins had been to India? He had said he had been to see their horses. He asked how his good friend Bahadur Shah Zafer, the Mogul Emperor, fared?

Many Muslims, in their tens of millions, still considered him the true ruler of India; the British running his empire for him, and their presence being due to his amity and on his sufferance. Perkins admitted he had not been grand enough to see the Emperor, but that he understood him to be hale and happy at this time.

The interior of the house in Khiva where the expedition was held as 'guests' of the Khan. Illustration III-XV-19

A Voyage Down The Oxus To Khodjeili The City Of Hajjis
And
The Disaster That Befell Us

Day 26 Thursday 27 July

We are up at dawn and brought into the nearest mosque to pray with Colonel Begi and his officers. We did well, having practiced these actions many times before, and we escaped any notice of course, as we made sure we were in the last course of the assembly, so that none could view us for imperfections.

Having done this, and finding that Colonel Begi would accompany us with ten men as far as the city of Khodjeili at the head of the delta, a city which is inhabited by descendants of those who are Hajis. It is there the Khan's representatives would secure for us sufficient camels to cross from the Aral Sea to wherever the Russians might lie.

Bannington was of the mind that we should not leave yet, until we had ascertained the health of our fellow countrymen. Perkins, Dobbins and Hynes disagreed, holding to the belief that any contact with them might lead us to being exposed, and we already had the burden of Nolta, so no effort was made to meet with them.

Bannington implored us that we should do more to assist the Englishmen before we left. Perkins replied again that he knew nothing on earth is more conducive to shortening a man's life than being found to have lied to and tricked an Eastern Khan. I would think this equal to trying to enter a violent man's marriage bed while he was there, or playing Russian roulette with a keg of black powder and a lit match.

So no, we would leave the matter of the three Britons outside our area of view.

So we saddled up, and left, after several delays, out of the same gate we had originally entered.

As we moved out, we had in our new luggage a screen, consisting of four stout poles and a fabric to allow Nolta, our 'Princess' to go to the lavatory without exposing his gender. In some cases, I was beginning to see the expedition as some sort of Shakespearean farce, with everyone having false identities; like a magnified Comedy of Errors or Two Gentlemen from Verona.

We made good time, and our march was uneventful. I was happy to see Colonel Begi was not interested in us at all, and he spent his time whipping his men to keep them moving, as a more slothful group of men I have not yet seen. They galloped well, then scattered everywhere, having a thousand reasons to do so, it would seem. The good Colonel ate with his men. We realised that he kept his distance, due to the 'woman' in our midst. That made me rather happy.

The right bank of the Oxus River. Illustration III-XV-20

The Colonel had brought with him a number of men who acted to cook meals, and that gave us a time to rest more. I had to take great care not to be seen writing, however and we could take no scientific measurements.

Day 27 Friday 28 July

In the afternoon, we made the city of Gourlen. Here the Colonel arranged for us to take passage on barges; very much like Thames lighters, which move down river by the use of men called *Gayigshi* or barge haulers, these poor wretches seemed the most degraded group we had yet seen. They did work no horse, oxen or donkey could do, marching along the swampy fringe of the river, dragging lighters, as the flow of the river was very slight indeed. The horses must have hated it, reminding them perhaps of the passage from Bombay. The river is five hundred yards wide here and shallow cliffs can be seen to the northeast. The town was another dirty uninteresting collection and there was nothing remarkable to write about.

The Colonel and I are on the same barge, so I will stop writing.

I have made a pole and attached my line, weight, and hook and plan to worship at the feet of the Oxus river god, and hope for fish. There were numerous sand bars in the river, causing many halts and delays.

Day 28-30 Saturday 29-31 July

No entry

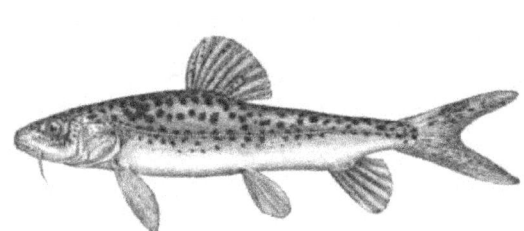

One of the fish Driscol caught which he though was Calanoida but was instead a Diptychus Severzovi. Illustration III-XV-21

Day 31 Tuesday 1 August

We have arrived in Khodjeili, but there are few camels here. Colonel Begi now has every official, everywhere, seeking camels; every *Mirab {Mayor}* in the delta is being harassed to find transports for us. We must wait, and are placed into a caravanserai, that is cleared of all other inhabitants. We put our Khivan cavalry-guard to work to clean it, but they are so bad at it, that we hire some locals, who then bring slaves, who clean it from top to bottom. We pay them when no one is looking. Horne I find flirting with Tartar looking girls, as they are not covered here, and they move around freely. As they have no shared language, it is a short flirtation.

During our voyage down the river, I had spent a great deal of time fishing, and had caught some twelve fish of an unknown type, but of the genus *Calanoida*, I would suspect.

Our float down the river was boring in the extreme. I had the Colonel next to me, and with only Dissanayake and Vickery on board with me, and his officers; this was a very tense time.

Dissanayake was concerned that while on the river, we could not do a service for the tenth Sunday after Pentecost.

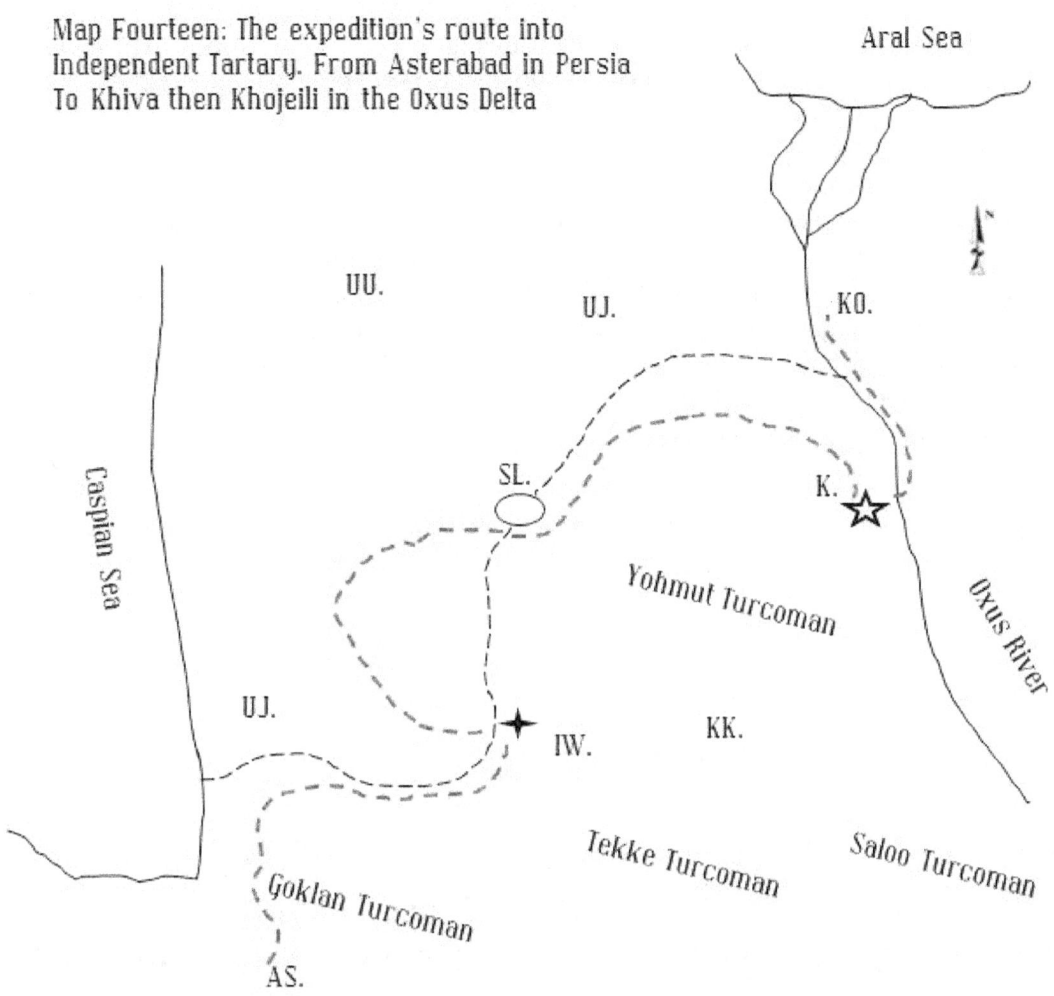

Map Fourteen: The expedition's route into Independent Tartary. From Asterabad in Persia To Khiva then Khojeili in the Oxus Delta

Aral Sea

UU.

UJ.

KO.

Caspian Sea

SL.

K.

Yohmut Turcoman

Oxus River

UJ.

IW.

KK.

Goklan Turcoman

Tekke Turcoman

Saloo Turcoman

AS.

L E G E N D

Expedition's route   — — —
K. Khiva
AS. Asterabad
O. Oxus River
KK. Kara Kum Desert
SL. Sarykamysh Lake
IW. Igdy Wells
KO. Khojeili
UU. Ust Urt
UJ. Uzboj. dried bed of
the Oxus

Day 32 Wednesday 2 August

This place is full of pious Khivans; a great change from the Khivans at the capital, and what changes do we note? They go to the Mosque when the *adhan {prayer call}* is sounded. Other than that, they are the same general type of degraded Easterner, perhaps a little bit cleaner.

From Nolta, we begin to learn some of the local language, for he had picked up several hundred words. We had not been studying language for some time, so the exercise is entertaining.

Day 33 Thursday 3 August ✝ ⌐ ✝

I heard a commotion just after Colonel Begi had reported that he had half the camels we would need, and a quarter of the camel men. We were all seated on matting, when I heard Dissanayake, who was on duty that day, and outside our dwelling on guard duty. We heard him issue a warning in Persian to stop, then some unaccountable noise, a vile curse in English and through the cloth, that made a curtain over the door, came striding in a man, wearing the rough approximation of European clothes, topped with a turban, and covered by the dust of the road. Despite the dust, one could see his eyes were aflame with fever. I had no idea who he was, until he spoke.

DAMN THE WHOLE LOT OF YOU I WILL SEE YOU ALL COURT MARTIALED!!

========

End of Volume III

Bombay to Persia and the River Oxus

Chronicle of the Middlecombe Expedition 1837-1838 with a Full Report and Narrative, on the Expedition's Departure from Bombay and travel though Persia and Turcomania to the Cities of Independent Tartary

========

Karen K. Wainwright, Driscol's confidante
Shown wearing clothes and necklace sent by him

Chapter Notes

Chapter XI notes:

1. "Le Hunte:" A bag somewhat like a Lister bag, of the type created by William Lyster to provide purified water, this however was probably just a canvas bag, which ,by evaporation, kept the water relatively cool and had no attached spout

2. "Kashgar:" Also known as Kashi a Chinese city in modern Xinjiang province; to have reached there, the expedition would have to have travelled north though modern Kashmir and Jammu, then penetrated the Pamir Mountains; a region virtually unknown to the Europeans of that time. This suggestion probably came from an armchair geographer, without the slightest consideration of the difficulty of doing so. It would have been a major effort just to get there

3. "Letters:" At this time, a letter could take up to two years to go each way. With the development of steam navigation, and the overland method, this transit time would drop to less than six months

4. "A purchase man:" he was either a man hired and sent out under another man's name to gain experience for the hirer, while they did some other task in England, or even went to another posting or just remained safe in England while gaining seniority. A more sinister version was that of a complete stranger impersonating the man for personal gain or for the purpose of spying. This may sound odd to modern ears, but then there were no photographs, no ID cards nor identifying numbers, databases or any way to determine if a person saying he was x wasn't so. Identification in this age was made by association with others already known, and by looking at clothes, accent and education, but all three of these could be affected or purchased. It was not

uncommon to have a servant's son, raised in a noble or middle class family, and having access to their knowledge, clothes and accent, to perpetrate such frauds

5. "Lazzaro Spallanzani:" looked at the results of John Needham's experiments with boiling broths, sealing them, and noting that they would cloud, supporting the idea of spontaneous generation. Spallanzani boiled the broth in a sealed container, from which the air had been removed, requiring no sealing afterwards; his experiments were instrumental in promoting widespread skepticism over the theory of spontaneous generation

6. "Broughton's:" Directions for fisticuffs was printed in 1743 and were the predecessor to the later and more famous Marquis of Queensberry rules which were formalized in 1867

7. "Shot:" Bar and double headed shot are ammunition for smoothbore cannon consisting of iron bars bound together and designed to spread apart after being fired. Double headed shot have a half a shot at each end of an iron bar, designed to cut enemy rigging and having a secondary anti-personnel role. They were notoriously inaccurate and could be fired with certainly, only at very close range

8. "Gwadar:" A city off the modern coast of Pakistan, but at the time that Driscol was there, it was controlled by Muscat Arabs and used as a port to transport spices, ivory and slaves. It was purchased by the Aga Khan in 1958 and then given to Pakistan

9. "Zanj Rebellion:" A Persian named Ali bin Muhammed in 869 AD led a revolt of African slaves, in what is now southern Iraq. The rebellion lasted for fourteen years before being crushed and Muhammed being slain

10. "Stone of Bologna:" The first known man-made luminescent material was fabricated in Italy during the 17th Century, under the names of Stone of Bologna. It was composed of a compound of ground barium sulfide and white stones, first found near Bologna by an Italian alchemist, Cascariolo, who amalgamated them to form a luminescent material that glowed at night, after being exposed to the Sun. Originally thought to have been the long sought for philosopher's stone, Bologna stone was shown to be the mineral barite, barium sulfate

11. "Results:" The 13th day of the Persian New Year falls on April 1 or April 2. This day, known for 2,600 years, is the oldest pranking holiday in the world, which has led some to believe that April Fools' Day has its origins in this Persian tradition

12. "Fluid:" At this time, the nature of electricity, and especially lightning, was not fully formed. It was held by many, based on the ideas of conflicting theories of Robert Symmer and Benjamin Franklin, that electricity and lightning bolts were of a 'liquid' nature. The debate at that time was over whether it was two fluids, or only one, the other unknown liquid being associated with electromagnetism. Driscol's friend Karen Wainwright was doing experiments on this subject when he left England

13. "Smith:" It is unclear to whom Driscol is referring to here but in his margin notes he wrote G. A. then the name Smith but there is no such person, the identification of the 'Smith' is difficult as his hand writing is particularly bad here. It has been suggested that the name Smith is in error and he is referring to Giovanni Arduino, 1714-1795 who wrote out the first classification of geological time and 'Smith' might be the word 'smart' or some other term

14. "Chesney:" An Irishman Francis Rawdon Chesney, artilleryman and explorer; he had arrived in Bushire in 1836 having just taken two disassembled steamers across Asia Minor, assembled them and then navigated the Euphrates to the Persian Gulf

15. "Boy:" In Driscol's time each Whit Monday, the people of Brockworth would meet on Cooper's Hill to roll an eight pound Double Gloucester cheese down the hill and the winner was he who caught it at the bottom - by running downhill at neck break speed

----

Chapter XII notes:

1. "Eeliauts:" or Iliyats, are a wandering tribe of Persia, and Central Asia. The name Iliyat is the plural of iel (*eel*), a nomadic tribe, equivalent to the Arabic kabilali. They are similar in some ways to the European Gypsy and viewed and treated in the same way

2. "Qisas:" In Islamic jurisprudence, instead of a murderer being executed, or going to jail, they can agree to pay blood money to the victim's family. The family though can reject this and demand the former harsher penalties

3. "Haydari & Ne'mat-Allahi:" These two names refer to mutually hostile urban moieties or kinships in Persia. From the late fifteenth century up until recent decades, a number of cities and towns of Iran were perceived as being divided into two groupings of adjacent neighborhood known by the names above. The respective inhabitants of these places would look upon the other with contempt and antagonism and these groupings would periodically clash in massive public fights. The origins of their names and the cause of the antagonism is not known to the participants and seems of no importance

4. "McNeill:" The British ambassador to Persia in Driscol's time was Sir John McNeill, a Scottish Laird, diplomat and doctor of medicine in the service of the Honourable East India Company's Bombay establishment, before being appointed to his post in Persia

5. "Cadet:" This identification was for the finest scholars produced by the East India Company Military Seminary, or more commonly known as Addiscombe College. They were given the best positions and early promotion

6. "Alamut and Khurrem-abad:" This is a region of Persia just south of the Caspian Sea on the slopes of the Alborz mountain chain

7. "Kater's:" This compass is the original prototype azimuth compass invented by Captain Henry Kater in 1811. However Driscol's use of this term may have been generic, just as a modern American will call a copier made by HP a "Xerox" machine

8. "Trebeck:" An English solicitor who was joined the Moorcroft expedition into northern India and Central Asia. He died of disease in August 30, 1825 while in Afghanistan

9. "Moorcroft's:" An earlier explorer who entered Independent Tartary in 1819 he and his expedition died in the attempt. At Andkhoy, in Turkestan, Moorcroft became ill and died in August 1825; Trebeck survived him by only a few days and also died. His papers were later recovered and published by H. H. Wilson, under the title of Travels in the Himalayan Provinces of Hindustan

and the Punjab, in Ladakh and Kashmir, in Peshawur, Kabul, Kunduz and Bokhara, from 1819 to 1825.

10. "Arthur Conolly:" Anglo-Irishman who was an expert on Central Asia and created the term the "Great Game" to label the diplomatic war between Russian and the British Empires over influence in Central Asia. In late 1841 he was captured and executed by the Khan of Bukhara for spying for the British Empire.

11. "Literature:" These fish would be described in 1901 by Kamensky - with no mention of Driscol

12. "Temperaments:" The four classical temperaments were Choleric or fire, Sanguine or air, Melancholic or earth and Phlegmatic or water

13. "Penicuik Experiment:" A breeding program in the late 19th century, that investigated the concepts of "telegony" and in this case, led to the hybrid Zebra horse mixtures

> Telegony: was a theory in heredity, that said offspring could inherit the characteristics of a previous mate of the female parent; thus the child of a widowed or remarried woman might partake of traits of a previous husband

14. "Raghes:" The modern city of Ray and to the Romans Rhagae, a large ruins to the south of Teheran; also called by the Persians *Shahr-e-Ray (City of Ray)* , with the oldest ruins going back eight thousand years

15. "Cevennes:" This part of France is noted for the people being 'unlearned', rude and uncivilized, located in the hills of south central France, it is dominated by the descendants of Huguenots

16. "Portrait:" Unfortunately Phileas Vickery died of appendicitis at Marseilles, in February 1838, but he did send word and the painting to the Vickery family of his discovery of Eduard Vickery

----

Chapter XIII notes:

1."Marlowe:" From the poem, The Passionate Shepherd to His Love by Christopher Marlowe (1599)

2. Portsmouth fire ship:" Referring to the 'ladies' who flocked to the sally ports of a newly arrived ship, seeking the favours of a sailor, the name arose from the burning sensations from the diseases that were often associated with after effects of a 'collision' with a such a fire ship

3. "Delights:" The boy would remember this, and as a young man made his way to India and became a doctor studying at the hospital Michaelson had helped to set up in Bombay, for he had remembered the name told him as a youth, he married into a Parsee family and his descendants are well known in the halls of medicine in modern India. His descendant would work with me at the Higher Colleges of Technology in Dubai in the 1990's. He requested his name not be used as his ancestors being Muslims (and he a Parsi) was not something to be proud of, or cast about, as apostates to Islam often suffer for this action even generations later

4. "Eighth Imaum:" In Persian Shia'ism there are twelve great Imams, of which he was the eighth. Imam Reza or Ali ibn Musaal-Ridha, claimed to be the seventh descendent of the prophet

Mohammad. There are also in Shia Fivers and Seveners or believers in those Imaums instead of the twelve Imaums.

5. "Lieutenant Wyburd:" An officer of the Indian Navy, a man noted for his proficiency in Persian and having lived for two years as a native in Arabia. He disappeared while traveling in mufti through Central Asia a few years before the Middlecombe Expedition arrived in Persia. He had been sent on a highly important and hazardous diplomatic appointment to Khiva. It was known that he had left Tehran under the name of Hajee Ahmet Arab, in the summer of 1835 for Asterabad, but after that, nothing more was ever heard of him. In 1845 it was reported that he had never reached Khiva, but on his way thither had been seized and put to death by the Ameer of Bokhara

6. "Eccles cakes:" This delight, which is made from flaky pastry, butter, nutmeg, candied peel, sugar and currants, was first produced and sold in the home town of Driscol in 1793

7. "Shihuh tribe:" A tribe thought to be a group of Indo-European isolates who had resisted the tides of Semitic Arabs who had swarmed over them centuries before. They had accepted Islam but had kept their own traditions and language. In modern times they are called 'people of the ax' as they carry that to differentiate themselves from the others around them

8. "Alison:" Probably a private traveller in Persia who never wrote about his experiences

9. "Yakhchal:" Ice houses made by the ancient Persians that act as an evaporative cooler for storing ice during the summer in the desert areas of Persia

10. "Asterabad:" In 1841, the Chief of Asterabad, sent to the Shah of Persia some ancient gold vessels and other curious and precious objects, which had been found in a mound within the town of Asterabad. A suggestion for the location of Zadracarta seems to be the site of Qal'a-ye Kandan. It is a large mound measuring 900 x 650 feet with a height of about 125 feet, found at the southwest corner of the city of Gorgan on the road to Sari

11. "Imam Musa al-Kazem:" The seventh of the twelve Imams much beloved by the Shia Persians, his full name was Musa ibyn ja'far al-Kadhim and born in Araba and of part African origins. He was poisoned in 799 AD by Harun al-Rashid

12. "Morphine:" had been isolated in 1804 and had been refined and sold by Merck since 1827

13. "Sasanian house:" A former royal dynasty of Persia defeated by the Arab invasion in 633 and dissolved in 651 AD

Chapter XIV notes:

1. "Sardines:" Children's game of hide and seek where only one hides and all the others hunt them. When found, the finder joins the hider and are soon packed in like……sardines, the game continues until the last hunter finds the 'sardines' the finder then becomes 'it' and the game starts again

2. "Réaumur scale:" An alcohol based thermometer for determining temperature. It was set at 0° for freezing and 80° for boiling it was superseded by the Fahrenheit and Celsius systems by the mid-19th century

3. "Answers:" Letters upside down or up? H, I, N, O, S, X, Z. Which lowercase letters look like capitols, C, O, P, S, U, V, W, X, Z and what letters are used as numbers in Latin, C, D, I, L, M, V, X

4. "Uzboy:" In 1819 the Russian explorer Andrei Nikolaevich Mouravieff stumbled upon the old bed of the Oxus at the wells of Besh-dishik, where he found it $\frac{1}{6}$th of a mile wide, with a high bank on the north facing the Ust Urt plains. On a later journey, he crossed the old river again at the salt springs at Tunuklu. In 1836, the Russian General Blaramberg had the opportunity of exploring the mouth of the old bed, where it once emptied into Balkan Bay on the Caspian Sea. In 1870 the Russians finally started a proper survey of the steppes east of the Caspian and the shrivelled bed of the Oxus

5. "Old Grape:" Means Earth and this idea would later become Baer's Law which, explained the Coriolis affect

6. "Tall:" This tower had written on it an inscription in the Sogdian alphabet, an alphabet derived from Syriac, the descendant script of the Aramaic alphabet

----

Chapter XV notes:

1. "Magister:" The German term for 'master'

2. "Ionian Islands:" These islands came under French dominion when their former owner, Venice was defeated by Napoleon. The British retained the islands for some time only transferring them to the nation of Greece in 1862

3. "Aether:" A theory that space was filled with substance that carried light, this was before the emergence of the wave theory of light however debate over this idea, continued up to modern times

4. "Bel-Bel:" A Russian turncoat who assisted the Khivans in making artillery; he later disappeared from history but was rumoured to have suffered a grisly fate

5. "David Urquhart:" A Scotsman who visited the region of the Caucasus in 1834 who was a social activist and became a supporter of Circassian independence from the Russian Czar

The

Appendixes

Appendix III-I: Driscol added into his journal a list of expeditions known to him to have entered the area of interest to the expedition plus other events of importance taken in part from; Henry Landsdell, Russian Central Asia, chronology, page 681. I have added a few 'future' items also

Table of events in Central Tartary prior to the Middlecombe Expedition	
Year	Event
1794	Visit of the oculist Blankennagel to Khiva
1800	First British mission to Persia under Captain Malcolm which was a success
1800	Consideration by Napoleon and Czar Paul to invade India
1803	Merv destroyed and its people deported to Bokhara
1802-1806	Russo-Persian war, won by Russia
1807	Scheme by Napoleon and Czar Alexander to invade India
1807	Treaty between France and Persia
1808	Second British mission to Persia under Captain Malcolm which failed
1809	Treaty between Great Britain and Persia
1811	Russian caravans proceed to Kuldja and Chuguchak
1813	Russian administration introduced into the Syr-daria (*Jaxartes River*) steppe
1813	Treaty of Gulistan between Russia and Persia loss of territory in their northwest
1814	Treaty of Teheran between Great Britain and Persia
1819	The Russian Ponomareff to the Turcoman
1819	The Russian Mouravieff to Khiva
1821	Mouravieff surveys the East Caspian coastline for a Russian port and visits Khiva
1824	First Russian caravan to Bokhara
1825	English explorer Moorcroft visits Bokhara but dies of disease in Afghanistan
1826	Allah Kuli Khan becomes Khan of Khiva
1826	Russian Menzikoff to Teheran
1826-1828	Second Russo-Persian war: Russia takes more of Persian territory in the north
1829	The Anglo-Irishman Conolly travels overland through Central Tartary to India
1831-32	English missionary Wolff visits Merv and Bokhara
1832	Scotsman Burnes visits Bokhara, Merv and Meshed
1833	Persians unsuccessfully attack the Afghan city of Herat
1834	Mohammed Shad comes to power in Persia
1834	Russians establish the port of Perovski on the Eastern shore of the Caspian
1835	Russian's Demaisons and Vitkovitch visit Bokhara
1834-1835	Russian Demaison and Vitkievitch visit Bokhara
1836	Russian fishing fleets begin operations in the Caspian
1836	Russian trading mission to the Turcoman
1837	Persia moves to attack the city of Herat again
1837-1838	Driscol and Middlecombe Expedition into Central Tartary
1837-1838	Persian attack on Herat; defeated with the help of English in the person of Pottinger
1838	Blaremberj''s exploration of the old bed of the Oxus, Uzboy
1838	Englishman Stoddart visits Bokhara
1838	Englishman Wood explores the upper Oxus River
1838-1842	Great Britain and Afghanistan at war, British defeat
1839	Ascent of the Upper Oxus by the English Lieutenant Wood
1840	General Perovsky's military expedition to Khiva
1841	Visit of Buteneff and others to Bokhara (*Abbott, Shakespear, and Conolly at Khiva*)
1842	Execution of British officers Stoddart and Conolly at Bokhara

Appendix III-II: The routes to the Aral Sea

Route 1

Route 2

Route 3

Route 4

This map reproduced from Driscol's note superimposes the considered routes on a map of Central Asia showing modern political boundaries - and showing the Aral Sea, as it was, not in its present dried up state.

Appendix III-III

May it please your Majesty to hear

That the King my master, aware of the strong ties of friendship and alliance which have existed between our two kingdoms for a generation has deputed me to bring forward to you these men who with your gracious permission will travel into Tartary on a course to bring them knowledge of those lands, its people and its situations back to me.

May the great disposer of all events grant your Majesty an increase of honour and prosperity and may the friendship and interests of England and Persia henceforward become inseparable.

Your brother

(Signed)

William the IV

King of England, etc.

Appendix III-IV: Babylonian cosmology & universe

The upright central line is the polar axis of the heavens and earth. The two seven-staged pyramids represent the earth, the upper being the abode of living men, the under one the abode of the dead. The separating waters are the four seas. The seven inner homocentric globes are respectively the domains and special abodes of Sin, Shamash, Nabu, Ishtar, Negal, Marduk and Ninib, each being a "world ruler" in his own planetary sphere. The outermost of the spheres that of Anu and Ea, is the heaven of fixed stars. The axis from centre to zenith marks "the Way of Ana'; the axis from centre to nadir "the Way of Ea" See Journal of American Oriental Society, volume xxii, page 138-144, xxiii, opposite page 388; and xxvi, page 84-92.

The quote above is from, The earliest cosmology, William Warren, Eaton & Mains, New York, 1909, page viii, see page 33-40 of the same reference for more information. Illustration Appendix IV-I

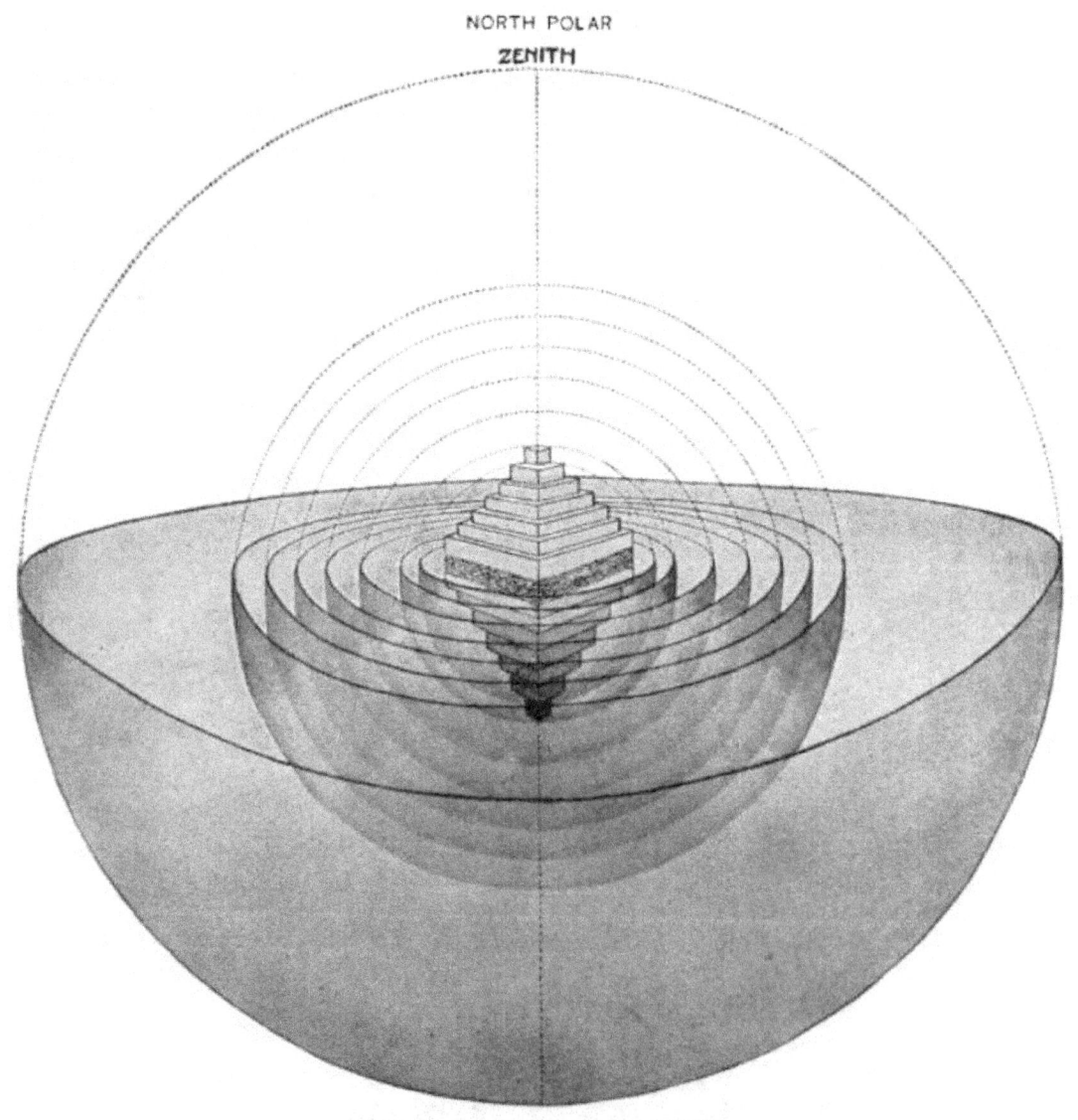

THE BABYLONIAN UNIVERSE

Appendix III-V: Driscol wrote, 'devised from what little I knew of the Turcoman, with what Abu Saman said, and later I confirmed it with the Dragoman and Saman himself:

328 BC Alexander the Great founds Merv (*Mary*)

420 AD Merv becomes a Christian city

704-748 The Turcoman rise up against the Arabs and overthrow them

749-874 Long war between the Arabs and Turcoman, the Turcoman aided by the Veiled Prophet of Kesh, Al-Muqanna who started a new sect of Muslims called the Khurramiyya, which existed until the twelfth century, when it disappeared after being frustrated by the failure of their prophet to return. However the Turcoman had broken free of Arab tyranny and was now free. Most Turcoman become Sunni by this time

1004 The Seljuk Turks arise and go on to set up a kingdom

1128 The Seljuk Turks power recedes

1220 The Mongol sack Merv and in doing so destroy the great dam which the flowed from the Aral Sea and to the Caspian

1505 The Uzbek arrive and fight the Turcoman

1570 The earth shakes and the bed of the Oxus is disturbed and it flow to the Caspian ends

1716-1717 Peter the Great sends a Russian army to conquer the region but they are betrayed and slaughtered

1794 Merv razed to the ground

1828 Russia becomes the owner of the Caspian Sea after the last war with the Persians by the signing of the Treaty of Turkomantchai. Russian traders are seen everywhere now however they have not yet been able to rid the sea of Turcoman raiders

Appendix III-VI: Overview of the skills and abilities of the members of expedition, note the inclusion of Hymison and Husher

Perkins Expedition Personnel			Ability or Talent				
Num.	Position	Rank & name	Persian	Written	Culture	Islam	Presence
1	Commander	Lieutenant Perkins	Good	Good	Excellent	Good	Good
2	Deputy Commander	Lieutenant Dobbins	Good	Poor	Good	Good	Good
3	Science & Survey	Ensign Driscol	Good	Acceptable	Excellent	Good	Excellent
4	Adjutant	Ensign Horne	Acceptable	Acceptable	Poor	Poor	Acceptable
5	Naturalist (Geologist)	Ensign Bannington	Acceptable	Good	Excellent	Excellent	Good
6	Surgeon	Asst. Surgeon Michaelson	Poor	None	Good	Good	Good
7	Quartermaster	Colour Sgt Hynes	Excellent	Good	Excellent	Excellent	Native
8	Secretary	(Sergeant) Mr Vickery	Acceptable	Poor	Excellent	Good	Native
9	Naturalist	(Private) Mr Dissanayake	Fair	Poor	Good	Poor	Poor
10	Surgeon	Dr. Nolta	None	None	None	Good	Excellent
11	-	Captain Hymison-Cecil	Excellent	Good	Poor	Non-existent	Non-existent
12	-	Lieutenant Husher	-	-	-	-	-

Appendix III-VII: A list drawn up by Driscol listing the armament of the various members of expedition showing what they would have been armed with at Igdy Wells, edited and added to by the editor

Weapons of the Middlecombe expedition at Igdy Wells and the Sullen Tower			
Member	Primary	Secondary	Tertiary but all men carried swords plus a dagger or knife but Nolta
Bannington	Holland & Holland double barreled percussion rifle, calibre not specified	Unknown	-
Dissanayake	India Pattern musket, .75 calibre 'Brown Bess', refigured to percussion	Unknown	-
Dobbins	Custom Indian made 4 bore single barreled hand cannon	Dickert rifle, single barrel flintlock of .45 calibre Double barrelled percussion rifle made by William Richard calibre unspecified	Two shotguns one of three 12 bore barrels and another of two barrels, 16 bore
Driscol	Danish combination; 10 bore shotgun .60 calibre rifle, both percussion	Lefaucheux 5 shot revolver of .51 calibre	Single shot 'derringer' and a Single shot percussion dueling pistol, .52 calibre
Horne	Sea Service Pattern percussion rifle, .75 calibre	Francotte doubled barreled .69 calibre percussion pistol	-
Hynes	Austrian Girandoni .46 caliber, 22 shot air rifle	Cavalry Carbine percussion rifle, .75 calibre	-
Michaelson	Never specified	Marriette, six-barreled percussion pepper pot pistol	Sword cane, he may also have carried one or more flintlock pistols
Perkins	William Chance & Son double barreled shotgun, 12 bore. Percussion	Colt 6 shot revolver, .28 calibre	Single shot percussion dueling pistol, .52 calibre
Vickery	German made double barreled smoothbore flintlock musket made from two Modele 1777 barrels, .69 calibre	Colt 6 shot revolver, .28 calibre	Single shot percussion dueling pistol, .63 calibre, javelins
Nolta was not at Igdy Wells but he used a number of weapons borrowed from others			
Nolta	-	-	Single shot percussion dueling pistol, .63 calibre

Appendix III-VIII: Modern recipe for Harvey Sauce

3 $^1/_3$ cup white vinegar
6 anchovies
3 TBSP Indian style soy
3 TBSP mushroom ketchup
2 heads of garlic,
1 $\frac{1}{2}$ TSP cayenne pepper
Red food dye

Crush anchovies and add to vinegar and all other ingredients, crushing garlic, place in sealable glass container, shake vigorously and each day repeat for two weeks.

Front piece: A journey through the Yemen and some general remarks upon that country, Walter Harris, William Blackwood and sons, London and Edinburgh, 1893, page 84

Chapter XI

III-XI-1: Indian shipping, a history of the sea-borne trade a history of the sea-borne trade and maritime activity of the Indians from the earliest times, Radhakumund Mookerji, Longman, Green and Company, Bombay, 1912, page 288

III-XI-2: Outing April-September 1886, Sampson Low & Co, London, page 330

III-XI-3: Old Deccan days or, Hindoo Fairy Legends, current in Southern India, M. Frere, John Murray, London, 1868, page 202

III-XI-4: British drawing of Indian labourers from Graphic Magazine 1873

III-XI-5: Turkistan, notes of a journey in Russian, Eugene Schuyler, Sampson Low, Marston, Searle & Rivington, London, 1876, page 184

III-XI-6: Asiatic costumes, R. Ackermann, Charles Wood and Son, 1828, page 84

III-XI-7: Illustrated India Its Princes and People, Upper, Central, and Farther India, Julia A. Stone, Hartford, Connecticut, American Publishing Company, 1877, page 565

III-XI-8: Birds' nesting in India, George Marshall, Published by the Calcutta Central Press Co., Calcutta 1877 page 162

III-XI-9: The Illustrated London News, February 17, 1876, page 1

III-XI-10: Kurrachee, Past, Present and future, Alexander Baillie, Thacker, Spink & Co., Calcutta 1890, page 203

III-XI-11: Kurrachee Harbour on the coast of Scinde, by Lieutenant G Carless, Indian Navy, 1838, page 45

III-XI-12: The Illustrated London News, July 25, 1857, page 112

III-XI-13: The rod in India, being hints how to obtain sport, Henry Thomas, Hamilton, Adams & Co., London, 1881, page 28

III-XI-14: Outing, Carr & Co. London, 1887, page 16

III-XI-15: Travels in Assyria, Media and Persia including a Journey from Bagdad by mount Zagros, J. S. Buckingham, Henry Colburn, London, 1829, page 428

III-XI-16: Sixty five plates of shipping and craft, Edward Cooke, London 1829, page 116

III-XI-17: Academy sketches, Edited by Henry Blackburn, W. H. Allen & Co, London, 1883, page 131

III-XI-18: Three years in the Libyan Desert, J.C. Falls, T. Fisher Unwin, London, 1913, page viii

III-XI-19: Travels in Assyria, James Buckingham, Henry Colburn, London 1829, page 47

III-XI-20: Outing and the Wheelman, Vol IV April 1884, The Wheelman Company, 1884, page 495

III-XI-21: Outing April-September 1886, Sampson Low & Co, London, page 330

III-XI-22: In the Eastern Seas, Or, William Kingston London, T. Nelson and Sons, 1872 page 241

III-XI-23: Through Turkish Arabia, Henry Cowper, W. H. Allen & Co., London, 1894, front piece

III-XI-24: The Parochial Missionary Magazine, George Trevor, Part I G. Bell London, 1849, page 37

III-XI-25: The Book of Shipwrecks, And Narratives of Maritime, No author, Boston, Charles Gaylord, 1836, page 511

III-XI-26: Abu-Shehr or Bushire, The American Cyclopedia, Volume III, George Ripley and Charles Dana, D Appleton and Company, New York, page 488

III-XI-27: Gazetteer of the Persian Gulf, Vol II, John Lorimer, Superintendent Government Printing, Calcutta 1908, page 343

III-XI-28: In the Kingdom of the Shah, Edward Treacher Collins, T. Fisher Unwin, London, 1896, page 54

III-XI-29: The royal cookery book, Alphonse Gouffe, Sampson Low, Son and Marston, London 1869, page 112

III-XI-30: An account of the manners and customs of the Modern Egyptians, by Edward Lane, John Murray, London, 1871, page 7

III-XI-31: Cuisine de tous les pays, Urbain Dubois, A la Librairie E. Dentu, Paris, 1881, page cccxi

III-XI-32: The Navy everywhere, Conrad Cato, Constable and Company, ltd, London, 1919, page 181

III-XI-33: Travels in Assyria, Media and Persia, James Buckingham, Henry Colburn 1829, page 316

III-XI-34: Outing, Carr & Co. London, 1887, page xxix

III-XI-35: The caravan route between Egypt and Syria, Ludwig Salvator, Chatto & Windus, London 1881, page 65

III-XI-36: The Kotal-e Doktar pass between Shiraz and Kazerun. Drawing by W. Kleiss. In idem, "Fortifications", Encyclopædia Iranica, online edition.

III-XI-37: Travels in Assyria, James Buckingham, Henry Colburn, London 1829, page 47

III-XI-38: The Earth and Its Inhabitants, India, Elisee Reclus, D. Appleton and Company, New York, 1881, page 11

III-XI-39: Caravan journeys Joseph Ferrier, John Murray, London 1857, page 151

III-XI-40: Travels in Assyria, James Buckingham, Henry Colburn, London 1829, page 47

III-XI-41: In the land of the lion and sun, C. J. Wills Ward, Lock and Co., London 1891, page 411

III-XI-42: Illustrierte Lander und Volkerkunde, Guitav Ritter, Verlagedruckerei Merkur, Berlin 1908, page 169

Chapter XII

III-XII-1: Tagbuch einer reise, in inner-Arabien, Julius Euting, E.J. Beill, Leiden, 1896, page 121

III-XII-2: That first affair, and other sketches J, A. Mitchell, John Wilson and Son, Cambridge, 1896, page xxi

III-XII-3: Glimpses of life and manners in Persia, Mary Sheil, John Murray, London, 1856, page 204

III-XII-4: Travels in Assyria, Media and Persia including a Journey from Bagdad by Mount Zagros, J. S. Buckingham, Henry Colburn, London, 1829, page 269

III-XII-5: In the Kingdom of the Shah, Edward Treacher Collins, T. Fisher Unwin, London, 1896, page 86

III-XII-6: History of Art in Persia - Georges Perrot, Charles Chipiez, London, Chapman and Hall, Limited, page 69

III-XII-7: In the Kingdom of the Shah, Edward Treacher Collins, T. Fisher Unwin, London, 1896, page 94

III-XII-8: Glimpses of life and manners in Persia, Mary Sheil, John Murray, London, 1856, page 190

III-XII-9: Image from Victorian advertisement in the 1870, London Illustrated news, author's collection and precise date lost

III-XII-10: Nadir Shah, Mortimer Durand, E. P. Dutton and Company, New York 1909, page 303

III-XII-11: Nadir Shah, Mortimer Durand, E. P. Dutton and Company, New York 1909, page 307

III-XII-12: In the Kingdom of the Shah, Edward Treacher Collins, T. Fisher Unwin, London, 1896, page 114

III-XII-13: My wanderings in Persia, T.S. Anderson, James Blackwood & Co, London 1880, page 77

III-XII-14: Through Persia on a side-saddle, Ella Sykes, John Macqueen, London 1901, page 36

III-XII-15: In the Kingdom of the Shah, Edward Treacher Collins, T. Fisher Unwin, London, 1896, page 170

III-XII-16: Astronomy for amateurs, Camille Flammarion, D. Appleton and Company, New York, 1915, page 14

III-XII-17: Yacht-reise in den Syrten, Ludwig Salvator, Druck und Verlag von Heinrich Mercy, Prague, 1874, page 108

III-XII-18: Glimpses of life and manners in Persia, Mary Sheil, John Murray, London, 1856, page 224

III-XII-19: Travels in Assyria, James Buckingham, Henry Colburn, London 1829, page 155

III-XII-20: A Voyage into the Levant, Joseph de Tournefort, London, 1741, page 284

III-XII-21: The Earth and its Inhabitants, Reclus, Southwest Asia, Vol. IV, Appleton & Co., New York, 1891, page 162

III-XII-22: Travels in Assyria, James Buckingham, Henry Colburn, London 1829, page 168

III-XII-23: A history of Persia, Percy Sykes, Macmillan and Co., London, 1921, page 307

III-XII-24: Travels in the regions of the upper and lower Amoor, Thomas William Atkinson, Harper & Bothers, New York, 1860, page 43

III-XII-25: Ten thousand miles in Persia, Percy Molesworth Sykes, Charles Scribner's Sons, New York 1902, page 190

III-XII-26: The caravan route between Egypt and Syria, Ludwig Salvator, Chatto & Windus, London 1881, page 16

III-XII-27: The Earth and its Inhabitants, Reclus, Southwest Asia, Vol. IV, Appleton & Co., New York, 1891, page 118

III-XII-28: My wanderings in Persia, T.S. Anderson, James Blackwood & Co, London 1880, page 213

III-XII-29: Cassells illustrated History of India, James Grant, Cassell & Company, Limited, London, no year, page 163

III-XII-30: My wanderings in Persia, T.S. Anderson, James Blackwood & Co, London 1880, page 219

III-XII-31: Journal of the British Embassy to Persia; embellished with numerous views taken in India and Persia, William Price, Kingsbury, Parbury, and Allen, London, 1825, page 190

III-XII-32: Sporting days in Southern India being reminiscences of twenty trips in pursuit of big game, chiefly in the Madras presidency, A. J. Pollock, Horace Cox, London, 1894, page 14

III-XII-33: Outing, Carr & Co. London, 1887, page 296

III-XII-34: From Batum to Baghdad, Walter Harris, William Blackwood and sons, London 1906, page 259

III-XII-35: Lives of the Lord Chancellors and Keepers of the Great Seal of England, John Campbell, Vol. IV, New York, James Cockcroft & Co, 1875 front piece

III-XII-36: In the land of the lion and sun, C. J. Wills Ward, Lock and Co., London 1891, page 91

III-XII-37: A ride to India across Persia and Baluchistán - Harry De Windt, London, Chapman and Hall, Limited 1891 page 104

III-XII-38: Persian children of the Royal family, Wilfrid Sparroy, John Lane, London 1902, page 12

III-XII-39: Southern Asia; Asia Minor and its borderlands; Arabia, Ascott Moncrieff, the Gresham Publishing Company, London, page 62

III-XII-40: Outing and the wheelman magazine October 1884, The Wheelman Company, Boston 1885, page 18

III-XII-41: Wikipedia commons

III-XII-42: Midnight marches through Persia, Boston, Lee and Shepard, 1879, page 186

III-XII-43: Travels in Mesopotamia, Vol 1, J. S. Buckingham, Henry Colburn, London, 1827, page 175

Chapter XIII

III-XIII-1: From the Black Sea through Persia and India, Edwin Lord Weeks, New York, Harper & Brothers Publishers, 1895, page 55

III-XIII-2: My wanderings in Persia, T.S. Anderson, James Blackwood & Co, London 1880, page 153

III-XIII-3: In the land of the lion and sun, C. J. Wills Ward, Lock and Co., London 1891, page 154

III-XIII-4: Persia, Samuel Benjamin, G.P. Putnam's Sons, 1888 page 10

III-XIII-5: The Earth and Its Inhabitants, India, Elisee Reclus, Vol. IV, D. Appleton and Company, New York, 1881, page 291

III-XIII-6: From the Black Sea through Persia and India, Edwin Lord Weeks, New York, Harper & Brothers Publishers, 1895, page 123

III-XIII-7: The last American, John Mitchell, Frederick A. Stokes Company, New York 1902, page x

III-XIII-8: The Earth and Its Inhabitants, Asiatic Russia, Elisee Reclus, D. Appleton and Company, New York, 1881, page 278

III-XIII-9: Travels to discover the source of the Nile, Volume V, James Bruce, J. Ruthven, London 1790, page 263

III-XIII-10: The earth and its inhabitants, Reclus, Southwest Asia, Vol. IV, Appleton & Co., New York, 1891, page 152

III-XIII-11: With star and Crescent, A. Locher, Aetna Publishing Company, Philadelphia 1889, page 13

III-XIII-12: The earth and its inhabitants, Reclus, Southwest Asia, Vol. IV, Appleton & Co., New York, 1891, page 128

III-XIII-13: The Earth and Its Inhabitants, Asiatic Russia, Elisee Reclus, D. Appleton and Company, New York, 1881, page 217

III-XIII-14: Proto-Elamite economic table from 3,000 BCE. Vallet, François. 1986. "The Most Ancient Scripts of Iran: The Current Situation." World Archaeology. 17, 3: 335-347. See: p. 337

III-XIII-15: Persia, the awakening east, William Cresson, J.J. Lippincott Company, London 1908, page 40

III-XIII-16: In the land of the lion and sun, C. J. Wills Ward, Lock and Co., London 1891, page 200

III-XIII-17: The earth and its inhabitants, Reclus, Southwest Asia, Vol. IV, Appleton & Co., New York, 1891, page 122

III-XIII-18: Travels in Assyria, Media and Persia including a Journey from Bagdad by mount Zagros, J. S. Buckingham, Henry Colburn, London, 1829, page 54

III-XIII-19: Across Asia on a Bicycle, Thomas Allen & William Sachtleben, The Century Company, 1894, page 91

III-XIII-20: Unknown provenance

III-XIII-21: Modern etchings, Charles Holme, The Studio LTD, London 1913, page 249

III-XIII-22: From the Black Sea through Persia and India, Edwin Lord Weeks, New York, Harper & Brothers Publishers, 1895, page 111

III-XIII-23: From the Black Sea through Persia and India, Edwin Lord Weeks, New York, Harper & Brothers Publishers, 1895, page 115

III-XIII-24: In the Kingdom of the Shah, Edward Treacher Collins, T. Fisher Unwin, London, 1896, page 230

III-XIII-25: Lillet; wine_thewhiskeyexchange.com, Shown with permission from III-XIII-26: Indian Racing Reminiscences - Matthew Horace Hayes, London, W. Thacker & Co. 1883, page 340

III-XIII-27: Outlines of the History of Art, Wilhelm Lubke, Dodd, Mead, and Company, New York, 1881, page 669

III-XIII-28: Opium plant porte-feuille des enfans, Vol I, no. 99 by Charles Fredercum, 1795 no page

III-XIII-29: The Indo-Chinese opium trade notes at an Opium factory at Patna, The Graphic, 24 June 1882, page 640, by LTC Walters Sherwill

III-XIII-30: Modern etching and engraving, edited by Charles Holme, London, 1902, page 245

III-XIII-31: The earliest cosmology, William Warren, Eaton & Mains, New York, 1910, page 12

III-XIII-32: A history of Persia, Percy Sykes, Macmillan and Co., London, 1921, page 381

III-XIII-33: Persia, Samuel Benjamin, G.P. Putnam's Sons, 1888 page 294

III-XIII-34: Travels in Assyria, James Buckingham, Henry Colburn, London 1829, page xxxi

III-XIII-35: Russia in Central Asia in 1889 and the Anglo-Russian Question, George N. Curzon, Longmans, Green and Co. London, 1889, page 64

III-XIII-36: Battles of the nineteenth century Vol II, Archibald Forbes, Cassell and Company, London, 1897, page 196

III-XIII-37: The Cossacks, William Cresson, Brentano's, New York 1919, page 229

Chapter XIV

III-XIV-1: From the Black Sea through Persia and India, Edwin Lord Weeks, New York, Harper & Brothers Publishers, 1895, page 45

III-XIV-2: The Russians in Central Asia, translated by John and Robert Mitchell, London, Edward Standford, 1865, page 42

III-XIV-3: From the Black Sea through Persia and India, Edwin Lord Weeks, New York, Harper & Brothers Publishers, 1895, page 21

III-XIV-4: Travels in Central Asia, Arminius Vambery, John Murray, London, 1864, page 316

III-XIV-5: Games for Family Parties, Mrs Valentine, Frederick Warne and Company, London 1861, page 90

III-XIV-6: From the Black Sea through Persia and India, Edwin Lord Weeks, New York, Harper & Brothers Publishers, 1895, page 53

III-XIV-7: The Vegetable Lamb of Tartary, a curious fable of the cotton plant, Henry Lee, Sampson Low, Marston, Searle & Rivington, London, 1887, page liii

III-XIV-8: With star and Crescent, A. Locher, Aetna Publishing Company, Philadelphia 1889, page 161

III-XIV-9: Travels and researches among the lakes and mountains of Eastern & Central Africa, James Frederick Elton, John Murray, London 1873, page 208

III-XIV-10: The Illustrated Horse Management, Edward Mayhew, Philadelphia, J. B. Lippincott & Co., 1865, page 216

III-XIV-11: The Arab Horse, Spencer Broden, Doubleday, Page & Company, New York 1906, page 86

III-XIV-12: Outing Vol. XXIX October 1896, The outing Publishing Company, New York, 1897, page 85

III-XIV-13: The Earth and Its Inhabitants, Asiatic Russia, Chicken, Elisee Reclus, D. Appleton and Company, New York, 1884, page 315

III-XIV-14: Travels in Central Asia, Arminius Vambery, John Murray, London, 1864, page 148

III-XIV-15: The Young Rajah, A Story of Indian Life and Adventure, William Kingston, London, Thomas Nelson and Sons, 1876, page 197

III-XIV-16: The story-book of the Shah, Ella Sykes, John MacQueen, London, 1901, page 86

III-XIV-17: The Earth and Its Inhabitants, Asiatic Russia, Elisee Reclus, D. Appleton and Company, New York, 1881, page 195

III-XIV-18: Arctic Adventures, William Kingston, London, George Routledge and Sons, 1882, page xii

III-XIV-19: Travels in Assyria, Media and Persia including a Journey from Bagdad by mount Zagros, J. S. Buckingham, Henry Colburn, London, 1829, page 238

III-XIV-20: Illustrations from the art gallery, Charles Kurtz, George Barrie, Philadelphia, 1893, page 99

III-XIV-21: Fairy Guardians, F. Willoughby, Macmillan and Co., London, 1875, page 146

III-XIV-22: The Earth and Its Inhabitants, Asiatic Russia, Elisee Reclus, D. Appleton and Company, New York, 1884, page 203

III-XIV-23: The Earth and Its Inhabitants, Asiatic Russia, Elisee Reclus, D. Appleton and Company, New York, 1884, page 223

III-XIV-24: The Earth and Its Inhabitants, Asiatic Russia, Elisee Reclus, D. Appleton and Company, New York, 1884, page 261

Chapter XV

III-XV-1: A journey through the Yemen and some general remarks upon that country, Walter Harris, William Blackwood and Sons, Edinburgh and London, 1893, page 88

III-XV-2: The Earth and Its Inhabitants, Asiatic Russia, Elisee Reclus, D. Appleton and Company, New York, 1884, page 263

III-XV-3: The young ladies treasure book, no author, Ward, Lock & Co., London, no year, page 176

III-XV-4: Travels in Mesopotamia, J. S. Buckingham, Henry Colburn, London, 1827, page 127

III-XV-5: III-XV-6: Unknown image from 19th century source. Citation lost in computer disk drive failure

III-XV-6: Journey to the North of India, Arthur Conolly, Richard Bentley, London, 1838, page 10

III-XV-7: The Earth and Its Inhabitants, Asiatic Russia, Vol 1, Elisee Reclus, D. Appleton and Company, New York, 1884, page 228

III-XV-8: A History of Persia, Percy Sykes, Macmillan and Co., Limited, London, 1915, page viii

III-XV-9: Southern Asia; Asia Minor and its borderlands; Arabia, Ascott Moncrieff, The Gresham Publishing Company, London, page 70

III-XV-10: The Earth and Its Inhabitants, Vol. 1, Asiatic Russia, Elisee Reclus, D. Appleton and Company, New York, 1884, page 290

III-XV-11: Russian central Asia, Volume II, Sampson Low, Marston, Searle and Rivington, London, 1885, page 290

III-XV-12: From the Black Sea through Persia and India, Edwin Lord Weeks, New York, Harper & Brothers Publishers, 1895, page 51

III-XV-13: The roving Englishman, G. Routledge & Co., London, 1856, page vii

III-XV-14: The Earth and Its Inhabitants, Vol. 1, Asiatic Russia, Elisee Reclus, D. Appleton and Company, New York, 1884, page 262

III-XV-15: Russian central Asia, Volume II, Sampson Low, Marston, Searle and Rivington, London, 1885, page 253

III-XV-16: Gazette des Beavx-arts, Courier European, Paris 1866, page li

III-XV-17: Old Deccan days or, Hindoo Fairy Legends, current in Southern India, M. Frere, John Murray, London, 1868, page 178

III-XV-18: The dungeons of old Paris, Tighe Hopkins, G. P. Putnam's Sons, New York, 1897, page 234

III-XV-19: A journey through the Yemen and some general remarks upon that country, Walter Harris, William Blackwood and Sons, Edinburgh and London, 1893, page 286

III-XV-20: Turkistna, notes of a journey in Russian, Eugene Schuyler, Sampson Low, Marston, Searle & Rivington, London, 1876, page 70

III-XV-21: Chinese central Asia, a ride to Little Tibet, Henry Lansdell, page 33

End piece

Biographical sketches of the Queens of Great Britain, Mary Howitt, Henry G Bohn, London, 1856, page 13

Appendix

III-IV: The earliest cosmology, William Warren, Eaton & Mains, New York, 1909, page viii

Appendix supplement

III-AS-1: Reproduced By permission of the David Rumsey Map Collection, Mitchell, Samuel Augustus, Map of Persia, Arabia, Turkey in Asia, Afghanistan, Beloochistan, 1880, David Rumsey Map Collection, www.davidrumsey.com.
III-AS-2: Central Asia, Travels in Cashmere, Little Thibet, Thomas Stevens, Charles Scribner's Sons, New York, 1892, page 300
III-AS-3: Zigzag journeys in India; or, The Antipodes of the Far East, a Collection of the Zenana Tales, Hezekiah Butterworth, Estes and Lauriat, Boston, 1887, page 229
III-AS-4: The Graphic magazine, March 26, 1870, page 388, 'Bombay Brokers and Traders'
III-AS-5: Russia in Central Asia in 1889 and the Anglo-Russian Question, George N. Curzon, Longmans, Green and Co. London, 1889, page 17
III-AS-6: A New Treatise on the Diseases of Horses, William Gibson, A. Millar, London, 1754, page 124
III-AS-7: The Armies of Europe, Illustrated, Fedor Von Koppen, William Clowes & Sons, limited, London, 1890, page 90

Sources of Ornamentation

Front inner & back pages

Documents diplomatiques, France Ministere des affaires estrangeres, Imprimerie Nationale, Paris 1880, page front page

Prologue

Indien, Emanuel Korff, Mansucript gedrudt, Saber'fde Buddrukerie, Magdeburg1893, page 371
Illustrierte Lander und Volkerkunde, Guitav Ritter, Verlagedruckerei Merkur, Berlin 1908, page 416, modified
Illustrierte Lander und Volkerkunde, Guitav Ritter, Verlagedruckerei Merkur, Berlin 1908, page 569, modified
Illustrierte Lander und Volkerkunde, Guitav Ritter, Verlagedruckerei Merkur, Berlin 1908, page 511, modified
The story-book of the Shah, Ella Sykes, John MacQueen, London, 1901, page 199
Floral Decorations for the Dwelling House, Anne Hassard, London, Macmillian and Co., 1876, page 28

Chapter XI

Illustrierte Lander und Volkerkunde, Guitav Ritter, Verlagedruckerei Merkur, Berlin 1908, page 57
A book of sea stories, Cyrus Brady, Hall & Locke Company, Boston, 1901, page 136
The outing magazine October 1906, The Outing press NY 1907, page 855
Tales of the sea, William Henry, G. Kingston, London, Gall & Ingles, no date, page 123
The outing magazine October 1906, The Outing press NY 1907, page 525
The art of Caricature, Grant Wright, The Bajer Taylor Co., New York 1904, page 22
Tales of the sea, William Henry G. Kingston, London, Gall & Inglis, no date, page 174
Old Deccan days or, Hindoo Fairy Legends, current in Southern India, M. Frere, John Murray, London, 1868, page 153
Brandy Station, Heros von Barcke and Justus Schelbert, Berline, Verlag Von Paul Kittel, 1893 page 19
History of Art in Persia, Georges Perrot, Charles Chipiez, London, Chapman and Hall, Limited, page 393
The dungeons of old Paris, Tighe Hopkins, G. P. Putnam's Sons, New York, 18977, page 266
La mode illustree Journal de la famille, A la Librairie de Firmin didot Freres, Paris, 1869, xxiv
Archibald Hughson, the Young Shetlander, William Kingston, London, Gall & Inglis, no date, page 102
Modern Persia, Mooshie G. Daniel, Henderson & Company, Toronto, 1898, page 46

Chapter XII

History of Art in Persia - Georges Perrot, Charles Chipiez, London, Chapman and Hall, Limited, page 407
The last American, John Mitchell, Frederick A. Stokes Company, New York 1902, page 37

The arch author's collection

Queen of the Adriatic, T. Nelson and Sons, London, 1869, William Daveport Adamas, page xxv

The Art of the Saracens in Egypt - Stanley Lane-Poole, London, Chapman and Hill, limited 1886, page 250

Primary education, 1914 magazine volume XXII, page 211

Ten thousand miles in Persia, Percy Molesworth Sykes, Charles Scribner's sons, New York 1902, page 91

Ten thousand miles in Persia, Percy Molesworth Sykes, Charles Scribner's sons, New York 1902, page 146

Ten thousand miles in Persia, Percy Molesworth Sykes, Charles Scribner's sons, New York 1902, page 503

Ten thousand miles in Persia, Percy Molesworth Sykes, Charles Scribner's sons, New York 1902, page 9

Ten thousand miles in Persia, Percy Molesworth Sykes, Charles Scribner's sons, New York 1902, page 199

History of Art in Persia - Georges Perrot, Charles Chipiez, London, Chapman and Hall, Limited, page 401

The history of a book, Annie Carey, Cassell, Peter & Galpin, London 1873, page 155

History of India, William Hunter, The Grolier Society, London, 1906, page xi

The Land of the Ganges and the Ghauts, Jabez Marrat, London, Charles H. Kelly, 1892, page 211

The History of Gibraltar, From the Earliest Period of Its Occupation by the Saracens, James Bell, London, William Pickering, 1845, page x

Chapter XIII

Ten thousand miles in Persia, Percy Molesworth Sykes, Charles Scribner's sons, New York 1902, page 100

A history of Persia, Percy Sykes, Macmillan and Co., London, 1921, page 610

The story-book of the Shah, Ella Sykes, John MacQueen, London, 1901, page 111

The Art of the Saracens in Egypt - Stanley Lane-Poole, London, Chapman and Hill, limited 1886, page 103

El Yèmen, tre anni nell'Arabia felice, Renzo Manzoni, Roma, Tipografi Eredi Botta, 1884, page 306

Cairo, sketches of its history, and social life, Stanley Lane-Poole, J.S. Virtue & Co., Limited, London, 1893 page 26

Hindu Tribes and Castes, Matthew Atmore Sherring, London, Trubner and Co, 1872, page 360

Floral Decorations for the Dwelling House, Anne Hassard, London, Macmillian and Co., 1876 page 124

London, a complete guide to the places of amusement, Henry Herbert Co., 1876, no author, page x

The story-book of the Shah, Ella Sykes, John MacQueen, London, 1901, page xl

Persian art, Murdoch Smith, Scribner, Welford, and Armstrong, New York 1877, page xx

Mirages et souvenirs, Hippolite Monplasir, Da Sociedade typographica Franco-Pontugueza, 1860, page 46

Floral Decorations for the Dwelling House, Anne Hassard, London, Macmillian and Co., 1876 page 163

Cartoons and caricatures of men, A.H. Dutton, Press of the Century printing company, Salt Lake City, 1907, page vii x 3

Les aventures de Jean-Paul Choppart, Paul Lauters, Publie par la societe des beaux-arts, Bruxelles, 1840, page 164

Women in all lands, Amand von Schweiger-Lerchenfeld, Chas. F. Roper & Co., New York, 1880, page 237

The Earth and its inhabitants, South and East Africa, Elisee Reclus, New York, 1882, page 424

Ten thousand miles in Persia, Percy Molesworth Sykes, Charles Scribner's sons, New York 1902, page 30

Ten thousand miles in Persia, Percy Molesworth Sykes, Charles Scribner's sons, New York 1902, page 576

Chapter XV

Stories from over the sea, Edinburgh, William P. Nimmo, 1873, page 58

Cairo, sketches of its history, and social life, Stanley Lane-Poole, J.S. Virtue & Co., Limited, London, 1893 page 54

Floral Decorations for the Dwelling House, Anne Hassard, London, Macmillian and Co., 1876 page 14

Cairo, sketches of its history, and social life, Stanley Lane-Poole, J.S. Virtue & Co., Limited, London, 1893 page 294

Cairo, sketches of its history, and social life, Stanley Lane-Poole, J.S. Virtue & Co., Limited, London, 1893 page 90

Warriors of the Crescent, William Henry Davenport Adams, New York, D. Appleton and Company, 1892, page x

In the Eastern Seas, Or, William Kingston London, T. Nelson and Sons, 1872 page 22

The Perfectly Good Cynic's Calendar, Ethel Grant, Paul Elder and Company, San Francisco, 1908, page 60

Celebrated women travellers, W. H. Davenport Adams, E.P. Dutton & Co., New York, 1903, page 112

The story-book of the Shah, Ella Sykes, John MacQueen, London, 1901, page lxvi

The art of Caricature, Grant Wright, The Bajer Taylor Co., New York 1904, page 89

Ten thousand miles in Persia, Percy Molesworth Sykes, Charles Scribner's sons, New York 1902, page 60

Ten thousand miles in Persia, Percy Molesworth Sykes, Charles Scribner's sons, New York 1902, page 361

Ten thousand miles in Persia, Percy Molesworth Sykes, Charles Scribner's sons, New York 1902, page 77

Chapter XV

Spherical ballooning, some of the requirements, Paul McCullough, page 1

Ten thousand miles in Persia, Percy Molesworth Sykes, Charles Scribner's sons, New York 1902, page ix

Ten thousand miles in Persia, Percy Molesworth Sykes, Charles Scribner's sons, New York 1902, page 274

The Land of the Ganges and the Ghauts, Jabez Marrat, London, Charles H. Kelly, 1892, page 253

Persian life and custom, Samuel Wilson, Fleming H Revell Company, New York 1895, page 2

Ten thousand miles in Persia, Percy Molesworth Sykes, Charles Scribner's sons, New York 1902, page 258

Voyage au Yemen, journal d'une excursion botanique faite en 1887, Albert Deflers, page 246

Academy sketches, ed. by H. Blackburn, W. H. Allen & Co., London, 1883, page 213

The buried cities of Campania W.H. Davenport Adams, T. Nelson and Sons, London, 1870, page lii

Overhead in a Garden El Catera, Oliver Herford, Charles Scribner's Sons, New York, 1900 page 28

Appendix and Notes

Persia, Samuel Benjamin, G.P. Putnam's Sons, 1888 page 306
Seaports of the Far East,historical and Descriptive, London, Allister Macmillian, W. H. and L Collingridge, 1907, page xv
Handbook of Information for the Colonies and India, Watson, Ferguson & Co., Brisbane, Warwocl & Sarsford, Printers, 1890, page 67 x 2
Gazette des Beavx-arts, , Courrier Europeen, Paris 1866, page 119

Appendix Supplement One

The play pictorial, Vol V, No author, Greening & Co, London 1905, page lxi
Academy sketches, ed. by H. Blackburn, page 214
The Diary of H.M. the Shah of Persia, During His Tour Through Europe in A.D. 1873 - Nasir al-Din Shah, London, Bradbury, Agnew & Co. page 343
The story-book of the Shah, Ella Sykes, John MacQueen, London, 1901, page vi
Floral Decorations for the Dwelling House, Anne Hassard, London, Macmillian and Co., 1876 page 20
The story-book of the Shah, Ella Sykes, John MacQueen, London, 1901, page 138
Anthologie japonaise, Leon de Rosny, Maisonneuve et cie, Paris, 1871, page 229
Scrolls, Monograms, Ornaments, Crests, Nathianiel Dearborn, Boston, N.S. Dearborn, 1869, page 32
Blackwoods magazine Jan 1871 x 3

Scrolls, Monograms, Ornaments, Crests, Nathaniel Dearborn, Boston, N.S. Dearborn, 1869, page 32
Persia, Samuel Benjamin, G.P. Putnam's Sons, 1888 page 306,
Seaports of the Far East, Historical and Descriptive, London, Allister Macmillian, W. H. and L Collingridge, 1907, page xv
Handbook of Information for the Colonies and India, Watson, Ferguson & Co., Brisbane, Warwocl & Sarsford, Printers, 1890, page 67 (modified)
Handbook of Information for the Colonies and India, Watson, Ferguson & Co., Brisbane, Warwocl & Sarsford, Printers, 1890, page 67 (modified)
Persia, Samuel Benjamin, G.P. Putnam's Sons, 1888 page 282
Bombay and Western India, A Series of Stray Papers - James Douglas, London, Sampson Low, Marston & Company, 1893, page 42
Academy sketches, ed. by H. Blackburn, page 214

End

The history of the Hawaiian mission press, Howard M. Ballou and George Carter, presented August 27, 1908, Honolulu, page 12

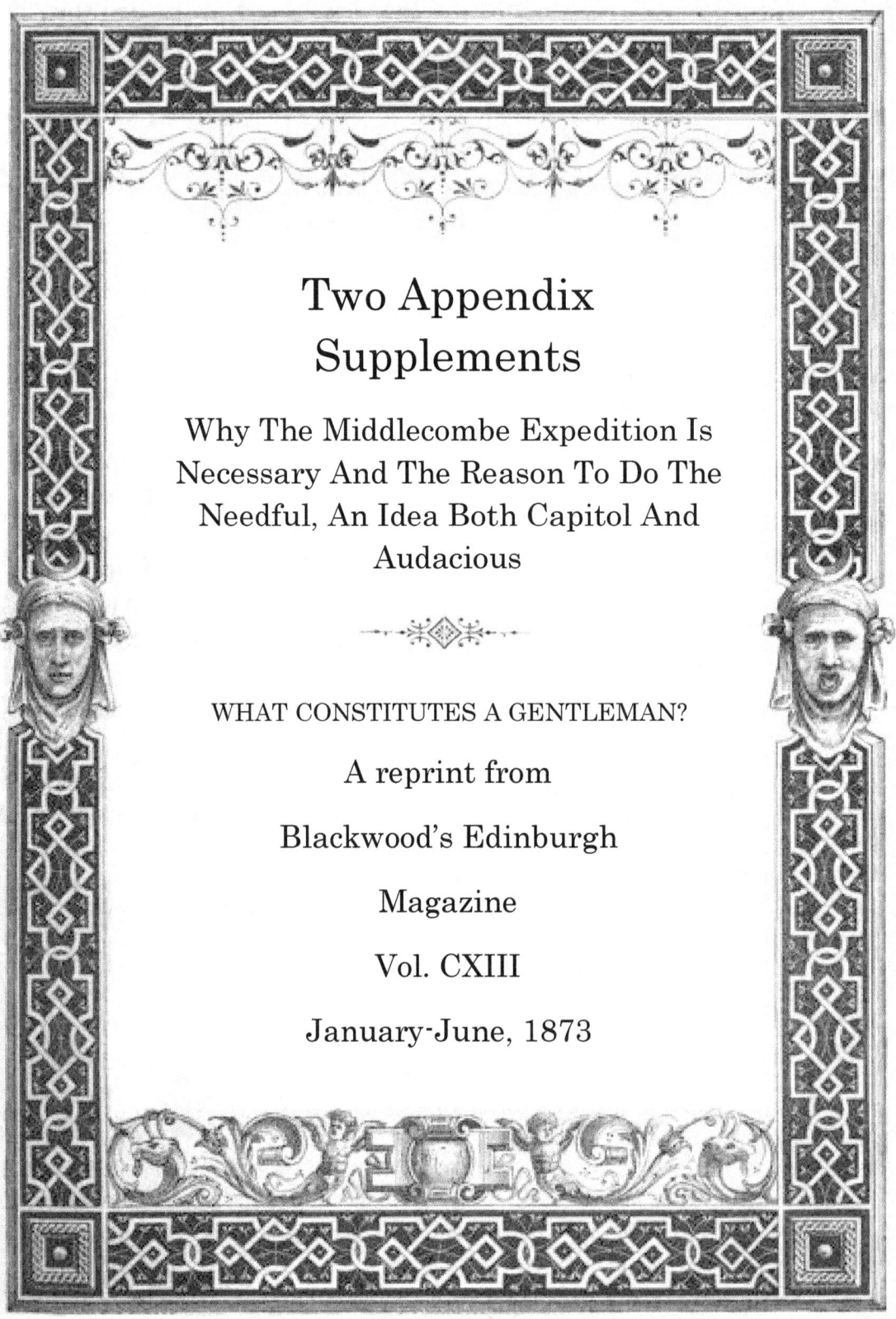

Two Appendix Supplements

Why The Middlecombe Expedition Is Necessary And The Reason To Do The Needful, An Idea Both Capitol And Audacious

— ❧ —

WHAT CONSTITUTES A GENTLEMAN?

A reprint from

Blackwood's Edinburgh

Magazine

Vol. CXIII

January-June, 1873

Appendix Supplement One

Why The Middlecombe Expedition Is Necessary And The Reason To Do The Needful, An Idea Both Capitol And Audacious

In 1836, it was announced in Parliament that exactly forty eight thousand, nine hundred and fifty four Britons were in the pay or employment of the Honourable East India Company, and that by their efforts, the land of Great Britain was greatly enriched. This was done by bringing good governance and trade to ninety-two million Indians. Yet expansion of this trade, and bringing good government, was in no way complete, for parts of Asia are still closed to our knowledge and our merchants, and the people are ground under by cruel tyrants, with trade throttled by corruption and ill-management, brigandage and excessive tariffs. Before merchants could overcome these great obstacles, it would be necessary that Great Britain have eyes on the ground, to see the lands unknown, to find the markets yet hidden, to understand the lay of the land, its people, rulers and methods of commerce.

The idea and need for the expedition arose first in the writings and deliberations of the Company[1] and were hastened by the passing in Parliament of the Government of India Act of 1833. The issues raised by this, and earlier Russian moves to invade the Independent Khanates of Independent Tartary[2], had given cause for great concern, that the creature that had crushed Napoleon's Grande Armee would now move towards the frontiers of India, and if in time of a European war, could challenge the basis of British power in the sub-continent. Also involved in this debate, but for singularly different motives, were concerns for scientific knowledge, British prestige and the empire's expansion. There were various private British organizations committed to obtaining more information about the region in question.

In the late 1820's, while serving in the Duke of Wellington's Cabinet, Lord Ellenborough issued a directive to the Political and Secret Department of the East India Company[3] to find the potential routes that attackers could approach India from the west and northwest. The East India Company will be referred to as the Company or by the initials of its full name; Honourable East India Company, or HEIC. How this was to be done was not explained and was left up to the Company to determine. Therefore they decided to dispatch officers to explore, map and study the peoples and resources of these areas. Thus informed they would be more able to formulate strategies to defeat any efforts to attack India. It was soon decided that to fully understand the possibility of such an attack, it would require that the Company look at the cities of Independent Tartary and it should gain knowledge of their power structures and political leanings.

In June 1835, a letter from William Hamilton, who was the president of the Geographical Society of London, was sent to John McNeill, who was then the newly appointed ambassador to Persia, and that is where the idea of the expedition first arose in print. The original letter was lost in the confusion of the withdrawal of the embassy during the crises of the siege of Herat, but its dominant point was;

> *...that an expedition of Company men should be sent into this region to ascertain with some certainty the full extent of Russian commercial, political and military penetration amongst the various native princes*

This letter had come about as the results of conversations between numbers of notable men at the College of Physicians' supper the September past. It was here that members of the Travellers' Club had met with certain nabobs returned from India, bringing with them tidings both of the newly commissioned Madras Club, but also a letter to one of them from the renowned Alexander Burnes[4]. This group of enthusiasts led by the British Navies' Admiralty Hydrographer, Francis Beaufort, concluded that such an expedition was not only needed, but a necessity. The British need for exploration, being built on an edifice of distrust and suspicions of Russian motives, were given great urgency in Wilson's seminal work[5].

The reader is asked to view the map on the following page. This shows how Independent Tartary was viewed in London at this time. Look at the upper right hand corner of the chart, where the title is, and it shows, pointed to by an arrow, a blank map in contrast to the well-known Turkish and Persian domains. It was this blank space on the map that the expedition would hopefully fill in. Illustration III-AS-1.

Reproduced By permission of the David Rumsey Map Collection

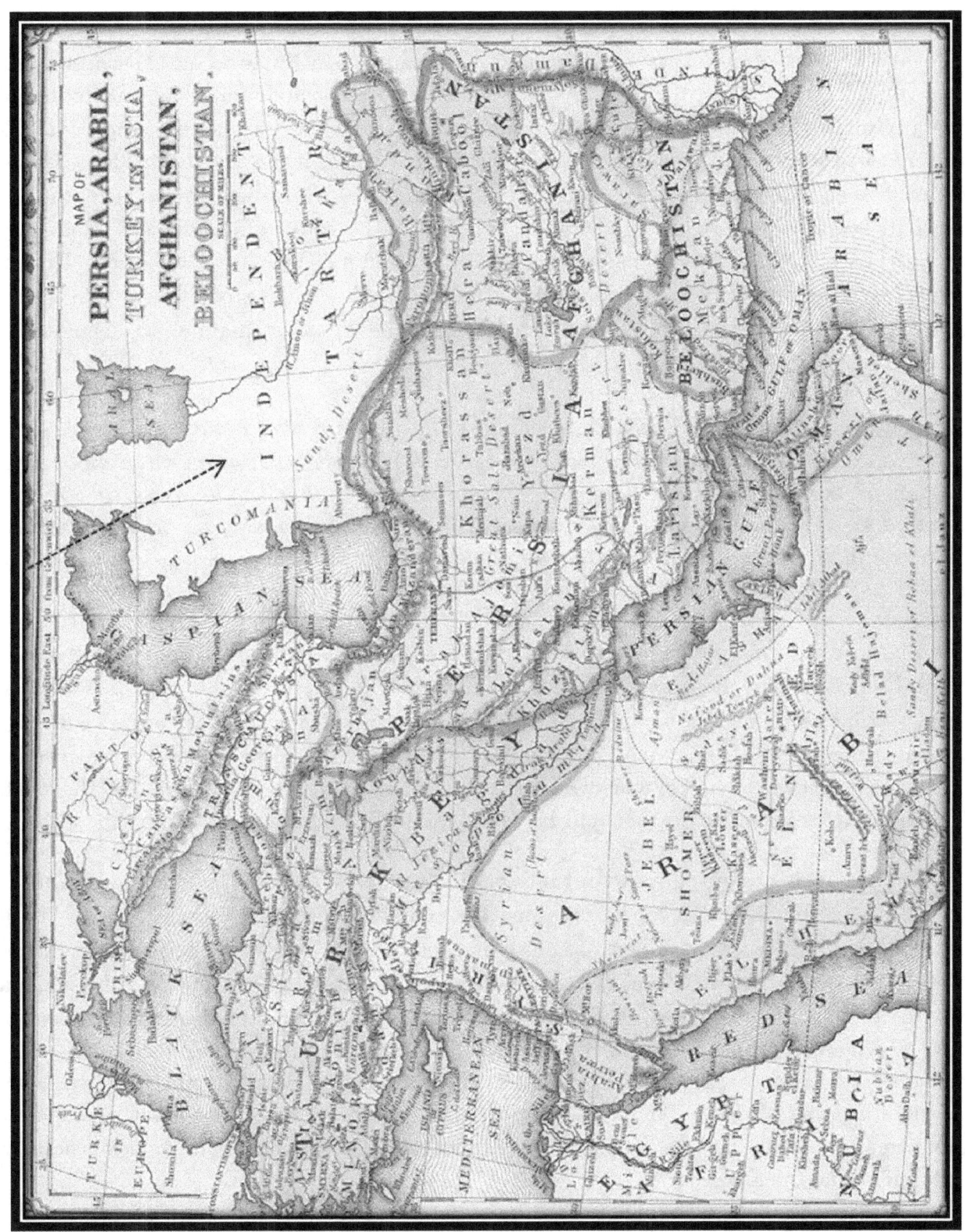

The Great Trigonometric Survey Enters the Stage

A Royal Engineer *{Lieutenant Perkins}*, late of India, was in England on leave from that organization noted in the title above. As he was of a well-respected family, he was invited to dine at Guildhall on Lord Mayor's day, a month or so after the Physician's supper. It was here that he received the necessary endorsements to proceed on the expedition. This charge was confirmed in a later meeting, where the details were determined in some depth, but due to its secretive nature, no papers were provided to the young officer; except a letter by the Secretary of the present chairman of the East Indian Company, Sir James Rivett-Carnac to those men in Bombay, Bengal and Madras, who could expedite the goal of the Lieutenant, and this letter addressed the issue in the broadest manner to disguise its import.

[Editor's note: There are no existing documents that explain why Perkins, of all persons, was chosen to lead the expedition. It was suggested, however, that someone in a powerful position in India wanted him out of India for reasons unknown; however this is idle speculation. At this time he was respected both for his surveying knowledge and resourcefulness, regardless of whether an occasional eye-brow had been raised about his social activities and growing reputation as a libertine or in modern terms a playboy]

This Lieutenant's next action was to prepare himself for the expedition, by speaking with oriental scholars, and thus, armed with a list of names and locations, he went in search of them, so that he could find what they knew about the peoples and places to be visited by the expedition. It was while visiting a Persian professor, that he encounters, by fortunate supervention, David Driscol, who was then preparing to depart England for the east. Perkins admired his pluck and thought he would be the first man to add to the expedition.

Lieutenant Perkins then set out to put into motion a way to address the following points of consideration. Before doing so, he obtained an audience with the Prime Minister, Lord Melbourne, where he obtained permission to proceed. He also met with the Commander-in-chief of the Army, Lord Hill, and by chance also with the Duke of Wellington, who while a private citizen at that time, was immensely influential, and he obtained the support of these two men. He also met with, briefly, the Secretary of State for Foreign Affairs *{The Viscount Palmerston}* who was noncommittal on the matter. He then met with the King and obtained his blessings and royal approval. Well-armed with authoritative support, signatures and seals, he was prepared to conduct the expedition with the permissions of Parliament and the King.

Determination Of Purposes For The Expedition

Our interests in this land of Tartary are manyfold; firstly there is a military concern, which must be the paramount point of apprehension. This imperative question must be answered at its soonest possibility. There are also many political considerations to include within this argument; the suppression of slavery in those lands, a question of scientific geography and a survey of the military topography of the region. Our secondary issues include the expansion of our markets and free trade into these unplumbed areas, especially looking to see which rivers are navigable and suitable for maritime trade. Additionally, this territory offers some products of interest to us, primarily horses for use with the Indian army. Those questions and observations will be considered after a limited review of previous attempts to explore the area of Independent Tartary and the Aral Sea.

Orientalists have long been involved in reshaping the map of Asia to suit various academic opinions of what the geography is, and how it could support their various theories on which tribe came from where, and who conquered who and when.

One main question had arisen between the geographers of Europe; did the Aral Sea drain into the Caspian? Earlier explorers had noted a dry delta on the eastern shore of the Caspian, but was it an intermittent river, or did the Oxus once flow into the Caspian? These questions were being hotly debated by geographers in several countries: most notably in Russia, France and England. Despite the answer to the questions having been provided by both English, native, and Russian reports, the question of a connecting river persist to this day. We will address this question in depth later in the paragraphs following.

The importance of this is as follows. If such a connection exists between the two great rivers, the Oxus and Jaxates of Tartary *{The modern Amu Darya and Syr Darya}* and the Aral, then by this unknown river to the Caspian, the Russians by way of the Volga river which empties into the Caspian may move men and equipment by water to the headwaters of those two rivers, which are close by the main entry routes to the sub-continent.

I will examine briefly the history of preceding explorations of the Aral Sea and its lands by the ancients and up to the present. This review of the previous knowledge is not exhaustive, but represents what was known to us in India and Persia while planning the expedition, and in some cases was taken from information that was at hand to men in England or Russia, but was not known, at that time, to the members of the expedition.

The ancient view of the world was that it was an island of land surrounded by the sea, which in fact it was. This encircling sea is now explored and has been made safe for trade by the Royal Navy.

Hecataeus of Miletus is credited with the creation of the idea of an encompassing ocean with the land within inhabited by variously named barbarians, while in the centre, were the civilized peoples.

To the revered ancients the lands where they lived was the *oikoumene*, while where the Aral Sea lies, was *terra incognito* and most probably inhabited by strange creatures and cruel barbarians. The maps by the Greeks, made by such great men as Dicaearcus, Eratosthenes, Herodotus, and Posidonius, show the Caspian Sea to be a large gulf of the great encircling ocean known as the Northern Ocean.

Eratosthenes, to his credit, attempted to map the lands beyond the *oikoumene* and in the east, he found the end of the world at the Ganges Delta, while in the west, it was the Ocean that became known as the Atlantic. He was limited in his abilities to map these regions, due to the unreliable nature of anecdotes told about it from peripatetic merchants, their tales, mendacities and descriptions, along with their statements of distances estimated in days needed to travel from one place to another. It was from these hints, that he tried to construct maps of the area, known now to us as Tartary, but he was hampered not only by this unreliable information, but also by his desire to uphold the Greek metaphysical belief of an *oikoumene*, with a length to breadth ratio of 2 to1 based on false considerations. In his day, the question of what lay beyond a mountains, to a Greek meant that he would ask some barbarian for the answer, to a Roman he might just ignore the question, or better yet conquer the people on the other side, while to an Englishman the answer is simpler, go there to see for himself, and if he failed to do so, then follow the Roman method.

In the book, *The Campaigns of Alexander*, Lucius Arrianus gave us our first hint of the Aral Sea and its connection to the Caspian. His writings brought up the idea of a river that flows into it from the east. He wrote in part,

> *It empties itself into the Caspian Sea in Hyrcania. Alexander marched for Marakanda, the Royal city of Sogdiana, moving thence to the Tanais. Like the Oxus, this river, too (according to Aristobulus the natives call it the Orexartes) rises in the Indian Caucasus and flows into the Caspian Sea. In the various writing of Alexanders' campaigns, no mention of the sea in question can be found.*

The Roman Strabo and Pliny added little to our knowledge of the Sea, as their concerns were for the trade routes, and in particular the much appreciated silk from Seres *{The China of our day}*. In the first century of our Lord, information was obtained about the Seresians, but no mention is made of the great lakes or seas of Independent Tartary.

In the maps of Claudius Ptolemy and Marinus the Tyrian, we find a presentation that might be considered as the Aral Sea, but as the publications of his work were adapted with new information over the centuries, it is ambiguous when the Aral Sea might have been added.

It may be that the Sea is represented in their map, but as the Caspian Sea is badly distorted, the identification of a lake to the east of it in the region of the Turan plain by the name Oxia Palus or Lacus Oxiana, is not proof that Aral Sea's location was known with any confidence.

It was the esteemed Persian geographer Abu Ishaq ibn Muhammad al-Farisi al Istakhri who produced a map in 1143, which one could evaluate as showing a lake to the east of the Caspian, which he called Khwarazm. Later, some local geographers nominated the lake as Horesm Lake after the kingdom of the area.

The Venetian map maker, Fra Mauro's map of 1457, shows a lake to the east of the Caspian, but it is unnamed. Where he obtained this geographical detail is not known.

Next the Arab historian Muhammad al-Idrisi produced a map known as the Tabula Rogeriana, which Lieutenant Perkins had the pleasure to see in the Bodleian Library at Oxford before the expedition. This copy was made in Cairo in 1553. He found it to be full of errors, but it did give a hint that the Aral Sea was known to a man who lived in the Mediterranean 1150 years after the birth of Jesus Christ, but that observation is one based on hindsight. The Arab geographers had a fair idea of the location of the lake by the 12th century and our more modern geographers did so only by the 16th, and as it was noted earlier, many questions still remain about the situation and location of the lake and especially what rivers, if any, flowed from it to the Caspian.

Other medieval Mohammedan historians wrote of a river called the Uzboj[6] in that region, which allegedly was a waterway used by traders who navigated it despite its treacherous course. It[7] flowed to the Caspian Sea from a lake to the east in Independent Tartary.

It was the French Jesuits, those perfidious monks who wandered the world to spread their popery, who brought back the first modern knowledge of the Sea. They had travelled to China, but had providentially lingered in the area of our interest and created a map of the region. They failed to note the Sea of our interest, but did find and document the existence of a river that ran into the Caspian Sea from the east, and furthermore they noted that it was fed by a lake, and that lake was fed by the Oxus[8].

We are most appreciative of the information obtained from our former enemies, the occupiers of Gaul[9], in particular the work of Pascal Gossellin, and his Geographie des Grecs analysee, ou les Systemes d'Eratosthene, de Strabon et de Ptolemee compares entre eux et avec nos connaissances modernes, printed during the phantasmagoria of the pit[10]. He was of a mind that the Oxus had once communicated with the Caspian and furthermore commerce was had with the Mediterranean and Black Sea by this way. These merchants would journey to the Caspian then steer south till they reached the mouth of the river Kur in the Caucasus. They would then sailed inland and use a portage to reach the source of the Rioni[11], and then by ship again into the Black Sea and Mediterranean. About the middle of the 17th century the Russians endeavoured to re-open this ancient route, but this effort was unsuccessful. His work seemed to confirm the opinions of the earlier Mohammedan geographers noted earlier.

It is a hope that this route could be reinvigorated once these lands have been freed from Ottoman and Persian ineptitude and tyranny over the Christian communities of Armenia and Georgia[12]. I am an ally to the idea of a modernisation and dismembering of the Ottoman Empire for reason of the promotion of Christianity, trade, medicine and good governance.

Father Brennan's document continues on the next page.

[Editor's note: Driscol added into his journal a list of expeditions known to him to have entered the area of interest to the expedition, I have added in a number of Russian expeditions then unknown to him and major political actions that affected the region and ultimately the expedition itself, see Appendix III-I]

Seclusion Of Independent Tartary

The reasons for this are manifest, the isolation of the area from Christian civilization, its hostility to outsiders, especially infidels, makes the region difficult to travel in. Furthermore, constant strife between the various sects of the Mohammedans makes the place no stranger to massacre and bloodshed, that would make our own acts of savagery seem less. Our own horrors of the Armagnac massacres, Joshua's slaughter of the Amalekites, or the Sicilian vespers[13] and the many other bloody acts in the annals of this world are still commonplace amongst the people and rulers of Tartary.

Although one might applaud the Russian advances as belonging to those of the greater Christian civilization, one must contemplate that Russian Civilization and their view of religion, is askance to European ideas and the true creed. For good or bad, it is now the Russians who have led modernity into Turan's lacustrine plains. It is due to them that nearly all the current information is derived. There are two camps[14] within European cartographers over the quality of this Russian material: One group is known as the 'Moselle' group from where they have meetings on occasion. This Moselle group is the more vocal of the two. It holds that the Russians are not to be trusted, and whatever information we receive has been distorted or filtered of any valuable military, geographic and natural science intelligence. The second group, that is called the 'The Elders' holds that the geographic and other scientific information is correct but that it is dated and reflects what the Russians knew a generation or more ago, and that the Czar is withholding both the scope and extent of his progress in all areas.

The idea that the Russians would not expand into this region is not credible. That the Czar, the Russian nobility, the church and the very soul of the people would not move to avenge the defeat of its army, the murder of a Prince of that nation by deception and oriental deceit, that it would not send scouts, nor survey the people and products of that region is by all accounts, preposterous. *Bis peccare in bello non licet, {to blunder twice in war is not permitted}* and it is a blunder to ever let a blow from an Oriental go unanswered, and doubly so when dealing with followers of the Mekkan fortune-teller *{The prophet Mohammed}*. For this reason alone, it is thought that the Russians will drive into Tartary if for no other reason than to revenge Prince Cherkassky, slain those many years ago by Tartary duplicity[15].

Yet this state of affairs appears to be the status quo. We cannot know whether the information obtained from Russian sources is pure, correct, or all of the pastry, as one might say. We will examine briefly the Empire of Russia's efforts in this distant arena.

In 1697 the Remezov map was printed, which is reported to have shown the Aral Sea or in the original Cyrillic alphabet it would be pronounce the Aralsko Sea. The origin of the Sea's name is unknown; speculation on this matter has consumed many printed sheets and has not yet been resolved. The Russian sources show that the each new explorer named it differently, some called it the 'Dark Blue' or the "Blue Sea', while in the 17th century the term 'Aral' Sea became more commonplace. The nomenclature may have derived from the word which means an island, perhaps a poetic view of it being an 'island' of blue water in the pitiless desert of the Turansk lowlands.

The first accurate geographic information on the location of this inland sea came from the work of a Muhammadan, Devlet Girei Murza, who had righteously converted to Christianity, so he might serve his Russian sovereign in the field of exploration; known now as Prince Alexander Cherkassky, he would do some work at the Sea before being consumed by perfidy, and he and his army destroyed by the ruler of Khiva. It is revenge for this army, which is the excuse often given for further advances of the Russians into Tartary. The army is said to have been lost in the following manner.

We have only the Russian sources for the first part of the tale, and for the second part, no sources at all. But after a march towards the city of Khiva, a battle was fought with the forces of that Ameer who they apparently defeated. The defeated Khivans are known to have then used guile to lure the feckless Russians to their destruction; with some four thousand Christian souls being slaughtered. What good that did come of the expedition, was that the east coast of the Caspian Sea was made known, and partially mapped.

In the same year, 1717, the Czar travelled to France, where he received word and confirmation from the French that the Oxus ran not into the Caspian but into the little known Aral Sea. Later, the French geographer Delilja placed the Aral Sea on an influential map; the original now unfortunately being lost. In 1730 the Swedish prisoner of war Philip Johann von Stralenberg[16] who was being held at Tobolsk, published the *Nova descriptio geographica Tattariae magnae,* which showed the region of the middle Jaxartes *{Syr Darya}* and the areas north of the Caspian and Aral Seas.

Other Russians, or those in their service, also began to provide geographical data on the sea, and the first sketches were provided. Notably, Lieutenant Dmitry Gladyshev and his surveyor Ivan Muravin visited the peoples who lived to the north of the Sea. Muravin provided some of the first scientific survey data about the area, and this data was later incorporated into a new map, printed in 1741, that showed parts of the Sea. A similar expedition by Soimonov and Rachtov, with the objective to conduct hydrographic studies of the sea, was also completed at that time.

The most recent Russian expeditions were led by the Russian Polkovnik *{Colonel}* Feodor Berg to the western coast of the Sea, and from whom we get the first astronomical survey data, and he produced the first topographical maps of the Ustyurt plateau, where the Aral Sea is situated. His efforts were the last fully known and documented Russian military expedition to the area. A Professor Eversman of Kazan University did do work of a natural history nature, and his work is much admired by those in that field in Great Britain. This work dates to fifteen years before the departure of the Perkins expedition *{the expedition's* *original name - why it became known as the Middlecombe expedition will be told in this volume}* to the east.

To help fill in the gaps from the Russians, we do have the book by the English trader Jonas Hanway, who wrote about the Caspian Sea trade, and made valuable comments on the lands to the east, but his accounts are nearly ninety years old. He also plotted on a map in his manuscript the former dry channel of the Oxus. Before him, a British Merchant named Jacky is said to have worked in the area, and was reported on by the Russian Gladychef, in 1742, who was the Russian envoy to the area. It is also reported that an English naval captain, named Elton, had accompanied a caravan into Central Asia, and he is said to have reconnoitered Lake Aral, but no word of this has ever been seen by any other authority in writing or orally about this man or his trip. Allegedly he died at his desk as he sat to write the book of his adventures. He is known to have made the trip with a view to promoting the establishment of a British naval flotilla upon it *{The Caspian Sea}*. Because no Englishman, recently, has been to these lands, the Russian accounts are discounted, acceptable to some but considered unacceptable by the two groups noted above for the reasons so stated. In the opinion of those men, only the viewing of these lands by an English Officer can confirm these Russian accounts, while other Europeans state that the Russian representation of the area is as they so say.

The most recent of English visitors to this distant land were:

1558 Jenkinson, a British master *{merchant captain}* explored the Caspian Sea

1723 A Captain Bruce surveyed the eastern shore of the Caspian

1738 and 1741 Captain Woodruffe and Elton journey separately to the Sea

1822 James B. Fraser travels in Korassan

1825 William Moorcroft passes through on his way to India dying in Afghan Turkestan after visiting Bokhara

1829 Lieutenant Arthur Conolly who traveled through Central Asia and Afghanistan and onto India in January 1831. *{He is well remembered for coining the phrase "The Great Game" to describe the Russian and British efforts in Central Asia.}*

1831 The missionary Joseph Wolff travels to Merv

1832 Lieutenant Alexander Burnes passes through Merv

Military Concern

It is our eastern possessions, which the Russians may have an interest in, which until now have been too distant and aloof from them, by way of an impassable geography and peoples hostile to their advance. It is more precise to say, that the Russians have long wanted to have it in their ability to attack us in India, in case a European quarrel would render such a measure expedient. Our undefeatable navy renders any attack by them on our Island impossible. Granting that they can operate against our continental allies with some effect, but Great Britain cannot be approached. Given that they have no way to defeat us in Europe, the only other card that can be played, would be whether they can, or hereafter will be able to bring an army of native levies strengthened by Cossacks and a core of Russian infantry, artillery and sappers to our frontier in India. If such an army would come, the faithless Native Princes and their peoples might be moved to rise against us. If they were to move against us, they might also seek the aid of Persia or Afghanistaun in a war against us based on religion. This move by evoking *Jihad* could be dangerous to us by inflaming the always smoldering and incendiary instincts of the Mohammedans in India to turn against us.

For what reason is our English knowledge of Russian actions and preparations against Independent Tartary so ill positioned? The Marshal of France Nicolas Maison[17] observed that if one were in St. Petersburg and sat quietly in Palkin's restaurant and were moderately conversant with the language, or spoke even just French, one would

> *....know within the hour the utmost details of the activities of all the ministries, the movements of the army, the latest sinkings in the navy, the scandals of the nobility and any other news worth knowing....*

The Russians do not hide their efforts, except by the feeblest of diplomatic misrepresentations. The writings of their military and of the influential members of their society are very open about their plans and purposes. We must at the earliest possible time gain strength by knowledge and only by our expedition can we gain said acquaintance and understanding of Tartary and the Russian moves there.

Suppression Of Slavery In Those Lands

In Britain we have undone slavery only since 1834, and some of these poor wretches are still being held in chains and not set to be released until three years hence by the action of the Slavery Abolition Act of 1833. This contemptible commerce is still greatly practiced in the land of the Tartary Khans. A noted and most notorious slave market for captured Russian and Persian slaves is centred in the Emirates or Khanates of Khiva, Bukhara and Samarkand. Tens of the thousands of innocent Christian Russian citizens and innumerable Persians are swept up each year for these markets; there are also reports that Indians are sold there. More information is needed as to how these abominable markets operate so that they can be confronted and ended. It is felt that once slavery is abolished in these regions, the men who run such large complex vocations can be diverted to more respectable trade in tea, sugar and textiles, supplied to them by British commerce. Removal of this detestable exchange will also remove from the Russians one of their given reasons for advancing into the region. If their slaves are freed by British actions, the motivation for their advance will lose one of its strongest incentives.

An enslaved Persian in Khiva. Illustration III-AS-2

Scientific And Military Geography And Topography

Despite the evidence provided, some questions remained as to what size of army could be supplied at the gates of India? Some answers to this have been provided by a number of British missions such as those by the heroic Moorcroft, Grant, Christie and Pottinger[18].

It is hoped that our expedition will answer a number of perplexing scientific and geographical questions and could also tackle certain military topographical inquiries.

It remains clear to any historian, that if invaders such as Alexander the Great, Afghanis, Arabs, Kushans, Mongols and Turks, were able to move through this area and attack India, others could too. The sturdy Russian soldier and his ally the Cossack need little in the way of supplies. What they do need can be provided by their local supporters, and the fertile plains of India, and in victory from our own depots. All they would need from Mother Russia are supplies for their artillery and capable officers.

An optimistic view of a future attack on India by Russian supported natives; the Elephant represents British India, the mahout the British Army and the poor man about to have his head crushed, an attacking Russian army. Illustration III-AS-3

Expansion of Our Markets and Free Trade

[Editor's note: I have deleted twenty pages on the commercial trade possibilities that the British hoped to find in Independent Tartary, these never came to anything as the cost to transport materials to Central Asia was prohibitive and there was a lack of customer desire for many of the British products. Much of the abridged material consists of comparing British methods of weights and measure to those in use in those regions. The weights and measures used there during that time were an overlap of different systems, each Khanate having its own systems, but mixed into it were Persian systems, the Chinese Shizhi system and Russian systems, to which the British wished to add in Rundlets, Tierces, Barrels and Firkins. Additionally there were discussions about the different forms of money, the Islamic banking system, and other aspects of setting up a British dominated financial and commerce zone in the area]

One area he also noted was the problem of brigands. In 1739 the first large Russian commercial caravan was sent into Tartary, and this was robbed by the Kirghiz tribe, prior to its arrival at Tashkent. It was just not infidel Russian caravans that were at risk, with a large Khivan caravan being looted on its return from Russia. These two examples were but isolated examples of the brigandage common to the place. Only the most heavily armed caravans, or those cavalcades prepared to pay heavy tolls and bribes, could transverse the area. The expense of this made the products brought in by them so costly, that only the wealthy could buy their merchandise.

Many sources were consulted; the most creditable being the Hindoo, Jews, Parsee and Muhammadan merchants who had already penetrated to most parts of the region in question and had also brought out of it a fair estimate of its treasures. Among those treasures was alum, which is used in leather tanning and for medicinal uses, culinary practices and as a skin whitener popular in India. Also available was agate, asbestos, coal, copper, gold, nitre, salt, and sulphur. The astute reader will note that contained in this list is all that is needed to produce gunpowder; which is produced by the competing Khans, but never in large quantities and often of inferior quality. The making of weaponry is limited to small arms, and all types of archaic edged weapons. The last cannons were said to have been cast in Samarkand some centuries prior; and French made 8 pounder cannons were laboriously dragged to Bokhara at a price equal to nearly three tons of tea.

> *Many of the cannons in Tartary are from the foundry of Tophane, the Ottoman armory in Istanbul, but there are pieces from every country that has every made a cannon. Due to the expense of casting iron, carved stone balls are commonly used still while those cannons which are cast are made of reinforced copper, brass or bronze*

> I am indebted to Major Gaspard Drouville[19] for this insight

Also produced in large quantities are, cereals, cotton, dyes, flax, hemp, millet, pulses, rice, sesame, tobacco, copious fruits to include grapes and from that wine, and swan's down. The greatest items from the area in terms of bulk are leather goods, cattle and horses.

They are in need of tea, sugar, pottery, textiles, woolen goods, manufacturers of all things, metal goods and all manner of scientific instruments and clocks.

Regrettably, in the past, the Empire had held to a mercantile vision for our colonies. Our economy had to be self-contained, and in bygone times this caused us to be discredited in the world markets. Instead we now are champions of the progressive theory of free trade, in which all the markets and trade of the world will move about in English bottoms {*ships*}, unrestricted by tariffs and government limitations and constraints. Great Britain is the mistress of the world's oceans and has the means to dispense commerce as it should be, and our industry is producing much that all men want. Is it not possible that in time, the rest of the nations will grant to us unchallenged domination of the world's business? I believe this is possible, but we must gain access to every corner before this can be achieved. One corner that is blind to our trade is Central or Independent Tartary.

The merchants of Independent Tartary, enamoured of British products, or so was the hope and belief. Illustration III-AS-4

Which Rivers Are Navigable And Suitable In Supporting Markets?

The Oxus is considered, according to the Mosaic and Mohammedan accounts, to be one of the places where the Garden of Eden may have been. The Jaxartes and Oxus were considered by the latter to have been two of the rivers than ran into Adam's paradise.

Our interest in the Oxus is such that its availability to transport the commerce of the world must be explored. From a military perspective, we must consider the possibility that the river known to run from northwest to south east points like a dagger towards India, and if used to convey Russian military supplies, could prove most dangerous to our situation in India. Additionally, it has been noted that Woods has already conquered the Indus with his steam craft[20].

The Jaxartes[21] River will be beyond our reach in this expedition, but its banks will be reached by the expedition after this.

As the English like to imagine Independent Tartary's benefiting from British trade. III-AS-5

Horses For Use With The Indian Army

In Independent Tartary, the horse is of supreme importance to the native, and there are a number of breeds in that area of interest to the British and Company Army. The most common breeds are the Argamak, Karabair, Kirghiz, Kokhandi, and the Uzbek. The first of these come from Arab stock and are fine animals, but this breed, although fast, lacks endurance and will not take the harness well. A good cavalry horse for use on the central plains, the Karabair is a mix between the Argamak and the Kirghiz which we will consider next and has the characteristics of both; the Kirghiz, which is the majority breed, is a tough well-legged horse, resistant to disease and fatigue. The excellent qualities of the Kirghiz horse have led to a proposal to use it for our cavalry remounts. The Kokhandi is a breed of the Kirghiz and also held in high esteem, but is rarer and more costly.

The Uzbek is a smaller, but much stronger horse, well adapted to travel, but is not considered suitable for war; being somewhat unreliable in situations involving the noise, frightfulness and chaos of war. It is estimated that there is more horseflesh in Central Asia than the combined horse populations of France and Great Britain. Such a reserve of cavalry supremacy cannot be allowed to fall into the hands of the Russian Cossacks and their regular cavalry regiment. It is said that even today the Russian Chevalier Guard regiment use only the Argamak horses exclusively, despite the cost and difficulty of securing them.

To the east, nearer Afghanistaun, one finds the much-esteemed Kataghani breed; so well thought of in Afghanistaun, that succeeding rulers have refused to allow their exportation, their breed being reserved to the service of that ruler's cavalry. Of the other breeds that could be of value also, the Badakhshan are notable for their stamina and might be serviceable as horses for the artillery. Zangskar ponies would also serve well with irregular cavalry.

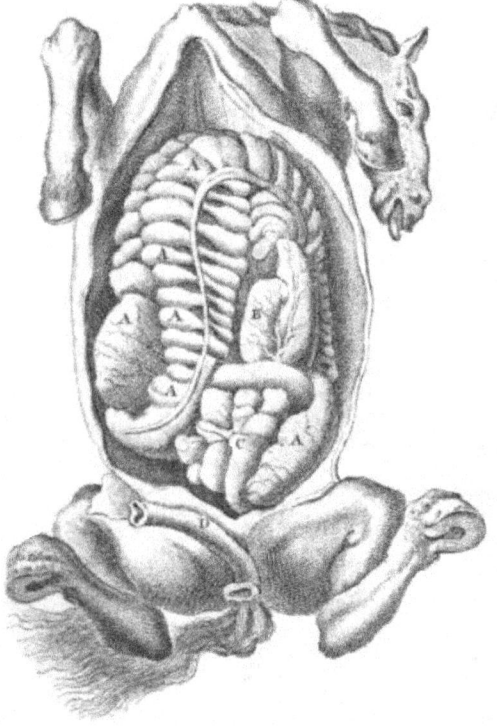

Perkins used this drawing to elucidate on various speculations about the 'internal operations' of a Tartar's horse that was thought to be different from others. Illustration III-AS-6

[Editor's note; I have deleted several pages on the myth then held by many in the west as truth that Central Asian horses could live on meat and had a different digestive system – horses can eat meat but most of the nutrient value passes through just like when we eat grass]

Conclusion

The Russians will, in our opinion, continue their steady advance to the frontier of India. They will, sooner or later, be in such a position to allow them to threaten our possession by an invasion from the northwest. In the eventually that England is embroiled in a European war or will not be willing to give in to the Russian desire to own Constantinople, then Russia will be able to open a front against England's Indian Empire.

[Editor's note: Driscol didn't view an advance into Central Asia by Russia with anything but the deepest suspicion but he did support the Czarist advance into Caucasus if it were to free the Christian Georgian and Armenian people from the Muslim yoke.

Driscol and Perkins didn't have access to the Indian Sanskrit records concerning Central Asia, nor the Chinese histories of their dominance and explorations of the region, and what they knew about the Aral Sea; these would not become widely known until later 19th century scholarship found them]

<u>End of the Father Brennan's document</u>

A Russian Grenadier of the Guard one of the fearsome Russians thought by the British to be bearing down on their outposts in India. The Russians did arrive at the boundaries of what had once been Imperial India - in 1980. Illustration III-AS-7

Appendix Supplement One notes:

1. "Company:" The Honourable East India Company, also known as the East India Company or more commonly as 'John Company', the EIC, HEIC or simply the 'Company'. A commercial company created by royal charter but not owned or directly controlled by the British Government. Its shareholders were, for the most part, drawn from the British political elite, and it actions supported the crown whenever possible. While initially concerned only with trade, it came to control vast territories, starting in 1757 until it was dissolved in 1874.

2. "Independent Tartary:" The idea of Central Asia as a distinct region of the world was only introduced in 1843 by the geographer Alexander von Humboldt. Prior to that, the area was ill defined. Driscol referred to it as Independent Tartary or sometimes Central Asia and we will follow his designations. The Russians of the time referred to it as 'Middle Asia'. The Russian viewed their exploration and expansion in the same way as the Americans did under the 'manifest destiny', but they called it the *stremlenie na vostok* the 'Drive to the East'. This expedition occurred prior to establishment of what would come to be known as the 'Great Game', a nomenclature assigned to it by Arthur Conolly, who would write about it to Sir Henry Rawlinson, in 1839

3. "Political and Secret Department of the East India Company:" Was a gentleman's name for an early form of an intelligence organization that used merchants, explorers, travellers, spies and diplomats to obtain information about those countries, and native princes, outside the present control of The Honorable East India Company, which it has an interest in. It was set up to administrate or advise the company on what actions to take in regards to the information it obtained

4. "Alexander Burnes:" From Driscol's notebook #3, he appears to have had a copy of that letter, but the envelope I was directed to in his papers contained only a torn heading, and a note from the unknown editor that it was missing. It doesn't show up in the papers of either Hamilton or McNeill. Burnes was an earlier player in the Great Game, the tussle over Central Asia by England and Russia. His views were valued, but he was lost early in life, being killed in Kabul in 1841 at the age of 36

5. "Wilson's seminal work:" Driscol is referring to Robert Wilson's paper titled, *A sketch of the Military and Political power of Russia in the year 1817*, published in the Quarterly Review of that year

6. "Uzboj:" Now called the Uzboy it dried up in the 17th century, causing the destruction of the riverine civilization on its banks. The river for reasons unknown, but most probably seismic, caused an uplifting of the land that shut off the river from its former channel. The flow was redirected by nature's hand into the Aral Sea

7. "It:" The Uzboy flowed some four hundred and sixty miles to the Caspian Sea from a lake, but it was the Sarykamysh Lake, which is formed well south of the Aral Sea by the Oxus River

8. "Oxus:" The river was known by many names to the Greeks. It was the Oxos to the Romans and British, to the Arabs it was the Jayhoun, to the Persians the Amudaryo from the name of the city Amul and the Persian word for river, to the Afghanis the Gozan, the ancient Indians knew it as the Vaksu River and in the modern world we call it the Amu Darya

9. "France:" Use of that phrase points to the writer being Driscol and reflected his distrust of France, the country of Napoleon, that his father had fought against and developed a dislike for in fighting against them for many years. At the same time, Driscol admired its culture, especially its food and people with great intensity; a classic love hate relationship

10. "Phantasmagoria of the pit:" The French revolution, the other name was a common reference to it in British thought, and reflected the middle and upper classes revulsion of it

11. "Rioni:" Known to the Greeks as the Cyrus and Phasis Rivers

12. "Georgia:" Parts of Georgia and Armenia were already freed of Ottoman and Persian influence at the time of this writing, but complete removal from Muslim control would take place well after the period these volumes cover

13. "Sicilian vespers:" A series of famous massacres: the first, the Armagnac massacres, were in 1418 and of a political nature between Burgundian and Armagnacs and led to the overthrow of the Armagnacs. The second, Joshua's slaughter of Amalekites in the Bible by God's command in 2 Samuel 15:2-8 and the third, the Sicilian Vespers, was the successful rebellion by Sicilians against a despotic French King

14: "Two camps:" In retrospect, Driscol may have been referring to the two main streams of thought on the matter, what would be called the 'forward policies' and the 'backwards' or 'masterly inactivity' policy and their supporters: the former to do aggressive actions like the expedition, while the latter group would prefer to do nothing and let the matter resolve itself

15: "Tartar duplicity:" He is referring to the destruction of the Russian army in 1717, when it attempted to advance on Khiva, he and this army were slaughtered by ruse and deceit

16. "Philip Johann von Stralenberg:" The Swedish and Russian crowns were involved in the Great Northern War, 1700-1721 at this time and he was prisoner for some years

17. "Nicolas Maison:" French ambassador to Russia, 1832-1835, this is 1st Marquis Maison, Nicolas Joseph Maison, and former Marshal of France and Minister of War

18. "Moorcroft, Grant, Christie and Pottinger:" Earlier British explorers of Persia, Baluchistan and Central Asia, their expeditions were a mixture of success and disaster

19. "Major Gaspard Drouville:" The Major was a French, mercenary, officer in the service of the Czar, who assisted the British trainers in Persia. This information seems to have come to Driscol or Perkins by letter or hearsay

20. "Steam craft:" Lieutenant John Wood had explored the Indus River in October 1835 using a ten horsepower steamboat

21. "The Jaxartes:" This river was also known as the Sayhoun, Yaxartes, Sirdaryo and in modern terms the Syr Darya

Appendix Supplement Two

The magazine article that follows covers the unexpected arrival of Master Driscol at the 52nd Regiment barracks. His arrival there has been the subject of several articles, which are listed in the index. This interest in Driscol's early life was caused by his later celebrity and notoriety. Driscol never made mention of the first day, other than to note the outcome, and not how it did occur. Later his mother, Mary Margaret Christensen Driscol would, in 1837, write to her relatives in Denmark, and she related many details of the auspicious turn of events. The key piece of information came from a PhD dissertation, presented at Victoria University of Manchester in the year 1931, by Joseph James Brennan *{A nephew of Father Brennan}*, which made a connection between one of the men in the Commander's office that day and the infamous Thomas Pitt, 2nd Baron of Camelford; known then and now as the 'Half-mad' Lord. Within it was cited the newspaper included below.

In some cases, conversation and descriptions have been added, to explain the comings and goings of the main characters in the story. I have combined all the sources mentioned above into an adaptation of the original Blackwood's magazine article, which was 90% accurate. All the footnotes are modern.

BLACKWOOD'S

Edinburgh

MAGAZINE.

VOL. CXIII.

JANUARY—JUNE, 1873.

AMERICAN EDITION—VOLUME LXXVI.

NEW YORK:

PUBLISHED BY THE LEONARD SCOTT PUBLISHING COMPANY,
140 FULTON ST., BETWEEN BROADWAY AND NASSAU ST.

—

1873.

WHAT CONSTITUTES A GENTLEMAN?

A remembrance on the matter in the form of a short essay with recollections of the words said. While much of the conversation had to be reconstructed from letters, and forty year old memories, it is thought to be as accurate as can be achieved so long after the event. The primary source for the reconstruction of what occurred is an account of the incident recorded by the daughter of the Adjutant that day, who remembered her father telling the story many, many times during his life.

TO SET THE SCENE

A lovely day at Custume Barracks in Athlone, Ireland in 1836

The commander of the Regiment was at his desk in earnest discussion about the cares of the day, the pending death of the King, the ascension of his young niece Victoria and the more important matters of the running of the Regiment.

A discreet knock drew the Adjutant to the closed door, from where he returned with a message in hand.

The animated conversation touched on the care of the officer's horses, the failings of the commissary and finally coming to momentary respite.

The Adjutant spoke, 'Sir this note has arrived for you at the front gate, it is from a former Sergeant Major of the Regiment, one Driscol'.

'DRISCOL'! Both the commander and another of the officers, a Captain who had served longer than any other in the Regiment and in his late forties, pronounced this as if the word was Christmas and they young boys.

'Let us see' said the commander, he took the note from the Adjutant in some haste and despite being ten years younger than the elderly Captain, the Lieutenant Colonel had some difficulty in finding a distance that he could read the small printed message.

As he read he related the contents to the other men in the chamber.

'He is well and hopes that the Regiment is well quartered and content with being in Ireland. He's sent his youngest son to us to enlist'.

The elder Captain, smiled, 'I'll have him for my company if you please, Sir'.

A younger Captain in the room, queried, 'who sir was Driscol'?

'Oh, well you have not heard the name then, Francis', referring to the elderly Captain, 'and I were young Ensigns when he was our top Sergeant. Saved my life on occasion and taught me my duties and responsibilities. He kept us on pace when we charged at Waterloo. By Jupiter that was a hot day'.

'Indeed', replied the younger Captain, 'then his sons should be of good blood then'.

The Adjutant cleared his throat 'ahem sir, our rolls are full sir, please remember the circular put out....'

'Yes, yes, call the Sergeant Major in if you please Adjutant'.

The sentry was sent for and the Adjutant sent him off to find the Regiment's key man.

The younger Captain continued, 'he had but the one son'?

'No, he and his wife, a Danish woman, lovely person, had a number of sons, well before our disagreement with Boney.' The Colonel thought for a moment, 'he retired most honourably in '22 or 23 if I recall.'

'1823, Sir, remember just before the Regiment was to be sent to Nova Scotia,' said the elder Captain.

'Yes, that was a cold and miserable time, was it not, yes he had served over thirty years, and retired most honorably to Manchester I believe'.

'Did he lose those sons, or why did they not grace us with their enlistment'?

'Well, as I hear it, they went to India I believe, but here comes the Sergeant Major'.

'SIR'?

'Sergeant Major, do you remember Driscol, Colour Sergeant Driscol. He also held your position also'? Stated the Colonel.

A rare smile came to the grim features of the Regimental Sergeant Major, 'but of course sir, I was but a drummer boy and he had my position for a while, until he went back to Colour Sergeant. Has the Regiment heard from him? I do hope it is not hard news'?

'The news is good, very good, yes, his son is at the gate and he has sent in a note from his father to request he be enlisted in the Regiment'.

The Sergeant Major nodded his agreement and added, 'It would be good to have another Driscol'.

The Adjutant peered disapprovingly at the Sergeant Major, who returned the silent admonishment in a way only a senior Non-commissioned officer can, when corrected by a staff officer.

'We're full up Sir, but we can certainly put him on the set aside list. If we have a run of fever, or are ordered overseas, we may have a spot open up. If not, it may be a year or so before he can take the King's shilling'.

'I'll give him a good meal in the Sergeant's canteen and a tour of the barracks with the corporal of the guard' said the Sergeant Major; eager to get at the boy and find out how Angus Driscol, his old mentor, was.

'Well done Sergeant Major, but send him here first. I'd like to see the boy and find out what Driscol has been up to myself. I last heard from him a few years ago, in regards to his response to those scandalous letters in the Times about what happened when Maitland stopped the French Guards[1]'.

'Yes he was always a quiet man about himself. Let us drain this boy for all he knows'.

The younger Captain in an aside the older, 'If he's any good I may have to fight you for him dear Francis'.

'Sword or pistol'?

'Nay, a hand of whist perhaps? With Dauber and Shaffer[2]'?

'Done and you bring the claret'.

The front gate was some distance away and during the interim, the conversation drifted to the possibilities of war, the younger men thinking a blow up with Russia was on the cards, while the older men held true to fearing a renewal of French aggression. The recent affaire of the coup d'état by Prince Louis-Napoleon, son of Napoleon's brother, Louis, King of Holland, to overthrown the French monarch was noted as a sign of French uncertainty and of war in the future.

'Francis', said the Colonel, 'if war comes to us, will you join us on campaign'?

'Of course sir, it would be my joy and duty'.

'Perhaps', the commander said, 'you would consider staying behind and command the depot'?

'Sir, no I must disagree, I've been most diligent in having my company well trained for this very opportunity'.

'And so they are', replied the Colonel, 'I believe our new Captain', referring to the younger Captain who had purchased his commission in the Regiment last year, 'would agree'.

'Most assuredly', said the younger Captain, despite his not liking to say it, sir, his company is the best drilled, his Sergeants are chocked full of vigour and his Lieutenants are examples of zeal. However, once I have resolved the matter of Ensign Mumpsimus[3]. I shall challenge his position as top company'.

At that name, the cast of every officer in the room darkened – a cold silence reigned for a moment, then the Commander continued.

'Francis, you should consider my proposal, we'll need skilled reinforcements and you are the man to do it, and also who else could we trust the Regiment's correspondence and accounts to? War is for the young Francis, plus what would Amelia and your daughters do if you go overseas? Perhaps also, if the war is prolonged, we'll need to raise another battalion, you'd be our man for that too'. He added hastily at the end, 'You might get a Brevet Majority[4] to do that'.

Francis thought for a moment, nodded and said, 'I shall study it Sir. I shall, but it will gall me greatly to see the Regiment march off to war without me being with you'.

'We must all do our duty to England'. Said the Colonel with some gravity in his voice.

Francis looked at all the officers, 'it will be your duty to deal with our enemies in the field, while I guard the eggs, and go home to a warm bed each night'.

A wave of laughter rang through the room.

At this moment the Corporal of the Guard announced his presence, by coming to attention, and slamming his boot on the floor.

'SIR, the Sergeant Major ordered me to bring this civilian to your office'.

'Very good, carry on Sergeant.'

The Corporal did so hoping that the Commander's inadvertent mistake in stating his rank was a portent of a promotion in the future.

Hat in hand, a well-dressed young man, tall, thin, with thinner blonde hair, and the wisp of a moustache, came into the room. Unexpectantly, he came to a perfect rendition of attention, and stated in a voice full of emotion.

'Reporting as ordered Sir'!

The Commander rose to his feet and put his hands on his hips, a poise he made when addressing the troops.

'Be at ease young man, you aren't in the service…yet, have a seat and tell us of your father, and yourself'.

The young man had been well trained by his father, and the idea of breaking the position of attention, while in the lofty proximity of a Lieutenant Colonel, and taking a seat as if he was about to chat with his aunts, left him motionless.

'Come, come to it lad take a seat'. Said the Colonel as he sat himself down.

'That's an order laddie', the Colonel was a Sussex man, but had recently taken up aspects of a Scotsman's speech, but not without adding another log to the fire of his oddities, that irked and annoyed his men and officers, despite their begruntled respect and affection for him.

'Yes sir'. He sat gingerly, fearful that he might break some unknown regulation or ordinance in doing so.

'Your name'.

'David Sir, David Driscol.'

'I see your mother in your face'.

'And his father in his frame', added the older Captain.

'Yes indeed, when were you born'?

'September 20th', then realizing the answer was insufficient he added quickly, '1817'.

'Tell us of your father and mother, David'. He pointed to elderly Captain Francis Webb, 'knew him in the Regiment, as did the Sergeant Major. Did you meet the Sergeant Major'?

'Yes Sir, I gave him my father's note'.

'Two notes I see, may I inquire as to what the differences in the notes were'? The colonel was suspicious of all things in his regiment, not so much as wishing to know everything but desiring to be able to acknowledge it and happily dismiss it as beyond his concern.

'The note asked about a number of men my father had known and how they fared'.

'And how did they fare?'

'Half are dead, a quarter retired, and the rest still in the Regiment'.

'Now tell us what your father has been up to this decade past'.

'He has done well Sir; my brothers are all honestly employed[5]. The tavern and inn do well as does the farm and industries our family has interests in'.

'Where has Driscol been up to this at'?

'Around the town of Eccles in Lancashire, near Manchester town'.

'His health'? Inquired Francis

'Excellent sir he was going to journey with me here but the concerns of business kept him at home'.

'You walked from Manchester'?

'Yes Sir, when not on the boat of course'.

The Adjutant noted to the younger Captain, The Honourable Vincent Rollingston-Smythe, in Latin, '*velocius quam asparagi coquantur*,' and added in English, 'not an easy journey for such young man'.

David turned to them and replied, although the comment was not directed at him, 'not that quickly gentleman it took four days and was *sine metu*'.

All the officers looked at one another, young working class men rarely speak Latin and they knew well the road and sea voyage from their barracks to Manchester; to take the journey in four days was a hard pace on foot.

'It would seem that you did well in your studies', said the Colonel.

'I did as best as I could'.

'You can read and write then', asked the commander; for a soldier who could read and write was rare in that day and age, and many a good sergeant was limited by his inability to do a report or read a message sent in battle.

'Of course sir', he said with a bit of a nervous grin.

'Not that we would doubt the word of a Driscol, but one must clarify the point in regards to your future duties'.

The Colonel turned to his bookcase, for this Colonel was no Guardsman and he read much on the topics of the day. He plucked from the neat stacks some poetry, poor stuff he thought, some translated French doggerel his wife had gifted to him and which he had not touched. He split the book open without a concern as to what it had opened on and handed the leather-bound book to the waiting young man, read from the top please.

The boy stood, shuffled his feet, coughs and began but fear had quieted his voice and they could but hear '...... the respected forgery...'

He coughed and began again but with a much stronger voice

'*Sans crainte du pressoir, le pampre tout l'été*'

After this line he closed the book and recited

'Boit les doux présents de l'aurore;
Et moi, comme lui belle, et jeune comme lui,
Quoi que l'heure présente ait de trouble et d'ennui,
Je ne veux point mourir encore[6]*'*.

He stood for a moment and handed the book back to the Colonel who glanced briefly at the contents.

'The book is a translation of French poems', he stated to no one in particular.

'By Chénier, his La Jeune Captive, but I didn't like the translation; I hope you don't mind my finishing it in French it sounds much better that way'.

'Not at all, you know it by heart'?

'Yes one of his best pieces, Sir' he added.

Captain Webb spoke up, 'Well, Mr Driscol you have surprised us, and you have hold of Latin and French what other languages have you mastered'?

'Mastered sir, none, but I can read and speak French, German, Danish and some Russian'.

Captain Rollingston-Smythe sat forward in his chair, 'Russian you say, how did you come by that'?

'My mother's family are Danish and have traded in the Baltic for many years – I learned from my Uncles and Aunts, who have dealing with them and two of my Aunts speak Russian being that they are of that race'.

'You can read that abomination they call an alphabet'?

'Cyrillic, yes Sir'.

'Astounding'.

'We accept that you are well educated then'? Said the Colonel looking at the other officers.

'I would like to think so, my father, mother and brothers were very determined that I receive a full and complete education'.

'In what areas are you best'?

'History is my favorite, less so maths, and of course military studies'.

'Military studies you say, what learning do you have there'?

'I've read General Clausewitz and all the British and French manuals on the service subjects'.

'Good lord' tittered, the Colonel, 'and what did you learn from Mr Clausewitz'?

David responded quickly, 'That war is unpredictable and one must plan for the unexpected'?

'Gracious and did you father teach you all a soldier needs to know'?

'Much of it, but I admit to lacking experience.'

'A moment', The Colonel called for the sentry and directed him to give his musket to the young man, who had remaining standing after his recitation.

He took it up in the correct manner and shouldered it properly.

'Can you present arms then to rest'?

'SIR' David proceed to do so, as his father would say, sharply, and crashed the musket butt down, glancing off his thin shoes but he held the twinge of pain well and carried the manoeuver off like he had done it a thousand times before – which he had.

'Well done, well done' said the Adjutant; a man well versed in his drill.

Captain Rollingston-Smythe piped in, 'What is the marching pace of the light infantry'?

'140 paces sir'.

'What is the coverage of a full strength company assigned the role of piquet'?

'450-900 yards sir, depending on the lie of the land, weather and time of day, Sir'.

'What is a Petard and what is its use'?

'A bomb of 6 of pounds black powder for blowing open gates and doors, Sir'.

'What is the bulge call to tell the men to gather at a designated place'?

'Assembly, Sir'.

'In a fight how does the light infantry differ from a line regiment'?

'We skirmish by fighting in pairs, so that one soldier can cover the other while loading while the others fire from formation by volley…Sir'.

'CAPITAL, well-done' said all three Captains, for the Adjutant was also a Captain, for they were amazed as the questions had been answered as quickly as they had been asked. Captain Webb had in particular swelled with pride when the young man had said, 'we' instead of, 'the' light infantry.

'Dauber and Shaffer don't now half of that', said Captain Webb.

'By Jove', returned Captain Rollingston-Smythe, 'they don't know any of it'.

All three nodded their heads together with an acknowledgement from the Colonel.

The Colonel had watched in silence, for the truth to be told, he hadn't known the answers to a number of the items himself.

'Ah, the Sergeant Major is here again, go with him master Driscol and he will feed you well, and when you depart, I'll have a message for you at the guard house to take back home to your father'.

David hesitated, for he had intended to stay and enter service.

The Colonel saw in his face the disappointment and quickly added. 'The Sergeant Major will explain our situation in the regiment it may be a year or more before we can take you on roster, with your legacy we would take you this day if we could, can you wait'?

David regained a full smile and could only nod. He returned, with a flourish, the musket he had been given, and moved to leave with the Sergeant Major, but he turned back on his heels and thanked all the officers for their time, in a way that would have brought great pride to his mother who had worked tirelessly on his manners.

Captain Webb spoke after David marched off, 'a remarkable young man wouldn't you say'?

'Yes, yes he will be an excellent soldier and perhaps even an outstanding non-commissioned officer'.

It was at this moment that fate strode into that room in Ireland, in the fickle guise that it had taken on for that day. The messenger made his rounds to the barracks and headquarters, carrying returns, orders, and the other flotsam and jetsam of the British Army of that day. One envelope was from the Commander, Scots Fusilier Guards and addressed to Commander of the 52nd by name.

The light infantry rarely if ever heard from a Guards regiment, so this letter was the first to meet the Adjutant's eye, while sorting the messages on the commanding officer's desk, and he handed it to him with some small gesture to indicate its importance.

'My, what would the lofty Guards want with us'? The Colonel said with a great deal of mockery in his voice.

Captain Rollingston-Smythe, who had relatives in the Guards and who, but for a slight indiscretion while on holiday at Spa, would have been too. He noted yet again the Commanding officer's affront to his social superiors and he felt it also to him in particular. The 52nd had had a number of peers of the realm in its ranks over the years and it still did; he made a note to complain once more about this to the Colonel – in private.

The Commander in question had opened the letter with a sterling knife; made for that purpose by a Maharashtra soonar[7]. He read a moment then let his hands and the letter thump down on the desk with a sign of distress, signaled to all by his twist of the head, and biting his lower lip. He never took

the Lords name in vain but he was close to fracturing that vow in this moment.

The Adjutant spoke first, 'may I ask what the difficulty is Sir'?

'The first line of the letter is in regards to Ensign Mumpsimus'.

Every man in office was well aware of the difficulties this officer had inflicted on the regiment; one noted for its most excellent mess[8] and its lively atmosphere.

Rollingston-Smythe said, 'what has the right bastard done now'?

'Captain Smythe', said the Commander, 'I'll not have you using such language about an officer of the regiment, even if his mother was probably a French hedge whore[9] and his father an ill-tempered Yorkshire lout'.

The Adjutant and Captain Webb had some silent amusement from the latest barrage in the war between the commander and captain, to whom the young Ensign belonged. He having purchased his commission last year, from a man who had transferred to India, and he had plagued the Captain with his injudiciousness and personal failings since then.

'However…. I read only the first line; I fear to read on as he probably shot one of the Guards' officer's wives or buggered the Colonel's horse'.

The Adjutant too had spent a large part of his time in correspondence dealing with the creditors, bailiffs, enraged officers, abused clergy and other petty officials that the Ensign had clashed with. Some men rode to hounds, some hunted, some fished, but Ensign Mumpsimus started quarrels with officials and tradesmen.

'Sir, should I deal with it'? Offered the Adjutant.

'If you would please….let me know if we need to convene a Court-Martial'. Said the Colonel with some venom as he cast the offending letter onto his desk.

Captain Rollingston-Smythe spoke up, 'sir, perhaps this latest incident will give us the opportunity to send the young gentleman on his way'?

The Commanding officer looked at the Captain and only smiled. 'Our mutual friend, the Ensign, is a cousin of some very powerful men. They are aware of his, shall we say, flaws, they are looking to us to bring the young man around so that he recognises his responsibilities and duties. In this we shall continue to the best of our abilities'.

'Sir, with all respect, he is less than worthless, unless the regiment needs a shiftless, quarrelsome, drunk'.

The Commander and the Captain had had this conversation many times and by convention the Colonel ended it by a slight rise of his hand.

'I understand your concern Captain Smythe'. Again, thought the Captain, he doesn't use my name properly, 'but we must carry on, so if you would please stop all that rot and we'll proceed. Personally I take no pleasure in keeping this man in the regiment BUT I know the extent of the patronage behind him. We imperil our careers if we move against him. I believe that if we are patient, the man will either grow up quickly, or take such actions that will deliver him out of our care'.

The Adjutant spoke; 'you are right once again Colonel'.

'Oh how is that'. He looked at the Adjutant, 'Did he indeed bugger the Guard regiment's mascot'?

The letter, which he had deftly plucked from the Colonel's desk, was now read and the Adjutant summarised the contents, 'Sir it is from the Guards to inform us that Ensign Mumpsimus is now Captain Mumpsimus of the Scots Fusilier Guards'.

'WHAT, he has not spoken with me on the subject of the selling of his commission, not even he can purchase another commission and sell his position here without my permission, or that of the Colonel of Regiment. Who the blazes has he sold it to, some London high boy with a desire for a whiff of country air'?

'Sir I'm sorry to inform you that your objection is not well placed'.

Captain Rollingston-Smythe stated firmly, 'let him go Sir we have no need of his type'.

'It is not done, not done at all, no gentleman would do this', replied the Colonel to his desk which he thumped to accent his anger.

Captain Rollingston-Smythe, 'he was no gentleman sir'.

The commander glared briefly at the Captain but refrained from escalating to a conniption fit.

Captain Webb spoke now to the Adjutant who had learned not to try to get a word in edgewise when the Colonel and the Captain were discussing the man in question. 'Adjutant, you said the Colonel's objection was wrong. What did you mean'?

The Adjutant and Captain Webb carried on a conversation while the Colonel and Captain Rollingston-Smythe argued over the Ensign, the rights of the regiment, tradition and custom versus the good of the regiment.

The Adjutant replied, 'The Colonel and the other Captain are engaged, you look like you wish to say more? For he had not heard what Webb had said'.

Webb repeated himself.

'Yes, the solution to the problem is in the second paragraph'.

With those words, the bickering between the Colonel and Captain subsided.

'Solution, there can be no solution; an officer cannot purchase a commission in another regiment without permission of the losing regiment, that has been the custom since the time of William and Mary'. Restated the angry Colonel.

'That is true sir, but the letter states it clearly, I also find it hard to believe that Ensign Mumpsimus would do this, but then he is no stranger to folly, and he has abandoned our commission'.

'He did what'? Said the two Captains together.

'He has abandoned our commission and returned it to the regiment, along with all the fittings in his quarters, and all manner of things'.

Captain Rollingston-Smythe was smiling now, 'but can he do that? I had not heard of a man doing that before'.

'Usually a Commission is sold by Harrington and Company[10] but in rare cases', said the Adjutant, 'if the man has no known relatives, or he so states that he wishes it, the commission reverts to the regiment. He probably did so to avoid having to get permission from us. By this way, we cannot block it'.

Captain Webb, 'so Mumpsimus has just given up the Commission, does he not lose its value'?

'Yes, my understanding is that we, us, the regiment now own it'.

Captain Webb stated in a tone of complete disbelief, 'But that Commission would have been worth two hundred pounds, good Lord, how could he do that?' So said a man, who during his military life had never had more than five pounds in his pocket, or entire personal fortune. He found this news unbelievable. The result of his poverty had left him a Captain for three decades, because he couldn't afford the cost of purchasing a Majority.

'Tis more like three hundred pounds these days', stated the Adjutant.

'Three hundred', remarked Captain Webb, 'A fortune! How could he do that? He had many things wrong with him, but he wasn't COMPLETELY mad'.

The Colonel leaned back in his chair. 'I suspect he disliked us, as much as we detested him, and if I recall, he had a substantial private income'.

The Adjutant interjected, 'I believe he, or should I say his father, made some five thousand pounds a year from rents'.

'Five thousand pounds', said Captain Webb still struggling to get the figure of three hundred from his mind.

Captain Rollingston-Smythe stated loudly, 'I can say with some certainty that his family income was well over thirty thousand pounds last year'.

'Good Lord', was all that Captain Webb could reply, which he did several times, each repetition growing softer, shaking his head with each voiced objection.

'So', the Colonel spread his arms, 'Adjutant we need confirmation of this absquatulation[11] by the Ensign'.

'I'll go to London on the morrow and deal with it personally as I know the head clerk who deals with such matters'.

'Thank you Adjutant', for the Colonel was aware of the many duties that beleaguered all Adjutants and especially his. He recalled his own time as an Adjutant as nothing more than a frenzy of activity, punctuated by errors that irked him to this day. What had his commander described it as, oh yes, he had said that he, the Colonel, then a newly minted Captain had shown more action and agitation than a courtyard full of Spanish officers who'd heard the wine wagon had been lost to enemy fire.

'Well, assuming that the punitive expedition by the Adjutant does well, we will be faced with not having the problem of Ensign Dunderhead[12]'. Said Captain Rollingston-Smythe with some happiness.

'We will need to arrange for a replacement for Ensign Mumpsimus', said the Colonel.

The Adjutant was a man who thought fast on his feet, which was why he was the Adjutant, a dull, inactive, man did not long survive in this position. A thought had occurred to him. For the Adjutant, while outwardly always concerned for the wellbeing of the Regiment and its officers and men, held another point of view surreptitiously, so closely held was this, that he himself didn't consciously acknowledge it. He was always concerned about his own future promotion, and as he was now a Captain, and would soon want to move up, the last thing he wanted was another officer buying into the Regiment, who would compete with him for the rare Major's position. The idea bursts into his mind like a mad thing, ran around a bit, and then presented itself as a viable possibility. What better way to prevent another extraneous officer coming into the regiment, a challenge to him! Undeniably it would, by a small fraction, lubricate his way to the Colonelcy.

He had thought of his cousin Harper, yes he would do fine, a gentleman, in good condition and a small private income, and looking for something to do. A bit of light infantry would do him good. Fortunately his sword as they say wasn't particularly sharp, nor did he have a lot of money. Once in the Regiment he'd be hard pressed to raise the money to buy a Lieutenancy, a Captaincy then a Majority. Besides, he would be beholden to his cousin for having obtained the position for him – for a low price too.

Sometimes the Adjutant just loved himself, which he did very much at that moment. He would become a hero to his greater family, gift the regiment with a fairly good officer and in particular, one who would be no threat to him. Ensign Mumpsimus had been a threat, for that man could have bought the Colonelcy with a snap of his fingers. He was now finished and for that, the Adjutant was doubly glad.

He quickly saw his chance, and the way to bring it to fruition, was through Captain Webb. The Captain was not only no threat to him, but he was also a man who could be relied on to go where he was directed; even if he didn't know he was being directed to what he might think was his own initiative. Captain Webb knew his cousin and had discussed at one time selling his Captaincy to him, or to anyone else who might want it, but it had only been the good Captain's flirtation with retirement. He couldn't do it for he lacked the money and he had yet to wean himself off his love for the regiment.

'Captain Webb, Francis, I meant to ask, the Driscol boy, his father's background was?' for it was his plan to use this question as a pathway to bringing up the name of his cousin Harper.

At that moment, a change came over the older officer, the annoyance; impertinence of the unexpected news from the Scots Fusilier Guards was gone. Driscol was back at the table and in this rich and pleasant

feast, the men were more interested in that, than the poor fare provided by Ensign Mumpsimus.

'Irishman but long lived in England wasn't he'? 'Catholic'? The Adjutant ventured.

'Anglo-Irish', Said Captain Webb, 'he and I were in the same company in the Peninsula for some time. He was instrumental in making me Corporal. That was before he was taken under secondment to Major, oh what was his name'?

'Scovell[13]', I believe said the Colonel.

'No, no', continued Webb answering belatedly the Adjutant query on Driscol, 'a true son of the Church of England, but like many in the war rather slack at times in his observance'.

The Adjutant was stymied he'd planned to bring up Harper, who was very Church of England, when Driscol's allegiance to Popery was brought up – but this had not happened, a misfire.

It was at this point, seeing that Captain Webb and the Colonel would soon be joined up in a long discussion of their days in the Peninsula, Captain Rollingston-Smythe made his leave, and went off to attend to his duties, which this day were slight. As he left, the Colonel, as he knew he would, launched into remissions of their glory days in Wellington's army in Spain. The good Captain had heard these tales before and was particularly taken aback by Captain Webb's seeming pride of having risen from the un-imposing rank of Sergeant to an Ensign's commission, due to his bravery in the storming of Badajoz in 1812 followed by an even greater act of heroism in the great battle of Salamanca, where he was given the rank of first, Lieutenant and later, Captain to replace those who had fallen. He was particularly annoyed that Webb as a ranker had been awarded a commission for valour in the field, as he had effectively been granted a pension. It was expected that he would sell his commission on, after a discreet interval, with his being set up for the rest of his life, but Captain Webb had not done that, regrettably. However Vincent {Captain Rollingston-Smythe} had to accept that he did like the old man, his aptitude for whist and his ability to command, were not to be questioned; he was just not a true gentleman.

And Captain Rollingston-Smythe was most correct; for over an hour, the two men went over the old battles, personalities, tragedies, regrets, scandals, wine, dark-eyed ladies and all the other detritus of memory that flowed from their experiences as young men at war.

The Adjutant shuffled his paper for he had heard most of it before, and he knew its course, and when the right phrase came, he planned to pounce and try again to bring up the subject of Harper.

'Excuse me gentleman what did you say'?

'Yes Adjutant', answered the Colonel.

'That last part about your difficulty in Santander[14]'.

Captain Webb explained, 'Oh yes, some of the other Regiments and Corps were taking too much in the way of supplies, our supplies mainly. We were getting very little, so I was dispatched as a shiny new Captain to deal with it, and Sergeant Driscol went with me. To shorten the story, while there, we ran into a horde of grasping officials, authorised looters and men busy, to our eyes, in preventing the army from obtaining their supplies. It was then that Lord Wellington himself came to sort out the mess. He was fortunate that he spoke with Driscol and I, for Driscol gave it to him straight as a rapier and his Lordship responded in kind.

He made Driscol a temporary Colonel of militia, Colonel of the Port of Santander, and gave him written orders to sort it out. He even arranged for a uniform of a sort; something a Don might wear a mixture of gaudy Spanish and Portuguese uniforms and a hat from a German Legionnaire. A great uniform it was, naval lieutenants quelled at its sight, merchant ship masters were known to jump into the sea to avoid a verbal attack from that partial Colonel who inhabited it. Quartermasters learned to run at the boom of his voice, and in two weeks, two weeks I swear, the port was as taut as a drum head To this day I find it remarkable.'

The Adjutant added quickly, 'but Francis you did your part too and I know a man…'

The Captain wouldn't be denied the end of his story and ran right over the Adjutant's attempt to conduct an ambuscade in the support of Harper. 'So I did', said the Captain, 'but it was astonishingly easy to point to "Wellington's creature" and get done what needed to be done, and get it done quickly.'

'So Angus Driscol, in a way, was an officer'? Said the Adjutant, for that piece of information had not come out before.

The Colonel opened his mouth to say something, halted, reconsidered, opened his mouth again, but then rose from his chair and began to pace.

'Francis, this son of Driscol, I was thinking what a fine young officer he would have made'.

Captain Webb snorted, 'He would and I'd take him as my Ensign in a moment, but he is not gentry, we have Dauber and Shaffer, pure gentry, good boys but with little in the way of military knowledge'.

Colonel stopped his pacing, 'that is true, so true'.

The Adjutant, had been thinking he could see another path to his objective, now spoke, 'Sir you know that I'm fastidious about my uniform'.

The Colonel replied, 'you support the families of three tailors, so yes I'd say you were quite an expert in tailors, but what of it'?

'I know clothes and I can say, without reservation that the clothes the boy had on were of top quality, not Savile Row[15], but not far from it. An excellent cut and the finest woolen weave'. He left off his remarks, as if the statement itself would imply what he meant.

The Colonel was slow on the uptake, 'That may be true but how is it germane to the situation? What are we discussing'?

The Adjutant saw his chance for a clever manoeuver, 'If we are speaking of men suited to be an officer, Francis do you remember Harper'?

Captain Webb came alive at this moment rising out of his chair, not an easy task for one of his age, somewhat portly and having suffered five wounds in his day; twice from ball, once each from shell, French bayonet and sabre.

'Gentlemen what did the boy say about his father's holdings'? Asked Francis ignoring the Adjutant's question as a thought had come to him.

'I believe he said he worked in an Inn and did farming'? Said the Colonel.

'I thought he said something about industry'? Said the Adjutant again halted in his attempt to bring up Harper.

'I'm of mind to speak to the boy again, but if as you say, Adjutant his clothes were well made, why would he walk here instead of ride or take the train[16]'?

Captain Webb, thought for a moment, 'I can think of several reason he would not ride; either we are wrong and the family couldn't afford a horse, or his father made him walk to strengthen his legs, a necessity for a light infantryman, it may also be that it was the boy's choice to husband his money and save it for future use instead of on a coach'.

The Colonel nodded while the Adjutant added his thought, 'my cousin Harper, Francis you met him, is fine horseman and he never walks anywhere, dresses well too'.

The Colonel said, 'If he intended to join up this day he'd have had no use for a horse in the light infantry. It would have been an encumbrance to sell it when one lives in a barracks common room'.

The Adjutant raised his voice and repeated, 'Sir about Harper'.

'What, who is Harper? Adjutant summon the sentry'. Then correcting his own command he said, 'True, let us ask the boy, SENTRY', he shouted in a manner not fully acceptable for a commander of the 52nd regiment.

The man appeared in short order and in some haste.

'Go to the Sergeant Major and inform him that Mr Driscol is to come back here before he departs'.

The Sentry presented his musket in salute and turned to go. The Colonel raised his voice to amend the order, 'Let the man finish his time in the Sergeant's mess'.

In due course the Sergeant Major appeared, 'Sir Mr Driscol is at the Guard post awaiting your letter. I have sent the sentry to bring him here'.

'Very good'.

An awkward moment passed, the Sergeant Major, who was not privy to the earlier discussion, was mystified as to why this boy would be needed again by the officers.

The Colonel asked the Sergeant Major, who was standing by the door, what he thought of the young man. 'Do you think he'd be a good Sergeant'?

'A bit thin, Sir, too much learning, I'd say, not enough work, he would be better as a school master, gunner or a sapper, but his hands are rough, so he's used to SOME work. With a bit of employment with us we will make him into superior light infantryman'.

'You don't fully approve of him Sergeant Major'?

'I do and don't – the boy shows promise. He'd be a very fine Sergeant in time but he would probably be dissatisfied if he were not promoted quickly. That delay can sour a man, drive him to drink and irresponsibility, perhaps even to become a heretic; seen it happen in India. Legacy men sometimes feel they deserve a position because their father had one. While in the light infantry only those who show they have zeal and industry is so promoted – while I'm the RSM'.

'And that', said the Adjutant, 'is why we need to speak to the boy again'.

The Sergeant Major was pleased. He never cared much for over educated men; too prissy and thinking all the time. Reading and writing was a needed skill, but poetry, science, or those other things that constituted culture, were not needed in his world. In his world, discipline and training in the military art was what was needed and he knew education didn't provide that. However, as the lad was Driscol's son, he would make him into a good soldier, and when the time came, and IF he measured up, a goodly Sergeant.

At that moment, he thought of the two most junior officers now in the Regiment, Dauber and Shaffer. He cringed, and almost shook his head, until he quickly realised he was amongst the officers, and tightened, suppressing the motion of his head. When he was with them he always strove to remain intensely 'on parade' and 'in the fight', never allowing himself to be distracted by his own thoughts. Despite his efforts at control, he wondered if old Angus had taught him full drill? Probably knowing Angus, as he had, he'd probably had him and his brothers doing a bit of square-bashing *{Marching in formation}*.

The younger Driscol now made an appearance.

Captain Webb, the Adjutant, the Colonel and the Sergeant Major focused their attention on him.

'Master Driscol thank you for coming so quickly'. Which was true, he'd almost run when the Corporal of the Guard informed him of his presence being requested in the commander's office.

'We had a few questions', said the Colonel.

'Sir' acknowledged David, expecting a torrent of military-related terms to test his knowledge.

'You mentioned that your father owned a farm and Inn, is that correct'?

The question was unexpected and Driscol hesitated, but swallowed and answered. 'Oh no sir, we have the Tavern, the Inn, the tailor shop and livery, plus of course the farm and my mother has a notions shop.'

'Really how much land do you have'?

'163 and a quarter acres'.

That raised a number of eyebrows amongst the men assembled, for that was a sizeable allotment of land.

'What is the land used for'?

'Half is pasture, a quarter we plant, and the rest is rented out to various people for farms and houses'.

'Your father is landlord it would seem then'?

'Yes, we have always bought land when we had profit from the other industries'.

'Master Driscol I must ask why you and your father didn't look to see if a commission could be bought'? Asked the Colonel.

David had been waiting a long time for that question; his father had instilled him with the right answer.

'Sir we did inquire, but no commission in the 52nd was available and the agents said that the price would be well beyond what we could afford. He also felt that borrowing the money would be unwise. My father has always disliked bankers and loansmen'.

'As he should', replied the Colonel, thinking to himself and you not being a gentleman would have prevented you from getting it anyway, pity, such a fine lad.

'So you'd like to be an officer but you cannot afford the price'?

'Yes Sir, regrettably that is true, but I have hopes of obtaining a commission in war, on the battlefield'.

'Rightly so', said Captain Webb who had done so himself.

'Well son' and the Colonel rose from his seat and extended his hand. Driscol hesitated a moment, but shook it firmly, and not like a wet fish as his father had warned him against.

'You take to your father and mother our best wishes. We will contact you as soon as a private soldier's position becomes available'.

'I will be happy to wait, Sir'.

The Adjutant secured the original letter and noted the postal address on it for Angus Driscol, Esquire.

'Esquire', Uppity Irish bastard isn't he, he thought.

David made his farewells and was setting off to the door when Captain Rollingston-Smythe came back in, from his round of inspections, which had not been up to his expectations.

'Ah, Driscol, you are still here', he said.

As they passed, the Captain stopped and shot out a question.

'Did your father receive the vote in the Reform bill of 1832 Mr Driscol'?

'Oh no sir', David began to walk again, then turned and pivoted and added 'he already had it'. With that said, he got into step with the Corporal of the guard, and in step, headed for the gate.

{The vote was based on property ownership and around 200,000 men could vote in the England of that time and it would seem that Driscol's father was eminently qualified}

The Colonel was sitting down and shaking his head.

'Too bad about that, he'd have made a fine Ensign'.

Captain Rollingston-Smythe raised his eyebrows in a questioning manner.

'You were speaking to Driscol's son about a commission, but his family couldn't afford one'?

The Adjutant added, 'he is a well formed boy but his father is no gentleman'.

'Not so', said Captain Rollingston-Smythe, 'did you not hear his reply to my question'?

He received but blank looks from the other men.

'Gentlemen, his father has the vote, and he had it before the act of 1832. That means he is middle class; a property owner, during the war[17] with Boney *{Napoleon}*. We had many tradesmen's sons as officers.'

Captain Webb thought about something, but declined to mention that his father had once been a milliner's shop assistant.

'That much is true', said the Colonel.

Captain Webb came away from his recollections of his father and declared, 'his family does have 160 plus acres'.

This went back and forth for some time until the Colonel put his hand up.

Gentleman, Gentleman, the matter is as it is, whether he is entitled to a commission in the 52nd is a question that the Colonel of the Regiment would decide along with the rest of the officers. We might agree amongst ourselves on the matter, but the hard truth is he cannot afford to buy a commission.

Looking at the Sergeant Major, 'but we will bring him into to Regiment as soon as we can'.

Captain Rollingston-Smythe raised his hand, like a student requesting the attention from his teacher.

'Sir, I would like to offer an idea, but first I must have an agreement from you'.

The Colonel looked at him and said slowly, 'yes but in what matter…'

'Should Driscol obtain a commission, may I request that he join my company'?

Captain Webb jumped in immediately, 'Wait, I would want him for mine, most assuredly, mine'.

'You have all you need' said Captain Rollingston-Smythe.

'Sir, do we have agreement of this'?

The Colonel looked at the younger Captain, he knew there was some trick to this, but he couldn't fathom what it might be.

'That decision would be based solely on the needs of the Regiment'. Pronounced the Colonel.

The Adjutant added, 'however, Sir with the loss of Mumpsimus, he will be short one'.

'Yes' said the Colonel, 'there is that'.

Captain Webb spoke up, firmly this time, 'Sir we have a marvelous opportunity here. We have his commission'.

The Colonel thought for a moment and finally it became clear to him what those Captains were babbling about.

'Adjutant could we give Driscol that Commission'?

'Absolutely not Sir, it will be Regimental property. What would the market makers say if we gave a commission away to a former Non-Commissioned officer's son? No, no the 52nd would not come off well in that'. May I suggest a man I know of the name of Harper…'

'Pity that', said the Colonel cutting off the Adjutant, 'but you are right in what you say Adjutant, a glance around the room showed confirmation of that stand. It was a notable idea but quite impractical'.

With that, the Sergeant Major excused himself, for he had a few men in the Regiment he needed to take down a peg; such was his obligation, and it was an obligation he rather enjoyed. He had said nothing during the discussion about Driscol. He considered that he would make a better Ensign than a private, but in general, the Sergeant Major had a poor view of the 52nd's officers, except for Captain Webb of course.

Captain Rollingston-Smythe helped Webb to his feet, and all were about to depart, when Captain Rollingston-Smythe had a most devious and at the same time delicious thought.

'Sir, the commission, may I purchase it'?

The Adjutant and Colonel looked at him, as did Webb who was sorting out his uniform.

'Well', said the Colonel, 'I'm sure you don't want to be an Ensign again so would it be for a friend or relative'?

'No Sir, I'll give it to Driscol – if it were that he was to come to my company'.

Captain Webb, 'Unfair Sir, you cannot bargain with a commission that way. If Driscol obtained a commission, I'd want him too, I'll send you Dauber'.

'Sir', Captain Rollingston-Smythe came to attention. 'I offer 300 pounds for the Ensign's commission held by the Regiment, this is an official offer made with no attempt at wit or frivolity'.

The Adjutant, 'we are not sure yet whether the action by Ensign Mumpsimus was correct, although I believe it is legal and in accordance with custom, we certainly cannot sell his commission until we have confirmation, and others may want the commission, the Regiment has a valued asset and must not squander it'.

'Then' said Captain Rollingston-Smythe, 'I ask for acceptance of my bid as first, and having standing without vexation'.

The Adjutant, who was versed in such things, understood what he meant, while the language left the Colonel wondering. 'Yes, we'll accept your bid for the Commission as first and most valid'.

'Then I also suggest that we treat it as a transaction completed, until such time that you confirm its actual legality'.

'No, no Captain Rollingston-Smythe, you go too far, it would be imprudent to proceed so far on something that may have no basis'.

The good Captain was about to reply, when running feet were heard outside the office. The sentry appeared in a moment.

'Sir, the Corporal of the Guard begs to report that the Colonel (Brigadier Sir William 'Red Jack' Fitzwilliam)[18] has entered the quadrangle'.

…and so fate and coincidence yet again came to effect the outcome of this day.

The officers commenced a rapid search for hats and dress swords, with only Captain Rollingston-Smythe standing ready, for he was already properly dressed, and for the record had never been found to be out of proper dress. While the Adjutant might spend more on clothes, Vincent wore them correctly at all times.

The Colonel's hat had been sat on at some point, and while restoring it to functionality, the sentry called the building to attention, and in strode the rather short, and slight, Colonel of the Regiment. His stock of long white hair was a note of disarray on an otherwise perfect uniform, heavy with gold braid. He walked with a limp, which demonstrated his many wounds and the reason for his retirement. Although he could walk a short distance, he could no longer sit a horse.

'Gentlemen good morning, how are the light bobs'? This was the Regiment's nickname, first used during the American War and later given to the Light Division in the Peninsula campaign.

They returned the greeting with great gusto, adding 'Sir', which they said in unison for the 52nd, was noted for its sharpness in such things.

'I apology Percy', he said to the Lieutenant Colonel commanding, 'I was going down to London and thought to see how the Regiment is'? He said that in such a way as to make his being in Ireland the result of some casual arrangement.

'All is fine sir'.

'At full strength? No sickness? Are the men taking to the rations?' Shall I try and get you overseas again'?

'Please, yes sir', said the Colonel although in truth he rather liked being here, rather than in some foreign place, and yes he considered Ireland not to be 'foreign' but a part of England.

There was a rather formalistic air to this exchange, the Colonel of the Regiment despite his years and convention, tended to show up at odd hours of the day and night, asking the same questions each time. Usually the unscheduled visits ended in a riotous time in the officers' mess, highlighted by the Colonel's retracement of a certain charge during the Maratha war and a visit to the 'Black hole' a notorious Poona brothel, a visit buried in metaphor and insinuations.

Captain Rollingston-Smythe at that moment decided to outflank the Colonel and Adjutant.

'Sir, there is one small *affaire* we need your opinion on'.

'Oh' and Fitzwilliam turned to the Captain of whom he knew nothing, except his name, which at the moment he couldn't remember. 'Yes man'?

'Ensign Mumpsimus has turned over his commission to the Regiment and I'd like to purchase it for a young man of some demonstrable talent'.

'That bloody fool has insulted the 52nd by returning his commission? Why I'll have the bounder cashiered'.

The Adjutant quickly briefed the Colonel of the Regiment on the actions of their allegedly former officer.

'Guards, well he is now equal to you Percy, so watch your step, and considering his family connections. I must watch mine too[19]'.

'The insolence of that man'! Said the Brigadier vehemently, with a stamp of his foot.

Captain Rollingston-Smythe politely cleared his throat.

'What, ah yes, who is the man, family of yours'? Said the Brigadier.

'No sir, a lusty[20] lad, well educated, knows his military skills and his family is middle class and has a history with our regiment'.

'Well he may be fine material, and I see that Captain Webb agrees, as does Percy, but no a middle class background is not quite good enough for the 52nd'.

The Colonel, Percy, placed his hand in an odd way on his sword, an old gesture to signify that you were approaching danger, used in social situations, in some regiments it meant, shut up, in others, that you were heading into an ambush, which attracted Fitzwilliam's attention. 'Sir, might you recall when you were in Peninsula. I must remind you of that time after that cavalry fracas, you were in as a supernumerary[21]?'

'Sahagun[22], of course why do you mention it'?

'Do you recall you had a Frenchman's sabre lodged in your foot'?

'Oh my, that was painful. My, I could barely see; the pain was so great. I didn't even note the slash on my back and head until the surgeon spoke of it. With that, he rubbed at the scar on his head that he had had for decades, for it still itched at times, and it itched like mad with the memory of it. 'I still have that sabre. It was a French officer's cavalry sabre with a fine hilt.'

'Yes I remember it looked Egyptian didn't it'?

'So it was'.

'But why do you mention it – other than for me to remember that great pain, damn your eyes, the mere mention of it makes my own eyes water again', and the Brigadier laughed followed quickly by all the others.

'Who removed it from your foot, and carried you to the surgeon, and took care of your horse (*for the Brigadier did love his horse*)'.

'Why yes a fine man, Sergeant, ah, ah'.

'Driscol, sir'.

'Yes that was man, tried to give him a guinea for his efforts, but he refused it, said he was only doing his duty'.

'It is his son whom Captain Rollingston-Smythe would like to buy the commission for'.

The Brigadier thought for a few minutes, pursed his lips and said.

'Smythe', damn, damn, damn, Rollingston-Smythe thought, another man who cannot remember my name, 'I won't allow it despite the connection, his being middle class – really is his father middle class now'? Really a Sergeant's son as an Officer, no, no that would not do at all, NO'.

Having had that confirmed, he nodded, thought and continued, 'we'd take a great deal of trouble and botheration if you were to buy that Commission and gift it in such a way. Why do you wish to do this Smythe? You were not in Peninsula? It shall be a burden if you do'.

'Sir, the lad is well educated in the art of war and knows Russian, and I believe we shall soon cross swords with Russia'.

'You want the best officers for your company, noble sediment, ah pardon, sentiment'.

'Nonetheless if men like Baronet Fuller-Eliot Drake, the Viscount of Arbuthnott, Baron Carder or the Duke of Richmond[23] were to object even your family would quell before their charge of righteous indignation, if a man of that background was sold a commission in our regiment'.

Captain Rollingston-Smythe had to admit to himself that might be the case, however he said nothing.

'As you have no standing in regards to Driscol, your purchase would be suspect. Did you plan to sell it to him or gift it to him'?

Rollingston-Smythe had not thought that far in advance, but said, 'I hope to give it to him and reclaim the value once he sold it'.

'Oh no, my good man. Far too commercial a transaction, selling commissions to the middle class and perhaps gaining a profit, they would eat you up like the cannibals they are'.

'There is nothing for it then', said the Brigadier who was deep in thought.

A resigned, but knowing sigh, came from Captain Webb and Rollingston-Smythe.

A moment passed as the Brigadier thought on, then he thought some more, even at this age his mind was quick, he had earned the epithet of Red Jack, short for red jacket, for coming into battle clad only in his white shirt but having it slashed to pieces, so it was soon red with his and the enemies blood. His men had said he did it deliberately, so as to not to be seen out of uniform.

The Brigadier thought some more, of the time at Sahagun, and of Sergeant Angus Driscol.

He then stopped, cursed in a most foul way and threw up his hands. 'How could I forget! His father was an officer if only for a day or so. He was awarded a battlefield commission TWICE. Each time he sold it for he was no officer by birth, education or action. Is that not true Captain Webb'?

Webb had forgotten that small piece of information, but yes, he then remembered it too, after the battles of Vitoria and Waterloo. He explained how Angus Driscol had sold off the commission as soon as it was awarded.

'WELL!' cried the Brigadier, 'That's sorted! As an officer, even if only for two days at most, he was granted two battlefield commission, which in my Bible, means he was an officer.

The others reminded him of the Duke of Wellington's making him a temporary Colonel of Militia. He nodded to that piece of information, which he had forgotten also.

'That is the whyfore, and therefore, by this, his son can follow him'.

'Adjutant you will come with me to London this day'.

'Sir, yes sir'.

'We'll deal with this Mumpsimus fellow, and then I'll buy the commission, if all is sorted and correct'.

'Percy, for the time being, treat this son of Driscol as a First Class volunteer, until we resolve the situation. If we don't get the commission, I'll take him on as my Aide-de-Camp, until it is sorted in some other way', with his place of employment being here with the regiment.

'Captain Smythe, I will give you the credit for the idea, but the Commission goes to Driscol from me. None of those men I mentioned, and dare I say, several of them will remember Driscol, none will dare question my gift as his father saved my life, or at least my foot, and we Fitzwilliamses value our feet! By Jove his father was an officer in this Regiment, and so shall his son be. If they do object, I will speak to the Viscount himself[24]. He was with us in the Peninsula, but I'm not sure he'd remember Driscol, but if he does…. If I can next week, I'll speak to the Duke[25] too. It is unfortunate that I missed Waterloo, and consequently I have no 'W' but my 'P'[26] is justly earned, and I was in India, which means much to the Duke. He will definitely remember Driscol, if not, this will not stand, but if we can obtain his nod or more importantly no shake of his head, all the others will fall in behind him over such a matter. Few men will stand against the Duke on matters of this sort'.

He stamped his foot, the previously wounded one, which had been burning from the old wound, but now had no feeling at all;

it was a way he had found to end a conversation and to also stop his wounded foot from falling asleep.

'Good day gentlemen. Smythe, give the Son of Driscol this', and he fished out a gold guinea[27]. Give him this with my compliments. His father refused an earlier one, but I insist he takes this, as he'll need it to buy his kit. As that pillock[28] Mumpsimus has left everything to the Regiment, give it all to this young man. Also Smythe if this goes badly for the Regiment I'll see you, and he turned and looked at the Colonel, the Adjutant and Captain Webb in turn, 'spend a few years in the red grave[29]'. At that point, in order to quell the ice-cold shudder that had run through these men, he gave a small laugh and left, followed by the Colonel and Adjutant, whose duty it was accompany him wherever he went, when he was on the barrack's grounds.

Captain Webb looked at Rollingston-Smythe.

'Well we had better get our new Ensign back and in uniform'.

'Wait, he is just to be a First Class Volunteer'.

'There will be in truth no difference'.

They both nodded. 'Done'.

Notes for the Supplement:

1. At the Battle of Waterloo in 1815, the 52nd were marched forward to defend against attacks by French cavalry. Their position was pivotal, and Napoleon, in a final blow against the center of the British line, sent in the undefeated Imperial Guard. The Guard was halted by the intense volley fire of Maitland's Brigade of Guards and, as they wavered, the commander of the 52nd, Sir John

Colborne, led a charge into the flank of the French Guards, which routed them, and subsequently, the rest of the French army

2. Dauber and Shaffer. Rodger Creswicke Shaffer born 1817 in Chadlington, England joined the 52nd Regiment in 1836 and served with the regiment until 1859, where he was assigned as the Deputy Quartermaster of Scotland and finished his career as the Lieutenant Governor of Guernsey. He died suddenly in 1864 after a hunting accident. Henry Jameson Dauber was born in Penzance, Cornwall in 1814 and served in her Majesty's navy as a Midshipman but having married; he returned to the land and took an Ensign's commission in the 52nd in 1835. His life was unfortunately shortened and ultimately lost due to an African fever he endured while on an expedition to the Chadda-Benueh River in West Africa in 1851

3. His name was of course was not Mumpsimus, but the unknown editor lined through the real name and replaced it with Mumpsimus for the magazine article. Some debate has gone on as to who this officer was, as the lined-out name was of a man who held no position in either the 52nd or the Guards. It is thought that the editor knew this and replaced the wrong name with another as a placeholder until the matter could be researched. In later parts of his journals, Driscol suggests that one of the men he came into conflict with, later in life, may have been this same man. However it was never explicitly stated. Mumpsimus was probably used here in the meaning of, 'An unreasonable man who wouldn't change his ways'. His name was probably Giles Augustus Herewith Cecil, but this fellow is a historical ghost. He remained in the Guards only a fortnight before selling his commission and boarded a ship for the wilds of Paraguay

4. Brevet Majority, brevet referred to a warrant or order stating a commissioned officer is allowed to hold a higher rank temporarily, but without receiving the pay of that higher rank, except when actually serving in that role. In this context, it meant a lower ranking officer obtaining such a position that would warrant his being a 'brevet' Major; a Major in name and status but not in pay or power, if outside the position he was now in

5. This was not completely true. One of the Driscol's five brothers was not gainfully employed, but the family never mentioned the black sheep of the family, Aaron, to outsiders

6. Chenier's poem La Jeune Captive, printed in La Jeune Tarentine in the Mercure newspaper of 22 March 1801

7. A *soonar* was a caste of silversmiths in India, and the item had been obtained by the Regiment while on service with the East India Company, during the Maratha wars

8. Mess, by this they didn't mean the food served at the officer's mess, but the genial environment and the respect and good will amongst the officers who dined there

9. French hedge whore, the French part of this term needs no comment as British officers of this time, despite their general appreciation of French culture, tended to label and associate the unmentionable in life with the French, or if particularly bad, the Spanish. A Hedge whore was a prostitute who worked in rural areas and wasn't associated with a town or brothel, low class

10. Selling of commissions. One of the companies that provided this service was Harringtons. The system to gain promotion was not one of merit, but one of recommendation and purchase. A man without training could purchase up to the rank of Lieutenant Colonel, although the regiment he

was purchasing the commission in could refuse the transaction. Abuses of the systems and patronage often overcame these objections. Wealthy and politically influential men could rise quickly. For example the notorious James Brudenell also known as Lord Cardigan had in 1824, at the age of 27, purchased a commission in the 8th King's Royal Irish Hussars. Making extensive use of the purchase of commissions system then in use, he became a Lieutenant in January 1825, a Captain in June 1826, a Major in August 1830 and a Lieutenant-Colonel, only three months later, on 3 December 1830. He obtained command of the 15th The King's Hussars at a cost of £35,000 in March 1832. So in six years, he went from civilian to Lieutenant Colonel

11. Absquatulation, a term of some confusion amongst scholars, thought to be an Americanism made up from a humorous rendering of pseudo-Latin. It is thought the term was not in common use in 1836 but may have been used in 1873 to deal with a long forgotten conversation. Its meaning is to 'move away while squatted' or 'to leave in a hurry or under a suspicious state of affairs'

12. Dunderhead, an insult directed at Ensign Mumpsimus, Dunderhead reflects on the named person's intelligence or abilities

13. George Scovell, a Major of modest birth who broke the French Imperial codes and was the hidden secret to Wellington's success in the Peninsula Campaign

14. Santander. A city and port in northern Spain that, in this context, was the port through which the British supplied their army in Spain once it was re-captured from the French

15. Savile Row, the fashionable street in London where the best in uniforms and clothes could be made for the discerning gentleman at high cost

16. Train, the writer was probably forgetful of the fact, since this was written nearly forty years after the events, that the railroad in fact, didn't exist at that time, in that part of Ireland. It would come some years later

17. During the Napoleonic war, the need for Officers, competent ones, meant commissions were commonly sold to the sons of tradesmen, merchant and others, not considered 'gentlemen'

18. Brigadier Sir William Fitzwilliam was a retired officer who held the honorary title of Colonel of the Regiment - a senior officer with a history with the unit who acts as its titular and honorary head. The Brigadier tended at times to forget he was retired. His position was symbolic & traditional and he had no commission to give orders, but did so based on tradition and their acceptance by the officers given them

19. An officer of the British Guards was considered to have a rank outside of the Guards equaling that of two levels higher, thus Captain Mumpsimus of the Scots Fusilier Guards, was now equal in rank to Lieutenant Colonel Percy Raddick - or better known by his nickname of the 'Olde Maiden'.

20. Lusty had the meaning of enthusiasm and keenness at this time in the 19th century, the sexual meaning came about early in the next century.

21. Supernumerary, an officer attached as a volunteer to a military unit. It was common for officers with vigour to seek confrontation with the enemy even when his own unit might be involved elsewhere

22. Sahagun; an engagement in which the 15th Light Dragoons (Hussars) defeated two French units in a notable charge over the frozen fields in Spain on the 12th of December 1808. In this case, his brother was serving with the 15th Dragoons, and he was probably invited along for the 'show'

23. All officers presently or formerly in the 52nd Regiment and aristocrats as of 1836

24. Viscount, General Rowland Hill, 1st Lord Hill commander and chief of the Army

25. Duke Arthur Wellesley, Duke of Wellington former and future commander of the British army and former Prime Minister; one of the most powerful men in England at that time

26. P & W's. The officer's list at this time had written next to each officer a 'P' or 'W'. 'W' stood for Waterloo and indicated the man had been at that essential engagement, 'P' meant, Peninsula and that the officer had spent time there during the Napoleonic wars. To have none was to be less than qualified; to have one was to be respected, to have both was to ensure your future success. The value of having the P & W next to one's name faded as age won in its endless conflict with the previous victorious veterans

27. Guinea, the gold military guinea was minted in 1813 for the specific use of the Duke of Wellington's Peninsula army. The local inhabitants would take no currency but gold, so 80,000 were manufactured to pay his army. They were the last gold coins minted by Great Britain. Their worth today is around 700 pounds or 1,000 dollars. As the coin would not have existed in 1808, the good Brigadier or the later writer may have misremembered the offering of a Guinea to Sergeant Driscol by the then Captain, he probably offered another type of gold coin; probably Spanish or Portuguese

28. Pillock, an idiot or worse from the Swedish pillicock, which entered the English language by way of Gustavus Adolphus of Sweden

29. White men's grave, or the red grave from the color of its soil, West Africa or specifically Sierra Leone; where illness would often claim a man's life with regularity and speed

Finis

Hello reader

A greeting to the readers who have come this far for you having done so is immensely appreciated. A long final word is always considered an unbearable irritation to the reader, who having finished a book must bear the editor's voice once more - therefore mine will be petite.

I must thank you for having traveled to Persia and beyond with Driscol, by reading this book, the third volume in a four volume set. I would enjoy hearing from you about your experience in Driscol's world. I was quite pleased when reading his journal, when I realized he would travel to Persia, for I went to that land in 1998. In that year I was working in Dubai. Iran of that period was a difficult place to get into safely, especially for an American, and especially one who was still a reserve army officer.

Yet I proceeded to a holiday destination on the island of Kish, which lies in the Persian Gulf. I remember that at this time the Arabs were pushing the 'Arabian Gulf' name meme again and there was a bit of heightened tension, but I went anyway. My fiancé was not willing to try the trip, as we were unmarried and the ultra-conservative Iranian government was not one to look kindly on social adventurism. So I proceeded alone. I arrived and was kept in the terminal for four hours unnecessarily, because some Iranian wrestlers had been similarly delayed when traveling to the USA. It was a boring terminal, but they did provide a fine curry for lunch.

The hotel was faded, the rugs stained and threadbare but the food was good and the bed had no other inhabitants. There was not much to do in Kish. I walked around its perimeter and viewed the helicopter rides (in a maintenance-famished Russian Helicopter) with unease. An abandoned ship on the shoreline was good indication of the excitement once to be had. Yet I kept busy. I hope if someone was tailing me that they were as bored as I was!

Driscol seems to have had a better time in Persia than I did and I am envious of him for that.

Please contact me at: anofficerofthecrown@gmail.com.

Wayne